Become our fan on Facebook **facebook.com/idwpublishing**
Follow us on Twitter **@idwpublishing**
Subscribe to us on YouTube **youtube.com/idwpublishing**
See what's new on Tumblr **tumblr.idwpublishing.com**
Check us out on Instagram **instagram.com/idwpublishing**

ISBN: 978-1-63140-617-1   19 18 17 16   1 2 3 4

X-FILES ARCHIVES, VOL. 2: SKIN & ANTIBODIES. JUNE 2016. FIRST
PRINTING. The X-Files ™ & © 2016 Twentieth Century Fox Film Corporation.
All Rights Reserved. IDW Publishing, a division of Idea and Design Works, LLC.
Editorial offices: 2765 Truxtun Road, San Diego, CA 92106. The IDW logo is
registered in the U.S. Patent and Trademark Office. Any similarities to persons
living or dead are purely coincidental. With the exception of artwork used for
review purposes, none of the contents of this publication may be reprinted
without the permission of Idea and Design Works, LLC. Printed in Canada.

IDW Publishing does not read or accept unsolicited submissions of ideas, stories,
or artwork.

COVER BY
MICHAEL STRIBLING

EDITED BY
JUSTIN EISINGER

EDITORIAL ASSISTANCE BY
LESLIE MANES AND
SARAH DUFFY

COLLECTION DESIGN BY
**RICHARD SHEINAUS/
GOTHAM**

Ted Adams, CEO & Publisher
Greg Goldstein, President & COO
Robbie Robbins, EVP/Sr. Graphic Artist
Chris Ryall, Chief Creative Officer/Editor-in-Chief
Matthew Ruzicka, CPA, Chief Financial Officer
Dirk Wood, VP of Marketing
Lorelei Bunjes, VP of Digital Services
Jeff Weber, VP of Licensing, Digital and Subsidiary Rights
Jerry Bennington, VP of New Product Development

For international rights, please contact licensing@idwpublishing.com

The X-Files created by Chris Carter.

FILES

ARCHIVES VOL. 2

SKIN page 1
by Ben Mezrich

ANTIBODIES page 185
by Kevin J. Anderson

based on the characters created by
Chris Carter

SKIN

By Ben Mezrich

ONE

Two hours after midnight, sirens tore through the cinder-block walls, shattering the momentary calm. There was the screech of rubber tires against pavement—the ambulances careening to a stop in the receiving circle—and the steady wail was joined by the shouts of paramedics as they unloaded their cargo. A second later, the double doors crashed open, and the vast room seemed to buckle inward, as a torrent of stretchers streamed across the tiled floor.

"Here we go!" someone shouted, and suddenly the emergency room came alive. Bleary-eyed doctors in white coats and pale-blue scrubs leapt forward, shouting for chem trays and surgical consults. Triage nurses in pink uniforms swirled between the stretchers, trailing IV wires and portable crash carts. At first glance, the room seemed gripped by chaos, but in reality, it was a highly controlled, intricate performance. The nurses and doctors played off one another like professional athletes, acting out their roles in kinetic bursts of harmony.

Huddled in a corner near the back of the ER, Brad Alger watched the unfolding spectacle with wide eyes. Although he had been on duty for less than twenty minutes, his scrubs were already thick with sweat. Red splotches covered the sleeves of his white doctor's coat, and his high-top Nikes had turned a strange, nearly violet color. His platinum-blond hair rose from his head in unruly locks, like a miniature sunburst. There were heavy bags under his glassy blue eyes, and he looked as though he hadn't slept in months.

He rubbed a damp sleeve across his forehead, then quickly stepped aside as a disheveled nurse pushed a crash cart up against the wall next to him.

"Christ," Alger coughed, his voice pitching upward, "it's knee-deep in here. I thought the first salvo was bad—but this is crazy. How many ambulances did they say were coming?"

"Twenty-two," the nurse answered, tossing a pair of blood-spattered gloves toward the floor. "Maybe more. At first, they thought there were only nine cars involved in the accident. Now they say it was more like thirteen."

Alger whistled. "Thirteen cars. At two in the morning."

"This your first Friday night?"

She had spiky dark hair and kind eyes. Alger guessed she was thirty, maybe thirty-five. He felt like a kid next to her, and he tried to take the fearful edge out of his voice. "My internship started on Sunday."

The nurse offered a sympathetic smile. "Welcome to New York."

She grabbed a clean pair of gloves from the crash cart and moved back into the fray. For the thousandth time in less than a week, Alger wondered what the hell he was doing there. A month ago, he had been a fourth-year medical student in Cincinnati, Ohio. His biggest worries had been his school loan payments and Kelly Pierce, his most recent ex. He had done a rotation in emergency back in Cincinnati—but he had never imagined anything like this.

The evening had started innocently enough. A few cardios, a handful of recent entrants into the knife-and-gun club, a half dozen respiratory gomers sneaking cigarettes under their oxygen masks. And then the call had come over the emergency room's intercom system. There had been a multicar accident on the FDR Drive; at least ten critical, another two dozen in bad shape. All available doctors had been summoned down from the hospital's other departments, and the emergency room had been put on full trauma-alert.

Alger had made the mistake of asking Duke Baker—the gargantuan, short-tempered chief resident—what that meant in English. The Duke had nearly busted a capillary berating him; the only English spoken in the Duke's emergency room took the form of four-letter words. Trauma-alert meant you tried not to kill anyone before dawn—and in the process, kept the fuck out of Duke Baker's way.

"Brad! Over here!"

Alger felt his pulse rocket as he caught sight of Dennis Crow. Tall, thin, with a shock of dark hair and freckles covering every inch of exposed skin. Crow was one of the four interns who had started with Alger, and the only one who seemed even more out of place. Born on a farm, trained at the University of Wisconsin—and completely in over his head at the big-city ER. In other words, he had the Duke's footprints all over his freckled ass.

At the moment, Crow was standing between two paramedics, at the head of a stretcher on the other side of the ER. The two paramedics were struggling with a convulsing patient as Crow worked an endo tube down the man's throat. Although both paramedics were big and burly, they were having a hell of a time keeping the patient still. One was fighting to get a Velcro restraint around the man's shoulders, while the other was using his weight against the patient's wrists.

Alger grabbed a pair of sterile latex gloves from the cart next to him and rushed forward. As he navigated across the room, he signaled for a crash cart, a portable EKG machine, and a chem tray. He reached Crow and the stretcher seconds ahead of the equipment and a nurse. He watched as Maria Gomez began pasting the circular electrodes from the EKG monitor across the patient's chest. She was a big woman, with thick folds of fat hanging from around her arms and neck—but her motions were fluid and practiced. Still, her brown eyes showed a spark of concern. Crow and Alger were both interns with less than a week of experience. No nurse in her right mind wanted to stand around and watch two kids playing doctor.

Alger pushed the thought away. He wasn't playing doctor—he *was* a doctor. He focused his attention on the patient in front of him.

Caucasian, maybe twenty-four, twenty-five years old. Tall, muscular, with chiseled, boxy features and glazed, bright blue eyes. A blond crew cut, military style. His shirt had already been cut away by the paramedics, and there was a tattoo on his upper right shoulder, some sort of dragon with red flames coming out of its mouth. No visible signs of trauma, none of the marks of injury that Alger would have expected from a car-crash victim.

He watched as Crow finally got the intubation tube past the man's epiglottis and into his throat. The man's chest swelled beneath the EKG electrodes, and Crow quickly attached an air tube to the top of the endo tube. As the patient's breathing resumed, he settled back against the stretcher, his eyelids rolling shut. Alger turned toward the paramedics. "What have we got?"

The larger of the two answered as he finished fastening the Velcro restraint around the patient's chest. "Found him collapsed, unconscious, in the break-down lane, maybe twenty feet from the site of the crash. No contusions, no visible signs of trauma. He convulsed twice in the ambulance—and just a few minutes ago he went into respiratory distress."

"Any history?"

The paramedic stepped back from the stretcher. "No ID, no wallet. Doesn't respond to any stimulus at all. He was conscious for a few minutes in the wagon—but we couldn't get him to answer any questions."

"Start him on any meds?"

The paramedic shook his head. "His pulse and BP seemed fine. Like I said, his breathing didn't go down until a few minutes ago."

"What about the EKG?"

"You'll be the first to see it. It was a real grab and dash at the scene. We had another in the same ambulance, in much worse shape. We're not even sure this one was involved in the accident—he might have been a bystander. Certainly doesn't look like he was thrown through a car windshield, or anything like that." He paused. "Okay, you guys got it from here?"

There was obvious hesitation in the paramedic's eyes. Alger felt his face flush red. He couldn't help how young he looked. He nodded, his expression bold. The paramedic turned and headed back toward the double doors. His partner gave Alger a tiny nod, then followed. It was up to the two interns now. Alger tossed a glance toward the Duke, huddled over a patient on the other side of the ER, then gritted his teeth. He was fresh—but he could handle this.

"All right, let's start with the basics. Airway, Breathing, Cardio."

He knew he sounded like an idiot to the experienced nurse, but he had to begin with what he knew—and that meant the ABCs of medicine. He watched the man's chest rise and fall, and knew that Crow had done a good job with the intubation. Then he turned toward the EKG—the cardiac monitor—and focused his eyes on the small screen on top of the waist-high steel cart.

"Holy shit," he whispered.

Crow followed his gaze, his eyes widening. The screen was covered with frantic green lines. "He's all over the place! It looks like his heart's doing cart-wheels! Is that V-fib?"

Alger stared at the screen, then shook his head. The man wasn't in arrest yet—but he was certainly close. Alger had never seen anything like it before. One second, the monitor showed an elevated cadence—and the next second a prolonged skip. One second he seemed to be in normal, sinus rhythm—and the next second he was bouncing through a combination of arrhythmias. Alger had no doubt that if the paramedics had seen such a bizarre EKG reading in the ambulance, they would never have handed this patient over to two interns. They would have brought him straight to the chief resident.

Alger turned back to the patient. The man looked calm, still unconscious, but there were visible spasms beneath his skin. His muscles seemed to vibrate in concert with the readings on the screen. No doubt about it, something weird was going on. "Jesus, this isn't good. What's his BP?"

Maria Gomez looked up from the blood-pressure gauge strapped around the man's right arm. "Two-twenty over one-twenty."

"What?" The nurse looked at the gauge again. She shrugged, her face slightly pale. "Two-twenty over one-twenty."

Alger coughed, his stomach churning. Two-twenty over one-twenty was extremely high. Along with the erratic heartbeat, it was a dangerous sign. The man's circulatory system was completely out of whack, and his heart was enormously overstimulated.

"An acute MI?" Crow tried. "Maybe a pulmonary embolism?"

Alger shook his head. The EKG didn't look like an MI or an embolism. Alger rubbed sweat out of his eyes. *Stay calm. Stay focused.* It was a mystery—but that was the thrill of the ER, wasn't it? Solving the mysteries? "Okay, we need a blood workup, a Chem 7—"

"His BP's rising!" Gomez blurted. "Two-fifty over one-fifty!"

Shit. How could his BP be rising? It was already off the map! Alger cursed. Thrill or no thrill—he knew it was time to bring the Duke over. Any second, this patient was going to arrest. Alger was about to call out across the ER when Crow shouted at him. "Now *that's* V-fib! That's definitely V-fib!"

Alger whirled back toward the EKG screen. The bright green lines had become completely disjointed and frantic, indicating that the man had gone into ventricular fibrillation. His heart was responding to random electrical impulses, and was no longer capable of pumping blood to the rest of his body. In other words, this patient was failing. Fast.

"BP dropping!" Gomez chimed in. "He's crashing!"

Alger leapt for the crash cart, while Crow called the Code. Normally, doctors and nurses would have rushed toward the crashing patient—but tonight there were so many tragedies filling the ER, the Code barely registered. Alger knew that the Duke would make his way over when he realized his two interns were in charge of the dying man—but Alger didn't have time to wait for the chief resident to take over.

He grabbed the defibrillator paddles off the crash cart and slipped them over his hands. He rubbed the conductive fluid over the pads, then scraped them together in a circular motion. He had no choice but to shock the man and pray that his heart resumed a workable rhythm. He had never used the paddles before—but he had watched the procedure a dozen times during medical school.

"Three hundred joules," he declared, trying to keep the emotion out of his voice. He knew three hundred was a high place to start—but this was a big, muscular guy. Probably worked out every day of his life. "Clear!"

Everyone stepped back from the stretcher. Alger pressed the paddles against the man's bare chest and hit the triggers with his thumbs. The man's body spasmed upward, then crashed back down onto the stretcher. Alger turned to the EKG machine.

Still nothing. He turned back toward Gomez, who was now standing by the defibrillator. "Three-sixty. Stat!"

"Jesus," Crow mumbled. "Where the hell is Duke?"

Alger ignored him. There wasn't anything the Duke could do at this point—either they got this guy's heart started again, or he was finished. Gomez upped the voltage, and Alger readied the paddles. "Clear!"

This time, the man arched a full four inches off the stretcher. His neck twisted back and his arms convulsed beneath the Velcro straps.

"Flat line!" Crow yelled. "He's down! Brad—"

"Again!" Alger shouted back. "Clear!"

He shocked the man a third time. The smell of burned flesh filled Alger's nostrils, and he frantically turned back to the EKG machine. Still nothing. He tossed the defibrillator paddles aside and leapt halfway up the stretcher, placing his palms roughly near the center of the man's chest. The muscles of his fore-arms contracted as he started the most vigorous CPR of his life. The man's chest felt strangely stiff beneath his fingers, his skin rough, almost leathery. He worked in near silence, the minutes ticking by as he tried to coax the man's heart back to life. He ignored the sweat running down his back, the ache in his arms and shoulders. His mind raced through everything that had just happened, searching for some reason why things had gone so drastically wrong. Was there anything he had missed? Was there anything else he could have done? Did he make the right choice when he went for the defibrillator paddles?

"Well?" he asked, desperate, already knowing the answer.

"Still nothing," Crow responded. "He's gone, Brad. You're just pumping beef."

Alger looked at the EKG screen, then back at Crow. He glanced at Gomez, who nodded. He felt his shoulders deflate, his arms going limp. *Damn it.* It had all happened so fast. He glanced toward the Duke, who was still working on a patient near the front of the room. Either he hadn't heard the Code, or he was handling an emergency of his own.

Alger swallowed, telling himself that he had done everything by the book. The Duke wouldn't have handled the situation any differently. The guy had gone into arrest less than two minutes after he had been wheeled into the ER. The paddles could have saved him—and they certainly didn't kill him. Still, Alger felt awful. *A man had just died in front of him.* He lifted his hands off the man's bare chest and took a step back from the stretcher.

Why the hell had he chosen emergency? He glanced up at the clock over the double doors. "Time of death—three-fifteen."

He peeled off his gloves as Gomez rolled the stretcher toward the elevator at the back of the room. The elevator was a straight shot downstairs to pathology, then onward to the hospital morgue. There would probably be an autopsy, because of the mysterious circumstances behind the man's death, and maybe the pathologist would be able to tell him what had really happened. But it wouldn't make any difference to the man on the stretcher.

Alger's face went slack as he watched Gomez push the corpse away. His eyelids suddenly seemed as if they were filled with lead. He felt Dennis Crow's hand on his shoulder. "We did everything we could. People die, and despite what the Duke might think—sometimes it's not our fault."

Alger looked at him, then toward the double doors at the front of the room. He sighed as he watched another stretcher skid into the ER.

\\\\\\\\\\\\\\\\\\\

Twelve hours later, Mike Lifton fought back nausea as Josh Kemper yanked open the heavy steel drawer. The thick scent of dead flesh mixed with the antiseptic chill of the refrigerated storage room, and Mike grimaced, wishing he had never agreed to accompany his classmate on the harvest.

"You get used to it," Josh said, as he pulled the cadaver drawer forward with both hands. Josh was tall, gangly, with oversize ears sticking out from beneath long, stringy brown hair. "It helps to remind yourself how much money you're making. Twenty bucks an hour beats the hell out of pouring coffee at Starbucks."

Mike tried to laugh, but the sound caught somewhere in his throat. He nervously pulled at the sleeves of his green scrubs, rubbing the soft material between his gloved fingers. He could feel the sweat cooling against his back, and he shivered, staring down over Josh's right shoulder.

The body in the drawer was wrapped in opaque plastic with a zipper up the front. Mike took a tiny step back as Josh drew the zipper downward. "Here we go. One stiff, medium rare."

Mike blinked hard, his mouth going dry. Then he ran a gloved hand through his short, auburn hair. He had worked with cadavers before; as a first-year medical student, he had poked and prodded enough dead bodies to fill a zombie movie. But he had never seen a body so *fresh*.

The man inside the plastic bag was unnaturally pale, almost a blue-gray color, with fuzzy blond hair covering his muscular chest. His eyes were closed, and his face was drawn, the skin tight against his cheekbones. Early rigor mortis had begun to set in, and his square jaw jutted stiffly forward, his neck arched back against the steel storage drawer. There were no obvious signs of injury, no gaping wounds or visible bruises. The only distinguishing mark was a colorful tattoo high up on the man's right arm.

"Nice dragon," Josh continued, pointing. "That's about three hundred dollars of wasted skin."

Mike shivered at the macabre thought. He knew that the part-time job with the skin bank was a good way to make money—and great practice if he decided to go into surgery after med school—but he couldn't help feeling ghoulish. His classmate's attitude didn't help matters. It was more than just cynicism bred by experience; Josh Kemper had been born without a deferential bone in his body. During his first year at Columbia Medical School, he had nearly gotten himself suspended for playing catch with a pancreas during anatomy section. No doubt, he was heading straight for a career in pathology.

Mike had always been more sensitive than his classmate. His first day of anatomy, he had nearly fainted when his professor had made the first "Y" incision. And although he had grown stronger over the past three years, he still had a long way to go before he was ready to hold a surgeon's scalpel.

"Aside from the tattoo," Josh continued, unzipping the bag the rest of the way, "he looks pretty good. Both arms, both legs. And the eye bank hasn't gotten here yet. He's still got both peepers."

Mike turned away from the corpse as he steadied his nerves. It's necessary and important work, he reminded himself. The human body was recyclable. And that meant someone had to do the recycling. Heart, liver, kidneys, eyes, skin—someone had to harvest the raw material.

Still, the thought didn't make it any easier. He bit down against his lower lip, trying not to count the steel drawers that lined three walls of the deserted storage room.

"If you're going to puke," Josh interrupted, "do it now. Once we're in the OR, we've got to keep things sterile."

"I'm not going to puke."

"Well, you look worse than our buddy here. Mike, you've got to get used to this sort of thing. It's just a hunk of meat. And we're the guys behind the deli counter."

"You're disgusting."

"That's why you love me. Check the toe tag." Josh started across the storage room, toward a filing cabinet by the far wall. "I'll get the chart."

Mike breathed through his mouth as he circled around the open drawer. *Don't overthink. Do your job.* He reached the back end of the drawer and pulled the plastic bag down on either side. The dead man's legs were long and muscular, covered with more downy blond hair. His feet were heavily callused, his toenails yellowed like an old man's. Mike wondered if he had suffered from some sort of fungus.

Now you're thinking like a doctor. He smiled inwardly, then searched the big toes for the tag. The skin above his eyes wrinkled as he realized it was missing. He searched the drawer beneath the man's callused heels, but there was no sign of the plastic ID. "Hey, Josh. I don't see the tag."

Josh returned from the other side of the room. He had a manila folder open in his gloved hands. "Sometimes it falls down below their feet."

"I'm looking everywhere. There's no tag."

Josh stopped at his side, cursing. He held the manila folder under his arm and lifted the corpse's feet with both hands. Working together, the two students searched the drawer, but came up empty.

"Fuck," Josh said. "This is just great. Eckleman is such a moron."

"Who's Eckleman?"

"The ME's assistant. He runs the storage room. Tags the bodies, makes sure the files are coded correctly. He's a big fat piece of shit, and he drinks." Josh retrieved the folder from under his arm and leafed through it with gloved fingers. "Derrick Kaplan. Caucasian, mid-thirties. Blond hair, blue eyes. Acute aortic dissection, died in the ICU."

Mike glanced down at the body in the drawer. "Well, he's blond, and he's got blue eyes. But he doesn't look like he's in his mid-thirties. Does it say anything about the tattoo?"

Josh shook his head. "No, but like l said, Eckleman is a moron. Look, this is locker fifty-two. Eckleman blows the tags all the time. Especially when the ER is jumping, and after the accident last night—"

"Josh, are you sure we shouldn't ask somebody? What if it's the wrong cadaver?"

Josh paused, rubbing a gloved finger under his jaw. He glanced toward the elevator in the comer of the room, where a stretcher waited to take the body up to the OR for the harvesting. Then he shrugged. "We've got consent, we've got a body. More importantly, we've got an OR reserved for the next hour. So let's go slice up some skin."

He turned, and headed for the stretcher. Mike glanced back at the dragon tattoo. He hoped his classmate knew what he was doing.

\\\\\\\\\\\\\\\\\\\\

"Watch carefully. I promise, you're going to like this."

Mike bit his lips behind a papery surgical mask, as Josh played with one of the saline bags that hung from the IV rack above the operating table. There was a sudden hiss as the infusion pump came alive. Mike watched, shocked, as the skin covering the dead man's chest inflated like an enormous water balloon.

"The saline empties into the subcutaneous base," Josh explained, pointing to the three other saline bags that stood at the corners of the operating table. "The pressure lifts the dermis up from the layer of fat underneath. Makes it easier to get a smooth cut."

Mike nodded, repulsed but fascinated. The cadaver's chest—shaved, prepped with Betadine, and inflated with saline—no longer looked human. The inflated skin was slick, smooth, rounded, a sort of beige color Mike had never seen outside of a J. Crew catalog. "Is this going to be bloody?"

"Not very," Josh answered, reaching into the surgical tray by the operating table. "Until we turn him over. Most of the blood has pooled along his back."

He pulled a shiny steel instrument out of the surgical tray, showing it to Mike. It looked like an oversize cheese slicer, with a numbered knob near the razor-sharp blade. "I'm going to set the dermatome for point-oh-nine millimeters. The goal is to get a piece that you can just barely see through."

He leaned forward, placing the dermatome right below the cadaver's collarbone. Mike considered looking away, then dug his fingers into his palms. In a few months he would be doing rotations in the ER, and he'd see things just as bad—or worse.

He watched as Josh drew the dermatome down across the man's chest. A trickle of dark, deoxygenated blood ran down into the chrome table gutters. The thin layer of skin curled behind the blade, and Josh deftly twisted his wrist as he reached the bottom of the cadaver's rib cage, slicing the strip of skin free. He lifted it gently by an edge and held it in front of Mike. It was nearly transparent, a little more than a foot in length.

"Open the cooler," Josh said, and Mike quickly found the plastic case by his feet. The cooler was a white-and-red rectangle, with the New York Fire Department seal emblazoned across two sides. Mike opened the cooler and retrieved a small tray filled with bluish liquid.

Josh put the slice of skin into the liquid, and Mike sealed it shut. The cooler would keep the skin fresh until it could be transported to the skin bank. There, it would be soaked in antibiotic liquid and stored indefinitely at minus seventy degrees Fahrenheit.

Josh went back to work on the man's chest. His strokes were deft and sure, and in a few minutes he had skinned most of the man's chest and abdomen, both arms, and both legs. He left a small circle around the dragon tattoo, which stood out like a colorful island against the whitish pink background of subcutaneous fat.

"Help me turn him over," Josh said, sliding his hands under the man's back. Mike moved to assist him, and together they heaved the body onto its side. Mike noticed a small, circular rash on the back of the corpse's neck.

"Josh, look at that."

Josh glanced at the rash. It was no more than three inches in diameter and consisted of thousands of tiny red dots. "What about it?"

"Was it in the chart?"

Josh finished turning the body over, then went back for the dermatome. "It's nothing. An insect bite. A random abrasion. Maybe we scratched him when we transferred him to the operating table."

"It looks kind of strange—"

"Mike, the guy's already dead. Someone else is out there with a really bad burn, and this guy's been generous enough to sign away his skin. So let's just do our job and get out of here."

Mike nodded, realizing that Josh was right. The man on the operating table had already gone through the ER. The doctors had tried to save his life, and there was nothing anyone could do for him anymore. But because of Josh, Mike, and the New York Fire Department, someone else was going to benefit from his death. Derrick Kaplan was finished—*but someone else needed his skin.*

Mike gritted his teeth, then gestured toward the dermatome in his classmate's hand. "If you don't mind, I'd like to give it a try."

Josh Kemper raised his eyebrows, then smiled behind his mask.

\\\\\\\\\\\\\\\\\\\'

One week later, in the private-care ward at Jamaica Hospital in Queens, Perry Stanton jerked twice beneath his thin hospital smock, then suddenly came awake. Dr. Alec Bernstein beamed down at him.

"Professor Stanton," Bernstein said, his voice affable, "good afternoon. You'll be happy to hear, the procedure was a complete success."

Stanton blinked rapidly, trying to chase the fog from his vision. Bernstein watched the little man with almost fatherly pride. He always felt this way with his burn patients. Unlike the face-lifts, breast augmentations, and other elective procedures that made up the bulk of his caseload, the burn patients filled him with pride.

Dr. Bernstein felt that pride as he gazed down at Stanton. A forty-nine-year-old associate professor of history at nearby Jamaica University, Stanton had been wheeled into the emergency room eight hours ago, a full-thickness burn covering most of his left thigh. A boiler had exploded in the basement of the university library, and huge drafts of superheated steam had literally flayed the skin from Stanton's leg.

Bernstein remembered getting the emergency summons; he had been right in the middle of a liposuction and had scrubbed out immediately. He had surveyed the damage and made a quick call to the skin bank. An hour later he had gone to work on Stanton's thigh.

Bernstein glanced up as a nurse brushed past him and attached a new bag of fluids to the IV rack above Stanton's bed. Teri Nestor smiled at the surgeon, then looked down at the slowly awakening professor. "You're going to be as good as new, Professor Stanton. Dr. Bernstein is the best the hospital has to offer."

Bernstein blushed. The nurse finished with the IV rack, then moved to the pair of large picture windows that looked out on the hospital parking lot two floors below. She fiddled with the blinds, and orange sunlight glinted off the twenty-inch television screen on the other side of the small private-care room.

Perry Stanton coughed as the light reached his pale, puggish face, and Bernstein turned his attention back to his patient. The cough bothered him; steam could easily damage lung capacity, and Stanton had shown some signs of respiratory distress when he first came into the ER. Stanton was a small man—barely five-four, no more than 120 pounds, with stubby limbs and diminutive features. It wouldn't take much steam to diminish his breathing ability to dangerous levels.

Bernstein had already put Stanton on IV Solumedol, a strong steroid that had helped ease his respiratory distress. Now he wondered if he should up the dosage, at least for the next few days. "Professor, how does your chest feel? Any problems breathing?"

Stanton coughed again, then shook his head. He cleared his throat, speaking in a slightly slurred voice. "I'm just a little dizzy."

Bernstein nodded, relieved. "That's because of the morphine. How about your thigh? Are you experiencing any pain?"

"A little. And it itches. A lot."

Bernstein nodded again. The morphine would keep the pain to a minimum, as the temporary transplant helped the burned area heal enough to allow a matched graft. The itching was a little uncommon, but certainly not rare.

"I'll up the morphine a bit, to take care of the pain. The itchiness should go away on its own. Now let me take a look at the dressing." Bernstein leaned forward and gently pulled Stanton's smock up, revealing the man's left thigh. The area of the transplant was covered by rectangular strips of white gauze. The gauze started just above his kneecap and ran all the way to the inguinal line, where the thigh met the groin.

Bernstein gently lifted a corner of the gauze with a gloved finger. He could just make out one of the small steel staples that held the transplanted skin in place. The skin was whitish yellow, and clung tightly to the nerveless subdermal layer underneath. "Everything looks fine, Professor. Just fine."

Bernstein pulled the hospital smock back down over the gauze. He decided he could ignore the itchiness, unless it got worse. Bernstein was slightly more concerned about something he had noticed a few hours ago, when he had checked on his sleeping patient for the first time since the transplant procedure.

"Professor Stanton, would you mind turning your head to the side for a moment?" Bernstein walked to the top of the hospital bed and leaned forward, staring at the skin on the back of Stanton's neck.

The small, circular rash was still there, just above Stanton's spine. Thousands of tiny dots, a blemish no more than a few inches in diameter. Some sort of local allergic reaction, Bernstein supposed. Nothing dire, but something he would have to keep his eye on.

Bernstein stepped back from the hospital bed. "You try and get some more sleep, and I'll have Teri up your morphine. I'll be back to check on you in a few hours."

Bernstein gave Teri the morphine order, then headed out of the private-care room, closing the heavy wooden door behind him. He turned an abrupt corner and entered a long hallway with white walls and gray carpeting. At the end of the hallway stood a coffee machine beneath a large scheduling chart.

He paused at the coffee machine, taking a foam cup from a tall pile by the half-filled pot. He poured himself a cup, noticing with a sideways glance that the hospital seemed quieter than usual, even for a Sunday afternoon. He knew there were three other doctors wandering the private-care hallways, and at least a dozen nurses. But at the moment, he was alone with his coffee, his patient, and his thoughts.

He took a deep sip, feeling the hot liquid against his tongue. Not hot enough to burn, to sear skin and cauterize vessels, but hot enough to spark his synapses, to send warning messages to his brain. A little hotter, and his brain would send messages back: Escape the heat before it has a chance to damage and destroy. A little hotter still, and there would be no time for messages. Perry Stanton probably never felt the steam—even now, his pain had nothing to do with the burned area, which had no surviving nerves. It had to do with the steel staples that held the temporary graft in place. But in a few weeks, the staples and the pain would disappear. The professor would leave Jamaica Hospital with little more than a scar and the memory of a wonderful plastic surgeon.

Bernstein smiled, looking up at the scheduling chart above the coffee machine. Then his smile disappeared as he ticked off the rest of his afternoon. A lift at four, a breast consult at five, a liposuction at five-thirty. All elective procedures. Bernstein sighed, taking another deep sip of coffee.

He was about to refill when a sudden scream ripped through the hallway. Bernstein's eyes widened as he realized that the scream had come from Perry Stanton's room.

He whirled away from the coffee machine. As he rushed down the hallway, the scream still echoed in his ears. A female scream, filled with terror. Bernstein had never heard anything like it before.

He reached the end of the hall and turned toward Perry Stanton's room. The heavy wooden door was still shut, and there were sounds corning from the other side: the splintering of wood, the crash of breaking glass, the thud of heavy objects slamming to the floor. Bernstein swallowed, glancing back down the hall. He could hear voices from around the next bend, and he knew that a dozen nurses, techs, and doctors would be there within the next few seconds. But from the sound of things, Perry Stanton and his nurse might not survive that long.

Bernstein was about to step forward when something hit the door hard, near the center, and the wood buckled outward. Bernstein jumped back, terror rushing through him. The door was made of heavy oak; what could have hit it hard enough to buckle the wood? He stared, waiting for the door to crash open.

It never happened. Seconds passed in silence; then there was the sound of running feet, followed by a loud crash. Bernstein overcame his fear and dived forward, his hand reaching for the knob.

The door came open, and Bernstein stopped. He had never seen such devastation before. The metal-framed hospital bed had been bent completely in half, and there was a huge tear down the center of the mattress. The television set lay on the floor, its screen cracked and smoking. Both picture windows had been shattered, and shards of glass littered the floor. My God, Bernstein thought, what could have done this? Some sort of explosion? And where was Perry Stanton? Then Bernstein saw the IV rack embedded halfway into the plaster wall to his left. His head swam, and he took a slight step forward.

His foot landed in something wet. He looked down, and a gasp filled his throat. There was a kidney-shaped pool of blood beneath his shoes. It took him less than a second to follow the blood back to its source.

Teri Nestor was lying halfway beneath the warped hospital bed, her legs twisted unnaturally behind her body. Both of her arms looked broken in numerous places, and her uniform was drenched in blood. Bernstein was about to check her vitals when his gaze slid up past her contorted shoulders.

His knees weakened, and he slumped against the nearest wall, covering his mouth. Still, he could not tear his eyes away from the sight.

It was as if two enormously strong hands had grabbed Teri Nestor's skull on either side—and squeezed.

TWO

Fox Mulder pressed a soggy hotel towel against the side of his jaw as he lowered himself onto the edge of the imitation Colonial-style bed. Most of the ice had already melted through the cheap cloth, and he could feel the cold teardrops crawling down the skin of his forearm. He lay back against the mattress, listening to the bray of the television in the background, letting the monotonous voices of the CNN anchormen mingle with the dull throbbing in his head. *A wonderful end to a wonderful afternoon.* He ran his tongue around the inside of his mouth and grimaced at the salty taste. Dried blood, mixed with the distinct, gritty flavor of processed cow manure. Well, he thought to himself, it could be worse. The bastard could have had good aim.

Mulder closed his eyes, massaging the ice-filled towel harder against the knot of muscle just below his lower gum line. He could still see the shovel flashing toward him, and the crazy glint in the Colombian's eyes. A few inches higher, and the shovel would certainly have cracked his skull open. Mulder only wished his partner, Dana Scully, hadn't cuffed the man so quickly after he had wrested the weapon away. A good, long scuffle would have given Mulder a chance to pay the Colombian back for the blow. And for the wild-goose chase that had led them to the deserted barn in the first place.

Still, Mulder had to admit, it wasn't entirely the Colombian's fault that he and Scully had spent the last two weeks wandering through upstate New York on what should have been a DEA assignment. Carlos Sanchez couldn't have known about the reports of mutilated livestock that had trickled in to the FBI over the past few months, or about the resulting case file that had been dropped on Mulder's cluttered desk in the basement of the Hoover Building—partly because the case's bizarre focus seemed to fit with Mulder's obsession with the unexplained, and partly because no other agent wanted to investigate a bunch of dead cows.

Sanchez couldn't have known about these things—because in truth, the case had had nothing to do with mutilated livestock. Mulder should have known from the beginning that the case had not been a bona fide X-File. Thirty-two cows with scalpel wounds across their abdomens was a cliché, not a paranormal mystery.

Mulder had not seen the clues until too late. When Scully had discovered evidence of old stitches beneath the wounds of the most recently mutilated cows, he should have begun to suspect something. Then, when he and Scully had determined that all the mutilated cattle had originated in the same breeding ranch just outside of Bogota, he should have made the final connection.

But it wasn't until he had stumbled into the abandoned barn on the back lot of Sanchez's farm that he had realized the truth. He had stared at the eviscerated carcasses piled high in the center of the barn, and the bloody, sealed bags of white powder drying in the hay—and the lightbulb had finally gone on. Bandez had been using the cows to transport cocaine into the U.S. The abandoned barn was a drug depository, with distribution routes leading straight down I-95 into Manhattan.

Before Mulder had finished digesting his discovery, Sanchez had come at him with the shovel. A minute later he had been lying on top of the Colombian in a pile of dried manure, while Scully made the arrest. He had nursed his aching jaw in silence during the winding ride back to the hotel, avoiding Scully's eyes. He hadn't needed to see her expression—he knew what she was thinking. Yet another debunked mystery, a mirage with reason at its core. Of course, it was her job to think that way. That's why she was there in the first place—to expose the scientific, rational truth behind Mulder's supposed enigmas. Sometimes even her silence was as subtle as a shovel to his jaw.

He heard the shower go on in the adjacent room and groaned, lifting himself back to a sitting position on the edge of the bed. His athletic, six-foot frame ached from a combination of exhaustion and frustration. He ran his free hand through his dark hair and tried to chase the fog out of his tired hazel eyes. It was almost time to leave. He and Scully had a long drive back to the airfield in Westchester, and if they were going to catch the last commercial flight back to Washington, they would have to break more than a few speed limits along the way. Of course, that was one of the perks of having federal plates and FBI badges. *Somebody else handled the speeding tickets.*

Mulder removed the soggy towel from his jaw and let it drop to the ugly beige carpet. The cramped hotel room stared at him, four white plaster walls glowing in the light of the twenty-inch television set. Aside from the television, the room contained a redwood dresser that was supposed to look like an antique, a desk with a fax machine and a telephone, and a closet Mulder had filled with blue and gray suits. Mulder's travel bag was under the desk, and his gun and badge were next to the phone, the straps of his shoulder holster trailing down behind the fax machine, swinging in the refrigerated breeze from the baseboard vents. Home on the road, another variation on a theme. Mulder and Scully had been there a thousand times before.

Mulder was about to get up and start packing his suits when something on the television screen caught his eye. He paused, momentarily forgetting the throb in his jaw. A reporter with frosted blond hair was speaking into a microphone as she wandered through what looked to be a hospital hallway. Behind her was a spiderweb of yellow police tape. Even through the tape, Mulder could make out the disaster scene in the room on the other side of the hallway; the torn, blood-spattered mattress, the IV rack sticking straight out of the wall, the destroyed, overturned television set, the shattered picture windows—and most disturbing of all, the strange indentation in the center of the half-open wooden door. It was the indentation that had caught his attention in the first place—because it seemed somehow familiar. Something he could almost place.

"The sheer violence of yesterday's tragedy has shocked local authorities," the CNN reporter droned into her microphone, "and a borough-wide search for Professor Stanton is presently in full swing. Still, this is little comfort to the family of nurse Teri Nestor…"

The picture on the screen changed as the reporter continued on, and Mulder found himself staring into a pair of intelligent blue eyes. The man in the enlarged photograph looked to be about fifty years old, with thinning brown hair and slightly oversized ears. Even from the cropped photo, Mulder could tell he was a small man; the angled tips of his shoulders barely made an impression through his professorial tweed jacket, and his neck was thin and roosterlike, devoid of muscle.

As the CNN reporter dribbled out sketchy details about the diminutive professor and the horrible murder of the young nurse, Mulder's thoughts swept back to the moment in the barn when the Colombian swung at him with the shovel. He remembered the violent glint in the Colombian's eyes. Then he looked again at Professor Stanton's photo. He was still staring at Stanton's kind blue eyes when the picture on the television changed again.

This time he was looking at a close-up of the destroyed hospital room. The mattress, the IV rack, the broken television set, the shattered windows—and the marred, half-open door. He took a step closer to the screen, hunching forward, his eyes focused on the strangely shaped indentation in the wood. Suddenly, he realized what he was looking at.

An imprint of a human hand, set a few inches deep into the heavy oak. Palm wide-open, fingers splayed outward. Mulder's eyes widened, as a question struck him. *What kind of force would it take to make an imprint of a hand in a heavy oak door?*

He turned and looked at the open door to his hotel-room closet. As the CNN report ended and the frosted blond reporter was replaced by an over-weight sportscaster, Mulder crossed to the closet and placed his hand flat against the cold wood. He gently slapped the door, keeping his fingers stiff. Then he slapped it again, this time hard enough to send shivers back into his elbow. He lifted his hand and looked at the wood. Nothing, of course.

His mind felt suddenly alive; this was the feeling he hadn't gotten with the mutilated cows, the driving sensation that had earned him the nickname "Spooky" in the basement hallways of the Hoover Building. To anyone else, the scene held nothing more than a pair of kind blue eyes, a demolished hospital room, and a mark on a wooden door. But to Fox Mulder, it was like cocaine in his veins. These unexplainable details carried the scent of an X-File.

He quickly moved to the small desk in the other corner of the hotel room and reached for the phone. He dialed the number for the New York FBI office from memory, and spoke quietly to the operator, detailing the request he wanted forwarded to the NYPD homicide division in charge of the Stanton investigation. Then he replaced the receiver and made sure his fax machine was in the autoreceiving mode.

He crossed back to the closet door, pausing along the way to retrieve the soggy towel he had dropped on the floor by the bed. He wrapped the towel around his open right hand and stood facing the unmarked wood.

He shut his eyes, drew back-and slammed his right hand into the center of the door. There was a sharp crack, and Mulder grimaced, the muscles in his forearm contracting. He pulled back and saw fractures in the surface of the wood, expanding outward from the point of impact. The cracks were notice-able—but nothing like the deep indentations he had seen in the CNN report. And even with the towel, his entire arm ached from the collision with the wood. He tried to imagine each finger in his right hand hitting with enough force to leave a dent.

A sudden knock interrupted his thoughts, followed by a muffled female voice. "Mulder? Is everything okay?"

Mulder quickly crossed to the hotel-room door and undid the latch. Dana Scully was standing in the narrow hallway, her rust-colored hair dripping wet. She was wearing a dark suit jacket open over an untucked white button-down shirt, and it was obvious she had dressed quickly. Her usually precise and formal appearance seemed momentarily frayed—from the drops of water that glistened against the porcelain skin above her collarbone, to the concerned look in her blue eyes. Although her hands were empty, Mulder could see the bulge of her holstered Smith & Wesson service revolver under the left side of her jacket; no doubt, had he delayed answering the door, she would have entered the room barrel first. "What's going on in here? It sounded like someone was brawling with the furniture."

Mulder smiled. "Not the furniture. Just the closet door. Sorry if I interrupted your shower." Scully stepped past him into the room. She smelled vaguely of honeysuckle, and there were still flecks of shampoo caught in the lilting arcs of her hair. She stopped in front of the closet door and took in the cracked dent in the center of the wood. Then she glanced at the wet towel still wrapped around Mulder's right hand. "That's an interesting way to ice a swollen jaw."

Mulder had almost forgotten about his injury. The swelling and the pain no longer seemed to matter. "Scully, how often do patients try to kill their doctors?"

Scully raised her eyebrows. Her body had relaxed, and she was working on the top two buttons of her white shirt. She stopped in front of the television set, the glow reflecting off her high cheekbones. "Mulder, we need to get packed and on the road if we're going to make it back to Washington tonight."

Mulder shrugged, then returned to his line of thought. "A patient wakes up from an operation, vulnerable, drugged up, exhausted—and the first thing he does is erupt in a violent rage. How often, Scully? Rarely? Almost never?"

Scully was looking at him intently. She recognized the familiar gleam in his eyes. But Mulder could tell—she didn't know where it was coming from, or why it had to happen here, in the middle of nowhere. It was late, she was tired, and perhaps a little frustrated from the long days they had spent on a case that had turned out as mundanely as she had expected. Certainly, she was ready to get back home to her apartment and what little life she had beyond the enveloping reach of her job. "What are you getting at, Mulder?"

Before Mulder could answer, a high-pitched warble reverberated through the room. The fax machine coughed to life, and Scully turned, startled. She watched as the pages began to slip quietly into the receiving bin. "Did someone kill a doctor?"

Mulder followed a few paces behind as she crossed to the fax machine. "Not exactly. A nurse named Teri Nestor. But he did more than kill her. He destroyed his recovery room. He shoved an IV rack through the wall. Then he put his right hand two inches into a heavy oak door."

Scully lifted up the first three pages and began to leaf through them. Mulder could see her analytical mind going to work as she read the preliminary forensic evaluation he had requested from the homicide investigation. As for himself, he didn't need the details to get himself inspired; his obsessive curiosity was already aroused. "They had the man's picture on CNN, Scully. A small, gentle-looking professor. The kind of guy who gave me better grades than I deserved in college because he didn't want to hurt my feelings."

Scully continued to read the pages coming out of the fax machine as she spoke from a corner of her pursed lips. It was obvious she had little interest in a case that had seemingly materialized out of nowhere. "People kill for many reasons. Sometimes they kill without reasons. And we both know that size doesn't matter. The human body can perform miracles of violence— when properly provoked. Drugs, fear, pain, adrenaline; all of these things can incite impressive acts of violence. And all of these things are closely associated with hospital stays. This looks like a local homicide investigation, not a federal case—"

Scully paused midsentence. Mulder noticed the sudden creases that appeared on her forehead. He looked at the page at the top of the pile in her hands and saw what appeared to be some sort of medical chart. The page was split into a dozen categories, with lists of numbers and long paragraphs of medical terminology. Mulder had only a rudimentary knowledge of medicine, and the numbers and paragraphs made little sense to him; but Dana Scully was an experienced physician. Before joining the FBI she had completed a residency in forensic pathology and had an expert's grounding in biology, physics, and chemistry. It was the initial reason she had been chosen to act as a foil to Mulder's fantastic quests. It was also part of the reason she had grown into much more than a foil; her rational, systematic approach often functioned as the perfect complement to Mulder's brash and impulsive investigative style.

"What is it?" Mulder asked, trying to read her unreadable eyes. He had requested the entire NYPD case file, and he had no way of knowing what Scully had stumbled upon.

"It's the preliminary autopsy report on the murdered nurse," Scully responded. "There's obviously been some sort of error."

Mulder waited in silence, as Scully continued reading the report. Finally, she looked up from the pages in her hands. "According to this autopsy report, Teri Nestor's skull was crushed with the approximate force of two vehicles moving at more than thirty miles per hour."

Mulder felt a chill move down his back. His instincts had been correct. Despite Scully's reservations, he had a feeling they weren't heading back to Washington just yet.

THREE

Two hours later, Dana Scully watched her own reflection shimmer against the steel double doors of a carpeted elevator, as glowing circular numbers ticked upward above her head. Mulder was standing a few feet to her left, testing his jaw with his right hand as his left foot tapped an incomprehensible rhythm against the elevator floor. Behind him, a medical student in blue-green surgical scrubs leaned heavily against the back wall, his eyes half-closed from exhaustion. Scully knew exactly how he felt. *The whole world dancing on your shoulders, and all you want to do is sleep.*

She threw a glance at Mulder, noticing the energy behind his features, the bright glint in his hazel eyes. Scully was amazed at her partner's stamina; it was already close to ten, and they had both been on their feet since 6:00 a.m. Scully felt ready to collapse—and she wasn't the one who had been hit in the face with a shovel less than eight hours ago.

Then again, she knew how Mulder's mind worked. The minute he had turned his focus toward the potential X-File, everything else had vanished. He had barely spoken about anything else during the long drive into Manhattan, and Scully had been forced to shelve the follow-up paperwork on the Bandez drug-distribution ring—at least for the time being. Inside, she doubted that she and Mulder would be sojourning in Manhattan for more than a few days. The findings reported in Teri Nestor's autopsy file were alarming—but Scully had no doubt there would be a simple, scientific explanation.

"Miracles of violence," Mulder intoned, continuing the suspended line of conversation they had begun in upstate New York. "Interesting choice of words, Scully. You think Perry Stanton is a miracle worker?"

"It was a figure of speech," Scully responded, keeping her voice low to prevent the med student in the back of the elevator from overhearing. "I merely meant that the human body is capable of amazing feats of strength. I'm sure you've heard the stories of mothers lifting cars to save their babies, or karate experts breaking bricks with their bare hands. There's no real magic involved; it's actually a matter of pure physics. Angles of impact, leverage, velocity. At the right speed, even a drop of water can shatter a brick."

"Or a skull?" Mulder asked, as the elevator slowed to a stop.

Scully shrugged. She had been mulling this over for the past few hours. Her initial shock at the details of the Stanton case had subsided, and she had already begun to analyze the situation as a scientist. "Perry Stanton is significantly bigger than a drop of water. The autopsy report, on its own, is inconclusive. I don't know how her head was crushed with such force—but I do know that it's within the realm of physics."

Before Mulder had a chance to respond, the double doors whiffed open, and Scully stepped out into a long hallway with shiny white walls. Mulder followed a few feet behind, his hands clasped behind his back. "Physics didn't kill Teri Nestor. Neither did a karate expert or a woman protecting a baby."

They turned an abrupt corner and continued down a similar hallway, moving deeper into the recovery ward. The air carried a familiar, antiseptic smell, and the sounds of hospital machinery trickled into Scully's ears: the steady thumping of respirators, the metallic beeps of EKG monitors, the vibrating whir of adjustable hospital beds. The sounds sparked a mixture of emotions in her; she had spent much of her adult life inside hospitals—first during the years of her medical training, then more recently during her near-fatal battle with cancer. As a scientist, she found comfort in a setting guided by the rigid laws of cause and effect. At the same time, she couldn't help but associate her surroundings with her past illness; as she passed the closed doors of a half dozen private rooms, she wondered how many patients were struggling in silence a few feet away, praying for the light of just one more morning.

"Here we are," Mulder interrupted, pointing. "The scene of the miracle."

Scully squared her shoulders as they approached the group of uniformed officers standing in front of yellow police tape. She counted at least three men and two women, all wearing NYPD insignia. One of the officers was interviewing a nurse in a pink uniform, while two others spoke to a young woman in jeans and a white, paint-stained T-shirt. The officers looked up as Scully and Mulder advanced the last few steps. Scully quickly slipped her ID out of her jacket pocket. "FBI. I'm Special Agent Dana Scully, this is my partner, Special Agent Mulder. We're looking for the detective in charge of the Stanton case."

The nearest officer looked Scully over with dark eyes. He was a large man, perhaps six-five, with scruffy black hair and a puggish nose. He gestured with his head toward the yellow tape. The door behind the tape was half-open, and Scully could just make out the hand-shaped indentation in the center of the wood. She kept her eyes on the indentation as she stepped gingerly through a break in the police tape. As she held the tape up for Mulder, he whispered his own evaluation into her ear. "I'd like to see the physics behind that, Scully."

Scully shrugged. "Give me a computer, a forensics lab, and a week—and I'm sure I could show you, Mulder."

They paused in the room's entrance. Scully's gaze was drawn first to the huge sheets of yellow paper taped over the shattered picture windows. To the right of the windows was a contorted steel shelving unit, in front of which sat the upended, demolished television set. The warped hospital bed sat in the center of the room, the torn mattress sticking straight out of the deformed steel frame. Two men in white jumpsuits were leaning over the mattress with handheld vacuums, collecting hair and fiber evidence. Behind the hospital bed, another man focused an oversize camera on the IV rack still embedded in the wall. His flash went off like a strobe light, making the scene even more gritty and at the same time surreal, like a Quentin Tarantino movie. Scully was surprised to see the forensics people still collecting evidence so long after the incident, another testament to the bizarre nature of the crime. The degree of damage was exactly as Mulder had described it from the CNN report. It certainly didn't look like the work of one man.

Scully felt Mulder's hand on her shoulder and followed his eyes to the floor just in front of where they stood. The chalk outline started somewhere beneath a corner of the bed frame, twisting violently through a circular patch of dried blood. *Teri Nestor's blood.*

"Judging from the suits, I presume you're the two FBI agents your Manhattan office warned us about," a gravelly voice erupted from behind the contorted shelving unit. Scully watched as a heavyset woman in a dark gray suit stepped into view. She was quite tall—perhaps six feet—with wide, muscular shoulders and frizzy dark hair. She had a clipboard in her gloved hands, and there were dark bags under her dull blue eyes. "Detective Jennifer Barrett, NYPD."

Scully made the introductions, noting the strength of the detective's handshake: *Those were paws, not hands.* Barrett towered over her concise, five-foot-three frame, and though the detective looked to be in her late forties, she had obviously spent a lot of time in the gym. Her intimidating size was aggravated by her unkempt hair and the largeness of her facial features. Scully wondered if Barrett suffered from some sort of genetic pituitary problem; she could tell from the look on Mulder's face that he was thinking along similar lines.

Scully broke the silence before it became awkward, and after a few pleasantries, turned the focus toward the case at hand. "It's our understanding that Perry Stanton is the only suspect in the murder. Is that based on the forensic evidence?"

Barrett nodded, gesturing toward the two jumpsuited men still huddled over the mattress. "From what we've gathered so far, Stanton was alone with the nurse when the murder took place. According to the plastic surgeon—Dr. Alec Bernstein—they were in the room for less than five minutes, with the door shut, when the violence started. Hair, fiber, and fingerprint surveys concur with Bernstein's story. Nobody entered the room through the door—and the windows are more than twenty feet above the parking lot."

"A long way up," Mulder commented from a crouch in front of the door. "And an equally long way down."

Scully glanced at him. He had his hand out in front of the indentation in the wood, his fingers mimicking the deep marks from a few inches away. Scully turned away from him and watched as Barrett crossed to the shattered windows. The detective pulled up a corner of the yellow paper. "The way down's a lot easier than the way up. The trick is in the landing. Stanton got lucky and hit some shrubs at the edge of the parking lot. We found torn pieces of his hospital smock in the branches, along with more of Teri Nestor's blood. Our manhunt is progressing rapidly through the borough—but so far, we've been unable to pick up his trail."

"So the professor woke up from an operation," Mulder said out of the corner of his mouth. "Tore up a hospital room. Crushed his nurse's skull.

Then fell out of a second-story window into a shrub. And he's still managing to evade a police search?"

Mulder had aimed the question at Scully, but it was obvious from the red blotches spreading across Barrett's face that she had misinterpreted Mulder's tone. She turned away from the window, crossed her thick arms against her chest, and set her mouth in an angry grimace. A heavy Brooklyn accent suddenly dribbled down the edges of her consonants. "Hey, you want to bring in your own forensics people? I'd be happy to hear an alternative story. Because the media's already crawling up my ass on this one. We've got the pathologist redoing the autopsy, we've had the fingerprint team in here a dozen times—and it's still coming up the same. One perp, one dead nurse, one manhunt. And I don't care how fancy you fibbies think you are—you're not going to find anything different."

Scully stared at the woman, stunned by her altered tone. Frustration was one thing—but this was outright hostility. Barrett obviously had issues with control and a temper to match her size. Not a pretty combination. Scully decided to intervene before Mulder could aggravate her further. "We're not here to get in the way of your manhunt, Detective Barrett—just to assist in catching the perp. As for Professor Stanton—is there anything in his history that could explain the sudden outbreak of violence?"

Barrett grunted, her anger slowly diffusing. "Model citizen up until the transplant procedure. No priors, not even a speeding ticket. Married sixteen years until his wife died last February. Teaches European history at Jamaica University, volunteers two days a week at the public library in midtown—an adult-literacy program."

"No history of alcohol or drugs?" Scully asked.

"An occasional glass of wine on weekends, according to his daughter, Emily Kysdale, a twenty-six-year-old kindergarten teacher who lives in Brooklyn. According to Mrs. Kysdale, her father is a shy but happy man. He is most content in the basement library of the university—which is where he got burned in the boiler accident."

"Certainly doesn't fit the psychotic profile," Mulder commented. He was standing by the horizontal IV rack, trying to gauge how deeply it was embedded in the wall. "According to the police report, he is five-four, weighs one hundred and eighteen pounds. Scully, how much do you think this IV rack weighs? Or that mattress?"

Scully ignored Mulder's questions for the moment. She couldn't tell whether he was baiting the detective—or merely curious. She nodded toward the clipboard in Barrett's hands. She recognized the hospital-style pages under the heavy metal clip. "Is that Stanton's medical chart?"

Barrett nodded, her eyes on Mulder as she handed over the chart. "The plastic surgeon—Dr. Bernstein—has gone through this with me a few times already. He says there was nothing medically abnormal about Stanton—and nothing that he thought would have provoked a psychotic episode. But something I've learned working homicide in New York for the past twenty years—people crack for no good reason."

The chart was six pages long, full of scrawled medical descriptions and evaluations. Stanton had arrived at Jamaica's emergency room with a full-thickness third-degree steam burn on his right thigh. He had also been complaining of difficulty breathing, and had been given IV Solumedol, a strong steroid. After his breathing had stabilized, he had been prepped and wheeled into an operating room. Dr. Bernstein had performed an escharo-tomy—cutting away the damaged skin around the burn to prepare it for transplant—and had then attached a section of donor skin over the burn site.

The procedure had gone off without a snag; Stanton had awakened in the recovery room, complaining only of mild discomfort. If all had gone well, the temporary graft would have remained over the area of the burn for two weeks, at which time Stanton would have received a permanent matched graft from another part of his body, most likely his lower back.

Although Scully wasn't a plastic surgeon, there didn't seem to be anything about the transplant procedure itself that would have caused Stanton's violent reaction. But there was something in the chart that struck Scully as a possible explanation.

She moved next to Mulder and showed him the indication on the chart. "Stanton was given a fairly large dose of Solumedol, Mulder. It's an extremely potent steroid. There have been numerous documented cases of patients reacting violently to steroids—sort of an allergic neurological response. Rare, but definitely not unique."

Mulder looked at the IV rack bisecting the air between them. "Steroidal rage? Scully, he was given the Solumedol before the transplant procedure—but didn't explode until hours later."

Scully shrugged. "It doesn't have to be an immediate reaction. The neuro-transmitters build up in the nervous system. The procedure itself could have aggravated his body's reaction—and when the anesthesia from the operation wore off, his psychosis detonated."

Mulder looked skeptical. "Wouldn't Dr. Bernstein have mentioned the possibility to Detective Barrett?"

Barrett was watching them from the window, her arms still crossed against her chest. She coughed, letting Scully and Mulder know she was still in the room. "I'm sure I would have remembered if he had. He's performing a laser surgery at the moment—but you can interview him again when he's finished."

Scully nodded. Mulder seemed dissatisfied with Scully's quick answer to Stanton's psychosis. As Scully watched, he pulled a pair of latex gloves out of his jacket pocket and slipped them over his fingers. Then he placed both hands gingerly against the IV rack. Barrett watched him with a smirk on her oversized lips.

"It's in pretty good. I tried for twenty minutes. I doubt you'll be able to do any better."

Mulder smiled at the challenge, then leaned back, using his weight against the rack. The muscles of his arms worked beneath his dark suit, and his face grew taut, sweat beading above his eyebrows. He tried for a full minute, then gasped, giving up. "I guess neither of us gets to be king."

There was a brief pause, then Barrett laughed. The sound was somewhere between a diesel engine and a death rattle. Scully was glad that Mulder's charm had broken through some of Barrett's hostility. As long as they were going to have to work together, it would help if they could interact in a civil manner. Scully cleared her throat. "As long as we're waiting for Dr. Bernstein—you mentioned Stanton's daughter? Perhaps she can bring us up to speed on Professor Stanton."

Barrett nodded. "Out in the hallway. The pretty thing with the finger paint all over her shirt. She's been here since her father was brought into the ER yesterday morning. She won't go home until Stanton is safely apprehended. Be careful with her; she breaks easily."

Scully inadvertently glanced at Barrett's huge hands. She wondered if Mulder was thinking the same thing. *In hands like those—who didn't break easily?*

"This is all too much to take. You have to believe me, he could never have done this. Never." Emily Kysdale stared into her cup of coffee as the cafeteria traffic buzzed behind her bowed shoulders. Mulder and Scully had chosen the relative anonymity of the cafeteria over the recovery ward, to give the young woman a chance to speak without the obvious presence of the uniformed police officers.

Emily was shaking horribly, and Scully could see the goose bumps rising on the bare skin of her arms. Scully felt the immediate urge to reach across the steel cafeteria table and touch her, to let her know that it would be all right—but she resisted. The truth was, it wasn't going to be all right. Emily's father had murdered a woman about the same age as she, a woman with a child and a husband. Even if the violence was caused by an allergic reaction, or a mental illness, or an uncontrollable fit—it was murder.

"Mrs. Kysdale," Mulder said, his voice quiet as he lowered himself into the seat next to Scully, "we need to ask you a few questions. I know this is hard for you, but we're trying to help your father."

Scully could feel the emotion behind Mulder's near monotone. She knew her partner better than anyone in the world, and she could guess at the thoughts running through his head. Emily was an attractive, fragile woman, with long, brownish-blond hair, a lanky figure, and watery green eyes. Her jeans and paint-splotched T-shirt were rumpled, and it was obvious she had not slept since the incident. Her agony was no doubt triggering something deep inside Mulder—perhaps memories of his own sister. He carried Samantha Mulder like an internal scar, always just below the surface of his skin. The unique circumstances of Samantha's disappearance—and Mulder's belief that she had actually been abducted by aliens—did not disrupt the prosaic and sincere nature of his pain. It was what drove his obsession with the unexplained, and Emily's distress would only solidify his resolve to find the truth—however fantastic that truth turned out to be.

"My father is a gentle man," Emily finally responded, looking directly into Mulder's sympathetic eyes. "He lived for his work, his quiet research. He has never been in trouble before. And he has never complained, never gets angry. Even when my mother passed away."

"Mrs. Kysdale," Scully said, "did your father ever suffer any symptoms that may not have been in his medical chart? Any viral diseases—either recently, or in the past?"

Emily shrugged. "Nothing abnormal. He's had the flu a few times this year. And a bout of pneumonia two years ago. He had his appendix out when I was younger—"

"What about allergies?" Scully was searching, but it was worth a shot. Anaphylactic shock involved the entire neurological system—very similar to a steroid reaction. If Stanton had a history of strong allergies, it might be more evidence for her Solumedol theory.

"Not that I know of," Emily answered. "Dr. Bernstein asked me the same question when they first brought my father into the ER. I had arrived just as they were administering something to help him breathe."

Scully perked up, glancing at Mulder. "The IV steroids."

Emily nodded. "I remembered he had been put on steroids during the bout with pneumonia. He hadn't had a problem with it then, so Dr. Bernstein said it wouldn't be a problem this time either."

Scully leaned back in her chair. She could hear Mulder's shoes bouncing against the tiled floor beneath the table. The new information didn't completely rule out the Solumedol—but it certainly made it less likely. Bernstein probably hadn't mentioned the Solumedol to Detective Barrett because Stanton had been put on it before, without adverse reaction. Still, Scully knew that people could develop sensitivities at any stage in life. Insect bites, shellfish, peanuts—and steroids—had been known to kill people who had never had any problem with these things before. The Solumedol, though more improbable, was still a possibility.

"When you saw your father in the ER," Mulder asked, changing tack, "did anything strike you as abnormal—either in his behavior or his appearance?"

Emily shrugged. "He had that awful burn on his leg. And he was slipping in and out of consciousness. But when he was awake, he seemed normal."

"And after the transplant procedure—"

"I never got a chance to see him after the procedure. I was in the waiting room when I heard what happened. I couldn't believe it. I still don't believe it."

"Mrs. Kysdale," Scully asked, "is there any history of mental illness in your father's family?"

Emily was momentarily taken aback by the question. When she finally answered, she sounded cautious, as if she realized for the first time that she was talking to two FBI agents. "Not that I'm aware."

Scully paused; as helpful as the young woman was trying to be, Emily Kysdale wasn't going to help them understand the cause of her father's violence. It was obvious from Emily's sudden change of tone: in Emily's mind, Perry Stanton was a victim, not a murderer. Scully could tell from the way Mulder was looking at her that he agreed.

Whatever the reason for his explosion, Perry Stanton was a criminal. The cause of Stanton's act was only important insofar as it established culpability. Even if the cause remained a mystery, it would not change the facts of the case, or Scully and Mulder's mission. Their job was to catch the perp who had killed Teri Nestor—and at the moment, the blame still lay solely on Perry Stanton.

"Mrs. Kysdale, do you have any idea where your father might be hiding? Anywhere the police may not know to look?"

Emily's entire body trembled, and she clenched her hands around the foam cup of coffee in front of her. She lowered her head, then took a deep breath and seemed to regain some level of control. "They've been to his apartment, his office, all of his friends' houses. They've scoured the university. They've looked everywhere he used to go—even the cemetery where my mother is buried. But I can't help them find him—because the man who killed that nurse isn't the man I know. My father isn't the man they're looking for."

Scully felt a weight inside her chest, as Emily's grief finally broke through her veil of reserve. Mulder had his reasons for empathizing with the woman's pain—and Scully had her own. *Her sister's murder, her own father's death.* She knew what it was like to lose a family member—and that was exactly what had happened to Emily Kysdale. The Perry Stanton she knew was gone.

Scully reached across the table and touched the young woman's hand. Then she rose, thanking her for her help. Mulder paused for a moment, watching the woman cry over her coffee. Then he followed Scully toward the elevator at the back of the cafeteria, which would take them up to the surgical ward—and Dr. Alec Bernstein. After the double doors slid shut, Mulder spoke softly. "I believe her, Scully. Her father isn't the man we're looking for."

"What do you mean?"

"You heard what she said—he was normal when he was wheeled into the ER. He was normal even after he was given the Solumedol. But he wasn't normal when he woke up after the operation. He should have been vulnerable, groggy, in pain; instead, he was capable of unbelievable violence, of a physical act we can hardly describe, let alone understand."

Scully tried to see the expression on his face, but all she got was his profile. He finished his thought as the elevator slowed to a stop on the fourth floor—the surgical ward. "Scully, something happened during that transplant procedure to change Perry Stanton."

Scully wasn't sure what he meant. "Mulder, the temporary grafting procedure is nearly as common—and certainly as safe—as an appendectomy. And it's mainly localized to the area of the injury—Stanton's right thigh."

But even as she said the words, a thought hit her. The transplant procedure involved Stanton's thigh—but certainly, there was interaction with his bloodstream and his immune system. Perhaps Mulder had a point: It wasn't impossible that Stanton had contracted something from the graft itself. She would have to review the literature—but she was certain she had heard about certain viral diseases being transferred in just such a manner. She believed there had even been cases of cancer being transmitted through grafts—specifically, lymphoma and Kaposi's sarcoma. It was rare, but possible. *The question was, what kind of disease could cause a psychotic episode?*

"Something like meningitis," Scully murmured, as the elevator doors opened. "Or even syphilis. Something that causes the brain to swell and affects the neurological system."

"Sorry?" Mulder said.

"If the temporary graft had been infected with a blood-borne virus," Scully explained, "Stanton could have contracted the disease through the transplant. There are many diseases that could lead to an explosion of violence."

"Scully, that's not what I meant. The violence was beyond the scale of any psychotic episode. Stanton didn't just catch a disease—*he transformed.* Into something his own daughter wouldn't recognize."

Scully knew that the words were more than hyperbole; Mulder's ideas were never limited by the laws of science. But Scully didn't intend to let him lead her toward another of his wild fantasies. At the moment, this was a medical mystery—not a fantasy. *This investigation was on her turf.*

She stepped out into the surgical ward. "Sometimes, Mulder, transformation is the nature of disease."

Scully peered through the glass window with genuine interest as Dr. Bernstein carefully navigated the laser scalpel across the surface of the patient's exposed lower back. The tool was pen-shaped, attached to a long, articulated steel arm containing a series of specially made mirrors. The arm jutted out of a four-foot-tall cylindrical pedestal next to Bernstein. A pedal by his heel allowed him to control the strength and depth of the beam.

"Interesting juxtaposition," Mulder said, his face also close to the window as he surveyed the small operating room. "A five-thousand-year-old art transcended by a five-year-old technology."

Scully watched as the red guiding light traced the edges of the enormous tattoo in the center of the patient's bared back. The red light shivered in the thin white smoke rising from the patient's skin as the outer cells vaporized under the intense, pinpoint heat. The patient was awake, but felt no pain; a local anesthetic was enough to deaden the area of skin beneath the tattoo. In fact, the procedure could hardly be considered surgical. Aside from Bernstein and the patient, there was only one nurse in the small operating room, monitoring the patient's blood pressure.

"I guess nothing is truly permanent anymore," Mulder continued. "Anything can be erased."

"It's a tattoo, Mulder. Hardly the raw material for a philosophical analogy." Scully controlled a wince as the laser seared away a beautifully drawn lion's head, then moved backward through a flowing brown mane. She thought about the image on her own lower back: a snake eating its own tail, the result of a moment of whimsy in a Philadelphia tattoo parlor during a solo field trip a little over a year ago. Sometimes, she hardly even remembered the tattoo was there; other times, she found comfort in the idea that she had found the courage to do something so unlike her perceived exterior. She was a skeptic—but never a conformist. *That was another part of what made her and Mulder work so well together.*

The procedure went on for another ten minutes; when Bernstein was finally finished, he looked up from behind his surgical mask and noticed Mulder and Scully on the other side of the viewing windows. He said something to the nurse, then shut off the laser scalpel and stepped away from the patient. As the nurse moved to wrap the sensitive area of skin in antiseptic gauze, Bernstein yanked his gloves off and crossed to the OR door. He pulled his mask down as he moved into the outer scrub room where Scully and Mulder waited.

"I'm guessing you're not here for a tattoo removal," Bernstein said, tossing his gloves into a nearby trash can as he crossed toward the double sinks at the other end of the rectangular room. He was a tall man, slightly overweight and balding, but with handsome features and remarkably sculpted hands. He was wearing surgical scrubs and matching green sneakers. "So how can I help you?"

"Sorry to interrupt, Dr. Bernstein. I'm Agent Scully, this is Agent Mulder. We're here about Perry Stanton."

Bernstein nodded as he ran water over his hands, carefully massaging his long fingers. Scully could see the troubled look in his eyes and the slight tremble in his round shoulders. "I'm not sure what I can tell you—beyond what I've already told Detective Barrett. Mr. Stanton was fine when I left him in the recovery room—and when I returned, he had already gone through the window. It was a horrid sight—something I don't think I'll ever forget. Or understand."

Scully could sense the disbelief in his words. He reminded her of the many physicians she had known during her medical training; he didn't quite know what to do with an experience beyond his expertise. Scully tried to make her voice as sympathetic as possible. "It's certainly a mystery, one we're working to understand. Along that line, I noticed that you ordered IV Solumedol to help Mr. Stanton's breathing—"

"Yes," Bernstein interrupted with a wave of his hand. "Detective Barrett called to ask me about the Solumedol after you spoke to her downstairs in the recovery room, and you're right, I should have made it clear to her in the first place. Personally, I don't believe the steroid had anything to do with his violent outbreak. He'd been put on similar steroids fairly recently—a bout with pneumonia, I believe it was three years ago. It's extremely unlikely that he would have developed such a fierce allergy in such a short time."

Scully nodded; she had asked the necessary question and had gotten the expected answer. The Solumedol still wasn't ruled out, but as Bernstein had said, it was an extremely doubtful cause. They needed to search for other answers.

Mulder took the cue as Bernstein turned away from the sink and grabbed a towel from a rack attached to the wall.

"Dr. Bernstein, what about the grafting procedure itself? Do you remember anything abnormal about the operation? Anything out of the ordinary?"

Bernstein vigorously dried his hands. "I've performed hundreds of similar transplants. There were no hitches at all. The procedure took less than three hours. I cleaned up the burn, flattened out the donor skin, and stapled it onto Stanton's thigh—"

"Stapled?" Mulder asked, his eyebrows raised. Scully could have answered, but she deferred to the plastic surgeon.

"That's right. The device is very similar to an office stapler—except the staples are heat sterilized and made out of a specially tempered steel. Anyway, I stapled the skin over Stanton's burn and wrapped the area in sterile gauze. I would have changed the dressing in three days—then removed the graft in about two weeks, when he was ready to accept a permanent transplant."

Scully had explained the procedure to Mulder after reading about it in Stanton's chart, but it was good for both of them to hear it again from the expert. After all, it had been a long time since Scully's surgical rotation, and she had spent only a few months studying transplant techniques.

"So the donor skin is only temporarily attached?" Mulder asked.

"That's right. The temporary graft isn't matched to the patient—because it's intended to be rejected after a period of a couple of weeks. Then we graft a piece of the patient's own skin over the wound. In the meantime, the donor skin decreases the risk of infection, and it helps indicate when the burned area is ready to accept a permanent transplant."

"If the temporary graft isn't matched to the patient," Scully interrupted, "what precautions are taken to make sure the graft isn't carrying something that could infect the patient with a communicable disease?"

Bernstein glanced at her. She could tell from his eyes that he had already given this some thought. Stanton had been his patient—and as unfair and illogical as it seemed, he was partially blaming himself for what had happened. "Truthfully, very few—on my end. The skin is transported to us from the New York Fire Department Skin Bank; the bank is responsible for growing bacteriological cultures, and for checking the skin for viral threats. But they themselves are guided by the medical histories provided by the donor hospital. There are a million things to look for, and it's impossible to cover every possibility. If a donor dies from something infectious, they don't accept his skin. But if he dies from an unrelated cause—and happens to be carrying something, there is a chance that it will be passed on through a transplant."

"A slim chance?" Mulder asked. "Or a serious risk? And could any of these transferred diseases affect a patient's brain? Enough to send him into a violent rage?"

"I would call it extremely rare," Bernstein replied, leaning back against the sinks. "But possible. For instance, undetected melanomas have been known to spread through transplant procedures. They grow downward through the dermis and into the blood vessels, then ride the bloodstream up into the brain. And certain viruses could jump through the lower layers of the epidermis into the capillaries; herpes zoster, AIDS, meningitis, encephalitis— the list is endless. But most of these diseases would have shown up in the donor patient. Such microbe-laden skin would never have been harvested in the first place."

Not on purpose, Scully thought to herself. But people made mistakes. And microbes were often tricky to spot, even by trained professionals. A million viruses could live on the head of a pin—and viruses were extremely hard to trace, or predict. "After the procedure, did Stanton exhibit any symptoms at all? Anything that might hint at a viral or bacteriological exposure?"

Bernstein started to shake his head, then paused. "Well, now that I think about it, there was one thing. But I can't imagine how it could be connected to such an outbreak of violence."

He rubbed the back of his neck with his hand. "A small circular rash. Right here, on the nape of his neck. It looked like thousands of tiny red dots. I assumed it was some sort of local allergic reaction—like an insect bite, only a bit larger. I'm not a specialist, but I can't think of any serious disease that presents like that."

Scully wasn't sure if the strange rash was connected—but she filed it in her memory. She was trying to think if there was anything else they needed from the plastic surgeon when Bernstein glanced at his watch, then let out a ponderous sigh. "I'm sorry, but I've got an emergency surgery scheduled to start in a few minutes. If you have any more questions, I'll be in OR Four down the hall. And if there are any breakthroughs in the case, please let me know. Teri Nestor was a personal friend—but Mr. Stanton was my patient. I know it's foolish, but I feel like I failed him somehow."

He excused himself and exited the scrub room. When he was gone, Scully turned toward her partner. Though it was now well past one in the morning, she felt a new burst of energy. Based on what they had learned in the past few hours, she felt sure they were moving closer to solving the case. It was an intriguing difference in personality: Mulder grew electric when faced with a mystery—while Scully was excited by the prospect of a solution. "I think it's pretty clear what we need to do next. While Barrett continues her manhunt, we have to track down the donor skin and find out if it was infected with anything that could have caused Stanton's violence. And we have to act quickly—we don't want any more of that harvested skin ending up on other patients."

Mulder didn't respond right away. Instead, he moved to the sink. Bernstein had left the faucet loose, and a stream of drops spattered quietly against the basin. Mulder reached forward and held his palm under the stream. "Scully, do you really think a virus can explain what happened in that recovery room?"

Scully paused, staring at the back of his head. They had both seen the same evidence, participated in the same interviews—but it was obvious their thoughts were moving in two different directions. *As always*. "Absolutely. Dr. Bernstein corroborated my theory. It's possible that Stanton caught something from the graft—something that could have affected his brain, and his person-ality. Once we track down the graft, we'll be able to find out for sure. And then we'll know how to deal with Stanton when we find him—and what precautions Barrett's officers need to take in bringing him in."

Mulder shut off the sink and dried his hand against a towel from the rack. "A microbe, Scully? That's how you want to explain this?"

"You have a better explanation?"

Mulder shrugged. "Whenever doctors run into a mystery they can't explain, they blame a microbe. Some sort of virus or bacteria, something you can see only through a microscope—or sometimes not at all. If you ask me, it's a convenient way of thinking. It's a scientist's way of pretending to understand something completely beyond his grasp."

"Mulder," Scully interrupted, frustrated, "if you have a better plan of action, I'm listening."

"Actually, I agree with you, Scully. We need to track down that graft. We need to find out what changed Perry Stanton into a violent killer. But I'm not so sure we're going to need a microscope to find what we're looking for."

Scully watched as he moved toward the door. "What do you mean?"

He glanced back at her. "It would take a pretty big microbe to crush a nurse's skull."

As Scully followed Mulder out into the hallway, she failed to notice the tall, angled man watching from the now-deserted operating room on the other side of the viewing windows. The man was dressed in a blue orderly uniform, most of his young face obscured by a sterile white surgical mask. His skin was dark and vaguely Asiatic, his black hair cropped tight beneath a pink anti-septic cap.

His narrow eyes followed the two agents until they disappeared from view. Then he reached into his pocket and pulled out a tiny cellular phone. He dialed quickly, his long fingers flickering over the numbered keys. A few seconds later, he began to speak in a low, nasal voice. The words were foreign, the tone rising and falling as the syllables chased one another through the thin material of the young man's surgical mask. There was a brief pause, then a deep voice responded from somewhere far away. The young man nodded, slipping the phone back into his pocket.

An anticipatory tremor moved through his shoulders. Then he grinned, his high, brown cheeks pulling at his mask. For him, the task ahead was more than an act of loyalty, or of duty—it was an act of nearly erotic pleasure.

His fingers curled together as he followed the two FBI agents out into the hospital hallway.

FOUR

Forty minutes later, Mulder shivered against a sudden blast of refrigerated air as he pursued the ample ME's assistant into the cold-storage room lodged deep in the basement of New York Hospital. It had been a relatively easy task to trace the skin graft back across the Fifty-ninth Street Bridge, but in the process he and Scully had run into the first sign that their investigation was not going to take a simple route—and at the same time, the first strike against Scully's growing belief that the case would soon be explained by a conventional medical query. As Mulder had predicted, Stanton's transformation would not be solved through a quick trip to the New York Fire Department Skin Bank.

"Missing," Scully had said, hanging up the phone as she and Mulder had exited through the Jamaica Hospital ER. "They're unable to locate the six trays of harvested skin from which Stanton's transplant was taken."

The administrator of the skin bank had assured Scully that the FBI would be notified the minute the missing trays had been located. He had also insisted that this was not a matter for alarm; the grossly understaffed and underfunded skin bank dealt with hundreds of pounds of skin on a weekly basis, and mistakes like this were not uncommon. And although he hadn't been able to find the harvested skin, the administrator had been able to give Scully the name and location of the donor corpse: Derrick Kaplan, a current inhabitant of the New York Hospital morgue.

While Scully had accepted the administrator's comments at face value, Mulder had felt his own suspicions rising. He didn't believe Stanton's behavior could be explained by any known microbe—and the missing skin seemed like too much of a coincidence. Still, he and Scully had been left with a lead to follow. While the NYPD continued their search for Perry Stanton, he and Scully would follow the skin graft back to its source.

After Scully had hung up on the skin bank, she and Mulder headed directly to New York Hospital. After a short stop at the front desk, they had located the ME's assistant half-asleep in his office two elevator stops below the ER. Short, unkempt, with curly blond hair and thick lips, Leif Eckleman was exactly the type of man Mulder had expected to find working the basement warren of a hospital morgue. Likewise, Mulder hadn't been surprised to see the neck of a half-empty fifth of Jack Daniel's sticking out of the open top drawer of the man's cluttered desk; alcohol went with the territory. Mulder tried not to pass any judgments.

"The two kids from the med school got here late Friday night," Eckleman mumbled, as he crossed the rectangular room to a set of filing cabinets standing flush against a cinder-block wall. His words were slightly slurred, but Mulder couldn't tell whether it was the alcohol or the fact that he had just been awakened from a deep sleep. "Josh Kemper, and a buddy of his—Mike, I think his name was. Used OR Six, upstairs in the surgical ward. Cleaned it up pretty good afterward. No complaints from the surgeons."

Eckleman pulled open one of the cabinets and began to search through the manila folders inside. Mulder watched Scully amble across the center of the room, her low heels clicking against the tiled floor. Her gaze was pinned to the wall of body drawers that stretched the entire length of the room. Mulder counted at least sixty—and he knew that this was only one of eight similar cold-storage rooms that made up the hospital's morgue. Even so, New York was a big city; hard to find an apartment, and probably equally hard to find a drawer.

"Here it is," Eckleman finally said, lifting a folder out of the cabinet. "Mike Lifton, that was the other kid's name. Both were in their third year at Columbia Med. They signed for your donor at three-fifteen a.m. Derrick Kaplan—Caucasian, mid-thirties, blond hair, blue eyes. Locker fifty-two."

Mulder was already moving toward the wall of drawers. Scully turned to Eckleman as Mulder scanned the numbered labels. "May I take a look at the file?"

Eckleman shrugged, handing her the folder. "Not much to see. Kaplan came into the ER complaining of chest pains, then died in the ICU of an aortic dissection. Had a donor card in his wallet. The skin boys got to him first, because the van from the eye bank got stuck in the mess on the FDR Drive. The big accident, you know. Collected seven bodies that same night, but only Kaplan had the vulture card."

"The vulture card?" Mulder heard Scully ask, as he finally located the steel drawer with the number fifty-two written in black Magic Marker across its cardboard label. "Is that what you call it?"

"You work down here, you get to be fairly morbid. In my opinion, there's nothing wrong with vultures. Damned efficient birds—they don't let anything go to waste. Not so different from the harvest teams, when you think about it."

Mulder wasn't sure he wanted to think about it. He grasped the handle beneath the numbered label and gave it a gentle yank. The drawer rolled outward with a mild, metallic groan. Mulder paused for a brief moment, then glanced at Scully. She was engrossed in Kaplan's folder. Mulder cleared his throat.

Scully looked up. Mulder pointed, and Scully's face momentarily blanched. The locker was empty. She quickly turned toward the ME's assistant. "Mr. Eckleman?"

Eckleman rubbed the back of his hand against his thick lips. Then he laughed, nervously. "Whoops. That's not good. You sure that's number fifty-two?"

Mulder rechecked the label. "Is there any chance the body was moved?"

Eckleman quickly crossed back to the file cabinet. "Shouldn't have been. But sometimes they get switched around. Especially on the busy nights. And Friday was a busy night. Seven bodies, like I said. And there's always a chance the kids put the body back in the wrong drawer."

He paused as he pulled a handful of files out of the cabinet. He began reading to himself, and Mulder crossed back to Scully, who was still looking through Kaplan's chart. "Anything significant, Scully?"

Scully shook her head. "Nothing noticeably viral. But we need the body to know for sure. Or, at the very least, a sample of his skin."

Mulder felt his adrenaline rising. First the missing trays at the skin bank— now the missing body. Then again, he didn't want to get ahead of himself. He glanced at the flustered, semidrunk ME's assistant; certainly, the man could have gotten the drawers mixed up.

"I'll check the other six that came in that night, and all of the empties. Odds are, we'll find our boy." Eckleman tucked the files under his right arm and hurried back to the storage wall. He began pulling open the drawers, humming nervously to himself as he worked. Mulder could tell the man was embarrassed. Perhaps this sort of thing had happened before. "Locker fifty-three is all right. Angela Dotter, one of the victims from the accident. Got a steering wheel right through her rib cage. Fifty-four and fifty-five look good, too. And here's another from the accident. Kid can't be more than twenty…"

Eckleman paused midsentence as the next drawer slid to a stop by his knees. He began mumbling, half to himself. The stack of files slipped out from under his arm, the pages fanning out as they hit the floor. "What the hell? This can't be right."

He reached forward, and the sound of a zipper reverberated through the room. Mulder moved forward as Eckleman hovered over the toe tag. "Derrick Kaplan. It's him. But this doesn't make any sense."

Mulder looked over the man's shoulder. The corpse was staring straight up, blue eyes wide-open. Mulder heard Scully exhale as she joined him next to the drawer. It was immediately obvious what was wrong with the body.

Derrick Kaplan wasn't missing any skin.

"Damn it," Eckleman said, again rubbing at his watery lips. "The little vultures must have skinned the wrong body."

"The wrong body?" Mulder asked.

Eckleman didn't respond. Instead, he bent down and began pulling open the bottom row of steel drawers: the empties. Each time he stared into another blank box, he cursed, each profanity more colorful and obscene than the last. "Can't blame this on me. No way can they blame this one on me. I didn't skin anybody. I wasn't even in here—"

Eckleman stopped, as he suddenly realized that he had reached the last drawer. "Well, son of a bitch. Unless they double-stacked it in one of the other drawers, it's not here."

Mulder looked at the row of open, empty drawers. He didn't know whether to be frustrated or intrigued. "Can we at least figure out which body is missing?"

"Probably the one that was originally slated for this drawer," Scully answered, pointing at Derrick Kaplan's corpse. "Didn't you say this was supposed to contain one of the seven brought in that same Friday night?"

Eckleman nodded, returning to the stack of folders he had dropped on the floor. His stubby fingers were trembling by the time he found the correct file. "A John Doe. Brought into the ER from the scene of the big car accident I told you about. Also blond, blue eyes—but mid- to early twenties. With a dragon tattoo on his right shoulder."

"Was the John Doe a trauma victim?" Scully asked. "Did he die from injuries sustained in the accident?"

There was a pause as Eckleman read through the file. Then he shook his head. "Actually, no. There were no signs of external injuries. The two interns who worked on him didn't know what killed him. He was scheduled for an autopsy at eight tomorrow morning."

Mulder and Scully exchanged looks. *A missing body, an autopsy less than five hours away.* The trail was getting more circuitous—and, despite their efforts, they still hadn't found an ounce of the original skin.

"I better go report this," Eckleman grumbled, heading toward the door. "Administrator Cavanaugh is going to have my ass for dinner. But I tell you, it isn't my fault. I didn't skin the wrong damn body."

Mulder watched him trudge out of the cold-storage room. Then he turned back toward Scully. She was looking through the John Doe's file. "These are big institutions we're dealing with—and it's very late at night. At two in the morning, things get lost. At eight in the morning, they tend to turn up. In the meantime, we have to speak to those med students. If something was transmitted from this John Doe to Perry Stanton—they're the obvious link."

With the John Doe's body missing and Perry Stanton still at large, the two med students were the *only* link. Mulder felt his pulse quicken as he glanced back at the empty storage drawer. Somehow, he found the steel rectangle more foreboding without a corpse inside. It was like digging in a graveyard and finding an empty coffin.

Despite Scully's words, Mulder did not believe the missing corpse was a coincidence. He was certain the John Doe's skin held the key to the tragedy in the recovery room. And he would not accept any explanation that did not expose what had really happened to Perry Stanton—no matter how rational it seemed.

FIVE

The broken glass glittered like an emerald carpet in the triangle of light, jagged green shards spread out across the black asphalt in the shape of a bloated July moon. Perry Stanton stood beneath a streetlamp at the edge of the curb, his thin shoulders heaving under his torn hospital smock. He could see bottle necks sticking out of the glass like phallic icebergs, the trace of an alcoholic's rage or a fraternity party that had overflowed into the dark Brooklyn streets. Stanton's mind whirled as the shards grew in his eyes, huge green thorns taunting him, daring him, begging him forward.

Suddenly, his mouth opened and a dull moan escaped into the night air. His bare feet curled inward against the sidewalk, and his spine arched back. The muscles in his thighs contracted, and he threw himself forward, diving headlong into the street. His body crashed down into the glass, and he rolled back and forth against the shards, his arms flailing wildly at his sides.

He could hear the hospital smock tearing, the glass crunching under his weight. *But he felt no relief.* The glass did nothing to stop the horrible itching. The shards should have ripped through his skin as easily as it ripped his thin smock—but the terrible crawling continued unabated. It felt as though every inch of his body was infested with tiny, hungry maggots. It was so bad he couldn't keep a single thought in his head, so bad that every command from his brain seemed to echo a thousand times before it found his muscles.

Lying flat on his back in the broken glass, he slammed his palms over his eyes and an anguished wail bellowed through his lungs. What the hell was going on? *What the hell was wrong with him?*

He felt something warm and wet against his closed eyelids, and he quickly pulled his hands away. His eyes opened, and he stared at his blooded palms. He quickly crawled to his knees, more tears burning at his eyes.

Even through the intense itching, he could still remember the woman's head between his palms. He could still hear the bones in her skull crunching as he had squeezed. He could still see her eyes bulging forward, the blood spouting out of her ears, her cheeks collapsing into her mouth—he could still feel her die between his palms. *Between his palms.*

And worst of all—he could still feel the rage emanating through his body. The rage that had overwhelmed his thoughts and his brain and made him leap up out of the hospital bed. The fierce anger that had started somewhere in the itching: an unbelievable heat, burning downward through his flesh. It had felt as if his veins and arteries had caught fire, his insides boiling under the intense flame.

Then the fiery rage had entered his skull and everything had gone white. He had seen the nurse leaning over him, and it was like looking through someone else's eyes. The rage had taken over, and he had grabbed her head in his hands.

After that, it had all happened so fast. The itching, burning rage had made him destroy everything within reach. And then a single thought had twisted through the agony—*escape.*

His head jerked back and forth as new tremors spiraled through his body. He shook the broken glass out of his smock as he staggered to his feet. Escape. Somewhere in what was left of his mind, he knew the command was not his own. It also came from somewhere in the horrible itching. *Somewhere in his skin.*

He had no choice but to obey. When he resisted, the itching only grew worse. He stumbled forward, his bare feet crunching against the glass. He wasn't sure where he was—but he knew he wasn't far ahead of the sirens or the shouts. He couldn't let them catch him. He knew what the itching and the rage would make him do if they caught him. *More skulls between his palms—*

A sudden screech tore into his ears, and he looked up through blurry eyes. He saw the yellow hood of a taxicab careening around the comer ahead of him, the startled driver leaning heavily on his horn. There was a brief, frozen second—then the front fender glanced against Stanton's left thigh.

The cab skidded to a sudden stop. Stanton looked down and saw the mangled hood still partially wrapped around his leg. He stepped back, his entire body beginning to shake. The itchiness swept up through his hips, across his chest, to his face. *No, no, no!*

The driver-side door came open, and a tall, dark-skinned man leapt out. He saw Stanton, and shouted something. Then he noticed his ruined cab. His eyes widened. "Mister, are you okay?"

Stanton's skin caught fire, and his mind turned white. He tried to fight back, tried to stop the commands before they reached his muscles. He tried to picture himself as he was before—gentle, kind, weak. He tried to focus on the image of his daughter, beautiful Emily, and his life before the transplant.

But the thoughts vanished as the maggots crawled through his skin. He lurched forward, his face contorted. The taxi driver stepped back, fear evident on his face. Somehow, Stanton managed to coax a single word through his constricted throat.

"Run."

The taxi driver stared at him. Stanton held out his hands as he staggered forward. The driver saw the blood on his palms, and realization hit him. He turned and ran screaming down the dark street.

Stanton stumbled after him, the single word still echoing through his brain. *Run. Run. Run!*

SIX

The sky had turned a dull gray by the time Mulder trudged up the stone steps that led to the arched entrance of the J. P. Friedler Medical Arts Building on the Columbia Medical School campus. He didn't need to look at his watch to know it was close to five in the morning; his muscles had that strange, wiry feeling that meant he was nearing twenty-four hours without sleep. He realized that he and Scully couldn't keep going like this for much longer. But until Perry Stanton was taken into custody, they were in a fierce race with the mysteries of the case.

Just minutes ago, Scully had phoned him with the latest news from Detective Barrett's manhunt. Stanton had wrecked a taxicab somewhere in northern

Brooklyn, and the driver had narrowly escaped with his life. The search was now focused on a five-block area, and Barrett was certain they would find Stanton within the next few hours.

Which meant it was all the more important for Mulder and Scully to keep barreling ahead. They had split up to reach the two med students as quickly as possible. Even so, Mulder prayed they would be quick enough. If Scully's theory was right, there was a dangerous, diseased man still raging through the streets of New York. And if Mulder was right—a disease didn't begin to explain the phenomenon they were chasing: *something that could transform a quiet, gentle professor into a vicious killer, with inhuman strength.*

It took Mulder a few minutes to reach the anatomy lab on the third floor of the vast stone building. He was out of breath as he exited the marble stairwell, and he paused for a moment by the double doors that led into the lab, leaning against the wall. He could see the cavernous room through a small circular window in the center of one of the doors. The room was close to fifty yards deep, rectangular, and contained two parallel rows of waist-high steel tables. Mulder could vaguely make out the bulky shapes on the tables; the bodies were wrapped in opaque plastic bags, and there were bright red plastic organ trays on carts attached to the stainless steel blood and fluid gutters that ran the length of each table. Mulder swallowed back a gust of nausea as he pressed his palm against one of the double doors. It was more physiological than mental; he had seen many dead bodies in his career, and he was not squeamish by nature. But the clinical nature of the anatomy lab triggered something primitive inside of him. Here, the human body was nothing more than meat. There was no room for philosophies of life, soul, or even God. Here, humanity was defined by bright red plastic organ trays and stainless steel fluid gutters.

He pushed the door inward and stepped inside the long laboratory. The strong scent of formaldehyde filled his nostrils, and he fought the urge to gag. His gaze roamed over the cadaver tables, jumping from bag to bag. Then he caught sight of his quarry, standing alone near the back of the room, bent over an open body bag. From that distance, Michael Lifton appeared to be tall, gangly, with short reddish hair and youthful features. He was wearing crimson sweatpants and a gray athletic T-shirt beneath a white lab coat. There was a thick book open on the cart at the head of the dissecting table, and Lifton seemed completely entranced by the open body in front of him. He didn't look up until Mulder was a few feet away, and when he did his eyes seemed glazed, far away. His eyelids drooped unnaturally low, and there was a slight tremble in his upper lip. *Was he ill? Or simply tired?* Lifton coughed, as the color returned to his cheeks. "Excuse me, I didn't hear you come in. Can I help you?"

Mulder shifted his gaze from Lifton's face to his bloodied gloves and the scalpel balanced between his thumb and forefinger. "Hope I'm not interrupting. I'm Agent Fox Mulder from the FBI. I tried your dorm room, but there was no one home. Your next-door neighbor told me I could find you here."

Lifton didn't move for a full second. Then he carefully set the scalpel down next to the open book. Mulder read the large-print heading that stretched across the two open pages: PARTIAL BOWEL RESECTION. His gaze slid to the open lower abdomen on the dissecting table. It looked like a bag over-flowing with black snakes. Mulder quickly moved his eyes back to the young man's face.

"The FBI?" Lifton asked, his eyes wide. "Am I in some sort of trouble?"

Lifton coughed again, and the sound was coarse, vaguely pneumatic. Mulder saw beads of sweat running down the sides of the kid's face. It looked like he was running a fever. "Are you feeling all right, Mr. Lifton?"

"Call me Mike. I've got a bit of a cold. And I've been working in here most of the night; the formaldehyde screws with my allergies. What is this about?"

Lifton's hands were trembling, and Mulder could not tell if it was nervous-ness or another sign of fever. He thought about Scully's microbe theory. Any minute, she would be arriving at Josh Kemper's apartment; would he be suffering from the same flu-like symptoms as the kid in front of Mulder? Were the symptoms just the beginning of something worse? "I need to speak to you about a skin harvest you and Josh Kemper performed last Friday night."

Lifton took a tiny step back from the dissecting table, his hands falling to his sides. "Did we do something wrong?"

Mulder could tell from Lifton's tone that he was not as surprised by the idea as Mulder would have suspected. "Well, we think you and Josh might have harvested skin from the wrong body."

Lifton closed his eyes, his cheeks pale. "I knew it. I thought something was wrong. But Josh insisted. He said Eckleman probably blew the tags. He said the body was close enough to the chart. Blond hair, blue eyes, no outward trauma."

"So what made you suspect it was the wrong body?"

Lifton sighed, using his forearm to wipe the sweat off of his forehead. "First, there was the tattoo. A dragon, on his right arm. And then there was the strange rash."

Mulder's instincts perked up. He remembered what Bernstein had told him about the rash on Stanton's neck. "What sort of rash?"

Lifton turned his head to the side. He pointed to a clear area of skin, right below his hairline. "Here, on the nape of his neck. A circular eruption, thousands of tiny red dots. Josh told me it was nothing—and it probably was. But if the guy had been in the ICU, it would have been in the chart. A straight shot from the ER, maybe it would have been missed. But not in the ICU."

Mulder nodded. The John Doe had gone straight from the ER to the morgue. Derrick Kaplan had spent time in the ICU before he died. Mike Lifton was a smart kid—but he had allowed himself to be bullied into performing the harvest, even though he had suspected it was the wrong body.

"After you finished the harvest," Mulder continued, "what did you do with the body?" Lifton looked at him. "What do you mean? We returned it to the morgue, of course."

"To the same locker?"

"Yes. Fifty something. Fifty-two, or fifty-four. I've usually got a good head for numbers, but I've been practicing in here nearly every night this week. Lack of sleep, you know. Screws with everything."

Mulder nodded. He hoped it was just lack of sleep that was affecting Mike Lifton. But he had to cover the bases—to prove or disprove Scully's theory. "We need to get you checked out by a doctor right away. There might be a chance that you caught something from the John Doe."

Lifton's face turned even paler. "What do you mean? Did he die from some sort of infectious disease?"

"We're not sure. That's why we need you to get checked out."

Lifton's entire body seemed to sag as he thought about what Mulder was saying. Then Mulder noticed another tremor move through Lifton's upper lip, followed by a heavy cough. "I think we should get you to an ER right away. Just to be sure."

He didn't know whether or not it was evidence of Scully's theory—but suddenly, he didn't like the way Mike Lifton looked. It seemed as though

Lifton's condition was deteriorating as he watched. As the student hastily repacked the open cadaver with trembling hands, Mulder hoped that Scully had gotten to the other med student in time.

\\\\\\\\\\\\\\\\

"Mr. Kemper! Mr. Josh Kemper!" Scully's voice reverberated off the heavy apartment door. "This is Agent Dana Scully of the FBI! The building superintendent is here with me, and if you don't answer the door, I'm coming inside!"

Scully could feel her heart pounding as she waited for a response. She glanced at the short, stocky man in the untucked gray T-shirt standing next to her, and nodded. Mitch Butler began fumbling through his oversize ring of apartment keys. Scully cursed to herself as she watched the super's stubby fingers struggling to find the correct one. *This was taking too long.*

Scully had called for an ambulance when she had first arrived at the Columbia-owned apartment building and found Kemper unresponsive to her attempts to get inside his room, but she knew it would be another few minutes before the paramedics would arrive. She had already lost valuable time rousing the grubby superintendent out of his apartment on the first floor; the trip upstairs to the fourth floor had been insufferably long.

"Here it is," Butler finally exclaimed, holding up a copper-colored key. "Apartment four-twelve."

Scully took the key from him and went to work on the lock. The door came open, and she rushed inside. "Mr. Kemper? Josh?"

The living room was small and almost devoid of furniture. There was a gray couch in one corner, facing a small television sitting on top of a cardboard box. A picture of two dogs wearing tuxedos took up most of the far wall, and dirty laundry invaded every inch of bare floor. Scully was reminded of her own med-school days—when even an hour for laundry would have been a gift from heaven. She had been a kid, like Josh Kemper—just trying to survive.

"How many rooms?" she shouted back toward the super, who was still standing in the entrance, breathing hard from the four flights of stairs.

"Just this one, the kitchen, and the bedroom. Through that door."

Scully headed for the open doorway on the other side of the living room. She passed through a small hallway and found herself in a tiny kitchen: porcelain-tiled floor, chipped plaster hanging from the walls, a light fixture that looked like it was older than the electricity that powered it. There was an open container of orange juice on a small wooden table in front of the refrigerator. *Otherwise, no signs of life.* Scully rushed across the kitchen and through another open doorway.

She nearly tripped on a pile of bedding, catching her balance against a large wooden dresser. There was a bare mattress in the middle of the room, covered with medical texts and science magazines. But still no sign of Kemper.

"The bathroom," she shouted back over her shoulder. "Where is the bathroom?"

"Off the bedroom."

Scully cursed, her eyes wildly searching the cramped space—then she saw the closed door, directly on the other side of the dresser, partially obscured by a sea of hanging colored beads. She shoved the beads aside and yanked the door open.

There he was. Shirtless, lying facedown on the floor, one arm crooked around the base of the toilet, the other twisted strangely behind his back. Scully dropped to her knees and put her hand against the side of his neck. No pulse. His skin felt warm to the touch, but it had a waxy appearance and had turned a blue-gray color. No doubt about it—Josh Kemper was dead. She gently unhooked his right arm from around the base of the toilet, noting the lack of rigor mortis in his joints. She used her weight to roll him over.

His eyes and mouth were open, an anguished expression frozen on his boyish face. His face and bare chest were slightly purple where the blood had pooled beneath his skin. Scully reached forward and pushed an errant lock of blond hair out of the way, then pressed her index finger against Kemper's cheek. The pressure caused a slight blanching of the area beneath her fingertip. When she moved her hand away, the discoloration returned. *Early nonfixed lividity.* That meant he had been dead less than four hours—perhaps three, but no less than two. From the anguished look on his face and the awkward positioning of his body, Scully guessed he had convulsed or stroked out. But there were no obvious wounds to his head or face, so it wasn't the fall that had killed him. It had been something else—something inside his body.

Scully had a sudden thought and tilted Kemper's head to the side. But the back of his neck looked clear. No red dots, no circular rash. Still, that didn't mean it wasn't the same disease that had sent Stanton into a violent fit.

She sighed, rising to her feet. She turned to the sink and turned the water faucet as hot as it would go. Then she grabbed a bar of soap and began working on her hands. She knew she had taken a risk by coming into the room at all—but she doubted it was anything airborne or even contagious to the touch. Airborne viruses deadly enough to kill a man Kemper's age were extremely rare—and if the John Doe had been an airborne carrier, there would have been many more victims by now. That meant it was probably something blood-borne. Those at risk included the interns who worked on him, the two med students, perhaps the paramedics who had brought him in, and Bernstein's surgical team at Jamaica Hospital.

"Ms. Scully?" The super's hack crept at her from somewhere in the bedroom. "Is everything all right in there?"

"Mr. Butler," Scully responded, "I need you to go downstairs and wait for the ambulance. I'll join you in a moment."

Scully listened as Butler's plodding footsteps trickled away. Then she finished washing her hands and pulled her cellular phone out of her breast pocket. Her shoulders sagged as she dialed Mulder's number. He answered on the second ring.

"Mulder, where are you?"

His voice sounded tinny through the phone's earpiece. "The ER at Columbia Medical School."

Scully glanced at the body on the bathroom floor. She could hear sirens in the distance, but she wasn't sure if it was through the phone or through the thin apartment walls. "I take it you found Mike Lifton?"

"Scully, he's not doing so well. When I brought him in, he was complaining of flu-like symptoms. Now the doctors tell me he's fallen into some sort of coma."

Scully nodded to herself. The symptoms fit with her earlier hypothesis. A viral threat, something that could cause cerebral swelling. The sort of disease that could also cause a psychotic fit and deadly convulsions. "We're going to have to notify the CDC immediately. They're going to want to track down anyone who's had serious contact with the John Doe. And they'll need to act fast—obviously, the infected subjects' conditions deteriorate rapidly."

Mulder went silent on the other end of the line. Scully wondered if he was still resisting the idea that a microbe was behind the case. Or had the med student's illness finally convinced him that a disease linked all of the elements of the case together? Then again, she doubted he would give in to reason that easily.

Finally, Mulder's voice drifted back into Scully's ear. "So Josh Kemper's pretty sick, too?"

Scully took a deep breath. "He's dead, Mulder. Whatever the John Doe was carrying—it progresses quickly."

"And you think it's the same disease that made Stanton kill Teri Nestor?"

"Yes. Like I said before, it's some sort of microbe that causes a swelling of the brain. And Mulder, whatever Stanton was capable of in that recovery room or out in Brooklyn this morning—I don't think he'll be putting up much of a struggle in a few more hours. This is a fast-acting disease."

Scully heard voices out in the apartment. The paramedics had arrived. "I'm heading back to the hospital with Kemper's corpse. I'll find out what this microbe is, Mulder. And after I do—we're both going to get some sleep."

For once, there was no argument from the other end of the line.

Less than ten minutes later, the EMS team had secured Josh Kemper's body in the back of the ambulance. As the double doors clicked shut and the heavy vehicle pulled away from the curb, a solitary figure stepped out from the narrow garbage alley that ran next to the apartment complex. His glossy, sable hair was hidden beneath a baseball cap, and his lithe body swam beneath a long, tan overcoat. His hands were buried in his deep pockets, with just a hint of white latex showing at the wrists.

He watched the ambulance roll quietly down the deserted street. He could just make out the red-haired FBI agent sitting in the front passenger seat. Her pale cheek was pressed up against the side window, a look of sheer exhaustion in her blue eyes.

The young, caramel-skinned man thought about the discovery Agent Scully was about to make. Certainly, it would chase the fatigue out of her pretty features. The young man smiled, carefully removing his right hand from his pocket. He twirled a tiny plastic object between his gloved fingers. The object was thin and cylindrical, the shape of a miniature ballpoint pen. The young man touched a plastic button on the edge of the object, and there was an almost imperceptible click.

A shiver of excitement ran through the young man's skin as he carefully examined the three-inch-long needle that had appeared out of one end of the object. The needle was thinner than a single hair, its point significantly smaller than a single human pore. At certain angles it seemed invisible—too small, even, to displace particles of the early-morning air.

So much more subtle than a gun or a razor blade—and at the same time, so much more effective. The young man closed his eyes, reliving the moment just five hours ago—the tiny flick of his wrist, the unnoticed brush of a stranger in a crowded late-night subway car. Then the second moment ten minutes later, in passing on the stairwell of the Columbia Medical School anatomy lab. A thrill pulsed through his body, and he sighed, wishing he could have watched the results himself.

But despite his love for his work—he had to adhere to at least a semblance of professionalism. His gloved finger again found the plastic button, and the tiny needle retracted. He carefully slid the pen-shaped object back into his pocket and strolled toward a blue Chevrolet parked a few feet down the curb.

The two FBI agents would be returning to New York Hospital. If he hurried, he could arrive just a few minutes behind Josh Kemper's ambulance. He had to stay close to the two agents—on the off chance that they were smarter than expected. If they started to get too close again—the young man smiled, fondling the pen-shaped object inside his pocket. Professionalism, he reminded himself. Still, he could feel the warm, almost sexual anticipation rising through his body.

In his heart, he hoped agents Scully and Mulder were absolutely brilliant.

SEVEN

Four hours later, a triangle of harsh orange light ripped Mulder out of a deep sleep. He sat straight up on the borrowed hospital cot in the cozy third-floor intern room, blinking rapidly. Scully came into focus, her red hair highlighted by the high fluorescent beams from the hospital hallway. She was wearing a white lab coat and gloves, and there was a plastic contact sheet in her right hand. The look on her face was somewhere between disbelief and dismay.

"We've found our microbe," she said, crossing into the room and dropping heavily onto the edge of Mulder's cot. She tossed the contact sheet onto his lap. "These are shots of the isolated virus taken by an electron microscope.

The sample came from cerebrospinal fluid tapped from a postmortem lumbar puncture on Josh Kemper."

Mulder looked at the contact sheet. He could see a tiny pill-shaped object multiplied a half dozen times in the different-angled shots. It looked so small, so innocuous.

"They woke me with the results from the lab twenty minutes ago," Scully continued. "But I went down there myself to check what they were saying. Because it's pretty hard to believe."

"What do you mean? Scully, what am I looking at?"

Scully took a deep breath. "Encephalitis lethargica. We've matched it up through the CDC's computer link. They're sending a specialist here this afternoon to confirm the diagnosis. But the EEGs and CT scans coincide. There isn't any doubt."

Mulder wasn't sure if he had heard of the disease before. "So it's a form of encephalitis? Isn't that similar to what you predicted—a disease that could cause brain swelling?"

"It is a strain of encephalitis—but Mulder, it's not at all what I expected."

Mulder waited for her to continue. She was staring at the contact sheet in his hands as if the pill-shaped virus might crawl right out into the intern room.

"Mulder," she finally stated, "there hasn't been an outbreak of encephalitis lethargica since 1922. The virus you're looking at has rarely been seen outside a laboratory in over seventy-five years."

Mulder raised his eyebrows. No wonder he hadn't recognized the disease. "How does this virus manifest? Does it fit the symptoms we've seen?"

Scully shrugged. "The disease starts similarly to the more common strains of encephalitis; causing fever, confusion, sometimes paralysis of one side of the body—and in some cases, convulsions, psychosis, coma, and death. But lethargica also induces incredible fatigue, which is why it's sometimes called the 'sleeping sickness.'"

Mulder nodded. He remembered Mike Lifton's drooping eyelids and glazed eyes. But Scully still hadn't told him anything that could explain how Stanton could have reacted with such inhuman strength. And there were still other inconsistencies that were not yet explained. "Scully, what about the circular rash on both the John Doe and Perry Stanton? Could that have been caused by encephalitis lethargica? And why wasn't it present on either of the med students?"

"The rash might be unrelated—perhaps a separate infection, one that's more difficult to catch. Remember, the med students did not have the same level of contact with the John Doe as Perry Stanton. Stanton got a slab of his skin stapled onto an open burn."

"That still doesn't explain Stanton's violent explosion. Neither of the med students reacted violently—"

Scully waved her hand. "Viruses can affect different people differently—and especially a virus like this. Lethargica attacks areas of the brain, as well as the meninges, the brain's covering. There's no way to predict how a specific individual might react. During the 1922 outbreak, forty percent of those infected died. This time, we're looking at a much worse percentage—but at least the disease has been confined to two people who had close contact with the carrier. That means the virus hasn't changed its mode of transmission."

Mulder pushed his feet off the side of the cot, stretching his calves. He was becoming more alert by the second. He hoped Scully was as refreshed as he was—because in his mind, the case was nowhere near over. "You mean it's blood-borne. Like HIV."

Scully nodded. "That's right. It's transmitted only by blood-to-blood contact. The 1922 version was also sometimes carried by mosquitoes, or biting flies—but that's extremely rare."

Mulder reached out and touched one of Scully's gloved hands. "Scully, both the med students were wearing gloves. How do you explain the blood-to-blood contact? A swarm of mosquitoes in the ER?"

"Latex gloves aren't a hundred percent protection. And a skin harvest is a messy procedure."

Mulder still thought it was remarkable that both students had become so sick—so quickly—while the plastic surgery team, which had worked invasively with the harvested skin, had remained healthy. "It doesn't seem right, Scully. Even if the virus links the med students to the John Doe—we don't have any proof of a link to Perry Stanton. If Dr. Bernstein was sick, maybe—but he's not. The only thing that connects the John Doe to Perry Stanton is the circular red rash."

Scully rose slowly from the cot and took the contact sheet out of Mulder's hands. "We won't know for sure until we've got Stanton in custody. I've explained the precautions to Barrett—gloves, surgical masks, limited contact—and she assures me they'll have him within the next hour. By then, the investigator from the CDC will be here to confirm the lethargica, and this tragedy will come to a close."

Mulder ran his hands through his hair. He didn't say what he was thinking—that this tragedy was nowhere near the final act. Likewise, he doubted even Barrett would have such an easy time bringing in a man who had shoved an IV rack a few feet into a hospital wall. Instead, he pressed his fingers against the side of his jaw, testing the stiffness. Then he rose from the cot. "Personally, Scully, I don't think the CDC is going to make this case any clearer. You can follow the lethargica angle as far as it's going to go; in the meantime, I'm going to find out more about our John Doe."

Scully raised her eyebrows. "Mulder, we've already gone through his chart a half dozen times. The interns didn't know what was wrong with him—and until we've got a body and an autopsy, there isn't much more we can discover about his death."

Mulder headed toward the door. "I'm not interested in how he died, Scully. I want to know how he ended up in a medical chart in the first place."

Mulder arrived in the ER just as the trauma team crashed through the double doors. He counted at least six people crowded around the stretcher: the burly chief resident, a surgical consult in green scrubs, two nurses—and at the tail end of the stretcher, two thickset men in dark blue paramedic uniforms. The smaller of the two was holding a bottle of blood above his shoulder as he raced to keep up with an IV tube attached to the patient's right thigh. The larger paramedic had an object delicately braced in both arms; the object was oddly shaped and wrapped in white gauze.

Mulder remained a few feet away as the stretcher passed through the center of the ER, toward the elevators that led up to the surgical ward. He caught a glimpse of the patient between the shoulders of the two nurses: thin, tall, writhing in obvious pain, tubes running out of every inch of bare skin. At first, Mulder couldn't tell what was wrong—then his gaze moved to the tourniquet wrapped tightly around the man's left forearm. He watched as the surgical consult took the gauze-covered object out of the paramedic's arms and lifted a corner of the white cloth.

"It's in pretty good shape," he overheard the paramedic say. "Landed under the track, which protected it from the train. Think you can reattach?"

The consult nodded, then continued on with the stretcher. The two paramedics stood watching as the rest of the group raced toward the elevator. Mulder shivered, then took his cue and stepped forward.

"Luke Canton?" he asked. He had gotten the name from the ER dispatcher. Canton and his partner had brought the John Doe into the hospital on the night of the thirteen-car accident. The dispatcher had described him as one of the best in the city.

Canton turned toward Mulder, looking him over. The paramedic was six feet tall, with wide shoulders, and reddish scruff covering most of his square jaw. He yanked off his bloody gloves and tossed them to the floor. "That's right. This is my partner, Emory Ross."

"I'm Agent Mulder from the FBI. That was a hell of a scene. Is he going to be all right?"

Canton shrugged. His face was grim, but there was something bright, deep in his blue eyes. This was his high—the adrenaline pump of medicine at its most raw. "Lost a fight with a subway car. But if the surgeon's any good, he'll keep his hand."

Mulder noticed splotches of fresh blood all over Canton's uniform. "Covered you pretty good. Was it like this with the John Doe you brought in last Friday night?"

Canton shook his head. "I figured that's what this is about. Heard through the grapevine he might have been carrying some sort of virus."

"It's a possibility," Mulder responded. He knew the CDC would probably be rounding up all of the possible risk candidates by midafternoon. He gestured at the blood on Canton's uniform. "Most likely something blood-borne."

Canton shrugged. "Well, then we're in the clear. The John Doe had no external wounds. No blood at all. Actually, we hardly had any contact with him—other than lifting him into the ambulance and working the Velcro straps. He didn't crash until he was in the ER. We didn't even intubate—the two ER kids took over, and we went back into the field. "

Mulder moved his gaze from Canton to his partner, Emory Ross. Neither one looked the least bit ill. "And you're feeling all right? No signs of fatigue or fever?"

Canton smiled. "I worked out for two hours this morning. Hit two-fifty-five on the bench. What about you, Ross?"

Ross laughed. He seemed much younger than Canton, and it was obvious from his eyes that he looked up to his wide-shouldered partner. "I played pickup basketball for forty minutes before our shift started. Didn't score very many, but I got a handful of rebounds."

Mulder felt relief, and a tinge of excitement. He wasn't a doctor, but it sounded as though the two paramedics were not going to be felled by lethargy. Mulder walked with the two men toward the changing rooms located in the corner of the ER, just beyond the admissions desk. "I was told the John Doe was brought in from the scene of a car accident on the FDR Drive?"

"That's right," Canton answered. "Found him unconscious but stable in the breakdown lane, maybe twenty feet from the lead car. We already had one of the drivers in our wagon—a woman with a pretty severe impact wound to her chest—but we decided to risk a second scoop. There were other ambulances on the scene, but the accident was as bad as it gets. Many more bodies than wagons."

Mulder watched as Canton grabbed a passing nurse by the waist. The young woman laughed, wriggling free. Mulder could tell that Luke Canton was well liked. "And he remained stable en route to the hospital?"

"Unresponsive," Canton answered. "But certainly stable. We doubted he was even involved in the accident itself; there were no exterior wounds you would expect from someone thrown from a crash, no bruises or cuts or anything—"

"Except the slight scratch," Ross chimed in as they reached the curtain that led to the changing room. "A circular little thing on the back of his neck. But it didn't look like much—I don't remember if we even bothered to tell the interns when we brought him in."

Canton tossed a glance at his partner, who quickly looked at the floor. Canton looked at Mulder. "It was a crazy night. We had to get right back to the accident for the walking wounded. I'm sure the kids spotted the little scratch on their own. Anyway, I doubt it had anything to do with why the guy died."

They pushed into the small changing room. There was a row of metal lockers on one side, three parallel wooden benches, a closet full of hangers, and a door that led to a shower room. Canton and his partner moved to their adjacent lockers. As they changed into clean uniforms, Mulder contemplated what Canton had just told him. His thoughts kept coming back to the scene of the accident, where the John Doe had been picked up. If he wasn't thrown from one of the cars, why was he unconscious in the breakdown lane, twenty yards away?

When the paramedics had finished changing, Mulder turned to Luke Canton. "I've already spoken to the dispatcher, and if it's all right with you, I'd like to borrow an hour of your time."

Canton raised his eyebrows. Then he glanced at his partner and shrugged. "If you've got the authority, I've got the hour."

Mulder grinned. He liked Luke Canton's attitude.

EIGHT

The ambulance seemed to float through the three lanes of New York traffic as Luke Canton navigated between the moving bumpers with an expert's grace.

Only twice did he have to reach above the dashboard and flick on the colored lights. Mulder watched the chain-link snakes of traffic slither by beneath the high side windows, amazed at how the cars stayed so close together at such high speeds. *Coordinated chaos.*

"It's not surprising when they crash," Canton said, reading his mind. "It's surprising when they don't. You know how many people die every year in cars?"

Mulder had an idea, but said nothing. Canton pointed to a dented pickup truck weaving through the lanes two cars away. "More than fifty thousand. About the same number as die from AIDS. Funny thing. We're quite willing to give up casual sex. But give up casual driving? No way."

Mulder felt his seatbelt tighten as Canton punched the brake, and the ambulance suddenly veered to the right. Mulder watched the guardrail grow closer as they rolled to a stop in the breakdown lane. The lane was actually more like a gully, stretching fifty yards along a curved section of rail. It was half the size of a regular lane, a few bare feet wider than the ambulance itself. Mulder saw a glimmer of broken glass a dozen yards ahead and the twisted remains of a rear bumper in the grass just on the other side of the railing. Other than the bumper and the glass, there were no visible signs of the accident. "Looks like it's been cleaned up pretty well."

"Should have seen it right after the accident. The whole Drive was cluttered with metal and glass. All three of these lanes were closed. The cars looked like crumpled socks. You couldn't even tell the front few apart. Found one woman sitting in the driver seat of the car ahead of her."

Mulder opened his door and stepped down onto the asphalt. The noise from the cars whizzing by was nearly deafening. A warm breeze pulled at his jacket, and the heavy smell of exhaust filled his nostrils. Canton came around the front of the ambulance and pointed to the area directly ahead of them. "The accident scene started here, with the last car up against the railing just ahead. A few more were piled together in the center of the highway; then the bulk of the accident was about thirty yards up. The lead car—a BMW roadster—was upside down and crumpled pretty flat, right in the center of the road."

Mulder slowly walked forward, his eyes moving back and forth across the pavement. He knew that natural exposure to the elements, and the sheer passage of time, had probably erased most of the evidence left behind by the thirteen-car accident. But he also knew that investigative work relied heavily on luck. "Was it possible to determine what caused the lead car to spin out?"

Canton nodded as they continued forward down the breakdown lane. "According to a witness from five cars back, a white van was careening wildly back and forth between lanes, just ahead of the BMW. The back doors of the van popped open, and the driver of the BMW panicked. She bounced off the guardrail, then flipped over. The next car—a Volvo—hit her head-on at sixty-five miles per hour. Then the others just piled on."

They reached the spot Canton had described as the rough area where the first car had spun out. Mulder turned to the guardrail and saw a huge, jagged tear in the heavy horizontal iron bars. Two dark tire tracks led up to the tear, and Mulder could imagine the driver's frantic efforts to stop the BMW. Obviously, those efforts had been too late. "Did the lead driver get a good look at the van?"

"Maybe"—Canton sighed, leaning against an unmarred section of the guardrail—"but she was decapitated by the front axle of the Volvo. Like I said, the only good witness was five cars back. All the police know was that the van was white, some sort of American model, and the back doors were open. There's an APB out on it now, but there are a lot of vans like that in this city."

Mulder nodded. He would talk to the police after he returned to the hospital, but he didn't expect them to have any answers. If the van ran from the scene of the accident, chances are the driver didn't want to be found.

"And the John Doe?" Mulder asked. "He was unconscious somewhere up here?"

Canton walked a few more paces, then pointed to a spot in the breakdown lane. Mulder stopped at his side. The spot was only ten yards ahead of where the lead car had gone out of control. Roughly where the van had been weaving back and forth. *With the back doors hanging open.*

Mulder knelt, looking at the pavement. Of course, there was nothing remarkable. It had been a week. Mulder moved his eyes along the ground, imagining the body sprawled out. "Facedown? Or faceup?"

"Sort of a fetal position," Canton said. "Lying on his side. His head was away from the road."

Mulder felt the pavement rumble beneath his knees as a heavy Jeep roared by in the closest lane. There was a clattering sound, and Mulder watched a foam cup bounce toward the guardrail. His thoughts solidified as the cup disappeared down the grassy slope on the other side. He rose and walked to the edge of the breakdown lane. He moved slowly along the guardrail—and paused at a spot a few feet away from where Canton was standing.

There was a small dent in the guardrail, just above knee level. Mulder bent down and peered at the dent. Then he looked back toward the highway. "Mr. Canton, how fast did you say the lead car was moving?"

"Probably around sixty-five miles per hour. That's my best estimate, from the damage."

"And the van was traveling at around the same speed when its back doors popped open?"

"That's right."

Mulder nodded. The positioning of the dent seemed about right. If the John Doe's body had fallen out of the back of the van, hit the pavement, rolled into the guardrail, then bounced back a few yards into the breakdown lane—it would have landed right where Canton was standing. The only problem with the theory was the condition of the John Doe's body. Both the paramedics and the medical student had corroborated what the interns had written in the chart: The John Doe had shown no signs of external trauma.

Mulder could hear the question Scully would ask the minute he told her his theory: How could a man fall out of a van moving at sixty-five miles per hour, dent a guardrail—and receive no external injuries?

Mulder didn't have an answer—yet. But he wasn't ready to discard the theory. The John Doe was linked to Perry Stanton, and Perry Stanton had performed amazing, inhuman physical feats. Wasn't it possible that the John Doe had been similarly invulnerable?

Mulder reached into his coat pocket and pulled out a sterile plastic evidence bag and a small horsehair brush. He leaned close to the dent in the railing and began to collect brush samples. He doubted he'd find anything—but there was always the chance some sort of fiber evidence would show up under analysis.

"What are you doing over there?" Canton asked, watching him. "I said we found the John Doe over here."

"I don't think the body started there, Mr. Canton. I think that was just Mr. Doe's final resting place. It's the journey between that interests me." Mulder was about to drop to the ground and get samples from the pavement, when his brush caught on a small groove in the railing. When he pulled the brush free, he noticed a few tiny strips of white cloth caught in the fine horsehairs. He held the brush close to his eyes and saw flakes of some sort of red powder clinging to the underside of the strips. The powder had a strong, moldy scent—somewhat like a loaf of bread that had been left in a damp cabinet too long. Mulder wondered whether the powder and cloth were related to the John Doe. It was possible that the groove in the guardrail had protected it from the elements. He took a second bag out of his pocket and put the strips inside. Then he crossed back to Canton. Canton was looking at him strangely.

"Why is the FBI so interested in this John Doe, anyway? Was he some sort of serial killer?"

"As far as we know," Mulder said, kneeling down to take more samples from the pavement, "he didn't do anything but die. Problem was, his skin didn't die with him."

Mulder didn't add the sudden thought that had hit him: Maybe it was his skin that was the killer. Not some microbe carried in his blood—as Scully had proposed—but his skin itself. Because that was the real common denominator. Not his blood, not a microbe, not a disease.

Skin.

Forty minutes later, Mulder entered the infectious disease ward at New York Hospital. The ward was really just a cordoned-off section of the ICU; two hallways and a half dozen private rooms with a self-contained ventilation system and specially sealed metal doors. The rooms were designed with various degrees of biosafety in mind: from the highest level of security, with inverse vacuums and specialized Racal space suits—to the more manageable, low-level rooms, with glove and mask guidelines, maintained under strict video watch by a staff of infectious disease specialists.

Mulder was directed to a low-level containment room near the rear of the ward. After donning gloves and a mask, he was led into a small private room. Scully was standing by a hospital bed, arguing in a determined voice. Dr. Bernstein, Perry Stanton's plastic surgeon, was sitting on the edge of the bed in a white hospital smock, a skeptical look on his face. There was an IV running into his right arm, and every few seconds he stared at the wire with contempt. It was obvious he didn't want to be there. And it was equally obvious that he wasn't the slightest bit sick.

"Look," he was saying, as Mulder came into the room, "I can assure you, there was no blood-to-blood contact during the transplant. I was masked and gloved. So were my nurses. I've done similar procedures on HIV-positive patients. I've never had any problems."

"Dr. Bernstein," Scully responded, "I didn't order this quarantine. The infectious disease specialist from the CDC has decided not to take any chances. Your surgical team is the highest-risk group—and this quarantine is just a logical precaution."

"It's not logical, it's pointless. We both know there's no real cure for lethargica. I can understand restricting my surgical schedule until after the incubation period ends. But why keep me and my staff cooped up in these cells?"

Scully sighed, then nodded toward the IV. "The specialist from the CDC has suggested you remain on acyclovir, at least through the incubation period. It has been shown to be effective in stopping some of the more common types of encephalitis."

Bernstein rolled his eyes. "Acyclovir has been effective only in encephalitis cases related to the herpes simplex virus. Lethargica isn't caused by herpes."

Scully nodded, then shrugged. "Dr. Bernstein, I'm not going to argue medicine with you. Your specialty is plastic surgery. Mine is forensic pathology.

Neither one of us is an infectious disease specialist. We should both defer to the expert from the CDC."

Bernstein didn't respond. Finally, a grudging acceptance touched his lips. He glanced at Mulder. "I guess I should do what she says."

Mulder smiled. "Usually works for me. Scully, can I borrow you for a moment?"

Scully followed him out into the hallway. After the door sealed shut behind them, she pulled down her mask. "Mulder, I've got some good news. Dr. Cavanaugh, the hospital administrator, has made some initial headway tracking down the John Doe's body. One of his clerks found a transfer form from Rutgers Medical School in New Jersey. Cavanaugh thinks the cadaver might have been mistakenly sent over for dissection. We'll know for certain within a few hours."

Mulder digested the information. He didn't think it was going to be as simple as that. "I'll hold my breath. In the meantime, I'd like you to take a look at something. Tell me if you have any idea what it is."

He reached into his pocket and pulled out the small bag containing the cloth strips and the red powder. Scully took the bag from him and carefully opened the seal. She looked inside, then scrunched up the skin above her nose. She shook the bag, separating some of the red powder from the strips of white cloth. Then she pressed her gloved fingers together against the sides of the bag—getting a sense of the powder's texture. "Actually, I think I have seen something like this before. From the scent and grain, I think the powder might be an antibacterial agent of some sort. The strips of cloth look like they could have come from a bandage. Where did you get this?"

Mulder's body felt light as his intuition kicked in. Now he was getting somewhere. "The accident scene where the John Doe's body was found."

Scully looked at him, then back at the red powder and the strips of cloth. It seemed as if she were suddenly doubting her own memory. "Before you jump to any conclusions, let me show this to Dr. Bernstein. He's a surgeon— he'll have a better idea of what this is."

They reentered the private-care room. Dr. Bernstein was lying on his back, his hands behind his head. "Back so soon? Have I been paroled?"

Scully handed him the plastic bag. "Actually, we're just here to ask for your opinion. Do you recognize this red substance?"

Bernstein sat up, shaking the bag in front of his eyes. He opened a corner of the seal and took a small breath. Then he nodded. The answer was obvious to him. "Of course. The Dust. That's what we call it. It's an antibacterial compound used during massive skin transplantations. We're talking about patients with at least fifty percent burns, often more. It's fairly cutting edge; very powerful, very expensive. Its use was only recently approved by the FDA."

Mulder crossed his hands behind his back. He felt a tremor of excitement move through his shoulders. *A powder used in skin transplants.* If it was connected to the John Doe, it was a stunning discovery, and a bizarre, striking coincidence. He cleared his throat. "Dr. Bernstein, how common is this Dust?"

"Not common at all," Bernstein said, handing the bag back to Scully. "I don't think it's used in any of the local hospitals. Certainly not at Jamaica. I spent part of last year out at UCSF, where I first got a chance to try it out. If you want more information, I suggest you contact the company that developed and markets it. Fibrol International. It's a biotech that specializes in burn-transplantation materials. I'm pretty sure their headquarters is nearby."

Mulder had never heard of the company before. He knew there were dozens, if not hundreds, of biotech companies located up and down the Northeast Corridor. He watched as Scully thanked Bernstein, then he followed her back out into the hallway. He could hardly contain his enthusiasm as he told her what he was thinking. "Scully, this is too much of a coincidence."

"Well—"

"A specialized transplant powder found at the scene where the John Doe was picked up," Mulder bulldozed along. "It might mean that the John Doe himself was a transplant recipient. Then his skin was harvested, passing along strange, unexplainable symptoms to Perry Stanton. The red powder—the Dust—might be the key to everything."

Scully squinted, then shook her head. "Mulder, you're jumping way ahead of yourself. You found this powder at the scene of the accident, a spot on a major highway leading out of Manhattan?"

"You heard Dr. Bernstein. This powder is rare and expensive. We need to talk to the people at Fibrol International, find out if we can trace—"

Mulder was interrupted by a high-pitched ring. Scully had her cellular phone out before the noise had finished echoing through Mulder's ears. Only a few people had Scully's number—and Mulder had a good guess who it was on the other end of the line.

Barrett, Scully mouthed. Her face changed as she listened to the tinny voice in her ear. When she hung up the phone, her eyes were bright and animated. "It's Stanton. An eyewitness saw him entering a subway terminal in Brooklyn Heights. Barrett wants to know if we want to be in on the arrest."

Mulder was already moving toward the elevators.

NINE

Susan Doppler closed her eyes, the scream of metal against metal echoing through her skull. Her body jerked back and forth—her tired muscles victimized by the rhythmic mechanical surf, as the crowded, steel coffin burrowed through the city's bowels. She had entered that near-comatose state of the frequent commuter, barely kept awake by the turbulent chatter of the rails resonating upward through her feet.

Like many New Yorkers, Susan hated the subway. But the forty-minute ride into Manhattan was a necessary part of her daily routine. A single mother at thirty-one, she could hardly afford cab fare—and there was no direct bus route from her home in Brooklyn to the downtown department store where she worked an afternoon shift. As long as her nine-year-old daughter needed child care and braces, she had no choice besides the underground bump and grind.

Today, the ordeal was worse than usual. The air-conditioning had gone out two stops ago, and Susan could feel the sweat rolling down her back. The air reeked of body odor and seasoned urine; every breath was a test of Susan's reflux control, and her throat was already chalky and dry from her labored search for oxygen. The car was packed tight, and Susan struggled to keep from being crushed between the two businessmen seated on either side of her. The man to her left was overweight, and his white shirt was soaked through with sweat. Worse still, the man to Susan's right was angled and bony, and every few seconds he inadvertently jabbed her with a knifelike elbow as he turned the pages of the newspaper tabloid on his lap.

Still, with her eyes tightly shut and her head lolling back against the rattling glass window, she could almost pretend she was somewhere else: a sauna in a city on the other side of the world; a steaming beach on an island in the middle of the Pacific; the fiery cabin of an exploding airplane hurtling toward the side of a mountain. *Anything was better than a crowded subway in the middle of July.*

Susan grimaced as she once again felt the sharp elbow poking into her right hip. She opened her eyes and glared at the emaciated businessman. He was tall, spidery, with grayish hair and furry eyebrows. He seemed completely engrossed in his tabloid, oblivious to anything but the colorful pictures of celebrities and freaks.

Susan turned away, frustrated, and rested her chin on her hand. Wisps of her long brown hair fell down against her cheeks, framing her blue eyes. Azure, her ex-husband had called them—back when he had cared. The prick. Her eyes narrowed as she chided herself for thinking about him. It had been over a year now, and he was no longer a part of her or her daughter's life. Her eyes were *blue*—not azure.

Susan's body stiffened as the subway car wrenched to the left, the lights flickering. When the flickering stopped, she found herself staring directly at the man seated across from her. The sight was so pathetic, she almost gasped out loud. *Only in New York.*

The man was hunched forward, his small, football-shaped head in his hands. His jagged little body was barely covered by a filthy smock, the thin material stained and torn and covered in what looked to be flecks of green glass. The man seemed to be trembling—probably crack or heroin—and his thinning hair was slick with sweat. As Susan watched, the man shifted his head slightly, and she could see that his lips were moving, emitting a constant, unintelligible patter. She caught a glimpse of his eyes—noting that they were blue, just like hers. Maybe even a little azure.

She turned away, repulsed. The man was obviously homeless, most likely mentally disturbed. Thankfully, he was too small to cause any problems. Still, Susan was glad she wasn't sharing his bench.

Then the elbow touched her hip again, and she cursed out loud. The spidery businessman finally noticed her, apologizing in a thick New Jersey accent. He folded his tabloid in half, carefully resting it sideways against his knees. As he lifted a corner to continue reading, Susan caught a glimpse of a large black-and-white picture on the back cover of the magazine. The picture was right below a huge headline in oversize type:

PSYCHO PROFESSOR ROAMS NEW YORK

Something ticked in Susan's mind, and she looked up from the tabloid. Her eyes refocused on the little, hunched man sitting across from her. She stared at the torn white smock, a warm, tingling feeling rising through her spine. Slowly, her mouth came open as she realized that it certainly could be a hospital smock.

She remembered the story she had heard on the news that morning. A little history professor had murdered a nurse and jumped out of a second-story window. She couldn't be sure—but there was a chance that same man was sitting right across from her.

She shifted against the seat, wondering if she should say something. Then a new sound entered her ears—the squeal of the brakes kicking in. They had reached the next stop. The subway car jerked backward, and the little man suddenly looked up. Susan locked eyes with him—and knew for sure. It was the psycho professor. *And he was looking right at her.*

Her jaw shot open, and an involuntary scream erupted from her throat. The professor's eyes seemed to shrink as his entire body convulsed upward. Suddenly, he was on his feet and coming toward her across the narrow car. Susan cringed backward, pointing, as the other passengers stared in shock. There was a horrible frozen moment as the professor stood over her, his hands clenched at his sides. Then the subway car stopped suddenly at the station, and an anguished look crossed his face.

He seemed to forget about Susan as he turned and lurched toward the open doors. His head whirled back and forth as he shoved people out of his way. A heavyset man in bright sweatpants shouted at him to slow down—then toppled to the side as the diminutive professor slammed past. A second later he was out onto the platform.

Susan leapt across the subway car and pressed her face against the window on the other side. She watched the little man reeling away from a crowd of onlookers—then she saw three police officers coming through the turnstiles. Relief filled her body as she realized there was nowhere for the professor to go.

The little man paused, watching the three officers coming toward him. Susan noticed that all three were armed—and wearing white latex gloves. The subway car had gone silent around her, as other passengers jostled for positions at the window.

The three officers fanned out in a wide semicircle, surrounding the professor. The little man made a sudden decision, and spun to his left, heading straight for the dark subway tunnel ahead of Susan's stopped train. One officer stood between him and the oval black mouth of the tunnel. Susan watched as the officer dropped to one knee, his gun out in front of him. He shouted something—but the little man kept on coming.

Susan gasped as she saw the look of determination spread across the police officer's face.

Officer Carl Leary held his breath as the little man barreled toward him. He could see the fury in the professor's wild blue eyes, the sense of pure, liquid violence. He knew he had no choice. In a second, the man was going to be on top of him.

His finger clenched against the trigger, and his service revolver kicked upward, the muscles in his forearms contracting to take the recoil. A loud explosion echoed through the subway station, followed by a half dozen screams from the open subway doors. Leary's eyes widened as he saw the little man still coming toward him. His finger tightened again, and there was a second explosion—

And then the little man was rushing right past him. Leary fell back against the platform, stunned. He had fired at point-blank range. How the hell could he have missed?

He watched as the professor disappeared into the subway tunnel. Then he felt a gloved hand on his shoulder. He looked up and saw the concerned look on his partner's sweaty face. Joe Kenyon had been riding shotgun in Leary's patrol cruiser for two years. They had seen everything there was to see in this crazy city—but, for once, both officers were at a loss for words.

"You okay?" Kenyon finally managed. His thick voice was hoarse from the excitement. "The psycho didn't bleed on you, did he?"

Leary shook his head as he checked the chamber on his service revolver. The barrel was still hot, and he could smell the gunpowder in the air. He counted the bullets, and confirmed that two were missing. Then he shrugged, running a hand through his shock of sweaty red hair. "The diseased little bastard's out of his mind. Came right at me."

"He won't get far," Kenyon murmured, looking back at the subway car. He watched as the other officer herded the passengers out of the stopped train. "I think you winged him pretty good. He'll make it twenty, twenty-five yards at the most."

Leary didn't respond. Kenyon must have been right. He couldn't possibly have missed at such close range. Then again, why hadn't the little man gone down? How could a guy take a hit at such close range and not go down?

He pushed the thought away as he reached for his two-way radio. He was about to call it in when Kenyon pointed toward the turnstiles. "Don't bother with the radio. Here comes Big-Assed Barrett and the two fibbies."

Leary watched the hulking detective and the two well-dressed agents as they strolled onto the platform. Then he turned back toward the dark subway tunnel. Whether he had winged the little bastard or not—Perry Stanton wasn't going to get away. *Not this time.*

TEN

Scully watched in clinical disgust as a rat the size of a basketball ran head-first into the stone wall to her right, bounced off, then scurried beneath the iron tracks.

She turned her attention back to the dark tunnel, maneuvering the crisp orange beam of her flashlight until she found the outline of Mulder's shoulders a few feet ahead. She could hear her partner's low voice over the rumble of the underground ventilation system, and she hurried her pace, closing the distance. Detective Barrett came into view, her huge form hovering just ahead of Mulder in the darkness. Mulder was pointing at the heavy revolver that hung from Barrett's right paw.

"He's not in control," Mulder was arguing. "Certainly, there are more humane ways to bring him in."

"He's a murderer," Barrett hissed back, "and I'm not going to put myself or my officers at risk. If you feel comfortable armed with a chunk of plastic and a battery, that's your prerogative."

Scully glanced down at the stun gun in her gloved left hand. She and Mulder had procured the nonlethal weapons at the FBI East Side armory on the way to the subway terminal. The device was about the size of a paperback book, no more than three pounds. The textured plastic handle felt warm through the latex enveloping Scully's fingers.

"The Taser is just as effective as a bullet," Mulder said. "It can disable a three-hundred-pound man without causing any permanent damage."

"I know what the manual says," Barrett shot back. "But have you ever aimed one of those toys at a junkie in a PCP rage? Roughly equivalent to poking a rattlesnake with a paper clip."

Scully cleared her throat. In her mind, the discussion was moot. The other three police officers were at least twenty yards ahead by now, and all were armed with high-powered service revolvers. Barrett had sent the officers ahead because two of them had worked for the Transit Police before and knew the tunnel layout. "Hopefully, there won't be any need for lethal force. Detective Barrett, how far does this tunnel go before we reach the next platform?"

"About half a mile," Barrett responded, heading forward again. "But there are numerous junctions leading off the main line. Construction adjuncts, equipment areas, voltage rooms; plenty of places for Stanton to hide. I've got teams guarding all the exits—but if we don't find him now, we'll have to call in the dogs and the search squads."

Scully took a deep breath, nearly choking on the dank, heavy air. She could imagine the fear and confusion Stanton was feeling as he ran through the darkness—his brain misinterpreting every signal from his nervous system, his psychotic paranoia sending him farther away from the people who were trying to help.

A few minutes passed in determined silence as they worked their way deeper into the tunnel. The ground was uneven around the tracks, covered in packed dirt and gravel. The walls were curved and roughly tiled, huge chunks of stone jutting out from a thick infrastructure of cement and steel.

Up ahead, Scully made out a sharp left turn. Beneath an orange emergency lantern stood one of the three police officers. The cop waved them forward, and Scully quickened her gait. She followed the turn up a slow incline and found herself at a junction between two tunnels. The subway track continued to the left, into the better-lit shaft. The other shaft angled into pure darkness, the walls and floor carved out of what looked to be jagged limestone.

"It's the new line," the officer explained. He was mildly overweight, and sweat ran in rivulets down the sides of his red face. "Still under construction. Leary spotted him 'bout thirty yards ahead. He and Kenyon went in after 'im."

Scully pointed her flashlight into the pitch-black shaft.

The hungry air swallowed the orange beam after only a few yards. She glanced at Mulder and Barrett. The under-construction tunnel was a dangerous place to chase the carrier of a rare, fatal disease. She contemplated asking Barrett to call for backup—when a thunderous crack echoed off the limestone walls.

Scully's stomach lurched as she recognized the echoing report of a police-issue nine millimeter. She saw Mulder dart forward, and quickly rushed to follow. She could hear Barrett and the overweight officer a few steps behind her, but she forced them out of her thoughts, concentrating on the dark floor beneath her feet. Her flashlight beam bounced over slabs of stone and chunks of rail, and she tried to keep her feet as light as possible. She saw Mulder cut sharply to the right and found herself stumbling up a narrow incline. She guessed it was some sort of construction access—perhaps leading all the way to the surface. If so, there would be a team of officers waiting at the top. If they had heard the gunshot, they would already be streaming inside—

Scully nearly collided with Mulder's back as he reared up, his flashlight diving toward the floor. Scully added her own orange beam and saw the officer curled up against the stone wall. She recognized the man's bright red hair and quickly dropped to one knee. She saw a thin pool of blood seeping out from just above Leary's right ear. She reached forward, feeling for the man's pulse.

"He's alive," she whispered, applying gentle but constant pressure to the bleeding head wound. "Looks like he got hit with something, probably a metal pipe or a heavy rock. Maybe a skull fracture."

"Gun's still in his hand," Mulder responded, also dropping to his knees. "The barrel's warm. Three bullets missing from the chamber."

There were heavy footsteps from behind, and Scully quickly looked over her shoulder. She watched Barrett lumber the last few steps, followed by the overweight officer.

"Christ," Barrett said, looking at the downed man. Then she glanced up the narrow, black incline that seemed to continue on forever. "Where the hell is Kenyon?"

Scully turned her attention back to the man in front of her, trying to get a better look at his wound. "I need a medical kit right away. And we've got to get paramedics down here immediately."

"There's a kit back at the junction," the portly cop said. Barrett nodded at him, and he raced back in the direction they had come from. Meanwhile, Mulder had taken a few more steps up the dark incline. He glanced back at Scully, and she nodded.

Mulder started forward, his stun gun out ahead of him. Barrett quickly moved past Scully and the downed officer. Her intention was obvious. Mulder gestured toward the revolver in her gloved right hand. "Just remember, one of your officers is somewhere up ahead."

Barrett nodded. Scully called after them, as they faded into the darkness, "I'll follow when the paramedics get here—and I'll make sure he doesn't double back and get away. That's if he hasn't already reached the surface."

"He's not going to reach the surface," Barrett responded.

"Why is that?" Scully asked.

"Because it's a dead end. They capped this construction access off with three tons of cement two weeks ago." Barrett's voice trailed off as she and Mulder moved out of range.

Mulder's chest burned as the adrenaline pumped through his body. His eyes were wide-open, chasing the orange beam from his flashlight as he navigated across the uneven tunnel floor. He could hear Barrett's heavy gasps from a few feet behind his right shoulder; every few seconds a curse echoed into his ears as she struggled to keep up.

A dozen yards into the tunnel, the air began to taste vaguely metallic, and a thick, mildewy scent rose off the limestone walls. The tunnel seemed to be narrowing as they neared the surface, the curved walls closing in like the inner curls of an angry fist. Mulder slowed his pace, motioning for Barrett to keep quiet. They were close to the dead end—and that meant Perry Stanton and the other officer had to be nearby.

The tunnel took a sharp right, and suddenly Mulder found himself in the entrance to a small, rectangular corridor. Mulder moved the flashlight along the walls and saw wires and steel cables running in parallel twists across the limestone. Every few feet he made out little dark alcoves dug directly into the walls.

"Generator room," Barrett whispered as she joined him in the entrance to the corridor. "They powered the excavation equipment from generators housed in those empty alcoves. The cement wall should be right on the other side of this corridor."

Mulder pointed his flashlight toward the nearest generator alcove. The space looked to be about ten feet deep, and at least three feet in diameter. Easily enough room for a diminutive professor. Or an officer's body.

Mulder raised his stun gun and slowly advanced into the corridor. His neck tingled as he swung the flashlight back and forth, trying to illuminate as much area as possible. Despite his efforts, he was surrounded by black air. After a few feet, he realized the danger he was in; Stanton could hit him from either side, and he'd never see him corning. He was about to turn back toward Barrett—when his right foot touched something soft.

He quickly aimed the flashlight toward the ground. He saw wisps of blue, marred by spots of seeping red. Then the orange beam touched the shiny curves of a police badge.

He was about to call for Barrett when there was a sudden motion from his right. He turned just as the shape hit him, right below the shoulder. His stun gun went off, sparks flying through the darkness as the twin metal contacts glanced off a limestone wall.

Mulder's shoulder hit the ground, and the air was knocked out of him. His hands opened, and the flashlight and stun gun clattered away. The flashlight beam twirled through the blackness, and he caught sight of Perry Stanton's face rearing up above him, a look of anguish in his blue eyes. Then he saw Stanton's hands, clenched into wiry fists, rising above his head. Stanton leaped toward him, and Mulder shouted, raising his arms, wondering why the hell he always seemed to lose his weapon at the worst time—when, suddenly, there was a high-pitched buzzing. Stanton froze midstep, his eyes widening, his mouth curling open. Convulsions rocked his body, his muscles twisting into strange knots beneath his skin. He arched backward, his knees giving out. He collapsed to the ground a few feet away, his arms and legs twitching. Then he went still.

Mulder crawled to his knees as Scully entered the corridor, the stun gun hanging loosely from her right hand. Barrett rushed out from behind her, her revolver uselessly pointed at Stanton's prone body. "I couldn't get a clear shot. Christ, he came at you so fast."

Scully hurried to Mulder's side. She was out of breath, sweat dripping into her eyes. "Are you okay? Leary regained consciousness shortly after we separated. I decided he could wait for the paramedics on his own."

"Good timing, Scully. And even better aim."

Scully smiled. "Actually, I didn't aim. I just fired. You got lucky and saved yourself a nasty hangover." Mulder gestured toward the cop lying in the middle of the corridor. "Officer Kenyon wasn't so lucky."

Scully followed her flashlight to the man and checked his pulse. Then she pushed his shoulder, turning him onto his side. She looked up, and Mulder saw the stricken look on her face. He glanced at the officer—and realized the man's head was facing the wrong direction. Stanton had twisted his neck 180 degrees, snapping his spinal column.

Barrett saw the dead officer and noisily reholstered her gun. "The damn animal. I don't care how sick he is. I'm gonna make sure he spends the rest of his life in a cell."

Mulder didn't respond to Barrett's angry comment. No matter how tragic the situation, he didn't believe Stanton was responsible. He thought about the anguished look in the professor's eyes—and the strange convulsions that had racked his body. It had almost seemed as if Stanton's muscles had been fighting his skin—struggling to tear through.

Mulder rose slowly and found his flashlight along the nearby wall. Then he trained the light on the downed professor. Stanton was lying on his back, his arms and legs twisted unnaturally at his sides. His eyes were wide open, his lips curled back. Mulder took a tentative step forward. *Something wasn't right.*

"Scully," he said, focusing the flashlight on Stanton's still chest, "I don't think he's breathing."

Scully stepped away from the dead officer. "He's just stunned, Mulder. The voltage running through the Taser contacts wasn't anywhere near enough to kill him."

Just the same, she moved to the little man's side and dropped to her knees. She carefully leaned forward, holding her ear above his mouth. Then her eyebrows rose, and she quickly touched the side of his neck with a gloved finger.

She drew her hand away, staring. Sudden alarm swept across her features. She tilted Stanton's head back, searching his mouth and throat for obstructions. Then she moved both hands over his chest and started vigorous CPR. Mulder dropped next to her, leaning over to give mouth-to-mouth. Scully stopped him with her hand. "Mulder, the lethargica."

Mulder shrugged her hand away. Even if she was right, and Stanton was infected with the blood-borne strain of encephalitis, Mulder knew the odds were enormously in his favor. Saliva, on its own, was not a likely carrier. And he couldn't get the vision of Emily Kysdale out of his mind. *Despite what he had done, this was a young woman's father.*

He pressed his mouth over Stanton's open lips and exhaled, inflating the man's chest. Scully continued the cardiac compressions, while Barrett stood watching. The minutes passed in silence, Mulder and Scully working together to bring the man back.

Finally, Scully stopped, leaning back from the body. Her red hair was damp with effort. "He's gone, Mulder. I don't understand. He didn't have a heart condition. He was strong enough to kill an officer. How could a stun gun have done this to him?"

Mulder didn't have an answer. As voices drifted into the corridor from out in the tunnel, a strange thought struck him. Leary had fired a total of three shots at Stanton—and hadn't slowed him down. Scully had hit him once with the electric stun gun, and he had died. Similarly, the John Doe had quite possibly fallen out of a moving van at seventy miles per hour, and had not received a scratch. Then two interns had shocked him with a defibrillator— *and he had died on the stretcher.*

"Scully," he started—but then stopped himself as a team of paramedics rushed a portable stretcher into the corridor. They were followed by a handful of uniformed officers. Barrett started shouting orders, and the paramedics rushed to the dead officer's side. Then they saw Stanton, and shouted for a second stretcher.

Mulder and Scully stepped out of the way as more paramedics moved into the corridor and lifted Stanton onto another stretcher. Scully watched with determined eyes. "I'm going to get to the bottom of this, Mulder. I'm going to perform the autopsy myself—and find out what really killed him."

Mulder felt the same level of determination move through him. Stanton was dead, but the case was far from over. Mulder was still convinced—Perry

Stanton may have killed a nurse and a police officer, but he was not a murderer. He was a victim.

Mulder had seen it in his anguished eyes.

ELEVEN

The digitized view screen flickered, then changed to a dull green color. Scully leaned back in the leather office chair, her arms stretched out in front of her. A radiology tech in a white lab coat hovered over her shoulder, his warm breath nipping at her earlobe. "Just another few seconds."

Scully tapped the edge of the keyboard beneath the screen, anticipation rising through her tense muscles. She pictured Stanton's body engulfed by the enormous, cylindrical MRI machine two rooms away. Mulder had remained with the body while she had accompanied the tech to the viewing room. They would regroup at the pathology lab downstairs, where they would be joined by Barrett and the investigator from the CDC.

"You want print copies as well, correct?" the tech asked, interrupting her thoughts. Scully nodded, and the tech hit a sequence of keys on a color laser printer next to the viewing screen. The young man was short and had thick, plastic-rimmed glasses. He was obviously enjoying her company—and the opportunity to show off his expertise with the MRI machine.

The MRI scan was not normal autopsy procedure, but Scully had decided to take every extra measure possible to understand what had happened to Perry Stanton. In truth, she couldn't help feeling a twinge of guilt at Stanton's sudden death. She knew it was not really her fault—but she *had* fired the stun gun. At the very least, she needed to know why his body had so fatally overreacted.

"Here we go," the tech coughed, pointing at the screen. The printer began to hum just as the screen flickered again, and suddenly the dull green display was replaced by a shifting sea of gray. The gray conformed roughly to the shape of a human skull, representing a vertical cross section taken through the direct center of Perry Stanton's brain.

It took Scully less than a second to realize that all of her previous assumptions had to be reevaluated. Even without the autopsy, she knew for a fact that Stanton had not died from anything related to the encephalitis virus. "This can't be right."

The tech glanced at the screen, then turned to the printer and pulled out a stack of pages. The pages showed the same image, multiplied four times at slightly different angles. "This is the sequence you ordered. The machine's been in use all morning—and nobody's had a complaint."

Scully took the pictures from him, looking them over. She had never seen anything like it before. There was no edema, none of the cerebral swelling she would have expected from encephalitis lethargica—but Stanton's brain was anything but normal. She reached forward with a finger and traced a large, dark gray spot near the center of the picture. It was the hypothalamus, the gland that regulated the nervous system—but it was enormous, nearly three times as large as normal. Surrounding the engorged gland were half a dozen strange polyp-type growths, arranged in a rough semicircle. In all her time spent in pathology labs, she had never seen such a manifestation.

She rose quickly from the leather chair, the pictures tucked under her right arm. She wanted to get to that autopsy room as soon as possible. She watched as the tech hit a few computer keys, sending the viewing screen back to its original green. "We'll keep the pictures on file for as long as you'd like. Just ask for me if you need a second look."

The young man winked from behind his thick glasses, but Scully was already moving out into the radiology wing. Her thoughts were three floors away, in a basement lab filled with plastic organ trays and steel fluid gutters.

\\\\\\\\\\\\\\\\\\\

Scully never made it to the autopsy room. She had taken three steps out of the elevator when she heard Mulder's angry voice echoing through the cinder-block pathology ward.

She found her partner blockaded in the long central hallway that ran down the center of the ward by three red-faced men wearing white lab coats. All of the coats had name tags, with tiny red seals that Scully recognized from her previous dealings with the CDC. Mulder's focus was the tallest man, a mid-fifties African-American with thick eyelids and speckled gray hair. The man had his arms crossed against his chest, a disdainful look in his eyes. His name tag identified him as Dr. Basil Georgian, a senior infectious disease investigator. Scully caught the tail end of Mulder's heated interchange as she arrived at his side.

"This isn't merely an infectious disease scare," Mulder was near-shouting. "It's an FBI investigation. You don't have automatic priority or jurisdiction."

Georgian shook his head. "That's where you're wrong. We've got two reported cases of encephalitis lethargica. That's all the jurisdiction we need. Your murderer is dead, Agent Mulder. He's not going to go anywhere. Our virus is still very much alive—at least in one coma victim. We've got to make sure that's where it stays contained."

Mulder turned to Scully. "These guys seem to think they're going to run off with our body."

Scully looked at Georgian. Georgian shrugged. "Our superiors in Atlanta have already spoken to your superiors in Washington. Everyone agrees that it's more appropriate for us to handle the autopsy in our biocontainment lab in Hoboken—where the microbe can be properly studied, handled, and contained. We'll send you the reports when we're finished. Lethargica doesn't come around often, and we intend to figure out what it's doing in New York."

Without another word, Georgian spun on his heels and headed down the hallway, flanked by his two associates. Scully could see Stanton's stretcher being wheeled through a pair of double doors another ten yards beyond them—most likely to an underground garage, where an ambulance was waiting. Mulder started after them, but she stopped him with an outstretched hand. "They aren't going to change their minds. And they do have priority. From an official stand-point, our investigation is finished. Our perp is in custody—so to speak."

Mulder sighed, shaking his head. *They'll send us their report?* That's ridiculous. This is our case."

"But the infectious disease makes it their concern. Mulder, I don't think we have much choice."

"So we just let it go?"

Scully didn't like the idea any more than he did. But they had to let the CDC scientists do their job. In the meantime, Scully still had the MRI scans. She pulled them out from under her arm and showed one of the views to Mulder. "While we're waiting for their autopsy report, we still have a lead to work with. This is one of the strangest MRIs I've ever seen. You see these polyps surrounding the hypothalamus?"

Mulder squinted, following her finger. To an untrained observer, the idio-syncrasy was fairly obtuse—but to Scully it was like a massive neon sign. "Given Stanton's sudden onset of psychosis, my guess is these polyps might have something to do with excess dopamine production. That would involve the hypothalamus—and explain the violence and disorientation."

"Dopamine," Mulder repeated. "That's a neurotransmitter, right? A chemical used by the nervous system to transmit information?"

Scully nodded. She wouldn't know for sure until she saw the CDC autopsy report, but it seemed a viable possibility. Still, it wasn't an explanation. "I'd like to run these pictures through the hospital's Medline system, see if anything like this has been reported before."

Mulder was still looking longingly in the direction of Stanton's body. "Scully, how many times have we worked with the CDC before?"

Scully raised an eyebrow. "A half dozen. Maybe more. Why?"

Mulder shrugged. "First the John Doe. Now Perry Stanton. It seems that people are going to great lengths to keep us from getting our hands on anyone involved in that skin transplant."

Scully resisted the urge to roll her eyes. "Mulder, I called the CDC about the lethargica—not the other way around."

Mulder gestured toward the MRI scans. "Does that look like lethargica?"

Scully paused. "The truth is, I have no idea what this is. That's why we need to find out if it's ever happened before."

Ten minutes later, Scully and Mulder huddled together in the corner of a cramped administrative office located one floor above the pathology ward. They had borrowed the office from a human-resources manager, bypassing any questions or possible red tape with a flick of their federal IDs. The office was sparse, containing little more than a desk, a few chairs, and an IBM workstation. In other words, it was a no-frills window into cyberspace.

The computer whirred as the inboard modem connected the two agents to the nationwide medical database located in Washington, DC. Scully was closest to the screen, and her face glowed a techno blue as she maneuvered a plastic track ball through a half dozen menus loaded with options and navigational commands. Mulder had already placed one of the MRI pictures into the scanner next to the oversize processor, and in a few minutes they would begin to search the hundred million stored files for any possible match.

"This search should cover any MRIs, CAT scans, or skull X rays with similar manifestations," Scully said. "The Medline system is linked to every hospital in the country, and many throughout the world. If there's an associated syndrome, we'll surely find something—"

She paused as the screen began to change. Suddenly, her eyes widened. Mulder read the notice at the top of the file that had suddenly appeared. "One match. New York Hospital, 1984."

Scully immediately realized the significance of the notice. As she skimmed the first paragraph of the file, her shock grew. The MRI scan had matched a pair of CAT scans taken on two inmates of Rikers Island in New York, shortly before their deaths. Both inmates had been part of some sort of volunteer experimental study performed in the early eighties. Even more stunning, according to the file, the study was conducted under the auspices of a fledgling biotech company located just outside Manhattan. Scully immediately recognized the company's name.

"Fibrol International," Mulder stated, his voice characteristically calm. "The same company that manufactures the red powder I found at the accident scene."

Scully didn't know what to say. She scrolled farther down the file and found the two CAT scans that had heralded the match. In both images, she saw the same unmistakable pattern of polyps surrounding an enlarged hypothalamus. At the bottom of the file she found a link to an attached file. She hit the link, and the CAT scans were replaced by a single page of official-looking text.

"It's a prosecutorial assessment," she said, reading the heading. "There was a criminal investigation into the man behind the experimentation—Fibrol's founder and CEO, Emile Paladin. But it looks as though it never came to trial. According to this, the experiment had been conducted with full permission from the inmates. There's no explanation of the cause of death—just that it was accidental."

"Look at this," Mulder said, tapping a paragraph lower down in the assessment. There was a brief description of the nature of the experiment. "Skin transplantation, Scully. The experiment had to do with a radical new method of skin transplantation."

Scully rubbed her scalp with her fingers. It was hard to believe. Perry Stanton's brain had been ravaged by the same polyps that had killed the two inmates. But Stanton had not been the subject of an experimental transplantation.

"The red powder," Mulder continued. "It's the link—and Fibrol is the common denominator. We've got to find this Emile Paladin."

"This happened fifteen years ago," Scully responded. "And Perry Stanton wasn't part of any radical experiment."

"Not directly. But the John Doe might have been. And Stanton's wearing his skin."

Scully shook her head. What Mulder was implying was extremely unlikely. What sort of mechanism could transfer such a fatal cerebral reaction—through nothing more than a slab of harvested skin? It didn't make medical sense.

Still, she didn't know what to make of the connection to Fibrol. They needed to find out more about the experiment that had killed the two prisoners. And Mulder was right, they needed to track down Emile Paladin.

Maybe he could tell them how a skin transplant could ravage a man's brain from the inside—and what any of this had to do with the encephalitis lethargica that had felled the two med students.

Maybe Emile Paladin had some idea what had really happened to Perry Stanton.

TWELVE

The huge crimson atrium spilled out in front of the electronic revolving door like blood from a gunshot wound. Mulder paused to catch his breath as he and Scully stepped from inside the moving triangle of smoked glass. Twenty yards ahead stood an enormous black-glass desk, staffed by three men in similar dark blue suits. Behind the desk, the walls curved upward in magnificent swells of stone to the paneled black ceiling lined with more than a dozen miniature spotlights, a synthetic night sky gazing down upon a mock vermilion desert carved out of imported marble.

The interior of the Fibrol complex was nothing like the nondescript, blank-walled three-storied boxes he and Scully had seen from the highway. Even when they had passed through the twin security checkpoints on the way into the parking lot, Mulder had not realized the extent of the building's architectural deception. From the outside, Fibrol's main offices seemed no different from the hundreds of other corporate headquarters lodged in the grassy foothills that surrounded New York City. But the interior decor told a story more in line with the S&P reports the agents had scoured after leaving New York Hospital. Fibrol had grown wealthy during the biotech boom of the late eighties, burgeoning into one of the nation's largest suppliers of burn-transplantation materials. Along with their most recent product—the antibacterial Dust—Fibrol held over three hundred patents on products in use at major hospitals and research centers. The company operated a half dozen burn clinics in the Northeast, and satellite offices in Los Angeles, Seattle, London, Tokyo, Paris, and Rome.

Mulder's shoes clicked against the polished marble as he and Scully bisected the huge atrium. He noticed a long glass case running along the wall to his right, containing strange-looking metal and plastic tools; each tool had a plaque explaining its use and date of development, and by the third scalpel-like object, Mulder realized the case was a visual history of the transplantation art. He looked more closely as he reached the last section of the case. He passed what appeared to be microscalpels and needles, lying next to a specialized microscope. To the right of the microscope, he recognized a laser device similar to the machine Dr. Bernstein had used to remove the tattoo.

Then he came to the red powder, spread out in three equal piles above a metallic plaque.

He paused, tapping Scully's arm. The plaque was dated thirteen months ago, and contained a single caption in gilded script:

Antibacterial Compound 1279
**Effective in reducing consequential septicity
after radical transplantation**

Mulder was about to ask for a medical definition of "consequential septicity" when a high voice impaled his right ear. "Agents Mulder and Scully? I trust you had no problem following my directions?"

Mulder looked up from the glass case. One of the blue-suited men had risen from behind the black desk. Just a kid, really—he looked no older than twenty-three, with short blond hair and an acne-covered face. His thin limbs were swimming in his suit. Scully nodded in his direction. "Are you the man we spoke to on the phone?"

The kid smiled, coming around the edge of the desk. "Dick Baxter. I set up your appointment with Dr. Kyle, our director of research. He's waiting in his office. I'll take you right to him."

Mulder and Scully shook Baxter's hand. Enthusiasm leaked out of the kid's every pore.

"Dr. Kyle?" Mulder asked. He remembered seeing Julian Kyle's name in the S&P files. Kyle was responsible for a number of Fibrol's patents, spanning back to the company's inception. Still, Mulder had hoped their FBI status would get them access to someone higher up than a director of research.

Then again, Mulder didn't yet know enough about Fibrol's leadership to complain. He and Scully had been hoping to find Emile Paladin still at the helm of the company—but to their surprise, they had discovered that Fibrol's founder and CEO had died in an accident overseas shortly after the experiment involving the Rikers Island prisoners. Since then, the company had gone through two acting CEOs, and at present no CEO was in place. Perhaps Julian Kyle was as close to the company's true leadership as Mulder and Scully were going to get.

"You asked to speak to the person in charge of our East Coast operations, didn't you?" Baxter continued. "Julian Kyle heads up all new projects at Fibrol. His finger is on the pulse of everything that goes on around here."

Mulder and Scully followed the young man as he strolled past the desk to an opaque glass door embedded in the marble wall. Baxter paused, pressing his hand against a plastic circular plate next to the door. There was a short metallic whir, and the door slid open, revealing a long corridor with matching crimson walls.

"Pretty high-tech," Scully commented.

"Infrared imaging," Baxter said, smiling proudly. "It's a lot more comfortable than a retinal scanner, and certainly more accurate than a thumb pad. Of course, it's much more expensive than either technology."

Mulder glanced back toward the spectacular front atrium. "Doesn't look like Fibrol is too concerned with expense."

Baxter laughed. "Not lately. We've got a number of major new developments coming down the pipeline. Already, our foreign division has tripled in revenues—just in the past two years. The new board of directors has decided to update our look, to reflect this new level of success. They've redesigned much of the complex; you should see the new labs in the basement—we're talking major high-tech."

Mulder raised his eyebrows, glancing at Scully as they followed the young man through the security door and into the long corridor. "You seem pretty excited about the changes. Is that why they have you working the door?"

Baxter laughed, pulling at the lapels of his blue suit. "Actually, I'm a Ph.D. student at NYU. I'm working here through the summer—but I hope to be hired full-time after I graduate. Maybe start as a junior scientist and claw my way up in the research department. Beats the hell out of academia, and you get to really see your work transformed into something useful."

Mulder kept his eyes moving as they sliced through the inner corridors of the complex. The place was built like a maze, and Mulder was reminded of the interior floor plan of the Pentagon. They passed many unmarked offices, each with opaque glass security doors. None of the doors had knobs. Instead, each was fitted with the same plastic handplate. A very efficient security system, probably routed through a computer center somewhere in the complex. Mulder also noticed closed-circuit television cameras at ten-foot intervals along the hallway ceiling. The cameras were painted the same crimson as the walls. He touched Scully's arm, pointing. "Fibrol seems to take its security fairly seriously. Cameras, infrared access panels, and the twin security checks on the way into the fenced parking lot."

Baxter overheard his comment and nodded vigorously. "Oh, yes. We're very concerned with keeping our work private. You'd be surprised at the sort of thing that goes on in the biotech industry. Theft, sabotage, corporate spying, Internet hacking—just last month we had an incident with the janitorial staff. A cleaning lady on the third floor was caught stealing the shredded paper from a central wastebasket."

"Shredded paper?" Scully asked.

Baxter had a serious look on his face. "A hacker employed by a rival biotech company could have extracted password information from the stolen garbage. Once inside our computer banks, there's no telling what sort of damage they could have done."

Mulder stifled a smile. It seemed he did not have a monopoly on paranoia. Then again, perhaps Baxter was right. Mulder knew that the biotech industry relied on its secrets to survive. Patents could only protect inventions that were already complete—every step along the way was a fierce race. And judging from the lavish front atrium with its expensive marble walls, the payoff could be impressive.

Baxter stopped in front of another glass door, again placing his palm against an infrared panel. After two clicks the door slid open, and Baxter gestured for the two agents to step inside. "Dr. Kyle will answer all your questions from here on out. I hope you enjoy your visit."

Mulder could see the sincerity in Baxter's eyes. The kid was nearly floating on the balls of his feet, not an ounce of cynicism in his slender body. As long as he kept his attitude, he'd probably go far in the corporate-industrial world. *Great brochure material.*

Mulder and Scully thanked him, and together they stepped into Julian Kyle's office.

"Damn it! Just stay where you are. I'll get them back on in a second."

Mulder stood frozen next to Scully in complete darkness, his skin tingling as his pupils tried to dilate. The lights had gone off the second the door had slid shut behind them. He had caught a brief glance of a stocky man in a white lab coat moving toward them across a large, well-appointed office— then everything had gone black. A second later, there had been a loud crash, followed by the sound of breaking glass.

"It's this new environmentally sensitive system," the frustrated voice continued from a corner of the room. "It's all Bill Gates's fault. He had to go and build that intelligent house, and suddenly every new designer wants to copy his technology. The system is supposed to shut off the lights when you *leave* the room—not when someone else enters. Hold on, here we go."

There was a metallic cough, and suddenly a panel of fluorescent lights flickered to life. The office was about thirty feet across, square, with two wide picture windows overlooking the parking lot and the same crimson walls that lined the building's corridors. There was a glass desk at one end of the airy room, covered with fancy computer equipment and neat little stacks of CD-ROMs. In front of the desk crouched a black leather love seat with high armrests. Directly to the left of the love seat, a display case's chrome frame lay surrounded by a pile of broken glass. Half-buried in the glass was a shiny plastic rectangle painted in colors running from pink to beige.

"Shit. If it's broken, I'm going to charge it to the board. This whole reconstruction was their idea. I thought we were doing fine with white walls, doorknobs, and light switches."

Julian Kyle swept out of the far corner of the room, his white coat flapping behind him. He was built like a fire hydrant, with solid shoulders, stumpy legs, and a cube-shaped head. His silver hair was cropped close to the planes of his skull, and his face was remarkably chiseled and unwrinkled for a man of his age. Sixty-five, Mulder guessed, but it was difficult to be sure. There was a vigorous spring in the doctor's step as he rushed to the destroyed display case and carefully reached for the large plastic object.

"Can we help?" Scully asked, as both agents moved forward. Kyle shook his head, carefully lifting the object and shaking away the broken glass. Mulder saw that it was some sort of model, made up of different-colored horizontal layers, each a few inches in height.

"An award from the International Burn Victim's Society," Kyle explained, reverently checking the model for scratches. "It's a three-dimensional cross section of an undamaged segment of human skin. See, it's even got the melanocyte layer—done in bronze leaf."

Mulder looked more closely at the model as Kyle placed it gently on an empty corner of his glass desk. The cross section was divided into three parts, showing the epidermis at the top, then the thick, beige dermis, and finally the white layer of subcutaneous fat. Tiny blood vessels and twisting branches of nerves curled through the middle section, winding delicately around tubular sweat glands and dark, towering follicles of hair. Mulder was struck by the intricacy of the skin's structure. He knew skin was an organ—the body's largest—but he had never considered what that meant. To Mulder, skin was just there. It could be rough or soft, porcelain like Scully's or stained and creased like the Cancer Man's.

Kyle noticed Mulder's focus as he moved to the other side of his desk. "Most people suffer from a misconception when it comes to skin. They assume it's something static, like a leather coat wrapped around your body to keep your skeleton warm. But nothing could be further from the truth. The skin is an amazing organ. It's in a constant state of motion; basal cells migrating upward to replace the dying epidermal cells, nerves reacting to inputs from the outside, blood vessels feeding muscles and fat, sweat glands struggling to regulate the body's temperature as the cells twist and stretch to accommodate movement. Not to mention the constant healing and recovery process, or the battle to stay moist and elastic."

Mulder lowered himself next to Scully onto the leather two-seater as Kyle took a seat behind the desk, holding his hands out in front of him, palms inward. He wriggled his fingers as if typing on an invisible keyboard. "We never notice our skin until there's something wrong with it. A cut, a rash—or a burn. Then we realize how important it really is. How much we'd be willing to pay to get it back to normal."

Mulder nodded, thinking of the building's front atrium. "Enough to import most of the marble in Italy."

Kyle laughed. Then his smile turned down at the corners, as he waved his hands at the walls on either side. "And have this entire complex dyed crimson. It had to be the worst decision this new board's ever made. Yes, we specialize in burn-transplant materials—but do we need the constant, fiery reminder on every wall in this damn complex? Still, they tell me that it impresses our foreign visitors, the corporate honchos from Tokyo, Seoul, and now Beijing."

"Sounds like business is good," Scully commented.

"Literally," Kyle beamed. "Our new product line is helping thousands of people survive transplants that would have seemed pointless just a few years ago. We've got new salve bandages, a whole new stock of microscalpels, an innovative new dry-chemical wrap—just to mention a few of our recent breakthroughs."

Mulder listened to the laundry list in silence. Julian Kyle seemed as enthusiastic about Fibrol as the kid at the front desk was—only Kyle's fervor had an edge of self-importance to it. It was as if he was telling them that Fibrol had accomplished these things directly because of his efforts.

"Actually," Scully said, as Kyle's monologue finally drew to a close, "it's your company's past that interests us at the moment. Specifically, an episode in 1984 involving two prisoners at Rikers Island."

Kyle raised his gray eyebrows. The motion pulled at the taut skin around his jaw, revealing a perfectly centered cleft. His face had an almost military bearing—and Mulder guessed he would have been just as comfortable in fatigues and an army helmet as he was in the white lab coat. "Forgive my surprise, Agent Scully. It's been a long time since anyone has asked about that. It's something we've put way behind us—ever since Emile's death."

The air in the small office had changed, as if the molecules themselves had somehow tightened along with Kyle's mood. Mulder tried to read the man's expression, searching for any sense of guilt or signs of hidden knowledge. But the man's surprise seemed sincere.

"It was an unfortunate incident," Kyle continued. "And I'm afraid I don't have much to tell you. Emile Paladin was a very private, controlling man. The experiment was entirely under his control, conducted in his own private clinic a hundred miles upstate. It had something to do with a new transplant procedure—but beyond that, I don't know any of the details."

Mulder saw the frustrated lines appear on Scully's forehead. She had expected a simple answer and, instead, they had run into another wall. Kyle spread his hands out against the desk, continuing in a casual voice. "After the criminal charges were dropped, Paladin announced the experimental procedure an unsalvageable failure and refocused the company toward the development of assistance products, rather than transplant techniques. Barely six months later, he died—but Fibrol continued to grow in the new direction."

Mulder shifted against the leather couch. Kyle had told them exactly what they already knew from the S&P reports. The blame had been shifted to Fibrol's founder, and since his death the company had moved in a different direction.

Scully cleared her throat, getting straight to the point. "Dr. Kyle, we have reason to believe that an individual died this morning from complications similar to those that killed the two prisoners. Do you have any idea how that might be possible?"

Kyle stared at her in shock. "Not at all. As I said, Paladin was the only one who knew anything about the experiment, and Paladin died almost fifteen years ago. I can't imagine how anything so recent could be connected."

Scully cocked her head. "We read that Paladin died in some sort of accident overseas?"

Kyle nodded. "A hiking accident in Thailand. It was his second home, ever since the Vietnam War. He had been stationed in a MASH unit, and after the incident he had wanted to take some time off in a serene, comfortable place. He had a home outside a little fishing village called Alkut, two hundred miles east of Bangkok. He died while climbing in the mountains around his home."

"And after his death," Scully interrupted. "Who inherited control of the company? Did he leave behind any family?"

"A brother. Andrew Paladin. But although Andrew is the major stockholder, he doesn't have any involvement with the company. You see, Andrew's what you'd call a recluse. He served in the Vietnam War about the same time as his brother, and in the early seventies an injury landed him in Emile's MASH unit in Alkut. After the war he settled in Thailand, and he hasn't left the country since."

"Is there some way we can get in touch with him?" Scully asked. "To see if he has any more information on Paladin's experiment?"

Kyle shrugged. "Not that I know of. He employed a lawyer in Bangkok around the time of his brother's death, but we haven't heard from him in more than ten years. From what I understand, nobody is even sure of his current address. But I'd doubt he'd be useful, even if you found him. As I said, Paladin was extremely independent. He kept his work private."

Kyle crossed his arms against his chest. To him, the interview was ending. But Mulder wasn't near finished. He leaned close to the desk, abruptly changing tack. "Dr. Kyle, tell us about Antibacterial Compound 1279."

For the first time in the short interview, Kyle's calm seemed to break. It was barely perceptible—a tightening of the skin around his eyes—and it vanished as quickly as it had appeared. But Mulder was acutely attuned to the signs of human discomfort—and he knew when someone suddenly found himself unprepared.

"The Dust?" Kyle responded. "I'm amazed you've even heard of it. We only received the patent last year. It's going to be one of our major market leaders within the next decade. Why are you interested in our antibacterial powder? It's a very recent development—it had nothing at all to do with Emile Paladin's work."

Mulder glanced at Scully. He had not mentioned any connection to Paladin's experiment—Kyle had made the jump himself. Scully followed Mulder's lead, her voice stiff but nonconfrontational. "Dr. Kyle, yesterday morning we found a sample of your powder in a breakdown lane on the FDR Drive."

Kyle wrinkled the skin above his eyes. Then he rubbed a hand against his jaw. "That's certainly strange. None of the New York hospitals are using the Dust yet. Still, I guess it could have come from a shipment between a couple of our clinics. Our largest burn center is twenty miles north of here, and we have a research laboratory down in Hoboken, New Jersey. It's something I can easily check out."

Scully nodded—but Mulder wasn't about to leave it at that. "We'd also like to consider another possibility. Could the Dust have been left behind by a recent transplant patient?"

Kyle stared at him in silence. Then he laughed curtly. "That's extremely unlikely. In fact, I'd say it's damn near impossible. The Dust is used only on radical transplant patients. These are not patients who get up and walk around. They can't even survive transport in ambulances. There's no way such a patient would be found out of a hospital. Not even for a moment."

Mulder was surprised by Kyle's adamant tone. Even if it was unlikely, was it really impossible that a burn clinic might have decided to transport a patient, despite the risks? "Well, perhaps you could show us some data on the powder, to help us understand. Maybe a list of the types of patients you've used it on—"

"I'm sorry," Kyle interrupted, rising from his chair. He was still smiling, but his eyes were now miles away. "But I really need to speak to the board before I can get to any of our records. I don't mean to be difficult—but this is a very competitive time for our company. I need to go through the proper channels before I release any proprietary information."

Kyle hadn't mentioned a search warrant, but it was obvious to Mulder that it would take a warrant to get the information he'd requested. The question was—was Kyle just being a good, loyal employee? Or was there something else going on?

Scully got up from the love seat first, and Mulder followed as Kyle hit an intercom buzzer on his desk, then strolled toward the couch. Mulder was much taller than the doctor—but still, Kyle cut an impressive, intimidating figure. As Kyle showed the two agents to the door, Mulder finally asked the question that had been on his mind since the beginning of the interview. "Dr. Kyle—I hope you don't mind my asking—but did you serve in the military?"

Scully glanced at Mulder, surprised by the question. But Kyle simply smiled. "For twelve years. I joined up in the mid-fifties. I was promoted to major during Vietnam. It's where I met Emile Paladin. I served under him in Alkut. It's where I was first introduced to the art of transplantation. I saw firsthand how important the skin could be—and how easily, and painfully, it could be damaged."

There was a near fanatic's determination in Kyle's eyes. Mulder had no doubt that Kyle would do anything necessary to protect Fibrol from danger—real or perceived.

"I'm sorry I couldn't be more helpful," Kyle continued, as he put his palm against the plate next to the door. "Mr. Baxter will show you back to your car. I'll be in touch if I find any more information for you."

The door hissed open, and Mulder and Scully were once again face-to-face with Dick Baxter. They followed the smiling young man back through the network of crimson hallways.

It wasn't until they were back in the privacy of their rental Chevrolet that Mulder finally told Scully what he was thinking. "Kyle knows something. About the red powder—and about Paladin's experiment. We need to keep digging."

Scully was momentarily silent, her hands on the dashboard in front of her. Finally, she shrugged. "It won't be easy. Emile Paladin died nearly fifteen years ago. According to Kyle, he took the secrets of his experiment with him."

Mulder wasn't going to accept anything Kyle had said at face value. Paladin might have died years ago—but his experiment was more than history. It was somehow involved in the Stanton case. "And what about the red powder? And the link to the John Doe?"

"I thought Kyle was pretty convincing. It could have fallen out of a shipment of medical supplies. The link with the John Doe is still unproven."

Mulder turned the ignition, and the car kicked to life. "Fibrol's involved; the MRI pictures don't lie. Stanton was another victim of Emile Paladin's transplantation experiment. And if Kyle can't tell us how that's possible, then we've got to find someone who can."

He could see that Scully was thinking along the same lines. As they were waved through the first security checkpoint at the edge of the parking lot, she put words to his thoughts. "Andrew Paladin. The recluse brother. He might have been the last person to speak to Emile Paladin before he died."

Mulder nodded, glancing at the boxlike complex shrinking rapidly in the Chevy's rearview mirror. They could spend weeks, even months, trying to crack through Fibrol's nondescript facade; but Mulder had a strong feeling that the answers they were looking for lay all the way on the other side of the world.

THIRTEEN

Left alone in his windowless office, Julian Kyle placed both hands flat on the cold surface of his glass desk, staring intently at the two imprints in the leather couch across from him. He wondered how many millions of plate-shaped epidermal cells rested in the microscopic canyons in the leather, how many millions of infinitesimal, cellular reminders of the FBI agents floated in the invisible drafts of air. He thought about Agent Mulder's dark, intelligent eyes, and Scully's determined, penetrating voice. He thought about the questions they had asked—and their reactions to his answers.

Kyle considered himself good at reading people—but the two agents were a mystery. Their texture was all wrong. They did not seem like the carbon-copy intelligence officers Kyle had dealt with many times in his career. They were smart, and they would not give up easily.

Kyle thought for a long moment, then reached beneath his desk and hit a small button located just above his knees. A few seconds later the door to his office slid open.

He watched as the tall young man with slicked-back sable hair slid into the room and tossed himself onto the couch, his long legs hooked nonchalantly over one of the armrests. The man's narrow eyes flickered playfully toward the shattered display case beside the desk, a smirk settling on his lips. "Having a bad day, Uncle Julian?"

Kyle grimaced as the man's heavy Thai accent trickled into his ears. He hated the artificial familiarity. He had watched the young man grow up—but thankfully, there was no physical relationship between them. Kyle considered himself a religious, moral man. This man was something altogether different. Warped. Perverted. Dangerous. *All of his father's sins—without any of his father's virtues.*

"We have a problem, Quo Tien," Kyle responded, keeping the conversation as short as possible. "The situation has not yet been contained."

The young man raised an eyebrow. Then he stretched his arms above his head. Kyle could see the sinewy muscles stretching beneath Quo Tien's caramel skin. An involuntary shudder moved through Kyle's shoulders.

He had served in Vietnam, had known many dangerous men; but the Amerasian man truly terrified him. He knew the pleasure Quo Tien took in his work, the sheer, almost sexual enthusiasm that accompanied his acts of silent violence. For years, he had witnessed the limitless exploitation of the child's perverse appetite.

He hated the fact that he, too, had taken part in that exploitation. And that conditions might force him to use the young man once again. "These two FBI agents aren't going to be easily dissuaded. They can't be allowed to get any closer."

"You worry too much," Quo Tien interrupted, running a hand through his dark hair. "They don't even have a body to work with. As long as we remain a step ahead of them, they'll have nothing but guesses."

Kyle rubbed his square jaw. Quo Tien was right—but Kyle didn't like to take chances. Especially so close to the final phase of the experiment. "At this stage, even guesses can be dangerous."

The Amerasian laced his fingers together, then shrugged. "As always, I eagerly await your orders."

Kyle searched the young man's eyes for some deeper meaning—but saw nothing but limitless black pits. He took a deep breath, slowly reaching for his phone. "It's not my orders you follow, Quo Tien. Don't you ever forget that. For both our sakes."

FOURTEEN

Scully watched the creases appear above Assistant Director Skinner's eyeglasses as he drummed his fingers against the open file on his desk. As usual, Scully felt stiff and uncomfortable in Skinner's wood-paneled office on the third floor of the FBI headquarters in Washington. Mulder looked much more relaxed on the shiny leather couch to her right, but she knew it was a well-practiced facade. Her own turbulent alliance with their supervisor did not compare to the chaotic, sometimes violent relationship between Mulder and the bald, spectacled ex-Marine who governed both their careers.

Well over six feet tall, Skinner had a professional athlete's body, chiseled features, and stone gray eyes. A perpetual frown was carved above his prominent jaw, and the packed muscles in his neck and shoulders struggled against the material of his dignified, dark suit. Power emanated from every inch of his body, and Scully had no doubt that Skinner could easily snap Mulder over one knee. At the same time, the man's brutish physique belied an intense and brilliant deductive mind; there wasn't much that went on in Washington Skinner didn't know about. That knowledge—and Skinner's ambiguous association with both the established military and the shadowy men behind the scenes—made him a natural target for Mulder's paranoia. Likewise, Mulder's unorthodox methods and nonconformist beliefs constantly antagonized Skinner, sometimes pushing him past the point of control. Scully prayed the afternoon meeting would be brief.

Skinner closed the file and crossed his arms against his chest. He shifted his gaze toward the window, letting the hazy sunlight play across the curves of his glasses. Behind him, Skinner's office was Spartan, another reflection of the AD's personality. Aside from the wood paneling and the pristine leather furniture, the only distinguishing possessions were a colorful U.S. wall map, and a framed photo of Janet Reno by the door. The map was covered in plastic pushpins, each representing an open federal case. Scully could not help but notice the large white pin jutting out of Manhattan.

"Red powder picked off of a highway and a few MRI scans," Skinner finally commented, still gazing out the window. "It's not much to go on. Especially when you consider the expense, and the red tape involved."

Scully nodded. "We wouldn't be here if there was any other way, sir. It's a unique situation. Perry Stanton's condition—a condition that caused him to commit murder—needs to be explained. At the moment, Agent Mulder and I believe that Fibrol is a dead end; even with a search warrant, it's doubtful we'll find any evidence of Emile Paladin's work, or any connection to the current MRIs. We believe that the only possible source of new information is in Thailand."

Skinner turned back from the window. "Andrew Paladin. The deceased subject's brother. You say he lives in the vicinity of a town called Alkut."

"It's a tiny fishing village on the southeastern coast," Scully continued. She had researched Alkut by airphone during the short shuttle flight from New York. "The population is around five thousand, mostly fishermen and their families. No tourist industry as of yet, because the town is still inaccessible by train or airplane. There's no local police force to speak of, and not much of a municipal structure. There's no way to reach Andrew Paladin through the local authorities."

Skinner nodded. "What about one of our foreign agencies? State Department, CIA, perhaps even the DEA? They've got people all over Southeast Asia."

Mulder coughed, crossing his legs. He avoided looking Skinner directly in the eyes. "Our investigation is still in a fetal stage, sir. Andrew Paladin is not the final step—just the necessary next step. It's not simply a matter of having him answer a few questions."

Skinner raised his eyebrows. He leaned back in his high-backed chair. "Agent Scully? Do you agree with Agent Mulder? Is Thailand the necessary next step?"

Scully took a deep breath. She did not relish the idea of traveling halfway around the world. But she knew there was little choice; Stanton's MRIs were impossible to explain—and as long as his death was a mystery, the case was still open. The only real clue they had was the connection to Fibrol and Emile Paladin's fifteen-year-old experiment. In New York, that translated to a corporate dead end; Julian Kyle could hide behind his board of directors for months, and the investigation would get nowhere. That had left them with two options: leave the case standing—or follow the only real avenue left open.

Scully met Skinner's gaze. She knew his decision would be based on her answer. "If we want to question Andrew Paladin about his brother's activities, we're going to have to do it in person. That's if we can find him at all."

Skinner paused, watching her expression. Finally, he nodded.

Twenty-one hours later, Scully's fingers dug into a thick faux-leather seat cushion as the 747 wide-body lurched upward, ambushed by turbulent swirls of dense black air. There was a sudden moment of weightlessness; then the plane rolled sickeningly to the right. Scully glanced toward the oval window next to her—but it was like staring into a pool of oil, shades of sable broken only by the distant flash of lightning.

"It's moments like these that make me glad I'm a believer," Mulder commented from the seat to Scully's right, nervously stretching his arms out in front of him. "I think I've discovered twelve new religions in the last five minutes alone."

"I'm still hanging on to the laws of aerodynamics and the statistics of air travel," Scully responded. "But if it gets any worse, I'll be getting my rosary beads out of the overhead compartment. This is pretty damn intense."

"Southeast Asia in July, Scully. The fun's just getting started. In a couple of weeks this will look like a calm spring evening."

Scully turned away from the window and tried to concentrate on the laptop computer resting precariously on her knees. The screen had changed from green to gray as the internal modem struggled to extract information from the static-ridden airphone link Scully had established before the storm set in. She tapped her fingers against the keyboard, trying to shake life into her fatigued muscles. It had been a long, tedious flight. Even in the relative comfort of Thai Airline's business class, twenty-two hours felt like an eternity.

But as she had told Assistant Director Skinner, there had been no other choice. They needed information, and the only true source was in Thailand.

"Andrew Paladin," Scully said out loud, as her laptop suddenly cleared. The picture took up half of the screen, and Mulder leaned closer to get a better look. Tall, muscular, with wide shoulders and a blond crew cut. Wearing a green infantry uniform, arms stiffly at his side. It was obviously an army recruitment photo, and Andrew Paladin had the dead look of a career foot soldier in his narrow blue eyes.

"He looks a lot heavier than his brother," Muider commented. "Wider in the shoulders, maybe a few inches shorter."

Scully nodded. They had already looked through a dozen photos of Emile Paladin, most taken around the time of the Fibrol scandal involving the prisoners. Emile Paladin had been a handsome man, long and thin, with intelligent eyes and an amiable smile. He had photographed well—and often. Especially in the years just before his death. But Andrew Paladin was a different story. "This is all I can find, Mulder. I've been through every data bank I can think of, and all I'm getting is an army recruitment photo and a paragraph of statistics. Born in upstate New York like his brother, served two years in South Vietnam before getting wounded in action. He was twenty-two years old at the time, and a pretty good soldier. Decorated twice for heroism, consistently good reports from his commanding officers. But after his injury, the reports end. He was sent to his brother's MASH unit in Alkut—and pretty much disappeared from record."

Mulder caught the side of the laptop as the airplane jerked hard to the left. "What about his wounds? Anything in his file about where he was hit—or how badly?"

Scully shook her head. She had skimmed Andrew Paladin's brief military file while Mulder had watched the third in-flight movie, *something about a family of talking cats*. "Well, his injuries were bad enough to take him out of the war. He received a medical discharge three months after arriving in Alkut. But there are no specifics in his file. It's odd, Mulder; the army is usually pretty good about this sort of thing. There should be some sort of medical chart, something the VA hospital system could refer to in case of future problems."

"Well," Mulder said, thinking out loud, "Emile Paladin was in charge of his brother's medical care, right? If he had wanted to keep the details off the record, he wouldn't have had much trouble."

Scully caught her breath as the lights in the cabin flickered, then resumed. The storm seemed to be getting worse, huge raindrops crackling against the Plexiglas double window. "Why would he want to keep his brother's medical state a secret?"

Mulder paused, as if debating bringing something out in the open. As usual, he decided not to edit his thoughts. "Emile Paladin might have had something to hide. He might still have something to hide."

Scully stared at him. "Mulder, Emile Paladin died fifteen years ago."

"Right on the tail of a scandal that could have landed him in jail—or threatened the company he had built."

Scully paused. "So you think the timing of his death is a bit convenient."

"And the circumstances, Scully. He died in an accident overseas. His recluse brother inherited controlling interest in his company—but remained completely invisible, without even an address or a phone number on record. A brother whose history seems to have ended more than twenty-five years ago—again, in mysterious circumstances."

Scully shook her head. "I agree that there are a lot of loose ends. But to suggest that Emile Paladin faked his death—for what reason, Mulder? And how does Andrew Paladin fit in?"

Mulder shrugged. "Perhaps Emile Paladin wanted to continue his research in secret. Perhaps his brother is helping him keep his work private. And perhaps, somehow, Emile Paladin let something leak out—something that caused Perry Stanton's rampage and death. Something that forced a cover-up that led to the murder of two medical students."

Scully leaned back in her seat, her thoughts as turbulent as the air outside. Mulder's paranoia had caused him to jump beyond the evidence—to conclusions he could not back up with facts. There was no reason to believe that Emile Paladin was still alive. Nor was there any way to connect the polyps inside Perry Stanton's skull with the deaths of the two medical students— much less classify their deaths as murder. But at the same time, Scully knew better than to discard Mulder's theory out of hand. His intuition—as insane as it often seemed—was unparalleled. "We're not here to chase a dead man, Mulder. We're here to find Andrew Paladin."

Mulder was about to respond when the 747 suddenly dipped forward, the cabin lights blinking three times. A heavily accented voice explained that the airplane was beginning its descent toward Bangkok International Airport. Mulder waited for the captain to turn his attention back to the storm before clearing his throat. "You're right. Andrew Paladin is where we have to start. But I don't think this investigation is going to end with a few answers from a recluse brother."

Scully let the thought sit in the air between them, as the airplane slipped downward through the frantic black air.

Six rows back, Quo Tien's long fingers crawled spiderlike down the window by his shoulder, chasing the teardrops of rain on the other side. He could just barely see the cluttered lights of Bangkok breaking through the cloud cover as the 747 sank toward the waiting runway. The sprawling metropolis evoked conflicting emotions inside of him; he thought about the years he had spent in the city's nocturnal alleys, practicing his art, keeping himself toned and in tune—waiting for the next call to service. For seven years, Bangkok had fed his existence—but only Alkut had ever been his home.

Tien was a half-breed, the son of an American soldier and a Thai prostitute; in his culture, that made him polluted, untouchable. Still, he had never cursed the nature of his birth. The distance between himself and the children he had grown up with had nothing to do with the muted color of his skin. It had always been a matter of appetite. *A matter of hunger.*

He thought about the two agents seated a few yards away from him, and his stomach churned, a heat dancing up through his body. A smile spilled across his thin face, and he closed his eyes, caressed by the rhythm of the storm.

\\\\\\\\\\\\\\\\\\\\

Twelve hours later, the rain was coming down in wide gray sheets as Mulder navigated a rented four-wheel-drive Jeep down a road rapidly changing from dirt to mud. Scully had a U.S. Army surplus map open on her lap, and she was struggling to match the surroundings with twenty-year-old military notations. Mulder could see that she was both tired and frustrated; every time the Jeep hit one of the crater-sized potholes that seemed to spring up out of nowhere, Scully let out a curse, strands of wet hair flopping into her eyes. In truth, Mulder sympathized with her worsening disposition. Hunched forward over the jerking steering wheel, sweat running down his back and chest, his fingers aching from the pitted road and the Jeep's over-taxed, circa 1960s manual transmission—he felt anything but fresh.

So far, Thailand was not the tropical paradise he had imagined. The beauty of the country had gotten lost somewhere in the midst of the rain, the oppressive heat, the choking humidity—and the increasingly primitive conditions. Mulder had already stripped down to his thin cotton shirt and trousers—and still his skin felt prickly where the material stuck to him, each breath catching in his throat as he strove to adapt to the nearly gelatinous air.

Ahead, the road seemed almost a living thing, serpentine twists of dark mud slithering between the lush green trees. The sky had long ago vanished behind a canopy of rain clouds, and the Jeep's fog lights danced like ghosts as Mulder fought to keep the vehicle from pitching into the encroaching forest on either side.

Physical conditions aside, it had been an exhausting twelve hours since he and Scully had landed in Bangkok. After deplaning, they had been met at the terminal by their military liaison, an army corporal in dress uniform with a permanent sneer embedded in his chiseled face. Timothy Van Epps was a career soldier with little time or regard for FBI agents so far from their jurisdiction—and it was obvious he had been given the assignment at the last minute, without his approval. After taking the agents to a small, lifeless office behind the airport customs desk, he had rushed them through a brief discussion of the present state of U.S. relations with the Thai monarchy, and had handed them a sheet of printed directions to Alkut. Along with the directions came a map of the tiny fishing village and the surrounding geography—and a disclaimer: "Things may be a hell of a lot different in real life than they appear on that piece of toilet paper. We haven't had much use for that area since Vietnam—so most of those notations are twenty-five years old at best. If you want, you can fax me an updated version when you're done with your little trip."

Mulder doubted the U.S. Army needed FBI agents to update its information—especially in a region of Southeast Asia where it had once deployed extensive military resources. It was much more likely that Van Epps had been ordered—or had taken it upon himself—to be less than helpful. Not because of some sort of overarching conspiracy—although Scully would have assumed that was where Mulder's line of thought was heading—but simply because it was in the military's nature. The military often saw the FBI as an errant little sibling—to be tolerated, but certainly not encouraged. Especially when the little brother wanted to join in the fun overseas.

After giving them the map and information, Van Epps had escorted them to a government sedan with diplomatic plates and transported them from the airport to Hua Lamphong, Bangkok's main train station. The trip had been mind-numbing after the tedious flight. The Thai capital redefined the notion of an urban jungle: narrow, tightly packed streets jammed with compact cars, open-air buses, bicycles, and moped rickshaws—and everywhere you looked, people, so many millions of people. Thai men dressed in white business shirts and women in silk dresses, children in dark school uniforms and monks in bright orange robes: a never-ending sea of people, bouncing through the sidewalks like balls in a pachinko machine. Rising up above the sidewalks, the buildings themselves were something out of a schizophrenic's dream. Glass-and-steel offices towered over ancient, golden-roofed temples, while apartment complexes sprang up on every corner, each a mixture of a half dozen different architectural styles: jutting spires, cubic balconies, curved white corners, levels constructed of wood, plaster, stone, and steel. The buildings seemed locked in a battle between old and new, and the only constant was growth—perpetual, throbbing, unstoppable.

Mulder and Scully never had a chance to digest the eclectic images; Van Epps squired them to the crowded train station, a fairly modern complex lodged near the center of the city. He had pointed them toward the right set of iron rails, then waved them on their way. Mulder had not minded the hands-off treatment; he did not trust men like Van Epps, nor did he enjoy having the military watching over his shoulder. He and Scully were now free to conduct their investigation on their own terms and timetable.

Soon the swollen city of Bangkok had given way to a lush green country-side of dense forests and unending rice fields, as the train had briefly wound its way into the interior of the country on its journey toward the southeastern coast. Mulder had spent much of the trip conversing—in a mixture of English and inadequate French—with a Thai farmer on his way back home after a three-week trip to the great capital. When Mulder had told the rugged-looking man their destination, he had reacted strangely, backing away while grabbing at something near the collar of his shirt. Mulder had seen it was an amulet of some kind—a common Thai accoutrement. The Thai were one of the most superstitious and spiritual people on Earth, and most Thai men wore at least one Buddhist charm. Still, Mulder wondered why the mere mention of Alkut had caused such a reaction.

When Mulder had pressed the farmer on the issue, the man mumbled something about *mai dee phis*—literally, "bad spirits," as Mulder's English-Thai dictionary informed him. For the rest of the trip, he had stared out the window, avoiding conversation.

The train had taken the two agents as far as Rayong, a gulf town surrounded by white-sand beaches and sprawling European-style resorts. A fishing village famous for its *nam plaa*—"fish sauce," the most popular condiment in Thailand—Rayong bristled with coffee shops and souvenir markets catering to the large number of tourists visiting the nearby newly finished resorts.

Mulder and Scully had rented the Jeep just outside the town limits and begun the long drive away from the tourist centers, trekking deeper into the untouched southern regions of the country. The roads had quickly gone from asphalt to dirt, the scenery from controlled, sandy beauty spotted by palm trees and waterfront hotels to uninhabited tracts of dense forest and rocky cliffs. The closer they got to Alkut, the worse the conditions; in some instances, it seemed as if they had driven right off the edge of civilization.

"The town shouldn't be much farther," Scully commented as she unfolded a corner of the map and gestured at a break in the trees just beyond Mulder's shoulder. "I think the Gulf of Thailand is directly down that slope. And that outcropping to the right—that leads straight up into the mountains. See Dum Kao—'the Black Hills.' A twelve-thousand-foot ascension to its highest peak, dropping off right into the border with Kampuchea. According to the map, the See Dum range encompasses an area of nearly two hundred square miles. Mostly unlivable and uncharted—rife with mud slides, avalanches, predators, and disease-carrying insects."

"Recluse heaven," Mulder said. "Hide out in a cave somewhere, eat a few indigenous animals for supper, have your recluse buddies over on the weekends to watch the mud slides—"

"Mulder!"

The Jeep tipped perilously forward as the dirt road suddenly disappeared in a descending tangle of thick vegetation and loose rocks. Mulder yanked the steering wheel hard to the right, fighting to keep the headlights facing forward as the Jeep tumbled down the steep embankment. Tree branches lashed at the side windows as rocks the size of basketballs shot up around the churning tires. There was a brief second of dead silence as the Jeep lurched over some sort of rotted trunk—then the tires crashed down against packed dirt.

Mulder slammed his foot against the brake. The Jeep fishtailed to the left, then skidded to a complete stop. Eyes wild, Mulder looked up—and saw that they were parked at the edge of a cobblestone road, facing a long, flat valley bordered on three sides by the rising forest. The Gulf of Thailand was no more than three hundred yards to the left, separated from the road by huge granite boulders and gnarled trees that looked like a cross between a palm and a birch. Mulder was momentarily stunned by the sight; the clear blue water stretched on forever beneath the sky, flat and glistening like a plane of opaque glass. Mulder could make out a long wooden dock fifty yards away, surrounded by brightly colored Chinese-style junks and smaller, motorized fishing boats. The rain did not seem to deter the fishermen—tiny shapes garbed in dark green, hooded smocks moved on the boats' decks and along the dock. Mulder watched for a full minute as four fishermen struggled with a tangled net hanging off the back of one of the junks. Then he turned his attention back to the road ahead as he carefully restarted the Jeep's engine.

"I think we've found Alkut," Scully commented, breathing hard. She lifted her hands off the dashboard and pushed her hair out of her eyes. Mulder followed her gaze, letting the Jeep idle as he surveyed the scenery.

The cobblestone road ran parallel to the Gulf, leading toward the center of the quiet fishing village. Beginning twenty yards ahead, low wooden buildings were spaced every few hundred feet along both sides of the road, with shuttered windows and colorful vinyl overhangs covered in huge Thai letters. Most of the buildings seemed to be commercial shops, but Mulder recognized a few traditional Thai houses, with thatched roofs and slanted outer walls. Most of the buildings stood on short wooden stilts, and Mulder had a feeling the town spent many weeks of the rainy season under a few feet of water.

Farther down the road, the commercial buildings and traditional houses seemed to cling closer together, spreading backward from the main road in dense pockets, some rising as high as two or three stories. People of various ages, shapes, and sizes moved between the buildings, and Mulder counted at least a dozen other cars in the vicinity—most even older and more dilapidated than the mud-spattered rented Jeep. The cars shared the road with brightly colored wooden rickshaws, attached to rusty bicycles with wide umbrellas sticking up from their handlebars. Like the fishermen out by the dock, nobody seemed to notice the rain. The rickshaws careened between the cars, the drivers shouting at one another in singsongy Thai syllables. A small group of children ran along the edge of the road ten feet ahead, a pair of barking dogs following behind. To their right, two old women haggled loudly over a line of dried fish spread across a huge blanket beneath one of the vinyl overhangs.

"It's certainly quaint," Scully said, as the Jeep rolled toward the center of town. "And quite different from Bangkok. It's hard to believe they're both part of the same country."

Mulder nodded. "It's a nation in transition. Bangkok is a microcosm of the whole—a totally modern, commercialized city with a preindustrial feel. Alkut, on the other hand, seems lodged much further in the country's past. Less than five thousand residents, probably no tourist industry to speak of. Just fishermen and their families. And maybe a couple of Westerners left over from the war."

As he spoke, his gaze settled on an elderly man standing by the edge of the road, a wide, toothless smile on his lips. The man wore three necklaces around his thin, bare chest, each supporting a tiny rectangular block of jade. *Amulets, like the one worn by the farmer on the train,* Mulder reminded himself: The country had more spirits per capita than anywhere else in the world. Men wore as many as a dozen amulets to guard against everything from disease to fishing accidents. Still, something about the old man unnerved Mulder. Not merely his relative indifference at seeing two *farangs* rolling into town—but something deeper, something in his smile and his dark eyes. It was almost as though he had been expecting the two agents.

Mulder shook his head, telling himself it was just the rain, the unending sheets of gray screwing with his perspective. The old man was simply friendly—like most Thais. The next few villagers they passed offered up the same genuine smile, and Mulder's suspicions trickled away. As the Jeep moved deeper into Alkut, he glanced at the map in Scully's hands. "See anything that resembles a hotel?"

Scully shrugged. "I'm sure we'll find something near the center of town. Nothing fancy—but we just need a place to dump our stuff. Then we can start tracking down Andrew Paladin."

Mulder tossed a quick glance at the forest that rose up above the town, leading into the foothills of the See Dum mountain range. He thought about the two hundred square miles of uncharted land surrounding Alkut. He wondered which was easier, tracking a recluse in all that expanse of wilderness—or trailing a man who had supposedly died fifteen years ago. He had a feeling that both searches would lead to the same goal—the truth behind what had happened to Perry Stanton.

\\\\\\\\\\\\\\\\\\

"This looks like the spot," Scully said, huddled next to Mulder beneath the skimpy overhang of a tired-looking palm tree. "According to the army's records, this clinic was built over the original location of Emile Paladin's MASH unit."

Mulder kicked water out of his right shoe, then pushed back a wet palm leaf to get a better look at the building before them. The clinic was low and rectangular, stretching along the muddy road for about twenty yards. The walls were made of aging yellow cinder blocks, and the roof was sloped and encircled by a patchwork of iron rain gutters, overflowing at the corners into huge wooden barrels lodged in the thick mud. There were a half dozen crude windows cut into the cinder-block facade, covered in thick sheets of transparent plastic. Above the nondescript main entrance was a carved, grinning Buddha sunk directly into the wall, beneath two rows of Thai lettering. The Buddha was plated in gold, seated with crossed legs, palms facing upward in what Mulder recognized as the southern, meditative style. According to the white-haired old man who ran the small hotel where Mulder and Scully had deposited their things, Buddhist monks had been running the clinic for nearly ten years.

"Mulder, check out the building across the street. Isn't that a church?"

Mulder turned to look at the small two-story structure that faced the clinic. The building was painted white, with a single conic steeple rising almost twenty feet above the slanted roof. The top of the steeple housed a small bell tower, but the bell was missing, along with a fair-sized chunk of plaster where the steeple met the church's slanted roof. The place looked as though it had been shut down a long time ago, and the front doors were covered in the same transparent plastic as the clinic's windows. "It doesn't look as if they're doing a very brisk business."

"Thailand is the only country in Southeast Asia never to have been a European colony," Scully commented. "Christianity never gained a foothold here."

Mulder turned away from the church and gestured toward an object just in front of the clinic. It was a small wooden dollhouse set on top of a cylindrical post. The miniature house was three feet long and half as high, and had obviously been constructed with great care. The walls were painted in bright colors, and the roof was tiled in strips of what looked to be pure gold. The tiny windows had polished glass panes, and even the doorknobs had been molded out of brass. Someone had recently placed mounds of fresh garlands around the base of the house, and two long sticks of incense leaked smoke past the tiny glass windows. "Christianity never had a chance. The indigenous religion is too strong."

Mulder started forward toward the little house and the entrance to the clinic. His shoulders involuntarily arched forward against the warm rain. "It's a spirit house, Scully. They're a common sight in any town in Thailand—even in Bangkok, the most sophisticated city in the country. They serve as the homes of the resident *phis*—spirits—of the particular building nearby."

Scully raised her eyebrows as they passed close to the spirit house. She leaned over the beautiful pressed flowers that peeked from the tiny windows. "You seem to know a lot about the Thai religion, Mulder."

Mulder smiled as they reached the door to the clinic. "I have an enormous respect for the Thai—always have. Their spirituality is extremely individualistic. In fact, the word *Thai* means 'free.' Their beliefs aren't a matter of doctrine—but of day-to-day observation. If they choose to placate a certain spirit, it's because they've witnessed the results of having that spirit become angry. Not because someone has told them it's the right thing to do."

Scully glanced at Mulder. He knew that she was trying to gauge whether or not he was serious. His face gave her no clues as he reached for the door to the clinic. "There's something to be said for a culture that's remained independent—without even a single civil war—for over eight hundred years."

The door came open, and Mulder felt cool air touch his wet cheeks. He ushered Scully out of the rain and shut the door behind them. They were standing at the edge of a wide rectangular hall with plaster walls and a cement floor. The place was well lit by a pair of fluorescent tubes hanging from the high tiled ceiling, and a crisp, antiseptic scent filled the air. More than a dozen litters were set up along the two sidewalls, complete with IV racks, medical carts, and the odd EKG machine. The litters were modern, with chrome frames, steel wheels, and thick hospital bedding. At least half the litters were occupied.

Buddhist monks in orange robes moved among the patients, followed by nurses in white Red Cross uniforms. Mulder noticed that the monks were wearing latex gloves and many had stethoscopes around their necks. All things considered, the place was sparser than a Western clinic, but seemed modern and efficient. Compared to the rest of the sleepy fishing village, the clinic was almost cosmopolitan.

Scully touched Mulder's shoulder, pointing toward one of the litters. Two monks hovered over the chrome rail, watching as a tall, blond Caucasian woman leaned close to the patient's chest. Mulder noticed that her jacket was different from the ones worn by the Red Cross nurses, longer in the back with an open front. Beneath the jacket, the woman was wearing light blue surgical scrubs.

"Looks like she's in charge," Scully said. "That's an MD's jacket. And the way she's wearing her stethoscope—she's trained in the U.S. At least through her internship."

As Mulder and Scully approached the litter, the woman stepped back, letting the two monks have a better look at what she had just done. Mulder's eyes shifted to the patient. The man was mid-forties, conscious, with his shirt tied down around his waist. A thin line of fresh sutures ran from his upper abdomen to just below his collarbone. Mulder could see the approval in Scullys eyes; the woman had done a good job closing the wound.

"We'll put him on antibiotics for three weeks," the woman said to the monks. "He should be as good as new. Unless he gets in the way of another swordfish hook."

The monks nodded vigorously, and the woman turned, noticing the two agents for the first time. "You two look like you're from out of town. I'm Dr. Lianna Fielding. Is there something I can help you with?"

Mulder slid his ID out of his pants pocket, watching Fielding's expression as she studied the FBI seal. She was tall—almost Mulder's height, with sharp features and narrow blue eyes. "I'm Fox Mulder, this is my partner, Dana Scully. We're U.S. federal agents, and we were hoping you could spare a moment of your time. Are you a full-time resident of Alkut, Dr. Fielding?"

Fielding pulled off her latex gloves and tossed them toward a plastic waste bin. "Actually, I'm attached to the local division of the Red Cross. I make a tour of all of the towns and villages in the area, teaching and assisting as much as I can. U.S. federal agents? You're rather far from home, aren't you?"

Scully had stepped next to the litter and was surveying the stitches. The two monks were next to her, conversing in quiet Thai. Mulder noticed that Scully was being careful to keep a respectable distance between herself and the monks, as Buddhist law dictated. "From your cross-stitching, Dr. Fielding, my guess is you trained in the States. Is that right?"

"Chicago. Are you a doctor?" Scully nodded. "Forensic pathology. But I'm not here in that capacity."

"We're investigating a case that goes back fifteen years," Mulder interrupted. "We're interested in finding two men connected to the MASH unit that used to be located on this spot. Emile and Andrew Paladin—"

Fielding coughed, then glanced at the two monks, who had both looked up at the mention of the names. "If you're federal agents, I'm sure you must know that Emile Paladin died a long time ago."

Mulder's instincts kicked in as he watched the two monks whispering to one another. Something about Emile Paladin's name had struck a nerve— fifteen years after the fact. Lianna Fielding noticed the change in Mulder's eyes and made an attempt at explanation. "Emile Paladin is a part of this town's history, Agent Mulder. His MASH unit was many of the townspeople's first real contact with the outside world. And as you probably know, the Thai have an extremely—creative—way of thinking. Things that are different inspire stories, legends—and fear. And from what I understand, Emile Paladin was indeed different."

Mulder felt his muscles tense. "How do you mean?"

Fielding started to answer when a commotion broke out near the doorway to the clinic. Mulder turned and saw an old man being half-carried toward a litter by two younger men in fishing gear. The old man was moaning in obvious, excruciating pain, clutching wildly at his leg. Without a word, Fielding quickly grabbed a fresh pair of gloves from a nearby cart and rushed past the two agents. She shouted something in Thai to one of the young men, and received a high-pitched response.

Fielding reached the litter a few steps ahead of Scully. Mulder saw that the old man's pants had been torn away below the knee. His right leg had turned a strange purple color and was speckled with circular blisters. Fielding spoke quietly to the man, trying to calm him, as a monk handed her a vial of clear liquid. She poured the liquid over the purple area, and Mulder caught the distinct scent of vinegar.

"Jellyfish," Scully commented, watching Fielding work. "Maybe a man-of-war. Incredibly painful, sometimes even fatally so. The vinegar fixes the nematocysts—stinging cells—onto the skin, to prevent further encroachment."

Fielding began applying a dry powder over the wound. "Meat tenderizer," Scully explained. "It makes the nematocysts stick together, and neutralizes the acid venom."

Fielding reached for a scalpel from a small tray held by one of the monks. She carefully began to scrape the top layer of skin off of the old man's leg. The man's pain seemed to lessen as she shaved away the nematocysts. Still, he seemed dazed, nearly catatonic. Mulder's thoughts drifted back to Perry Stanton as he watched Fielding work with the scalpel. He remembered the wild look in Stanton's eyes as he leapt at him in the subway tunnel. Stanton had been completely out of his mind, in agony—not so different from the old man on the litter.

Both were trapped in the torment of their own skin.

Finally, Fielding set the scalpel back on the tray and began to rinse the wound. As the patient settled back against the stretcher, Fielding turned toward Mulder. "As I was about to say, I'm not really the person you should be talking to. I'm not a native of this town—and I have no personal knowledge of either of the Paladins. But there is someone who might be able to help you. Allan Trowbridge, one of the clinic's founders."

Scully had her notepad out of her pocket and was shaking rainwater out of the binding. "Did Trowbridge know Emile Paladin?"

"Allan served as an orderly with the MASH unit during the war. He decided to settle in Alkut after the war ended. He helped set up this clinic—and was responsible for getting the Red Cross to send much of the equipment. He's very well respected in the community."

"Is he here at the clinic?" Mulder asked, his interest growing.

"Today is his day off. You can probably find him at home—I'll give you directions. A friendly warning, though; from what I've heard about Emile Paladin and his MASH unit, you aren't going to be making many friends, bringing up that past. Some things are better left alone."

Mulder raised his eyebrows. The cryptic statement was just the sort of thing to make him want to dig deeper.

FIFTEEN

Mulder's face caught fire from the inside, followed by a shrill ringing deep in his ears. He quickly reached for his drink, but his eyes were watering so much he couldn't find the glass. He opened his mouth to beg for help, but all he could manage was a fierce choking sound, somewhat akin to a chain saw cutting through bone.

His attempts at communication were met by a gale of laughter from the other side of the low wooden table. Allan Trowbridge slammed his beefy palms together, a huge smile on his lips. "Like I said, *som-dtam* is an acquired taste. Even the Thais treat the northern dish with respect."

Mulder finally found his glass of *bia*—Thai beer—letting the harsh bubbles chase the fire away. He rubbed the tears out of his eyes and looked at Scully, who was seated cross-legged on the wood-paneled floor next to him, her chopsticks hovering above the oversize dish. "Dive right in, Scully. Don't let me suffer alone."

Scully paused for a moment, then shrugged and lifted one of the noodle-like strips to her lips. The moment she closed her mouth, her eyes sprang open and red cauliflowers appeared on her cheeks. She coughed, grabbing Mulder's glass right out of his hand. Mulder turned back toward Trowbridge, who was thoroughly enjoying the show.

"You know," Mulder joked, "assaulting FBI agents is a federal crime. What did you say was in this concoction?"

Before Trowbridge could answer, his wife sidled up next to him, bowing softly as she took her seat at the low pine table. Her appearance was a striking contrast to her husband's. Trowbridge was a huge man, over six feet tall and at least 220 pounds. His barrel chest swelled against the table with each breath, and his bright red beard seemed to spring out over his square jaw like moss on a boulder. Rina Trowbridge, on the other hand, was a tiny woman—barely five feet tall, with thin, delicate features. Her jet-black hair was tied back behind her head in a complex system of buns, and she was wearing an elegant, jade green silk smock, buttoned at the throat.

"First," Rina said, her English draped in the velvet tones of her Thai accent, "we start with raw papaya. Then we add lime juice, a handful of chilies, dried shrimp, and tiny salted land crabs. The finished product is pounded in a pestle, and served as is. I apologize for the lack of warning—my husband is a sadist."

Mulder laughed. In truth, Allan Trowbridge seemed to be a genuinely amiable man. Despite Dr. Fielding's warnings, Trowbridge had not seemed upset by Mulder and Scully's arrival—or their front line of questions about Emile Paladin and the MASH unit. Instead of displaying any anger, he had immediately demanded that the two agents join him for lunch. His wife had happily added two settings to the table.

Mulder's gaze swept across the small living area as he gingerly scooped a small ball of *khao niew*—sticky rice—into his serving bowl. The narrow, wood-walled room had a warm and friendly feel to it, from the loosely woven hangings to the plush, faded crimson oriental carpet that covered most of the floor. There was a tall rattan bookshelf by the door, filled with medical manuals and Thai-to-English dictionaries. In the far corner, there was a small Buddhist shrine, complete with a four-foot-high golden Buddha seated cross-legged, palms up, on a marble pedestal. The Buddha was surrounded by unlit incense and dried garlands, and there were two sets of cloth slippers beneath the pedestal. No doubt, Trowbridge had picked up some of his wife's culture—and perhaps that accounted for his easygoing attitude. Along with their spirituality and superstitions, the Thai were also known for their relaxed way of life.

"You've come a long way to ask questions about ancient history," Trowbridge said as he picked at the last remnants of his meal—finally turning the conversation back to Mulder and Scully's entrance. "Emile and Andrew Paladin are a part of this village's past—but certainly not part of its present. I haven't spoken either of those names in a long, long time. And I don't know anything about Andrew Paladin's whereabouts. I've heard rumors that he lives up in the mountains—but I haven't seen him since the war. So I'm not sure how I can help you."

"But you did serve under Emile Paladin in the MASH unit?" Scully asked, still sipping Mulder's beer. "Dr. Fielding led us to believe that Paladin and his unit were not something Alkut was very fond of remembering."

Trowbridge nodded, his smile weakening slightly. "Well, it was a time of war. And Emile Paladin was an intimidating, obsessive man. He ran the MASH unit as if it was his private fiefdom. And to the villagers, who weren't used to the effects of modern warfare, sometimes the place seemed like a hell on Earth. And I guess that made Emile Paladin into some sort of devil."

Mulder paused, as he saw a tiny, inadvertent shiver move through Trowbridge's shoulders. It was the first crack in the man's amiable facade, and it made Mulder wonder—was there something hidden behind that smile? "What exactly do you mean?"

Trowbridge spread his hands against the table, his eyes shifting downward for a brief second. "Our MASH unit specialized in napalm injuries, Agent Mulder. They sent us the absolute worst of the worst—men with burns over fifty percent of their body. A steady stream of horribly scorched soldiers, most without faces. Without hair. Without skin. Men who should have died on the battlefield but had somehow survived—burned to the last inch of their humanity."

Trowbridge's voice wavered, and Mulder watched as his wife rose from the table and crossed to the golden Buddha in the far comer. She leaned forward and took a match from beneath the garlands. Carefully, she lit one of the sticks of incense.

"Emile Paladin was their doctor," Trowbridge continued, his smile now gone but his expression still light. "And they were his obsession. He spent his days and nights surrounded by those tortured souls. He hardly spoke to anyone."

Scully leaned forward, the beautiful cuisine suddenly forgotten. "Were you aware of what he was working on?"

Trowbridge glanced at his wife, who was lighting a second stick of incense. The enormous man took a deep breath, his face slightly paled. "Skin. He was searching for the perfect synthetic skin. Something that could trick the body's defenses, that would be accepted by the immune system, that could repair the damage from the napalm. It was his quest, the only thing that mattered to him. He would spend weeks locked in his research laboratory, working on his skin. By the end, the only one he allowed inside with him was his son."

Mulder turned toward Trowbridge, wondering if he had misheard. *Emile Paladin had a son?* Julian Kyle had not mentioned anything about a son. Nor had there been anything in the military or FBI files on Emile Paladin about progeny. Mulder shifted his head and saw that Scully was staring at Trowbridge with the same intensity.

"Paladin had a child?" she asked.

Trowbridge looked toward his wife again, who instantly met his gaze. The fear was plainly written across her face. She didn't want her husband to say anything more. But Trowbridge shook his head, turning back to the agents. It seemed that he wanted to tell the story—as if he had been waiting a long time to let it out. "The boy's name was Quo Tien. He was born to a prostitute who lived near the MASH unit. She died during childbirth, and Paladin took the child as his own. He raised the boy among his burned, tortured patients. As you can guess, the boy did not turn out well."

Mulder wasn't sure what that meant. He waited for Trowbridge to continue, but instead the big man leaned back from the table, his face sagging. He shook his head, as if chasing the memories away. "As I said, that's all ancient history. The war ended, the MASH unit closed up shop. Emile Paladin was forced to continue his research elsewhere. He and his son moved out of Alkut. And a few years later—as you know—he died."

End of story, Trowbridge seemed to want to add. But something in his eyes told Mulder the story was actually far from over. Mulder aimed his chopsticks at another ball of sticky rice. "A hiking accident. That's what we were told."

"And that's what's on the death certificate," Trowbridge said, speaking quietly. "He fell into a deep ravine while hiking in the mountains. During the war, he had often taken trips up See Dum Kao. He was an avid student of Thai mythology, and there are many ancient ruins in those mountains. But the terrain can be quite treacherous—and according to the story, Paladin broke his neck in a canyon near the range's peak. His body was greatly damaged by the fall—and picked clean by local wildlife."

Rina Trowbridge was bent in ritual prostration before the Buddhist shrine. She suddenly cleared her throat, drawing the attention away from her husband. When she turned away from the Buddha, her face was strangely stiff, her eyes smoldering. "My husband has not told you the entire story. My husband is afraid. We are both afraid."

Mulder was shocked by the sudden admission. The tension was as palpable as the strong scent of incense. Trowbridge whispered something in Thai to his wife. She lowered her eyes. Mulder felt Scully's hand on his arm— but he couldn't let things lie. His senses told him they were on the edge of something vitally important. "Mr. Trowbridge, if you're in some kind of danger—"

"It's nothing," Trowbridge loudly interrupted, not meeting Mulder's eyes. "An old wives' tale, a foolish myth, a farmer's superstition. Rumors—"

"They're not rumors," Rina Trowbridge declared, stepping toward the table. "*Gin-Korng-Pew* is not a rumor."

Mulder searched his memory for the words, but found nothing that matched. He could hear Scully moving uncomfortably next to him; she could tell they were about to delve into Mulder territory, and she wasn't happy about it. They were supposed to be searching for Andrew Paladin. But from the looks on Rina's and Allan Trowbridge's faces, Mulder knew, this was too important to pass over.

"It's a local legend," Trowbridge finally explained, though something in his face told Mulder that he was not as skeptical as his words, "dating back many centuries. Gin-Korng-Pew means, literally, the Skin Eater. It's the name of a mythical creature that supposedly lives in a cave at the base of the See Dum range."

"The Skin Eater?" Scully repeated.

"I know how foolish it sounds," Trowbridge responded, facing her. "But as the story goes, around three hundred years ago, bodies began to crop up around the town—minus their skin. Usually vagrants, sometimes farm animals, sometimes missing children—and always the corpses were found in the same state, completely skinned. A local cult grew up around the myste- rious deaths—and a small temple was even erected, out near the edge of town. Sacrifices were made, and about a century ago the corpses stopped appearing. According to the myth, Gin-Korng-Pew was sated; the creature went into an indefinite hibernation in his cave."

Rina lowered herself to her husband's side. "But his hibernation was inter- rupted. Twenty-five years ago—around the same time the MASH unit opened its doors—the skinned bodies began appearing again. First farm animals. Then a pair of brothers, lost on a hunting expedition. Then more and more villagers—poor souls who had wandered too far from home. Every week, it seemed, there was another skinned corpse found near the town. It got so bad, people were afraid to leave their houses. And of course, everyone knew it was because of the MASH unit."

Mulder did not need to see Scully's expression to know what she was thinking. But he was not so quick to dismiss the woman's story. In his experience, old wives' tales usually had a basis in facts. It just took a certain sort of vision to see those facts. "And why was that, Mrs. Trowbridge?"

"Emile Paladin had awakened the Skin Eater. Either through his hikes in the mountains—or because of the thousands of horribly tormented soldiers he brought to Alkut. He had awakened Gin-Korng-Pew after so many years. And the creature was hungry."

"And now?" Scully asked, trying to keep the skepticism out of her voice. "Are there still skinless corpses appearing around town?"

Rina Trowbridge shook her head. "Emile Paladin was their last victim. After his death, the creature returned to his hibernation."

Scully touched Mulder's shoulder as she rose to her feet. Mulder could tell—she had heard enough. "Thank you both for lunch, and for your time. I'm sorry we can't stay any longer, but we need to continue our search for Andrew Paladin."

Trowbridge nodded. "I'm sorry I can't help you there. You might try speaking to David Kuo—he's the only lawyer in town, and he probably had some connection to the Paladins at the time of Emile's death. His office is connected to the town hall. The small circular building a block past the clinic."

Mulder shook Trowbridge's hand and bowed to his wife, thanking her for the meal. He waited until he and Scully had reached the door before letting his thoughts form a question. "You mentioned a temple built to placate Gin-Korng-Pew. Does it still exist?"

Trowbridge seemed surprised by Mulder's interest. Maybe he had assumed that an FBI agent couldn't possibly put stock in such a story. He didn't realize that Mulder could have told him a hundred stories that were equally as bizarre—and all based on fact.

"At the very edge of town," Trowbridge answered. "A stone building with a domed roof. It is run by a cadre of monks in dark red robes—the cult of Gin-Korng-Pew. They keep the temple in order in case, well—"

"In case of his reawakening," Rina Trowbridge finished, her face serious. Mulder felt a chill that had nothing to do with the rain spattering down outside. No matter what Scully thought, he could not discount the story he had just heard.

Skinless corpses. A scientist whose life had been dedicated to the search for the perfect synthetic skin. And a few thousand miles away, a man who had murdered—and died—because of something that had been done to his skin.

These were the elements of an X-File.

SIXTEEN

Quo Tien watched from across the street until the two agents turned the corner, heading toward the center of town. Then he quietly approached the traditional wooden house. His long, thin body was draped in a flowing black smock, and his slicked-back hair glistened in the perpetual rain. There was a heavy burlap bag hanging from the belt around his waist, and a dark rucksack slung over his left shoulder.

When he arrived at the front steps leading up to the house, he reached into an inner pocket in his smock and withdrew a shiny steel straight razor with a molded plastic handle. The blade was three and a quarter inches long, the handle specially designed to conform to Tien's fingers. A surge of hunger swept through him as he climbed the low steps, his free hand forming a gentle fist. He knocked twice on the painted wood.

The anticipation was intense, as he listened to the heavy footsteps on the other side of the door. He kept his hands at his sides, the straight razor hidden beneath his oversized sleeve. He could feel the rain running in twisting rivulets down his exposed neck, and the anticipation multiplied, turning virulent. Patience. Patience. *Patience.*

A few seconds later, the door swung inward. There was a brief pause— then recognition snapped across Allan Trowbridge's face. His eyes went wide, his mouth jerked open and closed. He looked like a marionette with tangled strings. Tien smiled. "Hello, Allan. Mind if I come inside?"

Trowbridge's cheeks turned chalky white. His thick shoulders shook with fear. "Please. I didn't tell them anything. I swear—"

"My father taught me never to swear, Allan. It's a straight shot to hell."

Suddenly, Quo Tien's right arm whipped forward. The razor sliced through the soft skin beneath Trowbridge's jaw, digging back almost to his spine. The huge man's head lolled to the side, and a fountain of bright blood spattered against the open door.

Tien caught Trowbridge by the waist as the man's body teetered forward. A second later he had dragged Trowbridge through the entrance of his home, gently shutting the door with the heel of his foot. He laid Trowbridge's body on the floor, kneeling so close he could hear the blood gurgling out of the gash in the man's throat. As he watched the man die, an incredible heat moved through his groin. He moaned softly, his eyes rolling back in his head.

Then the wonderful feeling grew, as a softly accented voice rang out from an inner room in the house. "Allan? Is everything all right?"

Tien leaned back, rubbing the back of his hand against his lips. He unslung his rucksack and placed it lightly on the floor next to the body. Then he retrieved his straight razor and slipped it back beneath his sleeve.

"Everything is just fine," he whispered. "It's just an old friend stopping by to say hello."

He rose to his feet and slid quietly across the front entrance. He could hear the small woman approaching from around the corner, and he waited with his back against the wall, measuring the distance by the sound of her feet. When she was just a few feet away, he leapt forward, his body uncoiling like a striking snake.

Rina Trowbridge saw him and froze. Her pretty features contorted as she saw the razor flash out from beneath his sleeve. She tried to run—but he was too fast. His free hand caught her by the hair, and she was yanked backward. The razor arced toward her throat. There was a spray of blood—and her small body slumped back against his chest. He leaned close, so that his bloody lips were inches from her ear.

"Hello," he whispered, as he twisted the razor free.

SEVENTEEN

"Hello? Is anyone home?"

Mulder stood in the arched entrance to the stone temple, staring down a long, dark corridor with smooth, rounded walls and a packed-mud floor.

Although it was still mid-afternoon, shadows played across his shoulders, dribbling down against the tops of his waterlogged shoes. He glanced upward toward the canopy of tree branches that stretched, like living tentacles, over the domed roof of the building. It seemed as though the trees were clutching at the temple, malevolent green fingers trying to drag the brutalized stone back into the encroaching wilderness. Mulder smiled inwardly at his own dark thoughts.

It had not been difficult to locate the temple at the far edge of the village. After he had dropped Scully off at the town hail—a meandering wooden construct of offices and meeting rooms—he had simply followed the main cobblestone road to its conclusion, then taken a hard right toward the forest. Fifty yards from the road, he had caught sight of the charcoal-colored building jutting out from beneath the tree cover.

At first glance, the temple looked as if it had been carved from a single, mammoth boulder; the temple was shaped like the top half of an egg, with smooth outer walls that curved upward nearly twenty feet to the domed roof. The roof was tiled with alternating strips of gold and silver, and the walls were decorated with Thai script, white and black letters curling across almost every inch of the smooth structure. Just above the entrance was another statue of the Buddha, this one chiseled out of shiny green jade. Set against the massive temple, the Buddha looked helpless and forlorn, and Mulder wondered if the idol had been an afterthought. The Buddha did not seem to fit with the architecture of the temple, which seemed more archaic, a product of a totemic-styled cult rather than a religion based on philosophical enlightenment. Compared to the rest of Alkut, the egg-shaped temple had been built on an artificially impressive—and emotionally driven—scale: more evidence that there was real gravity behind the legend of the Skin Eater, at least in the minds of the villagers. *They had not skimped in their efforts to placate the beast.*

Mulder took a tiny step forward, listening to his own voice echoing back at him from the darkness. He had been surprised to find the heavy wooden door to the temple hanging partially open, and he had waited a full minute before allowing his curiosity to tempt him forward. He knew it was bad form to trespass on a religious shrine—but he couldn't wait forever. In half an hour, he was meeting Scully outside the town hall to discuss her progress with the lawyer—and Mulder had three centuries of myths to decipher in that short time. Even if David Kuo could help them track down Andrew Paladin, Mulder was sure that the legend of the Skin Eater was somehow involved.

His mind made up, he continued forward down the dark corridor. The air was dense and cool, a stark contrast to the sweltering atmosphere outside. The walls on either side were smooth stone, polished to the point of reflection. There were wooden torches that smelled vaguely of kerosene mounted every few feet along the walls, none of them lit—and Mulder chided himself for not carrying matches. Then again, he didn't know if it was proper etiquette to trespass into a temple waving a burning torch. Instead, he watched as his reflection dimmed, each step moving him farther from the gray light of the outside world.

A few yards before total darkness, Mulder came to a second door, covered in some sort of frayed cloth. Mulder felt around the face of the material, but couldn't find anything resembling a doorknob. The cloth felt strangely warm, and Mulder wondered if there was something burning on the other side of the door. He pressed both palms flat against the thin material and gave a gentle shove.

The door swung inward. A sudden wave of heat splashed against Mulder's face. The strong scent of burning oil hit his nostrils, and he stifled a cough. He blinked rapidly, his eyes watering from the strong smell. As his pupils adjusted to the flickering firelight, Mulder saw that he was standing at the mouth of a circular inner chamber, with a polished stone floor and high, roughly hewn rock walls. There was an ancient-looking clay altar in the center of the chamber ten yards ahead of him, a waist-high pedestal construction with a wide rectangular base. Bright flames leaped high into the air above the clay, barely contained by a red-hot steel bowl filled with flammable, pitch-black liquid. Just beyond the steel bowl, seeming to shiver in the intense heat of the flames, stood an enormous statue made of some sort of shiny black stone. The statue was like nothing Mulder had ever seen before.

"Gin-Korng-Pew," Mulder whispered, as his eyes rode up the face of the stone beast. The black statue had a long, ridged snout like an emaciated wolf. The lips were curled back to reveal multiple rows of razor-sharp fangs. Two five-foot-long, curved tusks jutted out from the stone creature's bottom jaw, crisscrossing together just below its flared nostrils. The beast's eyes were enormous, with bright red spirals instead of pupils. Hundreds of spaghetti-strand tentacles sprang out of its head, each tipped by a single curved claw. It was a nightmare turned to stone—and it set off something primal inside Mulder, something he couldn't begin to explain. Though he knew it was a statue, he had the sudden urge to run. At the same time, his muscles felt paralyzed, he couldn't turn away.

"Every culture has its monsters," a voice suddenly echoed in his ears. "But they are all cut from the same soul."

Mulder whirled toward the voice. He saw that the far wall of the chamber was lined with dark alcoves, dug directly into the rough stone. Each alcove was at least five feet tall, and it was impossible to gauge how deeply they were dug into the temple. As Mulder watched, a stooped figure stepped out of the center alcove. The figure was wearing a bright red monk's robe, tied around his bare shoulder. His bald head glistened in the light from the fire. He looked at Mulder—and Mulder realized that he recognized the monk's face.

It was the old man who had watched him and Scully drive into town. The man with the multiple amulets who had stood at the edge of the road, smiling as if he had expected them all along.

Mulder stared at the man, stunned. The old monk noticed his expression and laughed. "Are you more afraid of the statue, or of me?"

Mulder swallowed, trying to regain his composure. Scully would say it was a coincidence, of course. The old man was a member of the Skin Eater cult. He had been standing by the side of the road when they had driven into Alkut. No mystery, no magic. But the one thing Mulder didn't believe in was coincidence. He cleared his throat. "You speak English."

The monk nodded. "I spent three years at the university in Bangkok. As you can imagine, I was a theology major. My name is Ganon."

Mulder gestured toward the statue behind the flaming altar. "And is this the Skin Eater?"

Ganon paused, his gaze still pinned to Mulder's face. "Nobody alive has ever seen Gin-Korng-Pew. This statue is based on an ancient drawing found in a cave not far from this temple. Perhaps it is the creature. Perhaps it is a fairy tale, chiseled out of polished stone."

Ganon made a brief motion with his hand, and a teenage boy in a similar red robe stepped out of one of the other alcoves. Mulder wondered whether there was a roomful of monks behind the wall, waiting for Canon's cues. He shifted his eyes back to the old monk. "But you don't believe it's a fairy tale. You believe the monster is real."

Ganon shrugged, a coy smile on his lips. He snapped the fingers of his right hand, and the teenager quickly crossed the room to where Mulder was standing. The boy was extremely thin, almost emaciated, with an oblong, shaved head and sunken eyes. Without a word, the boy pulled a small glass vial out of his robe. The vial was filled with some sort of clear liquid, with tiny leaves floating inside.

"It is unimportant what I believe," Ganon said. "I am a lowly servant of this temple. My role is to keep that altar lit. And to offer my protection to those who seek it."

He nodded, and the emaciated boy opened the vial and poured a few droplets of the clear liquid into his palm. He approached Mulder and reached for Mulder's cheek. Mulder involuntarily drew back.

"Malku will not hurt you. The balm is a spirit repellent. It is designed to protect the skin. All who journey into the mountains surrounding Alkut must wear the balm—or risk a horrible fate."

Mulder raised his eyebrows as he let the boy rub the liquid into his cheeks. It had a strong scent, bitter like almonds, with a tinge of something sulfurous. "And you think I'm going to journey into the mountains?"

Ganon shrugged. "Again, it is unimportant what I believe."

Mulder narrowed his eyes, trying to read the expression on the old man's face. Meanwhile, the teenager stepped back, then placed the vial in Mulder's hand. "Take. Makes skin taste bad. Take."

Mulder watched as the boy turned and shuffled back toward his alcove. "Is that what the creature does—eat the skin? As its name implies?"

"As the story goes," Ganon answered, moving gracefully toward the altar, "skin is the source of its immortality. Gin-Korng-Pew feeds on the skin of the unlucky—to replenish itself. When it is asleep, it does not need to feed. Only when it is disturbed does it feel the hunger."

Mulder watched as Ganon reached the altar. He wasn't sure yet how the information fit into the case—but he knew it was significant. Skin is the source of its immortality. The words echoed through Mulder's thoughts. Somehow, the Skin Eater was connected to Emile Paladin—and through him, to Perry Stanton. Mulder had to fill in the links.

"So the MASH unit woke the creature and sent it on a hungry rampage," Mulder said. "Somehow, Emile Paladin upset the beast, and the town suffered because of him. Now the creature is once again in hibernation. Somewhere in the mountains."

Ganon did not respond. Instead, he reached beneath the altar and pulled out a long metal staff with a tiny cup on one end. He carefully dipped the end of the staff into the flammable liquid in the metal fire bowl and gently stirred in a circular motion. The flames rose higher, daggers of orange twisting like living ropes around the tusks of the monstrous statue.

"Somewhere in See Dum Kao," Ganon repeated, staring at the flames. "A vast cave called *Thum Phi*—the spirit cavern."

Mulder had a sudden, strange feeling that Ganon was hinting that he knew where Thum Phi was located; the old monk knew where the mythical beast lived.

Mulder looked at the glass vial in his hand. Then his gaze shifted to the statue of the Skin Eater. Maybe Ganon was just telling him what he had already guessed—that the answers he was looking for were in those mountains.

Waiting for him.

Thirty minutes later, Mulder found Scully sitting on the partially enclosed front steps leading up to the town hall, leafing through a manila folder. The steps bisected a small flower garden, row after row of colorful buds creeping up between high blades of bright green grass. The air was thick with the scent of foreign pollen, and Mulder's throat itched as he dropped down next to his partner. He ran both hands through his sopping-wet hair, glancing back at the entrance to the town hall behind them. Above the high double doors he saw two floors of shuttered windows, and near the thatched roof an iron rain gutter like the one he had seen ringing the top of the clinic.

Mulder had barely noticed the perpetual gray sheets on his quick walk back from the temple. His thoughts were still consumed by Ganon and the Skin Eater; when he closed his eyes to blink, he could see the creature's face, the wolfish snout, the crisscrossed tusks, the razor-clawed tentacles.

Scully finally looked up from the manila folder, noticing the expression on his face. "You look as if you just met the bogeyman."

Mulder smiled. "I think maybe I did. How was your visit with David Kuo? Anything interesting?"

Scully sighed. "He doesn't know anything about Andrew's whereabouts. He was Emile Paladin's lawyer—but only in name. He had very little contact with the man since the war, and almost zero contact with his brother."

"So what's in the folder?"

Scully patted it with her fingers. "Kuo retrieved this for me from the town hall records. It's the ME's file from Emile Paladin's autopsy. And before you start telling me about your bogeyman—Emile Paladin died from a broken neck. The pathologist estimated a fall of at least fifty feet."

Mulder's expression didn't change. He reached down past the edge of the steps and yanked a yellow flower out of the garden. The petals were almost as long as his fingers. "And what about his skin? Or lack thereof?"

"Again, no great mystery. His body was mutilated by three different types of predators—all readily identifiable by the teeth marks. Two types of wolf and a mountain lion."

Mulder nodded, yanking one of the petals free. He hadn't expected an autopsy report full of tusks and clawed tentacles. *It was never that simple.* "Sounds like Paladin made quite a picnic."

"The damage was so bad, the positive ID was made from a dental match. Two teeth, to be exact—a left front incisor and a right canine. But there was no doubt. It was Paladin. According to the report, Andrew claimed the body, and it was cremated a few days after the autopsy."

Cremated. Mulder leaned back against the steps, stretching his neck side to side. Scully rolled her eyes. "Mulder, the body was cremated *after* the autopsy, not before. There's no mystery here. Emile Paladin died in a hiking accident."

Mulder didn't respond. Scully exhaled, frustrated. "It's a myth, Mulder. A fairy tale. And it has nothing to do with our case. Perry Stanton didn't have his skin eaten by some beast. Neither did Emile Paladin."

Mulder nodded, tossing the yellow flower back into the garden. He still couldn't shake the idea that the Skin Eater was involved. He remembered what Ganon had told him—that the Skin Eater's source of power was its supply of skin. It coincided closely with his own theory about the source of Stanton's invulnerability, and his incredible athletic feats. And the timing of the Skin Eater's hunger—the link to the MASH unit and to Emile Paladin's presence in Alkut—was impossible to ignore. "I just don't think we can discount anything out of hand."

"Mulder," Scully started, but she was interrupted by a frightened shout from down the street. Mulder looked up to see a pair of orange-robed monks running toward them, their faces masks of terror. Mulder noted that both monks were wearing latex gloves. He realized he had seen them before. They were the two monks from the clinic.

"Quickly!" the larger of the two shouted. "Please! Terrible thing! Terrible thing!"

He waved his arms wildly, pointing down the cobblestone street. The second monk was babbling in Thai, and Mulder saw that there were tears in the corners of his eyes. Mulder rose quickly, following Scully down the steps. The monks nodded vigorously, then turned and rushed down the street. Mulder and Scully had to jog to keep up. The cobblestones were tricky to navigate, but there was no sidewalk, and the mud on either side of the street would have been even worse. Mulder kept his head down, ignoring the buildings that flashed by on either side, as he and Scully struggled to stay close to the sprinting monks.

"This sounds pretty serious," Scully shouted, as she leapt over a puddle of murky rainwater in front of a small, open-air shop selling bowls filled with fishtails. "How did they know where to find us?"

Mulder shrugged, narrowly avoiding a rusted bicycle lying at the side of the road a few feet past the fishtail shop. He thought about Ganon and the man's knowing eyes. But he decided it was probably nothing so mysterious. "It's a small town. And we're pretty hard to miss."

The monks turned an abrupt corner, winding out of the center of town. Residential homes sprang up on stilts to the left and right, triangular thatched roofs spitting rainwater toward the street in controlled, noisy waterfalls. With a start, Mulder realized the direction they were heading. "Scully, don't the Trowbridges live down the next street?"

Scully looked at him. Both agents hurried their pace, catching up to the monks. As they approached the Trowbridges' home, Mulder saw that a small crowd of people had gathered on the front lawn. Mostly women and young children, dressed in loose smocks and homemade sandals. The women were whispering to one another in worried voices, and Mulder made out the distinct sound of weeping. He swallowed, a dull feeling in his stomach. Then he saw Ganon at the edge of the crowd, and their eyes met. Ganon nodded, his mouth moving, the words disappearing in the gray rain. Mulder didn't need to hear them to know their sound.

"Gin-Korng-Pew."

EIGHTEEN

Scully squared her shoulders as she and Mulder worked their way through the crowd. Her face and body quickly took on the controlled veneer of a career federal agent as her left hand slipped to her shoulder holster, checking to see that the snap was undone. She could tell by the grim faces in the crowd that something horrible had happened, and she prayed that the thoughts streaking from her own imagination were way off base. Then she caught sight of the open door, stained in bright red blood—and her heart sank. There was no longer any doubt; they had arrived at a crime scene.

The two monks disappeared into the stilted house, but Scully stopped next to Mulder in the doorway. She surveyed the pattern of blood, how it spread upward along the inside of the wooden door. She then turned her gaze downward, to the crimson, river-like trail leading into the house.

"Carotid artery," she said, half to herself. The blood on the door was well above eye level, which meant the victim had been standing. From the angle and arc of the spatter, Scully knew it could not have been a bullet wound. It had been something sharp, like a knife or a razor blade.

"The kill was made here," she continued, slowly strolling forward. She followed the trail of blood, walking as lightly as possible. The blood had soaked into the fading oriental carpet, darkening the crimson material like spilled red wine. She tried to forget that just hours ago, she and Mulder had eaten lunch a few yards away. She needed to be objective, to remain clinically detached—

Mulder grabbed her shoulder, stopping her in the narrow hallway that led to the living area. His eyes were wide, and he was pointing toward the edge of the open main room. Scully saw Dr. Fielding hunched near the end of the trail of blood. Fielding was on her knees on the carpet, her face hidden in her hands. The two bodies were on the floor in front of her.

"My God," Scully whispered. She could hear her heart pounding as she plodded forward. Mulder kept his hand on her shoulder. They had both seen horrors before. Dozens of brutal crime scenes, corpses in states too miserable to describe. Still, the sight of the two bodies was difficult to take. Despite all of her training, despite everything she had seen—Scully wanted to turn away.

"Skinned," Fielding said, lifting her head out of her hands. "Every inch removed, along with a fair amount of muscle and interior tissue. I sent for you as soon as I got here. The police are on their way from Rayong; there aren't any full-time officers here in Alkut. I figured you were the next best thing."

"Christ," Mulder said, standing over the corpses. The entire living room seemed covered in blood. The oriental carpet beneath the bodies was saturated with it. There were bits of muscle and organs sticking to the legs of the low pine table where Mulder and Scully had eaten lunch. "It's them, right? Allan and Rina Trowbridge?"

Scully dropped to one knee, next to the larger corpse. It was like looking at an animal on a butcher's block—but the animal was human, and the butchering had been crude and brutal. She tried to re-create the event, using the cues of her profession. She imagined that the first incision had been made directly under the jaw. The face had been peeled back, the ears sliced off, the entire scalp removed in one piece. Then the attention had shifted to the trunk. An incision had most likely been made down the center line, the skin pared open to reveal the rib cage and the organs beneath. Multiple slashes had been necessary to skin the pelvic region, the legs, down to the feet.

Scully shifted her eyes to the second body. Rina Trowbridge had not taken nearly as long. Scully could see strands of Rina's silky dark hair stuck to the bloodied mass that had once been her face. Then she saw one of Rina's eyeballs hanging from a strand of optic nerve, and her jaw clenched. She needed to concentrate. This was a crime scene. *This was a crime.*

She turned her attention back to the larger corpse's pelvic area, and below. "Dr. Fielding, do you have an extra pair of gloves?"

Fielding nodded, fishing through the pockets of her coat. Scully took the gloves from her and slid them over her fingers. She reached forward, gently running her index finger over a piece of exposed tibia. There was a sharp groove right above the knee. She found similar grooves higher up, near the pelvic bone. Then she found a series of slightly less pronounced scratches around the hip joint. She paused, thinking.

"The place looks pretty trashed," Mulder commented, from somewhere behind her. He was carefully picking his way through the small house, searching for clues. Soon, the Thai police would arrive—probably along with government investigators from Bangkok. Scully knew that the FBI would not be welcomed in the investigation, certainly not of a crime of this nature—and not in a town with Alkut's history. Though the town was off the beaten trail, the nation of Thailand was a tourist's paradise. Heinous double murders—even in the sticks—did not make for good tourism.

So Mulder was using the time they had to conduct a quick survey of the crime scene. Likewise, Scully could not count on getting the results of an autopsy. She had to find answers right here, right now. "Dr. Fielding, do you see these grooves and these scratches?"

Fielding leaned closer. She had been momentarily overwhelmed by the sight of the bodies; she had known the Trowbridges, had spoken very highly of Allan. But in her heart she was a doctor. "The grooves look as if they were made by some sort of blade. A few inches long. But I've never seen scratches like those before."

Scully nodded. The grooves were easy. Any forensic pathologist could have identified the blade. "The grooves were made by a straight razor. Very controlled, practiced strokes."

"And the scratches?" Scully paused a moment longer. "I can't be sure. But I think the killer used a dermatome to skin these bodies."

"A dermatome?" Mulder asked. He had paused in front of the Buddhist shrine in the far corner. The shrine seemed the only thing in the room that hadn't been overturned. His surprised expression swam across the curved surface of the gold Buddha. "Isn't that the tool that skin harvesters use? Like a supersharp cheese slicer?"

Scully nodded. The dermatome had been set to an incredibly brutal depth—all the way through the subcutaneous layer of fat, almost to the bone. "Whoever did this was extremely skilled. He's had some level of medical training. And he's done this many times before."

"He?" Mulder asked.

"Possibly a she. But it certainly wasn't an it, despite what the crowd outside might think. These incisions follow a controlled, determined pattern. It isn't easy to skin a body. It takes practice and a fair amount of strength. More than that, it takes preparation. Someplace to put the skin, some way to carry it away from the scene."

"But why?" Fielding asked, her voice weak. "Why the Trowbridges—and why like this?"

Scully didn't answer the first part of Fielding's question. She had a sickening feeling that the Trowbridges were killed because of her and Mulder's investigation. Either because of something the Trowbridges had said—or because of something they had withheld. The second part of Fielding's question seemed even more obvious.

"To feed the legend," Mulder answered for her. He was leaning forward over the Buddhist shrine, both palms gently touching the gold statue's belly. It looked as though something about the idol was bothering him. "It's an easy cover for a double murder—and it turns Alkut against our investigative efforts. Two foreigners stirring up trouble—waking the beast once again, sending it on a deadly rampage. We're going to be on our own from here on out."

Fielding rose, taking a deep breath. "I'll go and speak to some of the neighbors. Perhaps someone saw something. In any case, there's nothing more I can do here. It's so bloody tragic. I keep remembering their wedding—how they looked into each other's eyes. Both of them were foreign to this place— she a transplant from the north, he from America. But they had found each other. That was all that mattered."

Fielding sighed heavily, rubbing at her eyes with the backs of her hands. Then she shrugged and quietly exited the house, leaving Scully and Mulder alone with the bodies.

Scully pushed Fielding's sentimental thoughts out of her head. It didn't help to see these bodies as people. With practiced clinical detachment, she ran her gloved fingers through the pool of blood covering most of the floor, trying to estimate the exact time of death from the consistency of the fluid. Without skin or forensic tools, she had nothing else to go by.

"We left them about three hours ago," she said out loud. "Whoever did this must have been waiting just outside. Probably watched us leave."

"Maybe he's out there now," Mulder commented. "Still watching us to see what we do next. Or maybe he thinks he's done what he came here to do— cut off our line of information."

Scully rose, slowly. She crossed to Mulder's side, watching curiously as he continued to rub the golden Buddha. The statue was three feet high, and looked as if it weighed more than fifty pounds. The gold was well polished, though there were dark hints where the smoke from years of burning incense had stained the soft metal. The Buddha's wide expression was peaceful and strangely content—despite the flecks of fresh blood sprinkled across its globular cheeks. "Mulder, I'm just glad you're not out there with them. I was expecting you to argue with my conclusions."

"Monsters don't search people's houses after they kill them," Mulder said, suddenly straining against the statue. "And they aren't superstitious enough to leave a Buddhist shrine untouched."

There was a loud metallic click, and the front of the statue came loose from its pedestal. Scully was shocked to see that the Buddha was attached to the back of its base by two oversized metal hinges. She stared at Mulder as he pushed the statue back, revealing a deep, rectangular hiding place.

"Mulder—how did you know?"

"Actually," Mulder responded, as he reached into the opening, "the lunch menu gave it away, even before Fielding's comments a few minutes ago. *Somdtam* and *khao niew* are northern delicacies. That led me to believe that Rina Trowbridge was a transplant from the northern regions of the country— which Fielding just verified. But this Buddha has his arms crossed at the waist, palms up. That's usually a southern representation of the master. It didn't make sense to me—until I saw the shrine untouched by our killer."

He pulled a thick envelope from the pedestal, then stepped back from the shrine. "A southern Thai wouldn't think to desecrate a shrine like this. That made it the perfect hiding place."

Scully was impressed. Mulder's eye for detail was truly amazing. She watched eagerly while he opened the envelope and peered inside. "Photographs," he said, evenly. "About a dozen, divided into two sets. And a few printed pages."

He reached inside and removed the photographs. The two sets were bundled separately with rubber bands. Mulder crossed to the low lunch table and spread the two sets out against the wood.

The first set that caught Scully's eye were almost as horrible as the two bodies on the floor. They were pictures of burned patients, lying naked on military-style hospital stretchers. Each picture had a date in the corner—and according to the notations, all were taken between the years of 1970 and 1973. "Full-thickness napalm burns," she commented. "At least seventy percent of their bodies. These patients were all terminal—if not postmortem."

She shifted her eyes to the second set of photos. These were of naked men as well, lying on similar hospital stretchers. But none of these men were burned. All seemed in perfect health. The second set of photos had dates as well—but all the dates were the same: June 7, 1975.

Scully tried to make sense of what she was looking at. "The stretchers look as though they could be MASH unit standard issue, circa Vietnam."

She paused, noticing that Mulder was frozen in place, staring at two of the photos. One was of a burn victim, the other of one of the unmarred men. He had placed the two photos next to one another on the table.

"Mulder?"

"Scully, look."

Scully leaned close, and realized that the burn victim's face was partially recognizable. When she shifted her gaze to the unmarred man—she realized they were photos of the same man. She reread the dates in the corners, then shook her head. "These dates must be incorrect. Burns like that don't heal. Even if he did somehow recover—he would have been covered in transplant scars."

Mulder didn't seem to be listening. He was carefully arranging the two sets of photos, burn victims next to their unmarred counterparts. An eye here, an ear there—he was using whatever clues he could find to pair them up. Some of the pairs seemed incontrovertible, others more like guesswork. But in every case, the effect was the same. A horribly burned body dated between 1970 and 1973, and a healthy body dated 1975.

When Mulder was finished, he looked at Scully. She shook her head. "I know what you're thinking. But it's impossible. Synthetic skin for limited transplantation, maybe. But nothing like this. Medicine isn't magic. This isn't medicine—this is raising the dead. These dates are wrong, Mulder."

Mulder tapped his fingers against the table. He didn't believe her—but he didn't have any proof to the contrary. Instead of responding, he turned back to the folder and removed the rest of its contents: two printed pages of paper.

The first page contained some sort of list. A row of names, numbers, and medical conditions, all divided into columns. Scully quickly recognized that the list was a hospital admission register. The figures were army serial numbers. And the conditions were all strikingly similar. Burns of various degrees, either from napalm or other chemical-based weapons. None of the patients had burns over less than fifty percent of his body. Most were charred beyond the seventy percent range—again, all were terminal.

"A hundred and thirty," Mulder said after a few moments, "all horribly burned, like the men in those pictures—"

Mulder stopped, his brow furrowed. He pointed at one of the names. Scully read it aloud. "Andrew Paladin. Napalm burns, full torso, sixty-eight percent of his face and legs."

"Another mistake?" Mulder asked. "Like the dates on those pictures?"

"It must be," Scully commented, nonplussed. "Or someone's created a long trail of lies. Andrew Paladin could not have survived his brother with burns like that. And if, somehow, he had survived—he'd be confined to a burn clinic, in permanent ICU. Not living as a recluse up in the mountains."

"Unless those pictures are real," Mulder said, as he turned to the second sheet of paper from the folder.

"Unless Paladin's search for his perfect synthetic skin was successful."

"Mulder—"

"Take a look at this," Mulder interrupted, not letting Scully stop him mid-fantasy. "It's a map. It looks similar to the map of the MASH unit we got from Van Epps. But this one's got a basement level."

Scully took the sheet of paper from him. Indeed, it was a map of the Alkut MASH unit. A second level was superimposed beneath the roughly drawn complex, showing a series of tunnels and underground chambers. The chambers were marked by numbers and letters—but there was no key, no explanation of what they meant. Still, it was significant. The official map of the MASH unit did not indicate the existence of an underground floor.

"It might still be there," Mulder said, his eyes bright. "The tunnels might still be down there, beneath the clinic. Maybe there's more evidence of Paladin's research."

Scully watched as Mulder gathered up the photos and list of wounded soldiers and shoved them back into the envelope. He folded the map in half and slid it into his pocket. It was obvious what he intended to do. He was going to head back to the clinic and see for himself.

"It's been twenty years," Scully said. "Even if the tunnels still exist, there won't be anything down there."

"It's worth a look." Mulder paused, gesturing toward the two mutilated bodies on the floor. "They died for a reason, Scully. They were hiding something—and I think we found it."

Scully envied his conviction, despite how baseless it seemed. "What did we find, Mulder?"

"Evidence of Paladin's success. And, perhaps, of his continued success. If the men on that list came into Alkut with seventy and eighty percent napalm burns—and came out like the healthy men in those pictures, then Paladin really did achieve a miracle. But that miracle might have had a price. Perry Stanton might have paid that price—along with everyone who got in his way. Indirectly, Allan and Rina Trowbridge might have also paid that price."

There were so many holes in Mulder's theory, it was barely a theory at all. *At least he hadn't mentioned anything about a mythical, skin-eating beast.* "Why would anyone keep something like this a secret? Why kill innocent people to cover up a miracle?"

"I don't know. But we won't find out standing around here."

Scully paused, thinking. Mulder had a point. They had leads to follow—even if the leads seemed insane. She made up her mind and took the envelope with the photos and hospital admission list out of his hands. "All right. As long as we're here, we'll follow this wherever it leads. You search for those tunnels. I'm going to find out what I can about the names on this list. If these men were casualties of the Vietnam War, I should be able to find files on them. If they died in Alkut, then there's a good chance Andrew Paladin died alongside them—and we just wasted a whole lot of federal money tracking down two dead brothers."

Mulder was already heading toward the door. Scully waited a few seconds before following him, her eyes drifting to the two mutilated bodies. Wordlessly, she crossed herself, then squeezed her hand tight around the tiny gold cross she wore around her neck.

The truth was, they *were* chasing a monster. The violent actions of Perry Stanton—the case that had brought them to Thailand in the first place—seemed to pale in comparison to the tragedy on the floor in front of her.

Like Mulder, Scully wanted to catch the monster. But she did not share Mulder's bravado. Staring at the two skinned bodies, she was gripped by a single, sobering thought.

If they got too close to the truth—the monster would be chasing *them*.

NINETEEN

Mulder's shoulders ached as he strained against the heavy steel equipment shelf, rocking it carefully back into place against the cinder-block wall. The tiny storage room was cramped and claustrophobic, a cluttered swamp of Red Cross surplus, outdated radiology machines, linens, and folded military cots. The walls were lined with off-white plaster, the ceiling covered in similarly colored tiles. A small fluorescent tube lodged in one corner of the ceiling gave the room a sickly yellow, hepatic glow.

The storage room was the fifth and last interior space Mulder had found within the clinic, and he had no idea where to go next. He had kicked every wall, stamped on every inch of floor—and he had not found anything resembling an entrance to an underground level.

He stepped back from the steel shelf, breathing hard. He was becoming more frustrated by the second. The investigation was at a critical point; the double murder had significantly raised the stakes. The Thai police had arrived from Rayong shortly after Mulder and Scully had shifted the Buddha back into place, and had confiscated both bodies for their own investigative efforts. Mulder had a sinking feeling that he and Scully did not have much time before the Thai authorities co-opted their case. As Scully had inferred, an FBI investigation of a vicious double murder did not make good copy for Thai tourism brochures.

Mulder hastily reached into his pocket and retrieved the folded map. He studied it for the hundredth time, trying to find some sort of physical logic. Since there were no notations of scale or direction, it was impossible to match the tunnels to the geography of the clinic. The MASH unit had consisted of more than a dozen free-standing structures. The triage room and the recovery ward were by far the largest of the buildings, followed by the command office and the barracks. The tunnels seemed to originate beneath the command office, with a second entrance just beyond the edge of the camp.

Mulder leaned back against the door to the small storage room, his eyes shifting to the sheer cement floor. He knew that the tunnels were down there—but he also knew it would take excavation equipment to get through that floor. If an entrance still existed, it wasn't inside the clinic.

He shoved the map back into his pocket and headed out of the storage room. There were three monks clustered around Fielding at the far end of the main room, speaking in hushed tones. The monks looked up as he moved past, and Fielding offered a weak smile. The entire town was shocked by the murder—and rumors about the reawakening of the Skin Eater were rapidly spreading from household to household. Mulder could feel the tension in the air, the sense that something ancient and terrifying had returned.

Shivering, Mulder cast a final look at the interior of the building, then stepped out through the front door. The rain had finally slowed to a light drizzle, and he could see breaks in the clouds above the high wooden steeple of the dilapidated church across the street. Mulder paused as the clinic door swung shut behind him, his eyes resting on the miniature spirit house just a few feet away. Someone had placed fresh flowers along the base, and there were more than a dozen sticks of incense jutting from the little windows. Even the post had been decorated, twists of garlands mingling with colorful silk tassels and strings of beads.

Mulder felt his muscles sagging as he thought about Trowbridge and his wife. Fielding had informed him when the police had carted the bodies off, and he had considered going after them—offering his support to the Thai investigation. But he knew it was pointless. It would be near impossible to explain the connection to Perry Stanton. And any reference to the Skin Eater or Paladin's miraculous research would be considered an offense. The Skin Eater was a village myth, a matter of belief—not of forensic science. As for Paladin's research, Mulder had nothing but a series of photographs as proof.

Still, he had to live with the guilt of the Trowbridges' deaths. They had been murdered because of their connection to the FBI investigation. In a way, Mulder and Scully *had* awakened the Skin Eater.

Mulder started forward, intending to head back to the hotel, where Scully was using her laptop computer to research the list of burned soldiers. But as he stepped past the spirit house he paused, bothered by something across the street.

There was a young man standing in the doorway to the Church. He was tall and thin, with slicked-back hair and caramel skin, wearing a long dark smock with baggy sleeves. He was leaning nonchalantly against the half-open church door, a serene smile on his thin face. As Mulder watched, the young man turned and slipped inside the church. The door clicked shut behind him.

Mulder felt his stomach tighten. There was something about the young man that bothered him. He wasn't sure—but he thought he recognized that caramel face. He had seen a similar man in line at customs in the airport in Bangkok. He couldn't be sure—but the young man might have been on the same flight from New York.

Mulder realized immediately what that might mean. Then another thought hit him, and he quickly retrieved the folded map from his pocket. He ran his eyes over the map, focusing on the distance between the major structures. He looked at the church, the way it was perched close to the road that separated it from the clinic, the way it seemed to have been built on a slight angle to accommodate the small plot of land beneath. He came to a sudden realization.

The area where the church was built could have also been part of the MASH unit.

He jammed the map back into his pocket and rushed into the street. His heart was racing, and his hand automatically went to his gun. He unbuttoned his holster and let his fingers rest on the grooved handle of his Smith & Wesson. If he was right about the young man's arrival in Thailand coinciding with his own, then there was a good chance he was heading toward a trap. But he couldn't risk losing a potential suspect in the Trowbridges' double murder. And a possible link to Emile Paladin's research.

He reached the door to the church, pressing his body against the nearby wall. There was a pile of transparent plastic a few feet away, and he remembered seeing the door covered when he and Scully had first arrived. He had assumed the church was closed down, out of use. It was a good cover for a research laboratory, especially in a place like Alkut. The Buddhist villagers had no use for a Catholic church, with their spirit houses and their Buddhist shrines.

Mulder took a deep breath, letting his heart rate slow.

He wished there was some way he could contact Scully—but he knew his cell phone was useless, since Alkut was out of his cell's satellite window.

He placed his free hand against the door and gave it a quick shove. The door swung inward, clanging against the inside wall. The sound reverberated through the air, indicating a wide, open space. Mulder drew his automatic, clicking back the safety.

He crouched low and maneuvered around the doorframe. The air was thick and musty, tinged with the distinct scent of rotting wood. Mulder was standing at the back of a long rectangular hall with a twenty-foot arched ceiling and wood-paneled walls. The walls were partially covered by a green-hued mural of the Last Supper, but many of the panels were missing, gaping holes in the place of holy guests.

Mulder quietly slid along the back of the hall, his eyes adjusting to the strange lighting. Huge stained-glass windows on either side cast rainbows across the wooden pews, revealing dark gashes where the benches had been randomly torn out from the floor. Near the front of the room, Mulder saw a tangle of wood that used to be the support beams of a stage. Rising up from somewhere near the center of the tangle was a row of rusted organ pipes, dented and twisted by age and the warm, moist air.

The hall seemed deserted; Mulder moved forward carefully, trying to keep track of the floor in front of his feet. As with the clinic, the floor was made of cement, though it looked as though there had once been carpeting; tufts of moldy green padding speckled the aisle between the pews.

Mulder had nearly reached the destroyed stage when his gaze settled on a pair of thick, forest green curtains hanging down along the back wall. Between the curtains was a door, attached at a disturbed angle by a single warped hinge. There was easily enough room between the door and the frame for someone to slip through.

Mulder hurried his pace, his gun trained on the dark opening. He could hear the blood rushing through his ears, and his knees burned from the controlled crouch. He reached the curtains and kneeled next to the broken door. The room on the other side looked small, dimly lit by a single, painted window. It seemed deserted as well, and Mulder slid inside, shoulder first.

It was some sort of priest's chambers. There was a low table in the center, and an overturned chair by the wall. A pair of crucifixes hung at eye level above the chair. Beneath the crucifixes stood a small shelf of sacramental items: a few cheap-looking goblets, a pair of candles, an empty wine bottle. Next to the shelf hung an enormous, faded tapestry, taking up almost half of the back wall. Mulder could make out the outline of three separate miracles imprinted on the tapestry, but the details had long since eroded.

Mulder slid toward the tapestry, his feet making as little sound as possible. The bottom of the tapestry was swinging, as if brushed by a gentle wind. Mulder grabbed a handful of the thick material and lifted.

He found himself peering into a dark, descending stairwell. The steps looked worn and scuffed, and Mulder could see they had once been covered in the same green carpeting as the front hall. He smiled, then narrowed his eyes. Caution demanded that he head back to the inn and get Scully— perhaps even contact Van Epps for some armed military backup. He had no idea what he was going to find in those tunnels.

But the longer he waited, the less chance he would find answers. The young man could easily slip away. Mulder shook away his reservations, bent low, and carefully slid beneath the tapestry. He slowly worked his way down the stairs, one hand gliding along the cold stone wall.

The stairs ended about twenty-five feet below the church, at the mouth of a long tunnel. The tunnel had porcelain-tiled walls, with steel support beams rising out of the cement floor at regular intervals. It looked roughly as Mulder had imagined; more modern and clean than the subway tunnels where he and Scully had found Perry Stanton, but certainly not the sort of thing you'd find in any urban mall in the U.S.

To Mulder's surprise, the tunnel was well lit by fluorescent light strips set every few yards into the curved ceiling. The lights meant two things; there was some sort of power source beneath the church, and the underground tunnels had not been abandoned twenty years ago with the rest of the MASH unit.

Mulder headed forward, calling on his training to keep his progress near silent. The air had a brisk, cavernous feel, and Mulder wondered if there was a ventilation system in place. He thought he could detect the soft hum of a fan in the distance, but he couldn't be sure.

Ten yards beyond the stairwell, the tunnel branched out in two directions. Mulder paused at the fork, his back hard against one of the steel struts rising up along the wall. To the left, the tunnel seemed to go on forever, winding like a snake beneath Alkut. To the right, the curved walls opened up into some sort of chamber.

Mulder shifted his gun to his other hand and retrieved his map one more time. He tried to place himself near one of the major chambers—but he couldn't be sure where he had entered the underground compound. His best guess was that he was a few feet from a large, oval room labeled C23. Judging from the distance he had just traveled, C23 appeared to be about fifty feet across.

Mulder decided it was worth investigating, and exchanged the map for the automatic. He held the gun with both hands, index finger beneath the trigger. Then he swung around the corner and through the entrance to the chamber.

He had accurately judged the dimensions of the room. The ceiling was higher than in the tunnels, curved like the inside of a tennis ball. As in the tunnels, the walls were covered in porcelain tiles, but the tiles had gone from light green to a much deeper, oceanic blue. The floor was still cement, and there were two steel posts in the center of the chamber supporting the high ceiling. At the back of the chamber was the opening to what looked to be another tunnel.

Mulder's eyes widened as he saw row after row of hospital stretchers taking up most of the sheer cement floor. Each stretcher was partially concealed by a light blue, circular plastic curtain. Next to the stretchers stood chrome IV racks trailing long yellow rubber IV wires.

The walls on either side of the chamber were lined with high-tech medical equipment—much fancier and certainly more expensive than anything he had seen in Fielding's clinic. He saw what looked to be an ultrasound station, a pair of EEG machines, and at least a dozen crash carts trailing defibrillator wires. Next to the crash carts stood an electron microscope, next to that a computer cabinet supporting a row of state-of-the-art monitors. The monitors' screens all emitted a blank blue light.

Across from the monitors stood a high glass shelf full of chemical vials and test-tube racks. Next to the shelf was a freestanding machine Mulder recognized as an autoclave, a steam sterilizing unit with a clear glass front and a digital control panel. The autoclave was about the size of a small closet, and the control panel was lit; the machine seemed to be in use. Between the sterilizer, the computers, and the various machines, this chamber was drawing a lot of power.

Mulder moved forward, counting the partially curtained stretchers. His eyebrows rose as he reached 130, closely packed together in groups of ten and twenty.

Altogether, the same number of stretchers as patients on the Trowbridges' list. Mulder reached the center of the chamber, his thoughts swirling. Was it possible that a group of horribly burned soldiers had been kept here, alive, for more than twenty-five years? Was it possible that Emile Paladin had truly discovered a miracle—

Mulder froze, as sudden footsteps echoed through the chamber. He spun toward the sound—and saw the thin young man standing at the entrance to the chamber. Now that there was less distance between them, he noticed that the man was of mixed origin. His eyes were narrow and dark, his face sharply angled. He was a good two inches taller than Mulder, and his lithe muscles looked like twisted ropes beneath his skin.

The young man's hands were hidden beneath the wide sleeves of his smock. Mulder made sure his gun was clearly visible. "I'm Agent Mulder of the American FBI. I'm going to approach, slowly. Don't make any sudden motions."

The young man smiled. There was a loud shuffling from somewhere behind Mulder's right shoulder. Mulder jerked his body to the side—and saw three men enter the chamber from the opposite entrance. All three were tall, and looked to be in their early twenties. They had matching crew cuts and seemed to be in excellent physical shape. They moved easily into the room, spreading out as they closed toward Mulder. The largest of the three strolled directly toward him, and Mulder noticed that he had something in his right hand: a syringe filled with clear liquid. Mulder aimed his gun at the man's chest. "Stay where you are."

The man continued forward. Mulder realized there was something off about his face. The man's eyes seemed strangely overdilated. He was looking right at Mulder—but he seemed somewhere else entirely, locked in some sort of daze.

"Not another step," Mulder warned, flipping the safety off his automatic. "I said stop!"

The two wingmen were within fifteen feet, now closing toward him. The man with the syringe was barely ten feet away. Mulder aimed directly at his chest. The man paused—but not because of the gun. He was looking at the syringe. He tapped it against his arm, knocking away an air bubble. *This was going to get ugly.*

Suddenly, all three men dived forward. Mulder fired twice, the gun kicking into the air. The lead man jerked back on his feet, then regained his momentum and continued toward Mulder. Before Mulder could fire again, incredibly strong arms grabbed his wrists, twisting his hands behind his back. The Smith & Wesson clattered to the floor.

He kicked out, trying desperately to twist free. The man with the syringe leaned over him, and he caught a glimpse of something that sent his terrified mind spinning. The man had a circular red rash on the back of his neck.

Mulder felt a sharp prick just above his collarbone. The three men suddenly released him, stepping back. Mulder's knees buckled, and he fell, trying limply to catch himself on the curtain around a nearby stretcher. The curtain snapped free, and he hit the ground. He heard laughter behind him, and he used all his strength to turn his head. The Amerasian was watching him, smiling. The smile seemed to extend at the corners, twisting and turning like a rope made of blood. Mulder tried to crawl away, but he couldn't get the commands to his muscles. His body had changed to liquid. Green clouds swept across his vision, and he felt the cold floor against his cheek. A second later, everything turned black.

Quo Tien shouted a blunt command, and the three drones started back toward the other side of the room. Tien watched their fluid progress, intrigued by their perfect muscle control, the lack of stagger in their walk. He remembered how it was in the beginning. The plodding, slow movements, the limited limb control. The progress was indeed impressive. But it was only partially complete. The drones represented only the first stage of the experiment. In a few hours, the final stage would begin. Twenty-five years of research funneled into a single operation—an operation that was going to make Tien immensely rich. And now there was nothing to stand in the way.

Tien turned his attention back to the FBI agent lying on the floor. A shiver moved through him as he flicked the straight razor out from beneath his sleeve. He could imagine the man's blood flowing just beneath his skin. He wanted to taste that blood, to feel it spread over his hands and lips.

He slid forward. The FBI agent was lying on his side, legs curled in a fetal position. His dark hair was spiked with sweat, and his face was drawn, his eyes moving rapidly beneath his eyelids. Tien dropped to his knees inches away. He ran a finger down the man's bare arm, feeling the slick sweat and the tense muscles beneath. He carefully lifted the razor.

"Tien. Put it down."

Tien looked up, anger flickering across his face. He watched as Julian Kyle strolled into the chamber. Julian was wearing a white lab coat over surgical scrubs. His hands were covered with latex gloves, and there was a heavy cooler under his right arm.

"Uncle Julian," Tien spat. "You're ruining my moment."

"He's an agent with the FBI," Kyle said, sternly. "It isn't as simple as that."

"It can be," Tien responded, glancing at the razor's blade. "This is Thailand, not the U.S."

"It doesn't matter. They'll send agents. The military will get involved. We can't risk the interruptions—not so close to the final experiment. And there's a better way."

Kyle raised the plastic cooler. Tien sighed, leaning back from the FBI agent's body. He knew the real reason for Kyle's reticence. Julian Kyle was weak. But there was logic in his words. "I guess it's not for either of us to decide."

Tien rose, sliding the straight razor back into his sleeve. In truth, both FBI agents had determined their own fate the minute they had entered Alkut.

"And the woman?" Kyle asked, setting the cooler down on one of the stretchers. "She's being dealt with as well?"

Tien nodded. "I sent a drone. He should be arriving at her room any moment."

"And one drone will be enough?"

Tien laughed. The drones were primitive compared to what was coming—but certainly, a single drone could handle the female agent. Kyle nodded, realizing it was true. It was just a matter of time before Dana Scully's body was laid out next to her partner's.

TWENTY

Scully watched from fifteen feet away as the small green lizard crawled across the perforated metal screen. The lizard had bulging black eyes, dark red spots, and a curved, tapered tail; probably some sort of Asian gecko, she mused, the remnants of some species of dinosaur too primitive to realize it was supposed to be extinct. At the moment, the gecko was doing its best to right evolution's mistake. Inches beneath the metal screen, a pair of propeller-shaped fan blades whirled by, pushing dense waves of humid air across the cramped hotel bedroom. As the gecko crawled across the circular mesh covering, its tail dangled precariously close to the blades. Any second, the fan would consume the little creature, spreading its bits and pieces across the room.

Jackson Pollock gone reptilian: In Scully's opinion, it certainly wouldn't hurt the hotel's spartan sense of decor. The squat, antique fan sat atop a teak bed table, next to a pair of twin-sized, water-stained mattresses. There was a loosely woven throw rug on the floor, and a warped wooden dresser by the closet door. A chest-high, rusting metal lamp stood a few feet from the desk where Scully sat, a single bulb flickering behind a goatskin shade as a tangle of exposed wires near the bottom of the base struggled noisily with the current coming out of the wall socket.

The desk itself was barely larger than the bed table, the chair designed for small Thai bodies. A perfect fit for Scully's concise frame, but Mulder would have had a hell of a time getting his long legs beneath the drawers.

Still, there was room in the closet for their bags, a phone jack, and an adaptable socket to plug in Scully's laptop computer. It was all she needed to link up with the FBI computer banks in Washington.

Scully rolled her shoulders back against the tight chair, shifting her attention from the doomed little dinosaur to the open laptop on the desk in front of her. The cursor blinked at her impatience, while the processor struggled to download her request to the data banks ten thousand miles away. She had laboriously plugged in the list of names—minus Andrew Paladin. Soon the computer would tell her if the men had indeed served in the Vietnam War. She had also asked for army registration photos, current addresses, and medical records; she knew how Mulder's mind worked, and she needed to be thorough. She intended to disprove the notion that these men had somehow survived horrific napalm burns.

Scully simply could not believe that Emile Paladin had invented some sort of miraculous synthetic skin—and had killed to keep its existence a secret. If Perry Stanton had died as the result of an experiment gone bad, it was a recent experiment, perhaps some re-creation of the procedure that had killed the Rikers Island prisoners. It was implausible to think that Stanton's death was somehow related to a twenty-four-year-old secret cure.

A series of beeps emanated from the laptop, and Scully sat up in her chair. The list of names began to spill across the screen, followed by concise FBI terminology. Scully furrowed her brow as she quickly interpreted the data. At first glance, the data confirmed her suspicions. The men were listed as casualties of the Vietnam War. But Scully noticed a strange discrepancy. The men were all registered as having been killed in action between 1970 and 1973; none was listed as having been transported to any army MASH unit, let alone the unit in Alkut.

Scully tapped her lips with her fingers. It didn't make any sense. She and Mulder had found a list registering dead men as admissions to the Alkut MASH. Either the list was a complete fabrication, or someone had falsified death records and admitted the men unofficially. Of course, the first case seemed more likely. The list was nothing more than a piece of paper—even if it had been found in the house of a viciously murdered couple.

Scully paused as the laptop screen changed color. Thumbnail pictures materialized along the horizontal—and by midscreen, she realized things were not as simple as they seemed. The photos had been lifted directly from army registration files, and at least three were clearly recognizable. They were the same photos she and Mulder had taken from the Trowbridges' envelope.

The photos weren't proof that the men had been admitted to the MASH unit—but they certainly implied a connection to Alkut. Scully leaned close to the screen, scanning the photos as they appeared, searching for more matches—

A sudden sound caught her attention, and she looked up from the screen. The sound had come from the other side of the bedroom door. A click of metal against metal, as if someone had tried turning the knob to see if it was locked.

"Hello?" Scully called, but there was no answer. "Mulder, is that you?"

Silence. Scully rose from the chair, her heart pounding. Her gun was in its holster, sitting on the bed table behind the propeller fan. She cleared her throat. "If someone's out there, please identify yourself!"

The doorknob exploded inward, a rain of wood splinters and mangled steel spiraling into the room. Scully jerked back, stunned, her hips slamming into the desk. A man was standing in the open doorway.

Tall, well built, with a crew cut and high, chiseled features. He was wearing a loose white shirt and military green slacks. His eyes seemed strange, his pupils overdilated. The muscles in his cheeks and jaw were slack, and Scully immediately thought of drugs—something depressive, perhaps a tranquilizer or an antipsychotic.

The man stepped into the room. Scully's eyes drifted downward, and she watched as he drew something out of the right pocket of his slacks. A hypodermic, with a three-inch-long syringe. Scully's pulse rocketed as she pressed back against the desk.

"Stay where you are," she said in her strongest voice. "I'm a U.S. federal agent."

The man didn't seem to hear her. He took another step forward, his dull eyes trained on her face. Despite his numb expression, his movements were gracefully fluid. Scully thought about her gun fifteen feet away—and realized he would reach her before she was halfway there. She had no way of knowing what was in the syringe, but she had to assume it was something lethal. She needed to disarm the man before going for her gun. She searched the room rapidly—and her gaze settled on the chest-high lamp a few feet past the edge of the desk. It looked heavy enough to cause damage, and close enough to reach. The exposed wires near the bottom of the base were menacing, but if she was careful, she could avoid electrocuting herself.

The man moved closer. He raised the syringe, shaking it until a droplet of liquid dangled pendulously from the point. Scully kept her eyes on the needle as she slid along the desk toward the lamp. She could hear her heart in her chest, and she took deep breaths, chasing the panic away.

As the man took another step forward, Scully suddenly leapt to the side, grabbing the lamp halfway up its metal base. Without pause, she swung the makeshift weapon in a sweeping arc, aiming for the hypodermic. The goatskin shade toppled away, revealing a naked bulb and more exposed wires. There was a flash of light as the bulb hit the syringe dead on. Then a rainbow of bright sparks burst into the air as the steel needle touched the light socket.

Scully dropped the lamp and dived for the bed table. She was halfway there when she realized the man wasn't chasing her. She turned and watched him convulse backward, the still-sparking lamp lying in front of him, smoke rising from the hypodermic in his hand. The man's knees suddenly went limp, and his body collapsed to the floor.

Scully stared, surprised. The syringe had only touched the light socket for a few seconds; the electric shock should have been strong enough to stun the man—but not enough to cause him serious harm. Scully grabbed her gun from the bed table and stepped cautiously toward him, the barrel aimed at his head. His arms were twisted unnaturally behind his back, his eyes wide open. His head was partially to one side, and Scully noticed a red rash on the back of his neck. Her cheeks flushed as she remembered that both Perry Stanton and the John Doe had had similar rashes.

She stopped a few feet from the collapsed man and lowered herself to one knee. Keeping the gun a careful distance away, she reached forward and checked his pulse.

Nothing. Scully grabbed the man's shoulder and rolled him over onto his back. His chest was still, his eyes shifting back in their sockets. Scully made a quick decision and slipped her gun into the back of her waistband. She began CPR, pressing as hard as she could against the man's muscular chest.

A few minutes into the CPR she realized it was pointless. The man was dead. As had happened with Perry Stanton, this man had been killed by a relatively small jolt of electricity. Although it was possible for a lamp to draw enough power to cause a cardiac arrest—it was definitely unlikely.

Scully shifted her gaze to the rash on the nape of the dead man's neck. She saw that it consisted of thousands of tiny red dots, arranged in a circular pattern. Like Perry Stanton's and the John Doe's rashes. And all three men had died after receiving electric shocks. Scully wondered—what would this man's autopsy show? She needed to get the body to an operating room. She hoped Fielding would let her use the clinic—

She froze, her gaze shifting to the syringe still clamped in the man's right hand. The clinic. Mulder was there, searching for the underground tunnels. If they had come for Scully, then they must have gone after Mulder as well.

A second later, Scully was on her feet and heading for the door.

TWENTY-ONE

Mulder tried to scream, but the beast was too fast. Its enormous black body hurtled toward him through the milky gray air. The monster landed on his chest, its heavy body crushing him back against the stretcher. The wolfish snout was inches from his face, and he stared in terror at the fiery red spirals that were the creature's eyes. The curved, crisscrossing tusks scraped together like kissing scimitars, while a stream of fetid yellow saliva dribbled against his cheeks.

Suddenly, the halo of clawed tentacles on top of the beast's head lashed forward. Mulder felt his skin being flayed away in burning white strips. Again and again the tentacles slashed at him, ruining his face, his neck, his chest. He writhed back and forth, trying to dodge the claws, but the beast was unrelenting. The Skin Eater had been disturbed—and he was hungry. He would tear at Mulder until every ounce of Mulder's skin had been removed. His tentacles and his tusks and his spiral eyes, slashing, gouging, gorging! Mulder convulsed upward with every ounce of strength, refusing to give in, refusing to let the beast have him so easily. He wasn't ready to die…

Mulder's eyes came open. His vision swirled, a wave of nausea working upward through his throat. He gagged, trying to lift himself to a sitting position—but his arms were pinned at his sides. He blinked rapidly, letting the yellowish light clear away the fog. He was staring at a curved stone ceiling, lined by fluorescent light strips. He shifted his head to the side and saw that he was surrounded by a blue plastic curtain. He realized immediately where he was. *The underground chamber.*

His head fell back against the stretcher. He blinked rapidly, fighting away the nausea. He did not know how long he had been unconscious, but from the lack of pain in his muscles, he guessed it was not more than a few hours. There was a black Velcro belt running around his chest and down beneath the stretcher, holding his arms in place. There was a similar restraint around his ankles. He could move his hands a few inches and wiggle his toes—but other than that, he was completely immobilized.

His thoughts shifted back to the violent attack. The three men had overpowered him without much effort.

He had fired two shots—could he have missed at point-blank range? Unlikely, but not impossible. And the circular red rash he had seen on the back of his attacker's neck? Was it the same rash that had been reported on both Perry Stanton and the John Doe? And how was it connected to the dazed, overdilated look in the man's eyes?

Mulder took a deep breath, calming himself. He didn't want to use up his energy building theories. He remembered the smiling young Amerasian man. There had been violence behind that smile—a sort of violence that Mulder well recognized. The same edge he had seen in dozens of serial killers throughout his career. *Controlled psychosis.* The Amerasian was a killer. Perhaps he was the young man Trowbridge had spoken about, Emile Paladin's son. Perhaps he had been responsible for the brutal double murder. Perhaps he was stalking Scully right now…

Mulder clenched his teeth and slammed his body back against the stretcher. He was helpless, impotent. He couldn't protect his partner. He couldn't even protect himself.

Or could he? He had a strange, sudden thought. He twisted his body a few inches beneath the Velcro strap and felt something hard and cylindrical in his right pocket—just within reach. Slowly, carefully, his fingers crawled toward the object.

With effort, he managed to get the vial free from his pants. Using his index finger and thumb, he went to work on the cap. It finally came free, and a bitter scent wafted up toward his nose. He remembered what the emaciated teenage monk had said when he had given him the balm: "Makes the skin taste bad." He thought about the monster in his dream, picturing the criss-crossing tusks. He shivered, gripping the vial tightly in his hand. Then he flicked his wrist upward toward his body.

He felt the transparent liquid splashing across his chest. A few drops touched his chin and neck, a few more landed on his shoulder and cheeks. The bitter, sulfuric scent burned at his nostrils. He knew Scully would have thought he was insane. He was in an underground research lab—not a monster's cave. But he couldn't shake the feeling that, somehow, the Skin Eater was involved. Either way, he wanted his skin to taste as bad as possible—

He froze, as footsteps reverberated through the stretcher beneath him. Someone was approaching the curtain from the other side. Mulder quickly pushed the empty vial beneath his leg, hiding it from view.

The curtain whipped back, and Mulder squinted at the apparition standing a few feet away. Over six feet tall, long-limbed, with narrow shoulders. The man was wearing light blue scrubs, latex gloves, and a white surgical mask. His hair was completely covered by a surgical cap. The only features Mulder could make out were the man's eyes. A flickering, almost transparent blue—like the base of a flame. Mulder swallowed, trying to appear calm. But those

eyes were almost as unnerving as never-ending spirals. Mulder wondered—
could this be Emile Paladin?

The man turned and said something in a quiet voice. There were other
people in the room, just out of view. Gloved hands held out a thin plastic tray.
The blue-eyed man took two objects from the tray and turned back to Mulder.

Mulder's gaze dropped to the man's hands. In the right, he held a steel
device shaped like an oversize stapler. Mulder remembered a conversation
from days ago, when he and Scully had questioned Perry Stanton's plastic
surgeon. Something about a stapler used in skin-transplantation procedures.
Christ. Mulder's eyes shifted to the man's other hand. He saw a long pair of
steel tweezers, delicately gripped around a four-inch strip of something thin
and yellow. The material looked organic and wet, as if it had just been
removed from some sort of preserving solution. *Washed and ready for transplantation.*

"Wait," Mulder whispered. He tried to regain his composure. "You're
making a big mistake. They'll send people looking for me."

The blue-eyed man shook the tweezers, and tiny droplets of liquid splat-
tered toward the floor. "Put him under. Now."

Suddenly, strong hands clamped a rubber gas mask over Mulder's mouth
and nose. He stared wildly at the square face leaning over him from the head
of the stretcher. The second man was also wearing a surgical mask, but
Mulder recognized the cubic shape of his head. *Julian Kyle. Here, in Thailand.*
Mulder held his breath, struggling violently against the old scientist's grip. But
the ex-military man was too strong.

"Take a deep breath," Kyle whispered into his ear. "You won't feel any pain."

Mulder arched his back against the Velcro strap. His lungs spasmed, but
still he held on. Kyle pressed the mask tighter against his face. "It has to be
this way."

Mulder saw spots in the corner of his vision, and suddenly he couldn't
fight any longer. He gasped, filling his lungs. A sweet taste touched the back
of his tongue, and his eyelids fluttered shut. He heard the material of his
slacks tearing, and he felt something touching his left calf. Something cold
and wet. *My god, my god, my god!* But he was helpless, fading fast. As he flirted
with consciousness, a faraway voice swirled in his ear.

"He won't cause us any more problems."

"And his partner?" came the response. There was a brief pause. When the first voice answered, it had a tinny, almost musical quality.

"Something went wrong. It was a mistake to send a first-stage drone on an unobserved mission. We need to send Tien—"

"Julian, we don't have time."

"But his partner—"

"Forget her," the first voice snapped. "We need to head back to the main lab and proceed with the final stage. The satellite link will allow us only a small window for our demonstration."

The voices disintegrated as Mulder's limp body settled back against the stretcher. Reality faded away to the rhythmic click click click of an oversize steel stapler.

TWENTY-TWO

Scully sat on the wet front steps of the clinic, staring in frustration at the blueprint open on her lap. It had been more than two hours since she had left the hotel, and still she had found no trace of Mulder. She had scoured every inch of the clinic, had questioned Fielding and her staff; Mulder had left the clinic the same way he had come—through the front door. He had found no underground tunnels, no hint of the basement floor.

But Scully knew better than to discount Mulder's ability to find what didn't seem to exist. After searching the clinic, she had headed straight to the records library in the town hall. While at the town hall, she had considered reporting the body in her hotel room—but had decided she didn't have time. She had to make sure Mulder was all right.

She ran her fingers across the center of the blueprint, tracing a shadowy line that she assumed represented Alkut's main road. She had found the blueprint in a booklet printed by the national Thai power company—an idea that had come to her while looking at the electrocuted man in her bedroom. Someone had dug power lines beneath the town's streets, which meant there had to be a better map of the town—and perhaps its underground—than the one provided by the U.S. military.

But after twenty minutes of trying to decipher the strange Thai notations and geographic cues that covered most of the power-company blueprint,

Scully was no longer sure that the map was going to provide much help. The town's buildings were represented by little more than numbered dots, connected by dark lines that could have been anything from dirt paths to paved highways. The only structures represented clearly on the blueprint were the power lines; the entire map was covered in spiderwebs of bright red ink, connected by larger blue trunks. The blue trunks seemed to be focused near the larger town buildings, such as the clinic and the town hall. Scully guessed they were the feeder lines, connected directly to the hydraulic power plant located a half mile beyond the north edge of town.

Scully flicked an oversize mosquito off the blueprint as her fingers reached the junction between the main road and the street where the clinic was located. The mosquito angrily buzzed off, leaving behind one of its front legs. Beneath the leg ran one of the blue trunks leading toward the clinic. Scully followed it with her eyes, her mind wandering to Mulder. *Damn it, where the hell are you?* In a few minutes she was going to have to put in a call to Washington, then another to Van Epps. On orders from Washington, the military would turn the town upside down searching for a missing FBI agent—and in the process, scare off any chance they had of solving the mysteries of the Stanton case.

Scully heard a buzzing in her right ear, and felt the injured mosquito land on her exposed neck. Even missing a leg, it would not give up. Like the lizard on the fan, it was a creature too simple to face reality. She was about to slap it away when her eyes involuntarily focused on a spot on the blueprint.

She saw that three of the blue trunks converged within a few centimeters of each other, somewhere close to the clinic. She leaned over the map, trying to decipher the exact location. She barely even noticed the sharp pinch as the mosquito dug its nose into her skin. Her head was spinning as she traced the few centimeters of map between the clinic and the three blue trunks. She suddenly looked up.

She stared at the decrepit building across the street. Then she moved her eyes from the steeple to the door to the heap of plastic sheeting next to the front entrance. She remembered how the sheeting had covered the door. She had assumed that the church was abandoned.

She turned back to the blueprint, oblivious of the bloated, sated mosquito that lifted off from her neck and flew past her face. The blueprint didn't make any sense—unless she and Mulder had both been looking in the wrong place. The thought was like a gunshot, sending Scully to her feet.

If she had read the blueprint right, there were three power lines feeding electricity to the abandoned church across the street.

TWENTY-THREE

Mulder's throat constricted, and he lurched forward, gasping for air. His skull throbbed, and he violently shook his head back and forth, desperate to silence the horrid ringing in his ears. Then his eyes came open—and memory crashed into him with a burst of fluorescent light.

He was lying on the same stretcher in the same underground chamber, but the Velcro straps were gone. The curtain was pulled back, and there was no sign of the blue-eyed man or Julian Kyle. As far as Mulder could tell, he was alone in the chamber. He noticed with a start that his clothes were gone; he was wearing a white hospital smock, and there was a thin rubber wire sticking out of his right arm. Eyes wide, he followed the rubber wire to a bottle of yellowish liquid hanging from the IV rack above his shoulder.

Without thought, he grabbed the wire and yanked it out of his arm. Thin drops of blood dribbled down his wrist, and he quickly applied pressure, cursing at the sharp pain. As he stared at the yellow liquid dripping from the detached IV wire, his entire body started to tremble. A strange, crawling feeling was moving up his left leg. It felt like a thousand worms twitching through his skin.

He clenched his teeth and yanked the smock up. A dozen oversize staples were sticking out from his calf, winding down toward his Achilles tendon. To his surprise, the yellow strip below the staples had shriveled into a hard mass, barely touching the skin beneath. Mulder quickly grabbed the withered slab and yanked as hard as he could. It tore free, dragging half the staples with it. Blood ran freely down his calf, but he barely noticed. He was staring at the failed transplant, relief billowing through him. As he pressed the slab between his fingers, it disintegrated to a fine dust. Mulder exhaled, watching the dust flow through his fingers to the floor.

"I've heard of a patient rejecting a skin transplant," he mused, "but never a transplant rejecting a patient."

He carefully tore a strip of material from the bottom of his smock and wrapped it tightly around his calf. The bleeding slowed, and although he could still feel the few remaining staples, he barely felt any pain. He thought about the balm he had splashed on himself, and how the transplanted skin had reacted. In his mind, connections were forming. But he still needed more information to convince himself that his theories were true.

He shifted his legs off the stretcher, ignoring the dull pounding in his skull. No worse than a bad hangover, he told himself—*a cup of coffee and you'll be as good as new.* His feet touched the cold cement floor, and a new shiver moved up through his shoulders. He felt exposed in the thin hospital smock, and he half expected the blue-eyed man to return with another slab of skin. This time, he would not have the balm to protect him. The transplant would stick—and then? He had a feeling he knew exactly what would happen. But he needed proof.

He rose, slowly, and staggered through the open curtain that surrounded his stretcher. The other stretchers that filled the chamber were still empty, and he noticed again that each had a single IV rack nearby, supporting similar bottles of yellowish liquid. As he moved past the stretchers, he scratched the tiny wound in his forearm, wondering how long he had been unconscious— and how much of the unknown substance was coursing through his veins.

He reached the far wall of the chamber and paused, his eyes shifting across the medical machinery. He was a few feet away from the electron microscope, and his gaze settled on the row of computer monitors nearby. As before, the monitors were all switched on, the screens glowing blue. Mulder noticed that the processors beneath the monitors were connected by a series of wires to the electron microscope. It was a situation he could not resist.

He ran his fingers along the boxlike microscope housing and found a pair of switches. He flicked both of them to the on position, and watched as the computer screens changed color. A second later, tiny, plate-shaped objects bounced across a background of swirling red. Mulder recognized the objects from the broken model in Julian Kyle's office. Epidermal cells, but there was something unnatural about the way they were moving—an almost violent cadence spurred by some unknown desire. The skin cells seemed—for lack of a better word—hungry.

Mulder chided himself. His body and mind had suffered extreme abuse in the past few hours, and he was letting his thoughts get carried away. He drifted past the computer screens—and noticed a small steel file cabinet by the last monitor. The cabinet was barely waist high, and he hadn't noticed it before. A thrill moved through him as he dropped to one knee. *File cabinets were an FBI agent's pornography.*

Mulder began rifling through the drawers. Within a few seconds, he had forgotten about the pounding in his skull and the blood still soaking through the loose tourniquet around his calf. All of his thoughts were trained on the pages that sped past his fingers.

He had reached the back half of the second drawer when he stopped, drawing out a familiar sheet of paper. It was the same list of 130 soldiers he had found beneath the golden Buddha. But in this list, there was a difference. One of the names was crossed off. Next to the name was a small, handwritten note:

Dopamine inhibitor deficiency, due to IV malfunction.
Began cardiac convulsions shortly after 2 a.m. en route to in-house demon-
stration. Drone escaped custody shortly afterward.

Mulder rocked back on his feet, rereading the words. He thought back to the three men who had assaulted him. He pictured their overdilated eyes, their faraway stares. *Drone* was a fitting description. He remembered the tail end of the conversation he had heard, just before he had lost consciousness. Kyle had mentioned something about sending a drone after Scully. The memory sent shards of fear down Mulder's spine—but then he remembered the last part of the conversation. Kyle had said that the drone—the "first-stage drone" had been unable to complete the mission. Then the other man had mentioned something about a final stage—and a demonstration. A demonstration that was going to take place at a main laboratory…

Mulder turned back to the file cabinet. Near the back of the same drawer, his fingers hit a thick sheaf of pages. As he lifted the sheaf free, he saw that the front page was another copy of the familiar list. But as he turned the pages, his pulse quickened. The list did not end at 130 names: It was sixteen pages long. Mulder quickly did the calculations. *Over two thousand soldiers.* All designated as napalm-burn victims brought to Alkut between 1970 and 1973. It was unthinkable. Two thousand men who should have died more than twenty-five years ago. His mind whirling, Mulder opened the last drawer in the file cabinet. The drawer was filled with photocopies of MRI scans. He pulled a handful free, leafing through them. The scans were cross sections of human brains, similar to the scans Scully had taken of Perry Stanton. Mulder was no expert, but he remembered what Scully had shown him, and he noticed some obvious similarities. As in Stanton's and the prisoners' MRIs, the brains in the scans had enlarged hypothalamuses. But as far as Mulder could tell, there were no polyps surrounding the augmented glands—

"Mulder!"

Mulder nearly dropped the scans as he whirled on his heels. He saw Scully rushing across the chamber. She had her gun out, and her eyes were scanning the room. Mulder tried to stand, but a rush of dizziness knocked him back to a crouch. In his excitement at finding the file cabinet, he had forgotten about the abuses his body had suffered. He leaned against the cabinet as Scully dropped to his side. She took in the hospital smock, then saw the bloodied tourniquet around his calf.

She quickly slid her gun back into its holster and put the back of her hand against his neck, checking his pulse. Her hand felt warm and reassuring. Mulder tried to smile. His head was pounding worse than before. But he wasn't going to give in to the pain. They were too close to solving their case. "I'm fine. A little elective surgery, that's all."

"Elective?" Scully asked, as her fingers probed beneath the edge of the makeshift tourniquet.

"As you can imagine, my vote was in the minority."

Scully's concern abated slightly as she discerned that the wound was minor. Then she shifted her attention to the small puncture where he had pulled out the IV wire. The anxiety returned to her face. "Do you know what you were given?"

"Over there, by the stretcher. The yellowish liquid. I think it was some sort of dopamine inhibitor."

Scully raised her eyebrows. "That would explain your sluggishness. But what makes you think that?"

Mulder showed her the first list, with the handwritten notation. "According to this, one of the transplant patients died from a lack of dopamine inhibitor. I believe all the transplant recipients have to get periodic infusions of the inhibitor—to keep them from going psychotic."

Scully stared at him. "All the transplant recipients. Are you implying—"

"They tried to transplant skin onto my calf. Thankfully, the procedure was a failure. But they didn't know that—and hooked me up to the inhibitor."

Mulder had made enormous jumps to come to the conclusion—but he knew he was on the right track. The blue-eyed man had tried to transplant skin onto his body—to turn him into a drone. They had left him with a dopamine-inhibitor drip. As Scully had explained back when she had first seen Perry Stanton's MRIs, dopamine was a neurotransmitter related to psychotic violence. Excess dopamine might also have explained the polyps surrounding Perry Stanton's hypothalamus.

Mulder handed Scully the MRI scans, and watched as she leafed through them. "The hypothalamuses are enlarged," she said, "like Stanton's. And look at this. The motor cortex has nearly doubled in size—while the amygdala has become almost nonexistent."

Mulder raised his eyebrows, confused. "The motor cortex and the amygdala?"

"The motor cortex is the part of the brain associated with involuntary reflex and motor control," Scully explained, still staring at the MRIs. "The amygdala is associated with personality and thought. If these MRIs are real, then the people whose brains have been photographed would be almost automatons—"

"Drones," Mulder interrupted. For some reason, Scully wasn't as shocked by the term as Mulder would have expected. Mulder shifted against the file cabinet. "They can follow simple commands—they can be controlled. Unless they don't get their dopamine inhibitor—and turn out like Perry Stanton."

Scully paused, still looking at the MRIs. "If your list is to be believed, our John Doe arrived here in Alkut—along with one hundred twenty-nine others—more than twenty-five years ago, burned almost to death. You're saying that all these men have been turned into drones?"

Mulder paused. He knew how insane it sounded. But he had his own experience to go from. They had tried to put the skin on him—*to transform him.* "That's just the beginning."

He showed her the list of two thousand names. Her eyes widened as she flipped through the pages. Two thousand men stolen from their families, turned into guinea pigs. Scully shook her head. "Impossible. The logistics alone would be incredible. These men would have to be kept in an intensive care facility. Someplace really big—with enough financing to last more than two decades. And for what purpose? Two thousand mindless drones—what's the point?"

Mulder slowly struggled to his feet, using Scully's arm for balance. "I don't think the drones are the final product. They were the first stage, the prototype. Paladin must be planning to create something much more valuable."

Scully exhaled. They had been through this before. She knew that death certificates could be faked—but Mulder had no real evidence that Paladin was still alive. Mulder thought about describing the blue-eyed man—but the surgical mask had hidden most of his features.

For the moment, Scully let the argument go and gestured toward the open chamber. "So you're convinced that Paladin's search for synthetic skin led to all of this."

Mulder paused. He had been developing a theory since his trip to the temple—but he knew that Scully would never buy into it. Still, he felt the need to tell her his thoughts. "It's not synthetic. It's scavenged."

He started across the chamber. Scully followed alongside. "What do you mean?"

"Trowbridge told us that Paladin was a devoted student of Thai mythology. I think Paladin knew about the Skin Eater before he ever came to Alkut. He went looking for the creature—and has been using its skin as the source of his transplants." To Mulder, it made perfect sense. Skin was the source of the Skin Eater's power. Skin was also the source of Perry Stanton's invulnerability, and his strength. Paladin had wandered in the mountains surrounding Alkut—and had found a way to make miracles.

Scully stopped near the row of computer screens. She stared, silently, at the unnatural epidermal cells migrating across the swirls of red. Finally, she shook her head. "It has to be synthetic, Mulder. Some sort of chemical structure that interacts with the patient's bloodstream, spreading into the muscle-control centers of the brain. An extremely elastic and inviolable substance—except to electricity. Electricity passes right through the skin into the nervous system itself, setting off a cardiac reaction."

Mulder raised his eyebrows. Stanton and the John Doe had both died from electric shocks. But Scully had not accepted the connection before.

"I had an encounter with one of these men," Scully explained. "In my hotel room. He went into cardiac arrest after shoving a hypodermic needle into a light socket."

Mulder nodded. Now he understood why she had been willing to accept his premise—if not his conclusions.

"If these men are just the beginning," Scully continued, "what's next?"

Mulder wasn't sure. But the sinking feeling in his gut told him where they would have to go to find out. "If Emile Paladin is experimenting on two thousand missing soldiers, he needs a private, secluded place to work. A place where no one would dare bother him."

Scully exhaled at his obvious attempt at melodrama. But Mulder was sure she was thinking along the same lines. As soon as he recovered his balance, they would be heading into the mountains that surrounded Alkut.

Searching for a secret intensive care unit—and a mythological lair.

TWENTY-FOUR

Scully sprawled next to Mulder against the fallen evergreen trunk, watching in awe as the three Thai guides hacked at the underbrush with their huge, curved machetes. All three men were bare to the waist, and their sinewy bodies glowed in the sweltering heat. A few feet away, the emaciated teenage monk guided their progress with abrupt flicks of his bony hand; even after seven hours of trekking upward through the dense tropical forest, he and the hired guides showed no sign of tiring. The sky had gone from orange to gray nearly an hour ago, and still they pushed forward, refusing to give up on the promise of reaching the mountain base before darkness set in.

"Very close," the teenage monk called over his shoulder, as he checked the sky with his eyes. "Trail ends over next hill."

Scully contained her enthusiasm. Malku had been making similar statements for the past three miles. What the teenage monk described as hills were actually small mountains covered in densely packed broadleaf evergreens, oak, laurel, and dipterocarps, a native Southeast Asian tree. And as far as Scully could tell, the "trail" was little more than a handful of disconnected breaks in the underbrush, separated by lush green barriers of tropical plant life.

Mulder noticed the skeptical expression on Scully's face, as he slipped off one of his combat boots and shook stones the size of marbles to the ground. A cloud of mosquitoes buzzed around his face, and he blinked rapidly, struggling to keep the irritating insects out of his eyes. "He knows where he's going, Scully. It's his religion, after all."

Scully glanced skeptically at her partner. It was a strange sight—Mulder in military camouflage, with combat boots and an assault rifle slung over his right shoulder. They had found the uniform and rifle at a shop next door to the town hall. Like the Jeep, the items were souvenirs of the Vietnam War—and both had been kept in surprisingly good shape. The uniform was frayed at the edges, and there were three quarter-sized holes in the lower back—but it fit Mulder's frame. He had balked at wearing the uniform until the shop owner had promised him that the original owner had survived his wounds.

The automatic rifle was a much easier decision. Mulder's gun had vanished with his clothes, and they did not have time to navigate the necessary channels in search of a replacement. Mulder's FBI training covered most models of assault rifles, including the CAR-15 slung over his shoulder. Basically, it was a shorter, carbine version of the M-16, chambered in 5.56 mm. The gun had come fitted with a single box magazine containing twenty rounds. The shopkeeper had done a good job keeping the machine oiled and clean, and it seemed battle-ready. A brutal weapon; surely capable of cutting through even the most durable synthetic skin.

"I don't share your confidence," Scully finally responded, focusing on the thin young monk. His jutting chin and narrow eyes made him look like some sort of plucked bird. "Even if the place we're looking for does exist, there are literally thousands of caves at the foot of See Dum Kao."

Mulder shrugged, pulling his boot back over his foot. He winced as the motion tweaked the edge of the fresh bandage around his calf. "You saw the map Ganon showed me in the temple. Malku has spent years memorizing its twists and turns. His whole life has been dedicated to understanding the legend of the Skin Eater. The cave is at the end of this trail."

Scully tightened the clasp holding her hair. It had been a struggle holding back her reservations when Mulder had brought her to Ganon and the Skin Eater temple. When the ancient monk had instructed his young apprentice to guide the agents to the legendary home of the Skin Eater, she had remained silent for one simple reason: The legendary mountain lair was their best bet for locating a private hospital large enough to hold two thousand burned soldiers. The myth was a good cover for unethical, radical experimentation. Emile Paladin could have set up some sort of private hospital during the war—and transferred control to Fibrol after his death. The company could have provided the funding necessary to keep the hospital functioning, while someone else—perhaps Julian Kyle—continued the transplant research.

But in no way did Scully give credence to the fairy tale itself. She had seen Allan and Rina Trowbridges' bodies. She had read Emile Paladin's death certificate. And she had found nothing in the underground laboratory that remotely suggested a connection to some sort of skin-eating beast. The skin sample that had been transplanted onto Mulder's calf had disintegrated into dust—and during microscopic analysis, the dust itself had decomposed beyond the molecular level, making any conclusions impossible. When Scully and Mulder had returned to the hotel before setting off for the mountains, they had found no trace of the electrocuted corpse. Scully assumed that the body had been discovered by the owner of the hotel and carted off along with the Trowbridges. She had unsuccessfully tried to track the body down by phone, and had finally accepted the obvious: another autopsy that would never take place.

All of the evidence pointed to a medical conspiracy: transplant experimentation with some sort of nefarious purpose, one valuable enough to kill for—and to spur a cover-up of violence and misdirection. In retrospect, Scully realized that their entire case had been watched, and to some extent guided, by sources unknown. From the missing John Doe to the outbreak of encephalitis lethargica, they had been steered away from the simple truth. In that, Mulder had been completely on target. The skin Perry Stanton had received was the source of his murderous rampage. But Scully was equally convinced that the source of that skin was science, not myth. And the people behind the skin were criminals: accessories to murder, conspirators who had at the very least falsified Vietnam War records—and at worst, kidnapped and experimented on American soldiers.

"Mulder, it's important that we keep focus. We're here to conduct a limited search of the area, to see if we can find traces of a major intensive care clinic or a laboratory. We're searching for criminal suspects—not monsters."

Mulder's response was cut off by a terrified shout that rang out from one of the machete-wielding guides. Mulder leapt to his feet, the assault rifle spinning expertly to his hands. Scully's Smith & Wesson seemed minuscule by comparison. The shouting changed to rhythmic chanting as the three guides backed away from the cleared underbrush. Scully moved between Mulder and the emaciated monk, her gaze shifting to the ground.

The skeleton was half-lodged in mud, curled in a fetal position. The bones were yellowish, obviously weeks old, and the skull was partially destroyed. Scully noticed the bowed shape of the spine and the short limbs. The skeleton wasn't human. "A gibbon. Dead at least a week."

"And picked clean," Mulder commented.

"By wildlife, yes. See the tracks in the mud over there? Cleft front hooves. Most likely a wild boar. Fierce animals. They're easily big enough to kill a gibbon."

Mulder dropped to one knee, looking over the skeleton. Malku was talking in quiet tones to the three other Thais, who had retreated a good ten feet back. One of them had slung his backpack full of camping supplies over his shoulders.

"Wild boars don't skin bodies," Mulder said.

"But jackals do," Scully responded. "There are at least two species indigenous to this area. Not to mention a number of feline carnivores, wolves, and flesh-eating insects."

Mulder nodded. They would need a zoologist to determine what had really happened to the gibbon. Mulder rose to his feet, then turned back toward the guides. Malku was pleading in a high-pitched voice, but the three guides were all shaking their heads. It was plainly obvious what was going on.

"They go back," Malku finally explained, his eyes sad. "Back to Alkut. They say I must lead them."

Scully glanced at Mulder, then at the underbrush. There was a break in the green, about the size of a person, extending beneath a thick canopy of branches. There was no telling how far the break continued. "I guess that doesn't give us much of a choice."

Mulder looked past her. "Malku, how much farther is the base of the mountain?"

"Not far. Just over hill."

"Mulder," Scully said, "this trail could continue for miles. It's going to be dark, and we don't know the area."

"Before I became unconscious, I heard Kyle and the other man talking about the upcoming demonstration. It's happening now, Scully. We can't head back to town."

Mulder pointed to one of the packs lying next to the fallen trunk. "We can carry what we need. Malku will come back for us. Right, Malku?"

The young monk bobbed his head. Scully bit her lower lip, thinking. She did not like the idea of heading farther into the forest on their own, especially so close to nightfall. But Mulder was right—if they didn't reach the mountain soon, there was no point in reaching it at all. She took a deep breath, tasting the steaming, wet air. "Another hour, Mulder. If we don't reach the mountain, we turn back."

\\\\\\\\\\\\\\\\\\\

"The key is in the wrist," Mulder grunted, bringing his machete down in a vicious arc. "Don't let the weight of the blade control your swing. Like golf, only this sucker will take your head off if you mistime your follow-through."

Scully swung her own machete, severing a branch almost half her length. Her body was slick with sweat, and her shoulders ached beneath the weight of the heavy assault rifle. Mulder was carrying the backpack containing enough rations for two days in the forest. Overkill—Scully hoped. It had been only forty minutes since Malku and the guides had turned back, and already the forest felt as if it was closing in on her, an enveloping crush of nature. Her ears were ringing with the strange whistles and calls of tropical birds and monkeys, and she no longer noticed the carpet of blood-sucking insects stuck to most of her exposed skin.

"It's getting pretty dark," she commented, as she stepped over the freshly cut branch and went to work on the next obstacle, a thick bush nearly twice her height. The effort seemed futile, and she was more than ready to turn back. All she could think about was a cool shower and a flight back to Washington. "We'll have to make camp soon—and wait for Malku to return. Unless you think we can find our way back ourselves."

Mulder moved alongside, slashing deep into the fingers of green. "I'm not ready to give up yet."

"It's not a matter of giving up," Scully said, chopping into the bush with frustrated swipes. "It's a matter of being reasonable—shit."

Scully watched as the machete slipped out from her sweaty fingers and somersaulted through a breach in the thick bush. The blade quickly disappeared from view, and a second later there was the loud clatter of metal against stone. Mulder's face brightened. "That sounded promising."

Scully did not argue. She delicately stepped after the machete, working her way between the minced branches. To her surprise, the other side of the bush opened into a narrow rock canyon leading steadily upward. The canyon was little more than shoulder wide, running between twenty-foot-high rock walls. It was impossible to tell if the canyon had been purposefully carved into the rocks or was a feat of evolution. The rock walls were rough, with sharp, jutting protuberances and clinging green vines. Ten feet ahead, the canyon twisted tightly to the right, making it impossible to see beyond a few feet— but it seemed the agents might have finally reached the edge of the forest.

"It's a pretty tight fit," Scully said. "We'll have to go one at a time."

It was an unpleasant thought—but they had come this far already. Scully slid the rifle off her shoulder and held it lightly in her hands. She had not used anything as powerful as the carbine since her days at Quantico, but she was mentally prepared to fire if it became necessary.

She quietly worked her way forward, Mulder a step behind. The rocks grew steeper on either side, until she could no longer see anything but the narrow incline ahead of her. She found herself turning sideways to fit through the walls, and every few seconds she felt a sharp pinch as she brushed against the jagged rock. She was getting scraped and bruised by the forward progress—and from Mulder's cursing behind her, she knew he was suffering as well.

"I'm beginning to know what a kidney stone feels like," he whispered, yanking off the heavy backpack to make more room for his body. Scully silenced him with her hand as she came to an abrupt turn in the canyon. The walls finally opened up into a brief, rock-strewn plain, stretching upward in a gentle slope. The ground was reddish brown, a combination of packed forest mud and thin gravel. Other than a few knee-high bushes, the ground was clear of significant obstructions. It was strange seeing so much empty space after the long trip through the tropical forest.

Just on the other side of the cleared, reddish plain, Scully saw sheer rock cliffs rising almost straight up, disappearing into the charcoal sky. The cliffs seemed staggeringly large, and she knew her and Mulder's forward progress was about to end. They had reached the base of See Dum Kao.

"Scully," Mulder whispered, his cheek almost touching hers. "Over there."

He gestured toward a huge black oval carved directly into the sheer cliff, about thirty yards away. It was the mouth of a vast cave, exactly as Ganon had described. *A foreboding sight.* The opening was at least twenty feet high, with a span nearly twice as wide. Twisting green vines hung down across the cave entrance like a living portcullis.

"It looks deserted," Scully commented.

"There's got to be another entrance," Mulder explained. "There's no way they move supplies back and forth the way we just came."

"Well," Scully said, shaking sweat out of her eyes. "Let's take a look."

She started forward, casting a glance at the sky. In a few more minutes they would be in total darkness. Isolated in the middle of nowhere, waiting for Malku to lead them back to Alkut. It was not a pleasant thought. On the bright side, at least night would bring relief from the overwhelming heat. If the cave were as deserted as it looked, they would have a place to camp out and wait.

They made short work of the rocky glade, angling along the sheer cliff toward the opening. See Dum Kao seemed to rise straight upward forever to Scully's right, a dagger stabbed deep into the dark skin of the sky. She wondered how many thousands of caves pockmarked the ancient mountain—and how many miles of subterranean caverns spread out like a hollow circulatory system beneath the stone.

She slowed as she reached the edge of the opening. One of the vines hung down just inches from her body, and she reached out, gently touching the thick green rope. Its outer layer was rough, speckled with tiny prickers like an elongated cactus. She looked up, searching for the plant's center, but she could no longer see the arched top of the cave entrance. She carefully unslung the automatic rifle and handed it to Mulder. Then she withdrew her handgun.

Without a word, Mulder slid between two of the vines and into the dark cave. Scully followed, noting how the air seemed to change instantly. The temperature dropped by at least ten degrees, while the humidity seemed to increase, causing an involuntary shiver to move down Scully's back. A dank, mossy smell filled her nostrils, and she fought the urge to cough. She knew there was a danger of inhaling poisonous gases—carbon monoxide, methane, even cyanotic compounds resulting from natural decomposition. But she hoped the wide opening kept fresh air circulating enough to provide sufficient oxygenation.

Beyond the entrance, the cave opened up into an oval chamber, similar in size to the laboratory beneath the church. Huge stalagmites rose up at random intervals across the red-mud floor, sparkling with crystal deposits. Some of the stalagmites were nearly fifteen feet tall—thousands, if not millions, of years old. The ceiling was shrouded in darkness, but Scully could make out the points of similar stalactites hanging down like dulled fangs. Directly across the room was another arched opening, leading deeper into the mountain. A yellowish light trickled across the stone floor, coming from somewhere beyond the second entrance. Scully could not tell for sure—but the light seemed artificial. Still, it was possible that some sort of natural aperture was directing reflected light through the cavern. Perhaps the moon had broken through the clouds, and its light was funneling through fissures in the surrounding stone.

Mulder touched her shoulder, pointing past one of the larger stalagmites to a cleared-out area by the far wall. A glint of reflected light caught her eye, and she held her breath. There was a large, rectangular object at the edge of the chamber. From the distance, it seemed to be made of glass.

Mulder advanced, the automatic rifle cradled in his arms. Scully weaved behind him, circumnavigating a huge stalagmite. As she moved closer to the reflection point, she saw an enormous glass tank running waist high along the wall. The tank was at least twelve feet long, perhaps four feet wide. A series of rubber tubes twisted out of the bottom of the tank, disappearing into holes drilled straight into the stone wall.

Scully's thoughts swirled as she stood next to Mulder, peering into the tank. It was half-filled with transparent liquid, and a strong scent wafted in Scully's nostrils. Salty and familiar. It reminded her of the many thousands of hours she had spent in bio labs during college, medical school, and beyond.

"Ringer's solution," she said, softly. "It's a biochemical solution used to keep organic cells alive. Tissue cultures, bacteria—"

"Transplant materials?" Mulder asked.

Scully shrugged. She was stunned by the sight of the tank. Now there was no doubt—the enormous mountain cave was the site of some sort of medical research. The long path from New York had led to this place in the mountains of Thailand—through the guidance of a religious cult and an ancient fairy tale. Scully reminded herself—there was logic behind it all. The myth of the Skin Eater was a cover story, much like the outbreak of encephalitis lethargica. "It's possible synthetic skin was kept in this tank."

"Maybe just the family pet," Mulder commented, reaching into the tank and touching the liquid inside. He took out his hand and shook the droplets toward the ground. Then he started toward the inner entrance. Scully followed, her nerves on edge. As they moved closer to the yellowish light, unnatural, vaguely mechanical sounds drifted into her ears. Soon the sounds reached a recognizable volume. She clearly made out the rhythmic pumping of respiratory ventilators, mingling with the hiss of liquid infusers and the beep of computer processors. She cautioned Mulder with her hand as they reached the entrance, and they spread out to either side, crouching low.

The inner room was at least four times as large as the initial chamber— massive and naturally domed, nearly the size of a football field. It was the largest underground cavern Scully had ever seen. Soft yellow light poured down from more than a dozen enormous spotlights hanging from steel poles suspended along the walls. And beginning just a few feet in front of Scully, stretching as far as her eyes could see—row after row of empty chrome hospital stretchers. The stretchers seemed to go on forever, parallel rows extending from one end of the cavern to the other.

"They're not here," Mulder whispered, slowly moving between the stretchers. "These stretchers are all empty—"

He paused midsentence. Then he pointed up ahead. There was a group of stretchers—between twenty and thirty—separated from the chrome sea, situated near the far end of the cavern. Each of the segregated stretchers was covered by a milky white oxygen tent.

Mulder rushed ahead, Scully a few feet behind. Their pace slowed as they reached the first oxygen tent. At the head of each tent stood a semicircle of medical carts; Scully recognized respirators and cardiac machines—but some of the other devices were foreign to her, and there were numerous infusion pumps attached to vessels full of unidentifiable chemicals. Tubes ran from the carts to valves attached directly to the plastic oxygen tents.

Scully followed Mulder through the maze of oxygen tents, counting as she went. Her approximation had been accurate; there were twenty-five tented stretchers. She took a deep breath and approached the closest plastic tent. She could hear the rhythm of the oxygen being pumped through the tubing—creating a pristine, sterile environment inside. She searched the outside of the plastic tent—and found a triangular flap held down by a steel zipper. She called Mulder over, and carefully undid the flap.

"My God," she whispered, as she stared through the thin transparent plastic viewplate beneath the flap. She was looking at a horribly burned face and upper torso. Nearly every inch of skin had been seared away, and in many places she could see straight through to the muscle and bone beneath. The patient was a patchwork of black, white, and red, with charred regions, exposed subcutaneous fat, and pulsing veins and arteries revealed to the sterile air. Both eyes were burned away, leaving blank sockets, and the patient's mouth was wide open—and missing all of its teeth.

But amazingly, the patient seemed to be still alive. Scully could see the mechanical rise and fall of his chest. She could watch the blood pumping through the body's circulatory system. Still alive—in a sense. More an organic machine than a human being. Blood pumping, lungs working, but brain function? Doubtful, if not impossible.

"This one's in the same condition," Mulder called to her from a few feet away. He had opened a similar flap on another oxygen tent. As Scully watched, he moved from stretcher to stretcher, carefully unzipping the flaps. "Twenty-five of them, all in similar states. The rest of the two thousand must have been moved, maybe to other holding areas."

Scully shifted her eyes to the semicircle of medical carts at the head of the stretcher. She listened to the symphony of life-support machinery. "We don't know that these twenty-five patients are from the list. And I'm not even sure there's any way to identify this man. No fingerprints, no teeth."

Mulder had paused by one of the stretchers. He peered down, then continued to the next. "None of these men has teeth—for that precise reason. But there's no doubt in my mind. These are Paladin's guinea pigs. And the rest are out there, somewhere. Waiting for the next phase."

Scully tore herself away from the stretcher and followed Mulder through the chamber. She thought about the man who had accosted her in her hotel bedroom. Had he once been like one of these patients, a skinless vegetable kept alive by tubes? It seemed impossible. The changes in Perry Stanton—in the MRIs she had seen in the basement of the church—these were changes she could fathom. Chemicals affecting brain structure, neurotransmitters affecting behavior, synthetic skin as a method of transmission. But Mulder was suggesting something completely different. *The raising of the dead.*

"No," Scully finally said. "These burns can't be healed. Not to that degree. Medicine isn't magic."

Suddenly, Mulder grabbed her arm and yanked her to the side. She gasped, nearly losing her footing. Mulder was pointing straight ahead. They were barely twenty yards from the back wall of the enormous chamber. A double door had been cut directly into the stone, and there was a circular viewing window set waist high in one of the doors, a few feet in diameter. Bright light poured through the window, and Scully could see movement on the other side.

"Over there," Mulder mouthed, pointing toward a pair of huge machines a few yards from the doors. Scully identified them as autoclaves: enormous steam sterilizers, each about the size of a small closet, with a transparent Plexiglas face. One of the autoclaves was open, its digital display glowing red, indicating that it was set on automatic and ready for operation. The other looked as if it had been recently used; Scully could see traces of the super-heated steam on the inside of the glass, and there were racks of syringes and scalpels glistening inside.

She crouched next to Mulder behind the second autoclave, craning her neck for a better angle through the viewing window.

"Looks like an operating theater," she whispered.

"Theater's the right word," Mulder responded. "Do you see the cameras?"

Scully nodded. From her angle, she could see at least three video cameras on tripods focused on the raised operating table on the other side of the window. A tall, thin man in surgical garb was speaking into one of the cameras, his face covered by a sterile white mask. Another man—squat, square, in similar surgical clothes—was hovering closer to the operating table. In his hands was an oversize plastic cooler, partially opened.

"Julian Kyle," Scully commented, snapping the safety off her Smith & Wesson. She didn't know what sort of surgery was going on in the other room, but she was ready to make an arrest. There were twenty-five burned patients on life support in a cave. *She certainly considered that probable cause.* "What do you suppose the cameras are for?"

"It's a satellite link," Mulder responded. His fingers had tightened against his automatic rifle. He was also preparing for the confrontation. "I heard them talking about it before I lost consciousness. They're demonstrating their procedure—probably to interested buyers."

"Do-it-yourself drones?" Scully asked. She still found the idea implausible. Nobody would go to this much trouble for mindless drones. Trained soldiers could fight circles around men who couldn't think. The drone who had accosted her was a perfect example. He had been unable to react to her surprise attack. How much money could an army of drones be worth?

"As I said before," Mulder responded, "the drones were just the first step. The procedure has been perfected—and the next stage is in that room."

Mulder's whisper had changed to an angry hiss. His objectivity was long gone. Looking at the twenty-five oxygen tents clustered together in the room like white ripples in a tormented ocean, Scully felt her own objectivity waver. She wanted answers as badly as her partner.

She nodded, and Mulder slid forward. Scully followed a step behind, her focus trained on the double doors. Another few seconds, and it would all be over.

TWENTY-FIVE

Quo Tien's face suddenly drained of color as he watched the two agents sweep out from behind the autoclave. He was standing twenty feet away, in the dark entrance to a secondary tunnel leading off from the main chamber. He could not believe the sight in front of him. The male agent—Fox Mulder, whose flesh Tien had almost tasted—had somehow escaped the effects of the transplant procedure. Now he and his partner were here, in Tien's play-ground—seconds away from ruining everything.

Tien's surprise rapidly turned to rage. This was his home. The agents' very presence was an abomination. This time, Uncle Julian would not get in the way.

Tien slid forward, his hands breaking free of his long sleeves. He had just returned from securing the last of the first-stage drones; in his left hand he held a compact stun gun, which had become a requirement since the debacle involving the drone in New York. *Better to kill a drone than let it escape*. His right hand embraced the hilt of his straight razor. The two agents were heavily armed—but Tien knew the razor and the stun gun would be enough.

The hunger screamed in his ears as he quickly closed the distance between them.

TWENTY-SIX

Scully saw the sudden flash of movement and jerked her head to the side. The thin young man was sprinting toward them, his lithe body cutting between the oxygen tents with amazing agility. His face was a mask of rage and violence, his eyes narrowed to black points. He looked more snake than human, his hands rising like fangs. Scully saw the sharp razor blade flashing under the yellow spotlights, then the stun gun—pointing right at her. She didn't have time to get her gun around, didn't even have time to scream. Instead, she did the only thing she could think of. She reached out and grabbed Mulder's shoulder.

The bolt of electricity hit her in the side, and there was an enormous popping in her ears. Her body lifted a few inches off the ground, and her muscles spasmed, sending her careening into Mulder. He jerked beneath her hand as half the electricity transferred to his body. The automatic rifle whirled out of his hands, clattering beneath a stretcher a few feet away. Together, they slammed into the stone wall, just inches from the double doors. Scully's skin felt as if it was on fire, her head spinning, black spots ricocheting across the plane of her vision. She felt Mulder roll free from beneath her, crawling toward his gun.

Her cheek touched the floor, and the room turned to liquid in front of her eyes. She blinked rapidly, struggling to remain conscious. She had avoided the full effect of the stun gun by grabbing Mulder—and she had warned him with the same stroke. But she had partially incapacitated them both. She managed to get her hands in front of her, lifting her face off the ground. She saw Mulder a few feet away, his hands inches from the rifle. Then she saw a long dark shape land on top of him, a shadow come to life. The shadow dragged Mulder back from the gun and spun him onto his back.

Scully shook her head, her vision clearing. The shadow flickered into three dimensions. It was the young man, straddling Mulder around his waist, the razor blade rising above Mulder's face. *Christ*. Scully clenched her jaw and launched herself forward. She slammed into the young man's back, knocking him off Mulder with her weight. Even before they hit the ground, the young man had twisted out of her grip. The back of his left hand caught the side of Scully's jaw, and she spun across the floor, crashing into a semicircle of medical carts. She tasted blood and felt the sharp pain of a pulled muscle daggering down her right side. She was lying against the legs of one of the occupied stretchers, staring up at the white-plastic oxygen tent. One of the carts had collapsed on top of her, and a cardiac machine was lying shattered next to her shoulder. A long plastic tube had yanked free from the machine, and Scully saw a sharp steel wire sticking out of the end of the tube. A trochar, used to insert an emergency cardiac balloon into a patient. Relief filled her as she realized that the machine had not been attached to the burn victim in the oxygen tent, that it was there in case of an emergency. Then her eyes focused on the trochar. The hollow steel wire was eight inches long, with an extremely sharp point.

Scully grabbed the trochar, yanking it free from the plastic tube. The sharp pain in her side sent tears to her eyes, as she struggled into a crouch. She spit blood, searching for Mulder and the young man.

She spotted them directly in front of the two autoclaves. Mulder was on his knees, his hands clenched around the Amerasian's wrists. There was blood pouring from a gash in Mulder's cheek, more blood from a deep cut in his left arm. The Amerasian clearly had the upper hand. The bloody razor blade was moving steadily toward Mulder's throat. The Amerasian's face was perfectly calm, the surface of a lake right before a storm. His lips twitched upward at the edges, a strangely erotic smile.

Scully clenched her hand around the trochar and hurtled forward. The Amerasian looked up at the last second, his eyes going wide. He tried to twist his body out of the way, but Mulder held on tight to his wrists, limiting his range of motion. The trochar caught the side of his shoulder and plunged through, ripping deep into his muscle, wounding him severely. A geyser of bright red blood sprayed Mulder's face, and he reeled back. The Amerasian lurched to his feet, his eyes wild. He staggered back, swinging the razor blade impotently through the air, his face draining as the blood fountained out of his deeply skewered shoulder. His feet tangled together, and he fell, crashing into the open autoclave. His weight sent the machine rocking backward, and the door swung shut.

There was a mechanical click, followed by a series of loud beeps. Scully's stomach dropped as she realized the machine was set on automatic. She lurched toward the control panel—but she was too late. She watched in horror as the Amerasian's body slumped against the transparent door, his knees buckling. Suddenly, a thunderous hiss erupted from the machine. Plumes of superheated steam exploded out of the half dozen sterilizing jets, hitting the young man from all four sides. His skin was instantly flayed from his body, tearing off in long, bloody strips. In less than a second he had been reduced to a skeleton shrouded in white steam.

Scully stared in shock, unable to turn away. Mulder staggered to his feet next to her, his hand over the wound on his left arm. "Karma," he said, simply. "Two thousand degrees of pure karma."

Scully looked at him. The blood flowed freely down his face from the cut in his cheek. Her own mouth ached, and she realized that one of her lower teeth was loose. "Was that Emile Paladin's son?"

Before Mulder could answer, there was the sound of a swinging door behind them. Scully turned, and saw Julian Kyle staring at them from in front of the double doors. He had the plastic cooler in his hands, and there was a shocked look on his face.

"Stay where you are," Mulder shouted, but Kyle was already sprinting across the chamber. Mulder ignored him, heading toward the double doors. The other man was presumably still inside the operating theater. "Scully, don't let him get away. He's got the skin!"

Scully thought about going after her gun, but decided she didn't have time to waste searching the chamber. Kyle was already near the secondary tunnel from where the Amerasian had entered the room. Scully raced after him, ignoring the pain in her side. She heard Mulder hit the double doors behind her, and she knew he was also unarmed.

She wondered how far they'd get on karma alone.

TWENTY-SEVEN

Mulder crashed through the twin doors shoulder first, bursting into the bright light. His boots skidded against the floor as he narrowly avoided a video camera set atop a tripod. The raised operating table was ten feet away, surrounded by surgical equipment. Anesthetic tanks stood by the head of the table, next to a respirator pump and two enormous canisters of oxygen. On the other side of the table, Mulder recognized the articulated arm and cylindrical housing of a high-powered laser scalpel, similar to the device he had seen used during the tattoo removal in the surgical ward at Jamaica Hospital. Next to the laser apparatus stood a defibrillator cart, next to that a cardiac monitor. Bright green mountains raced across the monitor, the fierce cadence of an overstimulated heart. Each peak sent a high-pitched tone echoing off the walls.

The blue-eyed man in the surgical mask stood frozen beside the monitor, a serrated steel scalpel in his right hand. Three separate video cameras were trained over his shoulders toward the operating table, and Mulder saw a spaghetti-sea of wires looping behind the cameras to an enormous receiver plugged into a generator by the wall. The cameras whirred in a quiet symphony of invisible gears.

"Sorry to interrupt the show," Mulder said, breathing hard in the doorway.

The blue-eyed man remained still, a strange calm moving across his features. He gently lowered the scalpel. His eyes shifted to the patient on the table in front of him. Mulder followed his gaze.

The patient was a work in progress. His bare torso was split into two distinct sections; his abdomen was still covered in terrible burns, a mix of white, black, and ruby red. But his upper pectorals, shoulders, neck, and face had been delicately reconstructed. The new, yellowish skin was pulled taut against his muscles and bone, giving off a jaundiced glow. At the edges of each newly transplanted section, Mulder could make out the thin staples—and spread around the staples, tiny flecks of red powder. *The Dust*—the antibacterial substance that had first connected their investigation to Fibrol, and Emile Paladin.

Beneath the fresh skin, the patient's face was unnaturally smooth, the features icily still beneath the anesthesia mask. His eyes were wide open, the same piercing blue as those of the surgeon by his side.

Mulder realized with a start that he recognized the patient's face. Andrew Paladin. He had found the recluse brother. He shifted his gaze back to the masked surgeon. The blue-eyed man moved slowly to one of the video cameras behind him, and hit a switch. The cameras stopped whirring. "You've disturbed a delicate procedure. This man could die because of you."

The voice was soft, almost melodic, tinged with confidence. He did not seem fazed by Mulder's presence.

"This man should have died a long time ago," Mulder responded, slowly moving around the operating table, his eyes flickering toward the scalpel. He could feel the warm blood still trickling down his jaw to his neck, staining the front of his camouflage. His wounded left arm hung uselessly at his side. "There are twenty-five just like him imprisoned in the next room. And there are close to two thousand more hidden somewhere, suffering the same horrid fate. Tortured souls, separated from their families for more than twenty-five years."

The blue-eyed man took a step back from the operating table, the scalpel poised expertly in his gloved hand. "Those men are alive because of me. My skin will give them a second chance—a way out from the torture."

Mulder shook his head, anger filling him. "You mean turn them into slaves—drones?"

The blue-eyed man backed between the two oxygen tanks as Mulder skirted the bottom corner of the operating table.

"No," Mulder continued, his anger turning his voice sharp. "That was just the first stage. Incapable of individual thought—willing, unthinking servants, following your orders. But the next stage—it's something much more advanced, isn't it? Much more *valuable*."

"This is beyond you," the blue-eyed man said, his voice indifferent, even clinical. "You can't possibly begin to understand."

Mulder felt his anger multiply. "I know that you've kept these men alive for the past twenty-five years. Medically, that seems impossible. So it must be the skin itself—or perhaps chemicals within the skin, that has made this longevity possible. You've used the skin to alter these men—to prepare them. For this *demonstration*."

Mulder paused, looking at the patient on the stretcher. Then he glanced at the cameras, then at the receiver by the wall. He assumed it was connected by a fiber-optic link to a satellite dish somewhere high in the mountains. "Soldiers—intelligent, invulnerable soldiers. That's what you're trying to create, isn't it? And you intend to sell them—to the military? To another government? Who's on the other end of the cameras?"

The blue-eyed man's face tensed as his left hand suddenly slipped into his coat pocket. When it reappeared, he was holding a small-caliber handgun. Mulder's chest constricted, and he took a step back. The cold glint in the man's eyes scared him almost as much as the gun.

"That's enough," he said, quietly.

It was more than a statement—it was a command. Looking at the man's face, at the intensity of his gaze, Mulder was struck by a sudden thought: This man was nothing like Julian Kyle. He might have worn a green uniform—but he had never been hard-line military. He was arrogant, egotistical, controlling; certainly, he was not a man who followed orders. His motivation came from within, from his own obsessions, his own unquenchable ego. Mulder glanced back at the cameras, at the operating table—and he realized it didn't make sense.

"It's not about money at all," he finally said. "The men who are funding you might think that's what you're after—but that's not it. You're chasing something else. Something much more powerful than money."

He thought about the twenty-five burn victims in the vast chamber, kept alive for twenty-five years. Then he thought about the first-stage drones—men who should have died during the Vietnam War, men who still appeared as young as they had the day they were injured. He realized that he and Scully had missed the point from the very beginning.

"Immortality," he whispered, his eyes widening. "Invulnerable soldiers are just the beginning. The skin is ageless. Timeless. Immortal—like the Skin Eater itself. That's what you're after, isn't it? Immortality—"

Mulder ducked to the left just as the gun went off. He felt something slam into his right shoulder, and he was whirled off his feet. He hit the floor, rolling as fast as his wounded body could manage. A second shot exploded against the floor by his feet, sending up a plume of shattered stone. Mulder scrambled the other way, his mind churning as he partially concealed himself beneath the raised operating table. He couldn't tell how badly he'd been shot, but a dull ache was moving through his shoulder, mingling with the pain from his slashed left arm. He could hear the blue-eyed man circling the operating table toward him, and he crawled in the opposite direction, struggling against the growing sense of panic. He had grossly misjudged the situation. He had let his adrenaline drive him carelessly forward. He had not counted on the hubris of a man who had turned a myth into a miracle. *A man who had spent his adult life searching for a way to beat death.*

"Two thousand regenerating sources of immortality," Mulder said, his voice low. "Including your own brother."

There was an audible cough, and Mulder's shoulders trembled. He had been correct all along. Emile Paladin was the man behind the surgical mask. Mulder leaned back against the operating table, the pain from his gunshot wound sapping his energy. Paladin's hubris was numbing—his accomplishments, overwhelming. Two thousand invulnerable soldiers, each to become a regenerating source of the transforming skin. A demonstration—and presumably, a sale of the product—to unknown forces within the Defense Department, men who had funded Paladin up until this point. Tinkering with the human species, an experiment that meddled with evolution itself—it was abominable. But there was nothing Mulder could do. He felt his head falling forward—when he noticed a rounded pedal just a few inches from his right foot. He followed the pedal to its cylindrical root, and realized he was lying a few feet from the base of the laser scalpel.

His heart slammed in his chest, the adrenaline rocking his body awake. He heard Paladin circling around the head of the operating table. He closed his eyes, imagining the man's position. He pictured the articulated arm with the attached laser, the way it pointed at a slightly upward angle. He set his jaw, tensing his aching muscles, forcing his body to coil inward. He counted the seconds, listening as the footsteps moved closer and closer and closer...

Suddenly, Mulder leapt out from under the operating table and rose to his full height. Paladin reared back, stunned, the gun sweeping upward. Before Paladin could pull the trigger, Mulder slapped at the steel arm with his open right hand. The mechanical arm sprang forward on its hinged springs, spinning wildly away from the cylinder. At the same moment, Mulder's foot came down hard on the control pedal and there was a loud, electric snap, like a leather belt pulled tight. The red guiding light flickered out toward a spot a few inches past the blue-eyed man's shoulder. Mulder's eyes went wide as he watched the light land directly on the rubber gasket at the top of one of the oversized oxygen tanks by the head of the operating table. Christ, he thought to himself. *Another miscalculation.* There was a moment of frozen time—followed by a blinding flash of white light.

Mulder was thrown backward as the oxygen tank exploded. A searing heat licked his face as a sphere of flame billowed out from the eruption point, instantly consuming Paladin from behind. The fiery sphere continued to expand, enveloping the operating table, licking at the canisters of anesthetic gas. Mulder crashed back into the wall, covering his head with his hands as a second explosion rocked the operating room. Metal shrapnel tore through the air, chunks of stone and steel pummeling the walls and floor. Something hit Mulder in the stomach, driving the air out of him. He doubled forward, gasping, the heat singeing the hairs on the back of his neck.

And just as suddenly, the heat evaporated as the oxygen burned out. Mulder staggered to his feet, staring at the devastated room. Medical machinery lay strewn against the walls, most of the devices charred beyond recognition. The video cameras lay mangled in the corners, lenses melted into crystal pools against the floor. The operating table itself had split down the middle—and Andrew Paladin was nothing more than a curled, blackened shape. The anesthetic gas inside his lungs had obviously ignited, engulfing him from the inside.

Mulder stumbled forward, his eyes searching for the man who had started it all. He stepped over the smoking remains of the cardiac monitor, wincing as the motion exacerbated the pain in his right shoulder. Still moving forward, he pulled open the buttons of his shirt and slid the material gently away from the wound. Relief filled him as he surveyed the slash of blood; the bullet had only nicked him, cutting through his skin but missing the muscle and bone beneath. His gaze moved back to the floor—and he stopped dead, his heart pounding in his chest.

"Mulder?" he heard from the entrance to the devastated operating room. "My God. What the hell happened in here?"

Mulder stared down at the blackened, mangled thing on the floor by his feet. "Emile Paladin. Though you'll have to take my word for it. There's even less of him to autopsy this time around."

Mulder looked up. Scully was gingerly touching a burned corner of the operating table. There was dried blood on her lower lip, and her red hair was matted with sweat.

"What about Julian Kyle? And the cooler of skin?"

Scully shook her head. "Kyle got away. The tunnels go on for miles into the base of the mountain. It could take days to search them all. We need to get back to Alkut and call Washington, then bring in Van Epps and the military."

"The military," Mulder repeated. He glanced at the ruined video cameras. Despite the horror he had just witnessed, an ironic smile inadvertently touched his lips. "The military may be less than helpful."

Scully shrugged. It was not the first time Mulder had made such a statement. Mulder sighed, frustration and fatigue tugging at his insides. The case was over—but they had little more evidence than when they had started. He knew it would be next to impossible to match the twenty-five soldiers with any of the names on the list. And by the time the military got involved, he doubted there would be any evidence of the 130 first-stage drones, or any trace of the rest of the two thousand burn victims. Without Kyle and the drones there was no remaining evidence of Emile Paladin's miracle skin—and no definitive proof of its source.

Scully seemed to have come to the same conclusion. She moved carefully into the room, her eyes focused on Mulder's shoulder wound. In many ways, she was a doctor first, a federal agent second. "We may never know the truth behind Paladin's synthetic skin. But we've put an end to his experiments."

Mulder wondered if it was true. Kyle had escaped with the synthetic skin. And the rest of the two thousand guinea pigs were still out there, somewhere. It was possible he could start again. Still, Julian Kyle wasn't Emile Paladin. It wasn't his experiment—and it wasn't his obsession.

Mulder sighed, letting Scully's expert fingers probe his bared shoulder. "Another case without closure, Scully. Without any hard evidence to take back with us."

Scully finished with his shoulder and stepped away, watching him rebutton his shirt. "Actually, on my way back to the chamber, I did find something. But I'm not sure what it means."

Mulder looked at her eyes. There was something there, deep beneath the blue. Something was bothering her. Mulder felt the fatigue disappear from his body.

"Show me."

Twenty minutes later, Mulder stood next to Scully in a small alcove near the center of the network of tunnels, staring up at two objects embedded in the stone wall. Mulder could feel his heart pounding in his chest.

Finally, Scully broke the silence. "I can think of a number of plausible explanations."

Mulder didn't respond. To him, no explanations were needed. Scully could break the objects down to their molecular level, stare at them under an electron microscope, bathe them in an acid bath, or weigh them on an atomic scale. She could subject them to every possible abuse in her scientific arsenal, and it wouldn't make any difference. To Mulder, the objects were an explanation in themselves. Their meaning was as terrifying, abrupt, and obvious as their appearance.

Mulder shivered, then slowly turned away. Scully remained behind, staring uneasily at the pair of crisscrossing, razor-sharp tusks.

TWENTY-EIGHT

Scully leaned back against the chain-link fence and shut her eyes. Even through her eyelids, she could see the lights: a caravan of flashing red and blue, a Christmas tree on its side stretching more than fifty yards beyond the edge of the cordoned-off runway. Although the sirens had been silenced because of the late hour and the proximity to Dulles International's main terminal, sound filled the night air: the rumble of diesel emergency vehicles, the shouts of medical personnel, the shrill squeal of steel stretcher wheels against pavement.

"It's like watching some sort of macabre carnival," Mulder commented from a few feet away. He was also leaning against the fence, his bandaged right arm resting in a sling against his chest. The razor wound on his cheek was covered by two strips of gauze, there was an Ace bandage around his left forearm, and heavy bags under his eyes. His stooped shoulders showed the effects of twenty hours in a plane and another ten in debriefing at FBI headquarters. "From here, it seems like a lot more than twenty-five ambulances."

Scully opened her eyes, watching the colored lights play across her partner's battered cheeks. She wondered if she looked as worn as Mulder. Her jaw still ached from Tien's backhand blow, and her eyesight had begun to blur from exhaustion. She had napped briefly on the plane, and had showered and changed at her apartment; but she knew it would take at least another week to recover fully from the rigorous case. It didn't help that there were still so many questions left unanswered. Sadly, lack of closure was not unfamiliar territory.

She rubbed the back of her hand across her eyes, clearing her vision. A hundred yards down the runway, beyond the ambulances, she could just make out the Boeing 727. A dozen high-intensity spotlights surrounded the curved fuselage of the plane, illuminating the military markings on the tail and wings. Both the front and back hatches of the plane were open, and bright orange mechanical hoists squatted beneath the openings, surrounded by medical technicians in light blue military uniforms. Scully watched as one of the hoists smoothly lowered a pair of stretchers from the front hatchway. Once the hoist had reached the ground, the medics spirited the stretchers to one of the waiting ambulances. Then the hoist rose back to the hatchway, ready for another pair.

Skinner had estimated that it would take only two hours to remove the patients from the specially outfitted plane. The expense of transporting the twenty-five burn victims—and for the years of medical care that would come next—fell squarely on the taxpayers. A VA hospital in Maryland had already been outfitted with the necessary life-support machinery, and a staff of full-time convalescent nurses had been hired. Frankly, Scully had been pleasantly surprised by the military's swift response to the situation. The first recon teams had arrived in Alkut only hours after she and Mulder had contacted Washington; led by Timothy Van Epps, three squadrons of Marines had quickly prepared the scene for transport. Meanwhile, Skinner had worked through the red tape in Washington, using Mulder and Scully's case report as a guideline for the upcoming analysis and management of the situation. Six hours later, the two agents were in an ambulance on their way to Bangkok. Scully had insisted that one of the burn victims be transported with her—perhaps in response to Mulder's growing paranoia at the military's swift presence.

The long journey to Bangkok had given Scully the opportunity to evaluate the patient firsthand. On closer inspection, the longevity of the napalm-burn victims seemed less miraculous than tragic. As she had suspected, the patient was in a vegetative state, in complete organ failure, kept alive by mechanical intrusion. Despite what Mulder had hypothesized, from a medical perspective there was no chance the patient would ever recover.

Still, Scully *had* discovered evidence that the patient's cellular structure had been infused with an unknown chemical—a strange, carbon-based molecule Scully had never seen before. The unknown chemical displayed two amazing characteristics: the ability to strengthen cell walls and to stave off fibroblast deterioration. Scully could only assume that the chemical was another synthetic breakthrough, like the red antibiotic dust. According to Mulder's theory, the chemical had "prepared" the patients for Paladin's radical transplant procedure. It would take years of further analysis to determine fully if that was true.

In the meantime, the military was considering her and Mulder's request for a regional search for the rest of the two thousand Vietnam casualties. Scully was pessimistic about the likelihood of a major operation ever taking place— after all, there wasn't any real evidence that the burn victims were still alive, nor was there much hope of tracking them down after so many years. Still, she could envision quiet diplomatic inquiries being circulated throughout Southeast Asia, and perhaps even a more wide-scale search of the mountains around Alkut.

She was more optimistic about the current efforts being made to match the twenty-five recovered patients to the list of casualties. Without teeth and distinguishing features, it would be difficult—but not impossible. DNA samples would be matched to blood taken from the casualties' surviving family members, and identities would be confirmed. The only obstacles were time and money, and the U.S. military had plenty of both.

"Isn't that Skinner?" Mulder interrupted, gesturing with his good arm. Scully saw a tall man separate from a group of uniformed officers fifty yards away, just beyond the rear ambulance. She easily identified the assistant director's broad shoulders and distinctive gait. Skinner was moving down the runway toward them, a heavy clipboard in his hands; Scully recognized the case file she and Mulder had prepared on the flight back to Washington.

"Maybe there's been some progress in the search for Julian Kyle," she said, hopefully. She and Mulder had sent out an international APB on the fugitive scientist, and had transferred his stats to Interpol and the Southeast Asian division of the CIA. Still, despite her hopes, she doubted Kyle would be apprehended anytime soon. Kyle was ex-military, and assuredly had the resources to hide in Asia indefinitely.

"I wouldn't hold my breath," Mulder commented, putting voice to Scully's thoughts. "From what the search teams reported after hitting Fibrol, I'd say Kyle planned for this contingency a long time ago."

Scully sighed, straightening her slacks as she pushed off the fence. Mulder's sentiments were accurate; there was little hope of finding Kyle or, for that matter, any evidence of a connection between Paladin's work and Fibrol International.

Three FBI search teams had descended on Fibrol's main complex just hours after Scully and Mulder had reported their findings to Skinner. Every office and laboratory had been thoroughly searched, every file cabinet and computer processor scoured for evidence. No links to Paladin or his experiments were found. Nothing to indict either Fibrol or Julian Kyle, and no indication that anyone at the company had previous knowledge of Emile Paladin's faked death or continued existence. Fibrol's board of directors had stood up to twelve hours of direct questioning—and not one member of the executive staff had shown evidence of the slightest deception, or any knowledge of Kyle's possible whereabouts. Paladin and Kyle had obviously been working alone. If, as Mulder maintained, they had been funded by sources within the Defense Department, the paper trail had long since vanished.

Still, the raid on Fibrol had not been a total waste of time. While going through Julian Kyle's office, the search team had found an unlabeled phone number in a locked drawer in his desk. The number had been traced to a studio apartment in Chelsea. The apartment had been deserted for at least a week, but the forensic specialists had found a number of hair and skin samples in the sink and shower drains matching similar samples taken from the cave at the base of See Dum Kao.

According to preliminary DNA matches, the apartment had belonged to Quo Tien, Emile Paladin's son.

Twenty minutes after the search team began to scour the apartment, they made a chilling discovery. Beneath a hinged tile in the apartment's bathroom, they had found a small vial of clear liquid and two specially manufactured, spring-loaded miniature syringes. Scully had recognized the description of the syringes from a *New England Journal of Medicine* article on microsurgery; they had been designed for intercapillary intrusions during microscopic surgical procedures. That in mind, she was not surprised when the clear liquid in the vial was identified as a rare viral sample suspended in a super-cooled chemical base. The search team had solved the mystery of the encephalitis lethargica outbreak.

"Kyle's long gone," Mulder continued, as he and Scully started toward the runway, intending to meet Skinner halfway. "And he took Paladin's skin with him. We're left with twenty-five unknown soldiers, a trail of brutal murders, a medically exonerated Perry Stanton—and, of course, a pair of tusks. In retrospect, I guess it's a pretty good ending to a three-hundred-year-old myth."

Scully avoided looking at her partner. They had been over the subject a dozen times. The tusks had been transported to the FBI headquarters along with Scully and Mulder's case file. Preliminary molecular dating had placed the age of the objects at approximately three hundred years—a fact that, on its own, was inconclusive. Elephants and wild boar were indigenous to the region, now as well as three hundred years ago. Although DNA analysis had not yet found a species match, there was a good chance the tusks belonged to a strain of elephant or boar that had since gone extinct.

"Maybe that's what Skinner wants to talk about," Scully finally responded, her voice low. They were now only a dozen yards from the assistant director, closing fast. "Maybe he wants to donate the tusks to a museum. Or better yet, sell them to pay for our little excursion."

"I'd rather mount them on the wall of my office," Mulder said. "A memento of our romantic journey to Southeast Asia. What do you say, Scully? We could split the pair."

"Thanks," Scully responded, her face stiffening as they met Skinner at the edge of the runway, "but I think they're more your style."

END

ANTIBODIES

By Kevin J. Anderson

ONE

DyMar Laboratory Ruins
Sunday, 11:13 p.m.

ate on a night filled with cold mist and still air, the alarm went off.
It was a crude security system hastily erected around the abandoned burn
site, and Vernon Ruckman was the only guard stationed to monitor the
night shift… but he got paid—and surprisingly well—to take care that no
intruders got into the unstable ruins of the DyMar Laboratory on the outskirts
of Portland, Oregon.

He drove his half-rusted Buick sedan up the wet gravel driveway. The bald
tires crunched up the gentle rise where the cancer research facility had stood
until a week and a half ago.

Vernon shifted into park, unbuckled his seatbelt, and got out to investigate.
He had to be sharp, alert. He had to scope out the scene. He flicked on the
beam of his official security flashlight—heavy enough to be used as a
weapon—and shone it like a firehose of light into the blackened ruins that
covered the site.

His employers hadn't given Vernon his own security vehicle, but they had
provided him with a uniform, a badge, and a loaded revolver. He had to
display confidence and an intimidating appearance if he was to chase off
rambunctious kids daring each other to go into the charred husk of the laboratory building. In the week and a half since the facility had been bombed, he

had already chased a few trespassers away, teenagers who ran giggling into the night. Vernon had never managed to catch any of them.

This was no laughing matter. The DyMar ruins were unstable, set to be demolished in a few days. Already construction equipment, bulldozers, steam shovels, and little Bobcats were parked around large fuel storage tanks. A padlocked locker that contained blasting caps and explosives. Someone sure was in a hurry to erase the remains of the medical research facility.

In the meantime, this place was an accident waiting to happen. And Vernon Ruckman didn't want it to happen on his watch.

The brilliant flashlight beam carved an expanding cone through the mist and penetrated the labyrinth of tilted girders, charred wooden beams, and fallen roof timbers. DyMar Lab looked like an abandoned movie set for an old horror film, and Vernon could imagine celluloid monsters shambling out of the mist from where they had lurked in the ruins.

After the fire, a rented chain-link fence had been thrown up around the perimeter—and now Vernon saw that the gate hung partially open. With a soft exhale of breeze, the chain-link sang faintly, and the gate creaked; then the air fell still again, like a held breath.

He thought he heard movement inside the building, debris shifting, stone and wood stirring. Vernon swung the gate open wide enough for him to enter the premises. He paused to listen carefully, then proceeded with caution, just like the guidebook said to do. His left hand gripped the flashlight, while his right hovered above the heavy police revolver strapped to his hip.

He had handcuffs in a small case on his leather belt, and he thought he knew how to use them, but he had never managed to catch anyone yet. Being a nighttime security guard generally involved a lot of reading, mixed with a few false alarms (especially if you had a vivid imagination)—and not much else.

Vernon's girlfriend was a night owl, an English major and aspiring poet who spent most of the night waiting to be inspired by the muse, or else putting in a few hours at the round-the-clock coffee shop where she worked. Vernon had adjusted his own biological cycle to keep up with her, and this night-shift job had seemed the perfect solution, though he had been tired and groggy for the first week or so.

Now Vernon was wide awake as he entered the burned-out labyrinth.

Someone was indeed in there.

Old ashes crunched under his feet, splinters of broken glass and smashed concrete. Vernon remembered how this research facility had once looked, a high-tech place with unusual modern Northwestern architecture—a mixture of glossy futuristic glass and steel, and rich golden wood from the Oregon coastal forests.

The lab had burned quite well after the violent protest, the arson, and the explosion.

It wouldn't surprise him if this late-night intruder was something more than just kids—perhaps some member of the animal rights group that had claimed responsibility for the fire. Maybe it was an activist collecting souvenirs, war trophies of their bloody victory.

Vernon didn't know. He just sensed he had to be careful. He stepped deeper inside, ducking his head to avoid a fallen wooden pole, black and warty with gray-white ashes where it had split in the intense heat. The floor of the main building seemed unstable, ready to tumble into the basement levels. Some of the walls had collapsed, partitions blackened, windows blasted out.

He heard someone moving stealthily. Vernon tilted the flashlight around, and white light stabbed into the shadows, making strange angles, black shapes that leapt at him and skittered along the walls. He had never been afraid of closed-in spaces, but now it seemed as if the whole place was ready to cave in on him.

Vernon paused, shone his light around. He heard the sound again, quiet rustling, a person intent on uncovering something in the wreckage. It came from the far corner, an enclosed office area with a partially slumped ceiling where the reinforced barricades had withstood most of the destruction.

He saw a shadow move there, tossing debris away, digging. Vernon swallowed hard and stepped forward, "You there! This is private property. No trespassing." He rested his hand on the butt of his revolver. Show no fear. He wouldn't let this intruder run from him.

Vernon directed his flashlight onto the figure. A large, broad-shouldered man stood up and turned toward him slowly. The intruder didn't run, didn't panic—and that made Vernon even more nervous. Oddly dressed, the man wore mismatched clothes, covered with soot; they looked like something stolen from a lost duffel bag or torn down from a clothesline.

"What are you doing here?" Vernon demanded. He flared the light into the man's face. The intruder was dirty, unkempt—and he didn't look at all well. Great, Vernon thought. A vagrant, rooting around in the ruins to find something he could salvage and sell. "There's nothing for you to take in here."

"Yes, there is," the man said. His voice was strangely strong and confident, and Vernon was taken aback.

"You're not supposed to be here," Vernon repeated, losing his nerve now.

"Yes, I am," the man answered. "I'm authorized. I... worked at DyMar."

Vernon moved forward. This was entirely unexpected. He continued to shine the flashlight, counting on its intimidation factor.

"My name is Dorman, Jeremy Dorman." The man fumbled in his shirt pocket, and Vernon grabbed for his revolver. "I'm just trying to show you my DyMar ID," Dorman said.

Vernon took another step closer, and in the glare of his powerful flashlight he could see that the intruder appeared sick, sweating... "Looks like you need to go to a doctor."

"No. What I need... is in here," Dorman said, pointing. Vernon saw that the burly man had pulled away some of the rubble to reveal a hidden fire safe.

Dorman finally managed to pluck a bent and battered photo badge out of his shirt pocket—a DyMar Laboratory clearance badge. This man had worked here... but that didn't mean he could root around in the burned wreckage now.

"That means nothing to me," Vernon said. "I'm going to take you in, and if you really have authorization to be here, we'll get this all straightened out."

"No!" Dorman said, so violently that spittle sprayed from his lips. "You're wasting my time." For a moment, it looked as if the skin on his face shifted and blurred, then reset itself to normal. Vernon swallowed hard, but tried to maintain his stance.

Dorman ignored him and turned around.

Indignant, Vernon stepped forward and drew his weapon. "I don't think so, Mr. Dorman. Get up against the wall—right now." Vernon suddenly noticed the thick bulges underneath the man's grimy shirt. They seemed to move of their own accord, twitching.

Dorman looked at him with narrowed dark eyes. Vernon gestured with the revolver. With no sign of intimidation or respect, the man went to one of the intact concrete walls that was smeared and blackened from the fire. "I told you, you're wasting my time," Dorman growled. "I don't have much time."

"We'll take all the time we need," Vernon said.

With a sigh, Dorman spread his hands against the soot-blackened wall and waited. The skin on his hands was waxy, plastic-looking… runny somehow. Vernon wondered if the man had been exposed to some kind of toxic substance, acid, or industrial waste. Despite the reassurance of his gun, Vernon didn't like this at all.

Out of the corner of his eye, he saw one of the bulges beneath Dorman's shirt squirm. "Stand still while I frisk you."

Dorman gritted his teeth and stared at the concrete wall in front of him, as if counting particles of ash. "I wouldn't do that," he said.

"Don't threaten me," Vernon answered quickly.

"Then don't touch me," Dorman retorted. In response, Vernon tucked the flashlight between his elbow and his side, then quickly patted the man down, frisking him with one hand.

Dorman's skin felt hot and strangely lumpy—and then Vernon's hand touched a wet, slick substance. He snatched his palm back quickly. "Gross!" he said. "What is this?" He looked down at his hand and saw that it was covered with a strange mucus, a slime.

Dorman's skin suddenly writhed and squirmed, almost as if an army of rats rushed along beneath the flesh. "You shouldn't have touched that." Dorman turned around and looked at him angrily.

"What is this stuff?" Vernon shoved the revolver back into his holster and, staring squeamishly at his hand, tried to wipe the slime off on his pants. He backed away, looking in horror at the unsettling movement throughout Dorman's body.

Suddenly his palm burned. It felt like acid eating deep into his flesh. "Hey!" He staggered backward, his heels skidding on the uneven rubble.

A burning, tingling sensation started at Vernon's hand, as if miniature bubbles were racing up his wrist, tiny bullets firing through his nerves, into his arms, his shoulders, his chest.

Dorman lowered his arms and turned to watch. "I told you not to touch me," he said.

Vernon Ruckman felt all of his muscles lock up. Seizures wracked his body, a thousand tiny fireworks exploded in his head. He couldn't see anymore, other than bright psychedelic flashes, static in front of his vision. His arms and legs jittered, his muscles spasmed and convulsed.

From inside his head he heard bones breaking. His own bones.

He screamed as he fell backward, as if his entire body had turned into a minefield.

The flashlight, still glowing brightly, dropped to the ash-covered ground.

Dorman watched the still-twitching body of the guard for a few moments before turning his attention back to the half-exposed safe. The victim's skin rippled and bubbled as large red-black blotches appeared in the destroyed muscle tissue. The guard's flashlight illuminated a brilliant white fan across the ground, and Dorman could see swollen growths, pustules, tumors, lumps.

The usual.

Dorman ripped away the last of the wall frame and the powdery gypsum from the burned Sheetrock to expose the fire safe. He knew the combination well enough, and quickly spun through the numbers, listening to the cylinders click into position. With one meaty, numb hand, he pounded on the door to chip free some of the blackened paint that had caked in the cracks. He swung open the door.

But the safe was empty. Somebody had already taken the contents, the records, and the stable prototypes.

He whirled to look at the dead guard, as if Vernon Ruckman somehow had been involved with the theft. He winced as another spasm coursed through him. His last hope had been inside that safe. Or so he thought.

Dorman stood up, furious. Now what was he going to do? He looked down at his hand, and the skin on his palm shifted and changed, like a cellular thunderstorm. He shuddered as minor convulsions trooped through his muscle systems, but taking deep breaths, he managed to get his body under control again.

It was getting harder every day, but he vowed to keep doing whatever was necessary to stay alive. Dorman had always done what was necessary.

Sickened with despair, he wandered aimlessly around the wreckage of DyMar Laboratory. The computer equipment was entirely trashed, all of the lab supplies obliterated. He found a melted and broken desk, and from its placement he knew it had been David Kennessy's, the lead researcher.

"Damn you, David," Dorman muttered.

Using all his strength, he ripped open one of the top drawers, and in the debris there he found an old framed photograph—burned around the edges, the glass cracked—and stared at it. He peeled the photo out of the remnants of the frame.

David, dark-haired and dashing, smiled beside a strong-looking and pretty young woman with strawberry-blond hair and a towheaded boy. Sitting in front of them, tongue lolling out, was the Kennessys' black Labrador, always the dog… The family portrait had been taken when the boy was eleven years old—before the leukemia had struck him. *Patrice and Jody Kennessy.*

Dorman took the photo and stood up. He thought he knew where they might have gone, and he was sure he could find them. He *had* to. Now that the other records were gone, only the dog's blood held the answer he needed. He would gamble on where they might go, where Patrice might think to hide. She didn't even know the remarkable secret their family pet carried inside his body.

Dorman looked back to the guard's dead body. Paying no attention to the horrible blotches on his skin, he removed the guard's revolver and tucked it in his pants pocket. If it came down to a crisis situation, he might need the weapon in order to get his way.

Leaving the cooling, blotched corpse behind and taking the weapon and the photograph, Jeremy Dorman walked away from the burned DyMar Laboratory.

Inside of him, the biological time bomb kept ticking. He didn't have many days left.

TWO

FBI Headquarters
Washington, D.C.
Monday, 7:43 a.m.

The bear stood huge, five times the size of an all-star wrestler. Bronze-brown fur bristled from its cable-thick muscles—a Kodiak bear, a prize specimen. Its claws were spread as it leaned over to rip a salmon from the rocky stream, pristine and uninterrupted.

Mulder stared at the claws, the fangs, the sheer primal power.

He was glad the creature was simply stuffed and on display in the Hoover Building, but even still, he appreciated the glass barrier. Mounting this beast must have been a taxidermist's nightmare.

The prize hunting trophy had been confiscated in an FBI raid against a drug kingpin. The drug lord had spent over twenty thousand dollars for his own personal hunting expedition to Alaska, and then spent more money to have his prize kill mounted. When the FBI arrested the man, they had confiscated the gigantic bear according to RICO statutes—since the drug lord had funded the expedition with illicit drug money, the stuffed bear was forfeited to the federal government.

Not knowing what else to do with it, the FBI had put the monster on display beside other noteworthy confiscated items: a customized Harley-Davidson motorcycle, emerald and diamond necklaces, earrings, bracelets, bricks of solid gold.

Sometimes Mulder left his quiet and dim basement offices where he kept the X-Files just to come up and peruse the display case.

Looking at the powerful bear, Mulder continued to be preoccupied, perplexed by a recent and highly unusual death report he had received, an X-File that had come across his desk from a field agent in Oregon.

When a monster like this bear killed its prey, it left no doubt as to the cause of death. A bizarre disease raised many questions, though—especially a new and virulent disease found at the site of a medical research laboratory that had recently been destroyed by arson.

Unanswered questions had always intrigued Agent Fox Mulder.

He went back down in the elevator to his own offices, where he could sit and read the death report again. Then he would go meet Scully.

She stood between the thick, soundproofed Plexiglas partitions inside the FBI's practice firing range. Special Agent Dana Scully removed her handgun, a new Sig Sauer 9mm. She slapped in an expanded clip that carried fifteen bullets, an extra one in the chamber.

She entered the code at the computer keypad at her left; hydraulics hummed, and a cable trundled the black silhouetted "bad guy" target to a range of twenty yards. She locked it into place and reached up to grab a set of padded earphones. She snugged the hearing protection over her head, pressing down her red hair.

Then she gripped her pistol, assuming a proper isosceles firing stance, and aimed at her target. Squinting and focusing down the hairline, she squeezed the trigger in an unconscious reflex and popped off the first round. She paid no attention to where it struck, simply aimed and shot again, firing over and over. Expended casings flew into the air like metal popcorn, clinking and rattling on the cement floor. The smell of burned black powder filled her nostrils.

She thought of those shadowy men who had killed her sister Melissa, those who had repeatedly tried to silence or discredit Mulder and his admittedly unorthodox theories.

Scully had to stay calm, maintain her firing stance, maintain her edge. If she let her anger and frustration simmer through her, then her aim would be off.

She looked at the black silhouette of the target and saw only the featureless men who had entwined themselves so deeply in her life. Smallpox scars, nose implants, vaccination records, and mysterious disappearances—like her own—and the cancer that was almost certainly a result of what they had done to her while she had been abducted. She had no way to fight against the conspiracies, no target to shoot at. She had no choice but to keep searching. Scully gritted her teeth and shot again and again until the entire clip was expended.

Removing her ear protection, she punched the button to retrieve the yellowish paper target. FBI agents had to re-qualify at the Quantico firing range at least once every three months. Scully wasn't due for another four weeks yet, but still she liked to come early in the morning to practice. The range was empty then, and she could take her time.

Later in the day, tour groups would come through to watch demonstrations as a special agent forced into tour guide service showed off his marksmanship skills with the Sig Sauer, the M-16, and possibly a Thompson submachine gun. Scully wanted to be long finished here before the first groups of wide-eyed Boy Scouts or schoolteachers marched in behind the observation windows.

She retrieved the battered target, studying her skill, and was pleased to see how well her sixteen shots had clustered around the center of the silhouetted chest.

Quantico instructors taught agents not to think of their mark as a person but as a "target." She didn't aim for the heart or the head or the side. She aimed for the "center of mass." She didn't aim to shoot the bad guys—she simply "removed the target."

Drawing her weapon and firing upon a suspect was the last possible resort of a good agent, not the proper way to end an investigation unless all other methods failed. Besides, the paperwork was horrendous. Once a federal agent fired her weapon, she had to account for every single shell casing expended—sometimes a difficult task during a heated running firefight.

Scully yanked the paper target from its binder clip and left the gunshot-spattered piece of support cardboard hanging in place. She punched the computer controls to reset the target to its average point, and then looked up, startled to see her partner Mulder leaning against the wall in the observation gallery. She wondered how long he had been waiting for her.

"Good shooting, Scully," he said. He didn't ask whether she was simply doing target practice or somehow exorcising personal demons.

"Spying on me, Mulder?" she said lightly, trying to cover her surprise. After an awkward moment of silence she said, "All right, what is it?"

"A new case. And this one is going to capture your interest, no doubt about it." He smiled.

She replaced her safety goggles on the proper hook and followed him. Even if they weren't always believable, Mulder's discoveries were always interesting and unusual.

THREE

Khe Sanh Khoffee Shoppe
Washington, D.C.
Monday, 8:44 a.m.

As Mulder led her out of the Hoover Building, Scully wondered about the new case he had found almost as much as she dreaded the coffee shop where he planned to take her. Even his offhanded promise, "I'm buying," hadn't exactly won her over.

They walked together past the metal detector, out the door, and down the granite steps. At all corners of the big, box-like building, uniformed FBI security teams manned imposing-looking guard stations.

Mulder and Scully passed alongside the line of tourists that had already begun to form for the first FBI tour of the day. Though most of the pedestrians wore the formal business attire typical in the bureaucratic environment of Washington, DC, the knowing looks told Scully that the tourists recognized them as obvious federal agents.

Other federal buildings stood tall around them, ornate and majestic—the architecture in downtown Washington had to compete with itself. Upstairs in many of these buildings were numerous consulting firms, law offices, and high-powered lobbyist organizations. The bottom levels contained cafes, delis, and newsstands.

Mulder held the glass door of the Khe Sanh Khoffee Shoppe. "Mulder, why do you want to take me here so often?" she asked, scanning the meager clientele inside. Many immigrant Korean families had opened similar businesses in the federal district—usually delicious cafeterias, coffee shops, and restaurants. But the proprietors of the Khe Sanh Khoffee Shoppe imitated mediocre American cuisine with a vengeance, with unfortunate results.

"I like the place," Mulder said with a shrug. "They serve coffee in those nice big Styrofoam cups."

Scully went inside without further argument. In her opinion, they had more important things to do… and she wasn't hungry.

Handwritten daily specials were listed on a white board propped on an easel near a large and dusty silk plant. A refrigerator filled with bottled water and soft drinks stood beside the cash register. An empty steam table occupied a large portion of the coffee shop; at lunchtime the proprietors served a cheap—and cheap-tasting—lunch buffet of various Americanized Asian specialties.

Mulder set his briefcase on one of the cleared tables, then bolted for the cash register and coffee line as Scully took her seat. "Can I get you anything, Scully?" he called.

"Just coffee," she said, against her better judgment.

He raised his eyebrows. "They've got a great fried egg and hash browns breakfast special."

"Just coffee," she repeated.

Mulder came back with two large Styrofoam cups. Scully could smell the bitter aroma even before he set the cup in front of her. She held it in both hands, enjoying the warmth on her fingertips.

Getting down to business, Mulder snapped open his briefcase. "This one will interest you, I think." He withdrew a manila folder. "Portland, Oregon," he said. "This is DyMar Laboratory, a federally funded cancer research center."

He handed her a slick brochure showcasing a beautifully modern laboratory facility: a glass-and-steel framework trimmed with handsome wood decking, support beams, and hardwood floors. The reception areas were heavily decorated with glowing golden wood and potted plants, while the laboratory areas were clean, white, and sterile.

"Nice place," Scully said as she folded the pages together again. "I've read a lot about current cancer research, but I'm not aware of their work."

"DyMar tried to keep a low profile," Mulder said, "until recently."

"What changed?" Scully asked, setting the brochure down on the small table.

Mulder removed the next item, a black-and-white glossy photo of the same place. This time the building was destroyed, gutted by fire, barricaded by chain-link fences—an abandoned war zone.

"Presumably sabotage and arson," Mulder said. "The investigation is still pending. This happened a week and a half ago. A Portland newspaper received a letter from a protest group—Liberation Now—claiming responsibility for the destruction. But nobody's ever heard of them. They were supposedly animal rights activists upset at some of the research the lead scientist, Dr. David Kennessy, was performing. High-tech research, and a lot of it was classified."

"And the activists burned the place down?"

"Blew it up and burned it down, actually."

"That's rather extreme, Mulder—usually those groups are just content to make their statement and get some publicity." Scully stared down at the charred building.

"Exactly, Scully. Somebody really wanted to stop the experimentation."

"What was Kennessy's research that got the group so excited?"

"The information on that is very vague," Mulder said, his forehead creasing. His voice became troubled. "New cancer therapy techniques—really cutting-edge stuff—he and his brother Darin worked together for years, in an unlikely combination of approaches. David was the biologist and medical chemist, while Darin came to the field from a background in electrical engineering."

"Electrical engineering and cancer research?" Scully asked. "Those two don't usually go together. Was he developing a new treatment apparatus or diagnostic equipment?"

"Unknown," Mulder said. "Darin Kennessy apparently had a falling-out with his brother six months ago. He abandoned his work at DyMar and joined a fringe group of survivalists out in the Oregon wilderness. Needless to say, he isn't reachable by phone."

Scully looked again at the brochure, but found no mention of the specific team members. "So, did David Kennessy continue the work even without his brother?"

"Yes," Mulder said. "He and their junior research partner, Jeremy Dorman. I've tried to locate their records and reports to determine the exact nature of their investigations, but most of the documents have been removed from the files. As far as I know, Kennessy concentrated on obscure techniques that have never been previously used in cancer research."

Scully frowned. "Why would anyone be so upset about that? Did his research show any progress?"

Mulder gulped his coffee. "Well, apparently the members of the mob were outraged at some supposedly cruel and unapproved animal tests Kennessy had performed. No details, but I suppose the good doctor strayed a bit from the rules of the Geneva Convention." Mulder shrugged. "Most of the records were burned or destroyed, and it's hard to get any concrete information."

"Anyone hurt in the fire?" Scully asked.

"Kennessy and Dorman were both reported killed in the blaze, though the investigators had trouble identifying—or even accounting for—all the body parts. Remember, the lab didn't just burn, it exploded. There must have been some kind of bombs planted. That group meant business, Scully."

"That's all interesting, Mulder, but I'm not sure why it's interesting to you."

"I'm getting to that."

Scully's brow furrowed as she looked down at the glossy print of the burned lab. She handed the photo back to Mulder.

At other tables, people in business suits hunched over, continuing their own conversations, oblivious to anyone listening in. Scully kept her senses alert out of habit as a federal investigator. A group of men from NASA sat at one table, discussing proposals and modifications to a new interplanetary probe, while other men at a different table talked in hushed tones about how best to cut the space program budget.

"Kennessy had apparently been threatened before," Mulder said, "but this group came out of nowhere and drew a big crowd. I've found no record of any organization called Liberation Now before the DyMar incident, until the *Portland Oregonian* received the letter claiming responsibility."

"Why would Kennessy have kept working under such conditions?" Scully picked up the colorful brochure and unfolded it again, skimming down the predictable propaganda statements about "new cancer breakthroughs," "remarkable treatment alternatives," and "a cure is just around the corner." She took a deep breath; the words struck a chord with her. Oncologists had been using those same phrases since the 1950s.

Mulder withdrew another photo of a boy eleven or twelve years old. The boy was smiling for the camera, but looked skeletal and weak, his face gaunt, his skin gray and papery, much of his hair gone.

"This is his twelve-year-old son Jody, terminally ill with cancer—acute lymphoblastic leukemia. Kennessy was desperate to find a cure, and he certainly wasn't going to let a few protesters delay his work. Not for a minute."

She rested her chin in her hands. "I still don't see how an arson and property-destruction case would capture your interest."

Mulder removed the last photo from the folder. A man in a security guard's uniform lay sprawled in the burned debris, his face twisted in a mask of agony, his skin blotched and swollen with sinuous lumps, arms and legs bent at strange angles. He looked like a spider that had been dosed with bug spray.

"This man was found at the burned lab just last night," Mulder said. "Look at those symptoms. No one has figured it out yet."

Scully snatched the photo and looked intently at it. Her eyes showed her alarm. "He appears to be dead from some fast-acting and exceedingly virulent pathogen."

Mulder waited for her to absorb the gruesome details, then said, "I wonder if something in Kennessy's research could be responsible? Something that didn't entirely perish in the fire…"

Scully frowned slightly as she concentrated. "Well, we don't know what exactly the arsonists did before they destroyed the lab. Maybe they liberated some of the experimental animals… maybe something very dangerous got loose."

Mulder took another sip of his coffee, then retrieved the papers from the folder. He waited for her to draw her own conclusions.

Scully let her interest show plainly as she continued to study the photo. "Look at those tumors… How fast did the symptoms appear?"

"The victim was apparently normal and healthy when he reported to work a few hours earlier." He leaned forward intently. "What do you think this guard stumbled upon?"

Scully pursed her lips in concern. "I can't really say without seeing it myself. Is this man's body being held in quarantine?"

"Yes. I thought you might want to come with me to take a look."

Scully took her first sip of the coffee, and it did indeed taste as awful as she had feared. "Let's go, Mulder," she said, standing up from the table. She handed him back the colorful brochure with its optimistic proclamations.

Kennessy must have performed some radical and unorthodox tests on his lab animals, she thought. It was possible that after the violent destruction of the facility, and with this possible disease outbreak, some of the animals had escaped. And perhaps they carried something deadly.

FOUR

State Highway 22
Coast Range, Oregon
Monday, 10:00 p.m.

The dog stopped in the middle of the road, distracted on his way to the forest. The ditch smelled damp and spicy with fallen leaves. Roadside reflectors poked out of the ditches beside gravel driveways and rural mailboxes. Unlike the rich spruce and cedar forest, the road smelled of vehicles, tires, hot engines, and belching exhaust.

The twin headlights of the approaching car looked like bright coins. The image fixated the dog, imprinting spots on his dark-adapted eyes. He could hear the car dominating the night noises of insects and stirring branches in the trees around him.

The car sounded loud. The car sounded angry.

The road was wet and dark, shrouded by thick trees. The kids were cranky after a long day of traveling... and at this point the impromptu vacation didn't seem like such a good idea after all.

The rugged and scenic coast was still a dozen miles away, and then it would be another unknown number of miles up the highway until they encountered one of the clustered tourist havens filled with cafes, art galleries, souvenir shops, and places to stay—each one called an "inn" or a "lodge," never a simple motel.

Ten miles back, they had driven past a lonely crossroads occupied by a gas station, a hamburger joint, and a rundown fifties-era motel with a pink neon NO flickering next to the VACANCY sign.

"We should have planned this trip better," Sharon said beside him in the front seat.

"I believe you mentioned that already," Richard answered testily. "Once or twice."

In the backseat, Megan and Rory displayed their intense boredom in uncharacteristic ways. Rory was so restless he had switched off his Game Boy, and Megan was so tired she had stopped picking on her brother.

"There's nothing to do," Rory said.

"Dad, don't you know any other games?" Megan asked. "Were you ever bored as a kid?"

He forced a smile, then glanced up in the rearview mirror to see them sulking in the back seat of the Subaru Outback. Richard had rented the car for this vacation, impressed by its good wheels, good traction for those mountain roads. At the start of the long drive, he had felt like SuperDad.

"Well, my sister and I used to play a game called 'Silo.' We were in Illinois, where they've got lots of farms. You'd keep watch around the countryside and call out every time you saw a silo next to a barn. Whoever saw the most silos won the game." He tried to make it sound interesting, but even back then only the tedium of the Midwestern rural landscape had made Silo a viable form of entertainment.

"Doesn't do much good when it's dark out, Dad," Rory said.

"I don't think there are any silos or barns out here anyway," Megan chimed in.

The dark trees pressing close to the narrow highway rushed by, and his blazing headlights made tunnels in front of him. He kept driving, kept trying to think of ways to distract his kids. He vowed to make this a good vacation after all. Tomorrow they would go see the Devil's Churn, where waves from the ocean shot up like a geyser through a hole in the rock, and then they would head up to the Columbia River Gorge and see waterfall after waterfall.

Now, though, he just wanted to find a place to spend the night.

"Dog!" his wife cried. "A dog! Watch out!"

For a frozen instant, Richard thought she was playing some bizarre variant of the Silo game, but then he spotted the black four-legged form hesitating in the middle of the road, its liquid eyes like pools of quicksilver that reflected the headlights.

He slammed on the brakes, and the new tires on the rental Subaru skiied across the slick coating of fallen leaves. The car slewed, slowed, but continued forward like a locomotive, barely under control.

In the back, the kids screamed. The brakes and tires screamed even louder.

The dog tried to leap away at the last instant, but the Subaru bumper struck it with a horrible muffled thump. The black Lab flew onto the hood, into the windshield, then caromed off the side into the weed-filled ditch.

The car screeched to a halt, spewing wet gravel from the road's shoulder. "Jesus Christ!" Richard shouted, slamming the gearshift into park so quickly the entire vehicle rocked.

He grabbed at his seatbelt, fumbling, punching, struggling, until the buckle finally popped free of the catch. Megan and Rory huddled in stunned silence in the back, but Richard popped the door open and sprang out. He looked from side to side, belatedly thinking to check if another car or truck might be bearing down on them.

Nothing. No traffic, just the night. In the deep forest, even the nocturnal insects had fallen silent, as if watching.

He walked around the front of the car with a sick dread. He saw the dent in the bumper, a smashed headlight, a scrape in the hood of the rental car. He remembered too vividly the offhanded and cheerful manner in which he had declined insurance coverage from the rental agent. He stared down now, wondering how much the repairs would cost.

The back door opened a crack, and a very pale-looking Megan eased out. "Daddy? Is he all right?" She peered around, blinking in the darkness. "Is the dog going to be okay?"

He swallowed hard, then crunched around the front of the car into the wet weeds. "Just a second, honey. I'm still looking."

The dog lay sprawled and twitching, a big black Labrador with a smashed skull. He could see the skid marks where it had tumbled across the underbrush. It still moved, attempting to drag itself into the brambles toward a barbed-wire fence and denser foliage beyond. But its body was too broken to let it move.

The dog wheezed through broken ribs. Blood trickled from its black nose. Christ, why couldn't the thing have just been killed outright? A mercy.

"Better take him to a doctor," Rory said, startling him. He hadn't heard the boy climb out of the car. Sharon stood up at the passenger side. She looked at him wide-eyed, and he gave a slight shake of his head.

"I don't think a doctor will be able to help him, sport," he said to his son.

"We can't just leave him here," Megan said, indignant. "We gotta take him to a vet."

He looked down at the broken dog, the dented rental car, and felt absolutely helpless. His wife hung on the open door. "Richard, there's a blanket in the back. We can move the suitcases between the kids, clear a spot. We'll take the dog to the nearest veterinary clinic. The next town up the road should have one."

Richard looked at the kids, his wife, and the dog. He had absolutely no choice. Swallowing bile, knowing it would do no good, he went to get the blanket while Sharon worked to rearrange their suitcases.

The next reasonably sized town up the road, Lincoln City, turned out to be all the way to the coast. The lights had been doused except for dim illumination through window shades in back rooms where the locals watched TV. As he drove through town, desperately searching for an animal care clinic, he wondered why the inhabitants hadn't bothered to roll up the sidewalks with sundown.

Finally he saw an unlit painted sign, "Hughart's Family Veterinary Clinic," and he swerved into the empty parking lot. Megan and Rory both sniffled in the backseat; his wife sat tight-lipped and silent next to him up front.

Richard took the responsibility himself, climbing the cement steps and ringing the buzzer at the veterinarian's door. He vigorously rapped his knuckles on the window until finally a light flicked on in the foyer. When an old man peered at them through the glass, Richard shouted, "We've got a hurt dog in the car. We need your help."

The old veterinarian showed no surprise at all, as if he had expected nothing else. He unlocked the door as Richard gestured toward the Subaru. "We hit him back up the highway. I... I think it's pretty bad."

"We'll see what we can do," the vet said, going around to the rear of the car. Richard swung open the hatchback, and both Megan and Rory clambered out of their seats, intently interested, their eyes wide with hope. The vet took one look at the children, then met Richard's eyes, understanding exactly the undertones here.

In back, the dog lay bloody and mangled, somehow still alive. To Richard's surprise, the black Lab seemed stronger than before, breathing more evenly, deeply asleep. The vet stared at it, and from the masked expression on the old man's face, Richard knew the dog had no hope of surviving.

"This isn't your dog?" the vet asked.

"No, sir," Richard answered. "No tags, either. Didn't see any."

Megan peered into the back to look. "Is he going to be all right, mister?" she asked. "Are we coming back to visit him, Daddy?"

"We'll have to leave him here, honey," he answered. "This man will know what to do with the dog."

The vet smiled at her. "Of course he'll be all right," he said. "I've got some special kinds of bandages." He looked up at Richard. "If you could help me carry him in back to the surgery, I'll let you all be on your way."

Richard swallowed hard. The way the old man looked right into his heart, he knew the vet must see cases like this every week, hurt animals abandoned to his care.

Together the two men reached under the blanket, lifting the heavy dog. With a grunt, they began to shuffle-walk to the back door of the clinic. "He's hot," the vet said as they entered the swinging door. Leaving the dog on the operating table, the vet went around the room, flicking on lights.

Anxious to be away, Richard stepped to the door, thanking the old man profusely. He left one of his business cards on the reception table, hesitated, then thought better of it. He tucked the card back in his pocket and hurried out the front door.

He rushed back to the Subaru and swung himself inside. "He'll take care of everything," Richard said to no one in particular, then jammed the vehicle into gear. His hands felt grimy, dirty, covered with fur and a smear of the dog's blood.

The car drove off as Richard desperately tried to relocate the peace and joy of a family vacation. The night insects resumed their music in the forest.

FIVE

Mercy Hospital
Portland, Oregon
Tuesday, 10:03 a.m.

The middle of morning on a gray day. Early mist hanging above and through the air made the temperature clammy and colder than it should have been. The clouds and gloom would burn off by noon, giving a blessed few minutes of sunshine before the clouds and the rain rolled in again.

Typical morning, typical Portland.

Scully didn't suppose it made any difference if she and Mulder were going to spend the day in a hospital morgue anyway.

In the basement levels of the hospital, the quiet halls were like tombs. Scully had seen the same thing in many hospitals where she had performed autopsies or continued investigations on cold cadavers in refrigerator drawers. But though the places were by now familiar, she would never find them comforting.

Dr. Frank Quinton, Portland's medical examiner, was a bald man with a feathery fringe of white hair surrounding the back of his head. He had wire-rimmed glasses and a cherubic face.

Judging by his friendly, grandfatherly smile, Scully would have pegged him as a charming, good-natured man—but she could see a tired hardness behind his eyes. In his career as a coroner, Quinton must have seen too many teenagers pulled from wrecked cars, too many suicides and senseless accidents, too many examples of the quirky nature of death.

He warmly shook Scully's hand, and Mulder's. Mulder nodded at his partner, speaking to the coroner. "As I mentioned on the phone, sir, Agent Scully is a medical doctor herself, and she has had experience with many unusual deaths. Perhaps she can offer some suggestions."

The coroner beamed at her, and Scully couldn't help but smile back at the kind-faced man. "What is the status of the body now?"

"We used full disinfectants and have been keeping the body in cold storage to stop the spread of any biological agents," the ME said.

The morgue attendant held out a clipboard and smiled like a puppy dog next to Quinton. The assistant was young and scrawny, but already nearly as bald as the medical examiner. From the idolizing way he looked up at the ME, Scully guessed that Frank Quinton must be his mentor, that one day the morgue attendant wanted to be a medical examiner himself.

"He's in drawer 4E," the attendant said, though Scully was certain the coroner already knew where the guard's body was stored. The attendant hurried over to the bank of clean stainless-steel refrigerator drawers. Most, Scully knew, would contain people who had died of natural causes, heart attacks, or car accidents, surgical failures from the hospital, or old retirees fallen like dead leaves in nursing homes.

One drawer, though, had been marked with yellow tape and sealed with stickers displaying the clawed-circle BIOHAZARD LABEL: 4E.

"Thank you, Edmund," the ME said as Mulder and Scully followed him to the morgue refrigerators.

"You've used appropriate quarantine conditions?" Scully asked.

Quinton looked over at her. "Luckily, the police were spooked enough by the appearance of the corpse that they took precautions, gloves, contamination wraps. Everything was burned in the hospital incinerator here."

Edmund stopped in front of the stainless-steel drawer and peeled away the biohazard sticker. A card on the front panel of the drawer labeled it RESTRICTED, POLICE EVIDENCE.

After tugging on a sterile pair of rubber gloves, Edmund grabbed the drawer handle and yanked it open. "Here it is. We don't usually get anything as curious as this poor guy." He held open the drawer, and a gust of frosty air drifted out.

With both hands, Edmund dragged out the plastic-draped cadaver of the dead guard. Like a showroom model revealing a new sports car, the attendant drew back the sheet. He stood aside proudly to let the medical examiner, Scully, and Mulder push forward.

Mixed with the cold breath of the refrigerator, the smell of heavy, caustic disinfectants swirled in the air, stinging Scully's eyes and nostrils. She was unable to keep herself from bending over in fascination. She saw the splotches of coagulated blood beneath the guard's skin like blackened bruises, the lumpy, doughy growths that had sprouted like mushrooms inside his tissues.

"I've never seen tumors that could grow so fast," Scully said. "The limited rate of cellular reproduction should make such a rapid spread impossible."

She bent down and observed a faint slimy covering on some patches of skin. Some kind of clear mucus… like slime.

"We're treating this as a high-contamination scenario. Our lab tests are expected back in another day or so from the CDC," Quinton said. "I'm doing my own analysis, under tight controls, but this is an unusual one. We can't just do it in-house."

Scully continued to study the body with the practiced eye of a physician analyzing the symptoms, the patterns, trying to imagine the pathology. The attendant offered her a box of latex gloves. She snapped on a pair, flexing her fingers, then she reached forward to touch the cadaver's skin. She expected it to be cold and hard with rigor—but instead the body felt warm, fresh, and flexible.

"When was this man brought in?" she asked.

"Sunday night," Quinton answered.

She could smell the frosty coldness from the refrigerator, felt it with her hand. "What's his body temperature? He's still warm," she said.

The medical examiner reached forward curiously, and laid his own gloved hand on the cadaver's bruised shoulder. The ME turned and looked sternly at the morgue attendant. "Edmund, are these refrigerators acting up again?"

The morgue attendant scrambled backward like a panicked squirrel, devastated that his mentor had spoken sternly to him. "Everything is working fine, sir. I had Maintenance check it just yesterday." He dashed over to study the gauges. "It says that the drawers are all at constant temperature."

"Feel his temperature for yourself," the ME snapped. Edmund stuttered, "No, sir, I'll take your word for it. I'll get Maintenance down here right away."

"Do that," Quinton said. He peeled off his gloves and went over to a sink to scrub his hands thoroughly. Scully did the same.

"I hope those refrigerators don't fall apart on us again," Quinton muttered. "The last thing I need is for that guy to start to smell."

Scully looked again at the cadaver and tried to picture what DyMar's mysterious research might have produced. If something had gotten loose, they might have to deal with a lot more bodies just like this one. What had Darin Kennessy known, or suspected, that had led him to run and hide from the research entirely?

"Let's go, Mulder. We've got a lot of ground to cover." Scully dried her hands and brushed her red hair away from her face. "We need to find out what Kennessy was working on."

SIX

Kennessy Residence
Tigard, Oregon
Tuesday, 12:17 p.m.

The house looked like most of the others on the street—suburban normal, built in the seventies with aluminum siding, shake shingles, average lawn, average hedges, nothing to make it stand out among the other middle-class homes in a residential town on the outskirts of Portland.

"Somehow, I expected the home of a hotshot young cancer researcher to be more... impressive," Mulder said. "Maybe a white lab coat draped on the mailbox, test tubes lining the front walkway... "

"Researchers aren't that glamorous, Mulder. They don't spend their time playing golf and living in mansions. Besides," she added, "the Kennessy family had some rather extraordinary medical expenses beyond what insurance would cover."

According to records they had obtained, Jody Kennessy's leukemia and his ever-worsening spiral of last-ditch treatments had gobbled their savings and forced them into taking a second mortgage.

Together, Mulder and Scully walked up the driveway toward the front door. Wrought-iron railings lined the two steps up to the porch. A forlorn, water-logged cactus looked out of place beside the downspout of the garage.

Mulder removed his notepad, and Scully brushed her hands down her jacket. The air was cool and damp, but her shiver came as much from her thoughts.

After seeing the guard's body and the gruesome results of the disease that had so rapidly struck him down, Scully knew they had to determine exactly what David Kennessy had been developing at the DyMar Laboratory. The available records had been destroyed in the fire, and Mulder had so far been unable to track down anyone in charge; he couldn't even pinpoint who had overseen DyMar's funding from the federal government.

The dead ends and false leads intrigued him, kept him hunting, while the medical questions engaged Scully's interest.

She wouldn't necessarily expect the wife of a researcher to know much about his work, but in this case there were extenuating circumstances. She and Mulder had decided their next step would be to talk to Kennessy's widow Patrice—an intelligent woman in her own right. In her heart, Scully also wanted to see Jody.

Mulder looked up at the house as he approached the front door. The garage door was closed, the drapes on the house windows drawn, everything quiet and dark. The fat Sunday *Portland Oregonian* lay in a protective plastic wrapper on the driveway, untouched. And it was Tuesday.

As Mulder reached for the doorbell, Scully instantly noticed the shattered latch. "Mulder… " She bent to inspect the lock. It had been broken in, the wood splintered. She could see dents around the knob and the dead bolt, the torn-up jamb. Someone had crudely pressed the fragments back in place, a cosmetic cover-up that would fool casual passersby from the street.

Mulder pounded on the door. "Hello!" he shouted. Scully stepped into a flowerbed to peer inside the window; through a gap in the drapes she saw overturned furniture in the main room, scattered debris on the floor.

"Mulder, we have sufficient cause to enter the premises."

He pushed harder, and the door swung easily open. "Federal agents," he called out—but the Kennessy home answered them only with a quiet, gasping echo of his call. Mulder and Scully stepped into the foyer, and both stopped simultaneously to stare at the disaster.

"Very subtle," Mulder said.

The home had been ransacked, furniture tipped over, upholstery slashed, stuffing pulled out. The baseboards had been pried away from the walls, the carpeting ripped up as the violent searchers dug down to the floorboards. Cabinets and cupboards hung open, bookshelves lay tipped over, with books and knickknacks strewn about.

"I don't think we're going to find anybody here," Scully said, hands on her hips.

"What we need to find is a housekeeper," Mulder answered.

They searched through the rooms anyway. Scully couldn't help wondering why anyone would have ransacked the place. Had the violent protest group struck at Kennessy's family as well, not satisfied with killing David Kennessy and Jeremy Dorman, not content with burning down the entire DyMar facility?

Had Patrice and Jody been here when the attack occurred?

Scully dreaded finding their bodies in the back room, gagged, beaten, or just shot to death where they stood.

But the house was empty.

"We'll have to get evidence technicians to search for blood traces," Scully said. "We'll need to seal off the site and get a team in here right away."

They entered Jody's room. The Sheetrock had been smashed open, presumably to let the searchers look between the studs in the walls. The boy's bed had been overturned, the mattress flayed of its sheets and fabric covering.

"This doesn't make any sense" Scully said. "Very violent… and very thorough."

Mulder picked up a smashed model of an alien spaceship from *Independence Day*. Scully could imagine how carefully and lovingly the twelve-year-old boy must have assembled it.

"Just like the DyMar attack two weeks ago," Mulder said.

Mulder bent over to pick up a chunk of broken gypsum board, turning it in his fingers. Scully retrieved a fighter jet model that had been suspended by fish line from the ceiling but now lay with its plastic airfoils broken on the floor, its fuselage cracked so that someone could pry inside. Searching.

Scully stood, feeling cold. She thought of the young boy who had already received a death sentence as the cancer ravaged his body. Jody Kennessy had been through enough already, and now he had to endure whatever had happened here.

Scully turned around and walked into the kitchen, mindful of the drinking glasses shattered on the linoleum floor and on the Formica countertop. The searchers couldn't possibly have been looking for anything inside the glass tumblers. They had simply enjoyed the destruction.

Mulder bent down next to the refrigerator and looked at an orange plastic dog food bowl. He picked it up, turning it to show the name VADER written in magic marker across the front. The bowl was empty, the food crumbs hard and dry.

"Look at this, Scully," he said. "If something happened to Patrice and Jody Kennessy… then where is the dog?"

Scully frowned. "Maybe the same place they are." With a long, slow look at the devastation in the kitchen, Scully swallowed hard. "Looks like our search just got wider."

SEVEN

Coast Range, Oregon
Tuesday, 2:05 p.m.

No one would ever find them in this cabin, isolated out in the wilderness of the Oregon coastal mountains. No one would help them, no one would rescue them.

Patrice and Jody Kennessy were alone, desperately trying to hold onto some semblance of normal life by the barest edges of their fingernails.

As far as Patrice was concerned, though, it wasn't working. Day after day of living in fear, jumping at shadows, hiding from mysterious noises... but they had no other choice for survival—and Patrice was determined that her son would survive this.

She went to the window of the small cabin and parted the dingy drapes to watch Jody bounce a tennis ball against the outside wall. He was in plain view, but within running distance of the thick forest that ringed the hollow. Each impact of the tennis ball sounded like gunshots aimed at her.

At one time the isolation of this plot of land had been a valuable asset, back when she had designed the place for her brother-in-law as a place for him to get away from DyMar. *Darin was good at getting away*, she thought. Scattered empty patches on the steep hills in the distance showed where clear-cutting teams had removed acres and acres of hardwood a few years before, leaving stubbled rectangles like scabs on the mountainside.

This cabin was supposed to be a private vacation hideout for relaxation and solitude. Darin had deliberately refused to put in a phone, or a mailbox, and they had promised to keep the location secret. No one was supposed to know about this place. Now the isolation was like a fortress wall around them. No one knew where they were. No one would ever find them out here.

A small twin-engine plane buzzed overhead, aimless and barely seen in the sky; the drone faded as it passed out of sight.

Their plight kept Patrice on the verge of terror and paralysis each day. Jody, so brave that it choked her up every time she thought about it, had been through so much already—the pursuit, the attack on DyMar... and before that, the doctor's assessment—terminal cancer, leukemia, not long to live. It was like a downward-plunging guillotine blade heading for his neck.

After the original leukemia diagnosis, what greater threat could shadowy conspirators possibly use? What could outweigh the demon inside Jody's own twelve-year-old body? Any other ordeal must pale in comparison.

As the tennis ball bounced away from the cabin into the knee-high weeds, Jody chased after it in a vain attempt to amuse himself. Patrice moved to the edge of the window to keep him in view. Ever since the fire and the attack, Patrice took great care never to let him out of her sight.

The boy seemed so much healthier now. Patrice didn't dare to hope for the remission to continue. He should be in the hospital now, but she couldn't take him. She didn't dare.

Jody halfheartedly bounced the tennis ball again, then once more ran after it. He had passed a remarkable milestone—their crisis situation had become *ordinary* after two weeks, and his boredom had overwhelmed his fear. He looked so young, so carefree, even after everything that had happened.

Twelve should have been a magic age for him, the verge of the teenage years, when concerns fostered by puberty achieved universal importance. But Jody was no longer a normal boy. The jury was still out as to whether he would survive this or not.

Patrice opened the screen door and, with a glance over her shoulder, stepped onto the porch, taking care to keep the worried expression off her face. Although by now, Jody would probably consider any look of concern normal for her.

The gray Oregon cloud cover had broken for its daily hour of sunshine. The meadow looked fresh from the previous night's rain showers, when the patter of raindrops had sounded like creeping footsteps outside the window. Patrice had lain awake for hours, staring at the ceiling. Now the tall pines and aspens cast afternoon shadows across the muddy driveway that led down from the rise, away from the distant highway.

Jody smacked the tennis ball too hard, and it sailed off to the driveway, struck a stone, and bounced into the thick meadow. With a shout of anger that finally betrayed his tension, Jody hurled his tennis racket after it, then stood fuming.

Impulsive, Patrice thought. Jody became more like his father every day.

"Hey, Jody!" she called, quelling most of the scolding tone. He fetched the racket and plodded toward her, his eyes toward the ground. He had been restless and moody all day. "What's wrong with you?"

Jody averted his eyes, turned instead to squint where the sunshine lit the dense pines. Far away, she could hear the deep drone of a heavily laden log truck growling down the highway on the other side of the tree barricade.

"It's Vader," he finally answered, and looked up at his mother for under-standing. "He didn't come back yesterday, and I haven't seen him all morning."

Now Patrice understood, and she felt the relief wash over her. For a moment, she had been afraid he might have seen some stranger or heard something about them on the radio news.

"Just wait and see. Your dog'll be alright—he always is."

Vader and Jody were about the same age, and had been inseparable all their lives. Despite her worries, Patrice smiled at the thought of the smart and good-natured black Lab.

Eleven years before, she had thought the world was golden. Their one-year-old son sat in his diapers in the middle of the hardwood floor, scooting around. He had tossed aside his action figure companions and played with the dog instead. The boy knew "Ma" and "Da" and attempted to say "Vader," though the dog's name came out more like a strangled "drrrr!"

Patrice and David chuckled together as they watched the black Lab play with Jody. Vader romped back and forth, his paws slipping on the polished floor. Jody squealed with delight. Vader woofed and circled the baby, who tried to spin on his diaper on the floor.

Those had been peaceful times, bright times. Now, though, she hadn't had a moment's peace since the fateful night she had received a desperate call from her husband at his besieged laboratory.

Up until then, learning that her son was dying of cancer had been the worst moment of her life.

"But what if Vader's lying hurt in a ditch somewhere, Mom?" Jody asked. She could see tears on the edges of her son's eyes as he fought hard against crying. "What if he's in a fur trap, or got shot by a hunter?"

Patrice shook her head, trying to comfort her son. "Vader will come home safe and sound. He always does."

Once again, Patrice felt the shudder. *Yes, he always did.*

EIGHT

Mercy Hospital
Portland, Oregon
Tuesday, 2:24 p.m.

Even through the thick fabric of her clumsy gloves, she could feel the slick softness of the corpse's inner cavity. Scully's movements were irritatingly sluggish and imprecise—but at least the heavy gear protected her from exposure to whatever had killed Vernon Ruckman.

The forced-air respirator pumped a cold, stale wind into her face. Her eyes were dry, burning. She wished she could just rub them, but enclosed in the anti-contamination suit, Scully had no choice but to endure the discomfort until the autopsy of the dead security guard was complete.

Her tape recorder rested on a table, voice-activated, waiting for her to say in detail what she was seeing. This wasn't a typical autopsy, though. She could see dozens of baffling physical anomalies just on first glance, and the mystery and horrific manifestations of the symptoms grew more astonishing as she proceeded with her thorough inspection.

Still, the step-by-step postmortem procedure had been established for a reason. She remembered teaching it to students at Quantico, during the brief period when the X-Files had been closed and she and Mulder had been separated. Some of her students had already completed their training through the FBI Academy and become special agents like herself.

But she doubted any of them would ever work a case like this one. At such times, falling back on a routine was the only way to keep her mind clear and focused.

First step. "Test," she said, and the red light of the voice-activated recorder winked on. She continued speaking in a normal voice, muffled through her transparent plastic faceplate.

"Subject's name, Vernon Ruckman. Age, thirty-two; weight, approximately one hundred eighty-five pounds. General external physical condition is good. He appears to have been quite healthy until this disease struck him down." Now he looked as if every cell in his body had gone haywire all at once.

She looked at the man's blotchy body, the dark red marks of tarlike blood pooled in pockets beneath his skin. The man's face had frozen in a contortion of agony, lips peeled back from his teeth.

"Fortunately, the people who found this body and the medical examiner established quarantine protocols immediately. No one handled this cadaver with unprotected hands." She suspected that this disease, whatever it was, might be exceedingly virulent.

"Outward symptoms, the blotches, the swellings under the skin, are reminiscent of the bubonic plague." But the Black Death, while killing about one-third of Europe when it raged through the population centers of the Middle Ages, had acted over the course of several days, even in its deadliest pneumonic form. "This man seems to have been struck down nearly instantaneously, however. I know of no disease short of a direct nerve toxin that can act with such extreme lethality."

Scully touched the skin on Ruckman's arms, which hung like loose folds of rubbery fabric draped on the bones. "The epidermis shows substantial slippage, as if the connective tissue to the muscles has been destroyed somehow.

"As for the muscle fiber itself… " She pushed against the meat of the body with her fingers, felt an unusual softness, a squishing. Her heart jumped. "Muscle fibers seem dissociated… almost *mealy*."

Part of the skin split open, and Scully drew back, surprised. A clear, whitish liquid oozed out, and she gingerly touched it with her gloved fingertips. The substance was sticky, thick and syrupy.

"I've found some sort of unusual… mucus-like substance coming from the skin of this man. It seems to have pooled and collected within the subcutaneous tissue. My manipulations have released it."

She touched her fingertips together, and the slime stuck, then dripped back down onto the body. "I don't understand this at all," Scully admitted to the tape recorder. She would probably delete that line in her report.

"Proceeding with the body cavity," she said, then drew the stainless-steel tray of saws, scalpels, spreaders, and forceps close to her side.

Taking great care with the scalpel so as not to puncture the fabric of her gloves, she cut into the man's body cavity and used a rib-spreader to open up the chest. It was hard work; sweat dripped down her forehead, tickling her eyebrows.

Looking at the mess of the guard's opened chest, she reached inside the wet cavity, fishing around with her protected fingers. Getting down to work, Scully began by taking an inventory, removing lungs, liver, heart, intestines, weighing each on a mass-balance.

"It's difficult to recognize the individual organs, due to the abundant presence"—perhaps *infestation* was a better word, she thought—"of tumors."

In and around the organs, Vernon Ruckman's lumps, growths, tumors spread like a nest of viperous worms, thick and insidious. As she watched, they moved, slipping and settling, with a discomforting *writhing* appearance.

But in a body this disturbed, this damaged, no doubt the simple process of autopsy would have caused a vigorous reaction, not to mention the possibility of contraction due to the temperature variations from the morgue refrigerator to the heated room.

Among the displayed organs, Scully found other large pockets of the mucus. Inside, under the lungs, she discovered a large nodule of the slimy, runny substance—almost like a biological island or a storehouse.

She withdrew a sample of the unusual fluid and sealed it in an Extreme Hazard container. She would perform her own analysis of the specimen and send another sample to the Centers for Disease Control to supplement the samples already sent by the ME. Perhaps the pathogen specialists had seen something like this before. But she had a far more immediate concern.

"My primary conclusion, which is still pure speculation," Scully continued, "is that the biological research at DyMar Laboratory may have produced some sort of disease organism. We have not been able to track down full disclosure of David Kennessy's experiments or his techniques, and so I am at a disadvantage to go on the record with any more detailed conjectures."

She stared down at Ruckman's open body, unsettled. The tape recorder waited for her to speak again. If the situation was as bad as Scully feared, then they would certainly need much more help than either she or Mulder could give by themselves.

"The lumps and misshapen portions inside Vernon Ruckman's body look as if rapid outgrowths of cells engulfed his body with astonishing speed." Dr. Kennessy was working on cancer research. Could he have somehow produced a genetic or microbial basis for the disease? she wondered. Had he unleashed some terrible viral form of cancer?

She swallowed hard, frightened by her own idea. "All this is very far-fetched, but difficult to discount in light of the symptoms I have observed in this body—especially if this man was visibly healthy mere hours before his body was found."

The period from onset to death was at a maximum only part of an evening, perhaps much less. No time for treatment, no time even for him to realize his fate...

Vernon Ruckman had had only minutes before a terminal disease struck him down. Barely even time enough to pray.

NINE

Hughart's Family Veterinary Clinic
Lincoln City, Oregon
Tuesday, 1:11 a.m.

Dr. Elliott Hughart was torn between intentionally putting the mangled black Labrador to sleep, or just letting it die. As a veterinarian, he had to make the same decision year after year after year. And it never got easier.

The dog lay on one of the stainless-steel surgical tables, still alive against all odds. The rest of the veterinary clinic was quiet and silent. A few other animals hunkered in their wire cages, quiet, but restive and suspicious.

Outside, it was dark, drizzling as it usually did this time of night, but the temperature was warm enough for the vet to prop open the back door. The damp breeze mitigated the smell of chemicals and frightened pets that thickened the air. Hughart had always believed in the curative properties of fresh air, and that went for animals as well as humans.

His living quarters were upstairs, and he had left the television on, the single set of dinner dishes unwashed—but he spent more time down here in the office, surgery, and lab anyway. This part was home for him—the other rooms upstairs were just the place where he slept and ate.

After all these years, Hughart kept his veterinary practice more as a matter of habit than out of any great hope of making it a huge success. He had scraped by over the years. The locals came to him regularly, though many of them expected free treatment as a favor to a friend or neighbor. Occasionally, tourists had accidents with their pets. Hughart had seen many cases like this black Lab: some guilt-ridden sightseer delivering the carcass or the still-living but grievously injured animal, expecting Hughart to work miracles. Sometimes the families stayed. Most of the time—as in this instance—they fled to continue their interrupted vacations.

The black Lab lay shivering, sniffing, whimpering. Blood smeared the steel table. At first, Hughart had done what he could to patch the injuries, stop the bleeding, bandage the worst gashes—but he didn't need a set of X-rays to tell that the dog had a shattered pelvis and a crushed spine, as well as major internal damage.

The black Lab wasn't tagged, was without any papers. It could never recover from these wounds, and even if it pulled through by some miracle, Hughart would have no choice but to relinquish it to the animal shelter, where it would sit in a cage for a few days and hope pathetically for freedom before the shelter destroyed it anyway.

Wasted. All wasted. Hughart drew a deep breath and sighed.

The dog shivered under his hands, but its body temperature burned higher than he had ever felt in an animal before. He inserted a thermometer, genuinely curious, then watched in astonishment as the digital readout climbed from 103 to 104. Normally a dog's temperature should have been 101.5, or 102 at most—and with the shock from his injuries, this dog's body temp should have dropped. The number on the read-out climbed to 106°F.

He drew a routine blood sample, then checked diligently for any other signs of sickness or disease, some cause for the fever that rose like a furnace from its body. What he found, though, surprised him even more.

The black Lab's massive injuries almost seemed to be healing rapidly, the wounds shrinking. He lifted one of the bandages he had pressed against a gash on the dog's rib cage, but though the gauze was soaked with blood, he saw no sign of the wound. Only matted fur. The veterinarian knew it must be his imagination, mere wishful thinking that somehow he might be able to save the dog.

But that would never happen. Hughart knew it in his mind, though his heart continued to hope.

The dog's body trembled, quietly whimpering. With his calloused thumb, Hughart lifted one of its squeezed-shut eyelids and saw a milky covering across its rolled-up eye, like a partially boiled egg. The dog was deep in a coma. Gone. It barely breathed.

The temperature reached 107°F. Even without the injuries, this fever was deadly.

A ribbon of blood trickled out of the wet black nostrils. Seeing that tiny injury, a little flow of red blood across the black fur of the delicate muzzle, made Hughart decide not to put the dog through any more of this. Enough was enough.

He stared down at his canine patient for some time before he shuffled over to his medicine cabinet, unlocked the doors, and removed a large syringe and a bottle of Euthanol, concentrated sodium pentabarbitol. The dog weighed about sixty to eighty pounds, and the suggested dose was about 1 cc for each ten pounds, plus a little extra. He drew 10 ccs, which should be more than sufficient.

If the dog's owners ever came back, they would find the notation "PTS" in the records, which was a euphemism for "Put To Sleep"—which was itself a euphemism for killing the animal… or putting it out of its misery, as veterinarian school had always taught.

Once he had made the decision, Hughart didn't pause. He bent over the dog and inserted the needle into the skin behind the dog's neck and quietly but firmly injected the lethal dose. After its enormous injuries, the black Lab didn't flinch from the prick of the hypodermic.

A cool, clammy breeze eased through the cracked-open door, but the dog remained hot and feverish.

Dr. Hughart heaved a heavy sigh as he discarded the used syringe. "Sorry, boy," he said. "Go chase some rabbits in your dreams… in a place where you don't have to watch out for cars."

The chemical would take effect soon, suppressing the dog's respiration and eventually stopping his heart. Irrevocable, but peaceful.

First, though, Hughart took the blood sample back to the small lab area in the adjoining room. The animal's high body temperature puzzled him. He'd never seen a case like this before. Often animals went into shock if they survived the trauma of being struck by a motor vehicle, but they didn't usually have such a high fever.

The back room was perfectly organized according to a system he had developed over decades, though a casual observer might just see it as cluttered. He flicked on the overhead lights in the small Formica-topped lab area and placed a smear of the blood on a glass slide. First step would be to check the dog's white blood cell count to see if maybe he had some sort of infection, or parasites in the blood.

The dog could have been very sick, even dying, before he'd been hit by the car. In fact, that could explain why the animal had been so sluggish, so unaware of the large automobile bearing down on him. A fever that high would have been intolerable. If the dog suffered from some major illness, Hughart needed to keep a record of it.

Out in the adjoining operating and recovery area, two of the other dogs began to bark and whimper. A cat yowled, and the cages rattled.

Hughart paid little attention. Dogs and cats made a typical chaotic noise, to which he'd grown deaf after so many years. In fact, he'd been surprised at how quiet the animals were when thrown together in a strange situation, penned up in a cage for overnight care. They were already smarting from spaying or neutering or whatever ailments had brought them into the vet's office in the first place.

The only animal he was worried about was the dying black Labrador, and by now the Euthanol would be working.

Bothered by the distracting shadows, Hughart switched on a brighter fluorescent lamp tucked under the cabinets, then illuminated the slide under his microscope with a small lamp. Rubbing his eyes first, he gazed down at the smear of blood, fiddling with the focus knob.

The dog should even now be drifting off to perpetual dreams—but its blood was absolutely *alive*.

In addition to the usual red and white cells and platelets, Hughart saw tiny specks, little silvery components... like squarish glittering crystals that moved about on their own. If this was some sort of massive infection, it was not like any microorganism he had ever before laid eyes on. The odd shapes were as large as the cells and moved about with blurred speed.

"That's incredible," he said, and his voice sounded loud in the claustrophobic lab area. He often talked to the animals around him, or to himself, and it had never bothered him before.

Now, though, he wished he wasn't alone; he wished he had someone with him to share this amazing discovery.

What kind of disease or infection looked like this? After a long career in veterinary medicine, he would have thought he'd seen just about everything. But he had never before witnessed anything remotely like this.

And he hoped it wasn't contagious.

This revamped building had been Elliott Hughart's home, his place of work, for decades, but now it seemed strange and sinister to him. If this dog had some sort of unknown disease, he would have to contact the Centers for Disease Control.

He knew what to do in the case of a rabies outbreak or other diseases that normally afflicted household pets—but these tiny microscopic... slivers? They were utterly foreign to him.

In the back surgery room, the caged animals set up a louder racket, yowling and barking. The old man noticed it subconsciously, but the noise wasn't enough to tear him from his fascination with what he saw under the microscope.

Hughart rubbed his eyes and focused the microscope again, blurring the image past its prime point and then back to sharp focus again. The glittering specks were still there, buzzing about, moving cells. He swallowed hard; his throat was dry and cottony. What to do now?

Then he realized that the barking and meowing inside the operating room cages had become an outright din, as if a fox had charged into a henhouse.

Hughart spun around, bumped into his metal stool, knocked it over, and hopped about on one foot as pain shot through his hip. When he finally rushed into the operating room, he looked at the cages first to see the captive animals pressed back against the bars of their cages, trying to get away from the center of the room.

He didn't even look at the black Lab, because it should have been dead by now—but then he heard paws skittering across the slick surface of stainless steel.

The dog got to its feet, shook itself, and leaped down from the table, leaving a smear of blood on the clean surface. But the dog showed no more wounds, no damage. It trembled with energy, completely healed.

Hughart stood in total shock, unable to believe that the dog had not only regained consciousness—despite its grievous injuries and the euthanasia drug—but had jumped down from the table. This was as incredible as the swarming contamination in the blood sample.

He caught his breath, then eased forward. "Here, boy, let me take a look." Quivering, the dog barked at him, then backed away.

TEN

DyMar Laboratory Ruins
Tuesday, 4:50 p.m.

Not long before sunset, a patch of bright blue sky made a rare appearance in the hills over Portland. Mulder squinted up, wishing he had brought along sunglasses as he maneuvered the rental car up the steep drive to the site of the DyMar Laboratory.

Much of the facility's structure remained intact, though entirely gutted by the fire. The walls were blackened, the wood support structure burned to charcoal, the office furniture slumped and twisted. Some overhead beams had toppled, while others balanced precariously against the concrete load-bearing walls and metal girders. Glass shards lay scattered among ashes and broken stone.

As they crested the hill and reached the sagging chain-link fence around the site, Mulder shifted the car into park and looked through the windshield. "A real fixer-upper," he said. "I'll have to talk to my real estate agent."

Scully got out of the car and looked over at him. "Too late to make an offer, Mulder—this place is scheduled to be demolished in a few days to make way for a new business park." She scanned the thick stands of dark pines and the sweeping view of Portland spread out below, with its sinuous river and necklace of bridges.

Mulder realized the construction crew was moving awfully fast, disturbingly so. He and Scully might not even be able to finish a decent investigation in the amount of time allotted to them.

He opened the chain-link gate; sections of the fence sagged and left wide gaps. Signs declaring DANGER and WARNING adorned the fence, marking the hazards of the half-collapsed building; he doubted those signs would discourage any but the meekest of vandals.

"Apparently Vernon Ruckman's death has proved a greater deterrent than any signs or guards," Scully said. She held on to the chain link for a moment, then followed Mulder into the burned area. "I contacted local law enforcement, trying to get a status on their arson investigation. But so far, all they would tell me is that it's 'pending—no progress.'"

Mulder raised his eyebrows. "A protest group large enough to turn into a destructive mob, and they can't find any members?"

The FBI crime lab was analyzing the note claiming responsibility. By late that evening they expected to have results on whoever was behind Liberation Now. From what Mulder had seen, the letter seemed to be a very amateurish job.

He stared at the blackened walls of the DyMar facility for a moment, then the two agents entered the shell of the building, stepping gingerly. The smell of soot, burned plastics, and other volatile chemicals bit into Mulder's nostrils.

As he stood inside the ruins, looking across the hilltop vista toward the forests and the city below, Mulder imagined that night two weeks earlier, when a mob of angry and uncontrolled protesters had marched up the gravel drive. He drew a deep breath of the ash-clogged air.

"Conjures up images of peasants carrying torches, doesn't it, Scully?" He looked up at the unstable ceiling, the splintered pillars, the collapsed walls. He gingerly took another step into what must have been a main lobby area. "A mob of angry people charging up the hill to burn down the evil laboratory, destroy the mad scientist."

Beside him, Scully appeared deeply disturbed. "But what were they so worried about?" she said. "What did they know? This was cancer research. Of all the different kinds of science, surely *cancer research* is something even the most vehement protesters will abide."

"I don't think it was the cancer part that concerned them," Mulder said.

"What then?" Scully asked, frowning. "The animal testing? I don't know what sort of experiments Dr. Kennessy was doing, but I've researched animal rights groups before—and while they sometimes break in and release a few dogs and rats from their cages, I'm unaware of any other situation that has exhibited this extreme level of violence."

"I think it was the type of research itself," Mulder said. "Something about it must have been very scary. Otherwise, why would all of his records be sealed away?"

"You already have an idea, Mulder. I can tell."

"David Kennessy and his brother had made some waves in the research community, trying unorthodox new approaches and treatments that had been abandoned by everyone else. According to Kennessy's resume, he was an expert in abnormal biochemistry, and his brother Darin had worked for years in Silicon Valley. Tell me, Scully, what sort of relationship could there be between electronics and cancer research?"

Scully didn't offer any of her thoughts as she poked around, looking for where the guard had been found. She saw the yellow-taped section and stood gazing at the rough outline of the body impressed into the loose ash, while Mulder ranged around the perimeter. He moved a fallen sheet of twisted metal out of the way and stumbled upon a fire safe, its door blackened but ajar. He called for Scully.

"Does it contain anything?" she asked.

Mulder raised his eyebrows and rummaged around in the sooty debris. "It's open, but empty. And the inside is dirty but not burned." He waited for that to sink in, then looked up at his partner. From her expression, it was clear she thought the same thing he did. The safe had been opened after the fire, not before. "Someone else was here that night, someone looking for the contents of this safe."

"That's why the guard came up here into the ruins. He saw someone."

Scully frowned. "That could explain why he was here. But it still doesn't tell us what killed him. He wasn't shot or strangled. We don't even know that he met up with the intruder."

"But it's possible, even likely," Mulder said.

Scully looked at him curiously. "So this other person took all the records we need?"

He shrugged. "Come on, Scully. Most of the other information on Kennessy's cancer research was locked away and classified. We can't get our hands on it. There may well have been some evidence here, too—but now that's gone as well, and a security guard is dead."

"Mulder, he was dead from a kind of disease."

"He was dead from some kind of toxic pathogen. We don't know where it came from."

"So whoever was here that night killed the guard, and stole the records from the safe?"

Mulder cocked his head to one side. "Unless someone else got to it first."

Scully remained tight-lipped as they eased around a burned wall, ducked under a fallen girder, and crunched slowly into the interior.

What remained of the lab areas sprawled like a dangerous maze, black and unstable. Part of the floor had collapsed, tumbling down into the basement clean rooms, holding areas, and storage vaults. The remaining section of floor creaked underfoot, demonstrably weakened after the fire.

Mulder picked up a shard of glass. The intense heat had bent and smoothed its sharp edges. "Even after his brother abandoned the research, I think Kennessy was very close to some sort of magnificent breakthrough, and he was willing to bend a few rules because of his son's condition. Someone found out about his work and tried to stop him from taking rash action. I suspect that this supposedly spontaneous protest movement, from a group nobody's ever heard of, was a violent effort to silence him and erase all the progress he had made."

Scully brushed her red hair back away from her face, leaving a little soot mark on her cheek. She sounded very tired. "Mulder, you see conspiracies everywhere."

He reached forward to brush the smudge from her face. "Yeah, Scully, but sometimes I'm right. And in this case it cost the lives of two people—maybe more."

ELEVEN

Under Burnside Bridge
Portland, Oregon
Tuesday, 11:21 p.m.

He tried to hide and he tried to sleep—but nothing came to him but a succession of vicious nightmares.

Jeremy Dorman did not know whether the dreams were caused by the swarms of microscopic invaders tinkering with his head, with his thought processes… or whether the nightmares came as a result of his guilty conscience.

Wet and clammy, clad in tattered clothes that didn't fit him right, he huddled under the shelter of Burnside Bridge, on the damp and trash-strewn shore of the Willamette River. The muddy green-blue water curled along in its stately course.

Years ago, downtown Portland had cleaned up River Park, making it an attractive, well-lit, and scenic area for the yuppies to jog, the tourists to sit on cold concrete benches and look out across the water. Young couples could listen to street musicians while they sipped on their gourmet coffee concoctions.

But not at this dark hour. Now most people sat in their warm homes, not thinking about the cold and lonely night outside. Dorman listened to the soft gurgle of the slow-moving river against the tumbled rocks around the bridge pilings. The water smelled warm and rich and alive, but the cool mist had a frosty metallic tang to it. Dorman shivered.

Pigeons nested in the bridge superstructure above, cooing and rustling. Farther down the walk came the rattling sound of another vagrant rummaging through trash cans to find recyclable bottles or cans. A few brown bags containing empty malt liquor and cheap wine bottles lay piled against the green-painted wastebaskets.

Dorman huddled in the shadows, in bodily pain, in mental misery. Fighting a spasm of his rebellious body, he rolled into a mud puddle, smearing dirt all over his back... but he didn't even notice.

A heavy truck rumbled overhead across the bridge with a sound like a muffled explosion.

Like the DyMar explosion.

That night, the *last* night, came back to him too vividly—the darkness filled with fire and shouts and explosions. Murderous and destructive people: faceless, nameless, all brought together by someone pulling strings invisibly in the shadows. And they were malicious, destructive.

He must have fallen asleep... or somehow been transported back in time. His memory had been enhanced in a sort of cruel and unusual punishment, perhaps by the wildcard action of his affliction.

"A chain-link fence and a couple of rent-a-cops does not make me feel safe," Dorman had said to David Kennessy. This wasn't exactly a high-security installation they were working in—after all, David had smuggled his damned pet dog in there, and a handgun. "I'm starting to think your brother had the right idea to walk away from all this six months ago."

DyMar had called for backup security from the state police, and had been turned down. The ostensible reason was some buried statute that allowed the police to defer "internal company disputes" to private security forces. David paced around the basement laboratory rooms, fuming, demanding to know how the police could consider a mob of demonstrators to be an internal company dispute. It still hadn't occurred to him that somebody might want the lab unprotected.

For all his biochemical brilliance, David Kennessy was clueless. His brother Darin hadn't been quite so politically naive, and Darin had gotten the hell out of Dodge—in time. David had stayed—for his son's sake. Neither of them understood the stakes involved in their own research.

When the actual destruction started, Jeremy recalled seeing David scrambling to grab his records, his samples, like in all those old movies where the mad scientist strives to rescue a single notebook from the flames. David seemed more pissed off than frightened. He kicked a few stray pencils away from his feet, and spoke in his "let's be reasonable" voice. "Some bone-headed fanatic is always trying to stop progress—but it never works. Nobody can undiscover this new technology." He made a rude noise through his lips.

Indeed, biological manufacturing and submicroscopic engineering had been progressing at remarkable speed for years now. Genetic engineers used the DNA machinery of certain bacteria to produce artificial insulin. A corporation in Syracuse, New York, had patented techniques for storing and reading data in cubes made of bacteriorhodopsin, a genetically altered protein. Too many people were working on too many different aspects of the problem. David was right—nobody could undiscover the technology.

But Dorman himself knew that some people in the government were certainly intent on trying to do just that. And even with all the prior planning and the hushed agreements, they hadn't given Dorman himself time to escape, despite their promises.

While David was distracted, rushing to the phone to warn his wife about the attack and her own danger, Dorman had not been able to find any of the pure original nanomachines, just the prototypes, the leftover and question-able samples that had been used—with mixed results—on the other lab animals, before their success with the dog. But still, the prototypes had worked... to a certain extent. They had saved him, technically at least.

Then Dorman heard windows smashing upstairs, the murderous shouts pouring closer—and he knew it was time.

Those prototypes had been his last resort, the only thing he could find. They had been viable enough in the lab rat tests, hadn't they? And the dog was just fine, perfectly healthy. What choice did he have but to take a chance? Still, the possibility froze Dorman with terror, uncertainty, for a moment—if he did this, it would be an irrevocable act. He couldn't just go to the drug-store and get the antidote.

But the thought of how those men had betrayed him, how they meant to kill him and tidy up all their problems, gave him the determination he needed.

After Dorman added the activation hormone and the self-perpetuating carrier fluid, the prototypes were supposed to adapt, reset their programming.

With a small *whumpp*, a Molotov cocktail exploded in the lobby, and then came running feet. He heard hushed voices in quiet discussion that sounded cool and professional—a contrast to the chanting and yelling that continued outside, the protests Dorman knew were staged.

Quickly, silently, Dorman injected himself, just before David Kennessy returned to his side. Now the lead researcher finally looked afraid, and with good reason.

Four of the gunshots struck Kennessy in the chest, driving him backward into the lab tables. Then the DyMar building erupted into flames—much faster than Jeremy Dorman could have imagined.

He tried to escape, but even as he fled, the flames swept along, closing in on him as the walls ignited. The shock wave of another large explosion pummeled him against one of the concrete basement walls. The stairwell became a chute of fire, searing his skin. He had watched his flesh bubble and blacken. Dorman shouted with outrage at the betrayal...

Now he awoke screaming under the bridge. The echoes of his outcry vibrated against the river water, ricocheting across the river and up under the bridge.

Dorman hauled himself to his feet. His eyes adjusted to the dim illumination of streetlights and the moon filtering through clouds above. His body twisted and contorted. He could feel the growths squirming in him, seething, taking on a life of their own.

Dorman clenched his teeth, brought his elbows tight against his ribs, struggling to regain control. He breathed heavily through his nostrils. The air was cold and metallic, soured with the memory of burning blood.

As he swayed to his feet, Dorman looked down at the rock embankment where he had slept so fitfully. There he saw the bodies of five pigeons, wings splayed, feathers ruffled, their eyes glassy gray. Their beaks hung open with a trickle of blood curling down from their tongues.

Dorman stared at the dead birds, and his stomach clenched, turning a somersault with nausea. He didn't know what his body had done, how he had lost control during his nightmares. Only the pigeons knew.

A last gray feather drifted to the ground in silence.

Dorman staggered away, climbing up toward the road. He had to get out of Portland. He had to find his quarry, find the dog, before it was too late for any of them.

TWELVE

Main Post Office
Milwaukie, Oregon
Wednesday, 10:59 a.m.

Mulder didn't feel at all nondescript or unnoticeable as he and Scully stood in the lobby of the main post office. They moved back and forth, pretending to wait in line, then going back to the counter and filling out unnecessary Express Mail forms. The postal officials at the counter watched them warily.

All the while, Scully and Mulder kept their eyes on the wall of covered cubbyholes, numbered post office boxes, especially number 3733. Each box looked like a tiny prison cubicle.

Every time a new customer walked in and marched toward the appropriate section of boxes, he and Scully exchanged a glance. They tensed, then relaxed, as person after person failed to fit the description, went to the wrong cubbyhole, or simply conducted routine post office business, oblivious to the FBI surveillance.

Finally, after about an hour and twenty minutes of stakeout, a gaunt man pushed open the heavy glass door and moved directly to the wall of P.O. boxes. His face was lean, his head completely shaven and glistening as if he used furniture polish every morning. His chin, though, held an explosion of black bristly beard. His eyes were sunken, his cheekbones high and protruding.

"Scully, that's him," he said. Mulder had seen various photos of Alphonse Gurik in his criminal file—but previously he had had long hair and no beard. Still, the effect was the same.

Scully gave a brief nod, then flicked her eyes away so as not to draw the man's suspicions. Mulder nonchalantly picked up a colorful brochure describing the Postal Service's selection of stamps featuring famous sports figures, raising his eyebrows in feigned interest.

The National Crime Information Center had rapidly and easily completed their analysis of the letter claiming responsibility for the destruction of the DyMar Lab. Liberation Now had mailed their note on a piece of easily trace- able stationery, written by hand in block letters and sporting two smudged fingerprints. *Sloppy.* The whole thing had been sloppy and amateurish.

NCIC and the FBI crime lab had studied the note, using handwriting analysis and fingerprint identification. This man, Alphonse Gurik—who had no permanent address—had been involved in many causes for many outspoken protest groups. His rap sheet had listed name after name of organi- zations that sounded so outrageous they couldn't possibly exist. Gurik had written the letter claiming responsibility for the destruction and arson at DyMar.

But already Mulder had expressed his doubts. After visiting the burned DyMar site, it was clear to both of them that this had been a professional job, eerily precise and coldly destructive. Alphonse Gurik seemed to be a rank amateur, perhaps deluded, certainly sincere. Mulder didn't think him capable of what had happened at DyMar.

As the man reached for P.O. Box 3733, spun his combination, and opened the little window to withdraw his mail, Scully nodded at Mulder. They both moved forward, reaching into their overcoats to withdraw their ID wallets.

"Mr. Alphonse Gurik," she said in a firm, uncompromising voice, "we're federal agents, and we are placing you under arrest."

The bald man whirled, dropped his mail in a scattershot on the floor, and then slammed his back against the wall of boxes.

"I didn't do anything!" he said, his face stricken with terror. He raised his hands in total surrender. "You've got no right to arrest me."

The other customers in the post office backed away, fascinated and afraid. Two workers at the counter leaned forward and craned their necks so they could see better.

Scully withdrew the folded piece of paper from her inner pocket. "This is an arrest warrant with your name on it. We have identified you as the author of a letter claiming responsibility for the fire and explosion at DyMar Labora- tory, which resulted in the deaths of two researchers."

"But, but—" Gurik's face paled. A thread of spittle connected his lips as he tried to find the appropriate words.

Mulder came forward and grabbed the bald man's arm after removing a set of handcuffs from his belt. Scully hung back, keeping herself in a bladed position, ready and prepared for any unexpected action from the prisoner. An FBI agent always had to be prepared no matter now submissive a detainee might appear.

"We're always happy to hear your side of this, Mr. Gurik," Mulder said. He took advantage of Gurik's shock to bring the man's arms down and cuff his wrists behind him. Scully read the memorized set of Miranda rights, which Alphonse Gurik seemed to know very well already.

According to his file, this man had been arrested seven times already on minor vandalism and protest charges—throwing rocks through windows or spray-painting misspelled threats on the headquarters buildings of companies he didn't like. Mulder gauged him to be a principled man, well-read in his field. Gurik had the courage to stand up for what he believed in, but he gave over his beliefs a little too easily.

As Mulder turned the prisoner around, escorting him toward the glass door, Scully bent down to retrieve Gurik's scattered mail. They ushered him outside.

It took thirty seconds, almost like clockwork, until Gurik began to babble, trying to make excuses. "Okay, I sent the letter! I admit it, I sent the letter—but I didn't burn anything. I didn't kill anybody. I didn't blow up that building."

Mulder thought he was probably telling the truth. Gurik's previous minor pranks had made him a nuisance, but could not be construed as a dry run for the destruction of an entire research facility.

"It's a little convenient to change your story now, isn't it?" Scully said. "Two people are dead, and you'll be up for murder charges. This isn't a few out-of-hand protest activities like the ones you've been arrested for in the past."

"I was just a protester. We picketed DyMar a few times in the past… but suddenly the whole place just exploded! Everybody was running and screaming, but I didn't do anything wrong!"

"So why did you write the letter?" Mulder asked.

"Somebody had to take responsibility," Gurik said. "I kept waiting, but nobody sent any letters, nobody took credit. It was a terrible tragedy, yeah! But the whole scene would have been pointless if nobody announced what we were protesting against. I thought we were trying to free all those lab animals, that's why I sent the letter…

"Some of us got together on this, a few different independent groups. There was this one guy who really railed against the stuff at DyMar—he even drafted the letter to the paper and made sure we all had a copy before the protest. He showed us videotapes, smuggled reports. You wouldn't believe what they were doing to the lab animals. You should have seen what they did to that poor dog."

Scully crossed her arms over her chest. "So what happened to this man?"

"We couldn't even find him again—he must have turned chicken after all. So I sent the letter myself. Somebody had to. The world has to know."

Outside the post office, Gurik looked desperately toward an old woody station wagon with peeling paint, touched up with spots of primer coat.

Boxes of leaflets, maps, newspaper clippings, and other literature crammed the worn seats of the station wagon. Bumper stickers and decals cluttered the car body and rear. One of the car's windshield wipers had broken off, Mulder saw, but at least it was on the passenger side.

"I didn't burn anything, though," Gurik insisted fervently. "I didn't even throw rocks. We just shouted and held our signs. I don't know who threw the firebombs. It wasn't me."

"Why don't you explain to us about Liberation Now?" Mulder asked, falling into the routine. "How do they fit into this?"

"It's just an organization I made up. Really! It's not an official group—there aren't even any members but me. I can make any group I want. I've done it before. Lots of activists were there that night, other groups, people I'd never seen before."

"So who set up the protest at DyMar?" Scully said.

"I don't know." Still pressed against the side of his car, Gurik twisted his head over his other shoulder to look at her. "We have connections, you know. All of us activist groups. We talk. We don't always agree, but when we can join forces it's stronger.

"I think the DyMar protest was pulled together by leaders of a few smaller groups that included animal rights activists, genetic engineering protesters, industrial labor organizations, and even some fundamentalist religious groups. Of course, with all my work in the past they wouldn't dare leave me out."

"No, of course not," Mulder said. He had hoped Gurik would be able to lead them toward other members of Liberation Now, but it appeared that he was the sole member of his own little splinter group.

The violent protesters had materialized promptly, with no known leaders and no prior history, conveniently turned into a mob that burned the facility down and destroyed all records and research… then evaporated without a trace. Whoever had engineered the bloody protest had so smoothly pulled together the various groups that even their respective members didn't know they were being herded to the same place at the same time.

Mulder thought it was very clear that the entire incident had been staged. "What were you fighting against at DyMar?" Scully said.

Gurik raised his eyebrows, indignant. "What do you mean, what were we fighting against? The horrible animal research, of course! It's a medical facility. You've got to know what scientists do in places like that."

"No," Scully said, "I don't know. What I do know is that they were trying to find medical breakthroughs that would help people. People dying of cancer."

Gurik snorted and turned his head. "Yeah, as if animals have any less right to a peaceful existence than humans do! By what standard do we torture animals so that humans can live longer?"

Scully blinked at Mulder in disbelief. How could you argue with someone like this?

"Actually," Mulder said, "our investigation hasn't turned up evidence of any animal experimentation beyond the lab rat stage."

"What?" Gurik said. "You're lying."

Mulder turned to Scully, cutting the protester off. "I think he's been set up, Scully. This guy doesn't know anything. Someone wanted to destroy DyMar and David Kennessy, while transferring the blame elsewhere."

Scully raised her eyebrows. "Who would want to do that, and why?"

Mulder looked hard at her. "I think Patrice Kennessy knows the answer to that question, and that's why she's in trouble."

Scully looked pained at the mention of the missing woman. "We've got to find Patrice and Jody," she said. "I suggest we question the missing brother, Darin, as well. The boy himself can't be too hard to find. If he's weak from his cancer treatments, he'll need medical attention soon. We've got to get to him."

"Cancer treatments!" Gurik exploded. "Do you know how they develop those things? Do you know what they do?" He growled in his throat as if he wanted to spit. "You should see the surgeries, the drugs, the apparatuses they hook to those poor little animals. Dogs and cats, anything that got lost and picked up on the streets."

"I'm aware of how... difficult cancer treatments can be," Scully said coldly, thinking of what she herself had endured, how the treatment had been nearly as lethal as the cancer itself.

But she had no patience for this now. "Some research is necessary to help people in the future. I don't condone excessive pain or malicious treatment of animals, but the research helps humans, helps find other methods of curing terminal diseases. I'm sorry, but I cannot sympathize with your attitude or your priorities."

Gurik twisted around enough so that he could look directly at her. "Yeah, and you don't think they're experimenting on humans, too?" His eyes were not panicky now, but burning with rage. He nodded knowingly at her. The skin on his shaven head wrinkled like leather.

"They're sadistic bastards," he said. "You wouldn't say that if you knew how some of the research was conducted!" He drew a deep breath. "You haven't seen the things I have."

THIRTEEN

Federal Office Building
Crystal City, Virginia
Wednesday, 11:30 a.m.

In a nondescript office with few furnishings, Adam Lentz sat at his government-issue desk and pondered the videotape in front of him. The tape still smelled of smoke from the DyMar fire, and he was anxious to play it.

Lentz's name wasn't stenciled on the office door, nor did he have a plaque on the new desk, none of the trappings of importance or power. Useless trappings. Adam Lentz had many titles, many positions, which he could adopt and use at his convenience. He simply had to select whichever role would allow him best to complete his real job.

The office had plain white walls, an interior room with no windows, no blinds—no means for anyone else to spy on him. The federal building itself sported completely unremarkable architecture, just another generic government building full of beehive offices for the unfathomable business of a sprawling bureaucracy.

Each evening, after working hours, Crystal City became a ghost town as federal employees—clerks and paper pushers and filing assistants—rushed home to Gaithersburg, Georgetown, Annapolis, Silver Spring… leaving much of the area uninhabited. Lentz often stayed late just to witness the patterns of human tribal behavior.

Part of his role in the unnamed government office had been to oversee David and Darin Kennessy's research at DyMar Laboratory. Other groups at the California Institute of Technology, NASA Ames, the Institute for Molecular Manufacturing—even Mitsubishi's Advanced Technology Research and Development Center in Japan—had forged ahead with their attempts. But the Kennessys had experienced a few crucial lucky breaks—or made shrewd decisions—and Lentz knew DyMar was the most likely site for a breakthrough.

He had followed the work, seen the brothers' remarkable progress, egged them on, and held them back. Some of the earlier experiments on rats and small lab animals had been amazing—and some had been horrific. Those initial samples and prototypes had all been confiscated and, he hoped, destroyed. But David Kennessy, who had kept working even after his brother left, had proved too successful for his own good. Things had gotten out of control, and Kennessy hadn't even seen it coming.

Lentz hoped the confiscated tape had not been damaged in the cleansing fire that had obliterated DyMar. His clean-up teams had scoured the wreckage for any evidence, any intact samples or notes, and they had found the hidden fire safe, removed its contents, and brought the tape to him.

He swiveled a small portable TV/VCR that he had set on his desk and plugged into a floor socket. He closed and locked his office door, but left the lights on, harsh and flickering fluorescent fixtures in the ceiling. He sat back in his standard-issue desk chair—he wasn't one for extravagant amenities—and popped the tape into the player. He had heard about an extraordinary tape, but he had never personally seen it. After adjusting the tracking and the volume, Lentz sat back to watch.

In the clean and brightly lit lab, the dog paced inside his cage, an enclosure designed for larger animals. He whined twice with an uncertain twitch of his tail, as if hoping for a quick end to his confinement.

"Good boy, Vader," David Kennessy said, moving across the camera's field of view. "Just sit."

Kennessy paced the room, running a hand through his dark hair, brushing aside a film of perspiration on his forehead. Oh, he was nervous, all right—acting cocky, doing his best to look confident. Darin Kennessy— perhaps the smarter brother—had abandoned the research and gone to ground half a year before. But David hadn't been so wise. He had continued to push.

People were very interested in what this team had accomplished, and he obviously felt he had to prove it with a videotape. Kennessy didn't know, though, that the success would be his own downfall. He had proven too much, and he had frightened the people who had never really believed he could do it.

But Lentz knew the researcher's own son was dying, which might have tempted him into taking unacceptable risks. That was dangerous.

Kennessy adjusted the camera himself, shoving his hand in the field of view, jittering the image. Beside him, near the dog's cage, the big-shouldered technical assistant, Jeremy Dorman, stood like Igor next to his beloved Frankenstein.

"All right," Kennessy said into the camcorder's microphone. A lot of white noise buzzed in the background, diagnostic equipment, air filters, the rattle of small lab rodents in their own cages. "Tonight, you're in for a *rilly big shew!*"

As if anybody remembered Ed Sullivan, Lentz thought.

Kennessy postured in front of the camera. "I've already filed my data, sent my detailed documentation. My initial rodent tests showed the amazing potential. But those progress reports either went unread, or at least were not understood. I'm tired of having my memos disappear in your piles of paper. Considering that this breakthrough will change the universe as we know it, I'd think somebody might want to give up a coffee break to have a look."

Oh no, Dr. Kennessy, Lentz thought as he watched, *your reports didn't disappear. We paid a great deal of attention.*

"They're management boobs, David," Dorman muttered. "You can't expect them to understand what they're funding." Then he covered his mouth, as if appalled that he had made such a comment within range of the camcorder's microphone.

Kennessy glanced at his watch, then over at Dorman. "Are you prepared, Herr Dorman?"

The big lab assistant fidgeted, rested his hand on the wire cage. The black Lab poked his muzzle against Dorman's palm, snuffling. Dorman practically leaped out of his skin.

"Are you sure we should do this?" he asked.

Kennessy looked at his assistant with an expression of pure scorn. "No, Jeremy. I want to just give up, shelve the work, and let Jody die. Maybe I should retire and become a CPA."

Dorman raised both hands in embarrassed surrender. "All right, all right—just checking."

In the background, on one of the poured-concrete basement walls, a poster showed Albert Einstein handing a candle to someone few people would recognize by sight—K. Eric Drexler; Drexler, in turn, was extending a candle toward the viewer. *Come on, take it!*

Drexler had been one of the first major visionaries behind genetic engineering some years before.

Too bad we couldn't have gotten to him soon enough, Lentz thought.

Vader looked expectantly at his master, then sat down in the middle of his cage. His tail thumped on the floor. "Good boy," Kennessy muttered.

Jeremy Dorman went out of range, then returned a few moments later holding a handgun, a clunky but powerful Smith & Wesson. According to records Lentz had easily obtained, Dorman himself had gone into a Portland gun shop and purchased the weapon with cash. At least the handgun hadn't come out of their funding request.

Kennessy spoke again to the camera as his assistant sweated. Dorman looked down at the handgun, then over at the caged dog.

"What I am about to show you will be shocking in the extreme. I shouldn't need to add the disclaimer that this is real, with no special effects, no artificial preparations." He crossed his arms and stared firmly into the camera eye. "My intention is to jar you so thoroughly that you are ready to question all your preconceptions."

He turned to Dorman. "Gridley, you may fire when ready."

Dorman looked confused, as if wondering who Kennessy meant, then he raised the Smith & Wesson. His Adam's apple bobbed up and down, exhibiting his nervousness. He pointed the gun at the dog.

Vader sensed something was wrong. He backed up as far as he could in the cage, then growled loud and low. His dark eyes met Dorman's, and he bared his fangs.

Dorman's hand began to shake. Kennessy's eyes flared. "Come on, Jeremy, dammit! Don't make this any worse than it is."

Dorman fired twice. The gunshots sounded thin and tinny on the video-tape. Both bullets hit the big black dog, and the impact smashed him into the mesh of the cage. One shot struck Vader's rib cage; another shattered his spine. Blood flew out from the bullet holes, drenching his fur.

Vader yelped and then sat down from the impact. He panted.

Dorman looked stupidly down at the handgun. "My God!" he muttered. "The animal rights activists would crucify us, David."

But Kennessy didn't allow the silence to hang on the tape. He stepped forward, delivering his rehearsed speech. He was running this show. Melodramatic though it might seem, he knew it would work.

"My medical breakthrough opens the doorway to numerous other applications. That's why so many people have been working on it for so long. The first researchers to make this breakthrough work are going to shake up society like you won't be able to imagine." Kennessy sounded as if he was giving a speech to a board of directors, while his pet dog lay shot and bleeding in his cage.

Lentz had to admire a man like that. He nodded to himself and leaned forward, closer to the television. He rested his elbows on the desktop. *All the more reason to make sure the technology is tightly controlled, and released only when we deem it necessary.*

On the screen, Kennessy turned to the cage, looking down with clinical detachment. "After a major trauma like this, the first thing that happens is that the nanocritters shut down all of the dog's pain centers."

In his cage, Vader sat, confused. His tongue lolled out. He had clumsily managed to prop himself upright. The dog seemed not to notice the gaping holes in his back. After a moment, the black Lab lay down on the floor of the cage, squishing his fur in the blood still running along his sides. His eyes grew heavy, and he sank down in deep sleep, resting his head on his front paws. He took a huge breath and released it slowly.

Kennessy knelt down on the floor beside the cage, reached his hand in to pat Vader on the head. "His temperature is already rising from the waste heat.

Look, the blood has stopped flowing. Jeremy, get the camera over here so we can have a close-up."

Dorman looked befuddled, then scurried over to grab the camera. The view on the videotape rocked and shook, then came into focus on the dog, zooming in on the injuries. Kennessy let the images speak for themselves for a moment, before he picked up the thread of his lecture.

"A large-scale physical trauma like this is actually easier to fix than a wide-spread disease, like cancer. A gunshot injury needs a bit of patchwork, cellular bandages, and some reconstruction.

"With a genetic disease, though, each cell must be repaired, every anomaly tweaked and adjusted. Purging a cancer patient might take weeks or months. These bullet wounds, though—" He gestured down at the motionless black Lab. "Well, Vader will be up chasing squirrels again tomorrow."

Dorman looked down in amazement and disbelief. "If this gets to the newspapers, David, we're all out of a job."

"I don't think so," Kennessy answered, and smiled. "I'll bet you a box of dog biscuits."

Within an hour, the dog woke up again, groggy but rapidly recovering. Vader stood up in the cage, shook himself, then barked. Healthy. Healed. As good as new. Kennessy released him from the cage, and the dog bounded out, starved for attention and praise. Kennessy laughed out loud and ruffled his fur.

Lentz watched in astonishment, understanding now that Kennessy's work was even more frightening, even more successful than he had feared. His people had been absolutely right to take the samples, lock them away, and then destroy all the remaining evidence.

If something like this became available to the general public, he couldn't conceive of the earth-shattering consequences. No, everything had to be destroyed.

Lentz popped out the videotape and locked it within a repository for classified documents. The fire safe at DyMar had protected this tape and the other documents with it, but unfortunately he knew with a grim certainty that they had not recovered every scrap, every sample.

Now, after all he had seen, Lentz finally understood the frantic phone call they had tapped, when David Kennessy had dialed his home number on the night of the explosive protest, on the night of the fire.

Kennessy's voice had been frantic, ragged. He didn't even let his wife speak. "Patrice, take Jody and Vader and get out of there—*now*! Everything I was afraid of is going down. You have to run. I'm already trapped at DyMar, but you can get away. Keep running. Don't let them… get you."

Then the phone recording was cut off before Kennessy or his wife could say anything else. Patrice Kennessy had listened to her husband, had acted quickly. By the time the clean-up teams got to their suburban house, she had packed up with the boy and the dog, and vanished.

After seeing the videotape, Lentz realized what a grave mistake he had made. Before, he had worried that Patrice might have a few notes, some research information that Lentz needed to retrieve. Now, though, the danger had increased by orders of magnitude.

How could he have missed it before? The dog wasn't just a family pet that the Kennessys couldn't bear to leave behind. That black Lab *was* the dog. It was the research animal, it carried the nanomachines inside its bloodstream, lurking there, just waiting to spread around the world.

Lentz swallowed hard and grabbed for the phone. After a moment, though, he froze and gently set the receiver back in the cradle. This was not a mistake he wanted to admit to the man in charge. He would take care of it himself.

Everything else had been destroyed in the DyMar fire—but now Adam Lentz had to call in all of his resources, get reinforcements, spend whatever time or money was necessary.

He had a woman, a boy, and, especially, their pet dog to track down.

FOURTEEN

Kennessys' Cabin
Coast Range, Oregon
Wednesday, 1:10 p.m.

The midday sunlight dappled the patches in the Oregon hills where the trees had been shaved in strips from clearcut logging. Patrice and Jody sat by the table in the living room with the curtains open and the lights switched off, working on a thousand-piece jigsaw puzzle they had found in one of the cedar window seats.

The two of them had finished a lunch of cold sandwiches and an old bag of potato chips that had gone stale in the damp air. Jody never complained. Patrice was just glad her son had an appetite again. His mysterious remission was remarkable, but she couldn't allow herself to hope. Soon, she dreaded, the blush of health would fade, and Jody would resume his negotiations with the Grim Reaper.

But still, she clung to every moment with him. Jody was all she had left.

Now the two of them hunched over the scattered puzzle pieces. When finished, the image would show the planet Earth rising over lunar crags, as photographed by one of the Apollo astronauts. The blue-green sphere covered most of the small wooden table, with jagged gaps from a few continents not yet filled in.

They weren't having much fun, barely even occupying their minds. They were just killing time.

Patrice and Jody talked little, in the shared silence of two people who'd had only their own company for many days. They could get by with partial sentences, cryptic comments, private jokes. Jody reached forward with a jagged piece of the Antarctic ice cap, turning it to see how the interlocking pieces fit in.

"Have you ever known somebody who went to Antarctica, Mom?" Jody asked.

Patrice forced a smile. "That's not exactly on the standard tour list, kid."

"Did Dad ever go there? For his research? Or Uncle Darin?"

She froze her face before a troubled frown could pass over her features. "You mean to test out a new medical treatment on, say, penguins? Or polar bears?" *Why not? He had tested it on Vader…*

"Polar bears live at the *North* Pole, Mom." Jody shook his head with mock scorn. "Get your data right."

Sometimes he sounded just like his father.

She had explained to her son why they had to hide from the outside world, why they had to wait until they learned some answers and discovered who had been behind the destruction of DyMar.

Darin had split from his brother after a huge fight about the dangers of their research, about the edge they were skirting. He had walked away from DyMar, sold his home, left this vacation cabin to rot, and joined an isolated group of survivalists in the Oregon wilds. From that point on, David had spoken of Darin with scorn, dismissing the usual misguided complaints by Luddite groups, like the one his brother had joined.

Darin had insisted they would be in danger as soon as more people found out about their research, but somehow David could not believe anybody but the technically literate would understand how significant a breakthrough he had made. "It's always nice to see that some people understand more than you give them credit for," David answered. "But I wouldn't count on it."

But Patrice knew he was naive. True, this wasn't the type of thing ordinary people got up in arms about—it was too complicated and required too much foresight to see how the world would change, to sort the dangers they feared from the miracles he offered. But some people were paying attention. Darin had had good reason to fear, good reason to run. Patrice's question now was who was orchestrating all this?

The demonstrators outside DyMar consisted of an odd mix of religious groups, labor union representatives, animal-rights activists, and who knew what else. Some were fruitcakes, some were violent. Her husband had died there, with only a crisp warning for her. *Go. Get away! Don't let them catch you. They'll be after you.*

Hoping it was just a temporary emergency, a flareup of destructive demonstrators, she had thrown Jody and the dog into their car, driving aimlessly for hours. She had seen the DyMar fire blazing on the distant bluff, and she feared the worst. Still not grasping the magnitude of the conspiracy, she had rushed home, hoping to find David there, hoping he had at least left her a message.

Instead, their place had been ransacked. People searching for something, searching for *them*. Patrice had run, taking only a few items they needed, using her wits and her fear as they raced away from Tigard, away from the Portland metropolitan area, into the deep wilderness.

She had swapped license plates several times in darkened parking lots, waited until near midnight and then grabbed a day's maximum cash from an ATM in downtown Eugene, Oregon; she had driven across town to another ATM, after midnight this time and therefore a new date, and gotten a second day's maximum. Then she had fled for the coast, for Darin's old, abandoned cabin, where she and Jody could go to ground, for however long it took for them to feel safe again.

For years she had worked freelance as an architect, doing her designs from home, especially in the last few months when Jody became more and more ill from his cancer and—worse—from the conventional chemo and radiation treatments themselves.

Patrice had designed this little hideaway as a favor for her brother-in-law several years ago. With rented equipment, Darin had installed the electricity himself, graded the driveway, cut down a few trees, but never gotten around to making it much of a vacation home. He had been too swallowed up in his eight-days-a-week research efforts. Corrupted by David, no doubt.

No one else would know about this place, no one would think to look for them here, in an unused vacation home built years ago for a brother who had disappeared half a year previously. It should have been a perfect place for her and Jody to catch their breath, to plan their next step.

But now the dog had disappeared, too. Vader had been Jody's last remaining sparkle of joy, his anchor during the chaos. The black Lab had been so excited to be out of the suburbs, where he could run through the forest. He had been a city dog for so long, fenced in; suddenly he had been turned loose in the Oregon forests.

She wasn't surprised that Vader had run off, but she always expected him to come home. She should have kept him on a rope—but how could she bear to do that, when she and her son were already trapped here? Prisoners in hiding? Patrice had been so afraid, she had stripped away the dog's ID tag. Now if Vader were caught, or injured somehow, there would be no way to get them back together—and no way to track them down.

Jody had taken it hard, trying his best to keep his hopes up. His every thought was a wish for his dog to return. Apart from his gloom, he looked increasingly healthy now; most of his hair had grown back after the leukemia therapies. His energy level was higher than it had been in a long time. He looked like a normal kid again.

But his sadness over Vader was like an open sore. After every piece he placed in the Earth-Moon jigsaw puzzle, he glanced through the dingy curtains over the main windows, searching the treeline.

Suddenly he jumped up. "Mom, he's back!" Jody shouted, pushing away from his chair.

For a moment, Patrice reacted with alarm, thinking of the hunters, wondering who could have found them, how she might have given them away. But then, through the open screen door, she could hear the dog barking.

She stood up from the puzzle table, astonished to see the black Labrador bounding out of the trees.

Jody leaped away from the table and bolted out the door. He ran toward the black dog so hard she expected her son to sprawl on his face on the gravel driveway or trip on a stump or fallen branch in the yard.

"Jody, be careful!" she called. Just what she needed—if the boy broke his arm, that would ruin everything. So far, she had managed to avoid all contact with doctors and any people who kept names and records.

Jody remained oblivious to everything but his excitement over the dog.

The boy reached his dog safely, and each tried to outdo the other's enthusiasm. Vader barked and danced around in circles, leaping into the air. Jody threw his arms around the dog's neck and wrestled him to the wet ground in a tumble of black fur, pale skin, and weeds.

Dripping and grass-stained, Jody raced Vader back to the cabin. Patrice wiped her hands on a kitchen towel and came out to the porch to greet him. "I told you he'd be okay," she said.

Idiotically happy, Jody nodded and then stroked the dog.

Patrice bent over and ran her fingers through the black fur. The wedding ring, still on her finger, stood out among the dark strands. The black Lab had a difficult time standing still for her, shifting on all four paws and letting his tongue loll out. His tail wagged like an out-of-control rudder, rocking his body off balance on his four paws.

Other than mud spatters and a few cockleburrs, she found nothing amiss. No injuries, no wounds. Not a mark on him.

She patted the dog's head, and Vader rolled his deep brown eyes up at her. With a shake of her head, she said, "I wish you could tell us stories."

FIFTEEN

Hughart's Family Veterinary Clinic
Lincoln City, Oregon
Wednesday, 5:01 p.m.

As they approached the veterinary clinic in the sleepy coastal town of Lincoln City, Scully could hear the barking dogs.

The building was a large old house that had been converted into a business.

The aluminum siding was white, smudged with mildew; the wooden shutters looked as if they needed a coat of paint. The two agents climbed the concrete steps to the main entrance and pushed open a storm door.

On their way to tracking down David Kennessy's survivalist brother, a report from this veterinarian's office had caught Mulder's attention. When Scully had requested a rush analysis of the strange fluid she had taken during the security guard's autopsy, the CDC had immediately recognized a distinct similarity to another sample—also submitted from rural Oregon.

Elliott Hughart had treated a dog, a black Labrador, who was also infected with the same substance. Mulder had been intrigued by the coincidence. Now at least they had someplace to start looking.

In the front lobby, the veterinarian's receptionist looked harried. Other patrons sat in folding chairs around the lobby beside pet carriers. Kittens wrestled in a cage. Dogs whined on their leashes. Posters warned of the hazards of heartworm, feline leukemia, and fleas, next to a magazine rack filled with months-old issues of *Time*, *Cat Fancy*, and *People*.

Mulder flashed his ID as he strode up to the receptionist. "I'm Agent Fox Mulder, Federal Bureau of Investigation. We'd like to see Dr. Hughart, please."

"Do you have an appointment?" The information didn't sink in for a few seconds, then the harried woman blinked at him. "Uh, the *FBI?*"

"We're here to see him about a dog he treated two days ago," Scully said. "He submitted a sample to the Centers for Disease Control."

"I'll get the doctor for you as soon as possible," she said. "I believe he's performing a neutering operation at the moment. Would you like to go into the surgery room and wait?"

Mulder shuffled his feet. "We'll stay out here, thanks."

Three-quarters of an hour later, when Scully had a roaring headache from the noise and chaos of the distressed animals, the old doctor came out. He blinked under bushy gray eyebrows, looking distracted but curious. The FBI agents were easy to spot in the waiting room.

"Please come back to my office," the veterinarian said with a gesture to a small examining room. He closed the door.

A stainless-steel table filled the center of the room, and the smell of wet fur and disinfectants hung in the air. Cabinets containing thermometers and hypodermic needles for treatment of tapeworms, rabies, and distemper sat behind glass doors.

"Now, then," Hughart said in a quiet, gentle voice, but obviously flustered. "I've never had to deal with the FBI before. How can I help you?"

"You submitted a sample to the CDC yesterday from a black Labrador dog you treated," Scully said. "We'd like to ask you a few questions."

Mulder held out a snapshot of Vader that they had taken from the family possessions at the ransacked Tigard home. "Can you identify the dog for us, sir? Is this the one you treated?"

Surprised, the veterinarian raised his eyebrows. "That's almost impossible to tell, just from a photograph like this. But the size and age look about right. Could be the same animal." The old veterinarian blinked. "Is this a criminal matter? Why is the FBI involved?"

Scully withdrew the photos of Patrice and Jody Kennessey. "We're trying to find these two people, and we have reason to believe they are the dog's owners."

The doctor shook his head and shrugged. "They weren't the ones who brought him in. The dog was hit by a car, brought in by a tourist. The man was real anxious to get out of here. Kids were crying in the back of the station wagon. It was late at night. But I treated the dog anyway, though there wasn't much cause for hope." He shook his head. "You can tell when they're about to die. They know it. You can see it in their eyes. But this dog... very strange."

"Strange in what way?" Scully asked.

"The dog was severely injured," the old man said. "Massive damage, broken ribs, shattered pelvis, crushed spine, ruptured internal organs. I didn't expect him to live, and the dog was in a great deal of pain." He distractedly wiped his fingers across the recently cleaned steel table, leaving fingerprint smears.

"I patched him up, but clearly there was no hope. He was hot, his body temperature higher than any fever I've seen in an animal before. That's why I took the blood sample. Never expected what I actually found, though."

Mulder's eyebrows perked up. Scully looked at her partner, then back at the veterinarian. "With severe trauma from a car accident, I wouldn't expect the temperature to rise," she said. "Not if the dog was in shock and entering a coma state."

The doctor nodded his head patiently. "Yes, that's why I was so curious. I believe the animal had some sort of infection before the accident. Perhaps that's why he was so disoriented and got struck by the car." Hughart looked deeply disturbed, almost embarrassed. "When I saw there was no hope, I gave the dog an injection of Euthanol—sodium pentabarbitol—to put him to sleep. Ten ccs, way more than enough for the body mass of a black Lab. It's the only thing to do in cases like that, to put the animal out of its misery… and this dog was in a world of misery."

"Could we see the body of the dog?" Scully asked.

"No." The veterinarian turned away. "I'm afraid that's impossible."

"Why?" Mulder asked.

Hughart looked at them from beneath his bushy gray eyebrows before glancing back down at his scrubbed-clean fingers. "I was working in the lab, studying the fresh blood sample, when I heard a noise. I came in and found that the dog had jumped off the table. I swear its forelegs were broken, its rib cage crushed."

Scully drew back, unable to believe what she was hearing. "And did you examine the dog?"

"I couldn't." Hughart shook his head. "When I tried to get to the dog, it barked at me, turned, then pushed its way through the door. I ran, but that black Lab bounded out into the night, as frisky as if he were just a puppy."

Scully looked at Mulder with eyebrows raised. The veterinarian seemed distracted by his own recollection. He scratched his hair in puzzlement. "I thought I saw a shadow disappearing toward the trees, but I couldn't be sure. I called for it to come back, but that dog knew exactly where he wanted to go."

Scully was astonished. "Are you suggesting that a dog struck by a car, as well as given an injection of concentrated sodium pentabarbitol… was somehow able to leap down from your operating table and run out the door?"

"Quite a lot of stamina," Mulder said.

"Look," the veterinarian said, "I don't have an explanation, but it happened. I guess somehow the dog… wasn't as injured after all. But I can't believe I made a mistake like that. I spent hours searching the woods around here, the streets, the yards. I expected to find the body out in the parking lot or not far from here… but I saw nothing. There've been no reports either. People around here talk about unusual things like that."

Scully changed the subject. "Do you still have the original blood sample from the dog? Could I take a look at it?"

"Sure," the veterinarian said, as if glad for the opportunity to be vindicated. He led the two agents to a small laboratory area where he performed simple tests for worms or blood counts. On one countertop underneath low fluorescent lights stood a bulky stereomicroscope.

Hughart pulled out a slide from a case where a dried smear of blood had turned brown under the cover slip. He inserted the slide under the lens, flicked on the lamp beneath it, and turned the knobs to adjust the lens. The old man stepped back and motioned for Scully to take a look.

"When I first glanced at it," the veterinarian said, "the blood was swarming with those tiny specks. I've never seen anything like it, and in my practice I've encountered plenty of blood-borne parasites in animals. Nematodes, amoebas, other kinds of pests. But these… these were so unusual. That's why I sent the sample to the CDC."

"And they called us." Scully looked down and saw the dog's blood cells, as well as numerous little glints that seemed too angular, too geometrical, unlike any other microorganism she had ever seen.

"When they were moving and alive, those things looked almost… I can't describe it," the old vet said. "They've all stopped now, hibernating somehow. Or dead."

Scully studied the specks and could not understand them either. Mulder waited patiently at her side, and she finally let him take a look. He looked at her knowingly.

Scully turned to the veterinarian. "Thank you for your time, Dr. Hughart. We may be back in touch. If you find any information on the location of the dog or its owners, please contact us."

"But what is this?" the doctor asked, following as Scully led Mulder toward the door. "And what prompted an FBI follow-up?"

"It's a missing persons case," Mulder said, "and there's some urgency."

The two agents made their way out through the reception area, where they encountered a different assortment of cats and dogs and cages. Several of the examining room doors were closed, and strange sounds came from behind them.

The veterinarian seemed reluctant to get back to his routine chaos of yowling animals, lingering in the door to watch them go down the steps.

Mulder held his comments until they had climbed back in the car, ready to drive off again. "Scully, I think the Kennessys were doing some very unorthodox research at DyMar Lab."

"I admit, it's some kind of strange infection, Mulder, but that doesn't mean—"

"Think about it, Scully." His eyes gleamed. "If DyMar developed some sort of amazing regenerative treatment, David might well have tested it on the pet dog." Scully bit her lip. "With his son's condition, he would have been desperate enough for just about anything."

She slumped into the seat and buckled her seatbelt. "But, Mulder, what kind of treatment could heal a dog from disastrous injuries after a car accident, then neutralize the effects of sodium pentabarbitol designed to put the dog to sleep?"

"Maybe something in the combined expertise of Darin and David Kennessy," Mulder said, and started the car.

She unfolded the state highway map, looking for the next stopping point on their search: the vicinity where Darin Kennessy had gone into hiding. "But, Mulder, if they really developed such a... miracle cure, why would Darin have abandoned the research? Why would someone want to blow up the lab and destroy all the records?"

Mulder eased out of the parking lot and waited as a string of RVs drove along the Coast Highway, before he turned right and followed the road through the small picturesque town. He thought of the dead security guard, the rampant and unexplained growths, the slime. "Maybe all of DyMar's samples weren't so successful. Maybe something much worse got loose."

Scully looked at the road ahead. "We've got to find that dog, Mulder." Without answering, he accelerated the car.

SIXTEEN

Mercy Hospital Morgue
Portland, Oregon
Thursday, 2:04 a.m.

Some people might have thought being alone in a morgue late at night would be frightening—or at least cause for some uneasiness. But Edmund found the silent and dimly lit hospital the best place to study. He had hours of quiet solitude, and he had his medical books, as well as popularized versions of true crime and coroner's work.

Someday he hoped to get into medical school himself and study forensic medicine. The subject fascinated him. Eventually, if he worked hard, he might become at least a first or second assistant to the county medical examiner, Frank Quinton. That was the highest goal Edmund thought he could reach.

Studying was somewhat hard for him, and he knew that medical school would be an enormous challenge. That was why he hoped to learn as much as he could on his own, looking at the pictures and diagrams, boning up on the details before he got a chance to enter college.

After all, Abraham Lincoln had been a self-educated man, hadn't he? Nothing wrong with it, no way, no how. And Edmund had the time and the concentration and the ambition to learn as much as he could.

Fluorescent lights shone in white pools around him on the clean tile floor, the white walls. The steel and chrome gleamed. The air vents made a sound like the soft breath of a peacefully sleeping man. The hospital corridors were silent. No intercom, no elevator bell, no footsteps from crepe-soled shoes walking down the halls.

He was all alone down here in the morgue on the night shift—and he liked it that way.

Edmund flipped pages in one of his medical texts, refreshing his memory as to the difference between a perforating and a penetrating wound. In a penetrating wound, the bullet simply passed into the body and remained there, while in a perforating wound, the bullet plowed through the other side, usually tearing out a larger chunk of flesh in the exit wound, as opposed to the neat round entry hole.

Edmund scratched the bald top of his head as he read the distinction over and over again, trying to keep the terms straight. On another page, he analyzed gunshot diagrams, saw dotted lines indicating the passage of bullets through the body cavity, how one course could be instantly fatal while another could be easily healed.

At least it was quiet here so he could concentrate, and when Edmund finally got all of the explanations clear in his mind, they usually stayed in place. The back of his head throbbed with a tension headache, but Edmund didn't want to get more coffee or take aspirin. He would think his way through it.

Just when he thought he was on the verge of a revelation, ready to grin with exhilarated triumph, he heard something moving… stirring.

Edmund perked up, squaring his shoulders and looking around the room. Only a week before, another morgue attendant had told him a whopper about a cadaver—a man decapitated in an auto accident—that had supposedly gotten up and walked out of the Allegheny Catholic Medical Center. One of the lights flickered in the left corner, but Edmund saw no shambling, headless corpses… or any other manifestations of ridiculous urban legends.

He stared at the dying bulb, realizing that its strobe-light pattern was distracting him. He sighed and jotted a little note for the maintenance crew. Maintenance had already double-checked the temperature in the refrigerator drawers, had added more freon, and claimed that everything in the small vaults—including 4E—was exactly the way it should be.

Hearing no further sound, Edmund turned the page and flipped to another chapter about the various types of trauma that could be inflicted by blunt weapons.

Then he noticed the sound of movement again—a brushing, stirring… and then a loud *thump*.

Edmund sat bolt upright, blinking repeatedly. He knew this wasn't his imagination, no way, no how. He had worked here in the morgue long enough that he didn't get easily spooked by sounds of settling buildings or whirring support machinery.

Another thump. Something striking metal.

He stood up, trying to determine the source of the noise. He wondered if someone was hurt, or if some sinister lurker had slipped into the quiet morgue… but why? Edmund had been at his station for the previous three hours and he had heard nothing, seen nothing. He could remember everyone who had entered the place.

Again, he heard a pounding, and a thump, and a scraping. There was no pretense of quiet at all anymore. Someone hammered inside a chamber, growing more frantic.

Edmund scuttled to the rear of the room with growing dread—in his heart, he knew where he would find the source of the noise. One of the refrigerator drawers—one of the drawers that contained a cadaver.

He had read horror stories in school, especially Edgar Allan Poe, about premature burials, people not actually dead. He had heard spooky stories about comatose victims slammed into morgue refrigerators until they died from the cold rather than their own injuries—patients who had been misdiagnosed, in a diabetic shock or epileptic seizures that gave all the appearance of death.

From his limited medical expertise, Edmund had dismissed each of these anecdotal examples as urban legends, old wives' tales… but right now there could be no mistaking it.

Someone was pounding from the *inside* of one of the refrigerator doors. He went over, listening. "Hello!" he shouted. "I'll get you out." It was the least he could do.

A RESTRICTED sign marked the drawer making the sounds, yellow tape, and a BIOHAZARD symbol. Drawer 4E. This one contained the body of the dead security guard, and Edmund knew the blotched, lumpy, slime-covered corpse had been inside the drawer for days. *Days!* Agent Scully had even performed an autopsy on the man.

This guy could not still be alive.

The restless noises fell quiet after his shout, then he heard a stirring, almost like… rats crawling within the walls.

Edmund swallowed hard. Was this a prank, someone trying to spook him? People picked on him often, called him a geek.

If this was a joke, he would get even with them.

But if someone needed help, Edmund had to take the chance.

"Are you in there?" he said, leaning closer to the sealed refrigerator door. "I'll let you out." He pressed his white lips together to squeeze just a little more bravery into his system, and tugged on the handle of 4E.

The door popped open, and something inside tried to push its way free. Something horrible.

Edmund screamed and fought against the door. He saw a strange twisted shape inside the unlit chamber thrashing about, denting the stainless-steel walls. The sliding drawer rocked and rattled.

A fleshy appendage protruded, bending around in ways no jointed limb would ever move… more like a stubby *tentacle*.

Edmund wailed again and used his back to push against the door, squirming out of the way so the groping thing would not be able to touch him. His weight was more than enough to force back the attack. Other protrusions from the body core, twisted lumps that seemed to have been arms or hands at one point, scraped and scrabbled for a hold against the slippery metal door, trying to get in.

A sticky coating of slime, like saliva, drooled from the inside ceiling of the drawer.

Edmund pushed hard enough that the door almost closed. Two of the tentacles and one many-jointed finger were caught in the edge. Other limbs—far too many for the normal complement of arms and legs—flailed and pounded, struggling to get out.

But he heard no sound from vocal chords. No words. No scream of pain. Just frantic movement.

Edmund pushed harder, crushing the pseudo-fingers. Finally they jerked and broke away, yanking themselves back into the relative safety of the refrigerator drawer.

Biting back an outcry, Edmund slammed himself against the steel door, shoving until he heard the latch click and lock into place.

Trembling with a huge sigh of relief, he fiddled with the latch to make sure it was solid. Then he stood in shock, staring at the silent refrigerator drawer.

He had a moment of blessed peace—but then he heard the trapped thing inside pounding about in a frenzy. Edmund shouted at it in panic, "Be quiet in there!"

The best thing he could think of was to rush to the temperature controls, where he dialed the setting as low as it could possibly go—to hard freeze. That would knock the thing down, keep it still. The refrigerators had just been charged, and the freezers would do their work quickly. They were designed to preserve evidence and tissue without any chance of further decay or handling damage.

Inside the coffin-sized drawer, the cold re-circulating air would even now be intense, stunning that thing that had somehow gotten inside where the guard's body was stored.

In a few moments he heard the frantic thrashing begin to subside—but it might have been just a ruse. Edmund wanted to run, but he didn't dare leave. He didn't know what to do. He couldn't think of any other way to deal with the problem. Cold… *cold*. That would freeze the thing.

The thumping and scrabbling slowed, and finally Edmund got up the nerve to hurry to the telephone. He punched a button and called Security.

When two hospital guards eventually came down—already skeptical and taking their sweet time, since they received more false alarms from night-shift morgue attendants than in any other place or any other time in the hospital— the creature inside the drawer had fallen entirely silent. Probably frozen by now.

They laughed at Edmund, thinking it was just his imagination. But he endured their joking for now.

He stood back, unwilling to be anywhere close by when they opened up drawer 4E. He warned them again, but they slid open the drawer anyway.

Their laughter stopped instantly as they stared down at the hideous remains.

SEVENTEEN

Ross Island Bridge
Portland, Oregon
Thursday, 7:18 a.m.

The bridge spread out into the early morning fog. Its vaulted and lacy metal girders disappeared into the mist like an infinite tunnel.

To Jeremy Dorman it was just a route across the Willamette River on his long and stumbling trek out of the city, toward the wilderness… toward where he might find Patrice and Jody Kennessy.

He took another step, then another, weaving. He couldn't feel his feet; they were just lumps of distant flesh at the ends of his legs, which themselves felt rubbery, as if his body were changing, altering, growing joints in odd places.

At the peak of the bridge, he felt suspended in air, though the dawn murk prevented him from seeing the river far below. The city lights of skyscrapers and streetlamps were mere fairy glows.

Dorman staggered along, focusing his mind on the vanishing point, where the bridge disappeared into the fog. His goal was just to get to the other side of the bridge. One step at a time. And after he succeeded in that task, he would set another for himself, and another, until he finally made his way out of Portland.

The wooded coastal mountains—the precious dog—seemed an impossibly long distance away.

The morning air was clammy and cold, but he couldn't feel it, didn't notice his sticky clothes. His skin crawled with gooseflesh, but it had nothing to do with the temperature, just the rampant disaster happening within all of his cells. As a scientist, he should have found it interesting—but as the victim of the change, he found it only horrifying.

Dorman swallowed hard. His throat felt slick, as if clogged with slime, a mucus that oozed from his pores. When he clenched his teeth, they rattled loosely in their gums. His vision carried a black fringe of static around the edges.

He walked onward. He had no other alternative.

A pickup truck roared by on the deck plates of the bridge. The echoes of the engine and the tires throbbed in his ears. He watched the red taillights disappear.

Suddenly Dorman's stomach clenched, his spine whipped about like an angry serpent. He feared he would disintegrate here, slough off into a pool of dissociated flesh and twitching muscles, a gelatinous mass that would drip down beneath the grated walkway of the bridge.

"Noooo!" he cried, a howling inhuman voice in the stillness.

Dorman reached out with one of his slick, waxy hands and grabbed the bridge railing to support himself, willing his body to cease its convulsions. He was losing control again.

It was getting harder and harder to stop his body. All of his biological systems were refusing commands from his mind, taking on a life of their own. He gripped the bridge rail with both hands and squeezed until he thought the steel would bend.

He must have looked like a potential suicide waiting to leap over the edge into the infinite murk of whispering water below—but Dorman had no intention of killing himself. In fact, everything he was doing was a desperate effort to keep himself alive, no matter what. No matter the cost.

He couldn't go to a hospital or seek other medical attention—no doctor in the world would know how to treat his affliction. And any time he reported his name, he might draw the attention of... unwanted eyes. He couldn't risk that. He would have to endure the pain for now.

Finally, when the spasm passed and he felt only weak and trembly, Dorman set off again. His body wouldn't fall apart on him yet. Not yet. But he needed to focus, needed to reestablish the goal in his mind.

He had to find the damned dog.

He reached into his tattered shirt pocket and pawed out the wrinkled, soot-smudged photo he had taken from the broken frame in David Kennessy's desk. Lovely young Patrice with her fine features and strawberry blond hair, and wiry, tousle-haired Jody grinning for the camera. Their expressions reflected the peaceful times before Jody's leukemia, before David's desperate drive for research.

Dorman narrowed his eyes and burned the picture into his brain.

He had been a close friend of the Kennessys. He had been Jody's surrogate uncle, practically a member of the family—far more than the skittish and rude brother Darin, that's for sure. And because he knew her so well, Dorman had a good idea where Patrice would think to hide. She would imagine she was safe there, since Darin had loved his secrets so much.

In the deep pocket of his tattered jacket, the revolver he had taken from the security guard hung like a heavy club.

When he finally reached the far end of the Ross Island Bridge, Dorman stared westward. The forested, fog-shrouded mountains of the coast were a long distance away.

Once he found them, Dorman hoped he could get away with the dog without Patrice or Jody seeing him. He didn't want to have to kill them—hell, the kid was already a skeleton, nearly dead from his leukemia—but he would shoot them, and the dog, too, if it became necessary. In the big picture, it didn't really matter how much he cared for them.

He already had plenty of blood on his hands.

Once again, he cursed David and his naiveté. Darin had understood, and he had run to hide under a rock. But David, hot-headed and desperate to help Jody, had blindly ignored the true sources of funding for their work. Did he really think they were giving DyMar all those millions just so David Kennessy could turn around and decide the morally responsible approach to its use?

David had stumbled into a political minefield, and he had set in motion all the events that had caused so much damage—including Jeremy Dorman's own desperate gambit for survival.

A gambit that was failing. Though the prototype samples had kept him alive at first, now his entire body was falling into a biological meltdown, and he could do nothing about it.

At least, not until he found the dog.

EIGHTEEN

Oregon Coast
Thursday, 12:25 p.m.

Mulder pulled up to the Mini Serve pump in the small, rundown gas station. As he got out of the car, he looked toward the glassed-in office and the tall, unlit CONOCO sign. He half expected to see old men sitting in rocking chairs on the porch, or at least someone coming out to offer Andy Griffith-like hospitality.

Scully got out of the car to stretch. They had been driving for hours up Highway 101, seeing the rugged coastline, small villages, and secluded houses tucked away into the forested hills.

Somewhere out here David Kennessy's brother had joined his isolated group of survivalists, and it was the same general area where the black Lab had been hit by the car. That made too great a coincidence for Mulder's mind. He wanted to find Darin and get some straight answers about the DyMar research. If Darin knew why DyMar had been destroyed, he might also know why Patrice had gone missing.

But further information on the survivalists was vague. The group, by its very nature, kept its exact location secret, without phones or electricity. Finding the camp might be as hard as finding Patrice and Jody.

Mulder popped the gas tank and lifted the nozzle from the pump. Then the office door banged open, but instead of a "service with a smile" attendant, a short potbellied man with a fringe of gray-white hair scuttled out.

"Hey, don't touch that!" the potbellied man snapped, wearing a stormy expression. "This ain't no self-serve."

Mulder looked at the gas nozzle in his hand, then at the Mini Serve sign. The potbellied man came over and grabbed the nozzle out of Mulder's grasp as if it were a dangerous toy in the hands of a child. The man slid the nozzle into the gas tank, squeezed and locked on the handle, then stepped back proudly, as if only a professional could be trusted with such a delicate operation.

"What is the problem, sir?" Scully asked.

The potbellied man glowered at her, then at Mulder, as if they were incredibly stupid. "Damn Californians." He shook his head after glancing at the license plate of their rental car. "This is Oregon. We don't allow amateurs to pump their own gas."

Mulder and Scully looked at each other from across the roof of the car. "Actually, we're not Californians," Mulder said, reaching inside his overcoat. "We're federal agents. We work for the FBI—and I can assure you that pumping gas is one of the rigorous training courses we're required to undergo at Quantico." He flashed his ID and gestured over at Scully. "In fact, Agent Scully here is nearly as qualified as I am to fill up a tank."

The potbellied man looked at Mulder skeptically. His flannel shirt was oil-stained and tattered. His jowls had been shaved intermittently, giving him a rugged, patchy appearance. He didn't seem the type ever to have dirtied his hands with knotting a necktie.

Scully drew out the photo of Patrice and Jody Kennessy. "We're searching for these people," she said. "A woman, mid-thirties, her son, twelve years old."

"Never seen 'em," the man said, then devoted his entire attention to the gas nozzle. On the pump, numbers clicked around and around in circles.

"They're also with a dog," Mulder said, "a black Labrador."

"Never seen 'em," the man repeated.

"You didn't even look at the picture, sir." Scully pushed it closer to his face across the top of the car.

The man looked at it carefully, then turned away again. "Never seen 'em. I got better things to do than to keep my eye on every stranger that comes through here."

Mulder raised his eyebrows. In his mind this man was *exactly* the type who would keep a careful eye on every stranger or customer who came through— and he had no doubt that before the afternoon was over, everyone within ten miles would hear the gossip that federal agents were searching for someone on the isolated stretches of the Oregon coast.

"You wouldn't happen to have any idea where we might locate a survivalist compound in this area?" Mulder added. "We believe they may have been taken there, to be with a family member."

The potbellied man raised his eyebrows. "I know some of those places exist in the hills and the thick forest—nobody in their right mind goes looking too close for them."

Scully took out her business card. "If you do see anything, sir, we'd appreciate it if you give us a call. We're not trying to arrest these two for anything. They need help."

"Sure, always happy to do my duty," the man said, and tucked the card into his shirt pocket without even glancing at it. He topped off the gas tank to an even dollar amount and then, maliciously, it seemed, squirted a few cents more into the tank.

Mulder paid him, got a receipt, and then he and Scully climbed back in the car. "People around here sure value their privacy," Mulder said. "Especially outside of the cities, Oregon has a reputation for harboring survivalists, isolationists, and anybody else who doesn't want to be bothered."

Scully glanced down at the photo in her hands, at Jody Kennessy's smiling face, and Mulder knew what must be occupying her mind. "I wonder why David Kennessy's brother wanted so badly to drop out of sight," she said.

After four more hours of knocking on doors, stopping at cafes, souvenir shops, and art galleries scattered along the back roads, Mulder wasn't sure they would get any benefit out of continuing their methodical search unless they found a better lead to the location of Darin Kennessy.

But they could either sit and cool their heels in their Lincoln City motel room, or they could do something. Mulder preferred to do something. Usually.

He picked up his cell phone to see if he could call Frank Quinton, the medical examiner, to check on any results of the analysis of the strange mucus, but he saw that the phone was out of range. He sighed. They could have missed a dozen phone calls by now. The wooded mountains were sparsely inhabited, often even without electrical utilities. Cellular phone substations were too widely separated to get reception. He collapsed the antenna and tucked the phone back into his pocket.

"Looks like we're on our own, Scully," he said.

The brooding pines stood dense and dominant on either side of the road, like a cathedral tunnel. Wet leaves, spruce needles, and slick moisture coated the pavement. Someone had bothered to put up an unbroken barbed-wire fence from which NO TRESPASSING signs dangled at frequent intervals.

Mulder drove slowly, glancing from side to side. "Not too friendly, are they?"

"Seems like they're overdoing it a bit," Scully agreed. "Anybody who needs that much privacy must be hiding something. Do you think we're close to the survivalist compound?"

Out of the corner of his eye, Mulder saw a black shape moving, an animal loping along. He squinted at it intently, then hit the brakes.

"Look, Scully!" He pointed, sure of what he saw in the trees behind the barbed-wire fence: a black dog about the right size to be the missing pet, looking at them curiously, then loping back off into the trees. "Let's go check it out. Maybe it's Vader."

He swung the car onto the narrow gravel shoulder, then hopped out. Scully exited into the ditch, trying to maintain her footing.

Mulder sprinted to the barbed wire, pushing down on the rusted strands and ducking through. He turned to hold one of the wires up for Scully. Off in the trees, the dog looked at them before trotting nervously away.

"Here, boy!" Mulder called, then tried whistling. He ran crashing after it through the underbrush. The dog barked and turned and bolted.

Scully chased after him. "That's not the way to get a skittish dog to come back to you," she said.

Mulder paused to listen, and the dog barked again. "Come on, Scully."

Along the trees even this deep in the woods he saw frequent NO TRES-PASSING signs, along with PRIVATE PROPERTY, WARNING—VIOLATORS WILL BE PROSECUTED.

Several of the signs were peppered with buckshot dents.

Scully hurried, but kept herself intensely alert, aware of the very real danger of excessive traps and the illegal countermeasures some of these survivalist groups were known to use. At any moment they could step into a hunting snare, snap a trip wire, or find themselves dropped into a trap pit.

Finally, as Mulder continued up the slope after the black dog, ducking between trees and wheezing from lack of breath, he reached the crest of the hill. A line of DANGER signs marked the area.

As Scully came close to him, flushed from the pursuit, they topped the rise. "Uh-oh, Mulder."

Suddenly dozens of dogs began barking and baying. She saw a chain-link fence topped with razor wire, surrounding an entire compound of half-buried houses, bunkers, prefabricated cabins, and guard shacks.

The black dog raced toward the compound.

Mulder and Scully skidded to a stop in the soft forest dirt as armed men rushed from the guard shacks at the corners of the compound. Other people stepped out of the cabins. Women peered through the windows, grabbing their children and protecting them from what they thought must be an unexpected government raid. The men shouted and raised their rifles, firing warning shots into the air.

Mulder instantly held up his hands. Other dogs came bounding out of the compound, German shepherds, rottweilers, and Doberman pinschers.

"Mulder, I think we found the survivalists we've been looking for," Scully said.

NINETEEN

Survivalist Compound
Thursday, 5:09 p.m.

"We're federal agents," Mulder announced. "I'm going to reach for my identification."

With agonizing slowness, he groped inside his topcoat.

Unfortunately, all the weapons remained leveled at him, if possible with even greater ire. He realized that radical survivalists probably wanted nothing to do with any government agency.

One middle-aged man with a long beard stepped forward to the fence and glowered at them. "And do federal agents not know how to read?" he said in a firm, intelligent voice. "You've passed dozens of NO TRESPASSING signs to get here. Do you have a duly authorized search warrant?"

"I'm sorry, sir," Scully said. "We were trying to stop your dog, the black one. We're searching for a man named Darin Kennessy. We have reason to believe he may have information on these people." She reached inside her jacket and withdrew the photos. "A woman and her boy."

"If you come one step closer, you'll be into a minefield," the bearded man said. The other survivalists continued watching Mulder and Scully with increased suspicion. "Just stay where you are."

Mulder couldn't imagine that the survivalists would let their dogs run loose if there were really a minefield around the compound... but, then again, it wasn't completely inconceivable either. He didn't feel like arguing with this man.

"Who are they?" one of the women asked, also holding a high-powered rifle. "Those two people you're looking for?" She looked at least as deadly as the men. "And why do you need to talk to Darin?"

Mulder kept his face impassive, not showing his excitement at learning they had finally tracked down the brother of David Kennessy.

"The boy is the nephew of Darin Kennessy. He desperately needs medical attention," Scully said, raising her voice. "They have a black Labrador dog. We saw your dog and thought it might be the one we were looking for."

The man with the beard laughed. "This is a spaniel, not a black Lab," he said.

"What happened to the boy's dad?" the woman asked.

"He was recently killed," Mulder said. "The laboratory where he worked— the same place Darin worked—was destroyed in a fire. The woman and the boy disappeared. We hoped they might have come here, to be with you."

"Why should we trust you?" the man with the beard asked. "You're prob- ably the people Darin warned us about."

"Go get Darin," the woman yelled over her shoulder; then she looked at the bearded man. "He's the one who's got to decide this. Besides, we have plenty of firepower to take care of these two, if there's trouble."

"There won't be any trouble," Scully assured them. "We just need some information."

A lean man with bushy cinnamon-red hair climbed up the underground stairs of one of the half-buried shacks. Uncertainly, he came closer, approaching the bearded man and the angry-looking woman.

"I'm Darin Kennessy, David's brother. What is it you want?"

Shouting across the fence, Mulder and Scully briefly explained the situa- tion, and Darin Kennessy looked deeply disturbed. "You suspected something beforehand, didn't you—before DyMar was destroyed and your brother was killed?" Mulder asked. "You left your research many months ago and came out here... to hide?"

Darin became indignant. "I left my research for philosophical reasons. I thought the technology was turning in a very alarming direction, and I did not like some of the funding... sources my brother was using. I wanted to separate myself from the work and the men associated with it. Cut loose entirely."

"We're trying to stay away from people like that," the man with the beard said. "We're trying to stay away from everything, build our own life here. We want to create a protected place to live with caring neighbors, with strong families. We're self-sufficient. We don't need any interference from people like you—people who wear suits and ties."

Mulder cocked his chin. "Did you folks by any chance read the *Unabomber Manifesto*?"

Darin Kennessy scowled. "I'm as repelled by the Unabomber's use of bomb technology as I am by the atrocities of modern technology. But not everything—just one facet in particular. Nanotechnology."

He waited for a beat. Mulder thought the rugged dress and homespun appearance of the man shifted subtly, so he could see the highly intelligent computer chip researcher hiding beneath the disguise. "Very tiny self-replicating machines small enough to work inside a human cell, versatile enough to assemble just about anything... and smart enough to know what they're doing."

Mulder looked at Scully. "Big things come in small packages."

Darin's eyes shone with fervor. "Because each nanomachine is so small, it can move its parts very rapidly—think of a hummingbird's wings vibrating. A swarm of nanomachines could scour through a pile of rubble or a tank of seawater and separate out every single atom of gold, platinum, or silver and sort them into convenient bins, all in total silence, with no waste and no unsightly mess."

Scully's brow furrowed. "And this was your DyMar work?"

"I started long before that," Darin said. "But David and I took our ideas in even more exciting directions. Inside a human body, nano-scouts could do the same work as white corpuscles do in fighting diseases, bacteria, and viruses. But unlike white corpuscles, these nano-doctors can also inspect DNA strands, find any individual cell that turns cancerous, then reprogram the DNA, fixing any errors and mutations they find. What if we could succeed in creating infinitesimal devices that can be injected into a body to act as 'biological policemen'—submicroscopic robots that seek out and repair damage on a cellular level?"

"A cure for cancer," Mulder said.

"And everything else."

Scully flashed him a somewhat skeptical look. "Mr. Kennessy, I've read some speculative pieces in popular science magazines, but certainly nothing that would suggest we are within decades of having such a breakthrough in nanotechnology."

"Progress is often closer than you think," he said. "Researchers at the University of Wisconsin used lithographic techniques to produce a train of gears a tenth of a millimeter across. Engineers at AT&T Bell Laboratories created semiconductors out of clusters containing only six to twelve atoms at a time. Using scanning tunneling microscopy, scientists at the IBM Almaden Research Center drew a complete map of Earth's western hemisphere only a fiftieth the diameter of a human hair."

"But there must be a limit to how small we can physically manipulate tools and circuit paths," Mulder said.

The dogs set up a louder barking, and the man with the beard went over to shush them. Darin Kennessy frowned, distracted, as if torn by his need to hide and deny all his technological breakthroughs and his clear passion for the work he had abandoned.

"That's only tackling the problem from one direction. Between David and myself, we also started to build from the bottom up. Self-assembly, the way nature does it. Researchers at Harvard have made use of amino acids and proteins as templates for new structures smaller than the size of a cell, for instance.

"With our combined expertise in silicon microminiaturization techniques and biological self-assembly, we tried to match up those advances to yield a sudden breakthrough."

"And did you?"

"Maybe. It seemed to be working very well, up until the time I abandoned it. I suspect my fool brother continued pushing, playing with fire."

"So why did you leave your research, if it was so promising?"

"There's a dark side, Agent Mulder," Darin continued, glancing over at the other survivalists. "Mistakes happen. Researchers usually screw up half a dozen times before they achieve success—it's just part of the learning process. The question is, can we afford that learning process with nanotechnology?" The woman with the shotgun grumbled, but kept her direct comments to herself.

"Just suppose one of our first nanomachines—a simple one, without fail-safe programming—happens to escape from the lab," Darin said. "If this one goes about copying itself, and each copy builds more copies, in about ten hours there would be sixty-eight billion nanomachines. In less than two days, the runaway nanomachines could take apart the entire Earth—*working one molecule at a time!* Two days, from beginning to end. Think of the last time you saw any government make a decision that fast, even in an emergency."

No wonder Kennessy's research was so threatening to people in well-established circles of power, Mulder realized. No wonder they might be trying to suppress it, at all costs.

"But you left DyMar before you reached a point where you could release your findings?" Scully asked.

"Nobody was ever going to release our findings," Darin said, his voice dripping with scorn. "I knew it would never be made available to society. David made noises about going public, releasing the results of our first tests with lab rats and small animals, but I always talked him out of it, and so did our assistant, Jeremy Dorman." He drew a deep breath. "I guess he must have come too close, if those people felt they finally had to burn down the lab facility and destroy all our records."

"Patrice and Jody aren't with you, are they?" Scully said, confirming her suspicions. "Do you know where they are?"

Darin snorted. "No, we went our separate ways. I haven't spoken to any of them since I came out here to join the camp." He gestured to the dogs, the guard shacks, the razor wire. "This wouldn't be scenic enough for them."

"But you are Jody's uncle," Mulder said.

"The only person that kid spent time with was Jeremy Dorman. He was the closest thing to a real uncle the boy had."

"He was also killed in the DyMar fire," Scully said.

"He was low man on the totem pole," Darin Kennessy said, "but he knew how to pull the business deals. He got us our initial funding and kept it coming. When I left to come out here, I think he was perfectly happy to step into my shoes, working with David."

Darin frowned. "But I had nothing more to do with them, not then and not now." He seemed deeply troubled, as if the news of his brother's death was just now breaking through his consciousness. "We used to be close, used to spend time out in the deep woods."

"Where?" Mulder asked.

"Patrice designed a little cabin for me, just to get away from it all."

Scully looked at Mulder, than at Darin. "Sir, could you tell us how we could locate the cabin?"

Darin frowned again, looking skittish and uneasy. "It's up near Colvain, off on some winding fire roads."

"Here's my card," Mulder said. "In case they do show up or you learn anything."

Darin frowned at him. "We don't have any phones here."

Scully grabbed Mulder's sleeve. "Thank you for your time."

"Be careful of the minefield," the man with the beard warned.

"We'll watch our step," Scully said.

Feeling tired and sweaty, Mulder was nonetheless excited by the information they had learned.

They made their way back through the thick woods past the dozens of warning signs to where they had parked their car at the edge of the road.

Scully couldn't believe how the survivalists lived. "Some people will do anything to survive," she muttered.

TWENTY

Kennessys' Cabin
Coast Range, Oregon
Thursday, 11:47 p.m.

On hearing Jody's cry, Patrice awoke from a restless sleep. She sat up in her narrow cot in the cabin's single back bedroom, throwing aside the musty-smelling blankets.

"Jody!"

The cabin was dark and too silent—until the dog woofed, once. She blinked the disorientation of sleep away and brushed mussed strawberry blond hair away from her eyes. She struggled free of the last tangles of blankets, as if they were a restraining net trying to keep her from the boy. He needed her.

On her way to the main room, she stumbled into an old wooden chair, hurt her foot as she kicked it away, then plunged blindly ahead into the darkness. "Jody!"

The moonlight gave just enough silvery light to guide her way once she got her bearings. On the sofa in the main room, she saw her boy lying in a sweat. The last embers of their fire in the hearth glowed red-orange, providing more wood smell than heat. After dark, no one should have been able to see the smoke.

For a moment the smoldering embers reminded her of the DyMar fire, where her husband had died in the raging flames. She shuddered at the thought, the reminder of the violence. David had been ambitious and impulsive and perhaps he had taken ill-advised risks. But David had believed passionately in his research, and he had tried to do his best.

Now he had died for his discoveries… and Jody had lost his father.

Vader sat erect close to Jody, a black guardian snuffling the boy's chest in concern. Seeing Patrice, Vader's tail thumped on the hardwood floor next to where one of the pillows had fallen. The black Lab pushed his muzzle into the blankets, whining.

Jody moaned and made another frightened sound.

Patrice stopped, looking down at her son. Vader stared back up with his liquid brown eyes, emitting another whine, as if asking why she didn't do anything. But she let Jody sleep.

Nightmares again.

Several times in the past week, Jody had awakened in the isolated and silent cabin, frightened and lost. Since the start of their desperate flight, he'd had good reason for nightmares. But was it his fear that brought on the dreams… or something else?

Patrice knelt down, and Vader squirmed with energy, pushing his nose against her side, anxious for her to reassure him. She patted him on the head, thumping hard, just the way he had always liked it. "It's okay, Vader," she said, attempting to soothe herself more than the dog.

With the flat of her palm, she touched Jody's forehead, feeling the heat. The boy stirred, and she wondered if she should wake him. His body was a war zone, a cellular battlefield. Though David had repeatedly denied what he had done, she knew full well what caused the fever.

Sometimes Patrice wondered if her son would be better off dead after all— and then she hated herself for even thinking such things…

Vader padded across the floor toward the fireplace, nosed around the base of a faded overstuffed chair, and came back to Jody's bedside with a slobber-soggy tennis ball in his jaws. He wanted to play, as if convinced that would make everything all right.

Patrice frowned at Vader, turning away from the sofa. "You've got so damned much energy, you know that?"

Vader whined, then chewed on the tennis ball.

She remembered sitting at home in their living room, back in the old suburban house in Tigard—now trashed and ransacked—with David. Jody, in extreme pain from his cancer, had soaked in a hot, hot bath, taken his prescription painkillers, and gone to bed early, leaving his parents alone.

Vader didn't want to settle down, though, and if his boy wouldn't play, then he would pester the adults. David halfheartedly played tug-of-war with the black Lab, while Patrice watched with a mixture of uneasiness and fasci-nation. The family dog was twelve years old already, the same age as Jody, and he shouldn't have been nearly so frisky.

"Vader's like a puppy again," Patrice said. Previously, the black Lab had settled into a middle-aged routine of sleeping most of the time, except for a lot of licking and tail-wagging to greet them every day when they came home. But lately the dog had been more energetic and playful than he had been in years. "I wonder what happened to him," she said.

David's grin, his short dark hair, and his heavy eyebrows made him look dashing. "Nothing."

Patrice sat up and pulled her hand away from him. "Did you take Vader into your lab again? What did you do to him?" She raised her voice, and the words came out with cold anger. "What did you do to him!"

Vader dropped the pull-toy in his jaws, staring at her as if she had gone insane. What business did she have yelling when they were trying to play?

David looked at her, hard. He raised his eyebrows in an expression of sincerity. "I didn't do anything. Honest."

With a woof, Vader lunged back with the pull-toy again, wagging his tail and growling as he dug his paws into the carpet. David fought back, leaning against the sofa to gain more leverage. "Just look at him! How can you think anything's wrong?"

But in their years of marriage, Patrice had learned one thing, and she had learned to hate it. She could always tell when David was lying...

Her husband had been focused on his research, bulldozing ahead and ignoring regulations and restrictions. He didn't consult with her on many things, just barged along, doing what he insisted was right. That was just the way David Kennessy did things.

He had been too focused, too involved in his work to take note of the suspicious occurrences at DyMar until it was too late. She herself had noticed things, people watching their house at night, keeping an eye on her when she was out with David, odd clicks on the phone line... but David had brushed her worries aside. Such a brilliant man, yet so oblivious. At the last moment, at least, he had called her, warned her.

She had grabbed Jody and run, even as the protesters burned down the DyMar facility, trapping her husband in the inferno with Jeremy; she barely made it into hiding here with her son. Her *healthy* son.

On the sofa, Jody fell into a more restful sleep. His temperature remained high, but Patrice knew she could do nothing about that. She tucked the blankets around him again, brushed straight the sweat-sticky bangs across his forehead.

Vader let the tennis ball thump on the floor, giving up on the possibility of play. With a heavy sigh, the dog turned three times in a circle in front of the sofa, then slumped into a comfortable position, guarding his boy. He let out a long, heavy animal sigh.

Comforted by the dog's devotion, Patrice wandered back to her cot, glad she hadn't awakened her son after all. At least she hadn't switched on any lights... lights that could have been seen out in the darkness.

Leaving Jody to sleep, she lay awake in her own cot, alternately growing too hot, then shivering. Patrice longed for rest, but she knew she couldn't let her guard down. Not for an instant.

With her eyes closed, Patrice quietly cursed her husband and listened for sounds outside.

TWENTY-ONE

Mercy Hospital Morgue
Portland, Oregon
Friday, 5:09 a.m.

Edmund was amazed at how fast the officials arrived, considering that they supposedly came all the way from Atlanta, Georgia. Their very demeanor unnerved him so much he didn't dare question their credentials. He was just glad that somebody seemed to believe his story.

Edmund had sealed drawer 4E after the previous night's incident and lowered the temperature as far as it would go, though nobody showed much interest in looking for the monsters that had given him the willies. He was waiting to talk to his mentor Dr. Quinton, who was busy analyzing the mucus specimen taken during the autopsy. He expected the ME any minute now, and then he would feel vindicated.

But the officials showed up first, three of them, nondescript but professional, with a manner that made Edmund want to avert his eyes. They looked clean-cut, well-dressed, but grim.

"We're here from the Centers for Disease Control," one man said and ripped out a badge bearing a gold-plated shield and a blurry ID photo. He folded the identification back into his suit faster than Edmund could make out any of the words.

"The CDC?" he stammered. "Are you here for... ?"

"It's imperative that we confiscate the organic tissue you have stored in your morgue refrigerator," said the man on the left. "We understand you had an incident yesterday."

"We certainly did," Edmund said. "Have you seen this sort of thing before? I looked in all my medical books—"

"We have to destroy the specimen, just to be safe," said the man on the right. Edmund felt relieved to know that someone was in charge, someone else could take care of it from here.

"We need to inspect all records you have regarding the victim, the autopsy, and any specimens you might have kept," the man in the middle said. "We're also going to take extreme precautions to sterilize every inch of your morgue refrigerators."

"Do you think I'm infected?" Edmund said.

"That's highly unlikely, sir. You would have manifested symptoms immediately." Edmund swallowed hard. But he knew his responsibilities. "But—but I have to get approval," he said. "The medical examiner has explicit responsibility."

"Yes, I do," Frank Quinton said, walking into the morgue and scanning the situation. The medical examiner's grandfatherly face clouded over. "What's going on here?"

The man on the right spoke up. "I assure you, sir, we have the proper authority here. This is a potential matter of national security and public health. We are very concerned."

"And so am I," Quinton said. "Are you working with the other federal agents who were here?"

"This… phase of the operation is out of their jurisdiction, sir. This outbreak poses an extreme danger without proper containment procedures."

The central man's eyes were hard, and even the ME seemed intimidated.

"Sir," the first man said, "we need to get an entire team in here to remove the… biomaterial from the refrigerator. We'll inconvenience you as little as possible."

"Well, I suppose… " Quinton's voice trailed off, sounding flustered as the three CDC men quickly ushered them both out of the quiet and clean room.

"Edmond, let's go for a cup of coffee," Quinton finally said, glancing uneasily over his shoulder.

Happy for the coroner's invitation—he had never been so lucky before—Edmund took the elevator and went to the hospital cafeteria for a while, still trying to recover. He kept seeing the many-tentacled creature trying to escape from the morgue refrigerator drawer.

Normally he would have had a thousand questions for the ME, checking details, demonstrating all the trivia he had learned from his midnight studies in the morgue. But Quinton sat quiet and reticent, looking at his hands, deeply troubled. He took out the card the FBI agents had given him previously, turning it over and over in his hands.

When they returned to the basement level an hour later, they found that the morgue had been scoured and sterilized. Drawer 4E had been ripped out entirely, its contents taken away. The men had left no receipt, no paperwork.

"We don't have any way to contact them to find out their results," Edmund said.

But the medical examiner just shook his head. "Maybe that's for the best."

TWENTY-TWO

The Devil's Churn
Oregon Coast
Friday, 10:13 a.m.

The ocean crashed against the black cliffs with a hollow booming sound like boulders dropped from a great height. The breeze at the scenic overlook whipped cold and salty and wet against Scully's face.

"It's called the Devil's Churn," Mulder had said, though Scully could certainly read the OREGON STATE SCENIC MARKER sign.

Below, the water turned milky in a frothing maelstrom as the breakers slammed into a hollowed-out indentation in the cliff. Sea caves there had collapsed, creating a sort of chute; as the waves struck the narrow passage head-on, it funneled the force of the water and sprayed it into a dramatic tower, like a water cannon blasting as high as the clifftops above, drenching unwary sightseers.

According to the signs, dozens of people had died at this place: unsuspecting tourists picking their way down to the mouth of the Churn, caught standing in the wrong place when the unexpected geyser of water exploded upward. Their bodies had been battered against the algae-slick rocks or simply sucked out to sea.

Station wagons, minivans, and rental cars were parked in the scenic area as families from out of state as well as locals came to stare down at the sea. Obnoxious seagulls screamed overhead.

A battered old vending coach stood open with aluminum awnings rattling in the breeze; a grinning man with a golf cap sold warmed-over hot dogs, sour coffee, bagged chips, and canned soft drinks. On the other side of the parking area, a woman with braids huddled in a down hunting vest, watching her handmade rugs flap vigorously on a clothesline.

Fighting back a headache and drawing a deep breath of the cool, salty breeze, Scully buttoned her coat to keep warm. Mulder went directly over to the cliff edge, eagerly peering down and waiting for the water to spray up. Scully withdrew her cell phone, glad to see that the signal here was strong enough, at last. She punched in the buttons for the Portland medical examiner.

"Ah, Agent Scully," Dr. Quinton said, "I've been trying to call you all morning."

"Any results?" she asked. After seeing the slide of the dog's contaminated blood at the veterinarian's, she had asked the medical examiner to look at his own sample of the slimy mucus she had taken during Vernon Ruckman's autopsy.

By the unsteady-looking guardrail, Mulder watched in fascination as a rooster tail of cold spray jetted into the air, curling up to the precipice, and then raining back down into the sea. She gestured for Mulder to come back to her as she pressed the phone tightly against her ear, concentrating on the ME's staticky words.

"Apparently something… unusual happened to the plague victim's body in the morgue refrigerator." Quinton seemed hesitant, at a loss for words. "Our attendant reported hearing noises, something moving inside the sealed drawer. And it's been sealed since you left it."

"That's impossible," Scully said. "The man couldn't still be alive. Even if the plague put him in some kind of extreme coma, I'd already performed an autopsy."

The ME said, "I know Edmund, and he's not the skittish sort. A little bit of a pest sometimes, but this isn't the kind of story he would make up. I was going to give him the benefit of the doubt, but…" Quinton hesitated again, and Scully pressed the phone closer to her ear, straining to hear the undertone in his voice. "Unfortunately, before I could check it out myself, some gentlemen from the Centers for Disease Control came in and sterilized everything. As a precaution, they took the entire refrigerator drawer."

"From the CDC?" Scully said in disbelief. She had worked many times with the CDC; and they were always consummate professionals, following official procedures rigorously. This sounded like something else entirely, someone else.

Now she was even more concerned about what she had learned earlier that morning when she called Atlanta to check on the status of the sample she had personally sent in. Apparently, their lab technician had lost the specimen.

Mulder came up to her, brushing his damp hair back, though the wind continued to blow it around. He looked at her, raising his eyebrows. She watched him as she spoke into the phone, keeping her voice carefully neutral. "Dr. Quinton, you kept a sample of the substance for your own analysis. Were you able to find anything?"

The ME pondered for a moment before answering. She heard static on the line, clicking, a warbling background tone. They still must be at the edge of reception for cellular transmissions. "I think it's an infestation of some kind," Quinton said finally. "Tiny flecks unlike anything I've seen before. The sample is utterly clotted with them. Under highest magnification they don't look like any microorganism I've ever seen. Squarish little boxes, cubes, geometrical shapes…"

Scully felt cold as she heard the ME's words, echoing what Darin Kennessy had told them at the survivalist camp.

"Have you ever seen anything like this, Agent Scully?" the ME persisted on the phone. "You're a doctor yourself."

Scully cleared her throat. "I'll have to get back to you on that, sir. Let me speak with my partner and compare notes. Thanks for your information." She ended the call and then looked at Mulder.

After she briefly recounted the conversation, Mulder nodded. "They sure were eager to get rid of the guard's body. Every trace."

Scully pondered as she listened to the roar of the ocean against the rocks below. "That doesn't sound like the way the Centers for Disease Control operates. No official receipt, no phone number in case Dr. Quinton has further information."

Mulder buttoned his coat against the chilly breeze. "Scully, I don't think that was the CDC. I think it could well be representatives from the same group that arranged for the destruction of DyMar Laboratory and pinned the blame on a scapegoat animal rights group."

"Mulder, why would anyone be willing to take such extreme action?"

"You heard Kennessy's brother. Nanotechnology research," he said. "It's gotten loose somehow, maybe from a research animal carrying something very dangerous. The mucus from the dead security guard sounds just like what we saw in the sample of the dog's blood—"

Scully put her hands on her hips as the sea wind whipped her red hair. "Mulder, I think we need to find that dog, and Patrice and Jody Kennessy."

Behind them the Devil's Churn erupted again with a loud booming sound. Spray shot high into the air. A group of children stood next to their parents at the guardrail and cheered and laughed at the spectacle. No one seemed to be paying any attention to the food vendor in his van or the braided woman with her handmade rugs.

"I agree, Scully—and after that report from the ME, I think maybe we aren't the only ones looking for them."

TWENTY-THREE

Tillamook County
Coast Range, Oregon
Friday, 10:47 a.m.

The cold rain sheeted down, drenching him and the roadside and everything all around—but Jeremy Dorman's other problems were far worse than a bit of lousy weather. The external world was all bad data to him now, irrelevant numbness. The forest of nerves inside him provided enough pain for a world all its own.

His shoes and clothes were soaked, his skin gray and clammy—but those discomforts were insignificant compared to the raging war within his own cells. Slick patches of the protectant carrier fluid coated his skin, swarming with the reproducing nanocritters.

His muscles trembled and vibrated, but he continued lifting his legs, taking steps, moving along. Dorman's brain seemed like a mere passenger in his body now. It took a conscious effort to keep the joints bending, the limbs moving, like a puppeteer working a complicated new marionette while wearing a blindfold and thick gloves.

A car roared past him, spraying water. Its tires struck a puddle in a depression in the road and jetted cold rainwater all over him. The taillights flickered red for an instant as the driver realized what he had done, and then, maliciously, the man honked a few times and continued weaving down the road.

Dorman trudged along the muddy shoulder, uncaring. He focused ahead. The long road curved into the wooded mountains. He had no idea how many miles he had gone from Portland, but he hoped he could find some way to hurry. He had no money and he didn't dare rent a car anyway, at the risk of someone spotting his identity. No one knew he was still alive, and he wanted to keep it that way. Not that he would trust his rebellious body or flickering depth perception if he was driving...

He shambled past a small county weigh station, a little shack with a gate and a red stoplight for trucks. Opaque miniblinds covered the windows, and a sign that looked as if it hadn't been changed in months said, WEIGH STATION CLOSED.

As Dorman trudged past, he looked longingly at the shelter. It would be unheated, with no food or supplies, but it would be dry. He longed to get out of the rain for a while, to sleep... but he would likely never wake up again. His time was rapidly running out.

He continued past the weigh station. Waterlogged potato fields sprawled in one direction, with a marsh on the other side of the road. Dorman headed toward the gentle uphill slope leading into the mountains.

Strange and unfathomable shapes skirled across his vision like static. The nanocritters in his body were messing around with his optic nerves again, fixing them, making improvements... or just toying with them. He hadn't been able to see colors for days.

Dorman clenched his jaws together, feeling the ache in his bones. He almost enjoyed the ache—a real pain, not a phantom side effect of having his body invaded by self-programmed machines.

He picked up his pace, so focused on keeping himself moving forward that he didn't even hear the loud hum of the approaching truck.

The vehicle grew louder, a large log truck half-loaded with pine logs whose bark had been splintered off and most of their large protruding branches amputated. Dorman turned and looked at it, then stepped farther to the side of the road. The driver flashed his headlights.

Dorman heard the engine growl as the trucker shifted down through the gears. The air brakes sighed as the log truck came to a halt thirty feet in front of Dorman.

He just stood and stared, unable to believe what had happened, what a stroke of luck. This man was going to give him a ride. Dorman hurried forward, squelching water from his shoes. He huddled his arms around his chest.

The driver leaned over the seat and popped open the passenger door. The rain continued to slash down, pelting the wet logs, steaming off the truck's warm grille.

Dorman grabbed the door handle and swung it open. His leg jittered as he lifted it to step on the running board. Finally he gained his balance and hauled himself up. He was dripping, exhausted, cold.

"Boy, you look miserable," the truck driver said. He was short and portly, with dirty-blond hair and blue eyes.

"I am miserable," Dorman answered, surprised that his voice worked so well.

"Well, then, be miserable inside the truck cab here. You got a place to go— or just wandering?"

"I've got a place to go," Dorman said. "I'm just trying to get there."

"Well, you can ride with me until the Coast Highway turnoff. My name's Wayne—Wayne Hykaway."

Dorman looked at him, suspicious. He didn't want his identity known. "I'm... David," he said. He slammed the truck's door, shoving his hands into the waterlogged pockets of his tattered jacket, hunched over and huddling into himself. Hykaway had extended his hand but quickly drew it back when it became obvious Dorman had no intention of shaking it.

The interior of the cab was warm and humid. Heat blasted from the vents. The windshield wipers slapped back and forth in an effort to keep the view clear. News radio played across the speakers of a far-too-expensive sound system, crackling with static from poor reception out here in the wilderness.

The trucker wrestled with the stick shift and rammed the vehicle into gear again. With a groan and a labor of its engines, the log truck began to move forward along the wet road uphill toward the trees.

As the truck picked up speed, Dorman could only think that he was growing closer to his destination every minute, every mile. This man had no idea of the deadly risk he had just taken, but Dorman had to think of his ultimate goal of finding Patrice and Jody and the dog. Whatever the cost.

Dorman sat back, pressed against the door of the truck, trying to ignore the guilt and fear. Water trickled down his face, and he blinked it away. He maintained his view through the windshield, watching the wipers tock back and forth. He tried to keep as far away from Wayne Hykaway as possible. He didn't dare let the man touch him. He couldn't risk the exposure another body would bring.

The cordial trucker switched off the talk radio and tried in vain to strike up a conversation, but when Dorman proved reticent, he just began to talk about himself instead. He chatted about the books he liked to read, his hobby of tai chi relaxation techniques, how he had once trained unemployed people.

Hykaway kept one hand on the steering wheel of the mammoth logging truck, and with the other he fiddled with the air vent controls, the heater. When he couldn't think of anything to say, he flicked on the radio again, tuning to a different station, then switched it off in disgust.

Dorman concentrated on his body, turning his thoughts inward. He could feel his skin crawling and squirming, his muscle growths moving of their own accord. He pressed his elbows against his ribs, feeling the clammy fabric of his jacket as well as the slick ooze of the nanomachine carrier mucus that seeped out of his pores.

After fifteen minutes of Dorman's trancelike silence, the trucker began to glance at him sidelong, as if wondering what kind of psychopath he had foolishly picked up.

Dorman avoided his gaze, staring out the side window—and then his gut spasmed. He hunched over and clenched his hands to his stomach. He hissed breath through his teeth. He felt something jerk beneath his skin, like a mole burrowing through his rib cage.

"Hey, are you all right?" the trucker said.

"Yes," Dorman answered, ripping the answer out of his voice box. He squeezed hard enough until he could finally regain control over his rebellious biological systems. He sucked in deep pounding breaths. Finally the convulsions settled down again.

Still, he felt his internal organs moving, exploring their freedom, twitching in places that should never have been able to move. It was like a roiling storm inside of him.

Wayne Hykaway glanced at him again, then turned back to concentrate on the wet road. He kept both hands gripped white on the steering wheel.

Dorman remained seated in silence, huddled against the hard comfort of the passenger-side door. A bit of slime began to pool on the seat around him.

He knew he could lose control again at any moment. Every hour it got harder and harder....

TWENTY-FOUR

Max's General Store and Art Gallery
Colvain, Oregon
Friday, 12:01 p.m.

Scully was already tired of driving and glad for the chance to stop and ask a few more people if they recognized Patrice and Jody Kennessy.

Mulder sat in the passenger seat, munching cheese curls from a bag in his lap and dropping a few crumbs on his overcoat. He plastered his face to the unfolded official road map of the state of Oregon. "I can't find this town on the map," Mulder said. "Colvain, Oregon."

Scully parked in front of a quaint old shake-shingle house with a hand-painted sign dangling on a chain on a post out front.

MAX'S GENERAL STORE AND ART GALLERY

"Mulder, we're in the town and I can't find it."

The heavy wooden door of the general store advertised Morley cigarettes; a bell on the top jingled as they entered the creaking hardwood floor of Max's. "Of course they'd have a bell," Mulder said, looking up.

Old 1950s-style coolers and refrigerators—enameled white with chrome trim—held lunch meats, bottled soft drinks, and frozen dinners. Boxes around the cash register displayed giant-size Slim Jims and seemingly infinite varieties of beef jerky.

T-shirts hung on a rack beside shelves full of knickknacks, most made from sweet-smelling cedar and painted with witty folk sayings related to the soggy weather in Oregon. Shot glasses, placemats, playing cards, and key chains rounded out the assortment.

Scully saw a few simple watercolor paintings hanging aslant on the far wall above a beer cooler; price tags dangled from the gold-painted frames. "I wonder if there's some kind of county ordinance that requires each town to have a certain number of art galleries," she said.

Behind the cash register, an old woman sat barricaded by newspaper racks and wire trays that held gum, candy, and breath mints. Her hair was dyed an outrageous red, her glasses thick and smudged with fingerprints. She was reading a well-thumbed tabloid with headlines proclaiming *Bigfoot Found in*

New Jersey, Alien Embryos Frozen in Government Facility, and even *Cannibal Cult in Arkansas.*

Mulder looked at the headlines and raised his eyebrows at Scully. The red-headed woman looked up over her glasses. "May I help you folks? Do you need maps or sodas?"

Mulder flashed his badge and ID. "We're federal agents, ma'am. We're wondering if you could give us directions to a cabin near here, some property owned by a Mr. Darin Kennessy?"

Scully withdrew the much-handled Kennessy photos and spread them on the counter. The woman hurriedly folded her tabloid and shoved it beside the cash register. Through her smudged glasses, she peered down at the photos.

"We're looking for these two people," Scully said, offering no further information.

Jody Kennessy smiled optimistically up from the photograph, but his face was gaunt and sunken, his hair mostly fallen out, his skin grayish and sickly from the rigorous chemo and radiation treatments.

The woman removed her glasses and wiped them off with a Kleenex, then put them on her face again. "Yes, I think I've seen these two before. The woman at least. Been out here a week or two."

Mulder perked up. "Yes, that's about the time frame we're talking about."

Scully leaned forward, unable to stop herself from telling too many details, so as to enlist the woman's aid. "This young man is very seriously ill. He's dying of leukemia. He needs immediate treatment. He may have gotten significantly worse since this photo was taken."

The woman looked down at Jody's photograph again. "Well, then, maybe I'm wrong," she said. "As I recall, the boy with this woman seemed pretty healthy to me. They could be staying out at the Kennessys' cabin. It's been empty a long time."

The woman rocked back on her chair, which let out a metal squeal. She pressed the thick glasses up against the bridge of her nose. "Nothing much moves around here without us knowing about it."

"Could you give us directions, ma'am?" Scully repeated.

The redheaded woman withdrew a pen, but didn't bother to write down directions. "About seven or eight miles back, you turn on a little road called Locust Springs Drive, go about a quarter of a mile, turn left on a logging road—it's the third driveway on your right." She toyed with her strand of fake pearls.

"This is the best lead we've got so far," Scully said softly, looking eagerly at her partner. The thought of rescuing Jody Kennessy, helping him out in his weakened state, gave her new energy.

As an FBI agent, Scully was supposed to maintain her objectivity and not get emotionally involved in a case lest her judgment be influenced. In this instance she couldn't help it. She and Jody Kennessy both shared the shadow of cancer, and the connection to this boy she'd never met was too strong. Her desire to help him was far more powerful than Scully had anticipated when she and Mulder had left Washington to investigate the DyMar fire.

The bell on the door jingled again, and a state policeman strode in, his boots heavy on the worn wooden floor of the general store. Scully looked over her shoulders as the trooper walked casually over to the soft drink cooler and grabbed a large bottle of orange soda.

"The usual, Jared?" the woman called from the cash register, already ringing him up.

"Would I ever change, Maxie?" he answered, and she tossed him a pack of artificially colored cheese crackers from the snack rack.

The policeman nodded politely to Mulder and Scully and noticed the photographs as well as Mulder's badge wallet. "Can I help you folks?"

"We're federal agents, sir," Scully said. She picked up the photographs to show him and asked for his assistance. Perhaps he could escort them out to the isolated cabin where Patrice or Jody might be held captive—but suddenly the radio at Jared's hip squelched.

A dispatcher's voice came over, sounding alarmed but brisk and professional. "Jared, come in, please. We've got an emergency situation here. A passing motorist found a dead body up the highway about three quarters of a mile past Doyle's property."

The trooper grabbed his radio. "Officer Penwick here," he said. "What do you mean by a dead body? What condition?"

"A trucker," the dispatcher answered. "His logging rig is half off the road. The guy's sprawled by the steering wheel, and… well, it's weird. Not like any accident injuries I've ever heard of."

Mulder quickly looked at Scully, intrigued. They both understood that this sounded remarkably like their own case. "You go ahead, Scully. I can ride out to the location of the body with Officer, uh, Penwick here and take a look around. If it's nothing, I'll have him take me to the cabin and meet up with you."

Uneasy about being separated from him, but realizing that they had to investigate both possibilities without delay, she nodded. "Make sure you take appropriate precautions."

"I will, Scully." Mulder hurried for the door.

The bell jangled as the trooper left, clutching his cheese crackers and orange soda in one hand as he sent off an acknowledgment on his walkie-talkie. He glanced over his shoulder. "Put it on my tab, Maxie. I'll catch you later."

Scully hurried behind them, letting the jingling door swing shut. Mulder and the trooper raced for his police vehicle, parked aslant in front of the general store.

Mulder called back at her, "Just see if you can find them, Scully. Learn what you can. I'll contact you on the cell phone."

The two car doors slammed, and with a spray of wet gravel the highway patrolman spun around and raced up the road with his red lights flashing.

She returned to their rental car, grabbing her keys. When she glanced down at the unit on the car seat, she finally noticed to her dismay that her cellular phone wasn't working. They were out of range once more.

TWENTY-FIVE

Kennessys' Cabin
Coast Range, Oregon
Friday, 12:58 p.m.

Outside the cabin, Vader barked. He stood up on the porch and paced, letting a low growl loose in his throat.

Patrice stiffened and hurried to the lace curtains. Her mouth went dry. She had owned Vader for a dozen years, and she knew that this time the dog was not making one of his puppy barks at a squirrel.

This was a bark of warning. She had been expecting something like this. Dreading it.

Outside, the trees girdling the hollow stood tall and dark, claustrophobic around the hills that sheltered them. The rough trunks seemed to have approached silently closer, like an implacable army… like the mob she had imagined surrounded DyMar.

The grassy, weed-filled clearing stirred in a faint breeze, laden with moisture from the recent downpour. She had once thought of the meadow as beautiful, a perfect set-piece to display the wilderness cabin to best effect—a wonderful spot, Darin had said, and she had shared his enthusiasm.

Now, though, the broad clearing made her feel exposed and vulnerable.

Vader barked again and stepped forward to the edge of the porch, his muzzle pointed toward the driveway that plunged into the forest. His black nostrils quivered.

"What is it, Mom?" Jody asked. From the drawn expression on his face, she could tell he felt the fear as much as she did. In the past two weeks she had trained him well enough.

"Someone's coming," she said.

Forcing bravery upon herself, she doused the lights inside the cabin, let the curtains dangle shut, then swung open the front door to stand guard on the porch. They had run here, gone to ground, without preparation. She had to count on their hiding place, since she had no gun, no other weapons. Patrice had ransacked the cabin, but Darin had not believed in handguns. She had only her bare hands and her ingenuity. Vader looked over his shoulder at her, then turned toward the driveway again.

Jody crowded next to her, trying to see, but she pushed him back inside. "Mom!" he said indignantly, but she pointed a scolding finger at him, her face hard. He backed away quickly.

The mother's protective instinct hung on her like a drug. She had been helpless in the face of his cancer, she had been helpless when his father was murdered by shadowy men pretending to be activists, the same people who had tapped their phones, followed them, and might even now be trying to track them down. But she had taken action to get her son to safety, and she had kept him alive so far. Patrice Kennessy had no intention of giving up now.

A figure appeared in the trees, approaching on foot down the long driveway bordered by dark pines, coming closer, intent on the cabin.

Patrice didn't have time to run.

She had taken Jody out to the coastal wilderness because of its abundance of survivalists, of religious cults and extremists—all of whom knew how to be left alone. David's own brother had joined one such group, abandoning even this cabin to find deeper isolation, but she hadn't dared to go to Darin and ask for protection. The people hunting them down would think to find David's brother. She had to do the unexpected.

Now her mind raced, and she tried to think of even the smallest misstep she might have made to tip off who she was and where she and Jody were staying. Suddenly she remembered that the last time she had gone into a grocery store, she had noticed the cover of a weekly Oregon newspaper depicting the fenced-off and burned ruins of DyMar Laboratory.

Surprised, she had flinched and tried to maintain her composure, cradling her groceries in front of the *TV Guides* and beef jerky strips and candy bars. The old woman with shockingly dyed red hair had looked up at her from behind smeared eyeglasses. No one, Patrice insisted to herself, would have put such a coincidence together, would have taken note of a woman traveling alone with her twelve-year-old son, would have connected all the details.

Still, the clerk had stared at her too intently…

"Who is it, Mom?" Jody asked in a stage whisper from the cold fireplace. "Can you see?" Patrice was glad she hadn't built a fire that morning, because the telltale wisp of gray-white smoke would have attracted even more attention.

They had made a plan for such a situation, that they would both try to slip away unnoticed and vanish in the trees, hiding out in the wooded hills. Jody knew the surrounding forest well enough. But this intruder had taken them by surprise. He had come on foot, with no telltale engine noise. And now neither of them had time to run.

"Jody, you stay back there. Take Vader, go to the back door, and hide. Be ready to run into the trees if you have to, but right now it'll be a tipoff."

He blinked at her in alarm. "But I can't leave you behind, Mom."

"If I buy you some time, then you can get a head start. If they don't mean any harm, then you don't have anything to worry about." Her face turned to stone, and Jody flushed as he realized what she meant.

She turned back to the door, squinting her eyes. "Now keep yourself out of sight. Wait until the timing's right."

With a grim expression on her face, Patrice crossed her arms over her chest and waited on her front porch to meet the approaching stranger. The terror and urgency nearly paralyzed her. This was the moment of confrontation she had dreaded ever since receiving David's desperate phone call.

The figure was a broad-shouldered man walking with an odd injured gait. He looked as if he had passed on foot through a car wash with open cans of waste oil in his arms. He staggered toward the cabin, but stopped dead in his tracks when he noticed her on the porch.

Vader growled.

Even from a distance, Patrice could see his dark gaze turn toward her, his eyes lock with hers. He had changed, his facial features distorted somehow—but she recognized him. She felt a flood of relief, a sensation she had not experienced in some time. A friend at last!

"Jeremy," she said with a sigh. "Jeremy Dorman!"

TWENTY-SIX

Kennessys' Cabin
Oregon Coast Range
Friday, 1:14 p.m.

"Patrice!" Dorman called in a hoarse voice, then walked toward her at an accelerated, somehow ominous pace.

She had bought newspapers from unattended machines on shadowy street corners, and had read that her husband's lab partner had also perished in the DyMar fire, murdered by the men who wanted to keep David's nanotech research from becoming public knowledge.

"Jeremy, are those men after you, too? How did you get away?"

The fact that Jeremy Dorman had somehow escaped gave her a flash of hope that perhaps David might have survived as well. But she could not grasp the thought; it slipped through her mental fingers. She had a thousand questions for him, but most of all she was glad just to see a familiar face, another person facing the same predicament as she was...

But something was very wrong about Jeremy's presence here. He had known to look for her and Jody in this cabin. She knew that David had always talked too much. Even his brother's secret hideaway would never have been a secret for long, after tedious hours of small talk in the laboratory, David and Jeremy together.

She was suddenly wary. "Were you followed? If they come after us here, we don't have any weapons—"

"Patrice," he interrupted her, "I'm desperate. Please help me." He swallowed hard… and his throat continued to move far longer than it should have. "I need to come inside."

As he stepped closer, the burly man looked very sick, barely able to move, as if suffering from a hundred ills. His skin had a strange, wet cast—and not just from the misty moisture in the air, but with a kind of slickness. Like slime.

"What happened to you, Jeremy?" She gestured toward the door, wondering why she felt so uneasy. Dorman had spent a great deal of time with her family, especially after Darin had abandoned the work and fled to his survivalist camp. "You look awful."

"I have a lot to explain, but not much time. Look at me, at the shape I'm in. This is very important—do you have the dog here as well?"

She remained frozen in place; then it was all she could do to step forward and grip the damp, mossy handrail. Why did he want to know about Vader, hidden inside with Jody? Even though this was *Jeremy*, Jeremy Dorman, she felt the need to be cautious.

"I *want* some answers first," she said, not moving from the porch. He stopped in his tracks, uncertain. "How did you survive the fire at DyMar? We thought you were dead."

"I was supposed to die there," Dorman said, his voice heavy.

"What do you mean, you were *supposed* to die there? On the phone, in his last message to me, David said the DyMar protest was some kind of setup, that it wasn't just animal rights people after all."

Dorman's dark, hooded eyes bored into her. "I was betrayed, just like David was." He took two steps closer.

"What are you saying?" After what she had been through, Patrice thought almost anything might sound believable by now.

Dorman nodded. "They had orders to make sure nothing would survive, no record of our nanotechnology research. Only ashes."

Patrice stood her ground, silently warning him not to approach closer. "David said the conspiracy went much deeper in the government than he had thought. I didn't believe him until I went back to our house—only to find it ransacked."

Dorman lurched to a halt ten feet from the porch, stopping in the weeds of the meadow. He walked away from the cleared driveway, on the trampled path toward the door of the cabin. "They're all after you now, too, Patrice. We can help each other. But I need Vader. He carries the stable prototypes in his bloodstream."

"Prototypes? What are you talking about?"

"The nanotechnology prototypes. I had to use some of the defective earlier generations, samples from the small lab animals, but many of those exhibited shocking… anomalies. I didn't have any choice, though. The lab was on fire, everything was burning. I was supposed to be able to get away, but this was the only way I could survive." He looked at her, pleading, then lowered his voice. "But they don't work the way they were supposed to. With Vader's blood, there is a chance I can reprogram them in myself."

Her mind reeled. She knew what David had been working on, had suspected something wrong with their black Lab.

"Where's Jody?" Dorman said, peering past her to see through the curtains or the half-closed door. "Hey, Jody! Come out here! It's all right."

Jody had always looked at Dorman as a friend of his father's, a surrogate uncle—especially after Darin had left. They played video games together; Jeremy was just about the only adult who knew as many Nintendo 64 tricks as Jody did. They exchanged tips and techniques for *Wave Race, Mortal Kombat Trilogy,* and *Shadows of the Empire.*

Before Patrice could collect her thoughts, understand exactly where the situation stood, Jody pulled open the cabin door, accompanied by his black dog. "Jeremy!"

Dorman looked down at Vader, delighted and relieved, but the dog curled back his dark lips to expose fangs. The low growl sounded like a chainsaw embedded in the dog's throat, as if Vader had some kind of grudge against Dorman.

But Dorman paid no attention. He was staring at Jody—healthy Jody—in amazement. The skin on Dorman's face blurred and shifted. He winced, somehow forcing it back into place. "Jody, you're… you're recovered from the cancer."

"It's a miracle," Patrice said stiffly. "Some kind of spontaneous remission."

The sudden predatory expression on Dorman's oddly glistening face made a knot in her stomach. "No, it's not a spontaneous remission. Is it, Jody? My God, you have it, too."

The boy paled, took a step backward.

"I know what your dad did to you." For some odd reason, Dorman kept his eyes fixed upon Jody and the dog.

Patrice looked at Jody in confusion, then an instant of dawning horror as she realized the magnitude of what David had done, the risk he had taken, the real reason why his brother had been so frightened of the research. Jody's recent good health was not the result of another remission. All of David's hard work and manic commitment had paid off after all. He had found his cure for cancer, without telling Patrice.

But in the space of an indrawn breath, her incredible joy and relief and lingering heartbreak tempered with fear of Jeremy Dorman. Fear of his predatory glances at Jody, of his unnaturally shifting features, his slipping control.

"This is even better than Vader." Dorman's dark eyes blazed, taking on a distorted look. "I just need a sample of your son's blood, Patrice. Some of his blood. Not much."

Shocked and confused, Patrice flinched, but stood defiantly on the porch, not moving. She wasn't going to let anyone touch her son. "His *blood*? What on earth—"

"I don't have time to explain to you, Patrice. I didn't know they meant to kill David! They were staging the protest, they meant to burn the place down, but they were going to move the research to a more isolated establishment." His face contorted with anger. "I was supposed to be their lead researcher in the new facility, but they tried to murder me, too!"

Patrice's mind reeled; her perception of reality was being assaulted from too many directions at once. "You knew all along they intended to burn the place down? You were part of the conspiracy."

"No, I didn't mean that! It was all supposed to be under control. They lied to me, too."

"You let David be killed, you bastard. You wanted the credit, wanted his research."

"Patrice... *Jody*, I'll die without your help. Right now." Dorman strode toward the porch with great speed, but Patrice moved to block his path.

"Jody, get back in the cabin—right now. We can't trust him! He betrayed your father!" Her voice was ice cold, and the boy was already frightened. He quickly moved to do as she asked.

Dorman stopped five feet away, glowering at her. "Don't do this. You don't understand."

"I know I've got to protect my son, after all he's been through. You're probably still working for those men, hunting us. I'm not letting you near him." She held her fists at her sides, ready to tear this man apart with her bare hands. "Jody, go out and hide in the forest! You know where to go, just like we planned before," she shouted into the gap of the half-open door. "Go!"

Something squirmed beneath Dorman's chest. He hunched over, covering his stomach and his ribs. Finally, he rose up with his eyes glassy and pain-stricken. "I can't... wait... any longer, Patrice." He swayed in his step, coming closer.

In the back of the cabin, the rear door banged shut. Jody had run outside, making a beeline for the forest. Inside, she thanked her son for not arguing. She had feared he would side with Jeremy and want to help the man.

Vader bounded around the side of the cabin after Jody, barking.

Dismissing Patrice, Dorman turned toward the back. "Jody! Come here to me, boy!" He trudged away from the porch over to the side of the cabin.

Patrice felt an animal scream build within her throat. "You leave my boy alone!"

Dorman spun about and withdrew a revolver from his pants pocket. He gripped it with unsteady hands, holding it in front of her disbelieving gaze. "You don't know what you're doing, Patrice," he said. "You don't know anything about what's going on. I can just shoot the dog—or Jody—and get the blood I need. Maybe that would be easiest after all."

His muscle control was sporadic, though, and he could not keep a steady bead on her. Patrice could not believe he would shoot her anyway. Not Jeremy Dorman.

With an outcry, she vaulted over the porch railing, throwing herself in a battering-ram tackle toward Dorman.

As he saw her charging him, he flinched backward with a look of horror on his face. "No! Don't touch me!"

Then she plowed into him, knocking his gun away and driving the man to the ground. "Jody, run! Keep running!" she screamed.

Dorman thrashed and writhed, trying to kick her away. "No, Patrice! Stay away. Stay away from me!" But she fought with him, clawing, pummeling. His skin was slick and slimy...

Without a word, Jody and the dog raced into the forest.

TWENTY-SEVEN

Kennessys' Cabin
Coast Range, Oregon
Friday, 1:26 p.m.

The dense trees clawed at him. Their branches scratched his face, tugged his hair, grabbed his shirt—but Jody kept sprinting anyway. The last words he heard were his mother's desperate shout. "Jody, run! Keep running!"

Over the past two weeks Patrice had drilled into him her fear and paranoia. They had made contingency plans. Jody knew full well that people were after them, powerful and deadly people. Someone had betrayed his father, burned down the whole laboratory facility.

He and his mother had driven away into the night, sleeping in their car parked off the road, going from place to place before finally arriving at the cabin. Again and again his mother had pounded into him that they must trust no one—and now it appeared that she might even have meant Jeremy Dorman himself. Jeremy, who had been like an uncle to him, who had played with him whenever he and his father could tear themselves away from work.

Now Jody didn't think; he just responded. He ran out the back door, across the meadow to the trees. Vader bounded into the fringe of pines ahead of him, barking as if scouting a safe path.

The cabin quickly fell behind, and Jody turned abruptly left, heading uphill. He hopped over a fallen tree, crunching broken branches and plowing through thick, thorny shrubs. Vines grabbed at the toes of his shoes, but Jody kept stumbling along.

He had explored these back woods in the last few weeks. His mother had hovered over him, making sure he didn't get into trouble or stray too far away, but still Jody had found time to poke around in the trees. He understood where he was supposed to go, how best to elude pursuit. He knew his way. He knew a few of the secret spots in the forest, but he didn't remember a hiding place that would be good enough or safe enough. His mother had told him to keep running, and he couldn't let her down.

If I buy you some time, then you can get a head start, she had said.

"Jody, wait!" It was Jeremy Dorman's voice, but it carried a strange and strangled undertone. "Hey, Jody—it's okay. I'm not going to hurt you."

Jody hesitated, then kept pushing ahead. Vader barked loudly and dashed under another fallen tree, then bounded up a rocky slope. Jody scrambled after him.

"Come here, boy. I need to talk to you," Dorman called from far back, near the cabin. Jody knew the man had just ducked into the trees, following him.

He paused for a moment, panting. His joints still ached sometimes with the strange tingly feeling, as if parts of his body had gone to sleep—but this discomfort was nothing like what he had experienced before, when the leukemia was at its worst, when he had honestly felt like dying just to stop the bone-deep ache. Now Jody felt healthy enough to go through with this effort—but he didn't want to keep it up for long. His skin crawled, and sweat prickled on his back, on his neck.

He heard Dorman lumbering through the trees, crashing branches aside, alarmingly close. How could the man have moved so fast? "Your mother wants to see you. She's waiting back at the cabin."

Jody hurried down a slope into a small gully where a stream trickled over rocks and fallen branches. Two days ago, as a game, he had skipped and hopped from stone to tree trunk to outcropping, crossing the stream and daring himself not to fall. Now the boy ran as fast as he could. Halfway across he slipped on a moss-covered boulder, and his right foot plunged into the icy water that chuckled along the banks.

He hissed in surprise, yanked his dripping foot back out of the stream, and continued across the stream. His mom had always warned him against getting his shoes wet… but right now Jody knew simple escape was much more important, was worth any sort of risk.

Dorman shouted again, "Jody, come here." He seemed a little more angry, his words sharper. "Come on, please. Only you can help me. Hey, Jody, I'm begging you!"

With his shoe soggy, Jody climbed back onto the bank. He heaved a deep breath to keep running. Grabbing a pine branch and getting sticky resin on his palm, he used it to haul himself up out of the gully to more level ground so he could run again.

He had a stitch in his side, which sent a sharp pain around his kidneys, his stomach, but he pressed his hand against the ache so he could keep fleeing. Jody didn't understand what was going on, but he trusted his fear, and he trusted his mother's warning. He vowed not to let Jeremy Dorman catch him. He paused in his tracks, gasping beside a tree as he listened intently for further pursuit.

Down the slope on the other side of the stream, he saw the heavy form of Jeremy Dorman and his tattered shirt. Their eyes met from across the great distance in the shadowy forest.

Seeing a complete stranger behind Jeremy's eyes, Jody ran with redoubled effort. His heart pounded, and his breath came in great gasps. He dove through clawing bushes that held him back. Behind him, Dorman had no difficulty charging through the underbrush.

Jody scrambled up a slope, slipping on loose wet leaves. He knew he couldn't keep up this incredible effort for long. Dorman didn't seem to be slowing at all.

He ran to a small gully, thick with deadfall and lichen-mottled sandstone outcroppings. The trees and shadows stood thick enough around him that he knew Dorman couldn't see him, and he had a chance to duck down in a damp animal hollow between a rotting tree stump and a cracked boulder. Twigs, vines, and underbrush crackled as he tried to huddle in the shelter.

He sat in silence, his lungs laboring, his pulse hammering. He listened for the man's approach. He had heard nothing at all from his mother, and he feared she might be hurt back at the cabin. What had Dorman done to her, what had she sacrificed so that he could get away?

Heavy footsteps crunched on the forest floor, but the man had stopped calling out now. Jody remembered playing chase games on his Nintendo system, how he and Jeremy Dorman would be opponents in death-defying races across the country or on alien landscapes.

But this was real, with a lot more at stake than a mere highest score.

Dorman came closer, pushing shrubs away, looking through the forest murk. Jody sat in tense silence, praying that his hiding place would remain secure.

In the distance Vader barked, and Dorman paused, then turned in a different direction. Jody saw his chance and attempted to slip away, but as he moved one of the fallen branches aside, a precariously balanced log crunched down into the brittle deadwood.

Dorman froze again, and then came charging toward Jody's hiding place.

The boy ducked down under the fallen trunk again, scuttled along next to the slick rock, and wormed his way out the other side of the gully. He stood up and raced off again, keeping his head low, pushing branches out of the way as Dorman yelled at him, fighting through the front of the thicket. Jody risked a glance over his should to see how close his pursuer had come.

Dorman reached up with a meaty hand, pointing toward him. Jody recognized a handgun at the same moment he saw a blaze of light flare from its muzzle.

A loud crack echoed through the forest. A chunk of splintered bark and wood exploded away from the pine tree only two feet above his head. Dorman had shot at him!

"Come here right now, dammit!" Dorman yelled.

Biting back an outcry, Jody scrambled away into the thick underbrush behind the tree that had protected him.

Through the forest murk, he heard Vader barking, whining as if in encouragement. Jody trusted his dog a lot more than he would ever trust Jeremy Dorman.

Jody ran off again, holding his side. His head pounded, his heart ran like a race car engine.

Back behind him, Dorman sloshed across the cold stream, not even trying to use the stepping stones. "Jody, come here!"

Jody fled desperately toward the sound of the barking dog—and, he hoped, safety.

TWENTY-EIGHT

Rural Oregon
Friday, 1:03 p.m.

The logging truck sat half off the road in a shallow ditch, its cab tilted at an odd angle like a metallic behemoth with a broken back.

As they drove up in the police cruiser, Mulder could tell instantly that something was wrong. This was more than a standard traffic accident. A red

Ford pickup sat parked on the shoulder beside the logging truck, and a man with a plastic rain poncho climbed out of the driver's side as Officer Jared Penwick pulled to a halt.

Studying the scene, Mulder spotted sinuous tire marks in the wet grass. The logging truck had weaved back and forth out of control before grinding to a stop here. A few raindrops spattered the police cruiser's windshield, and Jared left the wipers streaking back and forth. He picked up his handset, clicked the transmit button, and reported in to the dispatcher that they had arrived at the scene.

The man in the pickup truck waited beside his vehicle, hunched over in the plastic slicker as the trooper crunched toward him. Mulder followed, pulling his topcoat closed to keep himself warm. The wind and the rain mussed his hair, but there was nothing he could do about it.

"You didn't touch anything in there did you, Dominic?" Jared said.

"I'm not going near that thing," the man in the pickup answered with a suspicious glance at Mulder. "That guy in there is gross."

"This is Agent Mulder of the FBI," Jared said.

"I was just driving down the road," Dominic said, still keeping his eyes on Mulder, until he flicked his gaze toward the tilted log truck. "When I saw that truck there, I thought the driver maybe lost control in the rain. Either that, or sometimes truckers just pull off the road and sleep—not too much traffic on this stretch, you know—but it was dangerous the way he had parked. Didn't have an orange triangle set up around the back of the truck bed, like he should. I was going to chew his ass."

Dominic flicked rainwater away from his face before shaking his head. He swallowed hard. "But then I got a look inside the cab. My God, never seen anything like that."

Mulder left Jared to stand with the pickup owner as he went over to the logging truck. He held the driver's-side door handle and cautiously raised himself up by stepping on the running board.

Inside the cab, the driver of the truck sprawled back with his arms akimbo, his legs jammed up, and his knees wedged behind the steering wheel like a cockroach that had been sprayed with an exterminator's poison.

The pudgy man's face was contorted and swollen with lumps, his jaw slack. The whites of his eyes were gray and smoky, laced with red lines of worse-than-bloodshot veins. Purplish-black blotches stood out like leopard spots all over his skin, as if a miniaturized bombing raid had taken place in his vascular system.

The truck window was tightly rolled up. The rain continued to trickle off the slanted roof of the cab and down the passenger-side window. From inside, the windshield was fogged in some places. Mulder thought he saw faint steam rising from the body.

Still balanced on the running board, he turned back to the state trooper, who stood looking at him curiously. "Can you run the plates and registration?" Mulder asked. "See if you can find out who this guy was and where he might have been going."

It made Mulder very uneasy to see another hideous death so close to the possible location of Patrice and Jody Kennessy—so close to where Scully had gone to look for them.

The trooper came forward and took his turn peering through the driver's-side window, as if it were a circus peep show. "That's disgusting," he said. "What happened to the guy?"

"No one should touch the body until we can get some more help out here," Mulder said briskly. "The medical examiner in Portland has dealt with this before. He should probably be called in, since he'll know how to handle this."

The trooper hesitated, as if he wanted to ask a dozen more questions, but instead he trotted back to talk on his radio.

Mulder walked around the front of the truck, saw how the cab had shifted to the right, nearly jackknifing the vehicle. The splintered logs were still securely fastened by chains to the long truck bed.

If the driver had gone into convulsions and swerved the heavy vehicle off the road, luckily his foot had slipped from the accelerator. The log truck had come to a stop on this rise without careening into a tree or crashing over a steeper embankment.

Mulder stared at the grille of the truck as the rain picked up again. Trickles of water slithered down his back, and he shrugged his shoulders, pulling up the collar of his topcoat in an effort to keep himself a little drier.

Mulder continued walking around the truck, descending into the ditch. His shoes splashed in the water, and the weeds danced along his pant cuffs. Once he got completely drenched, he supposed, it wouldn't matter if the rain got any heavier.

Then he saw that the log truck's passenger door hung ajar.

He froze, suddenly considering possibilities. What if someone else had been in the truck, a passenger—someone with the driver, maybe even a hitchhiker? The carrier of this lethal biological agent?

Mulder walked carefully over to the open door, glancing behind him into the close trees, the tall weeds, wondering if he would see another corpse, the body of a passenger who had undergone similar convulsions but managed to stagger away and collapse outside.

But he saw nothing. The rain began to sheet down harder. "What did you find, Agent Mulder?" the trooper called.

"Still checking," he said. "Stay where you are."

The trooper called out again. "I've got the Portland ME and some other local law enforcement on their way. We'll have a real party scene here in a little while." Then, happy to let Mulder continue his business, Officer Penwick turned back to chat with the pickup driver.

Mulder carefully opened the heavy passenger-side door, and the metal swung out with a groan of hinges. He stepped back to peer inside.

The dead trucker looked even more bent and twisted from this perspective. Condensed steam had formed a halo across the windshield and the driver's-side door. The air smelled humid, but without the sour sharpness of death. The body hadn't been here for long, despite its horrible condition.

The passenger seat interested Mulder the most, though. He saw threads and tatters of cloth from a shirt that had been split or torn. Runnels of a strange translucent sticky substance clung to the fabric of the seat. A kind of congealed... slime, similar to what Mulder had seen on the dead security guard.

He swallowed hard, not wanting to get any closer, careful not to touch anything. This was indeed the same thing they had encountered before at the morgue. Mulder was sure this strange toxin, this lethal agent, was the result of Kennessy's renegade work.

Perhaps the unfortunate trucker had picked up someone and had become infected in close quarters. After the truck had crashed and the driver had died, the mysterious passenger had slipped away and escaped.

But where would he go?

Mulder saw a square of something like paper lying in the footwell beneath the passenger seat. At first he thought it was a candy wrapper or some kind of label, but then he realized it was a photograph, bent and half-hidden in the shadow of the seat.

Mulder withdrew a pen from his pocket and leaned forward, still careful not to touch any of the slimy residue. It was risky, but he felt a growing sense of urgency. Extending the pen, he reached in and drew the bent photo toward him. The edges were surrounded by other threads, as if the photo had fallen out of a shirt pocket during some sort of violent struggle.

He used the pen to flip over the photograph. It was a picture Mulder had not seen before, but he certainly recognized the faces of the woman and the young boy. He had seen them often enough in the past few days, had shown other photos to hundreds of people in their search for Patrice and Jody.

That meant whoever had been a passenger here in the truck, whoever had carried the nanotech plague, was also on his way, also connected to the woman and her son.

Headed to the same place Scully had gone.

Mulder tossed the pen into the truck, not daring to put it back in his pocket. As he hurried back around to the road, the trooper called to him from his patrol car, waving him over. "Agent Mulder!"

Mulder stepped away from the truck, wet and cold, feeling a deeper tension now. Distracted, Mulder went to see what Officer Penwick wanted.

"There's a truck weigh station a few miles back on this road. It's rarely open, but they have Highway Patrol surveillance cameras that operate automatically. I had somebody run them back a few hours to see if we could grab an image of this truck passing." Penwick smiled, and Mulder nodded at the man's good thinking. "That way we can at least establish a solid time frame."

"Did you find anything?" Mulder asked.

The trooper smiled. "Two images. One, we got the log truck barreling past—10:52 a.m. And a few minutes before that, we caught a man walking past. Very little traffic on the road."

"Can we get a video grab?" Mulder said eagerly, sliding into the front seat of the patrol car, looking down at the small screen mounted below the dash for their crime computer linkups.

"I thought you might want that," Penwick said, fiddling with the keypad. "I just had it up here... ah, there we go."

The first image showed the log truck heading down the road, obviously the same vehicle now stalled in the ditch. The digital time code on the bottom of the picture verified what the trooper had said.

But Mulder was more interested in something else. "Let me see the hitch-hiker, the other man." His brows knitted as he tried to think of other possibilities. If the nanotechnology pathogen was as lethal as he suspected, the trucker wouldn't have lasted long in close quarters with it.

The new image was somewhat blurry, but showed a man walking on the muddy shoulder, seemingly impervious to the rain. He looked directly at the camera, at the weigh station, as if longing to stop there and take shelter, but then he walked on.

Mulder had seen enough, though. He had looked at the file pictures, the DyMar background dossiers, the photos of the two researchers supposedly killed in the devastating fire.

It was Jeremy Dorman—David Kennessy's assistant. He was still alive.

And if Dorman had been exposed to something at DyMar, he was even now carrying a substance that had already killed at least two people.

He slid out of the front of the patrol car, looking urgently at the trooper. "Officer Penwick, you have to stay here and protect the scene. This is a highly hazardous place. Do not let anyone go near the body or even inside the cab of the truck without proper decontamination equipment."

"Sure, Agent Mulder," the trooper said. "But where will you be?"

Mulder turned toward Dominic. "Sir, I'm a federal agent. I need the use of your vehicle."

"My truck?" Dominic said.

"I need to reach my partner. I'm afraid she may be in grave danger." Before Dominic could argue with him, Mulder opened the door of the Ford pickup and extended his left hand. "The keys, please."

Dominic looked questioningly over at the state trooper, but Officer Penwick simply shrugged. "I've seen his ID. He is who he says." Then the trooper tucked his hat down against the rain. "Don't worry, Dominic. I'll give you a ride home."

The pickup driver frowned, as if this hadn't been the part that concerned him at all. Mulder slammed the door, and the old engine started with a comforting roar. He wrestled with the stick shift, trying to remember how to apply the clutch and nudge the gas pedal.

"You take good care of my truck!" Dominic yelled. "I don't want to waste time messing with insurance companies."

Mulder pushed down hard on the accelerator, hoping he would reach Scully in time.

TWENTY-NINE

Kennessys' Cabin
Coast Range, Oregon
Friday, 1:45 p.m.

Scully became disoriented on the winding dirt logging roads, but after making a cautious Y-turn on the narrow track, she finally found the driveway as described by Maxie at the general store and art gallery. She saw no mailbox, only a metal reflector post that bore a cryptic number designating a specific plot for fire control or trash pickup.

It was just a nondescript private road chewed through the dense underbrush, climbing over a rise and vanishing somewhere back into a secluded hollow. This was it, though—the place where Patrice and Jody Kennessy had supposedly been taken, or gone into hiding.

Scully drove down the driveway as quickly as she dared through mud puddles and over bumps. Up the rise on either side of her, the forest seemed too close. Branches ticked and scraped along the sideview mirrors.

She accelerated over a large bump, some long-buried log, and reached the top of the rise. The bottom of the car scraped on the gravel as she headed down the slope. Ahead of her, in a cleared meadow surrounded on all sides by dense trees, sat a single isolated cabin. A perfect place for hiding.

This modest, rugged home seemed even more out of the way and invisible than the survivalist outpost she and Mulder had visited the day before.

She drove forward cautiously, noticing a muddy car parked to one side of the cabin, where a corrugated metal overhang protected it from the rain. The car was a Volvo, the type a yuppie medical researcher would have driven—not the old pickup or sport utility vehicle a regular inhabitant of these mountains would have purchased.

Her heart raced. This place felt right: isolated, quiet, ominous. She had come miles from the nearest assistance, miles from reliable phone reception.

Anyone could hide out here, and anything could happen.

She eased the car to a stop in front of the cabin and waited for a few moments. This was a dangerous situation. She was approaching alone with no backup. She had no way of knowing whether Patrice and Jody were hiding voluntarily, or if someone held them hostage here, someone with weapons.

As Scully stepped out of the car, her head pounded. She paused for a moment as colors flashed before her eyes, but then with a deep breath she calmed herself and slammed the car door. "Hello?"

She wasn't approaching in secret. Anyone who lived in this cabin would have heard her approach, perhaps even before her car topped the rise. She couldn't be stealthy. She had to be apparent.

Scully stood beside the car for a few seconds, waiting. She withdrew her ID wallet with her left hand and kept her right hand on the Sig Sauer handgun on her hip. She was ready for anything.

Most of all, though, she just wanted to see Jody and make sure he got the medical attention he needed.

"Hello? Anybody there?" Scully called, speaking loudly enough to be heard by anyone inside the house. She took two steps away from the car.

The cabin seemed like a haunted house. Its windows were dark, some covered with drapes. Nothing stirred inside. She heard no sounds from within… but the door was ajar.

Beside the door she saw a fresh gouge in the wood siding, pale splinters… the mark from a small-caliber bullet.

Scully stepped up onto the slick wooden porch. "Anybody home?" she said again. "I'm a federal agent."

As she hesitated in front of the door, though, Scully looked to her left and spotted a figure in the tall grass beside the cabin. A human figure, lying still.

Scully froze, all senses alert, then approached to the edge of the porch, peering over the railing. It was a woman, sprawled on her chest in the tall grass.

Scully rushed back down the steps, then pulled herself to a halt as she looked down at a woman she recognized as Patrice Kennessy, with strawberry blond hair and narrow features—but the resemblance ended there.

Scully recalled the smiling woman whose photo she had looked at so many times—her husband a well-known and talented researcher, her son laughing and happy before the leukemia had struck him.

But Patrice Kennessy was no longer vivacious, no longer even on the run to protect her son. Now she lay twisted in the meadow, her head turned toward Scully and her expression grim and desperate even in death. Her skin was blotched with numerous hemorrhages from subcutaneous damage, distorted with wild growths in all shapes and sizes. Her eyes were squeezed shut, and Scully saw tiny maps of blood on the lids. Her hands were outstretched like claws, as if she had died while fighting tooth and nail against something horrible.

Scully stood stricken. She had arrived too late.

She moved back, knowing not to approach or touch the possibly contagious body. Patrice was already dead. Now the only thing that remained was to find Jody and keep him safe—unless something had already happened to him.

She listened to the wind whispering through the tall pines, a shushing sound as needles scraped against each other. The clouds overhead were thick with the constant threat of rain. She heard a few birds and other forest sounds, but the silence and abandonment of the place seemed oppressive, surrounding her.

Then she heard a dog bark off in the forest, a sharp excited sound—and a moment later came the distinctive crack of a gunshot.

"Come here right now, dammit!" She heard the words, a voice flattened by distance, made gruff with a threat. "Jody, come here!"

Scully drew her handgun and advanced toward the forest, following the sound of voices. Jody was still out here, running for his life—and a man who must have carried the plague, the man who had exposed Patrice Kennessy, was now after the boy.

Scully had to catch him first. She ran toward the forest.

THIRTY

Kennessys' Cabin
Coast Range, Oregon
Friday, 1:59 p.m.

No matter how far Jody ran, Dorman followed. The only shelter he could think of was the cabin, endlessly far back through the trees. The small building was not much of an island of safety, but he could think of no better place to go. At least there he could find some crude weapons, something with which to fight back.

His mother was resourceful, and Jody could be, too. He had learned a lot from her in the past weeks.

Jody circled through the trees in a long arc, looping around the meadow and approaching from the rear. Vader continued to bark in the trees, sometimes running close to Jody and then bounding off, as if ready to hunt or play. Jody wondered if the black Lab thought it was all some kind of game.

He continued stumbling along, his legs aching as if sharp metal pins had been inserted into his knees. His side was aflame with pain. His face had been scratched by sharp branches and whipping pine needles, but he paid no attention to the minor injuries; they would fade quickly. His throat was dry, and he couldn't draw in enough breath.

As quietly as he could move, he stumbled along without trails, without guidance, but after weeks of nothing to do but play in the woods, he knew how to find the cabin. Vader would follow him. Together they could get out of this, and his mother… if she was still safe.

From above, Jody could see the small building and the meadow ahead. He'd come farther than he had thought, but now he could see another car in the driveway. A strange vehicle.

He felt a rush of cold fear. Someone else had tracked him down! One of those others his mother had warned him about. Even if he succeeded in outsmarting Jeremy Dorman and escaping back to the cabin, would others be waiting there for him? Or did they mean to help? He had no way of knowing.

But right now his greatest fear was much closer at hand.

Dorman continued to charge after him like a truck, plowing through the trees and underbrush, closing the gap. Jody couldn't believe how fast the broad-shouldered man was moving, especially because the big lab assistant did not look at all healthy.

"Jody, please! I won't hurt you if you just let me talk to you for a second."

Jody didn't waste his breath answering. He ran back, arrowing toward the cabin, but abruptly came to a steep slope where a mudslide had sheared off the gentle hillside. Two enormous trees had uprooted, tumbling down and leaving a gash in the dirt like an open wound.

Jody didn't have time to go around. Dorman was approaching too fast, rushing along the hillside, holding onto trees and pulling himself along.

The slope looked too steep. He couldn't possibly get down it.

He heard the dog bark again. Halfway to the bottom, off to the left of the mudslide, Vader stood with his paws spread, his fur tangled with cockleburrs and weeds. He barked up at his boy.

With no other choice, Jody decided to follow. He eased himself over the lip of the mudslide and started to descend, using his hands, digging his fingers into the cold ground, stepping on loose rocks, and looking for support. He heard twigs snapping, branches crashing aside, as Dorman came closer.

Jody tried to move faster. He looked up and glimpsed the burly figure at the upper edge of the hillside. He gasped—and his hand slipped.

Jody's foot stepped on an unstable rock, which popped out of the raw dirt like a rotten tooth coming loose from a gum. He bit back an outcry as he began to fall.

He scrabbled with his fingers, digging into the mud, but his body slid down, tumbling, rolling, covering his clothes in dirt and mud. Rocks pattered around him.

As he bounced and slid, Jody saw Dorman standing at the lip of the mudslide, his hands outstretched like claws, ready to bend down and grab him—but the boy was too far away, still falling, still picking up speed.

Jody rolled, struck his side, and then his head—but he remained conscious, terrified that he would break his leg so that he couldn't keep running away from Dorman.

Dirt and rocks showered around him, but he didn't scream, didn't even cry out—and he finally came to rest at the bottom of the slide, up against one of the toppled trees. Its matted root system stuck out like a dirt-encrusted scrubbing pad. He slammed hard against the bark and lay gasping, struggling, trying to move. His back hurt.

Then, to his horror, he saw Jeremy Dorman bounding down the sharp slope up above, somehow keeping his balance. Dirt and gravel flew up from his feet as he stomped heavy indentations in the soft hillside. He waved the revolver in his hand in a threat to keep Jody where he was—not that Jody could have gotten up and moved fast enough anyway.

Dorman skidded to a halt just above the boy. His face was flushed… and his skin looked as if it were *crawling*, writhing, seething like a pot of candle wax slowly coming to a boil. Rage and exertion contorted the man's face.

He held the handgun up, gripping it with both hands and pointing the barrel directly at Jody. It looked like a cyclopean eye, a deadly open-mouthed viper.

Then Dorman's shoulders sagged, and he just stared at the boy for a few moments. "Jody, why do you have to make this so hard? Haven't I been through enough—haven't you been through enough?"

"Where's my mom?" Jody demanded, drawing deep breaths. His heart thumped like a jackhammer and his breath felt cold and frosty, like knives in his lungs. He struggled to get to his knees.

Dorman gestured with the revolver again. "All I need is some of your blood, Jody, that's all. Just some blood. Fresh blood."

"I said, where's my mom?" Jody shouted.

Dorman looked as if a thunderstorm passed across his face. Both the boy and the man were so intent on each other, neither heard the other person approach.

"Freeze! Federal agent!"

Dana Scully stood in the trees fifteen feet away, her feet braced, her arms extended and gripping her handgun in a precise firing position.

"Don't move," she said.

Scully had breathlessly followed the sounds of pursuit, the barking dog, the angry shouted words. When she came upon the hulking man who loomed too close over Jody Kennessy, she knew she had to prevent this man—this carrier of something like a deadly viral cancer—from so much as touching the boy.

Both the intimidating man and the twelve-year-old Jody snapped their glances aside to look at her, astonished. Jody's expression flooded with relief, then rapidly turned to suspicion.

"You're one of *them*!" the boy whispered.

Scully wondered how much Patrice Kennessy had told him, how much Jody knew about the death of his father and the possible conspiracy involving DyMar.

But what astonished her the most was the appearance of the boy. He seemed healthy, not gaunt and haggard, not at all pale and sickly. He should have been in the final stages of terminal lymphoblastic leukemia. Granted, Jody looked exhausted, battered… haunted perhaps by constant fear and lack of sleep. But certainly not like a terminal cancer patient.

Nearly a month earlier, Jody had been bedridden, at death's doorway. But now the boy had run vigorously through the forest and been caught by this man only because he had stumbled and fallen down a steep hillside.

The large man scowled at Scully, dismissed her, and tried to ease closer to the boy.

"I said don't move, sir," Scully said. Seeing the revolver hanging loosely in his hand, she feared he might take Jody in a hostage situation. "Put your gun down," she said, "and identify yourself."

The man looked at her with such pure disgust and impatience that she felt cold. "You don't know what's going on here," he said. "Stop interfering." He looked hungrily back down at the trapped Jody, then snapped his glance toward Scully once more. "Or are you one of them? Just like the boy says? Out to annihilate both of us?"

Before she could answer or question him further, a black shape like a rocket-propelled battering ram bounded from the underbrush and launched itself toward the man threatening Jody.

In a flash Scully recognized the dog, the black Lab that had somehow survived being struck by a car, that had escaped from the veterinarian's office and gone on the run with Patrice and Jody.

"Vader!" Jody cried.

The dog lunged. Black Labradors were not normally used as attack dogs, but Vader must have been able to sense the fear and tension in the air. He knew who the enemy was, and he fought back.

The burly man whirled, raising his gun and gripping the trigger with the sudden unexpected threat—but the dog crashed into him, growling and snarling, spoiling his aim. The man cried out, threw up his free hand to ward off the attack—and his finger squeezed the trigger.

The explosion roared through the quiet isolation far from the main road.

Instead of taking off Jody's head, the .38-caliber shell slammed into the boy's chest before he could hurl himself out of the way. The impact sprayed blood behind him, knocking the boy's lean frame back against the fallen tree, as if someone with an invisible piano wire had just jerked him backward. Jody cried out, and slid down the rain-slick bole of the tree.

Vader bore the gunman to the ground. The man tried to fight the dog off, but the suddenly vicious black Lab bit at his face, his throat.

Scully raced over to the wounded boy, dropped to her knees, and cradled Jody's head. "Oh my God!"

The boy blinked his eyes, wide with astonishment and seemingly far away. Blood bubbled out of his mouth, and he spat it aside. "So tired." She stroked his hair, unable to leave him to rescue the big man who had shot him.

The dog continued growling, snapping his jaws, digging his muzzle into the man's throat, ripping at the tendons. Blood sprayed onto the forest floor. The man dropped his smoking revolver and pounded on the black Lab's rib cage, trying to knock him away, but growing weaker and weaker.

Scully stared at where foamy scarlet blood blossomed from the center of Jody's chest. A hole with neat round edges stood out against a welling, pulsing lake of blood. She could tell from the placement of the wound that no simple first aid would do Jody any good.

"Oh, no," she said and bent down, tearing Jody's shirt wider and looking at the gunshot wound that had penetrated his left lung and perhaps struck the heart. A serious wound—a deadly wound.

He would never survive.

Jody's skin turned gray and pale. His eyes were closed in unconsciousness. Blood continued to pour from the bullet hole.

Leaning forward, Scully pushed aside her empathy for Jody, mentally clicking into her emergency medical mindset, slapping the heel of her hand on the wound and pressing down, pushing hard against the cloth of his shirt to stop the flow of blood. At her side, she could hear the dog continuing his attack on the fallen man—a vicious attack, a personal vendetta, as if this man had once hurt the dog very badly. Scully concentrated, though, on helping the boy. She had to slow the terrible bleeding from the bullet wound.

THIRTY-ONE

Kennessys' Cabin
Coast Range, Oregon
Friday, 2:20 p.m.

The sudden carnage astonished Scully, and time seemed to stop as the forest pressed around her, the smell of blood and black powder from the gunshots. The birdsong and the breeze fell silent.

She hesitated for only a moment before snapping back into her mindset as a federal agent. After pressing down her makeshift bandage, she stood up jerkily from the mortally wounded boy and ran over to the dog, who was still growling and snapping at the fallen man. She grabbed Vader by the skin of his neck, grappling with his strong shoulders and front forepaws to pull him away. His bloodied victim lay twitching in the mud, leaves, and twigs.

She tugged at the dog, dragging him away.

The dog continued to growl; and Scully realized the danger of throwing herself upon a vicious animal that had just ripped out the throat of a man. A killer. But the black Lab acquiesced and staggered away, sitting down obediently in the forest debris. Frothy blood covered his muzzle, and his sepia eyes were bright and angry, still fixed on the fallen form. Scully saw his red teeth and shivered.

She glanced down at the man who had held Jody at bay, who had shot the boy. His throat was mangled. His shirt hung in tatters, shredded as if it had burst from the inside.

Though he was obviously dead, the man's hand jittered and jerked like a frog on a dissection table, and his skin squirmed as if alive from the inside, the home of a colony of swarming cockroaches. Patches of his exposed skin glistened, wet and gelatinous… like the mucus Scully had found during her autopsy of Vernon Ruckman.

His skin also had an uneven darkish cast… but the blotches shifted and faded, mobile hemorrhages that healed and passed across his complexion. This man must be the carrier of the instantly disruptive disease that had killed Patrice Kennessy and Vernon Ruckman, and probably the trucker Mulder had gone to investigate. She had no idea who this was, but he looked oddly familiar to her. He must have some connection with DyMar Laboratory, with David Kennessy's research, and the radical cancer treatment he had meant to develop for his son.

As time seemed to stand still, Scully looked over at the black Lab to see if Vader might be suffering from the effects of the plague as well—but apparently the cellular destruction did not transfer readily across species boundaries. Vader sat patiently, not wagging his tail but focused intently on her reaction. He whined, as if daring her to challenge what he had done to protect his boy.

She whirled back toward Jody, who still lay gasping and bleeding from the bullet wound in his chest. She tore off more of his shirtsleeve and pressed the wadded cloth hard upon the open bubbling wound.

This was a penetrating wound—the bullet had not passed through the other side of Jody's back, but remained lodged somewhere in his lung, in his heart…

Scully couldn't imagine how the boy might survive—but she kept on treating him, doing what she knew best. She had lost fellow agents before, other people injured on cases—but she felt a unique affinity with Jody.

The twelve-year-old also suffered from a form of terminal cancer; both he and Scully were victims of the vagaries of fate, the mutations of one cell too many. Jody had already been given a death sentence by his own biology, but Scully didn't intend to let a tragic accident rob him of his last month or so of life. This was one thing she could control.

She fumbled in her pocket and pulled out the cellular phone. With shaking, blood-tipped fingers, she punched in the programmed number for Mulder's phone—but all she received was a burst of static. She was out of range in the isolated wooded hills. She tried three times, hoping for at least a faint signal, some stray opening of the electromagnetic window in the iono-sphere… but she had no such luck. It was almost as if someone was jamming her phone. Scully was alone.

She thought about running back to the car, driving it across the rugged meadows as close as she could get to the slide area, then rushing to Jody and carrying him to the car. It would be easier that way, if the car could travel over the wet and uneven meadow.

But that would also mean she'd have to leave Jody's side. She looked at the blood on her hands from pressing down on his gunshot wound, saw his pale complexion, and noted his faint fluttery breathing. No, she would not leave him. Jody might well die before she made it back here with the car, and she vowed not to let the boy die alone.

"Looks like I'll have to take you myself, then," she said grimly, and bent over to gather up the young man. "Above and beyond the call of duty."

Jody's frame was slight and frail. Though he appeared to have fought back the worst ravages of his wasting disease, he still had not put on much weight, and she could lift him. It was lucky they were close to the cabin.

Vader whined next to her, wanting to come close.

Jody moaned when she moved him. She tried not to hurt him further, though she had no choice but to get him back to her car, where she could drive at breakneck speed to the nearest hospital... wherever that might be.

She left the mangled and bloody form of the attacker lying on the trampled forest floor. The burly man was dead, killed before her eyes.

Later on, evidence technicians would come here and study the body of this man, as well as Patrice's. But that was in the future. There would be plenty of time to pick up the loose threads, to explain the pieces.

For now, the only thing that mattered to Scully was to get this boy to medical attention.

She felt so helpless. She was sure that whatever first aid she could give him—even whatever emergency room surgery the doctors could perform whenever she arrived at a medical center—would be too little, too late.

But she refused to give up.

In her arms, Jody felt warm and feverish. Incredibly hot, in fact. But Scully couldn't waste time thinking of explanations. She trudged ahead at her best speed, lugging him out of the forest, taking him to help. The black Lab followed close at her heels, silent and worried.

Jody continued to bleed, spilling crimson droplets along the forest floor, the grass, finally out to the clearing around the cabin. Scully focused her attention straight ahead and kept moving toward her rental car. She had to get out of here, had to hurry.

She looked off to one side as she bypassed the plague-ridden body of Patrice Kennessy. She was glad Jody didn't have to see his mother like this. Perhaps he didn't even know what had happened to her.

Scully reached the car and gently set the boy down on the ground, leaning his back against the back fender as she opened the rear door. Vader barked and jumped in, then barked again, as if urging her to hurry.

Scully picked up Jody's limp form and gently positioned him inside the car. Her makeshift bandage had fallen off, soaked with blood. But the bleeding from his huge wound had slowed remarkably, congealing. Scully worried that meant Jody's heartbeat was weak, at the edge of death. She pressed more cloth against the bullet hole, and then jumped into the driver's seat and started the car.

She drove off at a reckless speed up the bumpy dirt driveway, over the rise. She scraped the bottom of her car again as she headed back toward the logging road, but she accelerated this time, ignoring all caution.

The isolated cabin with all of its murder and death fell behind them. In the back seat, Vader looked through the rear window and continued barking.

THIRTY-TWO

Federal Office Building
Crystal City, Virginia
Friday, 12:08 p.m.

The phone rang in Adam Lentz's plain government office, and he grabbed for it immediately. Very few people knew his direct number, so the call had to be important, though it startled him from his quiet and intense study of maps and detailed local survey charts of the Oregon wilderness.

"Hello," he said, keeping his voice neutral.

Lentz listened to the voice on the other end of the phone, feeling a sudden chill. "Yes, sir," he answered. "I was about to have a progress report for you."

Indeed, he had put together a careful map of his ongoing search, a listing of all the attempts he had made, the professional hunters and investigators combing the wooded, mountainous area of western Oregon.

"In fact," Lentz said, "I have my briefcase packed and a ticket voucher. My plane leaves for Portland within the hour. I'm going to head up the mobile tactical command center there. I want to be on site so I can take care of things personally."

He listened to the voice, detecting no displeasure, no scorn, only the faintest background lilt of sarcasm.

The man didn't want a formal report. Not at this time. In fact, he tended to avoid anything on paper whatsoever, so Lentz verbally gave him a summary of what he had done to track down Patrice and Jody Kennessy and their pet dog.

Lentz looked at his topographical maps. With a flat voice he listed where the six teams had concentrated their searches, rattling off one after another. He did not need to make his efforts sound extravagant or impressive—just competent.

Finally, though, a hint of criticism came from the other end of the phone conversation. "We had thought all of the uncontrolled samples of Kennessy's nanomachines were destroyed. Your previous reports stated as much. This was a very important goal of ours, and I'm quite disappointed to learn that this isn't so. And the dog—that's a rather large mistake."

Lentz swallowed. "We believed those efforts had been successful after the fire at DyMar. We had sent sterilization crews in to retrieve any unburned records. We found the fire safe and the videotape, but nothing else."

"Yes," the man said on the phone, "but from the condition of the dead security guard—as well as several other bodies—we must assume that some of the nanomachines have now escaped."

"We'll get them, sir," Lentz said. "We're doing our best to track down the fugitives. Finding the dog should be no problem. When we complete our mission, I assure you, there won't be any samples remaining."

"That isn't a suggestion," the voice said. "That's the way it must be."

"I understand, sir," Lentz replied. "I've narrowed down my search, concentrating on a particular area in rural Oregon."

He rolled up the maps as he talked, folded other documents, and slid them into his briefcase. He glanced at his watch. His plane would be departing soon. He had only unmarked carry-on luggage, and he had papers that allowed him to bypass normal ticketing requirements. Lentz could take advantage of one of those empty seats the airlines were required to keep on all flights for important military or government personnel. His passes allowed him to move about at will with no written record of his travel plans or his movements. Such things were required in his line of work.

"And one last thing," said the man on the phone. "I've suggested this before, but I will reiterate it. You would do well to keep your eye on Agent Mulder. Make sure part of your team is specifically assigned to shadowing his movements, following everything he does. Eavesdrop on every conversation he has.

"You already have the manpower that you need, but Agent Mulder has a certain... talent for the unexpected. If you stay close to him, he may well lead you exactly where you need to be."

"Thank you, sir," Lentz said, then glanced at his watch again. "I need to get to National Airport. I'll remain in touch, but for now I've got a plane to catch."

"And a mission to accomplish," the man said without the slightest hint of emotion.

THIRTY-THREE

Kennessys' Cabin
Coast Range, Oregon
Friday, 3:15 p.m.

The red pickup truck Mulder had commandeered handled surprisingly well. With its big tires and high clearance, it ran like a steamroller over the potholes, puddles, and broken branches on the old logging road and the overgrown half-graded driveway that led back to the isolated cabin.

After seeing the dead trucker's body and the image of supposedly dead Jeremy Dorman on the surveillance videotape, he felt an urgency to find Scully, to warn her. But the cabin was quiet, empty, abandoned.

Leaving the truck and walking around, he saw fresh tire marks embedded in the soft mud and gravel. Someone had driven here recently and then departed again. Could Scully have gone already? Where would she go?

When he discovered the woman's body lying in the grass, he knew it was Patrice Kennessy, without a doubt.

Mulder frowned and stepped back away from her. Patrice's skin had been ravaged by the same disease he had just seen on the dead truck driver. He swallowed hard.

"Scully!" He moved with greater urgency. The scarlet blood spatters on the ground were obvious, bright red coins splashed in an uneven pattern.

With a sheen of sweat on his forehead, Mulder broke into a trot, looking ahead, then back down to the ground as he followed the blood trail back into the forest.

Now he saw footprints. Scully's shoes. Paw prints from a dog. His heart beat faster.

Mulder found his way to the base of a steep slope where a mudslide had gouged the hillside. Near one of the horizontal tree trunks Mulder saw the blood-smeared man with broad shoulders, tattered clothes, and a mangled throat ripped all the way down to the neck bone.

He recognized the burly man from the DyMar personnel photos, from the surveillance video at the truck weigh station. Jeremy Dorman—certainly dead now.

Mulder also smelled gunpowder beyond the blood. The dead man's hand clutched a service revolver. From the smell, Mulder could tell it had been recently fired—but Dorman didn't look as if he'd be firing it again anytime soon.

Mulder bent over to inspect the gaping wound in the man's throat. Had the black Lab attacked him?

But even as he watched, Dorman's mangled larynx and the muscle tissue and skin around it looked melted, smoothing itself over, as if someone had sealed it with wax. His throat injury was filled with translucent mucus, slime oozing over the mangled skin.

Around him, Mulder saw signs of a struggle where rocks and mud had slid down the slope. It looked as if someone had fallen over the edge, and then been pursued. He saw more of the dog's footprints, Scully's shoe prints.

And smaller prints—the boy's?

"Scully!" he called out again, but he heard no answer, only the rustle of pine trees and a few birds. The forest remained hushed, fearful or angry. Mulder listened, but he heard no answer.

Then the dead man on the ground lurched up as if spring-loaded.

His claw-like left hand grabbed the edge of Mulder's overcoat. Mulder cried out and struggled backward, but the desperate man clung to his coat.

Without changing his cadaverous expression, Jeremy Dorman brought up the revolver he held in his hand, pointing it threateningly at Mulder. Mulder looked down and saw the clutching hand, its covering of skin squirming, moving—infested with nanomachines?—slicked with a coating of slime. A contagious mucus… the carrier of the deadly nanotech plague.

THIRTY-FOUR

Oregon Wilderness
Friday, 4:19 p.m.

Fifty miles at least to the nearest hospital, along tangled roads through wooded mountains—and Scully didn't know exactly where she was going. She raced away as the lowering sun glittered through the trees, and then the clouds closed over again.

She kept driving, pushing her foot to the floor and wrestling with the curves of the county road, heading north. Dark pine trees flashed by like tunnel walls on either side of her.

In the backseat, Vader whimpered, very upset. Clumps of blood and foam bristled from his muzzle. She hadn't taken time to clean him up. He snuffled at the motionless boy on the seat beside him.

Scully remembered the brutal way the dog had attacked the hulking man who had carried the plague that killed Patrice Kennessy, who had threatened Jody. Now, despite the spattered evidence of dried blood on his fur, he seemed utterly loyal and devoted to guarding his master.

Before driving away from the cabin, she had checked Jody's pulse. It was faint, his breathing shallow—but the boy still lived, clinging tenaciously. He seemed to be in a coma. In the past twenty minutes Jody hadn't made a sound, not even a groan. She glanced up in the rearview mirror, just to reassure herself.

From the trees on her right, a dog stepped into the road in front of her, and she spotted it out of the corner of her eye. Scully slammed the brakes and yanked the steering wheel.

The dog bounded back out of sight, into the underbrush. She swerved, nearly lost control of the car on the slick road, then at the latest minute regained it. Behind her, in the rearview mirror, she saw the dark shape of the dog trot back across the road, undaunted by its close call.

In the backseat Jody gasped, and his spine arched with some kind of convulsion. Scully jerked the car to a stop in the middle of the road and unbuckled her seatbelt to reach back, dreading to find that the boy had finally succumbed to death, that he had reached the limits of endurance.

She touched him. Jody's skin was hot and feverish, damp with sweat. His skin burned. Sweat trickled along his forehead. His eyes were squeezed shut. Despite all her medical training, Scully still didn't know what to do.

In a moment the convulsion faded, and Jody breathed a little more easily. Vader nudged the boy in the shoulder and then licked Jody's cheek, whimpering.

Seeing him stabilized for the moment, Scully didn't dare waste any more time. She shifted back into gear and roared off, her tires spinning on the leaf-covered asphalt. Trees swallowed the curves ahead, and she was forced to concentrate on the road rather than her patient.

Beside her the cell phone still displayed NO SERVICE on its little screen. She felt incredibly isolated, like the survivalists in the group where Jody's uncle had gone to hide. Those people wanted it that way, but right now Scully would have much preferred a large, brightly lit hospital with lots of doctors and other specialists to help.

She wished Mulder were here. She wished she could at least call him.

When Jody coughed and sat up in the back seat, looking groggy but otherwise perfectly healthy, Scully nearly drove off the road.

Vader barked and nuzzled the young man, crawling all over him, slobbering on him, utterly happy to see Jody restored.

Scully slammed on the brakes. The car slewed onto the soft shoulder, and she came to a stop near an unmarked dirt road.

"Jody!" she cried. "You're all right."

"I'm hungry," he said, rubbing his eyes. He looked around in the backseat. His shirt still hung open, and though dried blood was caked on his skin, she could see that the wound itself had closed over.

She popped open her door and raced to the back of the car, leaving the driver's side open. The helpful chiming bell scolded her for leaving the keys in the ignition. In the back she bent over, grasping Jody by the shoulders.

"Sit back. Are you all right?" She touched him, checking his skin. His fever had dropped, but he still felt warm. "How do you feel?"

She saw that skin had folded over the gunshot wound in his chest, clean and smooth, with a plastic appearance. "I don't believe this," Scully said.

"Is there anything to eat?" Jody asked.

Scully remembered the bag of cheese curls Mulder had left in the front seat, and she moved around to the other side of the car to get it. The boy grabbed the bag of snack food and ate greedily, chomping handfuls as powdery orange flavoring covered his lips and fingers.

The black Lab wiggled and squirmed in the backseat, demanding as much attention as his boy could give him, though Jody was more interested in just eating. Offhandedly, he patted Vader on the shoulders.

Finished with the cheese curls, Jody leaned forward to scrounge around. Scully saw something glint. With a quiet sound, a piece of metal dropped away from his back.

Scully reached behind him, and Jody distractedly shifted aside to give her room. She picked up a slug—the bullet that had been lodged inside him. She lifted the back of his shirt, saw a red mark, a puckered scar that faded even as she watched. She held the flattened bullet between her fingertips, amazed.

"Jody, do you know what's happened to you?" she said.

The boy looked up at her, his face smeared with cheese powder. Vader sat next to him and laid his chin on Jody's shoulder, blinking his big brown eyes and looking absolutely at peace, enthralled to have the boy back and ready to pay attention to him.

Jody shrugged. "Something my dad did." He yawned. "Nanotech... no, he called them nanocritters. Biological policemen to make me better from the leukemia, fix me up. He made me promise not to tell anybody—not even my mom."

Before she could think of another thing to ask, Jody yawned again and his eyes dulled. Now that he had eaten, an overpowering weariness came over him. "I need to rest," he said, and though Scully tried to ask him more questions, Jody was unable to answer.

He blinked his heavy eyelids several times and then drew a deep breath, fading backward into the seat, where he dropped into a deep and restful sleep, not the shock-induced coma she had seen before. This sleep was healing and important for his body.

Scully stood back up and stepped away from the car, her mind reeling with what she had seen. The dull bell tone continued to remind her that she had her door open and the keys dangling in the ignition.

The implications astounded her, and she stood completely at a loss. Mulder had suspected as much. She would have been skeptical herself, unable to believe the cellular technology had advanced so far—but she'd witnessed Jody Kennessy's healing powers with her own eyes, not to mention the fact that he had visibly recovered from the terrible wasting cancer that had left him an invalid, weak and skeletal, according to the photos and records she had seen.

Scully moved slowly, in a daze, as she climbed back behind the steering wheel. Her head pounded. Her joints ached, and she tried to tell herself that it was just from the stressful several days of sleeping in hotel rooms, traveling across country, and not an additional set of symptoms from her own cancer, the affliction that had resulted perhaps from her abduction, the unfathomable tests that had been done on her... the experiments.

Scully buckled her seatbelt and pulled the door closed, if only to halt the idiotic bell. In the backseat, Vader heaved a heavy sigh and rested his head on Jody's lap. His tail bumped against the padded armrest of the rear door.

She drove off, slower this time, aimless.

David Kennessy had developed something wonderful, something astonishing—she realized the power he had tapped into at DyMar Laboratory. It had been a federally funded cancer research facility, and this work had a profound meaning for the millions of cancer patients each year—people like herself.

It was appalling and unethical for Dr. Kennessy to have given his own son such an unproven and risky course of treatment. As a medical doctor, she was indignant at the very idea that he had bypassed all the checks and balances, the control groups, the FDA analysis, other independent studies.

But then again, she understood the heartache, the desperate need to do *something*, anything, taking unorthodox measures when none of the normal ones would suffice. Was it so different from laetrile therapy, prayer healers, crystal meditation, or any number of other last-ditch schemes that terminal patients tried? She had found that as hope diminished, the gullibility factor increased. With nothing to lose, why not try everything? And Jody Kennessy had indeed been dying. He'd had no other chance.

However, prayer healers and crystal meditation offered no threat to the population at large, and Scully realized with a sick tenseness in her stomach that the risk was far greater with Kennessy's nanotechnology experiments. If he had made the slightest mistake in tailoring or adapting his "biological policemen" to human DNA, they could become profoundly destructive on a cellular level. The "nanocritters" could reproduce and transmit themselves from person to person. They could cause a radical outrage of growths inside other people, healthy people, scrambling the genetic pattern.

That would have been a concern only if the nanomachines didn't work properly... and Kennessy had brashly gambled that he had made no mistakes.

Scully set her jaw and drove along, tugging down the sun visor in an effort to counteract the flickering tree shadows that danced in an interlocking pattern across her windshield.

After the plague victims she and Mulder had seen, it appeared that something must have gone wrong—very wrong.

THIRTY-FIVE

Kennessys' Cabin
Coast Range, Oregon
Friday, 4:23 p.m.

The wounds in Jeremy Dorman's throat had sealed, and a tangible heat emanated from him, a pulsing warmth that radiated from his skin and body.

The supposedly dead man opened his mouth and formed words, but only a whispery gurgle came from his ruined voice box. He jabbed with the revolver and hissed words using only modulated breath. "Your weapon—drop it!"

Mulder slowly reached to the other side of his overcoat, found the handgun in its pancake holster. He dropped his handgun on the forest floor with a thump. It struck the mud, slid to one side, and rested against a clump of dried pine needles.

"Nanotechnology," Mulder said, trying to quell the wonder in his voice. "You're healing yourself."

"You're one of *them*," Dorman said, his voice harsh, his breath still grievously wounded. "One of those men."

Then he released his grip on Mulder's overcoat, leaving a handprint of slime that seeped into the fabric, spreading, moving of its own accord like an amoeba.

"Can I take off my coat?" Mulder asked, trying to keep the alarm out of his voice.

"Go ahead." Dorman heaved himself to his feet, still holding the revolver. Mulder shed his outer jacket, keeping only his dark sportcoat.

"How did you find me?" Dorman said. "Who are you?"

"I'm with the FBI. My name is Mulder. I've been looking for Patrice and Jody Kennessy. I'm after them, not you… though I would certainly like to know how you survived the DyMar fire, Mr. Dorman."

The man snorted. "FBI. I knew you were involved in the conspiracy. You're trying to suppress information, destroy our discoveries. You thought I was dead. You thought you had killed me."

Mulder would have laughed under any other circumstances. "No one's ever accused me of being involved in a conspiracy. I assure you, I had never heard of you, or David Kennessy, or DyMar Laboratory before the destruction of the facility." He paused. "You're contaminated with something from Kennessy's research, aren't you?"

"I *am* the research!" Dorman said, raising his voice, which was still rough and rocky.

Something in his chest squirmed beneath the tattered covering of his shirt. Dorman winced, nearly doubled over. Mulder saw writhing lumps like serpents, growths of a strange oily color that flickered into motion beneath his skin, and then calmed, seeping back into his muscle mass.

"It looks to me like the research still needs a little work," Mulder said.

Dorman gestured with the revolver for Mulder to turn around. "You have a vehicle here?"

Mulder nodded, thinking of the battered pickup. "So to speak."

"We're going to get out of here. You have to help me find Jody, or at least the dog. They're with the other one... the woman. She left me for dead."

"Considering the condition of your throat, that would have been a reasonable assumption," Mulder said, covering his relief at hearing confirmation that Scully had been here, that she was still alive.

"You're going to help me, Agent Mulder." Now Dorman's voice had an edge. "You are my key to tracking them down."

"So you can kill them both like you murdered Patrice Kennessy and the truck driver and the security guard?" Mulder said.

Dorman winced again as an inner turmoil convulsed through his body. "I didn't mean to. I had to." Then he snapped his gaze back toward Mulder. "But if you don't help me, I'll do the same to you. Don't try to touch me."

"Believe me, Mr. Dorman"—he glanced down at the slime-encrusted wounds on the man's exposed skin—"touching you is absolutely the last thing on my mind."

"I don't want to hurt anybody," Dorman said, his face twisted with anguish. "I don't. I never meant for any of this to happen... but it's rapidly becoming impossible not to hurt anyone else. If I can just get a few drops of fresh blood—preferably the boy's blood, but the dog might do—no one else needs to get hurt, and I can be well again. It's all so simple. Everybody wins."

For once Mulder let his skepticism show. He knew the dog had been used as some sort of research animal—but what did the boy have to do with it? "What will that accomplish? I don't understand."

Dorman flashed him a look of pure scorn. "Of course you don't understand, Agent Mulder."

"Then explain it to me," Mulder said. "You've got those nanotechnology machines inside your body, don't you?"

"David called them 'nanocritters'—very cute."

"The dog has them inside his bloodstream," Mulder guessed. "Developed by David and Darin Kennessy for Jody's cancer."

"And apparently Jody's nanocritters work just fine." Dorman's dark eyes flashed. "He's already cured of leukemia."

Mulder froze under the tangled, shadowy forest branches as he tried to digest the information. "But if… if the dog and the boy are infected, if the dog recovers from his injuries and Jody's healthy now—why are you falling apart? Why do you bring death to anyone you touch?"

Dorman practically shouted, "Because their nanocritters function perfectly! Unlike mine." He gestured for Mulder to march out of the forest, back toward the isolated cabin where he had parked the pickup truck. "I didn't have time. The lab was burning, and I was supposed to die, just like David. They betrayed me! I took… whatever was available."

Mulder's eyes widened, turning to look over his shoulder. "You used early generation nanocritters, the ones not fully tested. You injected yourself so your body could heal, so you could escape while everyone else thought you were dead."

Dorman scowled. "That dog was our first real success. I realize now that David must have immediately taken a fresh batch of virgin nanocritters and secretly injected them in his son. Jody was almost dead already from his leukemia, so what difference did it make? I doubt Patrice even knew. But after seeing Jody today—he's cured. He's healthy. The nanocritters worked perfectly inside him." Dorman's skin shuddered and rippled in the dim forest light.

"Unlike yours," Mulder pointed out.

"David was too paranoid to leave anything valuable within easy reach. He'd learned that much at least from his brother. I only had access to what remained in our cryostorage. Some of our prototypes had produced… alarming results. I should have been more careful, but the facility was burning around me. When the machines got into my system, they reproduced and adjusted to my genetics, my cell structure. I thought it would work."

As he trudged into the meadow, Mulder's mind raced ahead, sifting the possibilities. "So DyMar was bombed because someone else was funding your research, and they didn't want the nanotechnology to get loose. They didn't want David Kennessy testing it out on his pet dog or his son."

Dorman's voice carried a strange tone. "The cure to disease, the possibility of immortality—why wouldn't they want it all to themselves? They intended to take the samples to an isolation laboratory where they could continue the work in secret." He continued under his breath. "I was supposed to be in charge of that work, but those people decided to obliterate me as well as David and everyone else."

He gestured again with the revolver, and Mulder stepped carefully, swallowing hard as understanding crystallized around him.

The prototype nanocritters had adapted themselves to the DNA of the initial lab animals, but when Dorman had brashly injected them into himself, the cellular scouts were forced to adapt to completely different genetics: biological policemen with conflicting sets of instructions. The drastic shift must have knocked the already unstable machines out of whack.

Mulder continued to speculate. "So your prototype nanocritters are confused with conflicting programming. When they hit a third person, a new genetic structure, they grow even more rampant. That's what causes this viral form of cancer whenever you touch someone, a shutdown in the nervous system that grows like wildfire throughout the human body."

"If that's what you believe," Dorman said with a low mutter. "I haven't exactly had time to run a lot of tests."

Mulder frowned. "Is that mucus"—he carefully pointed at Dorman's throat, which was glistening with slime—"a carrier substance for the nanocritters?"

Dorman nodded. "It's infested with them. If someone gets the carrier fluid on them, the nanomachines quickly penetrate their body…"

The battered red pickup stood parked in the muddy driveway right in front of them now. As he walked, Dorman made every effort to avoid the fallen body of Patrice Kennessy.

"And now the same thing is happening to you as happened to your victims," Mulder said, "but much more slowly. Your body is falling apart, and you think Jody's blood will save you somehow."

Dorman sighed, at the end of his patience. "The nanocritters in his system are completely stable. That's what I need. They're working the way they should, not flawed with contradictory errors like mine. The dog's nanocritters are good, too, but Jody's are already conformed to human DNA."

Dorman drew a deep breath, and Mulder realized that the man had no reason to believe his own theory; he merely hoped against hope that his speculation was true. "If I can get an infusion of stable nanocritters, they'll be stronger than my warped ones. They will supersede the infestation in my own body and give them a new blueprint." He looked intensely at Mulder, as if he wanted to grab the FBI agent and shake his shoulders. "Is that so wrong?"

When the two men reached the old pickup parked in front of the cabin, Dorman told Mulder to take out his car keys.

"I've left them in the ignition," Mulder said.

"Very trusting of you."

"It's not my truck," Mulder said, making excuses, hesitating, trying to figure out what to do next.

Dorman yanked open his creaking door. "Okay, let's go." He slid onto the seat, but remained as far toward the passenger door as possible, avoiding contact. "We've got to find them."

Mulder drove off, trapped in the same vehicle with the man whose touch caused instant death.

THIRTY-SIX

Tactical Team Temporary Command Post
Oregon District
Friday, 6:10 p.m.

To Adam Lentz and his crew of professionals, the fugitives were leaving a trail of clues like muddy footprints on a snow-white carpet.

He didn't know the members of his team by name, but he knew their skills, that they had been hand-picked for this and other similar assignments. This group could handle everything themselves, but Lentz wanted to be on the scene in person to watch over them, to intimidate them… and to be sure he could claim the proper credit when this was all over.

In his line of work, he didn't get official promotions, awards, or trophies. In fact, his successes didn't even amount to tangible pay raises, though income was never a factor for him. He had many sources of cash.

He had flown into Portland, discreet and professional. He had been met at the airport and whisked off to the rendezvous point. Other team members converged at the site of a local police call, their first stop.

Their high-tech mobile sanitation van arrived, escorted by a black sedan. Men in black suits and ties boiled out of the open doors next to where a logging truck had swerved off the road. The report had come in over the airwaves, and Lentz's response team had scrambled.

A state trooper, Officer Jared Penwick, had remained at the scene. Next to him, huddled in the patrol car passenger seat—obviously not a prisoner—was an old man wearing a red wide-billed cap and a rain slicker. The man looked miserable and worried.

The men in suits flashed their badges and announced themselves as operatives from the federal government. They all wore sidearms. They moved quickly as a unit.

The doors to the cleanup van popped open and men in spacesuit-like anti-contamination gear clambered out, armed with plastic bags and foam guns. The team member in the rear carried a flamethrower.

"What's going on here?" Officer Penwick said, stepping toward them.

"We're the official cleanup team," Lentz answered. He hadn't even bothered to take out his badge. "We would appreciate your full cooperation."

He stood stoically out of range beyond the risk of contamination as the crew opened the truck driver's door and descended upon the victim with plastic wrapping. They sprayed thick foam and acid, using extreme decontamination efforts. They quickly had the dead trucker bundled, his arms and legs bent so he could be wrapped up like a dying caterpillar in a cocoon.

The trooper watched everything, wide-eyed. "Hey, you can't just take—"

"We're doing this to eliminate all risk of contamination, sir. Did you or this gentleman here"—he nodded toward the man in the rain slicker—"actually open up the truck cab or go inside?"

"No," Officer Penwick said, "but there was an FBI agent with us. Agent Mulder. One of your people, I suppose?"

Lentz didn't answer.

The trooper continued, "He commandeered this man's pickup truck and headed off. He said he had to meet his partner, which had something to do with this situation. I've been waiting here for"—he glanced at his watch—"close to an hour."

"We'll take care of everything from this point on, sir. Don't concern yourself." Lentz stepped back, shielding his eyes as the suited man with the flamethrower sprayed jellied gasoline inside the cab of the logging truck and then ignited it with a *whump* and a roar.

"Holy shit!" said the man in the rain slicker. He slammed the door of the patrol car as a wave of heat ruffled over them, sending clouds of steam from the wet weeds and asphalt.

"You'd best step back," Lentz said to the trooper. "The gas tank will blow at any minute."

They hustled away, ducking low. The rest of the team had gotten the trucker's body wrapped up and tucked inside a sterile isolation chamber within the cleanup vehicle. They would shuck their suits and incinerate them as soon as they got inside.

The log truck burned, an incandescent torch in the gray rainy afternoon. The gas tank exploded with a deafening roar, and all the men ducked just long enough to avoid the flying debris before they turned back to their work.

"You mentioned Agent Mulder," Lentz said, returning to the trooper. "Can you tell us where he's gone?"

"Sure, I know where he's headed." Officer Penwick said, still astounded at the fireball, how the men had so efficiently obliterated all the evidence. The sound of the fire crackled and roared, while the black smoke stank of gasoline, chemicals, and wet wood.

The trooper gave Lentz directions on how to find Darin Kennessy's cabin. Lentz wrote nothing down, but memorized every word. He had to restrain himself from shaking his head.

A trail like muddy footprints on a snow-white carpet…

The men climbed back into the black sedan, while the rest of the crew sealed the cleanup van and its driver started the engine.

"Hey!" The old man in the rain slicker opened the passenger door of the trooper's car and stood up. He shouted at Lentz, "When do I get my pickup back?"

If the image of Agent Fox Mulder driving around in a battered redneck pickup truck amused Lentz, his face betrayed no expression.

"We'll do everything we can, sir. There's no need to worry." Lentz then climbed into the sedan, and the team raced off to Kennessy's isolated cabin.

THIRTY-SEVEN

Oregon Back Roads
Friday, 6:17 p.m.

With a brief sigh from the backseat, Jody woke up again at dusk, refreshed, fully healed—and ready to talk.

"Who are you, lady?" Jody asked, startling her again. He woke up so quickly and fully. Vader sat up next to him, panting and happy, as if all was right with the world again.

"My name is Dana Scully," she said, intent on the darkening road. "Dana—just call me Dana. I was here looking for you. I wanted to make sure you got to the hospital before your cancer got any worse."

"I don't need the hospital," Jody said with a lilt in his voice that made it clear he thought the answer to that was plain. "Not anymore."

Scully drove on into the dusk. She hadn't been able to reach Mulder. "And why is it that you don't need a hospital?" Scully asked. "I've seen your medical records, Jody."

"I was sick. Cancer." Then he closed his eyes, trying to remember. "Acute lymphoblastic leukemia, that's what it's called—or 'ALL.' My dad said there were lots of names for it, cancer in the blood."

"It means your blood cells are being made wrong," Scully said. "They're not working properly and killing the ones that are."

"But I'm fixed now—or most of the way," Jody said confidently. He patted Vader on the head, then hugged his dog. The black Lab absolutely loved it.

Though Scully suspected the answers, she still had a hard time wrestling with the actual facts.

Jody suddenly looked forward at her with suspicion. "Are you one of those people chasing after us? Are you the one my mom was so afraid of?"

"No," Scully said, "I was trying to save you from those people. You were very hard to find, Jody. Your mom did a good job of hiding you." She bit her lip, knowing what he was going to ask next... and he did, looking around the backseat, suddenly realizing where he was.

"Hey, what happened to my mom? Where is she? Jeremy was chasing her, and she told me to run."

"Jeremy?" Scully asked, hating herself for so blatantly avoiding his question.

"Jeremy Dorman," Jody said, as if she should already know this information. "My dad's assistant. We thought he was killed in the fire, too, but he wasn't. I think there's something wrong with him, though. He said he needed my blood." Jody hung his head, absently patting the dog. He swallowed hard. "Jeremy did something to my mom, didn't he?"

Scully drew a deep breath and slowed the car. She didn't want to be distracted by any sharp curves or road hazards as she told Jody Kennessy that his mother was dead.

"She tried to protect you, I think," Scully said, "but that man, Mr. Dorman, who came after you... " She paused as her mind raced through possible choices of words. "Well, he is very sick. He's got some kind of disease. You were smart not to let him touch you."

"And did my mom catch the disease?" Jody asked.

Scully nodded, looking straight ahead and hoping he would still see her answer. "Yes."

"I don't think it was a disease," Jody said. He spoke bravely, his voice strong. "I think Jeremy has nanocritters inside him, too. He stole them from the lab... but they're not working right in him. His nanocritters kill people. I saw what he looked like."

"Is that why he was after you?" Scully asked. She was impressed by his intelligence and composure after such an awful ordeal—but his story seemed so fantastic. Yet, after what she had seen, how could he be making it up?

Jody sighed and his shoulders slumped. "I think those people are probably after him, too. We're carrying the only samples left, carrying them inside us. Somebody doesn't want them to get loose."

He blinked up, and Scully glanced in the rearview mirror, seeing his bright eyes in the fading light. He seemed terrified and innocent. She thought of the cancer ravaging him, how he faced a similar fate but a much greater risk than she herself did.

"Do you think I'm a threat, Dana? Are other people going to die because of me?"

"No." Scully said. "I've touched you, and I'm fine. I'm going to make sure you're okay."

The boy said nothing—it was hard to tell whether her words had the reassuring effect she intended.

"These 'nanocritters,' Jody. What did your dad say to you about them?"

"He told me they were biological policemen that went through my body looking for the bad cells and fixing them one at a time," Jody said. "The nanocritters can also protect me when I get hurt."

"Like from a gunshot," she said.

Scully realized that if the nanomachines were able to repair well-entrenched leukemia, a gunshot would have been simple patchwork. They could easily stop the bleeding, plug up holes, seal the skin.

Altering acute leukemia, though, was a monumentally more difficult task. The biological policemen would have to comb through billions of cells in Jody's body, a massive restructuring. It was the difference between a Band-Aid and a vaccine.

"You're not going to take me to a hospital, are you?" Jody asked. "I'm not supposed to be out in public. I'm not supposed to let my name get around anywhere."

Scully thought about what he had said. She wished she could talk this over with Mulder. If Kennessy's nanotechnology actually worked—as was apparent from the evidence of her own eyes—Jody and his dog were all that remained of the DyMar research. Everything else had been systematically destroyed, and these two in her backseat were living carriers of the functional nanocritters… and somebody wanted to destroy them.

It could be a grave mistake for her to take the boy to a hospital and entrust him into the care of other unsuspecting people. Scully had no doubt that before long Jody and Vader would fall into the hands of those men who had caused the destruction of DyMar.

As she drove on, Scully knew she couldn't let this boy be captured and whisked away, his identity erased. Jody Kennessy would not be swept under the rug. She felt too close to him.

"No, Jody," Scully said, "you don't have to worry. I'll keep you safe."

THIRTY-EIGHT

Oregon Back Roads
Friday, 6:24 p.m.

As the pickup truck droned on and the darkness deepened, at least Mulder didn't have to look at Jeremy Dorman, didn't have to see the sickening squirming and unexplained motion of his body.

After a long period of uneasiness, restlessness, and barely suppressed pain, Dorman seemed to be dropping into unconsciousness. Mulder could see that the former researcher, the man who had faced—and been seemingly killed by—the other conspirators, was in anguish. He clearly didn't have long to live. His body could no longer function with such severe ravages.

If Dorman didn't get his help soon, there would be no point.

But Mulder didn't know how much to believe the man's story. How much had he himself been responsible for the DyMar disaster?

Dorman lifted his heavy-lidded eyes, and when he noticed the antenna of Mulder's cellular phone poking from the pocket of his suit jacket, he sat up at once. "Your phone, Agent Mulder. You have a cell phone!"

Mulder blinked. "What about my phone?"

"Use it. Pull it out and dial your partner. We can find them that way."

So far Mulder had avoided bringing this monstrously distorted man anywhere close to Scully or the innocent boy in her possession—but now he didn't see any way he could talk himself out of it.

"Take out your phone, Agent Mulder," Dorman growled, the threat clear in his voice. "Now."

Mulder gripped the steering wheel with his left hand, compensating from side to side to maintain a steady course on the uneven road. He yanked out the phone and extended the antenna with his teeth. With some relief, he saw that the light still blinked NO SERVICE.

"I can't," Mulder said and turned the phone so that Dorman could see. "You know how far out we are. There aren't any substations nearby or booster antennas." He drew a deep breath. "Believe me, Mr. Dorman, I've wanted to call her many times."

The big man slumped against the passenger-side door until the armrest creaked. Dorman used his fingertip to rub at an imaginary mark on the pickup window; his finger left a tracing of sticky, translucent slime on the glass.

Mulder kept his eyes on the road. The headlights stabbed into the mist.

When Dorman looked at Mulder, in the shadows his eyes seemed very bright. "Jody will help me. I know he will." Dark trees flickered past them in the twilight. "He and I were pals. I was his foster uncle. We played games, we talked about things. Jody's dad was always busy, and his uncle—that jerk— told them all to go to hell when he had his fight with David and ran off to stick his head in the sand. But Jody knows I would never hurt him. He has to know that, no matter what else has happened."

He gestured to the phone lying between them on the seat. "Try it, Agent Mulder. Call your partner. Please."

The sincerity and desperation in Dorman's voice sent tingles down Mulder's spine. Reluctantly, without any faith that it would work, he picked up the phone and punched in Scully's speed-dial number.

This time, to his surprise, the phone rang.

THIRTY-NINE

Tactical Team Temporary Command Post
Oregon District
Friday, 6:36 p.m.

As the two vehicles toiled down the muddy rutted drive, Lentz couldn't believe they had missed the obvious connection all this time.

Earlier, they had quietly checked out the survivalist enclave where David Kennessy's brother Darin had gone to ground, thinking himself invisible and protected. But Patrice had not gone there. There was no sign of the dog or the twelve-year-old boy.

She had come instead to this land and this cabin, which had belonged to Kennessy's brother, purchased long ago and seemingly ignored. Focused on the red herring of the survivalist enclave, Lentz had not spotted this hiding place on any of their computer searches of where Patrice might have gone.

This cabin would have been a perfect place for Patrice to shelter her son and the dog. But now it appeared that someone had found them first.

The team again sprang out of their vehicles, this time fully armed, their automatic rifles and grenade launchers pointed toward the small, silent building.

They waited. No one moved—nobody inside, nobody on the team. They were like a set of plastic army men forever frozen in attack positions.

"Move closer," Lentz said without raising his voice. In the still-misty air, his words carried clearly. The team members shuffled about, exchanging positions, moving closer, tightening a noose around the cabin. Others sprinted around the back to secure the site.

Lentz flicked his glance around, confident that every member of the group had noticed the twin sets of fresh tire tracks on the driveway. Agent Mulder had already been here, as had his partner Scully.

One of the men shouted, gesturing toward a thick patch of tall grass and weeds near the front porch. Lentz and the others hurried over to find a woman's body sprawled on the ground, blotched from the ravages of rampant nanotech infestation. She had been tainted. The disease had gotten her, too.

The viral infestation was spreading, and with each victim the prospect for containment grew worse and worse. The team members had just barely thwarted an outbreak in the Mercy Hospital morgue, where the nanomachines had continued their work on the first victim, crudely reanimating some of the cadaver's bodily systems.

It was Lentz's job to ensure that such a close call never happened again. "They've gone," Lentz said, "but we've got more tidying up to do here."

He directed the teams in the cleanup van to put on fresh protective gear and prepare for another sterilization routine.

Lentz stood back and drew a deep breath, inhaling the resiny scent of the nearby forest, the damp perfume of the clean fresh meadow. He turned to one of the men. "Burn the cabin to the ground," he said. "Make sure nothing remains."

He turned to see the crew already swaddling Patrice Kennessy's body with the plastic and the foam. Another man took out pumping equipment and began to spray jellied gasoline around the exterior cabin walls, then made a special effort to douse the meadow where Patrice had lain.

Lentz didn't bother to stay and watch the fire. He went back to the car, where the radio systems connected to other satellite uplinks and receiving dishes, to cellular phone tapping or jamming devices and security descramblers.

Other members of the extended tactical squadron had been keeping tabs on Agent Mulder, and now Lentz required whatever information they could give him.

Mulder could be the one to lead them right where they needed to be.

FORTY

Oregon Back Roads
Friday, 6:47 p.m.

Scully's cellular phone rang in the quiet darkness of the car's front seat, like an electronic chipmunk chittering. She snatched it up, knowing who it must be, relieved to be back in touch with her partner at last.

In the rear of the car Jody remained quiet, curious. The dog whimpered, but fell silent. She yanked out the antenna while driving with one hand.

"Scully, it's me." Mulder's voice was surrounded by a nimbus of static, but still understandable.

"Mulder, I've been trying to reach you for hours," she said quickly, before he could say anything. "Listen, this is important. I've got Jody Kennessy with me. He's healed from his leukemia, and he's got amazing regenerative abilities—but he's in danger. We're both in danger." Her breath caught in her throat. "Mulder, he doesn't have the plague—he has the cure."

"I know, Scully. It's Kennessy's nanotechnology. The actual plague carrier is Jeremy Dorman—and he's sitting right here next to me... a little too close, but I don't have much choice at the moment."

Dorman was alive! She couldn't believe it. She had looked at the blood-soaked body, his hand still twitching. No human being could have survived an injury such as that.

"Mulder, I saw the dog attack him, tear his throat out—"

But then, Scully realized, she never would have believed young Jody could live after the gunshot wound he had received.

"Dorman's got the nanomachines in him as well," Mulder said, "but his are malfunctioning. Rather spectacularly, I'd say."

Jody leaned forward, concerned. "What is it, Dana? Is Jeremy after us?"

"He's got my partner," Scully muttered quietly to the boy.

Mulder's voice continued at the same time. "Those nanocritters are amazing things with remarkable healing abilities, as we've both seen. No wonder somebody wants to keep them under wraps."

"Mulder, we saw what happened at the DyMar Lab. We know people came in and confiscated all evidence of the dead security guard in the hospital morgue. I'm not going to let Jody Kennessy or the dog be captured, taken in, and somehow erased."

"I don't think that's what Mr. Dorman wants, either," Mulder said. "He wants to meet." She heard a mumbled discussion on the phone, Dorman saying something in a threatening tone. She remembered his gruff, dismissive voice from her confrontation with him in the forest, just before he had accidentally shot Jody. "In fact, he insists on it."

She pulled into a clearing at the side of the road. The trees were thinning, becoming scrubbier, and she looked down a shallow grade to a small city ahead. She hadn't noticed the town's name as she drove along, but from the direction she had been heading, Scully knew she must be nearing the suburbs around Portland.

"Mulder, are you all right?" she said.

"Dorman needs something from Jody. Some of his blood."

Scully interrupted. "I stopped him before… or at least I tried. I won't let Jody get hurt."

Mulder's voice fell silent for a few seconds on the phone, then she heard a scuffle. "Mulder! Are you all right?" she called out, wondering what was happening and how far away she was from helping him.

He didn't answer her.

As Mulder tried to think of something to say, Dorman finally gave up in frustration and reached over to snatch the telephone from Mulder's hand.

"Hey!" he said, then flinched away to keep from touching the slime-slick man.

Dorman cradled the cellular phone and pushed it against his fluctuating face. The skin on his cheeks glistened and squirmed. The mucus on his hands left sticky patches on the black plastic.

"Agent Scully, tell Jody I'm sorry I shot him," Dorman said into the phone. "But I knew he would heal, just like the dog. I didn't mean to hurt him. I don't want to hurt anybody."

He reached up to flick on the dome light in the pickup's cab so that Mulder could see the intent look on his face and the revolver still held in his hand. "You need to tell the boy something for me, please. I need to explain to him."

Mulder knew his own conversation with Scully was now over. He couldn't touch the telephone again, or else the nanocritters would infiltrate his body too and leave him a splotched, convulsing wreck like Dorman's other victims.

Dorman swallowed, and from the anguished look on his face and the yellow shadows cast from the dim dome light, Mulder thought perhaps the distorted man really was sorry for all that had happened. "Tell him his mother is dead—and it's because of me. But it was an accident: She was trying to protect him. She didn't know that just touching me would be deadly."

His lips pressed together. "The nanocritters in my body are going wrong, very wrong. They didn't heal her, like Jody's do—they destroyed his mother's systems, and she died. There was nothing I could do." He spoke faster and faster. "I warned her to stay away from me, but she"—he drew a deep breath—"she moved too fast. Jody knows how tough his mom was."

Dorman looked up, turning his gleaming, hooded eyes at Mulder.

Mulder kept driving. The red pickup rattled over a pothole, and a loose wrench in the rear bed clanged and bounced. He hoped one of the bumps would knock it free so he wouldn't have to hear the grating noise anymore.

"Listen, Agent Scully." Dorman's voice was soothing; his mangled voice box must have healed quite nicely. "Jody's nanocritters work just fine—and that's what I need his blood for. I think the nanocritters his dad gave him might be able to fix the ones in me. It's my only chance."

Dorman winced as his body convulsed again, and he tried not to gasp into the phone. The hand holding the revolver twitched and jerked. Mulder hoped his fingers wouldn't clench around the trigger and shoot a hole through the roof of the pickup.

"You saw how I look," he said. "Jody remembers what I was like, how everything was between us. Me and him playing *Mario Kart* or *Cruisin' USA*. Remind him about the one time I let him beat me."

Then he sat back, curling his mouth in a little bit of a smile, perhaps nostalgic, perhaps predatory. "David Kennessy was right. There are government men after us. They want to destroy everything we created—but I got away, and so did Jody and Vader. But we're marked for eradication. I'm going to die in less than a day unless my nanocritters can be fixed. Unless I can see Jody."

Mulder looked over at him. The broad-shouldered, devastatingly sick man was very persuasive. On the phone he could hear faint voices, a discussion—presumably Jody talking to Scully. By the expression on Dorman's face, Jody seemed swayed by the big man's arguments. And why not? Dorman was the only connection remaining to the boy's past. The twelve-year-old would give him the benefit of the doubt. Dorman's shoulders sagged with relief.

Mulder felt sick in the pit of his stomach, still not sure whether to believe Dorman or not.

Finally Dorman growled into the phone again. "Yes, Agent Scully. Let's all go back to DyMar. The lab will be burnt and abandoned, but it's neutral ground. I know you can't trick me there."

He rested the revolver in his lap, calmer and confident now. "You have to understand how desperate I am—that's the only reason I'm doing this. But I won't hesitate. Unless you bring Jody to meet me, I will kill your partner."

He raised his eyebrows. "I don't even need a gun. All I need to do is touch him." As if in an effort to provoke Mulder, he dropped the revolver onto the worn seat between them.

"Just be at DyMar." He punched the END button.

He looked at the sticky residue on the black plastic of the phone, frowned in disappointment. He rolled down his window and tossed the phone away. It bounced on the gravel and shattered.

"I guess we won't be needing that anymore."

333

FORTY-ONE

Mobile Tactical Command Center
Northwestern Oregon
Friday, 7:01 p.m.

Satellite dishes mounted atop the van tilted at different azimuths to tap into various relay satellites. Computer signal processors sifted through the complex medley of transmissions broadcast by hundreds of thousands of unsuspecting people.

The van sat parked at the terminus of a short dirt road that ended in a shallow dumping ground. Compost, deadwood, rotting garbage, and uprooted stumps stood in a massive pile like a revolutionary's barricade. Some farmer or logger had been tossing his debris here for years rather than pay a disposal fee at the county dump. PRIVATE PROPERTY and KEEP OUT signs offered impotent threats; Adam Lentz had far more serious methods of intimidation at his disposal.

No one had been out here for some time, though, especially not after dark. The men on the professional surveillance team had the area to them-selves—and with the black-program technology rigged into the van, they had most of North America at their fingertips.

Tree branches bristling with pine needles offered a mesh of camouflage overhead, and the thick clouds made the night dark and soupy, blocking the stars—but neither the trees nor the clouds hampered satellite transmissions.

The computers in the dashboard of the mobile tactical command center scanned thousands of frequencies, ran transmissions through voice-recogni-tion algorithms, searched for key words, targeted on likely transmission points.

They had continued their invisible surveillance for hours with no success, but Adam Lentz was not a man to give up. Unless he broached the subject himself, the rest of his team members would not dare to comment on the matter either.

Lentz was also not one to lose patience. He had cultivated it over the years, when patience and a cool lack of emotion as well as an absence of remorse had allowed him to rise to this unrecognized yet still substantial position of power. Though few people understood what he was all about,

Lentz was content with his place in the world, with the importance of his activities.

But he would have been much more content if he could just find Agent Fox Mulder.

"He can't know we're looking for him," Lentz muttered. The man at the command console looked over, his face stony, reflecting no surprise whatsoever.

"We've been very discreet," the man said.

Lentz tapped his fingertips on the dashboard, pondering. He knew Mulder and Scully had split up. Agent Mulder had seen the dead trucker whose body Lentz's team had cleanly eliminated. Both Mulder and Scully had been to Dorman's isolated cabin out in the hollow, which—along with the body of Patrice Kennessy—was now a pile of smoldering ashes.

Then they had fled, and Lentz believed either Agent Mulder or Scully had the boy Jody and his nanotech-infected dog.

But something else was spreading the plague. Patrice Kennessy and the boy had feared something. Was the dog going rampant? Had the nanomachines within it—as Lentz had witnessed so clearly and so brutally in the videotaped demonstration—somehow gone haywire so that they now destroyed human beings?

The prospect frightened even him, and he knew that his superiors were absolutely right in insisting that all such dangerous research be contained. Only responsible, authorized people should know about it.

He had to restore order to the world.

Outside, the awakening night insects in the Oregon deep woods made a humming, buzzing sound. Grasshoppers, tree bugs… Lentz didn't know their scientific names. He had never been much interested in wildlife. The hive behavior of humanity in general had been enough to capture his interest.

He sat back and waited, clearing his mind, thinking of nothing.

A man with many pressures, burdens, and dark secrets, Lentz found it most restful when he could make his mind entirely blank. He had no plans to set in motion, no schemes to concoct. He proceeded with his missions one step at a time.

And in this instance, he couldn't proceed to the next step until they heard from Agent Mulder.

The man at the command deck sat up quickly. "Incoming," he said. He pushed down his earphones and fiddled with switches on his receiver.

"Transmission number confirmed, frequency confirmed." He almost allowed himself a smile, then turned to Lentz. "Voice pattern match confirmed. It's Agent Mulder. I'm recording."

He handed the earphones to Lentz, who quickly snugged them in place. The technician fiddled with the controls and the recorder.

Lentz listened to a staticky, warbled conversation between Mulder and Scully. In spite of his own tight control over his reactions, Lentz's eyes went wide, and his eyebrows lifted.

Yes, Scully had the boy and the dog in her custody—and the boy had healed himself from a grievous wound... but the most astonishing news of all was that the organization's patsy, Jeremy Dorman, had not been killed in the DyMar fire after all. He was still alive, still a threat... and now Dorman, too, was a carrier of the rogue nanotechnology.

And so was the boy! The infestation was already spreading.

After various threats and explanations, Dorman and Agent Scully worked to arrange a time and a place where they could meet. Mulder and Scully, Dorman, Jody, and the dog were all falling right into his lap—if Lentz's team could set up their trap sufficiently ahead of time.

As soon as the cellular transmission ended, Lentz launched his team into motion.

Every member of his group was well aware of how to reach the burned-out ruins of the laboratory. After all, each one of the mercenaries had been part of the supposed protest group that had brought down the cancer research establishment. They had thrown the firebombs themselves, set the accelerants, detonated the facility so that little more than an unstable skeleton remained.

"We have to get there first," Lentz said.

The mobile van launched like a killer shark out of the dead-end dirt road and onto the leaf-slick highway, accelerating recklessly up the coast at a speed far from safe.

But a mere traffic accident was not enough to worry Adam Lentz at that moment.

FORTY-TWO

DyMar Laboratory Ruins
Friday, 8:45 p.m.

Back to the haunted house, Scully thought as she drove up the steep driveway to the gutted, fire-blackened ruins of the DyMar Laboratory.

Behind the clouds the moon spread a pearlescent glow, a shimmering brightness in the soupy sky overhead. On the hills surrounding DyMar, the forest had once been a peaceful, protective barricade—but now Scully thought the trees were ominous, offering cover for the stealthy movement of enemies, perhaps more violent protesters... or those other men that Jody feared were after him and his mother.

"Stay in the car, Jody." She walked to the sagging chain-link fence that had been erected to keep trespassers from the dangerous construction site. Nobody manned it now.

The bluff overlooking the sprawling city of Portland was prime business real estate, but she saw only the blackened ruins like the carcass of a dragon sprawled beneath the diluted moonlight. The place was empty, dangerous yet enticing.

As Scully passed through the open and too-inviting chain-link gate, she heard a car door slam. She whirled, expecting to see Mulder and his captor, the big man who had shot Jody—but it was only the boy climbing out of the car and looking around curiously. The black Lab bounded out next to him, anxious to be free, glad that his boy was healthy.

"Be careful, Jody," she called.

"I'm following you," he said. Before she could scold him, he added, "I don't want to be left alone."

Scully didn't want him to go into the burned ruins with her, but she couldn't blame him, either. "All right. Come on, then."

Jody hurried toward her while Vader bounded ahead, frolicking. "Keep the dog next to you," Scully warned.

Small sounds of settling debris came from the unstable site, structural timbers tugged by time and gravity. No damp breeze stirred the ashes, but still the blackened timbers creaked and groaned.

Some of the structural walls remained intact, but looked ready to collapse at any moment. Part of the floor had fallen into the basement levels, but in one section concrete-block walls stood tall, coated with fire-blistered enamel paint and covered with soot.

Bulldozers sat like metal leviathans outside the building perimeter. A steam shovel, Porta Potty outhouses, and construction lockers had been set up by the contractor in charge of erasing the last scar of DyMar's presence.

Scully thought she heard a sound, and proceeded cautiously toward the bulldozer. Fuel tanks sat near the heavy equipment. The demolitions crew had been ready to begin—and she wondered if the unusual rush to level the place had anything to do with the cover-up plans Dorman had talked about.

Then Scully saw a metal locker that had been pried open. A starburst of bright silver showed where a crowbar had ripped off the lock, just below the marking, DANGER: EXPLOSIVES.

Suddenly the darkness seemed much more oppressive, the silence unnatural. The air was cold and gauzy damp in her nostrils, with a sour poison of old burning.

"Jody, keep close to me," she said.

Her heart pounded, and all of her senses came fully alert. This meeting between the boy and Jeremy Dorman would be tense and dangerous. But she would make sure Jody got through it.

She heard the approach of another engine, a vehicle rattling and laboring up the slope, tires crunching on gravel. Twin headlights swept through the night like bright coins.

"Stay with me." She put a protective hand on Jody's shoulder, and the two stayed at the edge of the burned-out building.

It was an old red pickup truck patched with primer, rusted on the sides. The body groaned and creaked as the driver's door opened and Mulder climbed out.

Of all the unbelievable things she had witnessed with Fox Mulder, seeing her strictly suit-and-tie partner driving a battered old pickup ranked among the most unusual.

"Fancy meeting you here, Scully," Mulder said.

A larger form heaved itself out of the passenger side. Her eyes had adjusted to the dim light, and even the shadows could not hide that something was wrong with the way he moved, the way his limbs seemed to have extra joints, the way weariness and pain seemed ready to crush him.

Jeremy Dorman had looked bad before, and now he appeared even worse.

Scully took a step forward but kept herself in front of Jody. "Are you all right, Mulder?"

"For now," he said.

Dorman took a step closer to Mulder, who edged away in an attempt to keep his distance. The broad-shouldered man held a revolver in his hand... but the weapon itself seemed the least threatening aspect about him.

Scully drew her own handgun. She was a good shot and utterly confident. She pointed the 9mm directly at Jeremy Dorman. "Release Agent Mulder right now," she said. "Mulder, step away from him."

He did so by two or three steps, but he moved slowly, carefully, not wanting to provoke Dorman.

"I'm afraid I can't return your partner's weapon," Dorman said. "I've touched it, you see, and it's no use to anyone anymore."

"And I've also lost my jacket and my cell phone," Mulder said. "Think of all the paperwork I'm going to need to fill out."

Jody came hesitantly forward, standing close behind Scully. "Jeremy, why are you doing this?" he said. "You're as bad as... as bad as them."

Dorman's shoulders sagged, and Scully was reminded of the pathetic lummox Lenny from Of Mice and Men, who hurt things he loved without knowing why or how.

"I'm sorry, Jody," he said, spreading one hand while he gripped the revolver in the other. "You can see how this is affecting me. I had to come here. You can help me. It's the only way I know to survive."

Jody said nothing.

"Other people are after us, Jody," Dorman said. He took a step closer. Scully did not back away, maintaining herself as a barrier between them.

"We're being hunted by government officials, people trying to bury your dad's work so that no other cancer patients will ever be helped. No one else will be cured like you were. These men want to keep that cure for themselves."

He was so emphatic that the skin on his face shifted with his intense emotion. "The protesters that killed your dad, the ones who burned down this whole facility, were not just animal-rights activists. They were staged by the group I'm talking about. It was planned. It's a conspiracy. They're the ones who killed your father."

At that point, as if on cue, other figures appeared, shadowy silhouettes, men in dark suits emerging from the perimeter of the chain-link fence. They came out of the trees and the access road. Another group trudged up the steep driveway with bright flashlights blazing.

"We have evidence that suggests otherwise, Mr. Dorman," said one of the men in the lead. "We're your reinforcements, Agent Mulder. We'll take care of the situation from here."

Dorman looked around wildly and glared at Mulder, as if the agent had betrayed him.

"How did you know our names?" Mulder asked.

Scully backed away until she clutched Jody's wrist. "It's not that simple," she said. "We won't relinquish custody of this boy."

"I'm afraid you have to," the man in the lead said. "I assure you, our jurisdiction in this matter supersedes yours."

The men came closer; their dark suits acted as camouflage in the shadowy overhangs in the burned building.

"Identify yourselves," Scully said.

"These men don't carry business cards, Scully," Mulder said.

Jody looked at the man who had spoken. "What did you mean?" he said, his eyes gleaming. "What did you mean that they weren't the ones who killed my father?"

The man in the lead looked over at Jody like an insect collector assessing a prize specimen. "Mr. Dorman didn't explain to you what really happened to your father?" His voice held a mocking tone.

"Don't you dare, Lentz," Dorman said. His voice seethed. He had raised the revolver in his hand, but Lentz didn't seem at all bothered by the threat.

"Jeremy killed your dad, Jody. Not us."

"You bastard!" Dorman wailed in despair.

Scully was too astonished to respond, but it was clear to her that Dorman realized he would never convince the boy to help him, not now.

With a roar, swinging his too-flexible arms, Jeremy Dorman brought up the revolver in his hand, aiming at Lentz.

The other team members were much faster, though. They snatched their own weapons and opened fire.

FORTY-THREE

DyMar Laboratory Ruins
Friday, 9:03 p.m.

The hail of small-caliber bullets struck Jeremy Dorman, and he thrashed out his arms in a scream of pain—as his body suddenly went haywire.

Mulder and Scully both dove to one side, reacting according to their training. Jody cried out as Scully dragged him with her, scrambling toward shelter among the large construction equipment.

Mulder moved away, shouting for the men to hold their fire, but no one paid the slightest attention to him.

Dorman himself remained the focus of all the shooting. He had known these men wanted to take him down, though he doubted that they had known he was still alive before now. They did not know what had changed inside of him… how he was different.

Adam Lentz had betrayed him before: The people in the organization that had promised him his own laboratory, the ability to continue the nanotechnology research, had already attempted to destroy him. Now they were here to finish the job.

As two hot bullets struck him, one high in the shoulder and the other on the left side of his rib cage, the pain and adrenaline and fury destroyed the last vestiges of his control over his own body. He let slip his hold on the systems that had played havoc with his genetic structure, his muscles and nerves. He roared a wordless howl of outrage.

And his body *changed*.

His skin stretched like a trembling drumhead. Inside, his muscles convulsed and clenched. The wild tumorous growths that had protruded from his ribs, his skin, his neck, came loose, ripping their way through his already mangled shirt.

The mass of protrusions had fought themselves free one time previously, while he had been trapped with Wayne Hykaway in the logging truck. But that loss of control was nothing compared to the unleashed biological chaos he exhibited now, a wild-card reorganization that the nanocritters had found in his most primitive DNA coding.

His shoulders groaned, his biceps bulged, and his arms bent and twisted. Another whipping tumor crawled out of his throat from the base of his tongue. The skin on his face and neck ran like melting plastic.

The men in dark suits continued to fire at him, in alarm and self-defense now, but Dorman's bodily integrity was breaking down, mutating, able to absorb the impacts like soft clay.

From his position at the lead of the team, Adam Lentz reacted quickly, retreating to cover as the gunfire continued.

Dorman charged forward to attack the nearest dark-suited man with one twisted arm while tentacles whipped out in a hideously primeval mass from his body. His mind was a blur, filled with pain and static and conflicting images. The nerve signals he tried to send to his muscles had very little effect. Now his warped and rebellious body broke free, going on the rampage.

The government man's cool professionalism quickly degenerated into a scream as an explosion of fleshy protrusions, tentacled claws, a nightmare of bizarre biological abominations wrapped around his arms, his chest, his neck. Dorman squeezed and strangled, until the man broke like balsa kindling in his grasp.

Another bullet shattered Dorman's femur, but before he could collapse, the nanomachines knitted the bone together again, allowing him to charge forward to snare another victim.

The hot translucent slime covered Dorman's body, providing a vehicle for the seething nanocritters. He needed only to touch the enemy men and the cellular plague would instantly eradicate their systems—but his out-of-control body took great delight in snapping their necks, crushing their wind-pipes, folding up their rib cages like accordions.

The single tentacle whipped out of his mouth like the long sharp tongue of a serpent, lashing the air. He didn't know how to interpret his own senses anymore. He had no idea how much—or how little—humanity still remained within him.

For now he saw only the enemy, the conspirators, the traitors—and his buzzing, disintegrating brain thought only of killing them.

But even as he continued the struggle, Dorman felt disoriented. His vision blurred and distorted. The surrounding agents brought more weapons to bear. The bullet impacts drove him away, and Dorman stumbled backward.

A dim spark in his mind made him remember the DyMar laboratory, the rooms where Darin and David Kennessy had developed their fantastic work—work that even now had brought them to this threshold of disaster.

Like a wounded animal fleeing into its lair, Jeremy Dorman lurched into the burned wreckage, seeking refuge.

And the men with weapons charged after him.

FORTY-FOUR

DyMar Laboratory Ruins
Friday, 9:19 p.m.

As soon as Lentz and his team conveniently appeared, Mulder knew that these men were no "reinforcements," but a cleanup crew, minor players in the same conspiracy that he and Scully battled constantly. They had tracked Patrice and Jody, they had staged the violent protest that burned the lab down, they had ransacked the Kennessy home, they had confiscated the evidence in the hospital morgue.

Mulder could do without that kind of "reinforcement" any day of the week.

When the shots rang out, he was instantly afraid that he, Scully, and young Jody would all be mowed down in the rain of bullets. He ducked to one side, seeking shelter. Thanks to Dorman, he no longer had a handgun of his own, but Scully was still armed.

"Scully, stay with the boy!" he shouted. He heard the solid wet impact of bullets striking skin, and Dorman roared in pain.

Mulder scuttled along the darkened ground, ducking behind fallen beams and broken walls. He looked up as the ululating sound emanating from the ominous fugitive turned more bestial, less defined. Jeremy Dorman transformed into a monster before his eyes.

All the horrors of wild cellular growth, the reckless spread of a malignant cancer with a mind of its own, extended like some ill-defined creature that had lain dormant inside Dorman's cells. Now it spread forth, growing without a plan. *Like tract home developments approved by a bribed city council,* he thought.

And this cellular assault was unleashed with a predatory mind bent on attack and destruction.

From her vantage point, Scully couldn't see the details. She shielded Jody with her own body and ran over to the shelter of the nearby bulldozer. With the bright echoing sound of metal upon metal, bullets ricocheted from the armored side of the machine. Scully dove down into the shadows, knocking Jody to safety.

Mulder kept low, racing along the broken bricks and fallen timbers. He ran into the dubious shelter of the gutted structure of the DyMar Laboratory.

Dorman—or what was left of him—managed to grab two more of the attacking agents and kill them, using a combination of hands and tentacles, as well as the incredibly virulent plague that lived in the slime on his skin.

Gunfire continued to ring out, sounding like an out-of-control popcorn popper. Yellow pinpoints of light flew like fireflies in the darkness. Mulder could see that the dark-suited men had scattered to surround the entire perimeter. They closed in, driving Dorman back into the ruins.

As if it was part of a plan.

Mulder ducked beneath an overhanging archway, bristling with teeth of shattered glass, which had somehow remained standing even after the fire and the explosion.

Over by the bulldozer, Jody shouted in despair as his dog let out a long and nerve-grating chain of barks and growls. Raising his head, Mulder saw a dark shadow, the black Labrador, racing into the ruins. Vader barked and snapped as he pursued Jeremy Dorman.

Lentz's other agents also crept up to the labyrinthine wreckage, but they were wary now. Dorman had withstood their hail of gunfire, and he had already killed several of them. Two of the men had flashlights, bright white eyes that burned a white lance into the murk. Ash sifted down from where Dorman had stirred the debris. Mulder smelled the tang of soot and burned plastic.

One of the agents pinned Dorman with his flashlight beam, attempting to stun him like a deer facing oncoming headlights. With a grunt, the monstrous man shoved sideways against a support pillar, knocking a charred wooden pole down along with a shower of concrete blocks.

The agent with the flashlight tried to scramble back, but the wreckage fell on his upper leg. Part of the wall collapsed. Mulder heard the hard bamboo sound of a bone breaking. Then the dark-suited man, who had been so calm as he hunted down his victim, yelped in pain; he had a high-pitched bawling voice.

Somewhere inside the burned building, the dog barked.

Mulder tried to stay under cover, but he made plenty of noise as he tripped over fallen bricks and crunched broken glass. He ducked behind a slumped, charred desk as more gunfire rang out.

A bullet struck the office furniture, and Mulder let out a hiss of surprise. He could see Scully outside in the pearly gray of fog-muffled moonlight. She was holding the boy back, clutching his torn shirt. Jody continued to shout after his dog as the gunfire peppered the night with sharp sounds. Scully pushed Jody back down as a barrage of bullets struck the bulldozer again.

Another shot slammed into the desk near where Mulder hid.

He realized that these shots couldn't be accidental misfires, though they would be excused as such. To the men who had surrounded the DyMar site and tried to kill Dorman and Jody, it might prove advantageous if Agents Mulder and Scully were also "accidentally" caught in the line of fire.

FORTY-FIVE

DyMar Inferno
Friday, 9:38 p.m.

The trap had sprung. Not as neatly as Adam Lentz had hoped, perhaps, but still the results would be the same... if a bit messier.

Messes could be cleaned up.

The gunfire crackled in the night with sharp, deadly sounds, but none of the shots caused sufficient damage to take down Jeremy Dorman, their immediate target. Though Lentz's team members had standing instructions to use all the force necessary to capture the boy and the dog as well, Agent Scully had protected young Jody Kennessy. She had sheltered him with all the training and skills she had learned at the FBI Academy at Quantico.

Lentz and his men had undergone more rigorous training, though, in other... less accredited schools.

After the initial gunfire, he thought he had seen Agent Mulder also run for cover into the gutted building. No matter. Everything would be taken care of in time.

Jeremy Dorman's horrific transformation had captured the focus of the team members. Seeing several of their comrades slaughtered in the monster's murderous rage, they set out after him, grim-faced and murderous.

Though Lentz himself had ducked out of the way of Dorman and his plague-laced slime, he was still disappointed in how his team's cool efficiency had so quickly shattered into a backwash of vengeance. He'd believed that these men were the best and most professional in the world. If so, the world should offer better.

He heard the shrill cry of another man inside the burned ruins, and more gunshots rang out. The team had trapped Dorman inside the unstable facility. In that respect, at least, everything was going as smoothly as he had hoped.

Lentz stopped at the nearest tactical vehicle, reached into the front seat, and took out the demolition control. But he had to wait for the right moment.

His team had arrived a full twenty-five minutes before Agent Scully and the boy, but Lentz had not moved prematurely. It was so much more efficient to wait for everyone to reach the same rendezvous point.

Lentz's hand-picked demolitions men had used the blasting caps stored at the construction site, as well as other incendiaries and explosives they kept inside their cleanup van. Working in the precarious structure, his men had rigged sealed drums of jellied gasoline in the half-collapsed basement levels. When the drums exploded, flames would shoot up through the remaining floors and incinerate the rest of the DyMar building. No trace would remain.

Lentz didn't particularly want to obliterate his team members who had foolishly followed Dorman inside, chasing him in a cat-and-mouse routine among the falling-down walls. But they were expendable.

Each man had been aware of the risks when he signed up.

Agent Mulder had also vanished inside, and Lentz suspected that some of the gunfire was also directed at him. The team members would have taken it upon themselves to eradicate all witnesses.

Lentz had received clear instructions that Mulder was not to be killed. He and his partner Scully were already part of a larger plan, but Lentz had to make on-the-spot decisions. He had to set priorities—and seeing the rampaging thing unleashed from within Dorman's body had hardened him to the extreme necessity. If he had to, Lentz would make excuses to his superiors. Later.

Mulder and Scully both knew too much, after all, and this weapon, this breakthrough, this curse of rampant nanotechnology had to be controlled, no matter what the cost. Only certain people could be trusted with so much power.

And the time was now.

One of the other men rushed back to the armored cleanup van. His eyes were glazed; sweat bristled across his forehead. He panted, looking around wildly.

Lentz glanced over at him and snapped, "Control yourself."

The effect was like an electric shock running through the team member. He stopped, reeled for a second, then swallowed hard. He stood straight, his breathing resumed a normal rate almost instantly, and he cleared his throat, waiting for additional orders.

Lentz held up the control in his hand. A small transmitter. "Is everything prepared?"

The man looked down at the controls inside the van. He blinked, then answered quickly. His words were as fast and as crisp as the gunshots that pattered through the darkness.

"That's all you need, sir. It will set off the blasting caps and trigger the remaining explosives. On a parallel circuit, the jellied gasoline will ignite. Just push the red button. That's all you need."

Lentz nodded to him curtly. "Thank you." He took one last look at the blackened skeletal building and pushed the indicated button.

The DyMar Laboratory erupted in fresh flames.

FORTY-SIX

DyMar Laboratory Ruins
Friday, 9:47 p.m.

The shock wave toppled some of the remaining girders and the once-solid concrete wall. The metal desk sheltered Mulder from the worst of the blast, but still the hammer of heat pressed the heavy piece of furniture against the wall, nearly crushing him.

Flames swept upward, bright yellow and orange, moving rapidly, as if by magic. He'd thought most of the flammables would have been consumed in the first fire two weeks earlier. Shielding his eyes from the glare and the hot wind, Mulder could see from the magnitude of the blaze that someone had rigged the ruins to go up in an instant inferno.

The dark-suited men had planned for this.

Hearing a shriek of terror and pain, Mulder carefully raised his head, blinking his watery eyes against the furnace blast of the inferno. He saw one of the men who had hunted after him stumbling through the wreckage, his suit engulfed in flames. More gunshots rang out, frantic firepower among shouts and screams—and a barking dog.

The fire raced up along the wooden support beams. The heat was so intense, even the glass and broken stone seemed to have caught fire. The black Labrador had bounded into the building, gotten caught in the explosion, and was thrown against a wall. Vader's fur smoldered, but still he ran, casting about for something.

One of the overhead girders fell with a crash among the debris. Flames licked along the splintered edge.

Mulder stood up from behind the desk, shielding his eyes. "Vader!" he shouted. "Hey, over here!" That black dog was evidence. Vader's bloodstream carried functional nanotechnology that could be studied to save so many people, without the horrendous mutations Jeremy Dorman had suffered.

Mulder waved his hand to get the dog's attention, but instead another man trapped inside the wreckage turned and fired at him. The gunshot spanged against the desk and ricocheted onto one of the broken concrete walls.

Before the man could shoot again, though, the inhuman form of Jeremy Dorman crashed through the debris. The man with the gun tore his attention from Mulder—the easy target—to the monstrous creature. He didn't have time to make an outcry before several of Dorman's new appendages grasped him. With a twisted but powerful arm, Dorman snapped the man's neck, then discarded him.

At the moment, Mulder didn't feel inclined to shower the distorted man with gratitude. Shielding his eyes, barely able to see through the smoke and the blaze, he staggered toward the outside, needing to get away.

The dog was hopelessly lost inside the facility. Mulder couldn't understand why Vader had run into such a dangerous area in the first place.

The unstable floor was on fire. The walls, the debris... even the air burned his lungs with each gasping, retching breath he drew. Mulder didn't know how he was going to get out alive.

Scully clutched Jody's torn shirt, but the fabric ripped and pulled free as he lunged after his dog.

"Jody, no!"

But the boy charged after Vader. The men in the ambush continued shooting, but Dorman was killing them one after another. The black dog plunged directly into the crossfire. The twelve-year-old boy—perhaps a bit too confident in his own immortality, as many twelve-year-olds were—ran after him a few seconds later.

Scully dropped the useless scrap of cloth in her hand. Desperate, she stood up from behind the shelter of the bulldozer. Scully watched the boy run miraculously unharmed toward the charred walls of DyMar. With a loud ricochet, another bullet bounced off the heavy tractor tread; she didn't even bother to duck.

Bits of debris showered Jody, but he lowered his head and kept running. He stood screaming at the edge of the walls, looking at the barrier of flames. He ducked down and tried to get inside. She heard Mulder's voice call out for the dog, then more gunshots. The DyMar facility and all it stood for continued to burn.

So far, no police, no fire engines, no help whatsoever came to investigate the gunfire, the explosion, the flames.

"Mulder!" she shouted. She didn't know where he was or how he could get out. Jody ducked recklessly inside. "Jody!" she shouted. "Come back here!"

She ran to the threshold and squinted through the smoke. A girder tumbled as a ceiling collapsed, showering sparks. Part of the floor showed gaps and holes where the flames and the explosion beneath had weakened it, causing it to crack and tumble down in sections like a house of cards.

Jody stood half-balanced, flailing his hands. "Vader, where are you? Vader!"

Throwing all caution to the wind, needing to save the boy as if it were some measure of her own worthiness to survive, Scully hurried inside. She struggled ahead, taking shallow breaths. Most of the time, she held her eyes closed, blinking them open for a quick glimpse, then staggering along.

"Vader!" Jody called again, out of sight.

Finally Scully reached the boy's side and grabbed his arm. "We have to go, Jody. Out of here! The whole place is going to collapse."

"Scully!" Mulder shouted, his voice raw and ragged with the smoke and heat. She turned to see him making his way across the floor, stepping in flames and racing along. He swatted out a fire that smoldered on his trousers.

She gestured for him to hurry—but then a wall behind her crumbled. Concrete blocks fell to one side in a mound of cinders as a wooden support beam split.

"Hello, Jody…" Jeremy Dorman's tortured voice said as he pushed himself through the fire and debris of the wall he had just knocked down. The distorted man stood free, undisturbed by the heat raging around him. Embers pattered on his body, smoking on his skin and leaving black craters that shifted and melted and healed over. His body ran like candle wax. His clothes were fully involved in the fire that blazed around him, but his skin thrashed and writhed, a horror show of tentacles and growths.

Dorman blocked their way out. "Jody, you wouldn't help me when I asked—and now look what's happened."

Jody bit back a small scream and only glared at the hideously mutated creature. "You killed my dad."

"Now we're all going to die in this fire," Dorman said.

Scully doubted that even the swarming nanomachines could protect the boy from the intense flames. She knew for a fact, though, that she and Mulder had no such protection, mere humans, completely susceptible to the fire's heat and smoke. They were both doomed unless they could get around this man.

Mulder tripped and fell to one knee in the hot broken glass; he hauled himself up again without an outcry. Scully still had her handgun, but she knew that would offer no real threat against Dorman. He would laugh off her bullets, the way he had ignored the crossfire from the dark-suited men… the way he even now didn't seem troubled by the fire that raged around them.

"Jody, come to me," Dorman said, plodding closer. His skin roiled and rippled, glistening with slime that oozed from his every pore.

Jody staggered back toward Scully. She could see burns on his skin, scratches and bleeding cuts where debris had showered him in the explosion, and she wondered briefly why the small injuries weren't magically healing as his gunshot wound had. Was something wrong with his nanocritters? Had they given up, or shut down somehow?

Scully knew she couldn't protect the boy. Dorman lunged closer, reaching out to him with a flame-covered hand.

And then from a wall of burning wreckage to one side, where the light and the smoke made visibility impossible, the black Labrador howled and launched himself at the target.

Dorman spun about, his head twisting and swiveling. His broken, bent hands rose up, thrashing.

His tentacles and tumors quivered like a basket of snakes. The dog, a black-furred bulldozer, knocked Dorman backward.

"Vader!" Jody screamed.

The dog drove Dorman staggering into the flames, where bright light and curling fire rose up through ever-growing gaps in the floor, as if the pit of hell itself lay beneath the support platform.

Dorman yelped, and his tentacles wrapped around the dog. The black Lab's fur caught on fire in patches, but Vader didn't seem to notice. Immune to the plague Dorman carried, the dog snapped his jaws, digging his fangs deep into the soft flowing flesh of the nanotech-infected man.

Dorman wrestled with the heavy animal and both tumbled to the creaking, splintering floorboards. Dorman's left foot crashed through one of the flame-filled holes.

He cried out. His tentacles writhed. The dog bit ferociously at his face.

Then the floor collapsed in an avalanche of flaming debris. Sparks and smoke flew upward like a landmine explosion. With a howl and a scream, both Dorman and Vader fell into the seething basement.

Jody wailed and made as if to run after his dog, but Scully grabbed him fiercely by the arms. She dragged the boy back toward the opening, and safety. Coughing, Mulder followed, stumbling after her.

The flames roared higher, and more girders collapsed. Another concrete wall toppled into shards, then an entire section of the floor fell in, nearly dragging them with it.

They reached the threshold of the collapsing building, and Scully could think of nothing more than to push herself out into the fresh air, into the blessed relief. Safe from the fire.

The cool night seemed impossibly dark and cold as they fought their way from the flames and the wreckage. Her eyes burned, so filled with tears that she could barely see. Scully held the despairing boy, wrapping her arms around him. Mulder touched her shoulder, getting her attention as they stumbled away from the flames.

She looked up to see a group of men waiting for them, staring coldly. The survivors of Lentz's team held their automatic weapons high and pointed at them.

"Give me the boy," Adam Lentz said.

FORTY-SEVEN

DyMar Inferno
Friday, 9:58 p.m.

Mulder should have known the men in suits would be waiting for them at the perimeter of the inferno. Some of Lentz's "reinforcements" would have realized there was no need to endanger themselves—better just to hang around and let any survivors come to them.

"Stop right there, Agent Mulder, Agent Scully," the man in the lead said. "There's still a chance we can bring this to a satisfactory resolution."

"We're not interested in your satisfactory resolution," Mulder answered with a raw cough.

Scully's eyes flashed as she placed her arm protectively around the boy. "You're not taking Jody. We know why you want him."

"Then you know the danger," Lentz said. "Our friend Mr. Dorman just showed us all what could go wrong. This technology can't be allowed to be disseminated uncontrolled. We have no other choice." He smiled, but not with his eyes. "Don't make this difficult."

"You're *not* taking him," she said more vehemently.

To emphasize her point, Scully drew herself tall. Her face was smudged with soot; her clothes reeked of smoke and cinder burns. She stood defiantly in front of Jody, a barricade between him and their automatic weapons. Mulder wasn't sure if her body would block a hail of high-powered gunfire, but he thought her sheer determination just might stop them.

"I don't know who you are, Mr. Lentz," Mulder said, taking a step closer to Scully to support her stand, "but this young man is in our protective custody."

"I just want to help him," Lentz said smoothly. "We'll take him to medical care. A special facility where he'll be looked after by people who can... understand his condition. You know no normal hospital would be able to help him."

Scully did not budge. "I'm not convinced he would survive your treatment."

From below, finally, Mulder could hear sirens and approaching vehicles. Response crews with flashing red and blue lights raced along the suburb streets toward the base of the hill. The second DyMar fire continued to blaze at the top of the bluff.

Mulder stepped backward, closer to his partner. He kept his eyes nailed on Lentz's, ignoring the other men in suits.

"Now you're sounding like me, Scully," Mulder said.

"Give us the boy now," Lentz said. Below, the sirens were getting louder, closer.

"Not a chance in hell," Scully answered.

Fire engines and police cars raced up the hill, sirens wailing. They would reach the hilltop inferno in seconds. If Lentz meant to do something, it would be now. But Mulder knew if he did shoot them, he wouldn't have time to clean up his mess before the DyMar site became very public.

"Mr. Lentz—" one of the surviving team members said.

Scully took one step, paused a terribly long moment, then began to walk slowly away, one step at a time. Her determination didn't waver.

Lentz stared at her. The other men kept their guns trained.

Rescue workers and firefighters yanked open the chain-link gate, hauling it aside so the fire trucks could drive inside.

"You don't know what you're doing," Lentz said coldly. He eyed the arriving vehicles, as if still gauging whether he could get away with shooting the two agents and eliminating the bodies under the very noses of the rushing emergency crews. Adam Lentz and his men stood angry and defeated, backlit by the raging inferno that burned the remains of DyMar Laboratory to the ground.

But Scully knew she was saving the boy's life. She kept walking, holding Jody's arm. He looked forlornly back at the wall of flames.

As the uniformed men rushed to hook up hoses and rig their fire engine, Lentz's team stepped back, disappearing into the forest shadows.

Somehow the three of them managed to reach the rental car. "I'll drive, Scully," Mulder said as he popped open the driver's-side door. "You're a bit distracted."

"I'll keep an eye on Jody," she said.

Mulder started the engine, half-expecting that gunshots from the trees would ring out and the windshield would explode with spider-webbed bullet cracks. But instead, he managed to drive off, his tires spitting loose gravel on the steep driveway leading down from DyMar Laboratory. He had to flash his ID several times to get past the converging authorities. He wondered how Lentz would explain himself and his team… if they were found at all in the surrounding forest.

FORTY-EIGHT

Mercy Hospital
Portland, Oregon
Saturday, 12:16 p.m.

In the hospital, Scully checked and rechecked Jody Kennessy's lab results, but she remained as baffled after an hour of contemplation as when she had first seen the data.

She sat in the bustling cafeteria at lunchtime, nursing a bitter-tasting cup of coffee. Doctors and nurses came through, chatting about cases the way sports fans talked about football games; patients spent time out of their stuffy rooms with their family members.

Finally, realizing the charts would show her nothing else, Scully got another cup to go, and went to meet Mulder where he sat stationed on guard duty outside the boy's hospital room.

As she walked from the elevator down the hall, she waved the manila folder in her hand. Mulder looked up, eager for confirmation of the technology. He stuffed the magazine he had been reading back into its plain brown envelope. The door to Jody's room stood ajar, with the TV droning inside. So far, no mysterious strangers had come to challenge the boy.

"I don't know whether to be more astonished at the evidence of functional nanotechnology—or at the lack of it." Scully shook her head and pushed the dot matrix printouts of lab scans at Mulder.

He picked them up, glancing down at the numbers, graphs, and tables, but obviously didn't know what he was looking for. "I take it this isn't what you expected?"

"Absolutely no traces of nanotechnology in Jody's blood." She crossed her arms over her chest. "Look at the lab results."

Mulder scratched his dark hair. "How can that be? You saw him heal from a gunshot wound—a mortal wound."

"Maybe I was mistaken," she said, "Perhaps the bullet managed to miss vital organs—"

"But Scully, look at how healthy he is! You saw the picture of him with the leukemia symptoms. He only had a month or two to live. We *know* David Kennessy tested his cure on him."

Scully shrugged. "He's clean, Mulder. Remember the sample of dog's blood at the veterinarian's office? The remnants of nanotechnology were quite obvious. Dr. Quinton said the same thing about the fluid specimen I took during my autopsy of Vernon Ruckman. The traces aren't hard to find if the nanomachines are as ubiquitous in the bloodstream as they should be—and there would have to be millions upon millions of them in order to effect the dramatic cellular repairs that we witnessed."

Her first evidence that something was not as she suspected, though, had been Jody's recent scrapes, scratches, and cuts after the fire. Though not serious, they failed to heal any more quickly than other ordinary scratches. Jody Kennessy now seemed like a normal boy, despite what she knew of his background.

"Then where did the nanocritters go?" Mulder asked. "Did Jody lose them somehow?"

Scully had no idea how to explain it.

Together they entered Jody's room, where the boy sat up in bed, paying little attention to the television that played loudly in the background. Considering all he had been through, the twelve-year-old seemed to be taking the ordeal well enough. He gave Scully a wan smile when he saw her.

A few moments later, the chief oncologist bustled into the room, holding a clipboard in his hand and shaking his head. He looked over at Scully, then at Jody, dismissing Mulder entirely.

"I see no evidence of leukemia, Agent Scully," he said, shaking his head. "Are you sure this is the same boy?"

"Yes, we're sure."

The oncologist sighed. "I've looked at the boy's previous charts and lab results. No blast cells in the blood, and I performed a lumbar puncture to study the cerebrospinal fluid for the presence of blast cells—still nothing.

Very standard procedures, and usually very conclusive. In an advanced case such as his is supposed to be, the symptoms should be obvious just by looking at him—lord knows, I've seen enough cases."

Now the oncologist finally looked at Jody. "But this boy's leukemia is completely gone. Not just in remission—it's gone."

Scully hadn't honestly expected anything else.

The oncologist blinked his eyes and let his chart hang by his hip. "I've seen medical miracles happen... not often, but given the number of patients through here, occasionally events occur that medicine just can't explain. But this boy, who was facing terminal cancer only a month or two ago, now shows no symptoms whatsoever."

The oncologist raised his eyebrows at Jody, who seemed uninterested in the discussion, as if he knew the answers all along. "Mr. Kennessy, you're cured. Do you understand the magnitude of that diagnosis? You're completely healthy, other than a few scratches and scrapes and minor burns. There's absolutely nothing wrong with you."

"We'll let you know if we have any further questions," Scully said, and the doctor seemed disappointed that she wasn't quite as amazed as he was. A little too brusquely, perhaps, she ushered him out the door of the hospital room.

After the oncologist departed, she and Mulder sat at the end of Jody's bed. "Do you know why there's no trace left of the nanocritters in your bloodstream, Jody? We can't understand it. The nanomachines healed you from the gunshot wound before, they cured you of your cancer—but they're gone now."

"Because I'm cured." Jody looked up at the television, but did not care about the housewives' talk show going on at low volume. "My dad said they would shut down and dissolve when they were done. He made them so they would fix my leukemia cell by cell. He said it would take a long time, but I would get better every day. Then, when they were finished... the nanocritters were supposed to shut themselves down."

Mulder raised his eyebrows at Scully. "A fail-safe mechanism. I wonder if his brother Darin even knew about it."

"Mulder, that implies an incredible level of technological sophistication—" she began, but then realized that the entire prospect of self-sustaining biological policemen that worked on the human body, using nothing more than

DNA strands as an instruction manual, was also fantastically beyond what she had believed were modern capabilities.

"Jody," she said, leaning closer to the boy, "we intend to release these results as widely as possible." We need to let everyone know that you are no longer carrying any signs of the nanotechnology. If you're clean, there should be no reason why those men will continue to be after you."

"Whatever," he said, sounding glum.

Scully didn't waste her effort in a false cheeriness. The boy would have to deal with his situation in his own way.

Jody Kennessy had carried a miracle cure, not just for cancer but probably for all forms of disease that afflicted humanity. The nanocritters in his blood might even have offered immortality.

But with DyMar Laboratory destroyed, Jeremy Dorman and the black Lab swallowed up in the inferno, and David Kennessy and anyone else involved in the project dead, similar nanotechnology breakthroughs would be a long time coming if they had to be made from scratch.

Scully already had an idea of how the Bureau might keep Jody safe in the long run, where they could take him. It didn't make her feel good, but it was the best option she could think of.

Mulder, meanwhile, would simply write up the case, keep all of his records and his unexplained speculations, add them to his folders full of anecdotal evidence. Once again, he had nothing hard and fast to prove anything to anyone.

Just another X-File.

Before long, Scully figured, Mulder would need to install several more file cabinets in his cramped office, just to keep track of them all.

FORTY-NINE

Federal Office Building
Crystal City, Virginia
Sunday, 2:04 p.m.

Adam Lentz made his final report verbally and face to face, with no paperwork buffers between them. There would be no written record of this investigation, nothing that could be uncovered and read by the wrong sets of prying eyes. Instead, Lentz had to face down the man and tell him everything directly, in his own words.

It was one of the most terrifying experiences he had ever known.

A curl of acrid cigarette smoke rose from the ashtray, clinging like a deadly shroud around the man. He was gaunt, his eyes haunted, his face unremarkable, his dark brown hair combed back.

He did not look to be a man who held the eggshells of human lives at the mercy of his crushing grip. He didn't look like a man who had seen presidents die, who had engineered the fall of governments and the rise of others, who played with unknowing test groups of people and called them "merchandise."

But still, he played world politics the way other people played the game of Risk.

He took a long drag on his cigarette and exhaled the smoke slowly through parchment-dry lips. So far, he had said nothing.

Lentz stood inside the nondescript office, facing the man squarely. The ashtray on the desk was crowded with stubbed-out cigarette butts.

"How can you be so sure?" the man finally said. His voice was deceptively soft, with a melodious quality.

Though he had never once served in the military, at least not in any official capacity, Lentz stood ramrod straight. "Scully and Mulder have tested the boy's blood extensively. We have complete access to his hospital records. There is absolutely no evidence of a nanotechnology infestation, no microscopic machines, no fragments—nothing. He's clean."

"Then how do you explain his remarkable healing properties? The gunshot wound?"

"No one actually saw that, sir," Lentz said. "At least, no one on record."

The man just looked at him, smoke curling around his face. Lentz knew his answer wasn't acceptable. Not yet. "And the leukemia? The boy shows no sign of further illness, as I understand it."

"Dr. Kennessy knew the potential threat of nanotechnology—he was no fool—and he might have been able to program his nanocritters to shut down once their mission was accomplished, once his son was cured of his cancer. And according to the tests recently run in the hospital, Jody Kennessy is perfectly healthy, no longer suffering from acute lymphoblastic leukemia."

Eyebrows raised. "So he's been cured, but he no longer carries the cure." The man blew out a long breath of cigarette smoke. "We can be happy for that, at least. We certainly wouldn't want anyone else to get their hands on this miracle."

Lentz didn't answer, simply stood watchful and wary. In a secret repository, a building whose address was unknown, in rooms without numbers, drawers without markings, the Cigarette-Smoking Man kept samples and bits of evidence hidden away so that no one else could see. These tangible items would have proven enormously useful to others who sought the truth in all its many forms.

But this man would never share them. "What about Agents Mulder and Scully?" the smoking man said. "What do they have left?"

"More theories, more hypotheses, but no evidence," Lentz said.

The smoking man inhaled again, then coughed several times, a deep ominous cough that held a taint of much deeper ills. Perhaps he just had a guilty conscience… or perhaps something was wrong with him physically.

Lentz fidgeted, waiting to be dismissed or complimented or even reprimanded. The silence was the worst.

"To reiterate," Lentz said, speaking uncomfortably into the man's continued gaze. Languid smoke curled up and around, making a sinuous arabesque dance in the air. "We have destroyed the bodies of all the known plague victims and sterilized every place touched by the nanotechnology. We believe none of these self-reproducing devices has survived."

"Dorman?" the smoking man asked. "And the dog?"

"We sifted through the DyMar wreckage and found an assortment of bones and teeth and a partial skull. We believe these to be the remains of Dorman and the dog."

"Did dental records verify this?"

"Impossible, sir," Lentz answered. "The nanotechnology cellular growths had distorted and changed the bone structure and the teeth, even removing all the fillings from Dorman's mouth. We can't make a positive identification, even as to the species. However, we have eyewitness accounts. We saw the two fall into the flames. We found the bones. There seems to be no question."

"There are always questions," the man said, raising his eyebrows. But then, unconcerned, he lit another cigarette and smoked half of it without saying a word. Lentz waited.

Finally the man stubbed out the butt in the already overcrowded ashtray. He coughed one more time, and finally allowed himself a thin-lipped smile. "Very good, Mr. Lentz. I don't think the world is ready yet for miracle cures... at least not anytime soon."

"I agree, sir," Lentz said.

As the man nodded slightly in dismissal, Lentz turned, forcibly stopping himself from running full-tilt out of the office. Behind him, the man coughed again. Louder this time.

FIFTY

Survivalist Compound
Oregon Wilderness
One Month Later

The people were strange here, Jody thought... but at least he felt safe. After the ordeal he had recently survived, after his entire world had been destroyed in stages—first the leukemia, then the fire that had killed his father, then the long flight that ended with the death of his mother—he felt he could adapt easily.

Here in the survivalist compound, his Uncle Darin was overly protective but helpful as well. The man refused to talk about his work, his past... and that was just fine with Jody. Everyone in this isolated but vehement community fit together like interlocking puzzle pieces.

Just like the puzzle of the Earth rising above the Moon he and his mother had put together one of those last afternoons hidden in the cabin... Jody swallowed hard. He missed her very much.

After Agent Scully had brought him here, the other members of the heavily guarded survivalist compound had taken him under their wing. Jody Kennessy was an icon for them now, something like a mascot for their group—this twelve-year-old boy had taken on the dark and repressive system, and had survived.

Jody's story had only heightened the resolve of the compound members to keep themselves isolated and away from the interfering and destructive government they despised so much.

Jody, his Uncle Darin, and the other survivalists spent their days together in difficult physical work. All the members of the compound shared their own specialties with Jody, instructing him.

Still healing from the stinging wounds in his heart and in his mind, Jody spent much of his time walking the camp's extended perimeter, when he wasn't working in their gardens or fields to help make the colony self-sufficient. The survivalists did a lot of hunting and farming to supplement their enormous stockpile of canned and dried foods.

It was as if this entire community had been ripped up and transplanted here from another time, a self-sufficient time. Jody didn't mind. He was alone now. He didn't feel close even to his Uncle Darin... but he would survive. He had overcome terminal cancer, hadn't he?

The other members of the group knew to leave Jody alone when he was in one of his moods, to give him the time and space he needed. Jody wandered the barbed-wire fences, looking at the trees... but mainly just being by himself and walking.

A mist clung to the forest, hiding in the hollows, drifting like cottony fog as the day warmed up. Overhead, the clouds remained gray and heavy, barely seen through the tall treetops. He watched his step carefully, though Darin had assured him that there really was no minefield, no booby traps or secret defenses. The survivalists just liked to foster such rumors to maintain the aura of fear and security around their compound. Their main goal was to be left undisturbed by the outside world, and they would use whatever means necessary to accomplish that end.

Jody heard a dog bark in the distance, clear and sharp. The cold damp air seemed to intensify the sound waves.

The survivalists had many dogs in their compound, German shepherds, bloodhounds, rottweilers, Dobermans. But this dog sounded familiar. Jody looked up.

The dog barked again, and now he was more certain. "Come here, boy," he called.

He heard a crashing sound through the underbrush, branches and vines tossed aside as a large black dog bounded toward him, emerging from the mist. The dog barked happily upon seeing him.

"Vader!" Jody called. His heart swelled, but then he dropped his voice, concerned.

The dog looked unharmed, fully healed. Jody had seen Vader vanish into the flames. He had seen the DyMar facility collapse into embers, shards, and twisted girders.

But Jody also knew that his dog was special, just like he'd been before all the nanocritters in his own body had died off. Vader had no such fail-safe system.

The dog bounded toward him, practically knocking Jody over, licking his face, wagging his tail so furiously that it rocked his entire body back and forth. Vader wore no tags, no collar, no way to prove his identity. But Jody knew.

He suspected his uncle might guess the truth, but the story he would have to tell the others was just that he had found another dog, another black Lab like Vader. He would give his new pet the same name. The rest of the survivalists didn't know, and no one else in the outside world would ever need to find out.

He hugged the dog, ruffling his fur and squeezing his neck. He shouldn't have doubted. He should have kept watch, hoping, waiting. His mother had said it herself. The dog would come back to him eventually.

Vader always did.

END

BIOS

BEN MEZRICH worked variously as a cartoonist, legal researcher, and television production assistant before writing *Threshold*, his first novel. A 29-year-old Harvard graduate and *X-Files* fan, he lives in Boston.

KEVIN J. ANDERSON's first two *X-Files* novels, *Ground Zero* and *Ruins*, became national bestsellers. He is also the author of the critically acclaimed novels *Blindfold* and *Climbing Olympus* and the coauthor (with Doug Beason) of *Virtual Destruction*, *Ill Wind*, and *Assemblers of Infinity*. His work has been nominated for the Nebula and Bram Stoker Awards.

THE BIG 50

MINNESOTA TWINS

The Men and Moments that Made
the Minnesota Twins

Aaron Gleeman

TRIUMPH
B O O K S

Library of Congress Cataloging-in-Publication Data

Names: Gleeman, Aaron, author.
Title: The big 50 Minnesota Twins : the men and moments that made the Minnesota Twins / Aaron Gleeman.
Other titles: Big fifty Minnesota Twins
Description: Chicago, Illinois : Triumph Books, 2018.
Identifiers: LCCN 2016048653 | ISBN 9781629373775 (paperback)
Subjects: LCSH: Minnesota Twins (Baseball team)—History. | BISAC: SPORTS & RECREATION / Baseball / General. | TRAVEL / United States / Midwest / West North Central (IA, KS, MN, MO, ND, NE, SD).
Classification: LCC GV875.M55 G58 2017 | DDC 796.357/6409776579—dc23 LC record available at https://lccn.loc.gov/2016048653

This book is available in quantity at special discounts for your group or organization. For further information, contact:

Triumph Books LLC
814 North Franklin Street
Chicago, Illinois 60610
(312) 337-0747
www.triumphbooks.com

Printed in U.S.A.
ISBN: 978-1-62937-542-7

Design by Andy Hansen
All photos are courtesy of AP Images unless otherwise indicated.

To Judi, for never throwing out my baseball cards; to Jon, for teaching me that baseball was a worthy obsession; to Becky, for being the best thing to ever happen to me.

[Contents]

THE BIG 50

MINNESOTA TWINS

1

HARMON KILLEBREW

In the spring of 1954, a casual conversation at the ballpark between Washington Senators owner Clark Griffith and actual Idaho Senator Herman Walker turned into one of the most important moments in Minnesota Twins history. Walker told Griffith about a stocky high school kid from Payette, Idaho, who was crushing semi-pro pitching in the Idaho-Oregon Border League. Whatever he said must have made an impression, because Griffith sent Senators farm director Ossie Bluege across the country for an in-person look.

Once there, Bluege found that he wasn't alone. Idaho was suddenly overrun with scouts who had heard tales of the majestic home runs and had come to see 17-year-old Harmon Clayton Killebrew for themselves. He was the real deal, with plans to play baseball and football at the University of Oregon, so Bluege reported back to Griffith that the usually stingy owner needed to loosen the purse strings to land Killebrew. "Get him at all costs," Bluege later told the *New York Times*. "The sky is the limit."

For once, Griffith listened, shelling out a then-massive $30,000 bonus to beat the Red Sox and several other teams for the kid. Because of the rules surrounding high-priced amateur signings in the 1950s, so-called "bonus babies" had to be kept in the big leagues for two years instead of being allowed to develop normally in the minors. Killebrew immediately joined the Senators, officially becoming a major leaguer six days before his 18th birthday in June 1954. And then he collected dust.

Killebrew started just 22 games and received a total of 141

plate appearances from June of 1954 through June of 1956, hitting .205 with eight homers. He was a third baseman stuck behind All-Star Eddie Yost on the depth chart—and the Senators had All-Star Mickey Vernon winding down his career at first base. But in retrospect, the team with a combined 178–284 record probably could have found a bit more playing time for their high-priced prospect.

Finally allowed to develop freely once the two-year mandate ended in June 1956, he got his first taste of the minors and thrived. Killebrew played 70 games for Charlotte of the Single-A South Atlantic League, hitting .325 with 15 home runs and a .627 slugging percentage

"I didn't have evil intentions, but I guess I did have power."
— Harmon Killebrew

that was at least 100 points better than every other hitter in the league. Called back up to Washington in September for the first regular playing time of his big-league career, Killebrew hit .246 with one homer in 20 games.

Save for a few brief call-ups totaling 22 games, Killebrew spent most of 1957 and 1958 in the minors, where he led the Double-A Southern League in home runs as a 21-year-old in 1957 and hit a combined .280 with 48 homers and 148 walks in 266 games at Double-A and Triple-A. He had progressed from high-priced "bonus baby" to high-upside prospect, and in 1959 the Senators decided Killebrew was ready for primetime, trading Yost to the Tigers to clear a spot at third base.

Killebrew homered in his first game and never looked back, tying Rocky Colavito for the league lead with 42 homers and making his first All-Star team at age 23. He also ranked among the AL's top five in slugging percentage, total bases, RBIs, and walks. Killebrew was a fully-formed, middle-of-the-order monster, although in that era his high strikeout total was frowned upon—50 years later 116 strikeouts in 153 games would qualify more as a contact hitter—and his defense was very shaky at third base.

Killebrew split time between third base and first base in 1960 and was even better at the plate—upping his batting average, on-base percentage, and slugging percentage—but he missed 30 games with injuries. Even sitting out more than a month of the season, he still placed fifth in the AL with 31 homers. Despite his best efforts, the Senators were below .500 in 1960 for the seventh straight season. During that offseason the franchise moved from Washington to Minnesota and became the Twins.

His first year in Minnesota was spectacular, as Killebrew hit .288 with 46 homers, 107 walks, and 122 RBIs in 150 games. His home run

TWINS' LEADERS
IN OPS

minimum 2,500 plate appearances:

.901	Harmon Killebrew
.848	Kent Hrbek
.841	Rod Carew
.840	Bob Allison
.837	Kirby Puckett

total was good for "only" third in the league, because Roger Maris set the MLB record with 61 and teammate Mickey Mantle had 54. Six decades later no other Twins player has topped Killebrew's homer total from his first season in Minnesota. In fact, no other Twins hit even 40 homers until Brian Dozier more than five decades later. Killebrew did it that first year and then again in 1962, 1963, 1964, 1967, 1969, and 1970.

Killebrew's power was unmatched in his era—and it was one helluva era. He led all major leaguers in the 1960s with 393 homers, ahead of Hank Aaron with 375, Willie Mays with 350, and Frank Robinson with 315. In the American League from 1955–75, nearly one-third of all 40-homer seasons were by Killebrew, who reached 40 homers eight times in his first dozen seasons as a regular. His walk-drawing ability was also unmatched, as he led the 1960s with 970 walks when only one other player, Mantle, cracked 800.

At the time of Killebrew's retirement in 1975, his 573 career homers ranked fifth in MLB history and his 1,559 walks ranked seventh. Even now, after more than 50 years of bigger and bigger power numbers across baseball, Killebrew still ranks 12th in homers and 15th in walks. He's one of just nine players in baseball history with at least 500 homers and at least 1,500 walks, and of those nine only Babe Ruth, Barry Bonds, and Jim Thome have more homers and more walks than Killebrew.

Those league- and MLB-wide totals show Killebrew's sustained dominance as a walks-and-power savant at a time when that skill set was not yet fully appreciated and strikeouts drew more criticism than warranted. However, nothing drives home how amazing he was quite like Killebrew's place on the all-time Minnesota Twins leaderboards. He arrived in Minnesota as a superstar, writing and re-writing the team records on an annual basis, and six decades later no one (except Dozier, for one season) has pushed him off the lists.

TWINS' LEADERS
IN TIMES ON BASE

3,072	Harmon Killebrew
2,897	Joe Mauer
2,810	Kirby Puckett
2,718	Rod Carew
2,613	Kent Hrbek

Here are the Minnesota Twins' single-season home run leaders:

49	Harmon Killebrew,	1964
49	Harmon Killebrew,	1969
48	Harmon Killebrew,	1962
46	Harmon Killebrew,	1961
45	Harmon Killebrew,	1963
44	Harmon Killebrew,	1967
42	Brian Dozier,	2016
41	Harmon Killebrew,	1970
39	Harmon Killebrew,	1969

Here are the Minnesota Twins' single-season walk leaders:

145	Harmon Killebrew,	1969
131	Harmon Killebrew,	1967
128	Harmon Killebrew,	1970
114	Harmon Killebrew,	1971
107	Harmon Killebrew,	1961
106	Harmon Killebrew,	1962
103	Harmon Killebrew,	1966

He's also the Twins' leader in OPS—by more than 50 points—and slugging percentage, extra-base hits, times on base, and RBIs. Oh, and Killebrew never laid down a sac bunt. Not once. "He hit home runs like few people can in the category of height and distance," said Calvin Griffith, who took over for his father as Twins owner and general manager. "Harmon didn't hit many line drive home runs. He would hit the ball so blooming high in the sky, they were like a rocket ship going up in the air."

Killebrew's historic power came from a surprisingly short, compact right-handed swing that sent balls exploding off his bat. "When I was 14, and for the next four years, I was lifting and hauling 10-gallon milk cans full of milk," Killebrew told the *Washington Post* when asked to explain the source of his incredible power. "That will put muscles on you even if you're not trying." He was like upper-midwestern folklore come to life, an actual Paul Bunyan, wearing a Twins uniform instead of plaid.

TWINS' LEADERS
IN ISOLATED POWER

minimum 2,500 plate appearances:

.258	Harmon Killebrew
.225	Bob Allison
.207	Justin Morneau
.202	Tom Brunansky
.199	Kent Hrbek

Despite the "Killer" nickname—which certainly fit the pitch-crushing Killebrew on the field—he was a quiet, soft-spoken, kind man for whom no one ever had anything but praise as a person. "He was one of the few players who would go out of his way to compliment umpires on a good job, even if their calls went against him," longtime MLB umpire Ron Luciano wrote in his autobiography. "I'd call a tough strike on him and he would turn around and say approvingly, 'Good call.'"

Killebrew didn't drink or smoke, once joking—or maybe not—that his hobby was "just washing the dishes, I guess." American League pitchers might say his actual hobby was torturing them, but Killebrew did that for a living and few were ever better. In his second Twins season, 1962, he moved to left field and led the league in home runs (48) and RBIs (126) while placing second in OPS (.912) and third in the MVP voting. Killebrew led the league in homers again the next season (45) and the one after that (49).

He was on the way to another typically huge season in 1965, posting a .900 OPS through early August, when Killebrew suffered a dislocated elbow. Minnesota was running away with the AL pennant in a 102-win season. Killebrew returned to the lineup just six weeks later, shifting back to third base for the stretch run and World Series. Los Angeles' great pitching limited him to "only" one home run in the seven-game series—off Hall of Famer Don Drysdale in Game 4—but Killebrew led the Twins with an .873 OPS in a losing effort.

Killebrew came back to play all 162 games in 1966, batting .281 with 39 homers and a league-leading 103 walks to finish fourth in the MVP voting. And then he played every game again in 1967, leading the league in homers (44) and walks (131) while finishing runner-up for the MVP to Triple Crown winner Carl Yastrzemski of the Red Sox. Killebrew had played nine full seasons, leading his league in home runs five times and placing among the top five for the MVP award four times.

Killebrew got off to a slow start in 1968, hitting just .204 with 13 homers in the first half, but was chosen for a sixth straight All-Star game anyway. And that's where his poor start turned into a nightmare. Starting at first base, he stretched for an errant throw and tore his hamstring, saying later that he "heard it snap like a rubber band." He missed two months, rejoining the Twins in September for limited action as the team fell below .500. And then he went to work.

"A lot of people thought I was through," Killebrew told the *Los Angeles Times* a couple decades later. "But that injury was kind of a blessing in disguise for me. I worked harder in the winter than I ever did before, and I was in better shape the next season than I ever was in my life." Not only did Killebrew make a full recovery from a severe, potentially career-ending injury at age 33, he had the best season of his career and played in all 162 games as the Twins returned to first place under manager Billy Martin.

Killebrew batted .276 with a 1.011 OPS, leading the league in homers (49), RBIs (140), walks (145), and on-base percentage (.427). To draw 145 free passes, including a league-high 20 intentional, and still hit 49 homers and drive in 140 runs is astonishing. To do so for a division-winning team that finished below .500 the previous season *and* following a major injury...well, it's no wonder he was named MVP. Baltimore pitched around him in the ALCS, walking Killebrew six times in three games as the Orioles swept the Twins.

Another huge year followed in 1970, as Killebrew batted .271 with 41 homers, 113 RBIs, and 128 walks to finish third for the MVP. This time around Baltimore actually pitched to him in the ALCS, so Killebrew smacked two homers and posted a 1.203 OPS in another three-game sweep for the Orioles. His

TWINS' LEADERS
IN OPS VS. LEFTIES

minimum 800 plate appearances:

.935	Harmon Killebrew
.906	Kirby Puckett
.896	Bob Allison
.889	Brian Dozier
.869	Michael Cuddyer

TWINS' LEADERS
IN WIN PROBABILITY
ADDED AS HITTERS

55.6	Harmon Killebrew
34.3	Rod Carew
31.5	Kent Hrbek
27.3	Tony Oliva
27.1	Kirby Puckett
26.9	Joe Mauer

production declined in 1971, including a dip to 28 homers, but he still led the AL in RBIs (119) and walks (114). In mid-August he became the 10th member of the 500-homer club and then hit No. 501 in the same game.

Things were similar in 1972, at age 36, with 26 homers, 94 walks, and a top-10 slugging percentage. That offseason he underwent two leg surgeries, only to suffer a knee injury in June that required another surgery. Killebrew played just 69 games and hit .242 with five home runs. He returned to play 122 games in 1974, but hit just .222 with 13 homers in his final Twins season. Given the option to remain with the Twins as hitting coach or manage at Triple-A, he chose door No. 3 and was released.

Killebrew signed with the Royals one week later. Playing in Minnesota as a visitor for the first time, the Twins retired Killebrew's number and that night he homered against them. He homered 14 times for the Royals, but hit just .199 in 106 games and was released after the season. Killebrew announced his retirement the next spring and rejoined the Twins as an announcer. He was voted into the Hall of Fame in 1984, going into Cooperstown in the same class as the pitcher who served up his World Series homer, Don Drysdale.

During his Hall of Fame induction speech, Killebrew said this of his move to the Twin Cities from Washington in 1961: "I quickly learned that Minnesota was my kind of place and the fans there were my kind of people." He died of cancer in 2010, at age 74. Twins president Dave St. Peter issued a statement on behalf of the team, which began: "No individual has ever meant more to the Minnesota Twins organization and millions of fans across Twins Territory than Harmon Killebrew."

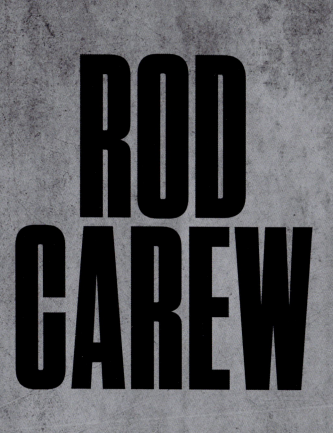

2

ROD CAREW

"Pure hitter" is an amorphous, subjective term that has essentially come to mean a player who posts big batting averages without big home run or strikeout totals. Once in a great while—or maybe just during Ted Williams' career—there's an overlap between the best offensive player and the best pure hitter, but if asked to think of the best "pure hitters" in baseball history, most fans will immediately picture low-power, high-contact, line-drive machines such as Tony Gwynn, Ichiro Suzuki, Wade Boggs, and Pete Rose.

And hopefully Rod Carew, who is one of the best pure hitters in baseball history. He won seven batting titles and, if he'd gotten just two more hits in 1976, would have won seven *consecutive* batting titles from 1972 to '78. Not only is he in the 3,000-hit club, Carew is one of just nine players in baseball history to come to the plate at least 10,000 times with a batting average above .325. Of those nine players, only Carew, Gwynn, and Boggs did so while starting their career after 1950.

Carew hit single-digit home runs in 17 of his 19 seasons, with a career-high of 14 and a career total of 92. He's one of two 3,000-hit club members with fewer than 100 homers and the other, Hall of Fame second baseman Eddie Collins, retired in 1930. Carew struck out 91 times as a rookie and then never struck out more than 81 times again, with fewer than 65 strikeouts in each of his final 14 seasons and fewer than 50 strikeouts in each of his final seven seasons. For his career he had 1,028 strikeouts and 1,018 walks.

Carew didn't so much hit the ball as use his bat to place the ball wherever he wanted it to be. His unique crouched stance—which you can see by way of the statue outside Gate 29 at Target Field—included holding the bat horizontally, even with his shoulder and nearly parallel to the ground, like a cross between a carpenter placing a level on a wall and a cat ready to pounce on its dinner. Sometimes he'd crowd the plate. Sometimes he'd sit all the way back in the box. Sometimes he'd go into an extreme crouch. He toyed with pitchers.

Carew read the defense like a quarterback before the snap and, if he spotted a mismatch, would torture them by dropping down a bunt into no man's land. He ranks fourth all time with 151 bunt hits and has the highest success rate among everyone with 75 or more—by far. Dan Fox of *Baseball Prospectus*, who later joined the Pittsburgh Pirates' front office, studied bunt hits throughout history and came to the conclusion that Carew's combination of volume and efficiency made him the best of all time.

TWINS' LEADERS IN REACHING BASE SAFELY 4+ TIMES

117	Rod Carew
110	Joe Mauer
94	Kirby Puckett
92	Harmon Killebrew
76	Chuck Knoblauch

"I get a kick out of watching a team defense me," Carew told the *New York Daily News* in 1979. "A player moves two steps in one direction and I hit it two steps the other way. It goes right by his glove and I laugh." He did an awful lot of laughing, hitting .300 in 15 seasons. He also continued to terrorize pitchers and defenders once on base, developing into a 40-steal threat after running sporadically early in his career, and swiping home an incredible 17 times—more than anyone since Ty Cobb.

Carew was born in Panama and grew up as a self-described "skinny, barefoot kid hitting a tennis ball with a broomstick on a quiet, dusty street." At age 14 he immigrated to New York with his mother, fleeing an abusive father. According to Carew, the coach at George Washington high school did not want him on the baseball team, so he played instead in a semi-pro league and caught the eye of a Twins scout named Monroe Katz, whose son was on the same team. After graduating, Carew signed with the Twins for $5,000 in June 1964.

He was fast and athletic, but a poor throwing arm limited Carew to second base from the start of his pro career. He hit .302 in the minor leagues, but totaled just two home runs in three seasons when Twins owner/general manager Calvin Griffith decided Carew was ready for the big leagues at 21. Griffith traded starting second baseman Bernie Allen to make room for Carew, telling *The Sporting News* that spring, "Carew can do it all.... He could be the American League All-Star second baseman if he sets his mind to it."

He did, and he was. Carew arrived in the majors during one of the most pitcher-friendly eras of all time. In his first season, 1967, the AL as a whole hit .236 and the league ERA was 3.23. Carew hit .292 as a rookie to rank sixth in the league and started the All-Star game, batting second in front of Twins teammates Tony Oliva and Harmon Killebrew. He was named Rookie of the Year, receiving all but one first-place vote, and the Twins won 91 games to finish tied for second in the American League.

Offense declined even further in 1968—with the league ERA slipping below 3.00—and pitching dominated so much that MLB lowered the mound after the season. Carew hit a career-worst .273 as a sophomore, but that was still 43 points above the league average and he again cracked the AL's starting lineup for the All-Star game. That would become an annual tradition for Carew, who was named to the All-Star team in each of his first 18 seasons as a major leaguer.

His breakout season came in 1969, as Carew hit .332 to win his first batting title by 23 points over Oliva. At the urging of aggressive manager Billy Martin, Carew stole home seven times—one shy of Cobb's single-season 1912 record. "Billy worked with me for hours on stealing home," Carew wrote in his autobiography. "He suggested I take a slow, walking lead. We had it timed to the split second. We also had the batters practice getting in the catcher's way, without being called for interference."

Carew got off to a spectacular start in 1970, becoming the first Twin to hit for the cycle on May 20 and batting .376 through late June. But he suffered a scary leg injury when Mike Hegan

TWINS' LEADERS IN REACHING BASE SAFELY 5+ TIMES

23	Rod Carew
17	Joe Mauer
14	Harmon Killebrew
13	Kent Hrbek
11	Kirby Puckett

of the Brewers slid hard into second base breaking up a double play on June 22. Carew underwent surgery to repair ligament damage and missed three months, returning in September for pinch-hitting appearances. He was healthy enough to play 147 games in 1971 but had a modest season by his own standards, hitting .307 with two homers.

TWINS' LEADERS IN ON-BASE PERCENTAGE

minimum 2,500 plate appearances:

.393	Rod Carew
.391	Joe Mauer
.391	Chuck Knoblauch
.383	Harmon Killebrew
.379	Matt Lawton

Carew won his second batting title in 1972, hitting .318, and then in 1973 kicked off one of the greatest "pure hitting" stretches in baseball history. He hit .330 or higher in each of the next six seasons—a combined .354 during the entire stretch—to win five batting titles and miss a sixth by two points. Never considered a strong defender, Carew transitioned from second base to first base late in 1975, made the full-time switch in 1976, and had the best season of his already brilliant career in 1977.

Carew hit .356 in April, .372 in May, and .486 in June. He was hitting .400 as late as July 10 and went into the break at .394. He hit .381 in the second half and finished at .388 for MLB's highest mark since Ted Williams. His average never fell below .350 after May 14 and never fell below .370 after June 2. Carew also set career-highs in doubles (38), triples (16), and homers (14). He led the AL in hits (239), on-base percentage (.449), runs scored (128), and OPS (1.019)—all of which were career-highs—and was named league MVP.

As a follow-up Carew hit .333 for his seventh batting title, again leading the league in on-base percentage with one season remaining on his contract. However, during that season Twins owner Calvin Griffith made headlines for his racist comments at a small speaking engagement, where he also called Carew "a damn fool" for his previous salary demands. Carew was furious, saying, "I will not ever sign another contract with this organization. I don't care how much money or how many options Calvin Griffith offers me.

TWINS' LEADERS IN TRIPLES

90	Rod Carew
61	Cristian Guzman
57	Kirby Puckett
56	Zoilo Versalles
51	Chuck Knoblauch

"I will not come back and play for a bigot," the normally soft-spoken Carew angrily told reporters. "I'm not going to be another nigger on his plantation. He respects nobody and expects nobody to respect him." That offseason the Twins shopped Carew around, nearly trading him to the Yankees before settling on a deal with the Angels in exchange for four players and $400,000. Carew signed a contract extension with the Angels and finished his career in California, hitting .314 with six All-Star appearances in seven seasons.

Griffith sold the Twins to Carl Pohlad in 1984, and Carew retired the next year. Five years after that he was inducted into the Hall of Fame on the first ballot and wearing a Twins hat on his plaque in Cooperstown. Carew hit .334 in 12 seasons for the Twins, winning seven batting titles and an MVP. His lifetime .358 average on balls in play is the fourth-highest of all time behind Ty Cobb, Shoeless Joe Jackson, and Rogers Hornsby, and his .339 average with runners in scoring position is second to only Gwynn. And no list of the best pure hitters in baseball history will ever be complete without Rod Carew.

KIRBY PUCKETT

After high school Kirby Puckett had just one baseball scholarship offer, from a junior college in Florida, so he stayed home in Chicago and worked at a Ford plant installing carpet in cars for eight dollars an hour. He got laid off from that job after three months and decided to attend a local tryout camp held by major-league teams, but the 5'8", 155-pound third baseman drew little interest. He did, however, catch the eye of Bradley University coach Dewey Kalmer, who offered him a scholarship. Puckett accepted.

In an effort to crack Bradley's lineup, Puckett shifted to the outfield and thrived, making the Missouri Valley All-Conference team as a center fielder. But he left school after one season to be closer to his family following his father's death. Puckett enrolled at Triton junior college, and that's where fate took over. Puckett was playing in a random summer league game in 1981, and one of the opposing players was Mike Rantz, whose father Jim Rantz was the Twins' assistant farm director.

Rantz had a lot of free time on his hands because MLB players were on strike, so he came to watch his son play. And then he saw Puckett and "scout" overtook "dad." Rantz recalled that Puckett "had something like four hits and made a great throw...and the best thing was that there were no other scouts in the stands to see him." Because the draft had already taken place, the Twins selected Puckett with the third pick in the (now defunct) January supplemental draft after non-luminaries Kash Beauchamp and Troy Afenir.

Puckett declined the Twins' initial offer of $6,000 and played for Triton, hitting .472 to lead the team to the Junior College World Series. Minnesota still held his rights, but only until the next draft, so the Twins upped their offer to $20,000 and he signed. He reported to Elizabethton of the rookie-level Appalachian League and hit .382 with 43 steals in 65 games against much younger competition. The next season Puckett moved up to Single-A and hit .314 with 48 steals in

138 games, winning California League player of the year.

By that point the Twins suspected that they had a real prospect on their hands, so Puckett jumped from Single-A to Triple-A in 1984, and 21 games later he was in the big leagues. He debuted against the Angels, in California, on

TWINS' LEADERS
IN DOUBLES

414	Kirby Puckett
401	Joe Mauer
329	Tony Oliva
312	Kent Hrbek
305	Rod Carew

May 8. Leading off and playing center field, Puckett went 4-for-5 with a stolen base, becoming just the 10th player in baseball history to notch four hits in a debut. Puckett had at least one hit in each of his first seven games and batted .393 with a total of 35 hits in his first 20 games. Hello, Kirby.

Puckett hit .296 in 128 games as a rookie, but failed to homer and drew only 16 walks in 583 trips to the plate. His sophomore season was similar, as Puckett hit .288 with four homers and 41 walks in 744 plate appearances. He was a diminutive 25-year-old with 17 homers in 513 games between the minors and majors, so Puckett seemed destined for a career as a speedy, singles-hitting machine. Instead, that offseason Puckett bulked up and worked with hitting coach/Twins great Tony Oliva on adding a leg kick to his swing.

He arrived at spring training with more than 210 pounds on his 5'8" frame, quipping to reporters: "What else can you do in Minnesota during the winter except eat?" And then he started to get fat on big-league pitching. Puckett topped his career homer total by mid-April and went deep 13 times in his first 33 games. He made the All-Star team, hit at least five homers in all but one month, and finished the year with 31 long balls. And Puckett didn't sacrifice batting average by adding power. In fact, he hit a career-high .328.

"Puckett just stands up there, belly over belt, bat looking like a tree limb...and whacks away at anything that looks like a strike," wrote Mike Downey of the *Los Angeles Times* late in Puckett's breakout year. Puckett's belly only got bigger, he never did stop swinging at anything, and the big leg kick became part of one of baseball's most recognizable swings.

Tom Kelly moved Puckett from the leadoff spot to No. 3 in the order and he followed up the out-of-nowhere 31-homer season in 1986 with 28 homers in 1987. It was a nearly identical all-around season, but this time Puckett's teammates gave him a lot more help and the Twins improved from 71–91 to 85–77, winning the AL West as he finished third in the MVP voting. Matched up against Detroit in the ALCS and St. Louis in the World Series, he hit .205 through 10 playoff games. For many great players, that would be the extent of their postseason experience and they'd forever be thought of as failing on the big stage. Joe Mauer, for instance, has played 10 career playoff games as of 2017.

Puckett got an extended opportunity because his teammates carried the slack enough for the team to keep chugging along and that's when Kirby Puckett, Postseason Legend was born. With the Twins down 3–2 against the Cardinals in the World Series, he was 4-for-4 with four runs scored in Game 6 and 2-for-4 with a double in Game 7. Minnesota had its first championship and the 5'8" non-prospect from Chicago whose career was nearly over before it even began was one of the biggest superstars in baseball.

For an encore, Puckett had the best year of his career in 1988, hitting .356 with 24 homers and 121 RBIs to again finish third in the MVP voting. He led the league with 237 hits and won a third straight Gold Glove award while ranking second among AL position players in Wins Above Replacement. Had the Twins made the postseason again Puckett probably would have been named MVP, but instead they placed a distant second despite winning six more games than the previous year.

Puckett's power disappeared in 1989, as he managed just nine homers in 159 games, but he hit .339 to win his first batting title, led the league in hits for the third season in a row, and signed a three-year, $9 million contract that made him baseball's highest-paid player. His production dipped in 1990, as his batting average fell below .300 with 12 home runs. Puckett was similarly good but not great in 1991—

"I was told I would never make it because I'm too short. Well, I'm still too short. It doesn't matter what your height is, it's what's in your heart."
—Kirby Puckett

until the playoffs, that is. Going from last place to first place, the Twins won the AL West and faced Toronto in the ALCS.

Puckett again started slow with one hit through two games, but then exploded for eight hits—including two homers—in the final three games as the Twins advanced to a second World Series. He was 3-for-18 (.167) in the first five games versus Atlanta and the Twins were down 3–2. What followed from Puckett and the Twins in Game 6 at the Metrodome was such a spectacular individual performance in such a magical game that simply saying the phrase "and we'll see you tomorrow night" is guaranteed to make Minnesotans smile.

As the legend goes, in batting practice Puckett told teammates: "Jump on my back today, I'll carry us." And boy did he. In the first inning, Puckett put the Twins up 2–0 with an RBI triple. In the third inning, with a runner on, he made a leaping grab at the wall—"The Catch"—to rob Ron Gant of extra bases. In the fifth inning, with the game tied, he put the Twins back in front with an RBI sacrifice fly. Atlanta re-tied the game, sending it to extra innings, and Puckett led off the 11th frame against left-hander Charlie Liebrandt.

Puckett feasted on left-handers throughout his career and hit .406 off them in 1991, so it was a bad matchup for the Braves that became worse when Liebrandt fell behind 2–1. On the fourth pitch Liebrandt hung a changeup and Puckett did what he'd done to bad changeups his entire life, hitting it over the fence in left-center field for a walk-off homer as Jack Buck (and John Gordon, on local radio) went nuts. Puckett pumped his fist rounding the bases and "tomorrow night" became one of the greatest games in baseball history.

Much like he did in 1988, Puckett had a tremendous encore in 1992, hitting .329 to lead the league in hits and total bases. And much like in 1988, he probably missed out on the MVP because the Twins missed the playoffs, finishing second to Dennis Eckersley in the voting despite leading the AL in WAR. A free agent for the first time after Twins owner Carl Pohlad rejected his five-year, $27.5 million offer, Puckett turned down more money elsewhere to stay in Minnesota...for five years and $30 million.

Now the second-highest-paid player in baseball, Puckett won All-Star game MVP honors in 1993, hit .317, and led the league in

RBIs while shifting from center field to right field in the strike-shortened 1994 season. He hit .314 with 23 homers in the strike-shortened 1995 campaign. In the Twins' final home game of 1995, a meaningless matchup between first-place Cleveland and last-place Minnesota, a high-and-tight pitch from starter Dennis Martinez struck Puckett in the face, breaking his jaw.

TWINS' LEADERS
IN HITS

2,304	Kirby Puckett
2,085	Rod Carew
1,986	Joe Mauer
1,917	Tony Oliva
1,749	Kent Hrbek

He headed into the next spring with a clean bill of health and hit .344, but one day in late March he woke up with blurred vision in his right eye. Placed on the disabled list to begin the season, Puckett was diagnosed with glaucoma and underwent multiple surgeries in an unsuccessful effort to save his career. Puckett announced his retirement on July 12, at 36 and just 10 months removed from one of the best seasons of his career. His number was retired by the Twins in 1997, and in 2001 he was a first-ballot Hall of Fame induction.

His abbreviated, 12-year career included 10 straight All-Star games, seven top-10 MVP finishes, six Gold Gloves, four hit titles, and two championships. He swung at everything and hit everything, batting .288 or higher each season and .318 overall. Puckett was well on his way to 3,000 hits despite not reaching the majors until age 24—his 2,304 hits are the fifth-most in baseball history through any player's first 12 seasons and he is ranked 52nd all time through age 35.

Puckett fared poorly in retirement, from both health and mental standpoints. He gained lots of weight and had a series of incidents in which he allegedly assaulted his wife and multiple other women. *Sports Illustrated* published a lengthy article in 2013 by Frank Deford detailing Puckett's off-field problems, which were far more numerous and serious than many Minnesotans wanted to believe. Puckett moved to Arizona, withdrawing from the spotlight, and suffered a fatal cerebral hemorrhage in 2006 at age 45.

No one played harder or smiled brighter than Puckett, whose great career was magnified by postseason heroics. He was the best, most charismatic and beloved player on the two best teams in Twins history. All of which made the sad way his career ended so crushing to fans and Puckett himself, and made the way his post-baseball life unraveled even more tragic. It's become commonplace to sweep Puckett's misdeeds under the rug, and a career like his can cover up almost anything in the eyes of many fans, but it shouldn't.

Puckett was an amazing baseball player and, in most circumstances and to most people, an amazing man, but he's also an example of why placing athletes on pedestals based on public personas can be a fool's errand. No matter the extent to which you believe various accusations, criminal charges, and lawsuits, Puckett was not the person everyone thought he was. His story is both remarkable and sad, just as he was both good and bad. Puckett was a flawed human being, not just a great baseball player, and neither negates the other.

BERT BLYLEVEN

Rik Aalbert "Bert" Blyleven was born in the Netherlands, which at the time had produced zero MLB players in nearly 50 years. His family moved to North America when he was a baby and Blyleven grew up in California, where he fell in love with baseball by listening to Vin Scully announce Dodgers games on the radio. During one broadcast his father, Joe Blyleven, heard Sandy Koufax tell Scully that he wouldn't let any child throw a curveball before age 13. Koufax had one of the best curveballs of all time. Bert Blyleven's was better.

Once he was cleared to start throwing it, Blyleven spent countless hours trying to mimic the left-handed Koufax, but as a right-hander. "My dad built me a mound in the backyard with a canvas backdrop," Blyleven told the *New York Times*. "I'd go back there and just throw and throw and throw until I developed it." And because Blyleven was mostly self-taught, he used a four-seam curveball grip rather than the two-seam norm. He grew to be 6'3" and had a plus fastball when the Twins made him a third-round draft pick in 1969.

It became immediately obvious to the Twins that Blyleven was a special talent and they moved him up to Triple-A to begin his second pro season. Blyleven had 63 strikeouts in 54 innings there when veteran Twins starter Luis Tiant suffered a year-ending fractured shoulder blade in early June. With the Twins in first place and fighting for their second consecutive division title, they called up Blyleven just two months after his 19th birthday and almost exactly one year after he was drafted.

Byleven took Tiant's spot in the rotation and debuted on June 5, 1970, as the league's youngest player, serving up a home run to the first batter, Lee Maye. That was the lone run he allowed in seven innings, striking out seven and walking one in a 2–1 win over Washington. He remained in the rotation for the rest of the year, throwing 164 innings with a 3.18 ERA and 135-to-47 strikeout-to-walk ratio as the Twins won 98 games and the division title. Blyleven ranked sixth among AL pitchers in strikeout rate.

As a sophomore, Blyleven became the workhorse of a Twins pitching staff that featured veterans Jim Kaat and Jim Perry, throwing 278 innings with a 2.81 ERA and completing 17-of-38 starts. He ranked among the AL's top 10 in ERA, strikeouts, innings, complete games,

MOST INNINGS IN TWINS HISTORY
THROUGH AGE 25

1,707	Bert Blyleven
1,036	Dave Boswell
891	Jim Kaat
866	Brad Radke
844	Frank Viola

and shutouts. At age 20 he was already an ace, although poor lineup and bullpen support on a 74–86 team left him with a mediocre 16–15 record in what would turn out to be the story of his entire career.

Blyleven threw 287 innings with a 2.73 ERA in 1972—ranking fourth in strikeouts and fifth in innings—but went just 17–17. He was even better in 1973, logging 325 innings with a 2.52 ERA and league-high nine shutouts, yet was just 20–17 and finished seventh in the Cy Young voting despite ranking second in ERA, second in strikeouts, and fourth in innings. Things continued that way for the next two-and-a-half years, with Blyleven throwing tons of innings with tons of strikeouts and a great ERA...while going 36–32.

Then in mid-1976, with Blyleven unhappy about his contract like so many stars forced to deal with Twins owner Calvin Griffith over the years, he was traded to the Rangers along with Danny Thompson for 23-year-old shortstop Roy Smalley, 25-year-old third baseman Mike Cubbage, 32-year-old former All-Star pitcher Bill Singer, and pitching prospect Jim Gideon. Gideon washed out and Singer was near the end of the line, but Cubbage played five seasons in Minnesota and Smalley went on to be the best shortstop in Twins history.

Blyleven had been publicly feuding with Griffith over his contract, and in his final Twins start he made an obscene gesture to the Metropolitan Stadium crowd as he walked off the mound in a complete-game loss. Texas gladly paid Blyleven what he wanted, which was a $100,000 bonus and a three-year contract worth

$150,000 per year. It was a bargain for a 25-year-old ace starter who'd averaged 290 innings with a 2.74 ERA over the previous five seasons.

He was good in Texas with a 2.72 ERA after the trade in 1976 and a 2.72 ERA in 1977, including a no-hitter against the Angels on September 22, 1977. However, late in 1977 he upset the Rangers by making another obscene gesture to a camera, and that offseason they traded him to the Pirates. Blyleven won a World Series with Pittsburgh in 1979, going 2–0 with a 1.42 ERA in three playoff games, but in early 1980 he demanded a trade due to what he called "non-support and lack of confidence from the manager" Chuck Tanner.

"I felt I had to speak up," Blyleven told the *Pittsburgh Post Gazette*. "If I didn't, maybe 20 years from now, I'd be wishing that I had spoken up. Or maybe 20 years from now I'll wish I hadn't spoken up." Speaking up was never a problem for Blyleven, who threatened to retire if he wasn't traded and left the team for two weeks in May. He rejoined the team for the remainder of the season and had his worst year, after which the Pirates traded him to the Indians that winter.

He spent four-and-a-half seasons in Cleveland, mostly without incident, but the Indians were one of the worst teams in baseball and by mid-1985 the assumption was that they'd trade the 34-year-old for prospects. Blyleven wanted a deal to his hometown Angels but settled for his stated "second choice": returning to the Twins. His attitude upon returning was much different because, as Blyleven explained, "Calvin [Griffith] is no longer here and times change." He later signed a contract extension with the Twins.

Blyleven pitched well down the stretch in 1985 and led the league with 272 innings in 1986, but allowed an all-time record 50 homers and had an ERA above 4.00 in a full season for the first time in his career. He allowed "only" 46 homers in 1987 and walked more than 100 batters for the first time at age 36, but posted a 4.01 ERA compared to the

TWINS' LEADERS
IN SHUTOUTS

29	Bert Blyleven
23	Jim Kaat
18	Camilo Pascual
17	Jim Perry
11	Dave Goltz

league average of 4.46 and chewed up 267 innings for a Twins team that lacked reliable starters beyond Frank Viola.

Minnesota scratched and clawed its way into the playoffs with an underwhelming 85–77 record and once there manager Tom Kelly—who was the same age

TWINS' LEADERS IN COMPLETE GAMES

141	Bert Blyleven
133	Jim Kaat
80	Dave Goltz
72	Camilo Pascual
61	Jim Perry

as Blyleven—leaned heavily on the Viola-Blyleven pairing. Blyleven started twice in the ALCS versus Detroit and twice in the World Series versus St. Louis, going 3–1 with a 3.42 ERA and just three homers allowed. He struggled for the Twins in 1988, going 10–17 with a 5.43 ERA, and then signed with the Angels as a free agent, finishing his 22-year career in California.

At the time of his retirement, Blyleven ranked third all time in strikeouts (3,701), ninth in innings (4,970), and 15th in wins (287), yet he failed to garner Hall of Fame support during his first decade on the ballot. Poor lineup and bullpen support had cost him entry into the 300-win club, left his record at a mediocre 287–250, and denied him awards and All-Star appearances that boost a candidacy. And while he later became known as a "prankster" and popular television announcer for the Twins, his early reputation as a malcontent lingered.

It wasn't until voters began to look beyond Blyleven's win-loss record that his candidacy took off. Blyleven has openly mocked sabermetrics, but the same stats he hates are what got him into Cooperstown, as his votes rose from 48 to 80 percent in four years. Blyleven had just one 20-win season, made only two All-Star teams, and had just three top-five Cy Young finishes, but his career Wins Above Replacement of 96.5 is the 11th-highest ever for pitchers and he ranked among the league's top five in pitching WAR a dozen times.

He spent 11 seasons in Minnesota, debuting at 19 and leaving for the second time at 37. His reputation changed almost as much as his homer rate by the second go-around, but the constants were his incredible durability and jaw-dropping curveball. "There were times when I looked for his curveball, got his curveball, and still didn't hit it," Paul Molitor told the *St. Paul Pioneer Press*. "He could start it literally almost behind your left shoulder and get it back to the plate."

Blyleven is the Twins' leader in strikeouts, complete games, shutouts, and pitching Wins Above Replacement while ranking second to Jim Kaat in wins and innings. He owns half of the Twins' top-10 single-season strikeout and innings totals, and his 1973—with 325 innings, 258 strikeouts, 25 complete games, nine shutouts, and a 2.52 ERA as a 22-year-old—is arguably the best pitching performance in team history. And 14 years later Blyleven and that curveball played a big role on the Twins' first championship team.

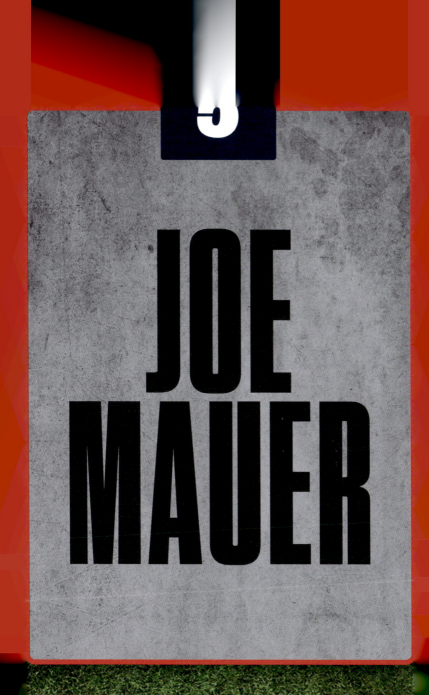

St. Paul native and Cretin-Derham Hall catcher Joe Mauer was the best high school athlete in the country in 2001—the nation's top-ranked quarterback, with a scholarship waiting to play for Bobby Bowden at Florida State even though it was unlikely because he was also the nation's top-rated baseball player. And as fate—or the pitching staff's 5.14 ERA in 2000—would have it, the Twins held the No. 1 pick in draft for just the second time in team history. There was one issue, however: Mark Prior.

Prior was so dominant at USC that the 6'5" right-hander was receiving "best college pitcher ever" hype, with talk of him skipping the minor leagues and going directly to the majors. There was also talk of him wanting a record-breaking signing bonus and viewing the Cubs, with the No. 2 pick, as a more desirable fit than the Twins. In the days leading up to the draft reports surfaced that negotiations between the Twins and Prior had stalled, and on June 5, 2001, the Twins selected Mauer.

Prior signed with the Cubs for a record $10.5 million, more than double Mauer's bonus, and initial criticism of the Twins grew louder as Prior reached the majors early the next season. He struck out 147 batters in 117 innings as a rookie and finished third in the Cy Young voting as a sophomore, going 18–6 with a 2.43 ERA and 245 strikeouts. Meanwhile, the Twins broke through as a division-winning team for whom a young ace atop the rotation could make a huge impact. Anyone who wanted Prior then definitely wanted him now.

Mauer began his career in rookie-ball, where he hit .400. He moved up to low Single-A in 2012—playing for Quad Cities of the Midwest League while Prior was starring in the majors—and hit .302. Mauer was living up to the hype. *Baseball America* ranked him as the game's fourth-best prospect heading into 2003, and then he hit .335 at high Single-A and .341 at Double-A. By the time that season was over Mauer was baseball's consensus No. 1 prospect at age 20 and

Prior was starting to break down physically.

Minnesota won back-to-back division titles in 2002 and 2003, with starting catcher A.J. Pierzynski hitting .300 in both seasons. Pierzynski was a 26-year-old All-Star and Mauer was the best prospect in baseball, so it was obvious that something had to give. Instead of sending Mauer to Triple-A in 2004 and delaying the catcher decision until midseason or maybe even 2005, general manager Terry Ryan traded Pierzynski to the Giants for Joe Nathan, Francisco Liriano, and Boof Bonser.

HIGHEST SINGLE-SEASON OPS IN TWINS HISTORY

1.031	Joe Mauer, 2009
1.019	Rod Carew, 1977
1.012	Harmon Killebrew, 1961
1.011	Harmon Killebrew, 1969
.966	Shane Mack, 1994

Like drafting Mauer over Prior, the trade was unpopular locally. And, like drafting Mauer over Prior, it was one of the best moves in Twins history even if it took a while to look that way. Pierzynski had a miserable first and only year in San Francisco, playing poorly and clashing with everyone before being cut. Nathan stepped into the closer role and became the best reliever in Twins history. For an all-too-brief moment Liriano was the best starter in baseball before injuries derailed him. Even with Bonser a bust, that's quite a haul.

Mauer debuted as the Twins' catcher on Opening Day of 2004, two weeks shy of his 21st birthday, and went 2–for–3 with two walks in a win. Suddenly no one seemed as upset by Pierzynski's departure. Unfortunately, the next day Mauer went chasing after a foul ball and tore his left knee, requiring surgery. It was a deflating blow, made worse by worries that knee surgery for a 20-year-old, 6′5″ catcher would have long-term ramifications. He was back within two months and hit well for 33 games, but was shut down in July.

He hit .308 with six homers and eight doubles in 35 games and threw out 40 percent of steal attempts—unheard of production for a 21-year-old rookie catcher—but soreness and swelling in the surgically repaired knee convinced the Twins to shut down Mauer for the season. Because of the knee injury Mauer hadn't played enough to exhaust his Rookie of the Year eligibility, so *Baseball America* again ranked him as the game's No. 1 prospect after an offseason Twins fans spent worrying about his future.

Mauer returned to play 131 games in 2005, logging 1,000 innings behind the plate while hitting .294 with nine homers and a 64/61 K/BB ratio. He even stole 13 bases in 14 tries, compared to allowing only 31 steals—with 23 caught stealing—by opponents. It was one of the best seasons ever by a 22-year-old catcher and especially impressive coming back from major knee surgery, yet many Twins fans still wondered if the injury and time off robbed them of seeing Mauer at full capacity.

Mauer put that to rest in 2006 by playing 140 games—120 of them behind the plate—and becoming the first catcher in American League history to win a batting title. At age 23 he hit .347 with 13 homers and 36 doubles, drew 79 walks versus 54 strikeouts, swiped eight bases and threw out 38 percent of steal attempts, made his first All-Star team, and placed sixth in the MVP voting. Meanwhile in Chicago, the Cubs got a 7.21 ERA in 44 innings from Prior in what would be the final season of his injury-wrecked career.

Two years after becoming the first AL catcher to win a batting title, Mauer hit .328 to win another one in 2008. He drew 84 walks with 50 strikeouts for a .413 on-base percentage, got his first Gold Glove, started the All-Star game, and placed fourth in the MVP voting. He was doing things catchers simply didn't do—he shut down opposing running games, he worked deep counts and drew walks with an incredible eye and unwavering patience, and when he zeroed in on a pitch in the strike zone he lined it into a gap in the defense.

TWINS' LEADERS IN MOST GAMES REACHING BASE SAFELY 3+ TIMES

401	Joe Mauer
379	Rod Carew
369	Harmon Killebrew
359	Kirby Puckett
297	Kent Hrbek

Mauer spent the winter of 2008 recovering from kidney obstruction surgery, which later gave way to back problems. He sat out spring training and began the year on the disabled list, missing all of April. Mauer returned on May 1 with one of the great runs ever, hitting .365 with 28 homers in 138 games for a league-high 1.031 OPS and a third batting title, equaling the combined total for all other catchers in baseball history. Minnesota went 74–59 with him in the lineup and won the division in a thrilling Game 163 over Detroit.

Mauer won the sabermetric triple crown by leading the league in batting average (.365), on-base percentage (.444), and slugging percentage (.587). He was the first catcher ever to do so and the first AL hitter of any position to do so since Hall of Famer George Brett in 1980. Despite sitting out the entire first month Mauer was named MVP and received all but one first-place vote, joining Ivan Rodriguez and Thurman Munson as the only AL catchers to win MVP in 50 years.

In the spring of 2010, with Mauer heading into the final year of his contract and the team moving from the Metrodome to Target Field, the Twins signed him to an eight-year, $184 million contract extension. Mauer had an excellent 2010 season, hitting .327 with nine homers, 43 doubles, more walks than strikeouts, and a .402 on-base percentage to finish eighth in the MVP voting. His performance was a near-perfect match for what he did in 2008, but the historic, MVP season and massive new contract had dramatically raised expectations.

In particular, exploding for 28 homers after failing to show big-time power as a prospect or in his first five Twins seasons had many people thinking Mauer was finally a slugger. He wasn't. His approach at the plate and swing mechanics were still made for line drives up the middle and to the opposite field, rather than long flies over the fence. Many of his 28 homers were wall-scrapers at the Metrodome and those were far tougher to come by at Target Field. Mauer was still the same hitter, but some people now saw that as a negative.

Mauer underwent offseason knee surgery, the recovery for which became a struggle and dragged into spring training. He was in the Opening Day lineup, but was clearly playing at less than full capacity and the Twins shut him down in mid-April. It would have been easy enough to simply say that Mauer was having difficulty coming back from surgery, but instead the Twins oddly treated his health like a mystery before deeming his issues "bilateral leg weakness." That term became a career-long punch line for detractors.

Mauer returned in mid-June, but struggled and finished with a .287 batting average and career-worst numbers across the board in 83 games. In two years Mauer had gone from beloved, hometown MVP winner to Minnesota's most-criticized athlete. He came back strong in 2012, hitting .319 in a career-high 147 games. It was a typically strong Mauer season, as he started the All-Star game, led the league with a .416 on-base percentage, and ranked 10th in OPS.

"Joe Mauer's the real deal. Not only is he a great player, but he's a great human being. He's the kind of guy you'd like to see be your son."
—Harmon Killebrew

He followed that up with a nearly identical season in 2013, hitting .324 with a .404 OBP through 113 games when disaster struck on August 19. Mauer suffered a concussion from a foul tip to the mask and was put on MLB's new seven-day concussion disabled list. He never returned to the lineup, as dizziness, nausea, blurred vision, sensitivity to light, and other common post-concussions symptoms repeatedly halted his rehab. Shortly after the season the Twins announced that the six-time All-Star catcher was moving to first base.

HIGHEST CAREER WINS ABOVE REPLACEMENT BY A NO. 1 PICK

118	Alex Rodriguez
85	Chipper Jones
84	Ken Griffey Jr.
53	Joe Mauer
43	Adrian Gonzalez

The hope was that getting out from behind the plate and away from the most physically taxing position in baseball would enable him to avoid further concussions, stay healthier overall, be in the lineup more, and up his production. Unfortunately, as was the case with MVP-winning teammate Justin Morneau just a few years earlier, the effects of Mauer's brain injury lingered for years after the concussion. He continued to have blurred vision and sensitivity to light, and his production at the plate dropped.

At the time of the concussion Mauer was hitting .324 with an .880 OPS. He'd hit .319 with an .861 OPS the previous season and was a 30-year-old career .323 hitter with an .873 OPS. In his first post-concussion season Mauer hit .277 with a .732 OPS and that was about where his production stayed before a stronger 2017. Mauer was still capable of weeks or even months looking like his old self, and he was still an above-average hitter overall, but he was quite clearly not the same player after August 19, 2013.

Mauer's career has been a lightning rod for criticism. First it was the decisions to draft him over Prior and make room for him by trading Pierzynski. Then he suffered a major knee injury right away. He bounced back to be the ultimate rarity, a batting title-winning catcher, and won an MVP with one of the best years the position has seen, at which point his lack of power and contract became targets. From there he had an injury-wrecked year and returned to form as a .320 hitter, only to suffer a career-altering brain injury at 30.

There may always be a sense that Mauer could or should have done more, and there's no question his time as an elite player was cut too short. However, his decade as a catcher is one of the best ever—he hit .323 with six All-Star games, three batting titles, three Gold Gloves, and an MVP by age 30. Among all catchers in history through age 30 only Mike Piazza had a higher AVG, only Mickey Cochrane had a higher OBP, and only Cochrane, Piazza, Bill Dickey, and Gabby Harnett had a higher OPS. They're all Hall of Famers.

Not only was he on a Hall of Fame path as of August 19, 2013, he was on track to be one of the 10 best catchers of all time and that shouldn't be brushed aside as he winds down his career at first base as a lesser but still valuable version of his old self. Mauer's career .329 batting average with runners in scoring position is the fourth-highest in baseball history, behind only Tony Gwynn, Rod Carew, and Miguel Cabrera, and he'll likely retire as the Twins' all-time leader in times on base while also ranking among the top three in hits, runs scored, extra-base hits, walks, intentional walks, and on-base percentage.

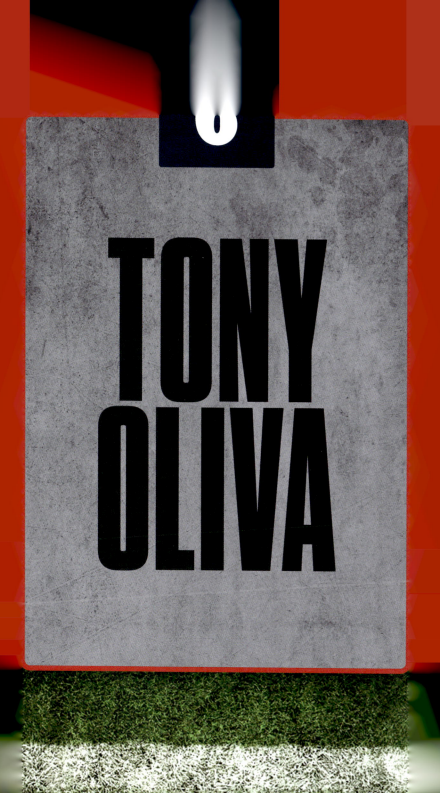

The most important name in Twins history that most fans have never heard uttered is Joe Cambria, an Italian-born scout who began working for Clark Griffith and the Washington Senators in the 1930s. Cambria spotted and signed Hall of Fame pitcher Early Wynn and Senators greats like Eddie Yost, Mickey Vernon, Walt Masterson, and George Case. And that was just in America. Cuban players became Cambria's specialty, and throughout the 1940s and 1950s he signed literally hundreds of teenage prospects from the island.

His track record for finding young talent—and, much to Griffith's delight, finding them cheaply—is unsurpassed in baseball history, and Cambria had become so entrenched in Cuba by the 1950s that the Senators essentially had a private pipeline to the best players. For instance, in 1951 he signed a Cuban pitcher named Camilo Pascual, and the story goes that the 16-year-old right-hander turned down $4,000 from the Brooklyn Dodgers to sign with Cambria for $175. Pascual was a five-time All-Star for the Senators and Twins.

Seven years later, just as Pascual was establishing himself as a Senators rotation fixture, Cambria signed a 16-year-old Cuban shortstop named Zoilo Versalles. Seven years after that Versalles was voted MVP of the American League while leading the Twins to their first World Series. But as great as Pascual and Versalles were—and as many other great players Cambria signed over the years from various countries—there's no question about the crown jewel of his scouting career. It was Tony Oliva.

Oliva was born in Pinar del Rio, which was also the birthplace of Cambria-signed pitcher Pedro Ramos, an All-Star left-hander for the Senators. Oliva's birth name was also Pedro, after his father, but in signing with Cambria and the Twins in February of 1961 he didn't have the necessary paperwork for a move to the United States by the start of spring training. His older brother Antonio did have a passport, and so Pedro Oliva took on that identity, left Cuba for America, and became Tony Oliva, professional baseball player.

Or at least that's how Oliva tells the story. There was always speculation that the identity switch took place because the Oliva signed by the Twins was the older brother—who was named after his father—and would benefit from being 19 rather than 22. Cambria may have even suggested it. Decades later Oliva's wife backed up that version, saying the 22-year-old Pedro believed he'd have a better chance of signing with the Twins and making it to the big leagues if he was seen as the 19-year-old Antonio.

TWINS' LEADERS
IN OPS BY A ROOKIE
minimum 500 plate appearances:

.916	Tony Oliva, 1964
.863	Jimmie Hall, 1963
.848	Kent Hrbek, 1982
.848	Tom Brunansky, 1982
.839	Marty Cordova, 1995

Whatever the case, Pedro "Tony" Oliva finally got to the United States after numerous delays and began his pro career in Wytheville, Virginia, of the rookie-level Appalachian League. Future major leaguers Frank Quilici and Ted Uhlaender were also on the team, but no one could keep their eyes off Oliva's sweet left-handed swing. He batted .410 with 81 RBIs in 64 games, all while dealing with the language barrier, and horrible working and living conditions for a dark-skinned foreigner in the largely segregated south.

Assigned to Charlotte of the Single-A South Atlantic League in 1962, he batted .350 with 17 homers and more walks (43) than strikeouts (32) in 127 games. Oliva was voted MVP over, among others, a 21-year-old Cincinnati Reds prospect named Pete Rose who had hit .330. Oliva's performance was so impressive that the Twins made him a September call-up and he went 4-for-9 (.444) with a double and three walks in his big-league debut playing alongside Pascual and Versalles.

Oliva's third pro season was a similar story. He starred in the minors, hitting .304 with 23 homers for Dallas of the Triple-A Pacific Coast League, and then returned to Minnesota only briefly as a September call-up. By that point Oliva was (officially) 24, with a

Tony Oliva's career in a nutshell: eight great seasons and eight knee surgeries.

three-year resume of crushing minor-league pitching from rookie-ball to Triple-A, and was 7-for-16 (.438) in limited major-league chances. Finally in 1964 the Twins decided Oliva was ready for the American League, but the American League wasn't ready for him.

Minnesota led all of baseball in both homers and runs scored in 1963, boasting one of the most powerful lineups the game had ever seen with All-Star sluggers Harmon Killebrew, Bob Allison, Jimmie Hall, Earl Battey, and Don Mincher. Yet in 1964, with the same cast back for what would be another league-leading offensive campaign, the Twins wasted no time inserting the Cuban rookie into the No. 3 spot in the order. Oliva collected multiple hits in each of the first five games and was an immediate superstar.

Oliva carried a .400 batting average into late May and finished the first half hitting .335 with 18 homers. Voted into the All-Star game by his peers as the AL's youngest player and starting right fielder, he hit second in the lineup ahead of Mickey Mantle, Killebrew, and Allison. Oliva kept rolling after the break and won the batting title with a .323 mark, also leading the league in hits, doubles, total bases, and runs. He was the easy choice for Rookie of the Year and was fourth in the MVP voting.

His raw rookie numbers say plenty, but it's important to note that Oliva did that damage at a time when pitching dominated. The league as a whole hit just .247 with a sub-.700 OPS in 1964, and five years later MLB lowered the mound to give hitters a chance. For a rookie to burst onto that scene hitting .323 with 32 homers and 84 total extra-base hits is incredible. It would be 20 years until another AL rookie topped 32 homers and five-plus decades later only Ichiro Suzuki has joined Oliva as AL rookies to win a batting title.

Within the context of Twins history there is no match for what Oliva accomplished as a rookie. He stands as the team's all-time rookie leader in hits, doubles, total bases, extra-base hits, batting average, slugging percentage, OPS, and runs scored—most of them by wide margins. His total of 6.8 Wins Above Replacement is not only the all-time Twins record for a rookie position player by more than 20 percent, it's one of the 10 best WAR totals posted by any Twins hitter, rookie or otherwise.

Oliva's home run total fell from 32 to 16 as a sophomore, but he hit .321 to win a second batting title and finished runner-up for the MVP award. The winner? His fellow Cambria-signed Twins teammate Zoilo Versalles. For the third straight season Minnesota's lineup led the league in runs scored and this time the pitching staff did its part too, as the Twins won 102 games and the AL pennant before falling to Sandy Koufax and the Dodgers in the World Series.

Oliva's production dipped somewhat from 1966–68, although that was partly due to an MLB-wide dearth of offense. He hit "only" .296 in that time period, which was actually the league's third-highest mark during that span behind Hall of Famers Frank Robinson and Carl Yastrzemski at .301. Oliva was runner-up for the 1966 batting title and placed third in 1968. He also won a Gold Glove award in 1966, as his range and strong throwing arm got some attention alongside his exceptional bat.

With the mound lowered and offensive levels rising, Oliva hit .309 in 1969 and .325 in 1970, finishing with the league's third-best mark both seasons as the Twins returned to the playoffs. MVP voters in 1970 gave first-place nods to seven different players, with Oliva sitting atop five ballots on the way to a runner-up finish behind Orioles slugger Boog Powell. Then in 1971 Oliva was in the midst of a career-year at age 32, batting .375 with 18 homers in late June, when he injured his knee diving for a ball in right field.

Oliva had bad knees for his entire career, undergoing three surgeries before turning 30, but it was that injury suffered on June 29, 1971, in Oakland that ended his days as an elite player. He returned for most of the second half and ended up hitting a career-high .337 for his third batting title, but following the injury Oliva's average slipped to .289 and he managed just four home runs in 58 games. He underwent surgery as soon as the season ended but continued to have pain and swelling at spring training six months later.

He began 1972 on the disabled list and remained there until mid-June, hitting .321 in 10 games before being shut down again. Oliva's season was over and he underwent a pair of surgeries designed to save his career at 33. That offseason the AL adopted the designated hitter, which was perfect timing for Oliva and his bad knees. He never saw an inning in the field again, but became the first DH to homer—off Hall of Famer Catfish Hunter in the 1973 opener—and played an average of 135 games per year from 1973–75.

Unfortunately, by that point most of the thunder in Oliva's bat was gone. He remained an above-average hitter during that three-season span as a full-time DH, but batted just .281 with 42 homers in 404 games for an OPS nearly 130 points below his 1962–71 prime. He was too hobbled in 1976 to play regularly even as a DH, so Oliva served mostly as a pinch-hitter and struggled in 128 plate appearances before retiring at age 37 as a lifetime .304 hitter.

Oliva's rookie season stands as one of the best ever and from that fantastic freshman campaign through 1971 he won three batting titles and led the league in hits five times in eight seasons, finishing runner-up for two MVP awards. During that span Oliva led the league in batting average, hits, doubles, and total bases while ranking among the top five in slugging percentage and OPS. He did that all despite bum wheels, and then those bum wheels finally did him in. Oliva was a Hall of Fame player with Triple-A knees.

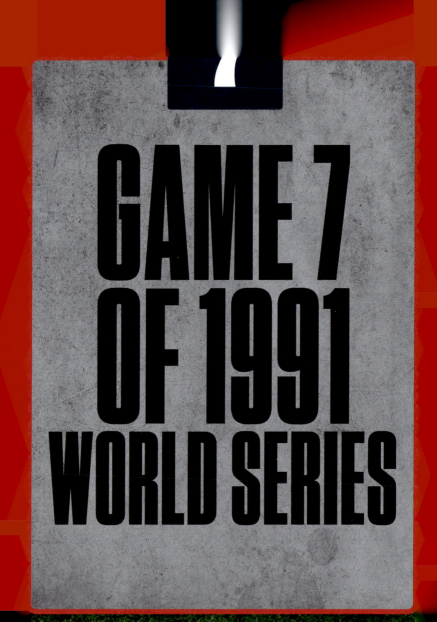

In the immediate, post-Game 6 euphoria, Jack Morris emerged from Kirby Puckett's glow to answer questions about his scheduled Game 7 start the next night from the throng of media assembled in the Twins' celebratory clubhouse. "I've pitched big games before," the 36-year-old five-time All-Star pointed out, matter-of-factly. "This is nothing new to me. We did what we had to do tonight. Now, we have to finish business."

It was, in fact, nothing new to Morris. He'd pitched in the World Series before, with the Tigers in 1984, posting a 2.00 ERA in a pair of complete-game victories over the Padres. But that was a long time ago, and from 1985-1990 he made just one playoff start, for the Tigers in 1987, when he lost Game 2 of the ALCS to the Twins. Plus, he'd never started a Game 7, in any playoff series, let alone the World Series. He had, however, started four times already in the 1991 postseason for the Twins, going 3–1 with a 3.08 ERA, including six innings of one-run ball against the Cardinals in Game 4 just four days earlier.

Morris was the most veteran of veteran pitchers by that point. He'd seen it all, spending 14 years as the workhorse of some very good Tigers teams before becoming a free agent and signing with his hometown Twins. Nothing was going to rattle him and, after several mediocre seasons in Detroit, the St. Paul native resurrected his career back in Minnesota by throwing 247 innings with a 3.43 ERA to place fourth for the Cy Young. He certainly had the confidence part down, gladly taking the baton and the spotlight from Puckett.

Problem was, John Smoltz felt pretty confident too. Smoltz was just 24 years old in 1991 and a half-dozen years from reaching the peak of his Cy Young-winning, Hall of Fame powers, but he was already damn good. He'd thrown 230 innings with a 3.80 ERA in the regular season, going 5–0 with a 1.38 ERA in his final eight starts, and the success carried over to the playoffs. Smoltz, unlike Morris, had pitched Game 7 before, hurling a shutout of the Pirates in the NLCS two weeks earlier to get the Braves to the World Series.

Once there, Smoltz tossed seven innings of one-run ball versus the Twins in Game 4—a Braves victory. He went on to be one of the best postseason pitchers of all time, reaching the playoffs nearly every season with Atlanta and going 15–4 with a 2.67 ERA over 209 career October innings. The young pitcher who matched up with Morris in Game 7 was just getting started on building that resume. Adding to the drama was that Smoltz grew up in Michigan as a Tigers fan and idolized Morris.

There were 275 total pitches thrown that night and any one of them could have changed the outcome of perhaps the greatest pitcher's duel in playoff history. Morris and Smoltz, the 36-year-old who'd been through it all and the 24-year-old who'd later go through even more, matched zero after zero after zero in an incredible showing of crisp, clean baseball. They kept swimming, side by side, out to deeper and deeper waters, until finally Braves manager Bobby Cox stepped in.

Smoltz had thrown 7.1 shutout innings, on 105 pitches, and with two runners on base the Hall of Fame manager opted against letting his young right-hander try to escape his own jam. Cox came out to remove Smoltz, who was clearly upset to be leaving the game and flipped the ball to his manager on the way off the mound. Left-hander Mike Stanton, who was brilliant in Game 6, came in and got out of Smoltz's mess without any runs scoring, but the Braves' fate was now in the hands of their bullpen.

Morris ran into his own trouble the next half inning, allowing a leadoff single to Lonnie Smith and a double into the left-center field

HIGHEST WIN PROBABILITY
ADDED BY A PITCHER IN A GAME 7

.845	Jack Morris, 1991 World Series
.823	Ralph Terry, 1962 World Series
.629	Steve Blass, 1971 World Series
.623	Johnny Podres, 1955 World Series
.615	Phil Douglas, 1915 World Series

gap by Terry Pendleton. It skipped up against the wall and likely should have scored Smith easily from first base with the go-ahead run, but it didn't. Smith hesitated at second base—either because Chuck Knoblauch and Greg Gagne deked him into believing they were turning a double play or, as he insisted later, he simply lost sight of Pendleton's hit in the hysteria. Smith advanced only to third base.

Morris got Ron Gant to ground out meekly to first base and—after Tom Kelly's lone mound visit of the entire game—intentionally walked David Justice to load the bases. Sid Bream then hit into a 3–6–3 double play, handled flawlessly on both ends by first baseman Kent Hrbek, who triumphantly spiked the ball into the turf to end the inning. Out of trouble and now swimming on his own, Morris kept going deeper and deeper, pitching a 1–2–3 ninth inning.

When the Twins failed to score off Stanton and closer Alejandro Pena despite staging a rally in the bottom of the inning, Kelly had a life-changing decision to make. Morris had thrown nine shutout innings—he'd also thrown 118 pitches, but Kelly didn't even track such things—and, if he pitched the 10th inning, it would be his 283rd of the season. No starter had stayed in past the ninth inning of a World Series game since Tom Seaver in 1969. All-Star closer Rick Aguilera was warmed up and ready to go in the bullpen.

Throughout his 15-year career as manager Kelly insisted on taking none of the credit for the Twins' success, with endless quotes attributed to him that essentially boiled down to: "If the players do well we win and if the players do poorly we lose." He pulled plenty

PLAYERS ON BOTH CHAMPIONSHIP TEAMS

Kirby Puckett
Kent Hrbek
Greg Gagne
Dan Gladden
Gene Larkin
Randy Bush
Al Newman

of strings, many of them brilliantly and in ways that made him a Minnesota legend, but he believed the manager was secondary. Within that context, it's not surprising that Kelly allowed Morris to talk him into another inning.

"He put his ass on the line by leaving me in there, and you don't realize it at the time," Morris told the *St. Paul Pioneer Press* two decades later. "You start reflecting back about the reality of the situation, and even me, if I was managing, I'd say to myself, 'Man, I've got Rick Aguilera, who's done a pretty damn good job. What do you do here?' And he did something that 99 percent of the baseball world wouldn't do, and without him doing it, I wouldn't be sitting here today."

Morris threw a 1–2–3 inning on a total of eight pitches, as if he'd done it before a dozen times, even blowing a fastball past Lonnie Smith for his eighth strikeout. "It was so loud it was almost peaceful," Morris recalled of the most pressure-packed game of all time. What would have happened if the Twins hadn't scored in the bottom of the 10th inning? Morris says he would have "wrestled" Kelly to stay in the game. Kelly says there was no doubt he would have sent Morris out for the 11th, and maybe more. It was his game.

Minnesota had the top of the lineup up against Pena, who was working his second inning after two scoreless frames in Game 6. Dan Gladden hacked at his first offering, an inside fastball, busting his bat and sending a looping ball into short left-center field. Left fielder Brian Hunter came up just short as the ball fell for a hit. As it bounced into center fielder Ron Gant's waiting glove, Gladden—full of hustle and adrenaline, his mullet waving in the wind—was already on his way to second base.

It was a "no, no, no...yes!" moment, where the bold decision seems crazy right up until it works. Gladden barreled into second base ahead of Mark Lemke's tag and they were in business. Third base coach Ron Gardenhire flashed the bunt sign to Knoblauch, who'd laid down just one sacrifice in his Rookie of the Year season. He executed flawlessly, forcing Pendleton to field the bunt as Gladden moved up 90 feet behind him. Puckett stepped to the plate, ready to be the hero again, but Cox intentionally walked him and Hrbek.

Bases loaded and one out, but instead of Chili Davis—the team leader in most offensive categories—it was light-hitting 24-year-old rookie Jarvis Brown, who pinch-ran for the designated hitter in the ninth inning. Kelly called on Gene Larkin, whose sore knee had limited him to bench duties in the postseason. Larkin couldn't run, but the switch-hitting outfielder/first baseman batted .293 with more walks than strikeouts against right-handed pitchers during the regular season and had a career .355 on-base percentage.

Cox brought the Braves' outfield way in, far enough that they could catch a fly ball and throw out the speedy Gladden at the plate. Larkin, who had sat on the bench for the past three-and-a-half hours watching one of the greatest games ever unfold, limped from the on-deck circle to the batter's box. Atlanta desperately wanted to turn a fourth double play of the game and anything hit on the ground would be trouble for Larkin. So he hit the ball in the air, on the first pitch, lashing a juicy, high fastball into the left-center field gap.

It was over from the moment ball met bat and Gladden, standing near third base, knew it. His feet touching the plate meant a second title in five seasons for the Twins, but before beginning that triumphant 90-foot trek he raised his right arm to the sky, tagging up out of pure instinct on a ball hit a mile beyond the nearest defender. Gladden skipped home, where Morris was waiting for him, exaggeratedly waving him in with his jacket still on because he was staying warm to pitch the 11th inning if needed.

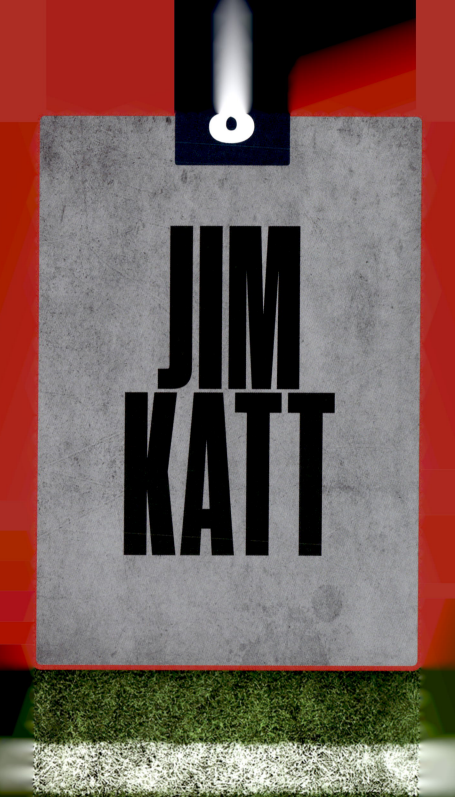

The story of how Jim Kaat ended up with the Twins is a simple one. When the franchise moved from Washington to Minnesota in 1961, he was a 22-year-old minor leaguer in the Senators' farm system who'd gotten knocked around in his first few stints in the majors. The story of how Kaat ended up with the Senators is much more interesting, in large part because it involves the unlikely pairing of a teenager turning down six times more money *and* listening to his parents' advice in doing so. Kaat was unique, right from the start.

Kaat was a freshman pitching for Hope College in his home state of Michigan when he attracted the attention of Washington scout Dick Wiencek, who invited him to a tryout in front of Senators manager Cookie Lavagetto. Kaat described in his autobiography how his father drove him to the tryout, where the left-hander threw to catcher Ed Fitz Gerald for 15–20 minutes. He did well enough that afterward Lavagetto said, "Kid, if you sign with us, you'll be in our starting rotation in three years." He was off, but not by much.

Wiencek presented Kaat with an offer for $4,000, but then a White Sox scout called to say he'd heard Kaat was thinking of signing and offered $25,000. Easy decision, right? Turns out, not really. Kaat's father was an avid baseball fan and knew all about the rule that forced "bonus babies" who signed for more than a certain amount to remain in the majors for two years regardless of how overmatched they were. It kept rich teams from hoarding young talent, but also often kept young talent from developing properly.

Why did Jim Kaat work so quickly on the mound? "If the game goes over two hours, my fastball turns into a pumpkin."

Kaat's father advised him to turn down the $25,000 from the White Sox and accept the $4,000 from the Senators, because being able to work his way up from the minors to the majors would be far more valuable over the long haul. Kaat noted that his father earned $72 per week at the time, so $25,000 was equal to six years of work and would have been life-changing money for the family. He signed for $4,000 and, on the day his parents took him to the airport, "John Kaat, tough as they come, broke down and cried" with joy.

Kaat reached the majors for the first time two years after signing—rather than spending two years in the majors as a "bonus baby"—and spent a total of four years in the minors. There was nothing special about his performance, including a 4.10 ERA at Double-A in 1959 and a 3.82 ERA at Triple-A in 1960, but Twins manager Cookie Lavagetto—who watched Kaat tryout for the Senators in 1957—decided to bring him north as part of the first Minnesota Twins roster in 1961.

Lavagetto was fired three months later, but Kaat remained in the Twins' rotation for the next 13 seasons and ranks as the team's all-time leader in wins and innings. Helluva way to spend $4,000, huh? There were some rough patches initially, as Kaat lost 17 games for a last-place team in his first Twins season, but the next season he threw 269 innings with a 3.14 ERA to make his first All-Star team at age 23 and Minnesota won 91 games with a young, exciting roster that quickly developed into a consistent contender.

Kaat was a huge part of the 1960s success, providing dependable, high-end, bulk innings atop a rotation that was often overlooked as the Twins' powerful lineup bashed opposing pitchers into submission. From his Twins debut in 1961 through 1971—a total of 11 full seasons—Kaat averaged 242 innings per year and failed to throw at least 200 innings just once. And he was far from just an innings-eater, posting a 3.23 ERA in a Twins uniform while preventing runs at a better-than-average rate in all but two seasons.

An outstanding athlete who wanted to play basketball out of high school, Kaat won 16 consecutive Gold Glove awards and also stood out among pitchers at the plate by hitting 16 homers and 44 doubles. Only five pitchers since 1950 have more extra-base hits. At the urging of legendary pitching coach Johnny Sain, Kaat also worked incredibly

TWINS' MOST GOLD GLOVE AWARDS

12	Jim Kaat, pitcher
7	Torii Hunter, outfield
6	Kirby Puckett, outfield
4	Gary Gaetti, third base
3	Earl Battey, catcher
3	Joe Mauer, catcher
3	Vic Power, first base
2	Zoilo Versalles, shortstop

fast on the mound, beginning his delivery within seconds of getting the ball back from the catcher. Kaat was very good, very durable, and very smart, adding value in all sorts of ways.

His best seasons came back-to-back in 1965 and 1966. In the first of those two years Kaat threw 264 innings with a 2.83 ERA as the Twins won 102 games and the AL pennant. In the World Series he was tasked with matching up against the best pitcher on the planet, Sandy Koufax. Three times, in fact. Kaat faced Koufax in Games 2, 5, and 7—all in the span of seven days. Kaat beat Koufax in Game 2, throwing a complete game and driving in more runs than he allowed, but struggled in Game 5 and was yanked early in Game 7.

Kaat was even better in 1966, reaching the peak of his powers at 27. He led the league in starts (41), innings (307), wins (25), and complete games (19) while ranking sixth with a 2.75 ERA. Minnesota slipped to second place, but the Twins were 26-15 (.634) with Kaat on the mound compared to 63-58 (.520) when anyone else started. He finished fifth in the MVP balloting and might have been a unanimous Cy Young winner, except 1966 was the final year the award wasn't split by league and Koufax won the lone MLB prize.

Kaat never again reached the same heights as 1965 and 1966, but from 1967-1971 he was an above-average starter who chewed up 240 innings per year. He got off to a great start in 1972 and was 10-2 with a 2.06 ERA on July 2 when he suffered a year-ending broken bone in his pitching hand while sliding into second base. He returned healthy in 1973 and was doing his usual thing with a 3.63 ERA in 166 first-half innings, but then Kaat went through a rough patch while the Twins tumbled down the standings.

He was traded to the White Sox in August in a move that could be explained partly by a 34-year-old not being key to a rebuilding effort and partly by ownership shedding a big salary. Kaat was fantastic for Chicago in 1974 and 1975, throwing 277 and 303 innings with a 2.92 and 3.11 ERA while winning 20 games in both years after previously doing so just once in Minnesota. From there he went to Philadelphia, New York, and St. Louis, extending his career to age 44 by shifting to the bullpen with modest success.

Kaat failed to make the Hall of Fame, but his 283 wins and 4,530 innings are each the third-most by any pitcher not in Cooperstown. Three different times with the Twins he finished with 17 or 18 wins when better lineup and bullpen support could easily have led to 20, and he's also missing a deserved Cy Young award. If his 283 wins included five or six 20-win seasons and a Cy Young, it's hard to imagine Kaat still being on the outside looking in, although certainly his case is built more on longevity than most.

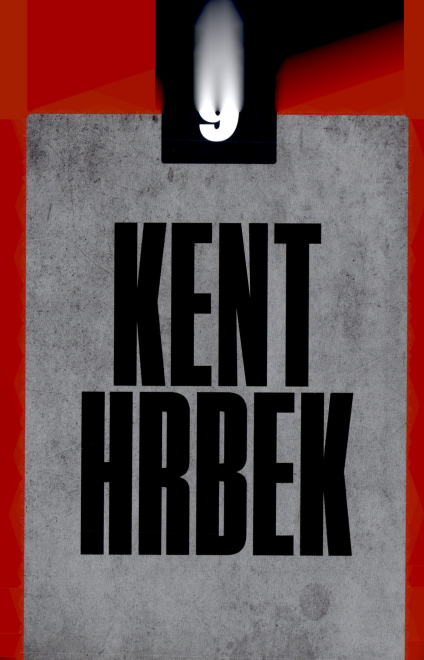

Kent Hrbek was born in Minneapolis one year before the Twins moved from Washington to Minnesota, and he grew up in Bloomington, right around the corner from Metropolitan Stadium. Picked by the Twins out of Bloomington Kennedy high school in the 17th round of the 1978 draft, he was all set to bypass the pros and attend the University of Minnesota before a last-minute increase in the front office's signing bonus offer from $5,000 to $35,000 changed his mind.

Rick Stelmaszek, who spent three decades coaching for the Twins, recalled that Hrbek "was a free spirit...like a labrador, all arms and legs." Hrbek made his pro debut in rookie-ball, but struggled while being limited by knee problems. Healthy in 1980, he hit .267 with 19 homers in 115 games at low Single-A. He also totaled more walks (61) than strikeouts (54), showing uncommon strike-zone control for a 20-year-old slugger in his first full season, which would later become a staple of his success with the Twins.

Hrbek broke out in 1981 with an incredible season at high Single-A, hitting .379 with 27 homers, 25 doubles, 111 RBIs, and 119 runs scored in 121 games while again posting a fantastic 59-to-59 strikeout-to-walk ratio. He was named MVP of the California League despite being one of the circuit's youngest hitters and earned a late-season Twins call-up, debuting at Yankee Stadium with a game-winning homer in extra innings after skipping Double-A and Triple-A. And he never did end up seeing any time in the high minors.

Hrbek had a huge spring training in 1982, which convinced the Twins to hand him the Opening Day job at first base as the team moved to the Metrodome with a roster packed with fellow rookies Tom Brunansky, Frank Viola, Gary Gaetti, Tim Laudner, and Randy Bush. It was hard to tell then, as the team lost 102 games, but several key building blocks were being put in place for future greatness and Hrbek was the best of the bunch, hitting .301 with 23 homers and 92 RBIs in 140 games.

He finished runner-up in the Rookie of the Year voting—sandwiched between future Hall of Famers Cal Ripken Jr. and Wade Boggs—and then posted nearly identical numbers as a sophomore. Hrbek broke out with a monster season in 1984, hitting .311/.383/.522 with 27 homers and 107 RBIs. Not many players on .500 teams generated heavy MVP support back then, but Hrbek was so impressive that he was runner-up in the balloting despite the Twins' modest 81-81 record.

Hrbek was hitting .335 at the All-Star break during a season in which he'd eventually be deemed the second-best player in the league by MVP voters, yet he was passed over for the All-Star team just like he was in 1983. The issue came to a head three seasons later in 1987, when Hrbek ended the first half with 23 homers and was again passed over for the All-Star team, this time for 29-year-old journeyman Pat Tabler of the Indians. Hrbek had an individual beef, to be sure, but he was more upset about the Twins being snubbed.

Minnesota was in first place at the break, boasting several standout performances in what would become a championship-winning season, but Kirby Puckett was the team's lone All-Star representative. "I accepted not making it when we weren't doing well, but this I don't accept," Hrbek explained to reporters at the time. "If those guys ask me to go again, they can kiss my butt. I played in my first All-Star game in 1982, and when I played in 1982 it was my last one."

Decades later, still hanging onto the All-Star grudge and sticking true to his Minnesota boy roots, Hrbek told the *St. Paul Pioneer Press* of his "kiss my butt" quote: "Minnesota sports don't get any kind of recognition at all. We were getting pissed on, so I figured I'd say

Once described as "the most human baseball player ever" by ESPN, Kent Hrbek went duck hunting before Game 7 of the World Series.

something and get a little upset about it.... I can't tell you who went instead of who, but it was enough to piss me off, and I just kind of said, 'Forget it, I don't need to go play in any of those.'"

True to his word, Hrbek's first and only All-Star selection came as a 22-year-old rookie in 1982 despite having several worthy campaigns after his 1987 promise. In fact, the very next season Hrbek hit .313 with 17 homers in the first half and finished the year batting .312/.387/.520 to rank among the league's top 10 in batting average, on-base percentage, slugging percentage, and homers. It was arguably his best season, although there wasn't much difference between Hrbek's best and Hrbek's worst—he was always very good.

Hrbek hit at least .270 with an OPS of at least .825 in all but one of his first 10 seasons, with an OPS low of .795 and a high of .934. He basically hit .285 with 25 homers and an .850 OPS like clockwork, always ranking solidly above average among first basemen at the plate. In fact, among all the big leaguers to start at least 750 games as a first baseman from 1980-1995 he ranked second in home runs and walks, third in RBIs and runs scored, and fifth in OPS. Hrbek was the model of high-end consistency offensively.

He mostly struggled in the playoffs, but came up big in one of the most important at-bats in Twins history. Game 6 of the 1987 World Series was a rough one for Hrbek until the sixth inning, when he stepped to the plate with the bases loaded and the Twins up 6–5. St. Louis brought in left-handed reliever Ken Dayley just to face him and Hrbek, who'd hit just .225 off lefties during the regular season and was 0-for–16 off them in the playoffs, crushed a first-pitch fastball to center field for a game-breaking grand slam.

A free agent following the 1989 season—a typically strong year in which Hrbek hit .272 with 25 home runs and an .872 OPS—he turned down larger offers to re-sign with the Twins for $14 million over five years. He remained productive in the first four years of the deal, posting an .827 OPS from 1990–93 and ranking second on the Twins in both homers and RBIs during their World Series-winning 1991 season. His hitting declined in 1994, and with the strike looming Hrbek pre-announced his retirement that August.

Hrbek's numbers were still respectable—with a .270 batting average and .773 OPS he was almost exactly a league-average hitter—but as a 34-year-old impending free agent with injury issues he opted to go out on his own terms. "My dad never got to retire," he said at the press conference. "That's why I wanted to retire. I want to do nothing until I'm tired of doing nothing and then I'll do something.… I feel decent, but it's still not there. I can't play first base like I used to."

As a big, middle-of-the-order bat on two World Series teams Hrbek was known for his offense, but he was also an outstanding, underrated defensive first baseman with softer hands and nimbler feet than his size suggested. Don Mattingly dominated the Gold Glove awards throughout his career, but Hrbek was a major asset in the field. Braves fans might even claim a little too major, but as Hrbek said of his "nudge" of Ron Gant in the 1991 World Series: "He fell on top of me. He pushed me over. That's the end of the story."

JOHAN
SANTANA

Snagging a 21-year-old Johan Santana via the Rule 5 draft is one of the greatest moves in Twins history, but it took a second, totally unplanned development to launch his career as one of the elite pitchers in team history. As is customary for Rule 5 picks, Santana spent his rookie season as a mop-up man, posting a 6.49 ERA with nearly as many walks (54) as strikeouts (64) in 89 innings. He spent the next season in a similarly low-leverage role, throwing 44 innings with a 4.74 ERA and 26/14 K/BB ratio before an elbow injury shut him down in mid-July.

Santana returned healthy in 2002, but after carrying the overmatched young left-hander on the MLB roster for two years the Twins decided he'd benefit from some more time in the minors. Demoted to Triple-A, he moved into the rotation and started working with the man who would change his life. Edmonton pitching coach Bobby Cuellar spent all of one month as a big leaguer, appearing in four games for the Rangers in 1977, but he pitched 11 seasons in the minors before becoming a well-traveled pitching coach and will forever be remembered in Minnesota as the man who taught Johan Santana his changeup.

Santana was 23 years old and had the potential to be a quality big-league pitcher thanks to a good fastball and slider, but to that point there wasn't much in the track record—with the Twins or in the minors—to suggest he was capable of being special. Cuellar preached to Santana the importance of trusting the changeup, not just as a much-needed third pitch but as a

TWINS' HIGHEST AVERAGE GAME SCORE

minimum 100 starts:

60.2	Johan Santana
57.8	Bert Blyleven
57.0	Camilo Pascual
55.7	Dave Boswell
54.9	Jim Perry

weapon that could be used in any count to any hitter. As his confidence with the pitch grew, Santana began to throw it more and more, and the results were immediately promising with 75 strikeouts and just 37 hits allowed in 49 innings at Triple-A.

Called up by the Twins in late May and inserted into the rotation a week later, Santana quickly became the best starter on a team that had Brad Radke, Eric Milton, Rick Reed, and Kyle Lohse. He made 14 starts, posting a 3.24 ERA with 98 strikeouts in 81 innings, and held opponents to a .212 batting average. And then in September, after seven innings of one-run ball in Santana's most recent start, the Twins demoted him to the bullpen. He thrived as a reliever down the stretch with a 1.50 ERA and 26 strikeouts in 18 innings, and the Twins decided to keep him in the bullpen to begin the next season.

It took until mid-July for the Twins to relent and allow the best pitcher on the team back into the rotation—appeasing the growing number of fans who'd begun a *Free Johan!* campaign on blogs and message boards—and Santana picked up right where he left off by going 8–2 with a 3.22 ERA and 92 strikeouts in 92 innings. It turns out that Santana magically transformed into one of the best starting pitchers in baseball basically from the moment he perfected the changeup under Cuellar's tutelage, but the Twins refused to fully buy into his greatness for another two years.

Finally in 2004 the notion of Santana not being in the rotation had reached absurd status, so the Twins made him a full-time starter for the first time...and he unanimously won the Cy Young award by going 20–6 with a league-best 2.61 ERA and league-high 265 strikeouts in 228 innings. Johan had been freed and boy did he live up to the hype, going 13–0 with a 1.21 ERA after the All-Star break for one of the greatest second-half pitching performances in baseball history. He broke the Twins' single-season strikeout record, set by Bert Blyleven in 1973, and led the league in nearly every major category.

He was equally excellent in 2005, throwing 232 innings with a 2.87 ERA and league-high 238 strikeouts, but poor lineup and bullpen support left him with "only" 16 wins. In a vote that now seems hilariously outdated the Cy Young award went to 21-game winner Bartolo Colon and his 3.48 ERA. Santana won his second unanimous

Johan Santana called his changeup "butterfly." Hitters had many less flattering names for it, usually as they walked back to the dugout.

Cy Young award the next season, capturing the traditional pitching triple crown by leading the league in wins (19), ERA (2.77), and strikeouts (245). Prior to Santana only Sandy Koufax, Roger Clemens, Greg Maddux, and Pedro Martinez had won multiple unanimous Cy Young awards.

After three seasons as a full-time starter he had two Cy Young awards along with a third he deserved to have won, plus two ERA titles and three strikeout titles. From the time he was recalled from Triple-A in mid-2002 through the end of the 2006 season, the Twins had a .729 winning percentage in games started by Santana compared to a .529 winning percentage in games started by everyone else. For a five-year stretch the Twins were the equivalent of a 120-win team with Santana on the mound. And while the team as a whole struggled mightily in the playoffs, Santana had a 2.93 ERA in five postseason starts.

By his own lofty standards Santana's performance slipped a bit in 2007. However, he was just four strikeouts short of leading the league for a fourth consecutive season and ranked sixth in innings and seventh in ERA. His "struggles" were a career-year for most pitchers, as Santana started the All-Star game and finished fifth in the Cy Young award balloting. He set the Twins' record with 17 strikeouts against the Rangers on August 19, allowing just two hits and zero walks in eight brilliant shutout innings. He had some rough outings in the six weeks that followed and Santana's final start of the season was cut short by rain after just three innings. It proved to be the final start of his Twins career, as well.

With one year remaining on Santana's contract and no sense that the Twins were willing to spend enough money to keep him in Minnesota long term, the front office—with Bill Smith in charge following Terry Ryan's decision to step down months earlier—spent the

TWINS' HIGHEST STRIKEOUT RATE

minimum 100 starts:

9.5	Johan Santana
9.1	Francisco Liriano
7.5	Dave Boswell
7.2	Scott Baker
7.1	Bert Blyleven

entire offseason shopping Santana to the Yankees, Mets, and Red Sox. Reports of prospect-packed offers swirled and ultimately on February 2 the Twins traded Santana to the Mets for Carlos Gomez, Deolis Guerra, Philip Humber, and Kevin Mulvey. Santana quickly inked a six-year, $137.5 million contract extension with

TWINS' HIGHEST ADJUSTED ERA+

minimum 100 starts:

141	Johan Santana
119	Bert Blyleven
116	Camilo Pascual
113	Brad Radke
113	Jim Perry

the Mets and just like that one of the best careers in Twins history was over.

The trade proved to be a disaster for the Twins, who got essentially zero value from the Guerra-Humber-Mulvey pitching prospect trio and misguidedly traded away Gomez at age 24 before he developed into an All-Star. It wasn't a great trade for the Mets, either. Santana was great early, winning an ERA title in his first season and posting a combined 2.85 ERA in his first three, but then injuries wrecked his career. He missed all of 2011, returned in 2012 to throw 117 innings with a 4.85 ERA—including a no-hitter—and then never pitched in the majors again. Santana got his first chance to be a full-time starter at 25, was the best pitcher in baseball from 25 to 29, and was done at 33.

CHUCK KNOBLAUCH

Things ended very badly for Chuck Knoblauch in Minnesota—and for his baseball career in general—but before their bitter divorce the Twins-Knoblauch marriage was a beautiful one for seven seasons. He came up in 1991, snagging the Rookie of the Year award on a veteran-filled championship squad, and later developed into one of the league's best all-around players—a .300-hitting, walk-drawing, base-stealing, Gold Glove–winning second baseman responsible for several of the most valuable seasons in Twins history.

Before any of that—and before any hot dog–related incidents at the Metrodome—he was an All-American shortstop at Texas A&M and the Twins' first-round draft pick in 1989. Knoblauch made quick work of the minor leagues, hitting .308 at Single-A after signing and moving up to Double-A as a 21-year-old in 1990, where he shifted from shortstop to second base and hit .290 with 23 steals and a .390 on-base percentage, grinding out twice as many walks (63) as strikeouts (31) in 118 games.

Knoblauch's power was very limited and he was still a bit shaky at the new position, but Twins second basemen—Al Newman, Nelson Liriano, and Fred Manrique—combined to hit just .238 in 1990 and the team jumped the 22-year-old from Double-A to the majors. It paid off in a huge way, as Knoblauch stepped into the lineup's No. 2 spot and hit .281 with 25 steals, more walks (59) than strikeouts (40), and a .351 on-base percentage to beat out Juan Guzman, Milt Cuyler, and future Hall of Famer Ivan Rodriguez for Rookie of the Year.

Knoblauch was even better in the playoffs, hitting .350 in the ALCS win over the Blue Jays and .308 in the World Series victory over the Braves. He stole six bases, collected 15 hits, and scored eight runs in 12 postseason games. And he forever secured his place in World Series highlights in the eighth inning of Game 7 by deking Lonnie Smith into thinking a double play was being turned on a double to the outfield. Smith stopped at third base instead of scoring to break a 0–0 tie. He was stranded, and the Twins won 1–0.

That's a tough act to follow as a sophomore, but Knoblauch hit .297 with 88 walks and a .384 on-base percentage, stole 34 bases, and scored 104 runs to make his first All-Star team at age 23. He had a bit of a down year in 1993, but broke out as a full-blown star in the strike-shortened 1994 season. Knoblauch hit .312 with 35 steals and an .841 OPS—up 125 points compared to 1991–93—while leading the league with 45 doubles in just 109 games. When the strike halted things he was on pace for the fourth-most doubles ever.

Following the strike Knoblauch upped his production even further in 1995, hitting .333 with 46 steals and a gaudy .424 on-base percentage that stood as the highest by a Twins player since Rod Carew's MVP-winning 1977 season. He ranked among the league's 10 best in OBP, runs scored, hits, doubles, triples, stolen bases, and times on base on the way to being fourth among AL position players in Wins Above Replacement and appearing on multiple MVP ballots. It was a spectacular all-around season.

Knoblauch was even better in 1996. An outstanding player at the absolute peak of his ability at age 27, he hit .341 with 13 homers, 35 doubles, and a league-leading 13 triples. He stole 45 bases, drew 98 walks while striking out 74 times, and scored 140 runs in 153 games. He ranked among the league's top five in AVG, OBP, runs, hits, steals, hit by pitches, and times on base. Wins Above Replacement pegged him as the third-best player in the entire league, behind only Ken Griffey Jr. and Alex Rodriguez.

Knoblauch's season is clearly one of the elite years in Twins history. Both his 140 runs scored and 314 times on base are the most in Twins history, his .448 on-base percentage is the second-highest behind only Carew in 1977, and his 98 walks are surpassed by only Harmon Killebrew and Bob Allison. Knoblauch hit .341/.448/.517 with 45 steals and plus defense at an up-the-middle position—his WAR total of 8.6 is the second-best in Twins history, sandwiched between MVP years by Carew and Joe Mauer.

Knoblauch and the Twins had been negotiating a potential contract extension for much of the season—while various trade speculation swirled—and in August the two sides agreed to a five-year, $30 million deal. It tied Kirby Puckett's extension four seasons prior as the largest in Twins history and made Knoblauch one of the league's highest-paid players. In announcing the deal, Knoblauch said, "I can't tell you how happy I am. This will finally end all the rumors and speculation." Suffice it to say, that was short-lived.

Knoblauch's great 1996 performance came for a 78–84 team and in 1997 the Twins fell even further, going 68-94 as memories of the 1987 and 1991 championships faded and any notion of contending vanished. He'd gone from being the rookie on a World Series winner to being the in-his-prime star on a rebuilding team and that didn't sit well with Knoblauch, who publicly requested a trade amid never-ending stories of his increasingly surly off-field behavior rubbing Twins teammates and officials the wrong way.

Shortly before spring training, Twins general manager Terry Ryan pulled the trigger on a trade that sent Knoblauch to the New York Yankees in exchange for $3 million and four minor leaguers—left-hander Eric Milton, shortstop Cristian Guzman, right fielder Brian Buchanan, and right-hander Danny Mota. "When you go public with a trade demand, it's very difficult to do anything," Ryan said at the time. "I had to do the best I could under the situation."

In retrospect Ryan did just fine, as Milton and Guzman became productive regulars for the Twins and even Buchanan turned into a part-time outfielder who was later traded to the Padres for Guzman's future replacement at shortstop, Jason Bartlett. Minnesota did well in trading Knoblauch, particularly under the circumstances, but a strong long-term return couldn't match the immediate pain of a homegrown, World Series–winning star forcing his way out at age 28 because he couldn't stand all the losing.

Knoblauch's production slipped in his first Yankees season, but he scored 117 runs atop MLB's best lineup and New York won 114 regular season games and the World Series. In the ALCS he helped hand the Indians a Game 2 victory by arguing with an umpire on a controversial play at first base as the ball trickled away and allowed the go-ahead run to score in the 12th inning. New York recovered to win the series and Knoblauch played a big part in their World Series sweep over San Diego, hitting .375 with a home run.

He bounced back offensively in 1999 and the Yankees won another title, but Knoblauch's defense started to become a problem. He committed a career-high 26 errors, doubling his total from the previous season, and Knoblauch's wild throws to first base became a major storyline. Some of the errant throws bounced, some fluttered, and some went sailing into the stands. He initially tried to downplay the obvious problems, saying, "When it doesn't have any effect on the score, it's just another play."

However, as the year wore on Knoblauch resorted to making sidearm throws against the wishes of Yankees manager Joe Torre, who eventually threw up his hands and told the *New York Times*, "Whatever we get with Knoblauch is what we get." Knoblauch's increasing inability to make routine plays could be brushed under the rug because the Yankees kept winning, but by mid-2000 his throwing problems had advanced to full-blown "yips" and Torre often moved him from second base to designated hitter.

New York won a third consecutive World Series in 2000, but by that point it was more in spite of Knoblauch. He hit just .236 in the playoffs and saw zero time in the field, making each of his starts at DH and getting benched in favor of journeyman utility infielder Jose Vizcaino for games played under NL rules. Yankees fans had come to despise him, but they still had nothing on Twins fans in that department. Knoblauch became a part-time player for the Yankees in 2001 and when he did play it was in left field.

All of which brings us to a May 2, 2001, game at the Metrodome. In the sixth inning, with the Twins leading the Yankees by three runs, fans in the left field stands started pelting Knoblauch with plastic beer bottles, golf balls, and—most famously—hot dogs on Dollar Dog night. Umpires pulled both teams off the field, and Twins manager Tom Kelly came out of the dugout and walked to the left field wall to beg fans to stop because the Twins were in danger of forfeiting. Kelly later escorted Knoblauch back to his position.

"It's been four years...they need to turn the page," Knoblauch said afterward, although in fairness by that point he had much bigger problems than whether Twins fans still held a grudge. Knoblauch, now a full-time left fielder at age 32, hit a career-worst .250 in the regular season and then batted .224 in the playoffs. New York made it to a fourth straight World Series, but lost to Arizona in seven games and Knoblauch was on the bench for the deciding game.

The five-year, $30 million contract Knoblauch signed with the Twins expired following the 2001 season and the Yankees made zero effort to retain him. He signed a one-year, $2 million deal with the Royals and hit .210 in what would be his final season. Years later, he made headlines again, first for being outed as a longtime steroid user and then for a series of domestic violence arrests. His induction into the Twins Hall of Fame, which had been scheduled for 2014, was canceled after Knoblauch was arrested for allegedly assaulting his ex-wife.

Knoblauch's career and personal life unraveled away from Minnesota, but he was correct about the state of the Twins at the time. They were consistently among the worst teams in baseball from 1993–2000. He wanted to play for a winner and the Yankees won four AL pennants and three World Series in his four seasons. His actual impact on all that winning was less and less each year, and ultimately he became an albatross with his once-great defense at second base making him a national punchline.

Everything unfolded like a deal with the devil that carried exorbitant interest rates. And perhaps fittingly, as Knoblauch's career was coming to a close, the Twins were emerging as winners again. They won 85 games in 2001 as Knoblauch fell fully out of favor with the Yankees. And in 2002—with Knoblauch washed up on a 100-loss Royals team—the Twins won the first of four division titles in five seasons. And it was thanks in a big way to going 14–5 against the Royals while Knoblauch watched (and hit .206).

His impact on Twins history was substantial—first overwhelmingly positive as the rookie sparkplug on a championship team and as one of the best all-around players in the league, then overwhelmingly negative by forcing a trade as the team collapsed around him, and then positive again as the return package from that forced trade began paying dividends in turning the Twins around. Few in Minnesota will ever remember Knoblauch fondly, and as a person they're absolutely right, but he was a helluva player in a Twins uniform.

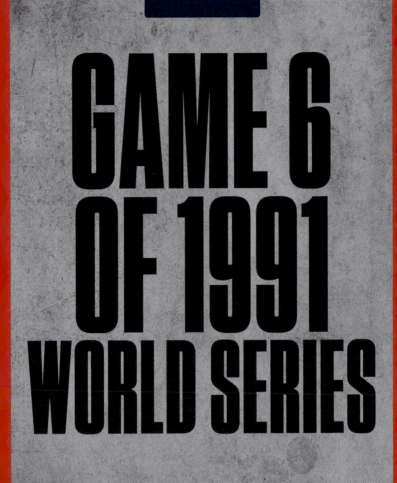

GAME 6 OF 1991 WORLD SERIES

Tom Kelly and the Twins had been here before, down 3–2 in the World Series and going back home to the Metrodome for Game 6 after three consecutive losses on the road. Just four years earlier, in fact. Back then they prevailed over St. Louis, staving off elimination despite having a shaky, inexperienced starting pitcher on the mound in a thrilling Game 6 and then riding a masterful veteran's pitching performance to victory in Game 7 for their first championship. The stage was set for history to repeat itself against Atlanta.

In the sequel, Scott Erickson would be playing the "Les Straker" role as a shaky Game 6 starter on a short leash. Erickson was a vastly superior pitcher to Straker, going 20–8 with a 3.18 ERA as a 23-year-old to place runner-up to Roger Clemens for the Cy Young, but Erickson struggled throughout the second half and had failed to make it out of the fifth inning in his previous two postseason starts. Counting the playoffs Erickson had a 5.20 ERA since the beginning of July, with noticeable drop-offs in velocity and command.

Just as Kelly said about Straker prior to Game 6 in 1987, the manager made it very clear that Erickson—who was also pitching on short rest—would be on thin ice right from the start. "Well, everyone tells me it's a go, but we're not going to fool around too much if things don't go well," Kelly told reporters before the game. "We're planning on Scotty giving us a good, solid six or seven innings, and we'll go from there. If he continues that same [bad] pattern, he won't be in there too long."

Tim McCarver, the CBS announcer who'd previously worked the 1987 World Series for ABC, felt there was one key difference between then and now: Atlanta's pitching. During the broadcast's opening segment McCarver noted that Steve Avery and John Smoltz were a far more imposing duo than John Tudor and Joe Magrane. Play-by-play man Jack Buck agreed and added that, because several key Cardinals were hurt in 1987, the Braves were the superior opponent. "It's like the Twins expect the Dome to beat Avery," he snarked.

Kelly made some changes to the lineup after playing three straight games under National League rules. Chili Davis was back at designated hitter after making a rare appearance as an outfielder in Game 5. Shane Mack, who was hitless in the World Series and had been benched for Davis in Game 5, was back in right field. Starting catcher Brian Harper was on the bench in favor of Erickson's personal catcher Junior Ortiz. Minnesota stacked the lineup with eight right-handed hitters and Kent Hrbek versus the left-handed Avery.

Early on, Erickson looked as shaky as feared. His first pitch of the game was well out of the strike zone and his third pitch nearly sailed over Lonnie Smith's head. He labored and put two runners on, but escaped the jam when left fielder Dan Gladden tracked down Sid Bream's two-out liner. In the bottom of the first inning the Twins' lineup went to work, providing Erickson with some breathing room and showing that they had a plan to beat Avery that went beyond the Metrodome magic.

Chuck Knoblauch fought off a high fastball, dumping a single to right field and bringing Kirby Puckett to the plate with one out. "He's been cold, cold, cold," Buck said, noting that Puckett was hitting just .167 in the series to that point. Moments later Puckett snuck a hard-hit grounder past third baseman Terry Pendleton and into the left field corner for a triple, driving in Knoblauch. Mack hit with two outs and broke his 0–for–15 slump with a broken-bat single into left field, scoring Puckett. Minnesota's bats had thawed.

In the top of the third inning Smith drew a leadoff walk and Pendleton sliced a would-be double down the left field line, but it landed foul by inches and brought Braves manager Bobby Cox out of the dugout to argue in vain. Pendleton grounded to first base, but the Twins couldn't turn a 3–6–1 double play. Ron Gant, who led the Braves with 32 homers, came up with a runner on and smashed a deep drive into the left-center field gap. It had extra-base hit written all over it, except it couldn't out-run Puckett.

The brilliance of "The Catch" is that it all came in one smooth motion. Puckett made a half-turn and ran fast to the wall—but didn't all-out sprint—and timed his jump perfectly. At age 31 his 5′8″ frame had plenty of extra pounds on it, but he elevated up against the plexiglass wall extension and snagged Gant's drive, sticking the landing and firing a strong, 200-foot throw back to first base that nearly doubled off Pendleton. First stunned and then ecstatic, the Homer Hanky–waving Metrodome crowd went nuts.

Minnesota narrowly escaped major damage, but two innings later Atlanta broke through against Erickson after peppering the bases with runners. Rafael Belliard reached base via an infield single and the Twins failed to turn Smith's tailor-made double play grounder into two outs when the ball got stuck in Knoblauch's glove. With double-barrel action in the bullpen as left-hander Mark Guthrie and right-hander Terry Leached warmed up quickly, Pendleton crushed the next pitch over Puckett's head in center field for a two-run homer.

In the bottom half of the inning the Twins re-took the lead. Dan Gladden won a lengthy battle with Avery for a leadoff walk, stole second base, and advanced to third base on a deep line out to right field from Knoblauch. Cox ordered the infield in with one out, but Puckett had no plans to hit a ball on the ground. He hacked at Avery's first pitch and sent a deep fly ball to center field for a sacrifice fly, scoring Gladden. Avery, the 22-year-old phenom who was 18–8 with a 2.38 regular-season ERA, allowed three runs six innings.

Erickson remained in for the top of the seventh inning, but gave up a leadoff single to Mark Lemke and was yanked at 101 pitches in favor of the left-handed Guthrie. A wild pitch, a walk, and an infield single followed, loading the bases with one out for another big Gant at-bat. Kelly had two right-handers warmed up in the bullpen and opted for his season-long setup man, Carl Willis, who'd allowed four runs in his four previous World Series innings.

Willis induced a hard grounder to shortstop, but Greg Gagne and Knoblauch could only get one out as Gant beat the return throw with his arms extended like a sprinter crossing the finish line. Tie game. Willis struck out David Justice to end the inning and then "Big Train" went into shutdown mode, setting Atlanta down in order in the eighth and ninth innings. Puckett tried to start an eighth-inning rally by singling and stealing second base but was stranded as the Braves' bullpen also stepped up in a big way.

Four relievers tossed back-to-back scoreless innings, as the Twins got great work from Willis and closer Rick Aguilera while the Braves got the same from Mike Stanton and closer Alejandro Pena. Deadlocked in the bottom of the 11th inning, Cox pulled Pena and brought in left-hander Charlie Liebrandt to face 3–4–5 hitters Kirby Puckett, Chili Davis, and Shane Mack. Extra innings force managers to make all sorts of suboptimal decisions and this was certainly far from a normal extra-inning game, but Cox's move was an odd one.

For one thing, Pena was the Braves' best reliever—posting a 2.40 ERA over 82 innings in the regular season before thriving in the playoffs—and had gone past 30 pitches fairly regularly. Beyond that he was right-handed, making him a good fit to face Puckett and Mack. Liebrandt, meanwhile, was a 34-year-old career-long starter who hadn't made a relief appearance in two seasons with the Braves. He was also a left-hander, off whom Puckett and Mack hit .406 and .350, respectively, during the season.

Why take out a right-handed closer and bring in a left-handed, soft-tossing starter to face the lineup's 3–4–5 hitters, each of whom will be batting right-handed against him? Cox was defiant when asked after the game to explain the move, noting, among other things, Liebrandt's regular-season win total as a starter and repeatedly saying, "Why not Charlie Liebrandt?" as if someone else might chime in with a more viable explanation he could then steal as his own.

With the Metrodome crowd chanting "Kirby! Kirby! Kirby!" he stepped to the plate and uncharacteristically worked the count in his favor at 2–1. Liebrandt turned to his favorite pitch, a circle-changeup.

Puckett's eyes lit up. He launched the pitch into orbit, by way of the left-center field gap, nearly blowing the roof off the Metrodome. "Into deep left-center, for Mitchell," began Jack Buck's famous, perfect call. "And we'll see you...TOMORROW NIGHT!"

"To tell the truth, I don't even know what I hit," Puckett told reporters in the clubhouse afterward, exhausted from carrying his team to victory both offensively and defensively, inning by inning. "A changeup, maybe. All I know is it was up." Liebrandt indeed hung his signature pitch, but not before Cox hung him out to dry in an extremely tough matchup. Puckett finished the game 3–for–4 with a triple, a single, a stolen base, a sacrifice fly, and a walk-off homer, plus one of the best catches in World Series history.

And he apparently called it, bringing the team together for a pregame clubhouse meeting and promising something special. "We were in a bad way. We needed someone to step forward in a major way," outfielder Gene Larkin revealed later. "He told us to jump on his back. Not many guys can talk the talk and walk the walk, but Kirby always could. After he spoke to us, we just knew that Kirby was going to do something special. We've seen him do that many times. That time it was on the biggest stage."

BRAD RADKE

Brad Radke was born in Eau Claire, Wisconsin, went to high school in Tampa, Florida, and was picked by the Twins in the eighth round of the 1991 draft. He fared well in the low minors and reached Double-A at age 20, struggling there during his first go-around in 1993. Sent back to Double-A in 1994, he threw 186 innings with a 2.66 ERA despite just 5.9 strikeouts per nine innings, making up for his lack of velocity and strikeouts by issuing just 34 walks in 28 starts in what would become the story of his entire career.

Radke was far from a top prospect at that point, but his ability to pound the strike zone with modest raw stuff caught the Twins' collective eye and in particular manager Tom Kelly, who took a liking to the slim right-hander. At age 22, the Twins had Radke skip Triple-A and jump to the major leagues, where Radke predictably struggled on the way to a 5.32 ERA. He continued to throw strikes, but his strikeout rate dipped to an absurdly low 3.7 per nine innings and big-league hitters teed off on all those high-80s fastballs in the zone.

Radke soaked up 181 innings in a strike-shortened season, but allowed a league-high 32 homers for a 56-88 team that had a hideous staff ERA of 5.76. Radke again allowed the most homers in the league as a sophomore, serving up 40 long balls, but bumped his strikeout rate from awful to merely bad at 5.7 per nine innings and sliced nearly a full run off his ERA while logging 232 innings. It was a turning point for Radke, who showed uncommon durability and control for a 23-year-old.

He took another step forward in 1997, tossing 240 innings with a 3.87 ERA in a

TWINS' FEWEST WALKS PER NINE INNINGS

minimum 1,000 innings:

1.6	Brad Radke
2.0	Kevin Tapani
2.1	Scott Baker
2.1	Jim Kaat
2.2	Nick Blackburn

hitting-dominated league where the average ERA was 4.56. Radke cut his home run rate by 50 percent, pushed his strikeout rate above the league average, and walked zero or one batter in 19-of-35 starts while never issuing more than three free passes. It was an outstanding season made famous by Radke winning 12 consecutive starts from June 7 through August 4 to tie the longest such streak by any pitcher since 1950.

In his final outing before the streak, Radke coughed up 13 hits as his ERA rose to 5.00. And then he didn't lose for two months, going 12–0 with a 1.87 ERA to make headlines and highlights across the country. He struggled for a bit once the streak was snapped, but Radke notched his 20th victory in remarkable fashion against the Brewers on September 21. He gave up a solo homer to the second batter of the game, Jeff Cirillo, and then went on to throw 9.2 straight scoreless frames in a 10-inning complete game. It's the last time a Twins starter has worked into extra innings.

Radke ranked just 14th among AL starters in ERA that season, but his historic streak and reaching the 20-win mark for a 68–94 team got him a third-place finish in the Cy Young balloting behind winner Roger Clemens and runner-up Randy Johnson. For the remainder of his career Radke suffered from playing on lots of bad teams that often failed to provide decent run support, leading to .500-or-worse records despite better-than-average work on the mound, but in 1997 it all clicked.

He never again approached 20 victories, but Radke topped 200 innings in all but one season from 1996 to 2005 and prevented runs at least 10 percent better than the rest of the league in all but two of those years. He was a durable, dependable strike-thrower, which made him the unquestioned Twins ace. It also made him the mold for the prototypical Twins pitcher—subpar fastball velocity and a mediocre strikeout rate, but impeccable control and a changeup that baffled sluggers looking to crush 88-mph fastballs.

For better or worse, the Twins spent the next two decades trying to find more Brad Radkes. He regularly led the league in first-pitch strikes and was able to challenge hitters because his changeup was so effective. "For all changeup pitchers, the key is making it look exactly like your fastball," Radke told the *Tampa Bay Times* in 2005. "The hitter has to have no idea the changeup is coming until they're already halfway through their swing."

Sometimes those challenges led to long homers—changeups that don't fool anyone tend to get punished, and first innings were especially troublesome for Radke—but he threw nearly 2,500 innings with an ERA that was 13 percent better than average because he wasn't afraid to live in the strike zone with raw stuff that lesser pitchers could never succeed with. From 1990-2010 only two pitchers threw 2,000 or more innings while walking 1.7 or fewer batters per nine innings: Greg Maddux (1.5) and Brad Radke (1.6).

To say Radke was a poor man's Maddux doesn't do either pitcher proper justice, because Maddux is one of the five best of all time and Radke is more accurately the rich man's version of every high school, college, and minor-league pitcher trying to figure out how to make it work with fastballs in the '80s. He's the uncommon crafty *right*-hander. Radke bridged the gap between the 1987 and 1991 championship teams and the run of division titles from 2002 to 2010, taking the mound every fifth day to provide some rare contender-quality pitching for a lot of losing Twins teams in the late 90s.

Johan Santana eventually surpassed Radke as team ace, but fittingly when the Twins finally made the playoffs in 2002 for the first time since 1991, it was Radke on the mound for Game 1. And it was also Radke on the mound for Game 5, when the Twins defeated the A's for what stands as their last playoff series victory. Overall in six playoff starts Radke posted a 3.60 ERA. In the last of those playoff starts, Game 3 of the 2006 ALDS, he was on borrowed time.

Radke had been pitching through a torn shoulder labrum for more than a year, somehow remaining effective despite an injury that typically requires surgery and a lengthy rehab process. Then late in 2006 he was diagnosed with a stress fracture in his shoulder, which made it almost impossible for Radke to pitch and even kept him from doing mundane off-field tasks like simply raising his arm to brush his teeth. He took a month off, returning in late September to throw five innings of one-run ball against the Royals to convince the Twins they could count on him in the playoffs.

Unfortunately all the guts in the world couldn't get Radke through Oakland's lineup, as he lasted just four innings and allowed four runs in a loss that ended the Twins' season. Sadder still, it was Radke's final game. He retired two months later, calling it a career at just 34 years old because he simply couldn't continue to pitch through the shoulder pain and wasn't interested in the long post-surgery rehab process. "There's not enough money in the world that's going to bring me back," he said at the retirement press conference. "I just don't want to do it. I'm shot, really."

Radke came in challenging hitters with high-80s fastballs and went out on his sword.

BOB ALLISON

Bob Allison was one of several fully formed, in-their-prime Senators stars who moved with the team to Minnesota in 1961. He'd won the Rookie of the Year award in 1959—smacking 30 homers to beat out future teammate Jim Perry—and his sophomore production remained solid despite failing to match his freshman excellence. He arrived in Minnesota at age 26 as one of the best right-handed sluggers in baseball, although he was second on his own team in that category behind Hall of Famer Harmon Killebrew.

Allison, much like Killebrew, struck out a ton for the 1960s, but made up for it with huge power and lots of walks. In his first five years with the Twins he averaged 30 homers and 90 walks per 150 games at a time when pitching dominated so much across MLB that the mound was lowered in 1968. During that five-year span of 1961–65, the only American Leaguers with more home runs (148) and more walks (442) than Allison were Killebrew, Mickey Mantle, Rocky Colavito, and Norm Cash.

That stretch included two of the best back-to-back years in Twins history, as Allison led the league in OPS in 1963 and then followed it up in 1964 by boosting his OPS nearly 50 points higher. He made the All-Star team in both seasons, but finished just 15th and 23rd in the MVP voting. In particular his 1963 season—when Allison hit 35 homers, drew 90 walks, and led the league in both OPS and runs scored while playing excellent defense in right field—is perhaps the most underappreciated great season in Twins history.

Allison led the league in OPS and Wins Above Replacement, yet 14 players—including Twins teammates Killebrew, Earl Battey, and Camilo Pascual—received more votes for MVP. Yankees second baseman Bobby Richardson, who hit .265 with three homers and an OPS nearly 200 points lower, finished higher in the balloting. "WAR" in 1963 had an entirely different meaning and even now-common statistics like on-base percentage and slugging percentage weren't widely cited, but…well, Allison was robbed.

And then it happened again the next season. Allison hit .287 with 32 homers and a .957 OPS that ranked third in the league behind Mickey Mantle and Boog Powell. He joined Mantle as the AL's only hitters with an on-base percentage above .400 and ranked fourth in slugging percentage. For all of that he finished 23rd in the MVP voting behind, among others, another sub-.650 OPS season from Richardson and multiple fellow sluggers who weren't within 100 points of his OPS.

Allison put together a three-year run from 1962 to '64 in which he led the league in runs scored while ranking second in homers and OPS; third in walks, on-base percentage, and slugging percentage; and fourth in RBIs while playing very good defense in the outfield. Add it all up and Allison led the entire American League in WAR from 1962 to '64, ahead of Killebrew, Mantle, Brooks Robinson, Al Kaline, Carl Yastrzemski, and all of the other household names from the era. Allison had to settle for being an after-the-fact superstar.

For all of the slugging he did, when Twins fans think of Allison, the most likely memory is his spectacular catch in Game 2 of the 1965 World Series. With a runner on first base and no outs in the fifth inning of a 0–0 game, Dodgers second baseman Jim Lefebvre lined a Jim Kaat pitch down the left field line. It looked like a sure extra-base hit and likely RBI, but Allison covered a tremendous amount of ground before making a sliding, backhanded catch. Kaat went on to throw a one-run complete game, beating Sandy Koufax.

Allison played fullback at the University of Kansas before signing with the Senators for $4,000 and was massive by 1960s standards at 6'4″ and 220 pounds, but he had enough range to log more than 1,600 innings as a center fielder. He primarily played right field and left field, where he combined outstanding instincts with a strong arm. Perhaps it's fitting that Allison's defense is etched in the minds of so many fans by way of his World Series grab, as being an asset in the field separated him from many other sluggers.

He was also a smart, efficient baserunner, swiping 40 bags while being caught just nine times between 1962 and '66, and ranking eighth in Twins history with 41 career triples. For a man Allison's size—and for a hitter with such prodigious home run, walk, and strikeout totals—having a skill set that also included plus defense and baserunning was a rarity that may help explain why his all-around value was so often overlooked. He was an All-Star-caliber player for a decade, ranking among the Twins' top 10 in homers, runs, and RBIs.

Sport magazine writer Leonard Schechter jokingly said of Allison in 1964: "Anyone can be successful in baseball if he follows the path of Bob Allison. All you have to do is be 6'4", strong as a weightlifter, handsome as a shirt model, have the personality of an honor graduate of Dale Carnegie, and also work your head off." Kaat, the beneficiary of the great catch in 1965, described Allison as having "the ideal body" and noted, "He was a hard-nosed player...he was always so fit, everyone marveled at his condition."

While playing in an old-timers' game at the Metrodome in 1987—just 13 years after his retirement—Allison began to notice coordination problems. Within a few years his health had deteriorated to the point that swinging a golf club became impossible and Allison was diagnosed with the neurodegenerative disorder ataxia. Not yet 60, he retired from an executive role with Coca-Cola, telling the *Arizona Republic* in 1991, "My coordination is gone. I can't walk. I can't talk. I can't write. I can't do anything."

Allison died in 1995 at age 60. His legacy lives on with the Bob Allison Ataxia Research Center at the University of Minnesota, where cerebellum disorders like the one that cut his life short are studied and treated. Many of his former Twins teammates, including Jim Kaat, helped raise money for the center.

TORII
HUNTER

Minnesota lost left-hander John Smiley to Cincinnati in free agency following the 1992 season and was awarded the Reds' first-round pick in 1993 as compensation, leaving the Twins choosing back-to-back at 20 and 21. They used the Reds' pick on Arkansas high school outfielder Torii Hunter and used their own pick on Georgia Tech catcher Jason Varitek. Hunter and Varitek combined to play 34 seasons in the majors, but Varitek never wore a Twins uniform whereas Hunter is one of the most beloved players ever to do so.

Varitek returned to college for his senior season rather than sign with the Twins, but the team convinced Hunter to pass up a scholarship to Pepperdine in favor of a $450,000 signing bonus. Billed as a tremendous raw athlete with unpolished baseball skills, Hunter looked the part in his pro debut, hitting .190 in rookie-ball. General manager Terry Ryan would say later that, at the time, he feared Hunter might get so discouraged that he'd give up on baseball and try football. He didn't, but his road to the majors was long and bumpy.

Hunter is one of the primary examples in Twins history of a top prospect needing time, coaching, patience, and multiple chances to fulfill his potential. Hunter did not light the minors on fire. He did not rise to the majors quickly. And once he did get to the majors, he did not stay for long at first. Or even at second or third. He had enough success at low Single-A in 1994 to put football out of his mind, but Hunter hit just .246 with seven homers at high Single-A in 1995 and .261 with seven homers at Double-A in 1996.

He was sent back to Double-A again in 1997 and was even worse, hitting .231 with eight homers for a New Britain team that also featured David Ortiz, Corey Koskie, and Doug Mientkiewicz. They all topped Hunter in OPS by at least 150 points. In fact, 11 different New

Britain hitters logged more than 150 plate appearances and Hunter was worse than all but two. Despite that, when the Twins needed a temporary roster reinforcement after trading outfielder Roberto Kelly in August, they called up Hunter for a one-game stay.

He debuted versus the Orioles on August 22, 1997, pinch-running for Terry Steinbach at first base and getting erased on Matt Lawton's game-ending double play. Hunter reached the majors at age 21, but it was merely a cup of coffee and the next season the Twins sent him back to Double-A for a third year. He was much better the third time around, hitting .282 with 10 homers in 82 games to earn a late-season promotion to Triple-A, where his .337 batting average and four homers in 28 games seemed to show a player breaking out.

The next spring the Twins handed Hunter the starting spot in center field and stuck with him all season, but he hit just .255 with nine homers, drawing only 26 walks in 422 trips to the plate. He remained the starter in 2000, but hit just .207 through late May and was demoted back to the minors. To that point Hunter's potential was based on defense and athleticism—he'd shown that he could run and throw and track down everything in the outfield, but at the plate it was low averages, modest pop, and poor strike-zone control.

That all changed following the demotion, as Hunter set the Pacific Coast League on fire for two months. Working under hitting coach Bill Springman—formerly the head coach at Pepperdine who recruited Hunter—he hit .368 with 18 homers in 55 games. *Baseball America* named him the PCL's best defensive outfielder and most exciting player, and in late July the Twins recalled him. He didn't miss a beat, hitting .332 in 53 games down the stretch. Finally, after seven seasons in the minors, Hunter was in the majors to stay.

Going into 2001 the Twins had 90-plus losses in four consecutive seasons and hadn't had a winning record in eight seasons. However, the young talent they'd amassed during that losing stretch was finally starting to take shape, with Hunter at the forefront. He emerged as one of the breakout stars of the 2001 season across baseball, winning the first of nine straight Gold Glove awards in center field and smacking 27 homers for the most by a Minnesota center fielder other than Kirby Puckett since 1963.

His plate discipline still needed plenty of work—as evidenced by 125 strikeouts and only 29 walks—and once he got behind in the count pitchers could make him chase sliders in the dirt, but Hunter was locked in against fastballs and pulverized hanging breaking balls. He was a bona fide slugging center fielder, which has always been and probably always will be a baseball rarity, yet Hunter's defensive excellence dwarfed anything he accomplished at the plate.

Hunter had high-end speed and athleticism, but what truly separated him from the pack was uncommon size and strength for a center fielder combined with a fearlessness rarely seen outside of the Knievel family. He sprinted into the gaps with complete disregard for his own safety and well-being, approaching a fly ball like a strong safety chasing down a running back. Hunter also had zero respect for the notion of fences determining what was or wasn't a home run, instead using them more as props in his robberies.

Voted into the 2002 All-Star game as the AL's starting center fielder, he forever secured his place in Midseason Classic highlights by leaping above the fence in Milwaukee to rob a first-inning home run from Barry Bonds, who couldn't help but laugh and then jokingly picked up Hunter as they made their way off the field. It was a star-making moment on a national stage and perfectly represented what Hunter meant to the Twins amid agonizing contraction talk in what would be their first playoff season since 1991.

Hunter was the MVP of that 2002 team, hitting .289 with 29 homers, 37 doubles, and 23 steals in 148 games while becoming a *SportsCenter* regular on defense. He even finished sixth in the league MVP voting, sandwiched between slugging superstars Jason Giambi and Jim Thome. That offseason Hunter and the Twins agreed to a four-year, $32 million contract that included a fifth-year team option, keeping him in Minnesota through age 31 in 2007.

For the next five seasons the Twins won three division titles and Hunter hit .271 with an .805 OPS, averaging 24 homers and 16 steals per year while sweeping the Gold Gloves. He never really learned to lay off those sliders in the dirt, failing to draw more than 50 walks

Torii Hunter has more Gold Gloves than every center fielder in baseball history except Willie Mays, Ken Griffey Jr., and Andruw Jones.

in a season, but Hunter's consistent pull-power made him a right-handed hitting force in the middle of the Twins' lefty-heavy lineup. He remained daring in center field after suffering a broken ankle at Fenway Park in 2005, but his range gradually shrunk.

Hunter hit free agency in the fall of 2007 at a time of great change for the Twins. Ryan stepped down as GM after the team's first losing season since 2000 and left overmatched replacement Bill Smith to make key decisions on Hunter and Johan Santana. Smith made only a face-saving three-year, $45 million offer to retain Hunter—who signed a five-year, $90 million deal with the Angels—and then traded Santana to the Mets for a package of prospects that included a new center fielder in Carlos Gomez.

"I didn't want to leave the Twins," Hunter said after joining the Angels. "I just felt like they were ready to leave me. They thought I was too old to do a five-year deal." Hunter revealed that multiple teams offered him five-year contracts, and the Rangers even upped their offer to include a sixth-year option. Within that context the Twins' three-year offer looked silly, but even in retrospect it's hard to blame Smith too much for not wanting to make a five-year commitment to a 32-year-old center fielder with diminished range.

Midway through the third season of the deal, Hunter shifted to right field for the Angels, which is exactly what the Twins were banking on. What the Twins, or even the Angels, couldn't possibly have expected is that Hunter would make up for some of the lost value defensively by upping his offensive production into his mid-30s. Hunter set career-highs in batting average (.299) and OPS (.873) in his first Angels season and hit .286 over the life of the five-year contract, compared to .271 over his final five Twins seasons.

He left the Angels as a 37-year-old free agent after 2012, signing a two-year contract with the Tigers, and again made everyone look silly for expecting a decline. By then Hunter's defense in right field was a major weakness, as his legs and body simply didn't have any juice left after all those battles with walls, but he batted .295 with a .783 OPS in Detroit. At age 39 he hit the open market again and went back to where it all started, signing with the Twins and contributing to a surprise 83-win season after five straight 90-loss years.

Ryan expressed interest in re-signing Hunter at age 40 despite a .702 OPS that was Hunter's worst mark since his rookie year, but he called it a career, saying he was "physically and mentally tired" while slumping in the second half. "Twins fans, you can't beat them," he said at the press conference. "That's my family. The city is my love." Hunter played 12 of his 19 seasons in Minnesota, winning seven Gold Gloves, making two All-Star teams, hitting 214 homers, and successfully taking the center field torch from Puckett.

FRANK VIOLA

Frank Viola was the Twins' second-round draft pick out of St. John's University in 1981 and less than one year later the 6'4" left-hander was in the majors. He took his lumps early on, going 11–25 with a 5.38 ERA in 336 innings through his first two years for two of the worst teams in Twins history, but in 1984 the young roster began to take shape and the 24-year-old Viola broke out. He threw 258 innings with a 3.21 ERA to finish sixth in the Cy Young balloting, being credited with 18 of the team's 81 wins.

Viola and the Twins both took a major step backward in 1985 and 1986, as he struggled to keep the ball in the ballpark and the team dipped back below .500 while firing manager Ray Miller and replacing him with Tom Kelly. Viola was 26 years old with a 4.38 career ERA, and the Twins had gone seven seasons without a winning record. But in 1987, with Kelly at the helm, Viola atop the rotation, and very little in the way of expectations for either, magic happened.

Viola won 17 games and logged 252 innings with a 2.90 ERA, striking out 197 batters with a deadly high fastball/diving changeup combination and perhaps most importantly slicing his home run rate by 20 percent. He again placed sixth in the Cy Young balloting and the Twins improved from 71–91 to 85–77, winning the American League West division title as Viola posted a 1.88 ERA in September to enter the postseason as the unquestioned ace of a staff that also featured 36-year-old future Hall of Famer Bert Blyleven.

Kelly rode Viola and Blyleven hard throughout the Twins' playoff run, starting them in four out of five ALCS games against Detroit and five out of seven World Series games against St. Louis. Viola started Game 1 and Game 4 in each series and the Twins were winners in three of the four games, but he pitched well just once and was shaky overall with a 5.01 ERA. He got knocked from Game 4 of the World Series in the fourth inning, taking the loss, and was then tasked with coming back on short rest to start Game 7.

Viola ran into trouble early, allowing a pair of second-inning runs on four singles. It was smooth sailing from there, however, as Viola faced one batter over the minimum for the next six innings—striking out six and walking none—before turning things over to closer Jeff Reardon with a 4–2 lead in the ninth inning. Reardon slammed the door with a 1–2–3 inning and the Twins captured their first championship in front of a raucous Metrodome crowd, with Viola being named MVP of the World Series.

Despite improving from 85 to 91 wins in 1988, the Twins missed the playoffs, but Viola did everything he possibly could to carry them back to October with one of the greatest individual pitching seasons in team history. After taking an Opening Day loss at Yankee Stadium, he went 24–6 with a 2.48 ERA in his final 34 starts, allowing just 18 homers in 250 innings. Viola was chosen by Kelly to start the All-Star game over reigning back-to-back Cy Young winner Roger Clemens and threw two perfect innings.

Viola kept rolling in the second half, finishing 24-7 with a 2.64 ERA in 255 innings for a team that was 64-63 without him on the mound. He received 27 of 28 first-place votes for the Cy Young award, with a lone ballot cast for A's closer Dennis Eckersley keeping him from being a unanimous winner. Most lefties are much worse versus right-handed batters, but Viola's circle-changeup had developed into such a weapon that he was actually more effective against righties than lefties in 1988.

Coming off a spectacular season and with just one year remaining on his contract, Viola and the Twins engaged in extension negotiations that dragged through spring training and into the regular season. He had a poor April while those talks became increasingly public, but eventually the two sides agreed to a three-year, $7.9 million deal that was in line with recent contracts signed by Clemens, Orel Hershiser, and Dwight Gooden. With that out of the way, Viola posted a 3.37 ERA in 18 starts from May 1 through the end of July.

However, the Twins had sunk to fifth place at 51–53 and minutes before the July 31 trade deadline general manager Andy MacPhail pulled the trigger on a blockbuster move that sent Viola to the Mets in exchange for five young pitchers. It was the first time in MLB history that a reigning Cy Young winner had been traded. Viola called the trade "a shock to me" just three months after signing a three-year contract, but the native New Yorker who grew up rooting for the Mets also described the move as "coming back home."

From the Twins' point of view left-hander David West was seen as the centerpiece of the prospect package, which also included right-handers Rick Aguilera, Kevin Tapani, Tim Drummond, and Jack Savage. "I know we gave up a lot, but he's one of the best," Mets manager Davey Johnson told the *New York Times*. "Any time we can get a player of this caliber, you have to make the trade." Locally, the Twins were criticized for once again trading away an expensive star player in what was viewed as a cost-cutting decision.

MacPhail tried to fend off criticism by telling the *Washington Post* that "the velocity of [Viola's] fastball was diminishing." Kelly downplayed Viola's importance by insisting "he never had the makeup to be a leader" and "players didn't follow him." One of those players, Twins first baseman Kent Hrbek, took it further by suggesting that Viola "had changed" and "started to make excuses.... I think the contract got to him." All of which fell at least somewhat on deaf ears, as Twins fans had heard similar stories about traded stars before.

Viola was fantastic for the Mets, posting a 3.32 ERA in the final two-and-a-half seasons of his three-year contract. He had a 3.38 ERA following the trade in 1988, won 20 games and finished third in the Cy Young voting in 1989, and made All-Star teams in both 1989 and 1990. He departed as a free agent after the 1990 season, spending three years with the Red Sox before winding down his career with the Reds and Blue Jays. Viola was exactly what the Mets had hoped to acquire—a veteran top-of-the-rotation pitcher in his prime.

And as painful as the move was at the time, trading Viola worked out brilliantly for the Twins even with his success in New York. West was a bust and neither Drummond nor Savage amounted to much in the big leagues, but Tapani capably replaced Viola in the rotation almost immediately and Aguilera stepped into the closer role with tremendous success. Their contributions played a crucial part in the Twins winning a second World Series just two years after trading Viola, and together they spent 18 years in Minnesota.

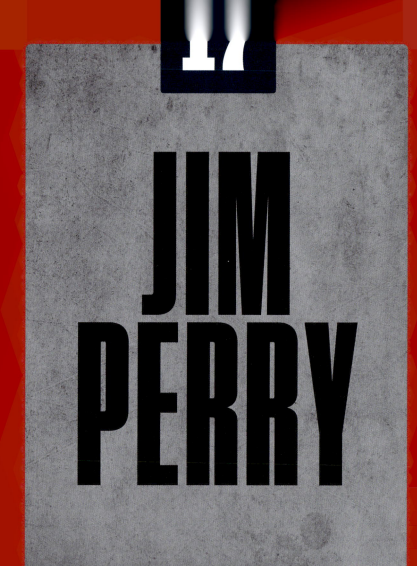

At the age of 20, Jim Perry left Campbell University is his home state of North Carolina to sign with the Cleveland Indians in 1956 and, after three seasons in the minor leagues, he was a surprise inclusion on the Opening Day roster in 1959. Perry spent the first half of the season in the bullpen, but manager Joe Gordon shifted the hard-throwing, 6'4" right-hander to the rotation in late July and in his first outing Perry threw a complete-game, two-hit shutout against Harmon Killebrew, Bob Allison, and the Washington Senators.

Perry ended up making 13 starts and 31 relief appearances on the season, throwing 153 innings with a 2.65 ERA despite a subpar 79-to-55 strikeout-to-walk ratio. He finished runner-up in the Rookie of the Year voting behind Allison, who would become Perry's teammate in Minnesota four years later. Perry was a full-time member of the rotation in 1960 and won an American League–high 18 games, but his 3.62 ERA was barely better than the league mark of 3.87 and he served up an MLB-high 35 homers.

Perry's strikeout-to-walk ratio was again poor at 120-to-91 and his measly strikeout rate of 4.1 per nine innings was particularly odd given his outstanding fastball velocity. Still, he was viewed as a very promising young pitcher and Perry made his first All-Star team in 1961 even though his 7–7 record, 4.18 ERA, and 44/42 K/BB ratio were unimpressive at the break. He fell apart in the second half, going 3–10 with a 5.30 ERA, and finished the season with nearly as many walks (87) as strikeouts (90) in 224 innings.

Another mediocre year followed in 1962, and in 1963 the

Indians demoted Perry to the bullpen. He was still just 27 years old and still threw hard, but Perry's poor control and inability to miss bats due to unrefined off-speed offerings threatened to stall his career. Perry pitched sparingly as a reliever, working mostly in mop-up or long-relief situations, and in mid-May the Indians traded him to the Twins for left-hander Jack Kralick. While not exactly a blockbuster swap at the time, the trade ended up being hugely important.

Kralick was 28 years old and had been a solid, innings-eating starter for the Twins, so it wasn't a shock when he was named an All-Star for the Indians in 1964. It also wasn't a shock when Perry spent 1964 in Minnesota's bullpen, throwing just 65 innings in mostly low-leverage spots. However, what came next was totally unexpected. Within three years Kralick's big-league career was over—he threw a total of only 156 innings after making that All-Star team with the Indians—and Perry's career was just getting rolling.

Perry spent the first three months of 1965 back in the bullpen because the Twins' rotation was stacked with the likes of Jim Kaat, Camilo Pascual, and Mudcat Grant. Perry finally got a shot to start again in early July, tossed a complete-game shutout against the Red Sox in his first game, and never looked back. Perry posted a 2.47 ERA in 135 innings down the stretch and, for the first time in his career, was able to put a little separation between his walk rate and strikeout rate. And it was all thanks to Johnny Sain.

Sain was an excellent starting pitcher for the Braves and Yankees, making three All-Star teams and finishing runner-up for the MVP award in 1948, but he's perhaps best known for his work as a pitching coach (and for being one of the stars of Jim Bouton's amazing book *Ball Four*). Sain joined the Twins in 1965 after a nasty breakup with the Yankees and his impact is impossible to deny, as the pitching staff shaved 78 runs off their 1964 total to rank third in the league.

Grant had a league-high 21 wins in a career that never saw him win more than 15 in any other season. Kaat posted his first sub-3.00 ERA in what would be a Hall of Fame-caliber career. Late-30s retreads Al Worthington and Johnny Klippstein formed a shutdown relief duo, and perhaps most impressively Perry emerged as a reliable starter. In true Sain fashion, he joined the lengthy list of people to clash with

Twins manager Sam Mele and was fired after 1966, but his work turning Perry into more than just a hard-thrower lived on.

Sain tweaked Perry's fastball to add more movement and got him to rely on a curveball that complemented the fastball and generated swinging strikes. And in doing so he gave Perry all of the credit, telling *The Sporting News* in late 1965: "I've never seen a man work so hard on his own. The coaches and manager have been getting the credit for the team leading the league, but it's effort like Perry's that put us there." And in this case "there" was the World Series, where the Twins fell to the Dodgers in seven games.

Sain moved on to Detroit, where the Tigers won the World Series in his second season as pitching coach thanks to a breakout, MVP-winning year by right-hander Denny McClain. Perry's breakout year came in 1969, when he went 20-6 with a 2.82 ERA in 262 innings while striking out 168 and walking just 57. He was third in the Cy Young award voting, behind McClain and Mike Cuellar, but then he came back just as strong in 1970 to snag the award by winning 24 games with a 3.04 ERA in 279 innings for a division winner.

His younger brother, Gaylord Perry, nearly matched Jim with 23 wins in 1970 and later won a pair of Cy Young awards on the way to the Hall of Fame. Jim and Gaylord Perry are the only brothers in baseball history to win Cy Young awards and their 529 combined victories—215 for Jim, 314 for Gaylord—trail only Phil and Joe Niekro as the all-time wins leaders among siblings. Jim and Gaylord Perry later pitched together for the Indians in 1974, winning 38 combined games.

On the surface the follow-up to his Cy Young–winning 1970 seemed to go well, as Perry made the All-Star team in 1971. However, his first-half performance was mediocre with a 4.10 ERA and his strikeout-to-walk ratio was slipping back to his pre-Sain days. Perry went 5–9 with a 4.40 ERA in the second half, finishing the year with the AL's most home runs and earned runs allowed. His strikeout-to-walk ratio, which had been 168-to-57 in 1970, deteriorated to nearly even at 126-to-102.

Perry turned in a similarly mediocre campaign in 1971 and was traded to the Tigers the next spring. He was traded twice more, first back to the Indians and then to the A's, and his career came to an end in 1975 at age 39. On the surface Perry's career path appears somewhat normal, but the prolonged struggles between the early promise he showed in Cleveland and the 30-something success in Minnesota shine a light on the impact good, smart coaching—or at least Johnny Sain—can have in turning talent into performance.

Perry spent a decade in Minnesota, winning a Cy Young award, finishing runner-up for another, and going 128-90 with a 3.15 ERA for some of the best teams in Twins history. His raw numbers are made to look better than they were by the pitching haven that MLB was in the 1960s—for example, his nice-looking 3.35 ERA in 1972 was actually worse than the league average of 3.06—but Perry's adjusted ERA+ of 113 with the Twins fits in the same range as Brad Radke (113), Jim Kaat (112), and Frank Viola (111).

JUSTIN MORNEAU

Minnesota whiffed on three consecutive top-10 draft picks from 1998 to 2000, wasting the only benefits of their prolonged losing on high-profile busts Ryan Mills, B.J. Garbe, and Adam Johnson. Garbe, the fifth overall pick in 1999, was a supposed five-tool outfielder from a Washington high school who never advanced past Double-A and retired at age 25. That same draft the Twins used their second-round pick on another high schooler, Indiana catcher Rob Bowen, who totaled 216 games in the majors and hit .209.

In the third round they drafted a third straight high school hitter and second straight high school catcher. This one worked out slightly better. Justin Morneau, a left-handed-hitting catcher from Westminster Secondary School in British Columbia, Canada, wasn't actually much of a catcher. *Baseball America*'s pre-draft scouting report noted that "his catching skills are marginal" and, after signing Morneau for a $290,000 bonus, the Twins played him at catcher in a grand total of 22 games, all in rookie-ball.

Morneau wasn't a catcher—he was a hitter—and two years later the Twins snapped their streak of terrible top-10 picks by snagging Joe Mauer anyway. Mauer and Morneau went on to become one of the best hitting duos in Twins history, each capturing an MVP award while perfectly complementing one another. Mauer grinded out at-bats, laced singles and doubles all over the field, and got on base constantly. Morneau, batting right behind Mauer, crushed doubles and homers while racking up huge RBI totals by driving Mauer in.

Morneau arrived first, in June of 2003, starting at designated hitter and batting cleanup in his debut when the Twins called him up to take at-bats from Matthew LeCroy. He was 22 years old and had hit .309 with 19 homers in 57 games between Double-A and Triple-A after coming into the season rated 14th on *Baseball America*'s prospect list. Morneau got off to a fast start, including a mammoth pinch-hit homer off the center field scoreboard in Milwaukee, but when he slumped in July the Twins sent him back to the minors.

Still not ready to hand Morneau a starting spot in 2004—when Mauer was the Opening Day catcher following the offseason A.J. Pierzynski trade—the Twins had him repeat Triple-A as a consensus top-20 prospect. He toyed with International League pitchers, hitting .306 with 22 homers and 23 doubles in 72 games, all while Minnesota stuck with light-hitting Doug Mientkiewicz at first base and split DH duties among LeCroy, Mike Ryan, and 36-year-old Jose Offerman.

Not until Mientkiewicz needed a disabled list stint for a wrist injury in mid-July did the Twins call up Morneau for extended action. He played so well, hitting .302 with three homers and three doubles in his first 10 games, that when Mientkiewicz returned from the brief DL stint the Twins kept Morneau around. And then a week later they decided it was Mientkiewicz who should go, trading the popular, slick-fielding first baseman to the Red Sox to clear the position for Morneau.

Already an awkward changing of the guard due to a reported rift between Mientkiewicz and manager Ron Gardenhire, the Twins playing the Red Sox at Fenwark Park added a surreal twist. Mientkiewicz walked across the field, put on the other uniform, and was in the lineup facing Morneau and the Twins hours after the trade was announced. He went on to win the World Series with the Red Sox as a part-time player, catching the final out, but by that time Morneau had established himself as a middle-of-the-order monster.

Morneau hit .271 with 19 homers and 17 doubles in 74 games, topping Mientkiewicz's career OPS with the Twins by 100 points, but then slumped for much of 2005 and ended up with a disappointing .239 batting average. He also started slowly in 2006, hitting just .208 in April, but Morneau broke through in early May and never stopped rolling. He hit .364 in June, .410 in July, and .345 overall in the second half, driving in 130 runs on the way to being named MVP in a tight vote over Derek Jeter of the Yankees.

In true M&M Boys fashion, Mauer hit .347 to win the batting title, adding 79 walks for a lofty .429 on-base percentage, and Morneau

"I focus on getting on base, he brings me home."
—Joe Mauer on Justin Morneau

smacked 34 homers and 37 doubles to cash in all of those RBI opportunities and get the MVP voters' attention. Mauer would get his MVP award three years later, but not before another huge RBI total garnered Morneau a runner-up finish in 2008 behind Dustin Pedroia of the Red Sox. (Mauer finished fourth that season, winning another batting title along with a .413 on-base percentage.)

Morneau was an RBI machine, combining big averages and power to all fields with a .400 OBP table-setter in front of him. He knocked in 130, 111, 129, and 100 runs from 2006 to 2009, trailing only Ryan Howard, Albert Pujols, and Alex Rodriguez during that four-year span in which he won an MVP and finished runner-up for another award while hitting .292/.364/.516 with an average of 30 homers and 35 doubles per 150 games. And then—after all of that—he had a career-year in 2010. For a while, at least.

During his MVP and MVP runner-up seasons, Morneau wasn't the league's best overall hitter and his all-around value lagged behind several other players in advanced metrics that account for defense/position, but he was really good and his RBI totals were really shiny. However, in 2010 he had the RBIs *and* gaudy overall production. He was a great player taking things to another level by becoming an elite offensive force in addition to an elite run producer.

He looked unstoppable, hitting .345 with 18 homers, 25 doubles, and 50 walks through 81 games for career-highs in on-base percentage (.437) and slugging percentage (.618). Not only was his 1.055 OPS a career-high, it beat his previous best mark by 120 points and ranked second in baseball behind only Miguel Cabrera. Morneau was 29 years old and playing by far his best baseball in the Twins' first year at Target Field, putting up numbers that dwarfed his MVP season. And then it all came crashing down on July 7.

During the eighth inning of a game against the Blue Jays in Toronto, Morneau singled to center field for his second hit. The next batter, Michael Cuddyer, hit a chopper to shortstop and Morneau slid hard into second base to break up the potential double play. Toronto second baseman John McDonald had to jump to get his throw off and in doing so kneed Morneau in the helmet. It appeared to be a relatively glancing blow, but Morneau lay prone on the ground for

TWINS' LEADERS IN OPS VERSUS RIGHTIES

minimum 1,500 plate appearances:

.896	Justin Morneau
.890	Tony Oliva
.889	Joe Mauer
.887	Harmon Killebrew
.879	Kent Hrbek

several minutes, clearly dazed, and then looked shaky walking off the field.

Initially said to be day-to-day, Morneau never played again that season—missing the final two-plus months and the playoffs—and was never the same once he did return from the concussion. He was limited to 69 games in 2011 and hit .229 with four homers while struggling with ongoing dizziness, sensitivity to light, and other common post-concussion symptoms. In the spring of 2012 he sounded on the verge of retirement, saying, "There comes a point where you can only torture yourself for so long."

His outlook improved enough that he decided to keep going. Morneau was healthy enough to play 134 games in 2012 and 154 games in 2013, but was a shell of his former self, hitting .263 with a .752 OPS compared to his .900 OPS from 2006 to 2010. His strikeouts rose, his walk rate went down, and his overall production was below average among first basemen and prone to lengthy slumps. After posting a winning record in all but one of Morneau's first eight seasons, the Twins lost 90-plus games in 2011, 2012, and 2013.

Late in 2013, with Morneau hitting .259 with 17 homers in the final season of a six-year, $80 million contract, the last-place Twins traded him to the Pirates for a pair of marginal prospects. Morneau failed to go deep in 25 games for Pittsburgh, but did make it back to the postseason for the first time since 2006. As a free agent that offseason he signed an incentive-laden deal with the Rockies and staged a bounce-back campaign with the help of Coors Field, hitting .319—with modest power—for his first batting title at age 33.

He was off to a similar start for the Rockies in 2014 when he suffered another concussion diving back to first base. He missed four months of action, returning in September to hit .338 in 22 games, but Morneau's long-term health became a bigger concern than his still-decent ability to hit a baseball. If anything, to hit .300-plus in his mid-30s after missing huge chunks of the previous four seasons with complications from a brain injury showed what a spectacular talent Morneau was before his career got derailed that day in Toronto.

Twins fans will forever imagine what could have been had Morneau stayed healthy, but they should also remember his incredible raw power, his ability to do damage spraying line drives from foul pole to foul pole, the little inhale he took in the moment just before bat met ball, the corkscrew follow-through that ended with the bat raised above his head, and the dynamic duo he formed with Mauer in the middle of the lineup. Justin Morneau deserved better, but he was still damn good.

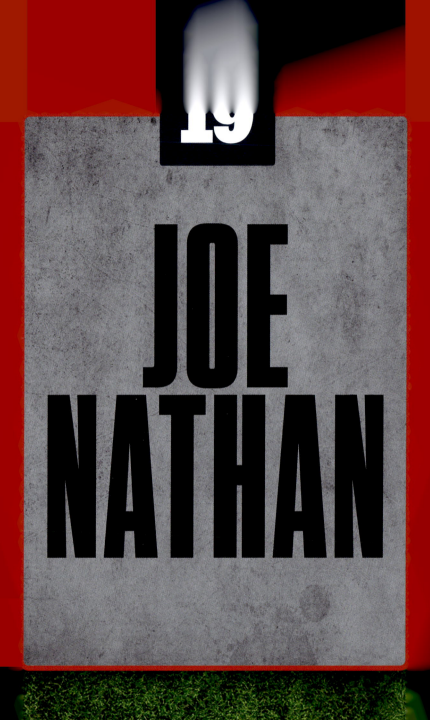

Things began to click for the Twins' bullpen in late 2001 when they demoted struggling closer LaTroy Hawkins to a setup role and gave ninth-inning duties to Eddie Guardado. Not only did Guardado thrive as the closer—locking down saves after spending the first decade of his career as a left-handed specialist and middle reliever—Hawkins went from a liability to a strength, kicking off what would become a fantastic 14-year run as a high-end setup man.

As a late-inning duo Guardado and Hawkins threw 148 innings with a 2.49 ERA in 2002 and 143 innings with a 2.33 ERA in 2003, playing a crucial part in Minnesota's return to prominence with back-to-back division titles. Unfortunately for the Twins they were both free agents following the 2003 season and all of that good late-inning work put re-signing them out of the team's spending range. Guardado joined the Mariners for three years and $13 million, and Hawkins signed a three-year, $9 million deal with the Cubs.

The bullpen cupboard wasn't totally bare, with right-hander Juan Rincon and left-hander J.C. Romero as in-house options to soak up some of those lost high-leverage innings, but the Twins made acquiring relief help an offseason priority. And in the process they pulled off one of the best trades in team history, acquiring three pitchers—starter prospects Boof Bonser and Francisco Liriano, plus big-league setup man Joe Nathan—from the Giants in exchange for catcher A.J. Pierzynski.

It was a controversial move at the time, because

TWINS' LEADERS IN
WIN PROBABILITY
ADDED AS RELIEVERS

24.6	Joe Nathan
10.3	Eddie Guardado
8.6	Rick Aguilera
6.5	J.C. Romero
6.4	Doug Corbett

Pierzynski was a homegrown, 26-year-old All-Star catcher coming off a season in which he hit .312. Giants general manager Brian Sabean portrayed the swap as a potential coup for San Francisco, saying, "It's not often you can send a right-handed reliever and two unproven prospects for a front-line, All-Star catcher.... While it didn't come easy to give up Joe [Nathan], we feel we've got some alternatives within the organization."

From the Twins' perspective, parting with Pierzynski saved money at a time when their payroll was under $60 million, but more importantly they had the consensus top prospect in baseball and one of the top catching prospects of all time waiting in the wings. General manager Terry Ryan felt that Joe Mauer was ready to make the jump from Double-A to the majors at age 21. Mauer's presence made Pierzynski expendable and the Twins made the smart, bold decision to cash him in at peak value.

Bonser was viewed by many as the centerpiece of the deal from the Twins' point of view. He was San Francisco's first-round draft pick in 2000 and had advanced to Triple-A as a 21-year-old, ranking 29th on *Baseball America*'s top-100 prospects list the previous year. Liriano was also seen as a very good prospect, but he'd thrown just 160 career innings at age 19 and missed most of 2013 with arm problems. Bonser was the top prospect, Liriano was the high-upside flier, and Nathan was the immediate bullpen help. Or so it seemed.

Things didn't quite go as planned, for the Twins or the Giants. Pierzynski's stint in San Francisco was a mess, as his OPS dropped nearly 100 points and he clashed with coaches and training staff before getting released after one season. Bonser reached Minnesota in 2006, but went 18-25 with a 5.15 ERA for the Twins and was finished as a major leaguer before turning 30. Liriano emerged as one of the elite pitching prospects in baseball and had an extraordinary rookie season for the Twins in 2006, but then blew out his elbow.

Meanwhile, the relative afterthought of the trade quickly grabbed hold of the closer role in spring training and became the best reliever in the history of the Twins. Nathan is the team's all-time leader with 260 saves—surpassing Rick Aguilera's total by six—and his 2.16 ERA is by far the lowest of anyone in a Twins uniform. He's also the Twins' leader in strikeout rate (10.9 per nine innings) and opponents' batting average (.186), blowing away the completion in both categories.

Nathan was so good, in fact, that placing his excellence within the context of the Twins short-changes him. He's simply one of the best relievers in baseball history and ranking eighth all time with 377 career saves is especially remarkable because on November 14, 2003—the day the Twins traded for him—Nathan was a 29-year-old ex-shortstop with a surgically repaired elbow and all of one career save. Heck, he'd only been a reliever for one year, moving to the bullpen following Tommy John elbow surgery.

Nathan was selected by the Giants—as a shortstop—in the sixth round of the 1995 draft. He'd starred at Stony Brook University for two seasons, hitting .391 with a .698 slugging percentage and 85 RBIs in 73 games. He was 6′4″ with good range and plenty of pop at the plate, and he even stole 13 bases. But his shortstop career was short-lived, as he hit .232 and committed 26 errors in 58 games at low Single-A after signing, at which point the Giants attempted to convince him to give pitching a try.

He hated the idea initially, sitting out the 1996 season rather than making the switch, but later reconsidered and took the mound in 1997 back at low Single-A. Just two years later Nathan was tossing seven shutout innings in his Giants debut, but he mostly struggled as a starter before blowing out his elbow in 2000. Nathan spent nearly all of 2001 and 2002 rehabbing in the minors, returning to the Giants in 2003 as a full-time reliever. He thrived right away, going 12–4 with a 2.96 ERA as the primary setup man on a 100-win team.

TWINS' HIGHEST STRIKEOUT PERCENTAGE

minimum 450 innings:

30.7%	Joe Nathan
26.2%	Johan Santana
23.6%	Francisco Liriano
23.0%	Tom Hall
20.5%	Rick Aguilera

Many of the best closers in baseball history have interesting origin stories, because until very recently most closers were starters who moved to the bullpen due to injuries or poor performances. The top four spots on the Twins' saves list—Nathan, Aguilera, Guardado, and Glen Perkins—are held by one-time starters who found much more success relieving. Even within that group Nathan's story still stands out, as a former Division III shortstop who converted to pitching and blew out his arm as a starter.

Traded at age 29 to a contending team overhauling its bullpen, Nathan saved 44 games with a 1.62 ERA and finished fourth in the Cy Young award voting. And then he did it again the next season and the next season and every year until his elbow gave out again in the spring of 2010. By that point Nathan had made four All-Star teams in six seasons with the Twins, averaging 41 saves per year at a 91 percent success rate with a 1.87 ERA and 518 strikeouts in 419 innings.

He missed all of 2010 recovering from a second Tommy John surgery, but fought his way back to reclaim the Twins' closer role in 2011 at age 36. Then he hit the open market as a free agent and left the Twins to sign a two-year, $14.5 million deal with the Rangers. He was brilliant in Texas, racking up 80 saves with 151 strikeouts in 129 innings and a 2.09 ERA in two seasons before moving on to the Tigers, where things unraveled for Nathan and he blew out his elbow for a third time at age 40.

For a decade—starting with his trade to Minnesota in 2004 and ending with his two-year Texas run—Nathan was a light-outs closer who saved an average of 38 games per season with a 2.38 ERA, 10.6 strikeouts per nine innings, and a .188 opponents' batting average. He posted a sub-3.00 ERA with at least 35 saves every season except for the time spent recovering from surgery and finished the 10-year stretch of 2004-2013 with numbers that compare to what Mariano Rivera did during the same time.

	SV	SV%	IP	ERA	SO/9	OAVG
Nathan	340	91%	592	2.14	10.8	.188
Rivera	369	91%	634	1.92	8.4	.208

Rivera was already on a Hall of Fame path by the time Nathan got his first closer job, but Nathan was Rivera's equal from 2004-2013. In the regular season, at least. Rivera raised his amazing performance to unthinkable heights in the playoffs and in doing so cemented his status as the greatest reliever ever. Nathan pitched in just 10 career playoff games and struggled in nearly all of them. He appeared three times for the Twins in the playoffs and two of them will forever give Minnesotans nightmares involving Alex Rodriguez.

It's a shame that a spectacular career as one of the greatest relievers in baseball history is skewed so much by what happened in 10 postseason innings, because for more than 900 regular season innings Nathan was every bit as dominant as any reliever short of Rivera. His career save percentage of 89.3 is the highest ever, slightly ahead of Rivera (89.1) and Trevor Hoffman (88.8), and Nathan also ranks among the top five relievers of all time in adjusted ERA+, Win Probability Added, and opponents' batting average.

GAME 7
OF 1987
WORLD SERIES

In sports, as in life, there are certain impossibilities. For instance, from now until the end of time no one else will ever become the best shooting guard in Chicago Bulls history or the best quarterback in New England Patriots history. No matter what happens from here on out, no one will ever be able to question which player traded from the Red Sox to the Yankees most haunts Boston fans. And there will never be a point at which a discussion among Twins fans about Game 7 pitching performances involves any kind of debate.

Michael Jordan. Tom Brady. Babe Ruth. Jack Morris. End of discussion, cease wasting any more time. Except here's the thing when it comes to Minnesota Twins history: Frank Viola also pitched one hell of a Game 7 in the World Series. And his came first, too. Not only is Viola's brilliant effort against the Cardinals in the deciding game of 1987 forever overshadowed in Twins history, it's one of the most overlooked playoff performances in baseball history, period.

"Game score" is a metric developed by Bill James to determine the quality of a pitching performance beyond simply innings and runs, by incorporating strikeouts, walks, hits allowed, and other key factors. The idea is to quantify dominance and run prevention, giving added credit to high-strikeout, low-baserunner games compared to starts in which a pitcher wriggled out of repeated trouble. Viola's "game score" for Game 7 in 1987 has been topped in Game 7 of a World Series just once since then—by Jack Morris in 1991.

Viola had been the Twins' ace all season, going 17–10 with a 2.90 ERA in 252 innings to finish sixth in Cy Young balloting, but he took the Game 4 loss as St. Louis knocked him out in the fourth inning with five runs. Back on the mound for Game 7 on short rest, he gave up two early runs as the Cardinals strung together four hits in the second inning. At that point his ERA in five postseason starts stood at 5.33, with 16 total runs allowed in 25 innings. And then, just like that, he was unhittable.

Viola set St. Louis down in order in the third, fourth, fifth, and sixth innings, erasing the one hit he allowed with a caught stealing. He gave up a double in the seventh inning, but retired the next two batters to escape the inning and then had a 1-2-3 eighth frame. Viola had thrown six straight scoreless innings, facing one batter more than the minimum, with six strikeouts and zero walks. And while he was making sweet music, the Twins' lineup was storming back to take the lead.

Cardinals manager Whitey Herzog chose rookie left-hander Joe Magrane to start Game 7 rather than turning back to veteran right-hander Danny Cox on short rest after his Game 5 victory. In explaining the decision before the game, Herzog said, "Let me put it this way—he'll be ready. We just want to get a few innings out of Magrane and stay in the game." Sure enough, with one out and a runner on in the fifth inning, Herzog pulled Magrane and brought in Cox to face Kirby Puckett, who lined the first pitch for a game-tying double.

Cox stayed in for the sixth inning, but was yanked after walking the first two batters and then got ejected for arguing with the home-plate umpire while leaving the mound. Todd Worrell replaced him and walked pinch-hitter Roy Smalley to load the bases. With two outs, Greg Gagne stepped to the plate in a tie game and delivered a go-ahead single. The lead grew to 4–2 thanks to an RBI double by Dan Gladden in the bottom of the eighth inning and Viola was ready to finish what he'd started, but manager Tom Kelly had other plans.

The biggest offseason move the Twins made heading into 1987 was acquiring All-Star closer Jeff Reardon from the Expos in a six-player trade. Minnesota had suffered through four-and-a-half years of Ron Davis blowing saves in the closer role, and general manager Andy MacPhail felt that in order for the young team to take a step forward, it needed a reliable veteran presence in the ninth inning. Reardon notched a league-high 41 saves in 1985, was an All-Star in 1985 and 1986, and had a 2.80 career ERA through age 30.

Reardon wasn't at his best in 1987, but still saved the second-most games in the league and received votes for both the Cy Young and MVP award. Viola, who'd witnessed firsthand the damage Davis could do when handed a late-inning lead, grew particularly fond of Reardon. "I told my wife when I left for spring training that we now had the guy who could make the difference," Viola said of Reardon. So when Kelly approached Viola in the dugout after the eighth inning to say the closer would be taking over, he understood.

"His exact words were, 'This is the way we've been doing it all year, so why change now?'" Viola revealed of his dugout exchange with Kelly, which began with the manager putting his arm around the ace left-hander. "Was I disappointed? That's a dumb question. Why should I be disappointed? Reardon is one of the best there is. It's a team game." Of course, as Ross Newhan of the *Los Angeles Times* pointed out, Viola said all of that while drenched in champagne and holding the World Series MVP trophy.

Reardon, working for the eighth time in 12 postseason games, put down the 3-4-5 hitters in the Cardinals' lineup and the Twins were champions for the first time. "This is just the greatest feeling in the world," Viola said. "I mean, we never even dared dream about this. We lost 102 games. We survived Calvin [Griffith]. We knew it was time to put up or shut up or they would start breaking up this nucleus. No one expected anything from us. We only expected it of ourselves."

CAMILO PASCUAL

Signed by the Washington Senators as an 18-year-old out of Havana, Cuba in 1952, Camilo Pascual made his big-league debut two years later. He struggled to throw strikes in his first two seasons, going 6–19 with a 5.23 ERA and 142-to-131 strikeout-to-walk ratio in 248 innings primarily spent as a long reliever. Pascual moved into the Senators' rotation in 1956 and began to rack up strikeouts with his world-class curveball, but went 14–35 with a 5.01 ERA over the next two seasons.

Pascual's first good season came as a 24-year-old in 1958, when he posted a 3.15 ERA and 146/60 K/BB ratio in 177 innings, leading the league in strikeout rate and finishing second in strikeout-to-walk ratio. Unfortunately, the Senators were an awful team, finishing dead last in the American League with a 61-93 record, and Pascual went just 8–12. Washington finished dead last again in 1959, but this time Pascual at least managed to win when he was on the mound.

He led the league with six shutouts and 17 complete games on the way to going 17–10 with a 2.64 ERA and 185/69 K/BB ratio in 239 innings. Pascual made his first All-Star team and ranked among the league's top five in ERA, wins, innings, and strikeouts. He was great again in 1960, making his second All-Star team while posting a 3.03 ERA and boasting the AL's top strikeout rate by a wide margin, but injuries limited Pascual to just 152 innings.

Tagged with the nickname "Little Potato" after his older brother, Carlos "Big Potato" Pascual, Camilo arrived in Minnesota along with the rest of the Senators when they became the Twins in 1961. He shook off prior arm problems to complete 15-of-33 starts while tossing 252 innings with a 3.46 ERA and AL-high 221 strikeouts. Unfortunately the Twins continued the Senators' tradition of awful play and Pascual went 15–16 despite leading the league with eight shutouts.

With a young core of 27-and-under players that included Harmon Killebrew, Bob Allison, Jim Kaat, Earl Battey, and Zoilo Versalles, the Twins emerged as a surprise contender in 1962 and finished second to the Yankees with a 91–71 record. Pascual was 28 by then, making him an elder-statesman among the team's big contributors, but led the charge by going 20–11 with a 3.32 ERA in 258 innings while pacing the AL in strikeouts, complete games, and shutouts.

As great as that performance was, Pascual was even better in 1963, going 21–9 with a 2.46 ERA in 248 innings while again leading the league in strikeouts and complete games. Thanks in large part to Pascual's second straight 20-win season—along with an MLB-best 225 homers from a scary lineup that had Killebrew, Allison, Battey, and Jimmie Hall all going deep 25-plus times—the Twins won 91 games for the second year in a row, this time finishing third in the AL.

Pascual and the Twins both declined in 1964, as the 30-year-old right-hander went 15–12 with a 3.30 ERA in 267 innings for a 79–83 team. The Twins came back stronger than ever in 1965, going 102–60 to capture the AL pennant, but Pascual wasn't as fortunate. After going 8–2 with a 3.06 ERA in a great first half, injuries limited Pascual to nine relatively ineffective second-half starts and he lost his World Series matchup with Claude Osteen of the Dodgers in Game 3.

A decade of buckling hitters' knees with his sweeping curveball had taken a toll on Pascual's right shoulder. He made 17 first-half starts in 1966, but posted a 5.07 ERA and then managed just 16 innings after the All-Star break. That winter the Twins sent Pascual and once-promising second baseman Bernie Allen to the *new* Senators for 35-year-old relief pitcher Ron Kline, who spent just one unremarkable season in Minnesota.

Pascual was no longer a durable, top-of-the-rotation workhorse able to rack up strikeouts, but he still had a little gas left in the tank for his return to Washington. He went 25–22 in 58 outings over the next

Ted Williams said that Camilo Pascual had "the most feared curveball in the American League."

two seasons, before getting off to a brutal start in 1969. Washington sent him to Cincinnati, where he gave up seven runs in seven innings before being released. Pascual bounced around after that, with brief stints as a reliever in Los Angeles and Cleveland.

His career fittingly ended with a strikeout, as Pascual got strike three past Earl Kirkpatrick in a scoreless ninth inning on May 5, 1971. That strikeout was the 2,167th of an 18-year career that saw him lead the league three times and finish second twice. Pascual possessed a good fastball, particularly in his prime, but it was his curveball that accounted for most of the whiffs. Tony Kubek, who struck out more against Pascual than any other pitcher, recalled facing him:

> He'd come straight over the top with it and it would just dive off the table. The spin was so tight, you couldn't identify the pitch until it was too late. It didn't flutter, it didn't hang, it just kept biting. When Pascual was right, nobody had a chance. That curve was unhittable.

Of course, when the curveball hung it also accounted for lots of homers. Pascual ranks 107th all time with 256 homers allowed—which is a huge total for someone who pitched most of his career in the pitcher-friendly 1960s—and he was among the AL's top 10 in homers allowed four times. Yankees superstar Mickey Mantle once said that Pascual and teammate Pedro Ramos "would laugh and rag each other about which gave up the longest home runs to me." Mantle went on:

> I hit two home runs into the tree beyond center field in old Griffith Stadium off Pascual, and Ramos is up waving a towel at Pascual while I'm rounding the bases. Later that year I hit one off the facade in Yankee Stadium off Ramos, and as I'm rounding third I see Pascual waving the towel at Ramos.

Although Pascual is often wrongly credited with being on the mound for it, Ramos served up what's generally considered one of the longest homers in baseball history against Mantle in 1956, the aforementioned shot that nearly exited Yankee Stadium. Mantle also smacked plenty of long bombs off Pascual, whom he took deep 11 times in total, but he viewed those homers differently: "I hit those off Camilo Pascual, one hell of a pitcher."

Pascual's career numbers are a mixed bag, with a 174–170 record and 3.63 ERA that was just slightly better than average in a pitcher-friendly era. However, he absorbed some beatings by debuting before he was likely ready, spent his first seven years pitching for horrible Senators teams, and then wound down his career away from Minnesota. In other words, his Twins-only career—which is what this book is all about—was far more impressive.

Pascual arrived in Minnesota with one of the greatest four-year runs in team history, winning 15, 20, 21, and 15 games while leading the league in strikeouts in the first three years and finishing second in the fourth. In six seasons with the Twins he made three All-Star teams, won 20 games twice, posted a 3.31 ERA in 1,284 innings, and went 88–57 for a .607 winning percentage that ranked as the best in team history until Johan Santana came around.

ROY SMALLEY

R oy Smalley was born into a baseball family. His father, Roy Smalley II, spent 11 years in the majors as a shortstop in the 1940s and 1950s, and his mother, Jolene Mauch, was the sister of longtime big-league manager Gene Mauch. And together they produced one hell of a player, as the younger Smalley starred on back-to-back national championship teams at USC and was drafted by four different MLB teams before finally signing with the Rangers as the No. 1 overall pick in 1974.

He skipped the low minors and jumped directly to Double-A as a 21-year-old, hitting .251 with 14 homers and 86 walks in 125 games. Smalley was called up to the majors a month into his second professional season and struggled, hitting .228 in 73 games for the Rangers, but the switch-hitting infielder hit .340 in 43 games at Triple-A that season and opened 1976 as Texas' starting second baseman. However, after a slow first two months the Rangers traded him to the Twins in a June 1 blockbuster.

Not many 23-year-old former No. 1 picks are traded just two years after being drafted, but the Rangers parted with Smalley—plus Mike Cubbage, Jim Gideon, Bill Singer, and $250,000 in cash—in order to get 25-year-old Twins ace Bert Blyleven, whose contract squabbles led to his exit from Minnesota. Blyleven went on to have a Hall of Fame career, but spent just one-and-a-half seasons with the Rangers and eventually returned to the Twins a decade after the trade.

Aside from the Hall of Fame part, Smalley had a

similar Twins career. He spent parts of seven seasons with the Twins, emerging as an All-Star shortstop before being traded to the Yankees in an April 1982 deal for Ron Davis, Paul Boris, and Greg Gagne, the latter of whom eventually replaced Smalley at shortstop. Then, after a few years with the Yankees and a half-season with the White Sox, Smalley was traded back to the Twins in February 1985 and finished his career in Minnesota.

Smalley's first go-around in Minnesota was without question his best, as he immediately took over as the starting shortstop in mid-1976 and hit .271/.353/.344 in 103 games for an 85-win team managed by his uncle, Gene Mauch. Shortstop was almost exclusively a defense-driven position in the 1970s, and Smalley's now-modest .697 OPS was actually 82 points above the American League average. He slumped back to the rest of the shortstop pack in 1977, hitting just .231/.316/.315 in 150 games.

Mauch stuck with his nephew and he responded with a big 1978, batting .273/.362/.433 with 19 homers, 53 total extra-base hits, and more walks (85) than strikeouts (70) in 158 games. Smalley's adjusted OPS+ of 122 led all MLB shortstops—with only Dave Concepción (114) and Robin Yount (110) also topping 100—and still stands as the best single-season mark by any shortstop in Twins history ahead of even Zoilo Versalles during his MVP-winning 1965 campaign.

It looked like Smalley was going to build on that great 1978 and take the next step to stardom in 1979 when he hit .341 with 15 homers, 65 RBIs, and a .959 OPS in the first half to make the All-Star team, but he slumped terribly in the second half, hitting just .185 to finish with a nearly identical-to-1978 overall line of .271/.353/.441. Despite the second-half fade he played all 162 games and led the league with 729 plate appearances, but Smalley's durable days were over.

He remained very productive during the next two seasons, hitting .274/.364/.415, but Smalley missed 29 games in 1980 and 53 games in the strike-shortened 1981 season because of back problems. Mauch was fired as manager in late 1980, and in 1981 owner Calvin Griffith publicly criticized Smalley for his alleged failure to treat the injury during the two-month strike. And four games into the 1982 season Smalley and his then-giant contract were traded to the Yankees.

Smalley split time between shortstop and third base in New York, forming quasi-platoons with Bucky Dent and one-time Twins prospect Graig Nettles while hitting .257/.346/.418 in 142 games. He was even better in 1983, hitting .275/.357/.452 in 130 games, but after a poor first half in 1984 the Yankees traded him to the White Sox for future Cy Young winner

TWINS' HIGHEST OPS IN GAMES STARTED AT SHORTSTOP

minimum 250 starts:

.744	Roy Smalley
.721	Leo Cardenas
.706	Jason Bartlett
.686	Zoilo Versalles
.686	Cristian Guzman

Doug Drabek. He hit .170 in 47 games for Chicago and that offseason Smalley was traded to Minnesota for the second time.

By that point Smalley was 32 years old and spent as much time at designated hitter as he did at shortstop, so there were no future Hall of Famers leaving Minnesota in the swap this time. In fact, neither player traded to the White Sox for Smalley played in the majors after the deal. And six months later the Twins re-acquired Blyleven from the Indians, teaming him with Smalley nine years after they were traded for one another.

Smalley still had plenty of gas left in the tank, at least offensively. He played some shortstop in 1985, but was primarily a DH while batting .258/.350/.419 in 382 games during the next three seasons. Those numbers may not seem like much from a DH by today's standards, but his .768 OPS was solidly above the 1985-1987 league average of .752 and Smalley's outstanding plate discipline remained a big asset as he drew 167 walks versus 197 strikeouts.

He went out on a high note, hitting .275/.352/.411 in 110 games as a part-time DH, occasional third baseman, and emergency shortstop in 1987, as the Twins won their first World Series. Smalley didn't play at all in the ALCS and was limited to pinch-hitting duties in the World Series as Randy Bush and late-season pickup Don Baylor split time at DH, but he made the most of a minor role by going 1-for-2 with a double and two walks against the Cardinals.

Smalley's career with the Twins is somewhat difficult to evaluate because he not only spent two multi-year stints with the team, they came a decade apart and he was a totally different player in each stint. In his twenties Smalley was a switch-hitting shortstop with great plate discipline and 20-homer power. In his thirties Smalley brought most of those same offensive skills to the table, except they came in the form of a slightly-above-average part-time designated hitter.

His final three years as a role player were valuable, and being on the World Series team in 1987 was no doubt the highlight of Smalley's career, but his strong standing in Twins history is largely due to the six-season run he had as their starting shortstop from 1976 to '81. During that time he hit .264/.350/.394 in 3,330 plate appearances, which was good for an adjusted OPS+ of 104. That led all MLB shortstops from 1976 to '81, followed by Garry Templeton (103), Dave Concepción (101), and Robin Yount (100).

During his first six-year stint with the Twins he was arguably the best-hitting shortstop in all of baseball, which is a remarkable feat that too often is overlooked because shortstops back then rarely put up the type of lofty raw numbers they do today. Not many players in Twins history can say they were the top hitter at their position for more than half a decade, and while his glove was never considered an asset, Smalley's all-around game makes him the best shortstop in Twins history.

GARY GAETTI

Selected by the Twins out of Northwest Missouri State University with the 11th overall pick in the 1979 draft, Gary Gaetti hit .257 with 14 homers and an .899 OPS in 66 games of rookie-ball after signing and then hit .266 with 22 homers, 24 steals, and an .820 OPS after moving up to Single-A in 1980. Gaetti made the leap to Double-A in 1981, hitting .277 with 30 homers and an .862 OPS in 137 games before the Twins called him up in late September.

Starting at third base and batting seventh against the Rangers on September 20, 1981, Gaetti blasted a homer off knuckleballer Charlie Hough in his first major-league at-bat. He then collected just four hits in his final 25 at-bats, but emerged from spring training the next season as the Opening Day third baseman on a 1982 team that also had a rookie at first base in Kent Hrbek and later included rookies Frank Viola, Tom Brunansky, and Tim Laudner in big roles.

The Metrodome opened on April 6, 1982, and "The Rat" christened it in style, going 4-for-4 with two homers and narrowly missing a third long ball off Mariners starter Floyd Bannister when he was thrown out at the plate trying to stretch a triple into an inside-the-parker. Gaetti never looked back after that, beginning his rookie year 10-for-17 with six extra-base hits while starting the first 13 games at third base, with former Rookie of the Year winner John Castino sliding over to second base.

Despite the fast start Gaetti hit just .230 with subpar plate discipline in 145 games as a rookie, leading to a ghastly .280 on-base percentage. However, he quickly established himself as an excellent defensive third baseman and his 25 homers immediately became the most ever by a Twins third baseman not named Harmon Killebrew. He put together a similar sophomore campaign, hitting .245 with a .309 OBP while smacking 21 homers, but fell off a cliff as a junior.

After more than 100 strikeouts in each of his first two seasons, Gaetti focused on making more contact at the plate in 1984. And he succeeded, whiffing just 81 times while upping his batting average to .262, but still posted a measly .312 OBP thanks to only 44 walks and saw his pop completely disappear. Despite playing all 162 games after hitting 46 homers during the previous two years, Gaetti went deep just five times in 588 at-bats for a lowly .350 slugging percentage.

At the time it would've been troubling to see a 25-year-old slugger's power vanish, but 1984 simply sticks out like a sore thumb in the context of his now-completed career. In fact, his 1985 season was nearly identical to his first two campaigns, as he hit .246 with a .301 OBP and 20 homers. At that point Gaetti was a 26-year-old with four seasons under his belt, three of them similar in their low-OBP, high-power skill set and one unique in its low-everything putridity.

What happened next is amazing, as seemingly out of nowhere he put together a three-year run that saw Gaetti become one of the best all-around third basemen in baseball. It started in 1986, with Gaetti batting .287 with 34 homers, 108 RBIs, and an .865 OPS while winning the first of four straight Gold Glove awards at third base. He followed that by hitting .257 with 31 homers and a .788 OPS for a 1987 team that shocked the baseball world by winning the World Series.

Not only did his 109 RBIs lead the team during the regular season, he homered in his first two playoff at-bats on the way to hitting .300 with a .650 slugging percentage against the Tigers to win the ALCS MVP. He slugged .519 versus the Cardinals in the World Series, homering in Game 2. He missed significant action in 1988 for the first time in his career, sitting out much of August with a knee injury, but he batted .301 with 28 homers and a .904 OPS in 133 games for his best season.

Sadly, like Cinderella's ride turning back into a pumpkin at midnight, Gaetti quickly ceased being an offensive force in 1989 and turned right back into the out-machine he'd been prior to 1986. In fact, his OBP became worse than ever because his plate discipline mysteriously went from bad to awful while he was trying on glass slippers. He batted just .251/.286/.404 in 1989 and .229/.274/.376 in 1990 before signing a four-year deal with the Angels as a free agent when the Twins made little effort to retain him.

Mike Pagliarulo and rookie Scott Leius replaced Gaetti at third base as a platoon, batting a combined .282/.342/.395 in 628 plate appearances while Gaetti hit just .246/.293/.379 in 634 trips to the plate for his new team. Along with the 50-point boost in OBP, the Pagliarulo-Leius duo cost less than a million bucks, compared to $2.7 million for Gaetti, giving the Twins money to sign free agents Chili Davis and Jack Morris on the way to their second World Series title.

Gaetti was a bust for the Angels, who released him in mid-1993. After latching on with the Royals he resurrected his career, smacking 35 homers in 1995. That earned him a multi-year deal from the Cardinals and he continued his resurgence with 23 homers in 1996. He dropped off in 1997, but then pulled his career out of the dumpster yet again in 1998, helping push the Sammy Sosa–led Cubs—and their front office boss, former Twins general manager Andy MacPhail—to the playoffs after being acquired in August.

Chicago handed Gaetti a starting job in 1999, but at age 40 the magic was finally gone. He hit .204 in 113 games, went 0-for-10 in an ugly stint with the Red Sox in 2000, and called it a career after 20 seasons. Bill James wrote in *The New Bill James Historical Baseball Abstract* that Gaetti is one of the few players in baseball history to avoid the traditional effects of aging, which tend to include a loss of speed, batting average, and defensive range, and an increase in plate discipline.

In ranking Gaetti the 34th-best third baseman ever, James noted how he bucked that trend completely, making up ground on superior third basemen who "all aged at a normal rate." He also wrote, "Gaetti is odd in two respects… His walk rate never improved at all, even an inch. Despite that, he aged at an exceptionally slow rate of speed…. There is no reason for a player like Gaetti to last until he is 40 years old, and not much precedent for it."

In other words, Gaetti was far from a Hall of Famer, but he's unique in that he never really got worse. Actually, that's not quite accurate. Gaetti did get worse, but he always got better again eventually. After two mediocre years to begin his career, he fell off a cliff and then inexplicably pumped out a great three-year stretch. Then he went back to being mediocre, falling into subpar territory while being released by the Angels, and again bounced back with the Cardinals and Cubs.

Taken as a whole, Gaetti's career isn't especially intriguing. He hit for a low average and didn't walk much, but he played great defense while staying very healthy, and hit a ton of bombs. What makes Gaetti's career so atypical and perhaps even downright fascinating is that there's seemingly neither rhyme nor reason to how the seasons were arranged. It's as if someone took 20 seasons, mixed them all together, randomly pulled them out one at a time, and arranged the new order into "Gary Gaetti."

Gaetti's place in Twins history varies wildly depending on how much of the focus is paid to his bad on-base skills or great defense. It's very difficult to be a great all-around player making an out 70 percent of the time, which Gaetti did in nearly all of his Twins seasons, but hitting 25 homers like clockwork helps and his defense was truly elite. Total Zone Rating pegs Gaetti as the eighth-best third baseman of all time, adding more than 130 runs above average with his glove. He was an out-machine on both sides of the ball.

Plus, he deserves some bonus points for that mustache.

24

COREY
KOSKIE

Corey Koskie was a star baseball, hockey, and volleyball player growing up in Manitoba, Canada and the Twins used their 26th-round pick in the 1994 draft to select him out of Kwantlen College in British Columbia. Koskie signed quickly and debuted at rookie-level Elizabethton as a 21-year-old but then spent one full year at each of low Single-A, high Single-A, Double-A, and Triple-A, failing to receive any midseason promotions despite consistently putting up excellent numbers.

After finally reaching Double-A as a 24-year-old in 1997, he hit .296 with 23 homers, 55 total extra-base hits, 90 walks, and a .939 OPS in 131 games to make the Eastern League All-Star team as the starting third baseman. He moved up to Triple-A in 1998, hitting .301 with 26 homers, 63 total extra-base hits, 51 walks, and a .904 OPS in 135 games before finally receiving his first in-season promotion in the form of a September call-up to Minnesota.

Frankie Rodriguez and Dan Serafini combined to give up 10 runs while recording six outs on September 9, so Koskie came off the bench to replace Ron Coomer at third base and struck out in both at-bats. Koskie saw his next action three days later, pinch-hitting for Chris Latham and singling to center field off Tim Worrell. He started seven of the final 15 games and didn't show much while going 4-for-29 (.138), but Koskie still broke camp with the Twins the next spring.

Koskie played sparingly through midseason, starting just 41 of the first 81 games in large part because manager Tom Kelly didn't think much of his defense at third base. Fewer than half of those starts came at third base and Koskie went six weeks without starting there as Coomer and Brent Gates manned the position. His sporadic starts came at designated hitter or in right field in place of an injured Matt Lawton, which allowed Koskie to at least show his bat was ready.

He hit .301 through 81 games as one of the few capable hitters on a team that was dead last offensively yet totaled just 189 plate appearances. By early July the Twins were 20 games out of the race, so Kelly decided to make Koskie the third baseman. He continued to sit against most lefties while starting 52 of the final 81 games, but more importantly each of the 52 starts came at third base. Koskie hit .310 with an .855 OPS overall to lead the Twins in batting average, on-base percentage, and slugging percentage as a rookie.

Looking back, it's amazing how quickly Koskie went from playing right field or DH to third base, because his defense wasn't considered strong enough to be an excellent defender there. Koskie never set foot in the outfield again and was the Opening Day third baseman in 2000, hitting .300 with an .841 OPS for an offense that was second-worst in the league. He joined Lawton and David Ortiz as the Twins' only above-average regulars and ranked fourth among AL third basemen in Wins Above Replacement.

After mastering third base defense and emerging as the Twins' top hitter Koskie moved on to developing his power. He homered once every 24 at-bats in the minors, including 20-homer seasons at both Double-A and Triple-A, and batted .298 with an .833 OPS through his first two full major-league seasons. However, he managed just 21 homers in 845 at-bats, including nine homers in 474 at-bats during his sophomore campaign.

That all changed in 2001 as Koskie put the finishing touches on his all-around game with the finest season of his career and the Twins had their first winning record since 1992. He batted .276 with 26 homers, 37 doubles, 103 RBIs, and an .850 OPS in 153 games and shockingly stole 27 bases at an 82-percent clip, trailing only Troy Glaus and Eric Chavez in Wins Above Replacement at third base. Along with Gary Gaetti in 1988, it's the top non–Harmon Killebrew year by a Twins third baseman.

Koskie's power dipped in 2002 and he missed time with a hamstring injury that proved to be a sign of things to come. Despite that, Koskie still managed to rank fourth among AL third basemen in WAR as the Twins won 94 games and the AL Central while advancing in the playoffs for the first time since 1991. A strained back limited him to 131 games in 2003 and the 20-homer power failed to resurface, but his AVG and OBP returned to their 2000–01 levels as he hit .292 and led the Twins in OPS.

Koskie turned 30 in mid-2003, but between a rapidly balding head and increasingly slow gait he had the look of an old man for whom doing nearly anything seemed to be a chore. He set a career-high with a .495 slugging percentage and smacked 25 homers in 2004, but saw his average dip to .251 while injuries sidelined him. Despite showing plenty of signs of wearing down, Koskie actually played his best down the stretch, slugging .607 from August 1 on as the Twins held off the White Sox and Royals to win the division.

He then came up big in the Twins' third straight trip to the postseason, batting .308 with a .474 on-base percentage in the ALDS while nearly becoming a hero against the Yankees. After winning Game 1 at Yankee Stadium behind Johan Santana's seven shutout innings, the Twins trailed 5–3 going into the eighth inning of Game 2. They rallied off Hall of Fame closer Mariano Rivera, cutting the lead to 5–4 and bringing Koskie up with runners on the corners and one out.

Luis Rivas pinch-ran for Justin Morneau, putting good speed on as the go-ahead run at first base, and Koskie slashed a Rivera fastball into the left field corner. Torii Hunter jogged home with the tying run and Rivas had a chance to claim a lead that could have put the Twins up 2–0 in the series heading back to Minnesota. Except the ball took a big bounce, hopping over the wall for a ground-rule double that kept Rivas locked at third base and the game tied at 5–5.

"They would have scored two, no doubt about it," Yankees catcher Jorge Posada said afterward. Instead, Rivas was stranded 90 feet from the plate and Alex Rodriguez's double scored Derek Jeter with the game-winning run in the 12th inning. Rather than Koskie's hit off Rivera putting the Yankees on the verge of elimination, one bounce wiped away his series-changing moment and the Twins lost back-to-back games at the Metrodome to end their season.

Koskie was an impending free agent, and that proved to be the final big hit of his career in Minnesota, as the Twins showed little interest in keeping him and he returned to Canada with the Blue Jays on a three-year, $16.5 million deal, thanking fans for their support with a full-page ad in the newspaper. After he missed 65 games with a broken thumb, the Blue Jays made Koskie available for pennies on the dollar and the Twins again passed despite a hole at third base they filled with Tony Batista.

Koskie ended up with the Brewers and got off to a strong start, hitting .261 with 12 homers, 23 doubles, and an .833 OPS through 76 games, but he suffered a concussion when he fell chasing a pop-up on July 5. Sadly, he never played again. Koskie was often criticized for his lack of durability, which is certainly fair to some extent and is part of his legacy given how things ended in Milwaukee. However, it's also likely overstated for his time in Minnesota.

He missed 44 games during his final season with the Twins, which was the lasting image that Koskie left fans with, but prior to that he had 550 plate appearances in four straight years and his 3,257 plate appearances rank 22nd in team history. Ignoring his rookie year, when Koskie was kept out of the lineup by a manager rather than by injuries, he averaged 138 games per season in Minnesota. For comparison, Torii Hunter averaged 141 games in seven years with the Twins after he became a full-time player.

Koskie led the Twins in WAR three times and ranked second twice before finishing third in his final year. During that time he consistently ranked among the AL's top half-dozen third basemen. He hit .280 with a .373 on-base percentage and .463 slugging percentage in Minnesota, which is good for a 115 adjusted OPS+ that ranks ninth among hitters with 3,000 plate appearances in a Twins uniform, ahead of some of the biggest names in team history.

A clubhouse favorite whose frequent pranks included filling an unsuspecting David Ortiz's underwear with peanut butter, Koskie spent part of his Twins career starring on horrible teams and then finished his time in Minnesota cultivating an "injury prone" label that he'll never shed. The end result is a career that goes down as one of the most underrated in team history and a player who should at the very least share the "best third baseman in Twins history" title with Gaetti.

Originally picked as a third baseman out of high school by the Cardinals in the 37th round of the 1980 draft, Rick Aguilera opted instead for college and became a pitcher. After three years at Brigham Young University, the California native was selected by the Mets in the third round of the 1983 draft and agreed to sign. Aguilera moved quickly through the minors, reporting to low Single-A after signing and finding himself at Triple-A to begin his third season.

After posting a 2.51 ERA in 11 starts at Triple-A the Mets called up Aguilera in June of 1985 and he was in the majors for good at age 24. He debuted as a reliever before moving into the rotation with a 3.35 ERA in 19 starts, but was overshadowed by 20-year-old Dwight Gooden, who followed up his Rookie of the Year award in 1984 with a Cy Young award in 1985. Also on that 1985 team was a 27-year-old utility infielder named Ron Gardenhire, who batted .179 in what would be his final big-league season.

Aguilera began 1986 alongside Gooden, Ron Darling, Sid Fernandez, and Bob Ojeda in the Mets' great young rotation, but was demoted to the bullpen and had to reclaim his rotation spot. He finished 10–7 with a 3.88 ERA in 142 innings for a 108-win team that ranks as one of the best in baseball history, spending the World Series run in the bullpen. Game 6 of the 1986 World Series is one of the most famous of all time, but few people recall Aguilera as the winning pitcher.

While the Twins were winning their own World Series in 1987, he blew out his elbow and missed most of 1988, coming back as a long reliever in 1989 after David Cone took his rotation spot. Aguilera was unhappy in a low-leverage relief role and asked to be traded, but before that could happen he thrived in the bullpen with a 2.34 ERA and 80 strikeouts in 69 innings through July. "The most amazing thing is that I'm actually learning to like being a reliever," Aguilera told *The Sporting News*.

Despite the change of heart, with the Mets clinging to contention and the Twins already out of it on the eve of the 1988 trade deadline, the teams completed a blockbuster swap. Frank Viola, the reigning Cy Young winner, went from Minnesota to New York for a five-player package of Aguilera, Kevin Tapani, David West, Tim Drummond, and Jack Savage. West was considered the premier prospect, but it turned out to be Tapani and Aguilera who made it one of the best trades in Twins history.

Aguilera got his wish by moving into the rotation following the deal, starting 11 games with a 3.21 ERA as Jeff Reardon had a third straight 30-save season as the Twins' closer. Those plans changed when Reardon left via free agency. Armed with a low-90s fastball, a hard-breaking slider, and a forkball that dropped off the table, Aguilera was the obvious choice to replace Reardon. "He's the most experienced we've got and the most capable strikeout pitcher," pitching coach Dick Such told the *Associated Press*. "He fits the bill."

When it became obvious during spring training that Aguilera would be taking over as closer he told reporters, "I was a little disappointed at first.... I was really excited about being able to start," but added, "I'll do it for the team." Things got off to a rough start when he blew his third save chance, serving up a walk-off three-run homer to Dante Bichette on April 14, but Aguilera recovered to convert 32-of-38 saves while posting a 2.76 ERA in 65 innings.

He made the first of three straight All-Star teams in 1991, tying Reardon's team record with 42 saves while posting a 2.35 ERA and 61/30 K/BB ratio in 69 innings as the Twins made their second World Series run in five seasons. A career .201 hitter with three homers in 139 at-bats, Aguilera became the first pitcher since Don Drysdale in 1965 to pinch-hit in the World Series when he flied out with two down and the bases loaded in the 12th inning of Game 3.

Moments later Aguilera took the Game 3 loss when Mark Lemke hit a walk-off single, but that was the lone postseason run he allowed while saving five of the Twins' eight playoff wins. He followed up the marvelous 1991 by ranking second in the league with 41 saves in 1992, and then saved 57 of the team's 124 wins between 1993 and 1994. When baseball returned in mid-1995 after the strike Aguilera was an impending free agent and the highest-paid pitcher on MLB's worst team.

He posted a 2.52 ERA in 25 innings through early July, saving 12 games despite the team's 19–44 start. On July 6, with Aguilera on the verge of becoming a 10-and-5 player who could veto any trades, the Twins sent him to the Red Sox for Frankie Rodriguez, a 22-year-old right-hander *Baseball America* ranked as the No. 36 prospect in baseball. Rodriguez proved to be a bust, going 25-32 with a 5.20 ERA in 509 innings during four seasons in Minnesota.

Aguilera notched his first Red Sox save the next day, against the Twins, at the Metrodome. He converted 20-of-21 saves to help the Red Sox win the AL East, but saw his only playoff action in Game 1 of the ALDS, serving up a game-tying homer to Albert Belle as a 100-win Indians team blitzed through on the way to the World Series. That offseason Aguilera returned to Minnesota as a free agent on a multi-year deal with a lower annual salary than he made the previous year.

Unsatisfied with the shaky rotation led by 23-year-olds Rodriguez and Brad Radke, manager Tom Kelly made Aguilera a starter again. Kelly had every reason to worry, as Twins starters combined for a 5.48 ERA, but changing Aguilera's role at age 34 proved to be a mistake. An arm injury allegedly suffered while lifting a suitcase limited Aguilera to one start in the first 60 games and he had a 5.42 ERA before a hamstring injury ended his season in early September.

Aguilera moved back to the bullpen and saved 64 games for a pair of sub-.500 teams during the next two seasons, but blew 18 saves and saw his ERA rise to 4.00. He began 1999 pitching as well as ever at 37, with a 1.27 ERA in 21 innings, but the Twins were once again the AL's worst team and he got just eight save chances through 40 games. He was traded to the Cubs on May 21 for minor-league pitchers Kyle Lohse and Jason Ryan. Ryan was a bust, but Lohse became a solid starter before wearing out his welcome.

Gone for good this time, Aguilera had 37 saves and a 4.31 ERA in two seasons with the Cubs to finish his 16-year career. Aguilera became the Twins' all-time saves leader when he notched No. 109 in 1992, but 20 years later Joe Nathan surpassed his total of 254. Aguilera blew at least a half-dozen saves in each of his seven full seasons as the Twins' closer and converted 82 percent of his saves in Minnesota, which is mediocre by modern standards. By comparison, Nathan converted 90 percent of his saves with the Twins.

However, it's important to note Kelly used Aguilera much differently than Gardenhire used Nathan. Nathan inherited a grand total of 63 baserunners in seven seasons with the Twins, which works out to one per eight innings. Aguilera inherited 38 baserunners in his first year as closer alone, and then 37 and 40 more in the next two years. In all, Aguilera inherited 207 runners during his time in Minnesota, which works out to one every three relief innings.

The vast majority of Nathan's saves involved starting an inning with a clean slate, but Aguilera often saved games he entered with runners on base. That goes a long way toward explaining his seemingly mediocre save percentage and Aguilera also deserves credit for stranding more than three-fourths of the baserunners he inherited. For a guy who never wanted to be a reliever, his 318 career saves ranked eighth in baseball history at the time of his retirement.

GAME 6 OF 1987 WORLD SERIES

With their season hanging in the balance after three straight losses in St. Louis, the Twins returned home for a must-win Game 6 of the World Series at the Metrodome, where they were an MLB-best 56–25 during the regular season and 4–0 in the playoffs. In the opening segment of ABC's broadcast, announcer Tim McCarver noted the Homer Hanky-waving crowd's power. "I can't really think of a team since the 1961 Yankees who have more of a home-field advantage than the Minnesota Twins." He was right.

Throughout the playoffs Twins manager Tom Kelly did everything he could to negate the team's weak rotation depth, turning to his only reliable veteran starters, Frank Viola and Bert Blyleven, whenever possible even on short rest. However, for Game 6 he ran out of ways to avoid going deeper into the rotation and Les Straker, a 28-year-old rookie who'd finally reached the majors after 10 seasons in the minors for three different teams, got the call. Kelly assured everyone that Straker's leash should and would be short. He was right.

With left-hander John Tudor starting for the Cardinals, the Twins stacked the lineup with eight right-handed bats and one left-handed hitter, Kent Hrbek. He'd struggled all season versus lefties, hitting .225, and went 0-for-4 in Tudor's previous start. Kelly dropped Hrbek down in the lineup for Game 6 but didn't bench him, believing Hrbek's game-changing power—he led the Twins with 34 homers and a .934 OPS in the regular season—would find a way to make a difference even with unfavorable matchups. He was right.

With slugging first baseman Jack Clark injured, the nine hitters in the Cardinals' lineup combined for just 38 homers in the regular season. By comparison, Hrbek, Gary Gaetti, Tom Brunansky, and Kirby Puckett each topped 25 homers for the Twins. Tommy Herr, batting third in the Cardinals' lineup, homered twice in 598 plate appearances, but when Straker hung him a slider in the first inning, the switch-hitting second baseman crushed it into the upper deck for a 1–0 lead.

In the bottom of the first inning the Twins answered right back, as Dan Gladden led off with an excuse-me double squibbed down the first base line and Kirby Puckett knocked him in with a line drive on the first pitch he saw. Puckett came around to score via Don Baylor's opposite-field single on a high fastball and the Twins led 2–1. And then things began to unravel, as the Cardinals tied the game at 2–2 in the second inning thanks partly to second baseman Steve Lombardozzi misplaying a potential double play grounder.

Hrbek led off the bottom of the second inning with a long fly ball into the gap in right-center field. Right fielder Curt Ford, who'd already had some issues in the first inning, seemed to lose sight of the ball for a moment, so center fielder Willie McGee came charging over to make the catch…and dropped it. Hrbek was running at less than full speed and made it only to second base, where he was promptly picked off by Tudor. Back-to-back singles followed, but the Twins failed to score in what could have been a big inning.

Straker ran into trouble in the fourth frame, as Clark fill-in Dan Driessen banged a double off the right field baggy and McGee singled, taking third base when Puckett airmailed the cutoff man. With the bullpen stirring, Terry Pendleton hit a chopper to first base and beat Straker to the bag, scoring Driessen. That was it for Straker, who compounded his shaky pitching by not hustling to cover first base. Kelly brought in left-hander Dan Schatzeder, a 32-year-old veteran who was acquired from the Phillies in June.

Two batters later Jose Oquendo put the Cardinals up 4–2 with a sacrifice fly. Schatzeder remained in the game for the fifth inning, giving up another run that began with an Ozzie Smith walk and ended with a McGee single. Cardinals manager Whitey Herzog unloaded nearly his entire clip by that point, pinch-hitting for his starting right fielder and starting first baseman on the way to taking a 5–2 lead. It was unnervingly quiet in the Metrodome as Tudor took the mound for the bottom of the fifth inning, but that changed in a hurry.

Puckett lined a leadoff single to center field and Gaetti golfed a double into the left field corner, making it 5–3. Suddenly it was St. Louis' bullpen stirring, but Herzog stuck with Tudor against designated hitter Don Baylor. Once an MVP slugger, the 38-year-old was on his last legs and failed to homer for the Twins after they got him from the Red Sox on September 1. He'd homered 331 times before, though, and when Tudor hung a first-pitch changeup Baylor deposited it into the left field seats for a two-run, game-tying bomb.

The notion of quiet no longer existed inside the Metrodome, but the Twins weren't done yet. Herzog left Tudor in for one more batter, Tom Brunansky, who singled for the fourth hit in the span of six total pitches. On came left-hander Ricky Horton, who recorded two outs and then allowed a line-drive single to Lombardozzi that scored Brunansky with the go-ahead run. With a 6-5 lead, Kelly was finished messing around and summoned setup man Juan Berenguer from the bullpen for a 1-2-3 top of the sixth inning.

Greg Gagne, who'd made a great defensive play at shortstop the previous half-inning, led off with a chopper off the plate to his Hall of Fame counterpart and for once The Wizard couldn't make the impossible play. Right-hander Bob Forsch replaced Horton and walked Puckett. Both runners advanced on a passed ball, Gaetti popped out, and Herzog ordered Baylor intentionally walked to load the bases. Brunansky popped up the first pitch. With two outs and the bases loaded in the sixth inning of a 6–5 game, up stepped Hrbek.

And in came lefty Ken Dayley, who'd started warming up four batters earlier just in case Hrbek batted in a key spot—or *the* key spot. Hrbek was 0-for-16 off lefties in the playoffs after hitting .225 against them in the regular season, and Dayley hadn't allowed a homer to a left-handed hitter all season. Herzog got exactly the matchup he wanted. But on the first pitch Hrbek finally got the fastball *he* wanted and absolutely unloaded on it, sending a grand slam over the 408-foot sign in center field. Game over. Bring on Game 7.

CESAR
TOVAR

Cesar Tovar signed with the Cincinnati Reds out of Caracas, Venezuela, as an 18-year-old in the winter of 1959 and batted .304, .338, and .328 in his first three pro seasons. He moved up to Triple-A in 1963 and hit .297 with 115 runs scored while showing good speed and excellent gap power, but he was blocked from moving up in Cincinnati by the likes of Pete Rose and Vada Pinson. He remained at Triple-A in 1964 and slumped, hitting .275 with a .379 slugging percentage.

In December of 1964, with a young nucleus of hitters already in place from a 92-win season, Cincinnati shipped Tovar to Minnesota in exchange for 23-year-old left-hander Gerry Arrigo. It was an oft-debated deal at the time, because parting with young southpaws has never been viewed in a positive light and Arrigo was coming off a rookie season that saw him go 7–4 with a 3.84 ERA and 96 strikeouts in 105 innings split between the rotation and bullpen.

With incumbent second baseman Bernie Allen struggling to bounce back after knee problems ended his 1964 season, Tovar was given a long look in spring training and headed north with the team, making the Opening Day roster as a reserve. Tovar saw just 13 at-bats in a month with the Twins and was sent back down to Triple-A in mid-May, where he batted .328 with a .523 slugging percentage in 102 games before returning to the big leagues in September.

Tovar didn't see any postseason action as the Twins won the American League pennant with a 102–60 record before falling to the

Dodgers in the World Series. In fact, hours after Sandy Koufax struck out Bob Allison to end the 1965 season, the *New York Times* reported that Twins owner/general manager Calvin Griffith was "not satisfied with their top second base candidates" and "would be active in the trading market...seeking a second baseman."

Talking to the *Los Angeles Times* early that spring, manager Sam Mele called second base "my only infield problem," and an article in the *Chicago Tribune* two weeks later suggested that the position was a three-way battle for Allen, Frank Quilici, and Jerry Kindall. Meanwhile, Tovar was seeing some work at second base, but also played the other infield spots and center field, where he was viewed as a potential platoon partner for the lefty-hitting Jimmie Hall.

Sure enough, Allen began the 1966 season as the starting second baseman and Tovar didn't find his way into the lineup anywhere for three weeks, finally starting both games of a Sunday doubleheader in center field on May 1. Allen's poor play and health issues eventually opened the door for Tovar to see significant action at second base and he ended up starting 73 games there despite not getting his first chance at the position until late June.

In addition to starting 73 times at second base, Tovar also saw 27 starts at shortstop and 16 starts in center field, combining to hit a modest .260 with 16 steals and a .660 OPS in 527 trips to the plate. When the Twins traded Hall to the Angels that winter Tovar was needed more as a center fielder in 1967, starting 60 times there, but also started 56 times at third base and 31 times at second base, while seeing occasional action at shortstop and in the outfield corners.

While most fans have come to think of a "utility man" as someone like Denny Hocking or Nick Punto—a capable backup at multiple spots—Tovar was more like an everyday player who just didn't know where he was going to play on a given day. Tovar batted just .267 with a .690 OPS in 1967, but ranked among the AL's top five in at-bats (649), runs scored (98), hits (173), doubles (32), and triples (7) while grabbing headlines for his finish in the MVP voting.

Tovar finished a surprising seventh in the balloting, ahead of stars like Tony Oliva and Frank Robinson, but more importantly he received the lone first-place vote that eluded Triple Crown winner Carl

Yastrzemski of the Red Sox, keeping him from being a unanimous winner. After initially remaining anonymous despite media scrutiny, Max Nichols of the *Minneapolis Star* was revealed as the guilty party. Not only wasn't Tovar even in the same ballpark as Yastrzemski in 1967, in hindsight it ended up being one of Tovar's worst seasons.

With offense insanely low in 1968 before the mound was lowered the next year, Tovar batted .272 with a .698 OPS while ranking among the AL's top five in hits, runs scored, steals, and doubles. He also made his mark as the second player in MLB history to play an inning at all nine positions in one game. Tovar was the starting pitcher in a 2–1 win over the A's on September 22, striking out Reggie Jackson and moving around the diamond for this box score line/scoring nightmare: *Tovar p, c, 1b, 2b, ss, 3b, lf, cf, rf*

He was even better in 1969, hitting .288 with 45 steals—including back-to-back steals of home with Rod Carew on May 18—and then hit .300/.356/.442 with 120 runs scored in 1970. Even those career-best numbers seem unspectacular by today's standards, but like other raw stats from the 1960s and '70s, context is key. Not only did he lead the league in doubles while ranking among the top 10 in runs scored, hits, and total bases, Tovar did so in a horrible hitting environment.

In other words, not all .300/.356/.442 lines are created equal. Tovar played for the Twins from 1965 to 1972, and during that time the AL as a whole batted .255/.327/.382. Had he instead played for the Twins from, say, 1995 to 2002, the AL as a whole would have hit .271/.341/.432 for a difference in overall production of about 10 percent. If you adjust his 1965–72 numbers to the 1995–2002 offensive levels, what you get instead is a .310 hitter with an .800 OPS, including a high OPS of .850 in 1970.

Suddenly that 1970 campaign is a monster season and Tovar is a perennial .300 hitter. His era-adjusted numbers also show a textbook aging curve in that he started slowly at age 25, peaked from 27–29, and gradually declined into his early 30s. Interestingly, as Tovar improved offensively, he also stopped moving around the diamond so much defensively. Tovar was primarily an outfielder by 1970, starting 125 games in center field and another 21 in left field compared to a total of just 10 starts as an infielder.

After hitting poorly as the primary right fielder on a 77-win team in 1972, the Twins traded Tovar to the Phillies for Joe Lis, Ken Sanders, and Ken Reynolds that offseason. Just as Arrigo never amounted to much after going to Cincinnati in exchange for Tovar back in 1964, none of those three provided much value to the Twins. Tovar hit .268 with a .692 OPS in Philadelphia, splitting time at third base with a struggling 23-year-old rookie named Mike Schmidt.

Tovar was one of the first *super* utility men, a manager's dream who could be plugged into the lineup anywhere while hitting for a good average, controlling the strike zone, and stealing bases. It's hard to accurately quantify that type of high-level versatility, even if everyone knows the value exists beyond the standard stats. And those standard stats were still damn good, as Tovar ranks among the Twins' all-time top 10 in steals, hits, and runs scored.

EARL BATTEY

Signed by the White Sox in 1953 out of a Los Angeles high school, Earl Battey made his MLB debut in 1955 at age 20. He collected a pair of hits in a five-game cup of coffee, but didn't see his first extended action in the big leagues until 1957. Battey then spent the next three seasons serving as Sherm Lollar's backup in Chicago, playing sparingly behind the seven-time All-Star while batting just .209 in 413 total plate appearances.

In the last of those three seasons backing up Lollar, a 24-year-old Battey lost playing time to another 24-year-old catcher, rookie Johnny Romano. Romano hit .294/.407/.468 in 53 games to overtake Battey for the second spot on the depth chart during Chicago's run to the World Series. Meanwhile, the 34-year-old Lollar was showing no signs of slowing down, turning in his second straight 20-homer, 80-RBI season while batting .265 with a .796 OPS in 140 games.

Lollar had been one of the Amerian League's best catchers for a decade, so the White Sox decided to stick with him. That offseason, owner Bill Veeck dealt Romano and 24-year-old first baseman Norm Cash to the Indians for a four-player package that included Minnie Minoso. Then two weeks before Opening Day the White Sox sent Battey and 22-year-old first baseman Don Mincher, plus $150,000 in cash, to the Washington Senators for Roy Sievers.

The trades paid immediate dividends, as both the 33-year-old Minoso and 34-year-old Sievers gave Chicago two strong seasons before leaving, but the moves were long-term disasters for the White Sox. Cash batted .361 with 41 homers and 132 RBIs for Detroit in 1961 and went on to make five All-Star teams. While not quite the hitter that Cash became, Mincher made two All-Star teams and hit .249/.348/.450 with 200 homers for his career.

Romano, who went on to make a pair of All-Star teams while batting .255/.354/.443 during his 10-year career, immediately took over as the Indians' starting catcher, hitting .272/.349/.475 in 1960 while the

35-year-old Lollar hit just .252/.326/.356 for the White Sox. Similarly, 1960 also saw Battey become an instant starter for the Senators, winning the AL Gold Glove award while batting .270/.346/.406 with 15 homers during the team's final season in Washington.

They moved to Minnesota and became the Twins in 1961, and Harmon Killebrew starred by hitting .288/.405/.606 with 46 homers and 122 RBIs. While he was putting together the first of what would be seven 40-homer seasons, Battey was establishing himself as one of the premier all-around catchers. Battey, now 26, won his second straight Gold Glove award and hit .302/.377/.470 with 17 homers while starting 127 games and catching more than 1,100 innings.

Battey declined in 1962, hitting .280/.348/.393, but won his third consecutive Gold Glove and made the first of four All-Star teams. He bounced back to have the best season of his career in 1963, hitting .285/.369/.476 with 26 homers while catching a league-leading 1,237 innings in a league-high 142 starts and finishing seventh in the MVP voting. Yankees catcher Elston Howard won the MVP, but Battey produced similar numbers—.285 with an .845 OPS, compared to .287 with an .870 OPS—while batting 55 more times in 12 more games.

Battey declined in 1964, hitting a still-solid .272/.348/.407, but bounced back in 1965 to finish 10th in the MVP voting. Twins teammates Zoilo Versalles and Tony Oliva finished one-two in the balloting and pitcher Mudcat Grant placed sixth, with Battey hitting .297/.375/.409 as the team won 102 games and the AL crown before falling to the Dodgers in the World Series. He caught all seven games despite running neck-first into a railing chasing a foul ball in Game 3.

Despite being just 30 years old, 1965 proved to be Battey's final great season as weight problems, injuries, and big workloads caught up to him. He hit .255/.337/.327 in 1966 but split time with Russ Nixon and Jerry Zimmerman in 1967, batting .165. After retiring he worked with inner-city kids in New York before going to college at age 45, graduating Summa Cum Laude. He then became a high school teacher and coach in Florida before dying from cancer in 2003.

Battey's relatively brief career ended shortly after his 30th birthday. One of his best years came in Washington for the Senators, yet for four decades he ranked as the best catcher in Twins history. His raw offensive numbers during seven seasons in Minnesota (.278 AVG, .356 OBP, .409 SLG, 76 homers) look solid and the multiple Gold Glove awards tell the story of his defensive reputation, but without a closer look at Battey's career it's easy to undersell his impact.

His entire career was spent in one of the lowest-scoring eras ever and he played a position that was the most physically demanding and often home to no-hit defensive specialists. Battey was a stud on both sides of the ball, logging a huge number of innings, frequently catching one of the league's best pitching staffs, throwing out a high percentage of steal attempts, and putting up numbers offensively that were far more impressive than they initially appear.

For instance, when Battey hit .285/.369/.476 with 26 homers in 1963, the AL as a whole hit just .247/.312/.380. Go forward 40 or 50 years and Battey's line in 1963 was the same as hitting around .310 with a .925 OPS, and he would have cleared 30 homers with ease. As it stands, he ranked among the AL's top five catchers in Wins Above Replacement in each of his six full seasons with the Twins. Overall from 1961 to '65, only Elston Howard and Joe Torre topped Battey in WAR for catchers.

Battey was never especially mobile to begin with and became perhaps MLB's slowest player once age, the rigors of five straight 1,000-inning seasons defensively, and excess weight from a goiter problem sapped him of whatever limited quickness he once had. Despite that, Battey never lost his amazing arm and remained the league's best-throwing catcher throughout his career. Battey allowed just 226 stolen bases in more than 6,700 innings at catcher for the Twins.

Allowing one steal for every 30 innings during the run-heavy 1960s is amazing enough, but he also gunned down nearly 40 percent of steal attempts. Teams rarely tested him despite the huge steal totals being posted throughout baseball, yet Battey still managed a league-leading caught-stealing total three times. He also led the league in pickoffs four times, including 15 in 1962. That season Battey allowed 34 steals and picked off or threw out 42 runners.

29

SHANE
MACK

When asked about a college freshman named Shane Mack by a *Los Angeles Times* reporter in 1982, UCLA coach Gary Adams looked right into his crystal ball and didn't pull any punches:

> I really believe that Shane Mack is going to be one of the greatest UCLA players of all time. He reminds me so much of Jackie Robinson, but his fire is inside, not outside like Jackie. He's not flashy like Jackie was. He just does the job and produces. I've never had such a quick learner. He realizes his shortcomings and that's why they don't last very long. You make the most of what you have, and he does. He has everything, all the tools. I'll tell you something, Shane isn't going to be just a major leaguer, but a super major leaguer.

Adams was right. After hitting .306 as a freshman, Mack emerged as one of the elite players in all of college baseball, hitting a conference-best .419 as a sophomore and then batting .352 as a junior. Mack was a first-team All-American in both seasons, and leading up to the 1984 draft there was heavy debate over whether Mack or USC slugger Mark McGwire should be the first player chosen.

An article in the *Los Angeles Times* on June 4, 1984 carried the headline MACK OR MCGWIRE COULD BE CHOSEN NO. 1, and quoted Dodgers scouting director Ben Wade as saying, "You've got two of the best in the country over at USC and UCLA." The next day the newspaper described Mack as "the finest all-around player in college baseball" and declared he was "at or near the top of virtually every major-league club's scouting list."

On draft day the Mets surprised everyone by taking high school outfielder Shawn Abner with the first selection, which turned out horribly. McGwire dropped to the A's with the 10th pick, while the

Padres were thrilled when Mack fell into their lap 11th overall. After playing for the United States' silver-medal-winning team in the 1984 summer Olympics, Mack bypassed his final year of eligibility and began his professional career in 1985.

Mack spent the bulk of his first two years at Double-A. He moved up to Triple-A late in 1986, hitting .362 in 19 games at hitter-friendly Las Vegas. Mack stayed there in 1987 and hit .333 with five homers while going 13-for-13 stealing bases in 39 games when a torn biceps tendon forced veteran first baseman Steve Garvey to the disabled list and San Diego called up Mack. He stayed with the Padres all season and received regular playing time against left-handed pitching, hitting just .239 in 105 games.

Mack began 1988 back at Triple-A and spent the year shuttling between San Diego and Las Vegas. He hit just .244 in 56 games with the Padres, but tore up the Pacific Coast League with a .347 average and 10 homers in 55 games. Mack was back at Triple-A again in 1989 when an elbow injury ended his season after 24 games. That winter the Padres left the 26-year-old Mack off their 40-man roster and the Twins snatched him up in the Rule 5 draft.

Mack made the Opening Day roster in 1990 but played sparingly early on. In mid-July, with Mack hitting over .300 and the Twins playing under .500, manager Tom Kelly finally gave him a shot. Splitting time between all three outfield spots, Mack responded by hitting .306 in July before slumping in August, and then finished the year by batting .432 with 17 RBIs and six steals in September. Overall he hit .326/.392/.460 with eight homers, 13 steals, 44 RBIs, and 50 runs in 353 plate appearances.

Kelly was still hesitant to make Mack an everyday player in 1991, but he started 61 times alongside Kirby Puckett in right field while also getting 16 starts subbing for Puckett in center field and 38 starts playing left field in place of Dan Gladden. Mack had a huge year, hitting .310/.363/.529 in 143 games to rank among the AL's top 10 in slugging percentage and OPS. Thanks in large part to Mack, the Twins went from worst to first, winning the AL West with a 95–67 record after finishing dead last the previous year.

Mack hit .333 with three RBIs and four runs in the five-game ALCS win over Toronto, but then went 0-for-15 with seven strikeouts in the first four games of the World Series against Atlanta. After pulling Mack in a Game 3 double-switch—leading to closer Rick Aguilera pinch-hitting in the 12th inning—Kelly gave designated hitter Chili Davis the Game 5 start in right field. Back home and playing under AL rules, Mack returned to the lineup for Game 6 and went 2-for-4 with a first-inning RBI single.

For the first time in his career Mack was given a chance to be a true everyday player in 1992. Starting 150 games and playing primarily left field, Mack hit .315/.394/.467 with 16 homers and 26 steals to rank among the AL's top 10 in batting average, on-base percentage, and runs. He fell to .276/.335/.412 in 1993 and missed the first month of 1994 with shoulder problems, but bounced back to hit .333/.402/.564 to rank among the AL leaders in average and slugging percentage.

An impending free agent when the strike ended the 1994 season, Mack took a guaranteed payday in Japan once the work stoppage dragged into the offseason. In January of 1995 he signed the biggest contract in the history of Japanese baseball—a two-year deal with the Yomiuri Giants worth $8.1 million American. In retrospect it's natural to question his decision, but Mack was already 31 when he became a free agent for the first time, the strike continued into 1995, and that was incredible money for a non-superstar back then.

It's easy for Mack to get lost in the long shadows of Puckett, Chuck Knoblauch, Kent Hrbek, and the rest of the 1991 lineup, but for five years he was one of the best, most underrated players in baseball. A great athlete who covered tons of ground wherever the Twins put him, Mack hit for big averages with plus speed and had overlooked power. Among all MLB outfielders to play at least 500 games from 1990-94, only Barry Bonds, Ken Griffey Jr., Rickey Henderson, and David Justice had a better OPS.

30

DAVE
GOLTZ

Pelican Rapids born and Rothsay raised, Dave Goltz was a 1967 fifth-round pick who became the first native Minnesotan drafted by the Twins to reach the majors with them. After going 38–18 with a 2.69 ERA in 460 minor-league innings, Goltz made his major-league debut on July 18, 1972, tossing 3.2 scoreless innings in relief of Ray Corbin against the Yankees. He soon moved into the starting rotation and posted a 2.67 ERA in 91 innings as a 23-year-old rookie.

Goltz began his second season pitching out of the bullpen before sliding back into the rotation late in the year, finishing with a disappointing 5.25 ERA in 106 total innings. Following the poor sophomore performance, Goltz was demoted to the minors in 1974 but was quickly called back up after going 3–1 with a 3.30 ERA in four starts at Triple-A. Goltz joined the rotation full time at that point, going 10–10 with a 3.25 ERA in 174 innings.

In his fourth season, Goltz established himself as a durable innings eater, logging 243 innings while going 14–14 with a 3.67 ERA. He turned in a nearly identical year in 1976, going 14–14 with a 3.36 ERA in 249 innings to become the only pitcher in MLB history with double-digit wins and an exactly .500 record in three straight seasons (10–10, 14–14, 14–14). More statistical oddity than anything else, the streak nonetheless snapped in a big way the next season.

Known for being a slow starter, Goltz had a 4–16 career record in March and April, compared to 109–91 in all other months. That trend was never more evident than in 1977, when he was 0–2 in five April starts and 20–9 with a 3.30 ERA for the remainder of the year. He was remarkably consistent once on track, winning four games in each of the first four months and three games in September before grabbing his 20th with a complete-game victory on October 2.

Goltz completed 19 of his 39 starts in 1977, including one-hitting Boston on August 23, and he tossed 303 innings to rank second in the league behind only Orioles ace Jim Palmer. He tied Palmer and Dennis Leonard for the league lead with 20 wins, but finished just sixth in the Cy Young voting thanks to his eighth-ranked ERA (3.36) and modest strikeout total (186). A 6′4″ right-hander with a heavy sinker-slider combo, Goltz relied more on inducing ground balls than missing bats.

He managed just 887 strikeouts in 1,638 innings with the Twins for basically a league-average rate, but Goltz did a fantastic job keeping the ball on the ground and in the ballpark. In fact, when compared to the average rates, no pitcher in Twins history allowed home runs less often than Goltz, who served up 119 in total or one per 14 innings. For comparison Camilo Pascual, another outstanding Twins starting pitcher, coughed up 123 homers in nearly 400 fewer innings.

When Goltz threw 303 innings in 1977—a total that's been topped just twice in team history—29 different big-league pitchers served up more long balls. Goltz was even better at suppressing homers in 1978, giving up one every 18 innings, but he got off to another slow start and then fractured his ribs during an on-field scuffle in an April 22 game with the Angels in which he didn't even pitch. Goltz started just once in May, but went 14–7 with a 2.27 ERA after returning in June.

With free agency looming following the 1979 season, Goltz got the Opening Day assignment for the third straight year. He beat the A's, throwing the first 8.1 of what would be 251 innings that ranked seventh in the league. However, he allowed a league-high 282 hits on the way to a 14–13 record and 4.16 ERA. He then left the Twins by agreeing to a free agent deal with the Dodgers that was worth a then-substantial $3 million over six seasons.

Goltz uncharacteristically got off to a good start in Los Angeles, hurling back-to-back shutouts of the rival Giants in April 1980, but then he fell apart. He finished 7–11 with a 4.31 ERA overall, went 2–7 with a 4.09 ERA while being yanked from the rotation in 1981, and was cut a month into 1982. Goltz signed with the Angels and pitched relatively well as a long reliever, but shut it down for good with a torn rotator cuff after beginning the next year 0–6 with a 6.22 ERA.

Goltz's lack of strikeouts meant he wasn't flashy—he had just one truly Cy Young-caliber year, and the Twins hovered within five games of .500 in all but one of his eight years in Minnesota. All of that's why he's seemingly an overlooked part of team history and why you'd stump a lot of fans asking them for the pitcher who ranks sixth in Twins history in wins, innings, and starts.

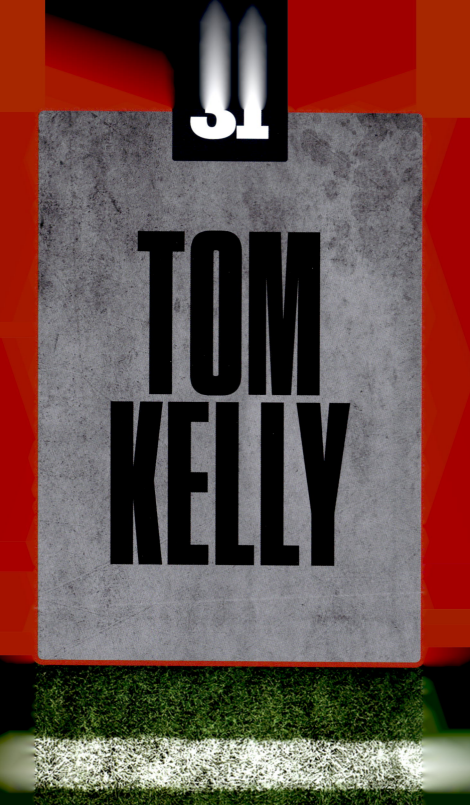

Tom Kelly was born in Graceville, Minnesota, and raised in New Jersey, getting drafted in the eighth round by the Seattle Pilots expansion team in 1968. Kelly played first base and the outfield, hitting well in rookie-ball after signing, but then struggled at Single-A and Double-A. He was released after three years and signed with the Twins as a minor-league free agent, reporting to Double-A in 1971. Kelly lacked power, but he controlled the strike zone well and hit .294 with a .413 on-base percentage in 100 games.

Kelly moved up to Triple-A in 1972 and hit .280 with 10 home runs and 70 walks in 132 games for Tacoma, where he stayed for four years. He wasn't really a prospect, but Kelly was a solid minor leaguer who topped an .800 OPS each season from 1971 to '77, usually with .400 on-base percentages and more walks than strikeouts. In the middle of Kelly's fourth Triple-A season, the Twins called him up to replace Craig Kusick at first base. He batted .181 in 49 games and was sent back down. And that was it for his big-league career.

Kelly spent another three seasons at Triple-A, including a stint as player/manager, before starting his full-time managing career at Single-A. He was 28 years old and managing a roster that included one 27-year-old, two 26-year-olds, and three 25-year-olds, which speaks to just how much Kelly struck everyone as manager material from Day 1. He was promoted to the Twins' staff as the third base coach in 1983, working under Billy Gardner and then Ray Miller.

Late in the 1986 season, with the Twins in the American League cellar, general manager Andy MacPhail fired Miller and named Kelly the interim manager. Kelly was just 35, but his age and inexperience certainly wasn't going to bother the 33-year-old MacPhail. Seen as a player's manager, the hope was that Kelly could relate to the young roster, several of whom he coached in the minors. Minnesota went 12–11 down the stretch, but owner Carl Pohlad reportedly wanted to hire former Cubs manager Jim Frey for the full-time job.

MacPhail pushed for Kelly, in part because he believed in him and in part because hiring the veteran Frey likely would have meant ceding some decision-making power. Kelly got the job, but only a one-year contract. Suffice it to say that his job security was quite a bit stronger by the time that year was up. Not viewed as contenders coming into the year and out-scored during the regular season, the Twins won 85 games and the AL West title, clinching the division with a week to spare.

They beat the 98-win Tigers in the ALCS and the 95-win Cardinals in the World Series while the baseball world kept wondering how Kelly's squad was winning. There was a secret sauce, sure, but it was clear that he'd drilled the young team on fundamentals and playing hard every day after no winning seasons in seven years. "We wanted to make the players, when they left the clubhouse, have a good attitude about coming back the next day.... [so] that they wanted to put the uniform on," Kelly told the *Minneapolis Star Tribune*.

Just as MacPhail suspected, Kelly was a player's manager who hit the right notes with a group that grew up together. "He was so excited to see a guy tag up on a fly ball or break up a double play or just play right," Kirby Puckett said of Kelly's approach to managing. "He didn't ask for nothing that you couldn't give. He just tried to get the best out of every individual in their own way. He didn't put everybody in the same category because I'm different than Hrbek and Hrbek is different than Gaetti."

Kelly and the Twins improved by six games in 1988 but missed the playoffs, followed by back-to-back losing seasons in 1989 and 1990. By the time 1991 rolled around, MacPhail had rebuilt nearly the entire roster in an effort to bring in young talent and new veterans, with only seven players left from 1987. Kelly worked his magic on the new group, with key holdovers like Puckett and Kent Hrbek, and the Twins went from worst to first by winning 95 games and the AL West. He was named Manager of the Year.

No longer the underdogs, the Twins had baseball's second-best record and out-scored their opponents by 124 runs. They blitzed through the 91-win Blue Jays in the ALCS, winning 4–1, and then outlasted the 94-win Braves in Game 7 of arguably the greatest World

Series of all time. Kelly was 40 years old with two championships and a career .528 winning percentage, including a 16–8 mark in the playoffs, yet he remained in the dugout during each celebration and never failed to deflect any credit aimed his way.

"My players make me look smart or stupid," Kelly told *Sports Illustrated*. "I just try not to screw things up. You've got to have the horses to go to the post." Kelly's old-school approach included throwing daily batting practice, which he loved almost as much as he hated talking to the media. "I have enough common sense to realize I'm not intelligent," he claimed. "I realize that if I keep talking, I'll eventually say something dumb. So I don't give myself a lot of opportunities to open my mouth and stick my foot in it."

Kelly's various quirks became somewhat less charming as the team fell from contention. They won 90 games but missed the playoffs in 1992, and then the magic vanished as the pipeline of young talent dried up and key veteran contributors began to retire or move on to other teams. MacPhail even left following the 1994 season, taking a higher-profile, larger-payroll job running the Cubs' front office. Kelly and the Twins had a losing record every season from 1993 to 2000, the last four of which were 90-loss campaigns.

Only a manager who wins two World Series in his first five full seasons could possibly keep the job amid eight straight losing years. While Kelly certainly received his fair share of criticism, particularly when it came to his handling of young players once he was no longer their contemporary, there was also an understanding that the payroll shrinking made it difficult to put a team on the field capable of winning consistently. Considering the talent Kelly had to work with, who could truly tell if he was doing a bad job?

As the calls for a new voice grew louder, the Twins' latest young roster came together for a breakout 2001 season, jumping out to a shocking division lead before fading down the stretch. They finished in second place at 85–77—the same record they had in Kelly's first full season as manager in 1987. Building blocks were in place with Torii Hunter, Jacque Jones, Brad Radke, Corey Koskie, Eric Milton, A.J. Pierzynski, and Cristian Guzman, plus Johan Santana and Michael Cuddyer getting their feet wet.

Kelly was still relatively young at 51, and the team seemed set up for a prolonged run of contention. He voluntarily stepped down as manager five days after the season came to a close, ending what was the longest tenure by any manager or head coach in American pro sports at 15 years. At the press conference Kelly indicated that he considered retiring one year earlier, but he "wanted to do it for one more year" after he "heard more than once that some people had thought the game had passed me by."

Pohlad had offered him a new contract, for the length of his choosing, but Kelly knew he'd had enough, citing burnout as a reason for his decision. "It was a lot of hard work, but I believe we've found the right combination of people," he said of the Twins' future. "I believe the ball club is now set and ready to go in the right direction." He was right, as the Twins won the AL Central in 2002—under rookie manager Ron Gardenhire, the third base coach on Kelly's staff—and a total of six division titles in the next nine seasons.

In the years that followed, Kelly's name occasionally popped up in managerial rumors, but he never expressed any interest in returning to the dugout, staying true to what he said the day he stepped down in Minnesota: "If I was going to do that again, I would just stay here. I'm going to try to manage my bank account and golf score." Kelly called it a career with a 1,140-1,244 (.478) record in 15-plus seasons, which can be broken down into six years of winning followed by eight years of losing and then an 85-win sendoff.

The extreme nature of Kelly's career makes evaluating his overall track record difficult. He won two World Series in his first five seasons and had a .530 winning percentage in his first seven years. And then he went eight straight seasons without a winning record, often ranking as one of the very worst teams while clashing with high-profile youngsters like David Ortiz and Todd Walker. Did he lose the magic or did the Twins' iffy decision-making and lack of spending make it nearly impossible for him to work that magic?

It's obvious what Kelly would say, because he said it often. "My players make me look smart or stupid."

32

ZOILO VERSALLES

Washington signed 18-year-old Zoilo Versalles out of Havana, Cuba in 1958 and rushed him to the big leagues nearly five months before his 20th birthday. Versalles debuted on August 1, 1959, starting at shortstop against the White Sox and going 0-for-4 with three strikeouts and an error as the Senators' leadoff man. He saw limited action down the stretch in 1958, hitting .153 in 59 at-bats spread over 29 games, and then batted .133 in 45 at-bats the next season.

Versalles arrived in Minnesota along with the rest of the team when the Senators became the Twins in 1961 and immediately stepped in as the starting shortstop, notching two hits and two steals in a 6–0 win over the Yankees on Opening Day. Despite being a 21-year-old rookie with 104 career at-bats, Versalles started each of the first 15 games and went on to hit .280/.314/.390 in 129 games for a Twins team that finished near the bottom of the league with a 70–90 record.

At first glance a .704 OPS doesn't look like much, but all shortstops combined for a .682 OPS in 1961, meaning Versalles' bat was above average for his position as a 21-year-old rookie. And much like his first full year, Versalles' entire career can be better appreciated by placing his raw numbers within the context of both the era in which he played and the position he manned. Rarely did Versalles post raw numbers that would turn heads today, but for a shortstop in the pitcher-friendly 1960s, he was an excellent hitter.

He never topped the .280 batting average from 1961 and hit above .260 just twice more, but

One of the most unlikely MVPs in sports history, Zoilo Versalles was the AL winner the same year that Willie Mays won NL honors.

he made up for it by adding significant power. After going deep just seven times in 510 at-bats as a rookie, he homered 17 times in 1962 to kick off a four-season stretch with double-digit long balls. From 1961 to '65 he led all shortstops with 73 homers. Contrary to the past two decades or so, the shortstop position back then was simply not played by guys capable of hitting the ball out of the park.

All of which is what made the two-year run Versalles put together starting in 1964 so impressive. Playing in 320-of-324 games, the man they called "Zorro" hit .266 with a .447 slugging percentage, 39 homers, 22 triples, 78 doubles, 41 steals, 141 RBIs, and 220 runs scored. During that two-year span Versalles ranked second among all MLB hitters in doubles and runs, eighth in extra-base hits, and 10th in steals and total bases. That kind of offensive production was largely unheard of from a shortstop at that time.

If you adjust Versalles' raw 1964–65 totals to fit the recent offensive environment, he comes out batting .280-.300 with a slugging percentage well over .500—a true slugging shortstop like, say, Troy Tulowitzki or Miguel Tejada. The second of those two seasons was Versalles' finest and one of the most memorable years in Twins history. After finishing 79–83 in 1964, the Twins waltzed through the AL in 1965, posting a 102–60 record that still stands as the team's all-time best.

Versalles was the shortstop and leadoff man in 155 of the 162 games, hitting .273 with 19 homers, 27 steals, and a .781 OPS while winning a Gold Glove and leading the league in runs scored, doubles, extra-base hits, and total bases. He was particularly outstanding in the second half, batting .303/.349/.500 after the All-Star break, including .353 in August and .337 in September as the Twins put away the White Sox and Orioles to take the AL pennant.

And while most of the Twins' hitters flailed away at Sandy Koufax and the Dodgers in a World Series loss, Versalles put the finishing touches on his great season by batting .283 with three extra-base hits, three runs scored, and four RBIs in seven games. Versalles blew away the competition in the AL MVP voting by receiving 19-of-20 first-place votes, with the lone dissenter casting a ballot for Twins teammate Tony Oliva, who finished a distant second.

MVP WINNERS
IN TWINS HISTORY

Zoilo Versalles	1965
Harmon Killebrew	1969
Rod Carew	1977
Justin Morneau	2006
Joe Mauer	2009

Decades later it became popular to use Versalles' MVP as a way to identify and attack perceived flaws within sabermetrics, the thinking seemingly being that because his raw stats weren't jaw-dropping in 1965, most "stat-heads" probably believe Versalles receiving the award was some sort of travesty brought about by the unenlightened. If you're a Twins fan harboring resentment toward stats-based analysis, it's tempting to set up that argument. "Versalles was great in 1965, but those dorks with their calculators don't think so!"

The premise that those who scrutinize numbers don't view Versalles' season as special is flawed because of a failure to realize that any stat-head worth a damn looks past raw stats. Versalles' stats aren't eye-popping at first glance, but the goal of sabermetrics is to place stats like that in proper context. Depending on circumstances, that means looking beyond oft-quoted numbers like batting averages and RBIs, adjusting for era and offensive environment, and making additional positional adjustments.

Wins Above Replacement, the most common advanced metric for evaluating a player's all-around contributions, pegged Versalles as the American League's best player in 1965. In fact, his total of 7.2 WAR that season also would have led the league in 1962, 1959, 1952, 1950, and...well, you get the idea. He was a Gold Glove–winning, power-hitting shortstop who played every day. WAR is designed to fully appreciate exactly that type of player.

Deserving or not, Versalles followed his MVP season with two ugly years, hitting .249/.307/.346 in 1966 and .200/.249/.282 in 1967 as back problems plagued him. No amount of contextual adjustments make those hitting lines pretty, and in November of 1967 the Twins sent Versalles and Mudcat Grant to the Dodgers for Johnny Roseboro, Bob Miller, and Ron Perranoski. Grant still had some strong years left in his arm, but Versalles was done as an effective player.

He batted .196 in 122 games as the Dodgers' starting shortstop in 1968 and was left unprotected in the expansion draft that winter, going to the upstart San Diego Padres. Traded to the Indians a month later, Versalles batted .226 in 72 games as a utility man before being let go, and ended the season with a stint back in Washington for the new Senators. He spent 1970 in the Mexican League before signing with the Braves in 1971, batting .191 in his final season.

Versalles went from a 25-year-old MVP to losing a fight against the Mendoza Line within two years and never recovered, which perhaps fuels some of the perception that he wasn't a deserving MVP. His career was among the worst ever for an MVP winner and his decline was sudden, but none of that takes away from the quality of a brief peak that ended in 1965 with one of the greatest years in Twins history, for one of the greatest teams in Twins history.

KEVIN TAPANI

Kevin Tapani played 13 seasons in the big leagues, winning 143 games and earning around $35 million, yet his entire baseball career almost never was. In an interview with his alma mater, Central Michigan University, here's how Tapani described the odd set of circumstances that led to his playing college baseball:

> I just signed up for school at CMU and had planned on being an ordinary student. When I went to orientation, I found out that Dan McReynolds was the Dodger scout in the Midwest and he told me they were going to hold a tryout camp. While at the Dodger camp, Coach Keilitz was sitting in the stands and he came down to me and said, "I see that you're enrolled here. Would you be interested in coming out for the team?"
>
> I said, "Yeah, that would be great." So, school started and by the time I got here, I had missed the first week of fall ball. I was sitting in my dorm room and coach called and asked if I were still interested in coming out for the team. I told him I sure was and when the season [started], I would be there. Coach then told me the season had already started. So, he said if I wanted to do it, show up the next day. I went out and ended up making the team in the fall.

Not only did Tapani go from being an un-recruited, last-minute walk-on to being the team's ace, after four years at CMU he was selected by the A's in the second round of the 1986 draft (two picks after the Twins took Oklahoma State right-hander Jeff Bronkey, who won two games in the majors). Tapani went 6–1 with a 2.48 ERA in 11 starts at Single-A in his pro debut and then went 10–7 with a 3.76 ERA in 24 starts at Single-A in his second year.

In December of 1987, he was part of a massive three-team trade involving the A's, Dodgers, and Mets that saw Bob Welch, Alfredo

Griffin, Jay Howell, and Jesse Orosco each change teams. Tapani went from Oakland to New York in the deal, joining an organization that had a big-league starting rotation packed with young, established pitchers in Dwight Gooden, David Cone, Ron Darling, and Sid Fernandez.

With so many young starters ahead of Tapani, the Mets moved him to the bullpen and sent him to the minors until calling him up in 1989. Tapani debuted on the Fourth of July with four innings of relief after starter Bob Ojeda was knocked out in the first inning. Tapani appeared in two more games over the next two weeks, both as a reliever. Then on July 31 he was traded again, this time going to Minnesota along with Rick Aguilera, David West, Tim Drummond, and Jack Savage for Frank Viola.

It was very controversial at the time because Viola was the reigning Cy Young award winner thanks to a 24–7 record in 1988, and he was instrumental to the Twins' championship in 1987. Viola had a 3.31 ERA for the Mets. Despite his post-trade success, however, the swap is one of the best in Twins history. West, Drummond, and Savage never amounted to much in Minnesota, but Tapani and Aguilera became outstanding pitchers and key members of the staff that helped lead the Twins to another World Series title in 1991.

After acquiring Tapani from the Mets, the Twins sent him back to Triple-A, where he had a 2.20 ERA in six starts. He was recalled when rosters expanded in September and made five starts down the stretch, winning his first two games in a Twins uniform and posting a 3.86 ERA. With his days in the minors over, Tapani began 1990 in the rotation and made 28 starts, going 12-8 with a 4.07 ERA while leading a 74–88, last-place team in wins and strikeouts.

It all came together for the Twins and Tapani in 1991, as he won 16 games with a 2.99 ERA in 244 innings to rank among the league's top 10 in all three categories, finishing seventh in the Cy Young balloting. The amazing thing is that Tapani went 0–6 with a 5.35 ERA in May, which means over the rest of the season he went 16–3 with a 2.54 ERA before surprisingly struggling in the postseason by going 1–2 with a 6.11 ERA in four starts.

He did come up big against Tom Glavine in Game 2 of the World Series, holding Atlanta to two runs over eight innings before turning things over to Aguilera for the save. Tapani was never again as good as he was in 1991, but during the next three seasons he was a dependable innings eater who twice ranked among the league's top 10 in wins. Tapani went 39–33 with a 4.31 ERA over the three-year span, leading the Twins in wins each year.

He had a .541 winning percentage from 1992 to '94, whereas the Twins won at a .479 clip when Tapani didn't figure in the decision. After the strike was settled in 1995 he started badly, going 6–11 with a 4.92 ERA. At the July 31 trade deadline, with the Twins holding MLB's worst record at 30–56 and Tapani just months from free agency, they shipped him and reliever Mark Guthrie to the Dodgers for Ron Coomer, Greg Hansell, Jose Parra, and Chris Latham.

In contrast to snagging both Tapani and Aguilera in the four-player haul for Viola, only Coomer provided any sort of usefulness to the Twins from the Tapani haul. The deal was a bust for Los Angeles too, as Tapani struggled in a half-season with the Dodgers and then inked a one-year contract with the White Sox that winter, going 13–10 with a 4.59 ERA in 1996. He stayed in Chicago for the final five seasons of his career, going 51–50 with a 4.66 ERA for the Cubs.

Tapani is an underrated figure in Twins history because, unlike many of the team's top pitchers, his best years came in a hitter-friendly era. That hurts his raw totals, especially compared to pitchers from the low-offense 1960s and 1970s, but his 75–63 record with the Twins was very good considering how awful some of the teams he played on were. He was incredibly durable, his peak season is among the best in team history, and his 4.06 ERA was better than it looks.

BRIAN DOZIER

Brian Dozier "ruined" what had been one of the more startling leaderboards in Minnesota Twins history. For more than 40 years, the Twins' single-season home run leaders looked like this:

49	Harmon Killebrew	1969
49	Harmon Killebrew	1964
48	Harmon Killebrew	1962
46	Harmon Killebrew	1961
45	Harmon Killebrew	1965
44	Harmon Killebrew	1967
41	Harmon Killebrew	1970
39	Harmon Killebrew	1966

And then Dozier's monster second half in 2016 happened, and now there's this:

42	Brian Dozier	2016

Much like the rest of his career, nothing about Dozier's leaderboard-joining 2016 season went as expected. He struggled down the stretch in 2015 and got off to a poor start in 2016. At that point, Dozier had hit just .205 with a .282 on-base percentage and .354 slugging percentage in the span of 11 months and 127 games from July 1, 2015 to May 31, 2016. Dozier was a replacement-level player for nearly an entire calendar year. And then, starting on June 1, 2016, he went on a power binge the likes of which have rarely been seen from middle infielders in baseball history.

Dozier hit .294/.358/.631 with 37 homers in 109 games from June 1 through the end of the 2016 season, finishing with 42 home runs. Not only did that break up Killebrew's monopoly on the Twins' leaderboard, it set the all-time American League record for homers by a second baseman and was one short of setting the all-time MLB mark. His 37 home runs *after* June 1 would have ranked fourth all time for AL second basemen. He did in four months what only Robinson Cano and Alfonso Soriano have ever done in a full season.

Dozier is one of the unlikeliest sluggers ever, a marginal prospect who showed little power in the minors, didn't reach the big leagues until age 25, and struggled offensively and defensively once he got there. Five years later he rewrote the AL record books and nearly hit as many homers in one season (42) as any previous second baseman had totaled in his entire Twins career (44, by Rod Carew). And his power was hardly a one-year wonder. Dozier hit more home runs than any MLB second baseman from 2013 to 2017. It's what happened before 2013 that made it so unlikely.

Dozier was the Twins' eighth-round pick in the 2009 draft after a college career at Mississippi State that saw the 5′10″ shortstop hit just four homers as a senior and a total of 16 homers in four seasons. He was a "senior sign" and agreed to a $30,000 bonus that was $120,000 less than the player picked before him and $75,000 less than the player picked after him. "More of a solid college shortstop than a big pro prospect" is how *Baseball America*'s pre-draft scouting report described him. And that's exactly what he looked like early on.

Dozier spent his first full season split between low Single-A and high Single-A, hitting .275 with five homers in 127 games. He controlled the strike zone well just as he had in college, with more walks (60) than strikeouts (57), but had a punchless .349 slugging percentage facing low-minors pitchers as a 23-year-old with tons of college experience. Dozier repeated high Single-A the next year, a sure sign that the Twins viewed him more as organizational depth or, if things went well, a light-hitting utility infielder.

Dozier beat up on the younger competition in his second go-around in Fort Myers, hitting .322, but managed just two homers in 49 games before a promotion to Double-A. He continued to hit well there, and even showed a little pop for the first time with seven home runs in 78 games, but then stumbled out of the gates the next year in his first taste of Triple-A. He was hitting .232 with two homers in 48 games when the Twins surprisingly summoned Dozier to the majors to replace 38-year-old Jamey Carroll at shortstop in mid-2012.

It went poorly. Dozier played shortstop nearly every day for three months, but his range and arm strength were both revealed as lacking for the position and he hit just .234/.271/.332 in 82 games before being demoted back to Triple-A and replaced by Pedro Florimon in August. In the spring of 2013 the Twins shifted Dozier from shortstop to second base and gave him the Opening Day job, but it was a similar story. He looked more at home defensively, but hit .223/.278/.314 with three homers through mid-June.

At that point, Dozier was a 26-year-old second baseman with a .409 slugging percentage in the minors and a .325 slugging percentage in the majors, including a grand total of just 25 homers in nearly 2,200 plate appearances as a pro. There was absolutely nothing about his skill set, physical size, or track record to even hint at what came next: Dozier started hitting for power, essentially overnight. He homered four times in a five-game stretch, nearly equally his career total of five homers through 102 games. And then he was rolling.

Dozier hit 15 home runs, plus another 29 doubles, in 93 games from mid-June through the end of the 2013 season. No second baseman in Twins history had ever topped 14 homers in any season. From there, Dozier morphed fully from high-average, low-power utility infielder to low-average, walk-drawing, hard-swinging slugger, hitting .242 with 23 homers, 89 walks, and 129 strikeouts in 156 games the next year. He took that approach to yet another level in 2015, hitting .256 with 19 homers in the first half to make his first All-Star team. And then—*poof!*—it was gone.

He hit .210 with a .359 slugging percentage in the second half and then began 2016 by hitting .202 with a .329 slugging percentage in April and May. One explanation offered at the time was that Dozier's transformation into a dead-pull slugger who feasted on high fastballs only worked until pitchers made adjustments, with a theory being that Dozier was unable or unwilling to make adjustments of his own. He was moved to the bottom of the batting order and even benched for a few games, but Dozier remained confident in the face of increasing criticism.

"The results will come," Dozier told the *Minneapolis Star Tribune* near the end of May. "It's not about shooting singles the other way. It's a lot more than that, so I've got to make adjustments." And he was right, the results did come. In one of the more remarkable in-season turnarounds in Twins history, Dozier's slugger switch flipped back on as soon as the calendar flipped to June. During the final four months of the season, Dozier led the league in slugging percentage (.631) and hit 37 homers while no other hitter in baseball had more than 33.

Many people couldn't resist the temptation to assume that Dozier had listened to all of the critics and dramatically changed his all-or-nothing, swing-hard-in-case-you-hit-it approach. He hadn't. All but two of the 37 homers were pulled, and his pull rate during those four magical months was MLB's second-highest and well beyond his career norms. If anything, he'd thrived by being even more pull-heavy and taking even bigger, more upper-cut, worse-intentioned hacks at high fastballs and hanging breaking balls.

Dozier got off to a slow start in 2017—although nowhere near as slow as 2016—and once again heated up in June and July. He couldn't quite match his record-breaking homer total, but Dozier topped 30 homers for the second straight season and did so while ranking among the five most pull-heavy hitters in the league. In addition to crashing Killebrew's leaderboard party, he created his own list to dominate. Here's the Twins' single-season leaderboard for home runs by a second baseman:

42	Brian Dozier	2016
34	Brian Dozier	2017
28	Brian Dozier	2015
23	Brian Dozier	2014
18	Brian Dozier	2013

Dozier is literally the only slugging second baseman in the history of the Twins, and one of the team's best sluggers, regardless of position. Prior to Dozier, no Twins hitter other than Killebrew had ever surpassed 35 homers, and in the decades between Twins hitters doing it hitters on other teams did so 385 different times. Not bad for a former eighth-round pick who signed for $30,000 and was stuck repeating Single-A at age 24. And not bad for a player who rejected the Twins' half-century fetishizing of opposite-field hitting to forge his own path to power.

1965 TEAM

he first great season in Twins history was 1965 and, if not for Sandy Koufax's record-breaking, era-defining otherworldliness, the 1965 club might be remembered as the best in team history. It was the only Twins team to win 100 games, going 102–60—including 51–30 at home and on the road—to capture the American League pennant going away over the White Sox and Orioles in a season that saw Metropolitan Stadium host the All-Star game and lead the AL in attendance. In short, Minnesota was the center of the 1965 baseball universe.

Five seasons after the former Senators' arrival from Washington, the Twins were a well-established offensive powerhouse, leading the league in homers and runs scored in 1963 and 1964. They boasted unmatched right-handed slugging in Harmon Killebrew and Bob Allison, balanced nicely by lefty thumpers Tony Oliva, Jimmie Hall, and Don Mincher. And yet it was shortstop Zoilo Versalles who stepped forward to win MVP of the league in 1965, receiving all but one first-place vote.

Minnesota led the league in offense for a third straight season in 1965, scoring 774 runs to top second-place Detroit by nearly 100. However, that wasn't much different than their 737 runs in 1963 or 767 runs in 1964. Everyone knew they could hit. What changed from 1964 to 1965 that propelled the Twins from 79–83 to 102–60 was pitching, as the rotation foursome of veterans Mudcat Grant, Jim Kaat, Jim Perry, and Camilo Pascual combined for 127 starts with a .682 winning percentage and 3.03 ERA.

Grant won a league-leading 21 games and threw 270 innings with a 3.30 ERA, including a league-high six shutouts. Kaat led the league with 42 starts and threw 267 innings with a 2.83 ERA and 18 wins. Pascual was limited to 27 starts by an injury, but went 9–3 with a 3.35 ERA in 156 innings. Perry, who spent most of the previous season in the bullpen after coming over from Cleveland in a trade, joined the rotation in July with a complete-game shutout and posted a 2.45 ERA in 17 starts down the stretch.

Minnesota had a high-powered lineup and a deep, standout rotation. And thanks to shrewd scrap-heap pickups the previous season, they also had a dominant late-inning bullpen duo. Al Worthington and Johnny Klippstein were journeymen in their late 30s who'd bounced around from team to team before they landed with the Twins as low-wattage acquisitions. And then in 1965 the 36-year-old Worthington emerged as an elite closer, with 10 wins, 21 saves, and a 2.13 ERA. Klippstein, at 37, went 9–3 with a 2.37 ERA as his setup man.

Eight different pitchers threw 75 or more innings for the Twins in 1965—the four veteran starters and the bullpen duo, plus swingman rookies Dave Boswell and Jim Merritt—and all of them posted an ERA of 3.40 or better. Owner/general manager Calvin Griffith assembled a roster with high-end talent and quality depth, giving manager Sam Mele the personnel to withstand Killebrew's dislocated left elbow and Pascual's arm surgery that knocked both stars out for one-third of the season.

They sent six players to the All-Star game at Metropolitan Stadium, with Killebrew and Gold Glove–winning catcher Earl Battey starting for the American League and Versalles, Hall, Oliva, and Grant appearing as reserves. Killebrew blasted a two-run homer off Reds ace Jim Maloney. At the break, the Twins held a five-game lead and pulled further away with an AL-best 49–31 record in the second half. Playing in their former home against the new Senators in Washington, they clinched the AL pennant on September 26.

And then they ran into the Los Angeles Dodgers and, more specifically, the best pitching staff in baseball led by one of the greatest pitchers of all time at his absolute peak. Walter Alston's club hadn't dominated the NL quite as much as the Twins had on the AL side in the regular season, going 97–65 to narrowly edge the rival Giants. Their lineup hit fewer homers all season (78) than the Twins hit in the first half (91), but the Dodgers' pitching was unreal. Minnesota's staff was damn good and Los Angeles allowed *80 fewer runs*.

Koufax won his fourth straight ERA title, going 26–8 with a 2.04 ERA while completing 27-of-41 starts and racking up an unfathomable 382 strikeouts in 336 innings. He received every first-place vote for the MLB-wide Cy Young in the final year before the award was split between the leagues, and was a close runner-up for MVP behind a 50-homer season by Willie Mays. Don Drysdale and Claude Osteen, working in Koufax's shadow, combined for 38 wins and a 2.78 ERA in 595 innings. Their team ERA, in 1,500 innings, was 2.81.

Koufax would be forced into retirement by an arthritic left elbow one year later, but the Dodgers rode him like few other pitchers in baseball history down the stretch and in the World Series. He started three of the seven games *after* stepping aside for Game 1 at Met Stadium due to the Jewish holiday Yom Kippur. Drysdale started instead and the Twins got to him for seven early runs—including homers by Versalles and Mincher—as Grant allowed two runs in a complete-game victory.

Game 2 saw Koufax make a rare start on full rest. He matched zeroes with Kaat for five innings, but the Twins broke through for two runs in the sixth inning with the help of Jim Gilliam's error at third base. They added three more runs off relief ace Ron Perranoski—who years later became the Twins' closer—and Kaat tossed a complete game aided in a big way by Bob Allison's sliding catch in left field. Minnesota had won both games at home, beating Drysdale and Koufax to take a 2–0 lead to Los Angeles.

They would score just two total runs in three games at Dodger Stadium, as Osteen hurled a shutout in Game 3 and Koufax whiffed 10 in a four-hit shutout in Game 5. In between, Grant struggled in a Game 4 defeat to Drysdale. Momentum had shifted to the Dodgers, who held a 3–2 series lead going back to Minnesota. Grant kept the Twins' season alive in Game 6 by throwing a complete game, allowing just one run despite pitching on two days' rest.

It all came down to a Game 2 and Game 5 rematch between star left-handers Koufax and Kaat, who split their first matchups to a draw. Kaat, working on two days' rest, was lifted after giving up two runs in the fourth inning. Worthington, Klippstein, Merritt, and Perry combined for six shutout innings of relief, but it was too late. Koufax was never going to give up one run, let alone three. He tossed his second straight complete-game shutout of the powerful Twins lineup, again striking out 10 and allowing just three hits.

There's no shame in losing to Koufax, who had a 0.38 ERA in the World Series and a 0.92 ERA in his last 10 starts dating back to the regular season. As a team—from top to bottom, up and down the roster—the Twins were perhaps better than the Dodgers, but no one was better than Koufax and no team was beating them the way he pitched in Game 5 and Game 7. Decades later the Twins won two World Series behind Frank Viola and Jack Morris in Game 7, but the best team in Twins history couldn't slay the dragon in 1965.

30

TOM BRUNANSKY

Taken by the Angels with the 14th overall pick in the 1978 draft out of a California high school, Tom Brunansky held out while he debated accepting a scholarship to play football at Stanford University. According to a July 6, 1978 article in the *Los Angeles Times*, here's how Brunansky ultimately settled on baseball:

> Brunansky was invited to the Angels–Kansas City game June 26 where [owner] Gene Autry was waiting to meet him. Autry told Brunansky he wanted him to meet a special friend, who turned out to be [Richard] Nixon, an Angel fan who was making a rare appearance at a game. Brunansky said that Nixon told him that he would enjoy himself tremendously playing baseball and would be fortunate to join an organization headed by as fine a man as Autry.
>
> The introduction to the club owner and the former president made a lasting impression, but Brunansky went ahead with plans to spend the rest of that week at Stanford getting oriented to the football program. When he returned, the Angels were ready with a new offer. After four hours of discussion at the Brunansky home, a contract was signed.

Persuaded by Richard Nixon to bypass football, Brunansky hit .332 in rookie-ball after signing and then had three straight 20-homer seasons in the minors—one each at Single-A, Double-A, and Triple-A— all before his 21st birthday. The last of the three came after Brunansky began the 1982 season with the Angels, hit .152 in 11 games, and was quickly sent back down to beat up on minor-league pitching for a bit longer. He did just that, hitting .332 with 22 homers and 81 RBIs in 96 games at Triple-A.

Brunansky began the 1982 season back at Triple-A and was hitting just .205 with one homer when he was traded to Minnesota in mid-

May, along with Mike Walters and a bunch of cash, for Doug Corbett and Rob Wilfong. He was immediately handed an everyday job in the majors by the Twins and turned in a fantastic rookie season, hitting .272/.377/.471 with 20 homers, 30 doubles, and 71 walks in 127 games while splitting time between right field and center field.

MOST HOMERS IN TWINS HISTORY THROUGH AGE 26

162	Tom Brunansky
117	Kent Hrbek
110	Justin Morneau
94	Harmon Killebrew
80	Zoilo Versalles

Despite that strong production, Brunansky was somewhat overlooked because the Twins also broke in fellow power-hitting rookies Kent Hrbek (23 homers) and Gary Gaetti (25 homers) that same year. Frank Viola and Randy Bush were also rookies on that same 1982 squad, and the core of a championship team was quietly being built despite a 60–102 record. Brunansky was the youngest player on the roster.

A walks-and-power hitter before that was appreciated as much as it is today, Brunansky was an underrated player because it was easy to get caught up in his low batting averages. He never batted above .260 for the Twins after his rookie year, but he blasted at least 20 homers in each of his six full seasons in Minnesota, leading the team in long balls three times. He also led the team in walks twice.

Brunansky ranked among the league's top 10 in home runs in 1983, 1984, and 1987, and from 1982 to '87 only Dwight Evans (175), Eddie Murray (175), and Dave Winfield (165) had more homers than Brunansky (162) among AL hitters. Brunansky made his lone All-Star appearance in 1985, but his best season in Minnesota was likely 1987, when he hit .259/.352/.489 with 32 homers in 155 games and then put the Twins on his back against the Tigers in the ALCS.

In five games versus Detroit, he batted .412 with two homers, four doubles, and nine RBIs as the Twins bashed the Tigers into submission before defeating the Cardinals in the seven-game World Series. Despite what his low batting averages and big power might suggest,

Brunansky was far from a plodding slugger. He actually played good defense in right field, had a fantastic arm, and could be counted on to play nearly every game.

While far from the team's best player, Brunansky's strengths epitomized the 1987 team in that he played solid defense and hit the ball over the fence. Brunansky (32), Hrbek (34), and Gaetti (31) each topped 30 homers that year, with Kirby Puckett adding 28 more as the Metrodome gained its "Homerdome" nickname. Remarkably, after that power-laden 1987 lineup, the Twins waited another 20 years for their next 30-homer season from anyone. That year was also the last full season Brunansky played for the Twins.

After he got off to a slow start in 1988, hitting .184 with one homer in 14 games, the Twins shipped Brunansky to those same Cardinals for Tommy Herr. It was a strange move—Gaetti called it "like a cold shower and a slap in the face at the same time." While the Twins had a need at second base, Herr was 32 years old and just wasn't all that good. And in retrospect it looks even worse, often being remembered as one of the worst moves in franchise history.

Brunansky continued to put up good numbers for another few seasons while Herr complained about being in Minnesota, played poorly, and was dealt to Philadelphia, along with Tom Nieto and Eric Bullock, for Shane Rawley in another disappointing move in the offseason. Brunansky had two more 20-homer seasons after leaving the Twins and was sent from the Cardinals to the Red Sox for Lee Smith in 1990. In retirement he rejoined the Twins, first as a minor-league instructor and then as a major league hitting coach.

Michael Cuddyer was the Gatorade National High School Player of the Year in 1997 and the Twins selected the power-hitting shortstop from Virginia with the ninth overall pick. He debuted the next season at Single-A and the "power-hitting" part immediately proved accurate, but the "shortstop" part was a stretch. Cuddyer batted .276 with 56 extra-base hits in 129 games as one of the youngest players in the Midwest League, but he committed an obscene 61 errors.

High error totals are common for young shortstops in the minors, but in Cuddyer's case they were coupled with a lack of range, and the Twins shifted him to third base the next season. He continued to commit a ton of errors there, but his arm strength provided hope that third base could be his long-term home and Cuddyer's bat drew most of the attention anyway. He had a breakout season at Double-A in 2001, hitting .301 with 30 homers and 75 walks in 141 games as a 22-year-old, earning a September call-up to Minnesota.

Sent to Triple-A in 2002, he hit .309 with 20 home runs in 86 games to earn an extended call-up to Minnesota. Cuddyer held his own as a 23-year-old rookie, batting .259 with a .740 OPS in 41 games, but found himself back in the minors the next season. It was the same story in 2003, as Cuddyer crushed Triple-A pitching and fared reasonably well in the big leagues, but the Twins stopped short of fully committing to him in part because they weren't quite sure where to play him defensively.

Cuddyer was seemingly a prospect forever. *Baseball America* rated him as one of MLB's top 100 prospects in five different seasons, twice placing him in the top 20. By the time Cuddyer reached Triple-A he was playing first base, right field, and left field in addition to third base, and he even saw some time at second base when the Twins got wise to Luis Rivas' flaws. Cuddyer wasn't suited for the infield, but faking it as a second baseman got his foot in the door and finally in 2005 he established himself as a regular.

For the next eight years he was the right-handed thump in the middle of a lineup that was always heavy on left-handed hitting, doing his best to make southpaw relievers pay a toll for facing Joe Mauer and Justin Morneau in the late innings. Cuddyer batted .290 with an .869 OPS versus lefties while in a Twins uniform, which stands as the fourth-best OPS in team history off southpaws behind Harmon Killebrew, Kirby Puckett, and Bob Allison. If a left-handed pitcher threw him a fastball in the zone or hung a slider, he punished it.

The same lack of speed and first-step quickness that led to Cuddyer moving away from the infield kept his range limited in right field, but the position switch unleashed the full scope of his arm strength on runners silly enough to test him. Cuddyer gunned down 11 runners in 2006 and 19 runners in 2007, at which point teams got smart enough to stop testing him. He also continued to shift around the diamond quite a bit, moving to first base when Morneau was hurt and filling in as needed at second base and third base.

Offensively there was far more consistency to Cuddyer's game, as he could generally be counted on to hit .275 with 20 homers, 60 walks, and an .800 OPS. In a decade with the Twins his OPS was never higher than .870 and fell below .750 just once, in 2008 when he struggled with injuries. His biggest years came in 2006 and 2009, when he topped an .850 OPS, and Cuddyer made his lone All-Star team as a member of the Twins in 2011 despite what was good but typical production at age 32.

Following that 2011 season he became a free agent and signed a three-year, $31.5 million deal with the Rockies, where calling Coors Field home allowed him to offset a decline in power by boosting his batting average. His top batting average in any Twins season was .284 and his career mark in Minnesota was .272, but Cuddyer hit .331 in 2013 to win the batting title and followed that up by hitting .332 in 2014. From there he moved on to the Mets with a two-year, $21 million deal, but retired after one season due to a knee injury.

It's difficult to have a firm grasp of Cuddyer's career value with the Twins, because he was a consistently good but not great hitter on a team that featured MVP-caliber bats in Mauer and Morneau. Beyond that, he also moved around so much defensively—and had limitations at every position—that his contributions on that side of the ball are tough to pin down. Cuddyer also earned constant praise as one of the Twins' leaders and loudest clubhouse voices—featuring lots of magic tricks—which is impossible to quantify.

Among all right-handed hitters in Twins history, only Harmon Killebrew, Torii Hunter, Bob Allison, Kirby Puckett, and Gary Gaetti have more home runs and more RBIs than Cuddyer, and of that group only Killebrew, Allison, and Puckett have a higher OPS. He was one of the Twins' top prospects of the 2000s and performed well from his first day to his last day, even if it took the team longer than warranted to find him an everyday spot in the lineup.

BRIAN HARPER

B ill James once wrote that Brian Harper "should have had a much better career than he did.... He lost a lot of his career to other people's stupidity." Harper languished in the minor leagues for years despite putting up big numbers, and even when he reached the majors it was in a very limited role that led to Harper bouncing around into his late 20s. Finally, general manager Andy MacPhail and the Twins took a flier on him and ended up looking very smart while fitting Harper for a World Series ring.

Harper was the Angels' fourth-round draft pick in 1977 and hit .293 with 24 homers at Single-A in 1978, followed by .315 with 14 homers and 37 doubles at Double-A in 1979. Then, at 21 years old, he hit .350 with 28 homers, 45 doubles, and 122 RBIs at Triple-A in 1980—a monster season for a young catcher. That should have made Harper a building block player, but instead the Angels traded him to the Pirates, who already had plenty of catching depth.

In an effort to simply get into the lineup *somewhere*, Harper spent some time at first base and in the outfield, but he played sparingly and went long stretches in the minors. Pittsburgh traded him to St. Louis, which was followed by stints with Detroit and Oakland. Through age 27, he had received a grand total of 390 at-bats in the majors spread over eight years and five teams, all while crushing minor-league pitching at every stop. He was a lifetime .308 hitter in the minors, including .311 in nearly 2,000 plate appearances at Triple-A.

Harper was released by the A's after 1987 and the Twins signed him to a minor-league deal in January 1988 with the intention of making him the regular catcher at Triple-A, but Harper ruined those plans by hitting .353 in 46 games there to all but force the Twins into giving him a shot. He went 9-for-22 (.409) with three doubles in his first six starts and suddenly—a decade into hitting like a good player and being treated like a scrub—Harper found a team that was willing to believe.

Given a chance to split time behind the plate with Tim Laudner during the final four months of the 1988 season, Harper hit .295 with a .772 OPS in 60 games. And just like that, he had himself a full-time gig. Laudner moved

TWINS' LOWEST STRIKEOUT RATE

minimum 2,500 plate appearances:

4.8%	Brian Harper
6.3%	Mickey Hatcher
6.7%	Cesar Tovar
8.1%	Butch Wynegar
9.4%	Tony Oliva

to the bench in 1989 and Harper batted .325 while starting 86 times at catcher and another 15 times at designated hitter. That was the first season of a five-year run that saw Harper consistently rank as one of the elite offensive catchers in baseball.

During that five-year period Harper was the only catcher in baseball to hit over .300. He also ranked among the position's top five in on-base percentage, slugging percentage, OPS, hits, doubles, runs scored, and RBIs. The man could always hit. The only difference was that the Twins were finally giving him a chance to prove it. He hit at least .295 with an OPS above .750 every season from 1988 to 1992, and the secret to Harper's success was a remarkable ability to avoid strikeouts and put the ball in play with authority.

Harper's strikeout numbers either appear to be misprints or look like they came from the 1800s: 16 in 1989, 27 in 1990, 22 in 1991, 22 in 1992, and 29 in 1993, all while topping 400 plate appearances every season. Combined from 1988 to 1993, he struck out a total of 128 times in 2,691 trips to the plate. Just for some context, nearly 1,000 players in baseball history have struck out more than 128 times in a single season. While with the Twins he whiffed an average of 29 times per 600 plate appearances, which is just silly.

He also rarely walked, which is less of an issue when you never strike out and hit .300 every season. To quote James on Harper again, "He was slow, didn't have real power, didn't walk, and didn't throw well, but he could hit .300 in his sleep." Harper was the

American League's best catcher from 1989 to '93, hitting .307 with a .772 OPS to top the league-average production for the position by about 12 percent. He led full-time catchers in Wins Above Replacement in that span.

The knock against Harper, even after he'd proven himself as a .300-hitting machine for a World Series–winning team, was that he was terrible defensively and especially dreadful at controlling the running game. His own manager, Tom Kelly, would freely make jokes about Harper's defense and it's easy to see that the defensive reputation probably played a big part in why it took so long for a team to give him a chance in the majors. However, the actual numbers tell a slightly different story.

From 1988 to 1990, he threw out 35 percent of steal attempts, which was solidly above the league average of 31 percent. For comparison, Laudner's career mark with the Twins was a shade under 30 percent, including just 27 percent in 1988–89. What likely cemented Harper's reputation as a poor thrower was his 22 percent caught stealing rate in 1991. The season everyone remembers was Harper's worst, and backup Junior Ortiz gunned down 46 percent in limited duty.

Plus, the Blue Jays and Braves ran a ton on Harper in the playoffs, going 11-for-14 in 12 games. Harper made up for much of that by going 13-for-39 (.333) with four doubles at the plate, but the idea that you could easily run on him stuck for the rest of his career. He allowed the league's most steals in 1992 and 1993, which added to the image everyone now had of him as a noodle arm. However, while teams were running on Harper like crazy, he actually threw out a very respectable 31 percent in 1992 and 33 percent in 1993.

Harper certainly had a mediocre arm and at times struggled gunning down runners, but more often than not he did just fine. "Harper wasn't a terrible thrower" will always be a tough sell to Twins fans, but the numbers can only lie so much. Jack Morris, who relied on strong-armed catchers to limit the running game in Detroit, noted that Harper took him aside in 1991 and worked with him to focus more on holding runners. "Harp was the first guy to teach me the need for the slide step," Morris told the *St. Paul Pioneer Press*.

It's a shame that Harper didn't latch on with the Twins earlier. He consistently produced big numbers in the minors, and given a chance he could have basically doubled the limited major-league career he had. He could hit in his sleep and did so whenever and wherever he got a shot to play regularly from 1979 to 1994, but Harper totaled just 1,001 games in the big leagues and received more than 400 plate appearances just five times—all from Kelly and the Twins.

ANDY MacPHAIL

Twins owner Calvin Griffith served as the team's de facto general manager dating back to the Washington Senators days. One of Griffith's closest confidants was Howard Fox, who joined the franchise in the 1940s, first as the PR director and traveling secretary in Washington and then as executive vice president in Minnesota. He'd spent five decades in the organization when Griffith sold the Twins to Carl Pohlad in 1984, and as part of the sale Griffith ordered Fox promoted to team president and general manager.

For more than a year, Fox held those titles and Pohlad created a vice president of player development role to bring in Andy MacPhail, the Houston Astros' assistant GM whose father Lee MacPhail and grandfather Larry MacPhail are Hall of Famers as front office executives. MacPhail truly ran the team, and in 1985 he was officially named GM. In the decades that followed, young GMs became common, but in 1985 a 32-year-old MacPhail taking over the Twins made headlines. "Boy Wonder" was the nickname that stuck.

"I wanted a new, fresh, young look, and somebody who wouldn't get caught up in old thinking," Pohlad explained. And so MacPhail set about overhauling a notoriously old-school organization that hadn't posted a winning record since 1979 and hadn't made the postseason since 1970. The losing continued in 1985 and 1986, but there was plenty of young talent in place with Kirby Puckett, Kent Hrbek, Frank Viola, Gary Gaetti, Tom Brunansky, Greg Gagne, and Randy Bush all 27 years old or younger.

MacPhail made three important roster moves following the 1986 season to bolster a team that went 71–91, adding Giants outfielder Dan Gladden and Expos closer Jeff Reardon via trades and signing journeyman reliever Juan Berenguer. His most important decision was at manager, where MacPhail replaced Ray Miller with Tom Kelly late in 1986 and gave Kelly the full-time job for 1987. Just as Pohlad bet on the 32-year-old MacPhail as GM, MacPhail was in turn betting on the 36-year-old Kelly as his partner in building a winner.

Puckett, Hrbek, Gaetti, and Brunansky emerged together as slugging stars, combining for 125 homers as the Twins' lineup improved by 50 runs. Viola stepped up as the ace of the rotation, with 36-year-old Bert Blyleven logging 251 innings in the second spot and late-inning duties being handled by the new Reardon-Berenguer bullpen duo. The Twins' pitching staff improved by 35 runs. It was far from a great team, as evidenced by an 85–77 record and being out-scored on the year, but it was good enough in a weak AL West.

MacPhail would say later that 1987 "was a mad scramble" as the young pieces joined a few veteran additions to form a team that was much greater than the sum of its parts in a frantic, storybook October. They snuck into the playoffs with a negative run differential and the American League's fifth-best record, facing a 98-win Tigers team in the ALCS and a 95-win Cardinals team in the World Series. None of that mattered, because the Twins simply refused to stop winning games and series they weren't supposed to win.

MacPhail's hand-picked, out-of-the-box choice for manager pulled the right strings and pushed the right buttons, including riding Viola and Blyleven extremely hard throughout the playoffs rather than trusting the rest of the Twins' shaky rotation. His three offseason pickups were all key contributors, including Gladden batting .314 with six extra-base hits and eight runs scored in 12 playoff games and Reardon closing out the World Series with a 1–2–3 ninth inning in Game 7. "Boy Wonder" was no longer said in jest.

That shine had a short shelf life, however. That offseason MacPhail swapped Brunansky to the just-defeated Cardinals for second baseman Tom Herr, which proved to be one of the worst trades in Twins history. Minnesota failed to make the playoffs in 1988 despite improving to 91–71 because the AL West toughened up, and then the Twins fell to 80–82 in 1989 and 74–88 in 1990. MacPhail was again tasked with turning around a losing team, but this time the roster was stocked with veterans from the World Series run.

Determining that the Twins needed an influx of young talent, MacPhail made the hugely unpopular decision to trade Viola, the reigning Cy Young award winner, to the Mets for a four-prospect package in mid-1989. Viola was great in New York, but the GM's gamble paid off when both Rick Aguilera and Kevin Tapani developed into building blocks for the pitching staff. Tapani essentially replaced Viola in the rotation and Aguilera replaced Reardon in the closer role, becoming one of the best relievers in baseball.

Gaetti left as a free agent following the 1990 season and MacPhail put together a platoon to fill his big shoes—homegrown rookie Scott Leuis versus left-handers and veteran free agent signing Mike Pagliarulo versus right-handers. It worked, as Twins third basemen combined to hit .274 with a higher OPS than Gaetti while being paid one-third as much. With those savings MacPhail brought in a pair of high-profile—by the Twins' standards, at least—free agents in starter Jack Morris and designated hitter Chili Davis.

Morris resurrected his career at age 36, throwing 247 innings and winning 18 games with a 3.43 ERA before forever planting himself in World Series lore with one of the greatest pitching performances of all time in Game 7. Davis was the most productive hitter in the lineup, leading the Twins in homers (29), doubles (34), walks (95), RBIs (93), and OPS (.893). Homegrown starter Scott Erickson became a star at 22 as the Cy Young award runner-up, and 1989 first-round draft pick Chuck Knoblauch won Rookie of the Year.

Not every move MacPhail made was good, but he showed the ability to adjust and adapt by making tough calls on departing stars, acquiring young talent from outside, developing homegrown talent within the farm system, and filling out the roster with free agents big and small. The first championship was a young team winning when they didn't know any better. The second title was MacPhail building and rebuilding a World Series roster. "It was validation of a true baseball organization," he said later. "I take more pride in 1991."

Much like in 1988, the Twins were a good team that failed to make the playoffs in 1992, and then things went downhill in a hurry. They lost 91 games in 1993 and had a losing record when the strike halted things in 1994. MacPhail had two seasons remaining on his contract, but Pohlad granted the Cubs' interview request and Chicago hired the now 41-year-old, two-time World Series–winning GM as president and CEO. Pohlad offered a raise and ownership stake to stay, but MacPhail had his mind made up.

MacPhail, who had been so masterful navigating the always murky low-payroll waters, was now ready to move on to a bigger market. "It would have been safe and secure, financially and reputation-wise, to stay in a small market and wring my hands and say, 'Oh, gee, there's only so much we can do here. Isn't it a shame?'" MacPhail told the *Chicago Tribune* after taking the Cubs job. "But security and comfort aren't exactly what you should be aspiring to at 41."

He spent more than a decade with the Cubs, taking the team to the playoffs just twice in an up-and-down run. MacPhail then moved on to Baltimore, where his father had been GM, but presided over even less success before leaving on his own accord. A few years later he joined the Phillies' rebuilt organization as team president, running a fourth team as one of the elder statesmen among front office bosses. Like his father and grandfather, "Boy Wonder" is a baseball lifer.

40

LARRY HISLE

Philadelphia selected Larry Hisle in the second round of the 1965 draft out of an Ohio high school, and in 1968 he made the Opening Day roster at age 20. Demoted back to the minors in late April, he hit well at Triple-A before his season was cut short when doctors diagnosed him with hepatitis. According to a July 13, 1968 article in the *Washington Post*, "Doctors sent Hisle to his home in Portsmouth, Ohio, and ordered him to follow a strict protein diet and get plenty of rest."

After taking nearly a year off Hisle had another impressive spring training in 1969 and was the Phillies' center fielder and leadoff man on Opening Day. He batted just .159 in April, but the Phillies stuck with him and watched as Hisle hit .266/.338/.459 with 20 homers and 18 steals to finish fourth in the Rookie of the Year balloting. Hisle fell off in his second year, hitting just .205, and when he got off to another slow start in 1971 the Phillies demoted him to Triple-A.

Hisle hit .328 with a .597 slugging percentage in 62 games there, but struggled again when the Phillies called him up near the end of 1971. Philadelphia traded him to Los Angeles for Tom Hutton during the offseason and Hisle spent all of 1972 at Triple-A, hitting .325/.410/.561 in 131 games. He was traded to St. Louis that offseason, and after spending less than a month as property of the Cardinals they shipped him to the Twins for Wayne Granger.

In two years Hisle had gone from being one of the game's most promising young players to being a minor leaguer with his fourth club. But landing in Minnesota turned his career around. Rather than spend yet another season at Triple-A, the Twins handed Hisle the starting job in center field. He went 4-for-5 as the Opening Day leadoff man, hit .304/.360/.609 overall in April, and finished his comeback season at .272/.351/.422 with 15 homers in 143 games.

Hisle was even better in 1974, hitting .286/.353/.465 with 19 homers while splitting time in all three outfield spots. Those numbers may not look particularly great, but it was a low-offense era and Hisle's seemingly modest .465 slugging percentage ranked ninth in the American League. Hisle was on track for the best season of his career in 1975, batting .314/.361/.518 with 17 steals through 57 games when a bone spur in his elbow forced him to the disabled list.

To make room on the roster for Hisle's return from the DL three weeks later, the Twins sent down first baseman Tom Kelly, who hit just .181 in 49 games during what would be his only season in the big leagues. After just one start and a few pinch-hitting appearances, Hisle was sidelined again. This time he missed nearly two months, returning to play 15 games in September, and finished the year at .314/.376/.494 with 11 homers and 17 steals in 80 games.

Hisle bounced back to play 155 games in 1976, and while his .272/.335/.394 mark isn't overly impressive even considering the era, he did hit 14 homers while driving in 96 runs and stealing 31 bases. Then in 1977, with free agency just around the corner, Hisle had the best year of his career. He hit .302/.369/.533 with 28 homers and a league-leading 119 RBIs to make his first All-Star team and finish 12th in the MVP balloting. (Twins teammate Rod Carew hit .388 to take the award.)

The timing was perfect for Hisle, who received several big offers when he hit the free agent market that winter. Hisle said at the time that he was interested in staying with the Twins, but talks reportedly broke down over some complicated contract details that included a loan and bonus money. Hisle eventually decided to sign with the Brewers, inking a six-year deal worth a then-massive $3.1 million. According to a November 19, 1977, article in the *New York Times*:

[The deal] put the 30-year-old outfielder in a financial league with Catfish Hunter of the Yankees (five years, $3.5 million), Mike Schmidt of Philadelphia (six years, $3.36 million) and Reggie Jackson of the Yankees (five years, $2.9 million).

In the same article, Hisle described his decision to leave Minnesota:

I had enjoyed my five years in Minnesota and it wasn't going to be easy for me to pack up and leave everyone. The Twins mentioned the fact that they really wanted me and they made me an offer, but I had decided 100 percent that Milwaukee would be the place to play.

Hisle was well worth the money in his first year with the Brewers, hitting .290 with 34 homers and 115 RBIs to finish third in the MVP voting behind Red Sox slugger Jim Rice and Yankees ace Ron Guidry. He was on his way to a similarly outstanding 1979 season when disaster struck on April 20. A throw from left field resulted in a torn rotator cuff that basically ended his career. A series of surgeries and rehab attempts left him unable to raise his right arm.

After suffering the injury in 1979, he played just 67 more games before finally giving in to the pain. Hisle's career with the Twins was short and sweet, with 662 games spread over five seasons, yet he's all over the team leaderboard. Hisle ranks among the team's top 20 in batting average, slugging percentage, on-base percentage, homers, steals, and RBIs, with a top-10 mark in adjusted OPS+, and his 1977 is one of the top years by any outfielder in Twins history.

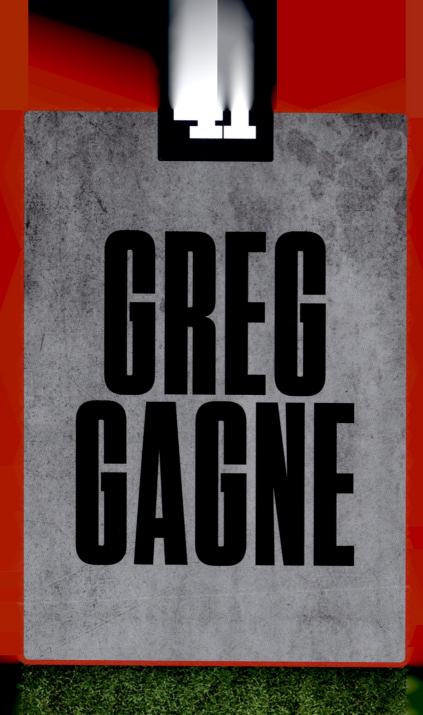

A week into the 1982 season the cost-cutting Twins traded starting shortstop Roy Smalley to the Yankees for All-Star setup man Ron Davis, Paul Boris, and a 20-year-old prospect named Greg Gagne. At the time Davis was clearly considered the big name coming back to Minnesota in the deal, but he flopped in the closer role and Boris was a non-factor. Gagne ended up being the real find as Smalley's eventual replacement.

Gagne spent 1982 hitting poorly at Double-A, but the former fifth-round draft pick from Massachusetts bounced back at Triple-A in 1983. Gagne batted .255/.323/.462 with 17 homers in 119 games there as a 21-year-old and also got his first taste of the big leagues with a brief stint in June as an injury replacement and later a September call-up. He struggled, managing just three hits in 27 at-bats, and found himself at Triple-A again in 1984.

Gagne put together another strong season there, hitting .280/.374/.441 with nine homers in 70 games, but he didn't make it back to Minnesota until rosters expanded in September and then he merely sat on the bench once he got there. Tired of trotting out guys like Ron Washington, Houston Jimenez, and Lenny Faedo, the Twins turned to a 23-year-old Gagne as their starting shortstop in 1985.

He batted just .225 with two homers in 114 games as a rookie and missed time with injuries in May and August. In his absence, the Twins turned to Smalley, who had returned that offseason in a trade for Ron Scheer and Randy Johnson (no, not that one), but back problems forced Smalley to be a designated hitter in 1986 and the Twins went with Gagne on a full-time basis at shortstop.

He came up with a solid sophomore campaign, hitting .250/.301/.398 with 12 homers in 156 games to rank 15th among all major-league shortstops in Wins Above Replacement. In the second-to-last game of the season, Gagne hit inside-the-park homers in each of his first two at-bats against Chicago starter Floyd Bannister, and

In the history of the Minnesota Twins, only Kirby Puckett (5) has more postseason home runs than Greg Gagne (4).

then smacked a triple off reliever Gene Nelson in his third at-bat to come 90 feet short of an all-time record.

After committing an AL-worst 26 errors in 1986, he had a team record 47-game errorless streak in 1987. He also hit .265/.310/.430 with 10 homers in 137 games as the Twins defeated the Tigers in the ALCS and beat the Cardinals in the World Series. Gagne hit just .229 in 12 playoff games, but had three homers and four doubles, scored 10 runs, and delivered the sixth-inning, broken-bat single to left field that drove Tom Brunansky in as the go-ahead run in Game 7 of the World Series.

He had three fairly mediocre years from 1988 to '90 and then hit .265/.310/.395 in 1991 as the Twins again won the World Series. This time Gagne hit just .195 in 12 postseason games and had just one homer, but it was a big one. With the Twins clinging to a 1–0 lead in the fifth inning of Game 1 versus Atlanta, Gagne launched a three-run homer off Charlie Leibrandt that provided all the breathing room Jack Morris needed in a 5–2 win.

Gagne became a free agent after 1992 and signed a three-year deal with Kansas City. He gave the Royals three solid years and then finished his 15-year career with two NL seasons playing for the Dodgers. Gagne retired at age 35. He was a starting shortstop in the major leagues from the moment the Twins handed him the job in 1985 to the moment he hung up the spikes in 1997, logging nearly 15,000 innings at the position. Dating back to 1980, only 13 players started more games at shortstop than Gagne with 1,649.

Shortstop became more of an offensive position after Gagne's retirement, making his raw numbers look paltry in comparison. However, take a closer look back at his decade in Minnesota and Gagne was more valuable than his .677 OPS suggests. Perhaps the biggest key to seeing Gagne's value is in understanding the difference between baseball in the 1980s and baseball today, after players like Alex Rodriguez, Derek Jeter, Miguel Tejada, and Nomar Garciaparra revolutionized the way shortstops are viewed.

Meanwhile, during Gagne's time with the Twins, the average shortstop hit just .252 with a .655 OPS, which is 50–100 points lower than what has been the norm since 2000. If you take Gagne's career numbers with the Twins and add that same 10 percent increase to them, you get something along the lines of .275/.320/.425. Jimmy Rollins, an MVP-winning shortstop for the Phillies who'll likely get some Hall of Fame support, is a career .264/.324/.418 hitter.

Gagne still wouldn't light up a stat sheet, but those adjusted numbers are a lot more palatable. And then you have his defense, which was excellent regardless of era. He never won a Gold Glove, as Alan Trammell and Tony Fernandez dominated the award in the 1980s, but Gagne is widely considered the best defensive shortstop in Twins history and Total Zone Rating pegs him as seven runs above average per 150 games in Minnesota.

Despite the speed and athleticism needed for his defensive range, he was awful swiping bags. Historically bad, in fact. He was 79-for-134 (59 percent) for the Twins, and no one else in team history with at least 50 steals is under 60 percent. And he was somehow even worse after leaving, including a 10-for-27 mark in 1994. Seriously. Overall he was 108-for-204, which at 53 percent is the second-worst rate ever for those who attempted 200 steals, behind Lou Gehrig.

42

JIMMIE HALL

Jimmie Hall signed with the Senators as an 18-year-old in 1956, but he didn't make it to the big leagues until three years after the team moved from Washington to Minnesota and became the Twins. As a 25-year-old rookie in 1963, he initially served as a reserve outfielder on a team that had veterans Harmon Killebrew, Bob Allison, and Lenny Green established as starters. Hall struggled early on, hitting just .188 in 80 at-bats through the end of May.

Hall got his big break when Green was injured in June. It wasn't quite Lou Gehrig replacing Wally Pipp, but Hall stepped in as the starting center fielder and had a huge rookie year. At a time when pitching dominated, Hall hit .260/.342/.521 and smacked 33 homers to break Ted Williams' then-record for AL rookies. Despite ranking among the league's top 10 in slugging percentage, homers, OPS, runs scored, and total bases, Hall finished just third in the Rookie of the Year balloting behind Gary Peters and Pete Ward.

His adjusted OPS+ of 136 in 1963 not only ranked seventh in the AL, it's a number that only 15 different Twins have topped since. What made Hall's rookie year particularly impressive was that he ended up with those outstanding overall numbers despite playing sporadically and poorly through the first two months. Then from June 1 on, Hall batted .273/.354/.556 with 31 homers and 77 RBIs in 116 games. Hall's rookie breakout was more than enough for him to supplant Green as the Twins' center fielder.

In the 13th game of the next season Hall, Killebrew, Allison, and 25-year-old rookie phenom Tony Oliva hit four consecutive extra-inning homers in a 7–3 win over the A's. While not an outstanding defensive foursome—Allison played mostly first base that season—they combined to blast 138 homers. The Twins led the AL with 221 homers while no other team reached 190. Despite all of that power, the Twins won just 79 games in 1964 because of a mediocre pitching staff and some tough breaks.

Hall turned in a solid sophomore season, batting .282 with 25 homers while making his first All-Star team, but was involved in an incident that may have led to his early decline. Playing center field on May 27 versus the Angels, he led off the fifth inning and was hit on the cheek by a pitch from southpaw Bo Belinsky. Hall immediately exited the game, but returned to the lineup about a week later and played well for the remainder of the season while wearing a protective flap on his batting helmet.

However, there's some speculation that the beaning ultimately led to his being timid and ineffective versus left-handed pitchers, and it could help explain why he was finished as a productive player by his sixth season. That theory has some holes in it. First and foremost is that he struggled against southpaws prior to the beaning, like many lefties do, hitting just .235 off them as a rookie. Beyond that, whatever negative impact the incident had on his hitting ability certainly didn't show up for several years.

In fact, Hall had arguably his best all-around year in 1965, making his second All-Star team while setting career-highs in batting average, on-base percentage, and RBIs. In large part thanks to Hall's excellent season, the Twins went 102–60 to win the pennant by seven games and then matched up against the Dodgers in the World Series. Los Angeles' three-man rotation included a pair of dominant lefties in Sandy Koufax and Claude Osteen, so Twins manager Sam Mele decided to bench Hall in five of the seven games.

The move was somewhat understandable considering how good Koufax and Osteen were and how bad Hall was against lefties, but his center field replacement, Joe Nossek, was one of MLB's worst bats and hit just .228 off lefties himself. Hall started the two games righty Don Drysdale pitched, going 1-for-7 with five strikeouts, Nossek went 4-for-20, and Koufax tossed a Game 7 shutout to win the series. Hall remained a power threat in 1966, homering 20 times in 356 at-bats, but hit .239 for his worst season in four years.

Hall was phased out in center field, giving way to rookie Ted Uhlaender, and was used as a platoon player and bench bat. Shortly after the season he was traded to the Angels along with Don Mincher and Pete Cimino for Dean Chance and Jackie Hernandez. Chance was the Twins' ace for two years and Mincher went on to have a solid post-Twins career. As for Hall, despite being only 29, he had exactly one more decent season left in him. Hall batted .249 with 16 homers in 129 games for the Angels in 1967.

Hall stuck around for another three years, playing for four teams while hitting .208 in 618 plate appearances. He flamed out quickly, but Hall's impact on the Twins was significant. He packed 98 homers into just four seasons in Minnesota despite playing at a time when big offensive numbers were rare—and played a passable center field while doing so.

BUTCH WYNEGAR

Butch Wynegar was Joe Mauer before there was a Joe Mauer. A switch-hitting high-school catcher from Pennsylvania, the Twins selected Wynegar in the second round of the 1974 draft. He tore through the minor leagues, leading the rookie-level Appalachian League with a .346 batting average in 60 games after signing and hitting .314 with 19 homers, 112 RBIs, and 106 runs scored in 139 games at Single-A in 1975.

That was enough for the Twins to bench Glenn Borgmann, skip their stud prospect past both Double-A and Triple-A, and enter 1976 with Wynegar as the starting catcher despite the fact that he celebrated his 20th birthday during spring training. Wynegar was an immediate success, starting 137 games behind the plate and another dozen as the designated hitter while batting .260/.356/.363 with 10 homers, 21 doubles, 79 walks, and 69 RBIs.

Wynegar began the year batting sixth in the lineup, spent some time hitting fifth, and ended up in the cleanup spot for much of the season. His raw numbers may not look like much, but for a 20-year-old catcher in 1976 they were amazing. In fact, if you adjust Wynegar's numbers from 1976 to the typical 2000s offensive environment, his rookie season looks an awful lot like Mauer's first full season in 2005:

	Year	G	PA	AVG	OBP	SLG	OPS+
Wynegar	1976	149	622	.275	.375	.435	109
Mauer	2005	131	554	.294	.372	.411	107

Add in the fact that Wynegar was actually two years younger than Mauer was in 2005 and possessed a similarly outstanding throwing arm, and it's easy to see why he was considered an extremely special player. Wynegar missed out on winning the Rookie of the Year award because Mark Fidrych turned in one of the greatest rookie seasons in baseball history, but he did manage to receive the only two first-place votes that Fidrych missed. Wynegar also became the youngest player ever to be selected to the All-Star team.

Wynegar had a nearly identical sophomore season, making his second All-Star team. An article in the *Los Angeles Times* on June 8, 1976 called Wynegar "this year's Fred Lynn" and also quoted Twins owner Calvin Griffith as saying that Wynegar was "going to be so good it's fantastic." Within the same article, A's manager Chuck Tanner said Wynegar had "one of the best swings for a young kid that I've ever seen." And here's an excerpt from an article that appeared in the *Washington Post* on June 5, 1977:

> "He's the most complete catcher in the American League," said Houston scout Harry Craft. "He doesn't hit yet like Thurman Munson or maybe Carlton Fisk, but considering everything, he's the best of the three."

Unfortunately, by his 22nd birthday Wynegar's best days were already behind him. He threw out 45 percent of steal attempts in 1978, but hit just .229 with four homers in 135 games. He bounced back somewhat in 1979, hitting .270, but Wynegar dropped off again in 1980, hitting .255 with five homers in 146 games. Despite looking so promising early on, he had essentially become a typical good-glove, no-hit backstop, playing nearly every day.

Wynegar's durability left in 1981, too, as he hit .247/.322/.280 and played just 47 games. The Next Big Thing at 21, he was suddenly 26 and hadn't improved a bit. His swing never produced the big batting averages people expected and his power declined at a time when the rest of baseball's soared. After hitting .209 in 24 games to start 1982, the Twins traded Wynegar to the Yankees, along with Roger Erickson, for John Pacella, Larry Milbourne, and Pete Filson.

They'd traded Roy Smalley to the Yankees in April and dumping another high-priced veteran wasn't a popular move. Ron Davis, who arrived in the Smalley deal, told the *Washington Post*, "If anybody should be traded, it's the owner. All he's worried about is money. There ain't no future for this team." Griffith's response was to call Davis "a New York counterfeit," which likely stung quite a bit considering he had just blown a game against the Red Sox the day before.

Wynegar spent a total of six seasons with the Yankees, and ended his career with two seasons as a backup catcher after being traded to the Angels in December of 1986. Wynegar's career was an odd one, and there are certainly plenty of interesting lessons that can be learned from it, one being that young superstars in the making—and especially young catchers who log over 1,000 innings per year behind the plate right away—don't always turn out that way.

It's not that Wynegar was bad—*The New Bill James Historical Baseball Abstract* rates him as the 65th-best catcher in baseball history—but rather that he peaked early and then suffered from not living up to the substantial hype. Had his career been shaped differently, with the poor seasons at 20/21 and peak years at a more typical age, he'd be viewed in a better light. Instead, he'll have to settle for being one of those "what could have been" players.

44

RON GARDENHIRE

In the spring of 1987, the Twins had a three-way battle for the utility infielder job between Ron Washington, Al Newman, and Ron Gardenhire. Each fit roughly the same profile as skinny, light-hitting, good-fielding backup options with limited upside. Washington was the incumbent, spending the previous six seasons in Minnesota as a part-timer, but he was 35 and the Twins wanted alternatives. They acquired Gardenhire from the Mets and Newman from the Expos in minor offseason trades.

Rookie manager Tom Kelly chose Newman, who spent the next five seasons as a quasi-regular for the Twins, averaging 375 plate appearances per season and winning a pair of World Series despite hitting .231 with zero homers. Washington was released and latched on with the Orioles. Gardenhire stayed with the Twins at Triple-A, where he hit .272 with six homers in 117 games. He wasn't called up, spending a second straight season entirely at Triple-A after parts of five years in the majors with the Mets. He then called it a career.

Just as Kelly immediately became a manager in the Twins' farm system after retiring as a player and later joined Minnesota's staff as third base coach, the Twins hired Gardenhire to manage their Single-A team in 1988 and added him to the big-league staff as third base coach in 1991. He was a 33-year-old rookie coaching a World Series team with a handful of veteran players older than him, but Gardenhire remained in that role and worked under Kelly for 11 seasons.

Kelly stepped down as manager shortly after the 2001 season and general manager Terry Ryan talked about looking outside the organization for potential replacements, but it was widely assumed that the job would go to Gardenhire or Paul Molitor, the Minnesota-born Hall of Famer who'd spent three seasons as Kelly's bench coach. Molitor later withdrew his name from consideration, citing the Twins' uncertain future amid contraction rumors, and Gardenhire was named manager in January, three months after Kelly's retirement.

Gardenhire got a two-year contract with a third-year team option, which he called "pretty neat...they didn't have to do that." He was right, as Kelly received only a one-year deal when he was named full-time manager. Ryan saw things differently than his predecessor, Andy MacPhail, explaining, "How can you put a manager in place for only a year? I told ownership we can't put him in a situation where he's set up to fail." Of course, Ryan was also quick to point out, "we're not paying him like Joe Torre."

Gardenhire's task was clear. Take over a young team that had made significant progress in Kelly's final season—going 85-77 after seven straight losing years—and keep things headed in the right direction. Many pieces were already in place as quality big leaguers, including Torii Hunter, Brad Radke, Corey Koskie, Jacque Jones, Eddie Guardado, Eric Milton, Cristian Guzman, A.J. Pierzynski, and Doug Mientkiewicz. Most of Kelly's staff remained, with only Molitor and longtime pitching coach Dick Such departing.

Gardenhire replaced Molitor as bench coach with Steve Liddle, replaced Such as pitching coach with his old minor-league roommate Rick Anderson, and replaced himself as third base coach with...Al Newman, who sent Gardenhire down the path toward coaching by beating him out for the utility infielder gig in 1987. Gardenhire was much different than Kelly, particularly in terms of on- and off-field demeanor, but the Twins picked up where they'd left off in 2001 and took another step forward to run away with the AL Central.

In the playoffs for the first time since 1991, the Twins topped the A's before losing to the Angels in the ALCS under a hail of Adam Kennedy homers. Gardenhire finished third in Manager of the Year voting, which would become a regular occurrence as he placed among the top three without winning the award in six of his first eight years.

Winning playoff series would not become a regular occurrence. Minnesota won six division titles in his first nine years, but the ALDS win over Oakland in 2002 would stand alone as playoff series won.

The collection of homegrown building blocks that Kelly handed over to Gardenhire soon added star power in Joe Mauer, Justin Morneau, Johan Santana, and Joe Nathan. His team had a winning record in all but one season from 2002 to 2010, never falling below 79 wins, and their dominance over the rest of the AL Central division is startling. Minnesota won 803 games from 2002 to 2010, which is 36 more than the White Sox, 99 more than the Indians, 138 more than the Tigers, and 206 more than the Royals.

However, they never got over the hump of being a good regular season team that ruled a weak division. They surpassed 92 wins just three times and had a 2–15 postseason record after 2002, losing in the opening round each time. In particular, Gardenhire never beat the Yankees. New York was a powerhouse and made plenty of teams look inferior, but their mastery of the Twins was extreme. Over a 13-year span Gardenhire had a 28-76 record and .269 winning percentage versus the Yankees, compared to .517 against other teams.

Gardenhire's team won the AL Central only to be dispatched by the Yankees in the first round in 2003, 2004, 2009, and 2010. The last two of those first-round knockouts were sweeps and 2010 marked the end of the Twins' success under Gardenhire, even if they didn't realize it for a while. That season the Twins moved into Target Field, set a team attendance record, and won 94 games with a league-best 48–26 record in the second half, as Gardenhire was finally voted Manager of the Year after five runner-up finishes.

Matched up with the Yankees again, the Twins opened the ALDS at home and grabbed a 3–0 lead in Game 1, only to be out-scored 17–4 after that in another sweep. "This is not much fun at all, to come up here, being knocked out, knowing your season is over with, again after three games," Gardenhire said after Game 3. "We've had that a few times. Right now we're in a little rut here. We can't seem to put it together. We have to do some more searching, trying to figure out how to get it done, because we definitely can do it."

Gardenhire never got another shot. Injuries wrecked the 2011 season, as the Twins lost 99 games after expecting to contend like they had for a decade. And then it got worse. Much worse. Years of poor drafting, misguided trades, and rotten injury luck led to a complete collapse, with four straight 90-loss seasons. Gardenhire appeared understandably beaten down. Gone was his sarcastic, folksy charm, replaced by a robotic cliché-giver unable to make sense of the constant ineptitude. He seemingly aged two decades in four years.

In baseball history only two managers kept their jobs after four straight 90-loss seasons: Connie Mack and Tom Kelly. Gardenhire did not join them, parting ways with the Twins after 2014. Officially he was fired, but it sure didn't feel that way as he attended the press conference and was in relatively good spirits, cracking a few smiles. He was relieved, both of his duties and to be done losing. Five weeks later Gardenhire was replaced by the man he was up against for the job 13 years earlier, Paul Molitor.

There are many similarities in how Kelly and Gardenhire became managers and they're the two most successful in Twins history, but their success came in opposite ways. Kelly won and won big right away, with a World Series in his rookie season and another title in his fifth year, but he had a losing record in 10-of-15 seasons. Gardenhire never won big, but the Twins were AL Central champions six times in his first nine years and never dipped below 79–83...until the bottom fell out in his 10th year.

Kelly will forever be remembered for what his teams did twice, which is reach the top of the mountain. Gardenhire will forever be remembered for what his teams could never do, which is beat the Yankees and go climbing. Infrequently great trumps consistently good, which is why—math be damned—a .507 winning percentage by Gardenhire shrinks next to a .478 mark by Kelly. That's perhaps unfair to Gardenhire, who presided over the Twins' most sustained success in history, but fans who saw those Yankees losses know nothing is fair.

SCOTT BAKER

Brad Radke's success led to two decades of the Twins packing the starting rotation with control artists, and no one represented the team's post-Radke generation of low-velocity, fly-ball, strike-throwing pitchers more than baby-faced right-hander Scott Baker. Picked out of Oklahoma State in the second round of the 2003 draft, Baker reached Triple-A in his first full season as a professional and was called up to Minnesota for his big-league debut less than 24 months after being drafted.

Baker had a strong 54-inning showing filling in for various injured veterans as a 23-year-old rookie, but when his sophomore campaign got off to a rough start, the Twins demoted him back to the minors. He spent much of 2006 at Triple-A and began 2007 there as well when the Twins bypassed him for a rotation spot out of spring training in favor of scrap-heap veterans Ramon Ortiz and Sidney Ponson. Baker consistently shut down Triple-A hitters and in late May the Twins finally gave him another chance in place of Ponson.

This time Baker was ready for success, establishing himself as a dependable mid-rotation starter. Armed with a low-90s fastball and sharp-breaking curveball, Baker posted a 4.26 ERA in 144 innings at a time when the average ERA in the American League was 4.50. He took a perfect game into the ninth inning against the Royals on August 31, losing the perfecto when leadoff man John Buck walked and losing the no-hitter a batter later when Mike Sweeney singled into center field. Baker had to settle for a one-hit shutout.

Baker was a full-time member of the rotation in 2008, starting 28 games with a 3.45 ERA in 172 innings. He began the 2009 season on the disabled list and then struggled initially upon returning, but Baker still finished with an even 200 innings and was brilliant in the second half with an 8–2 record and 3.28 ERA. Picked as the Opening Day starter in 2010, he again struggled early before going 5–0 with a 3.18 ERA down the stretch to finish with a 4.49 ERA in 170 innings overall.

The only pitchers in Twins history with more starts and a higher winning percentage than Scott Baker are Johan Santana, Camilo Pascual, and Jim Perry.

Because of late-season elbow problems Baker had to compete for a rotation spot in 2011. He secured the job and pitched as well as ever with a career-best 3.14 ERA and 3.8-to-1 strikeout-to-walk ratio, but Baker spent much of the second half on the disabled list with more elbow issues that proved much more serious than the Twins believed at the time. He made his last start on August 8 and sat out more than a month before appearing twice as a reliever in September.

Baker's elbow problems remained the next spring and he began the year on the disabled list. Things got worse when he tried to rehab the injury and further examination revealed that Baker needed Tommy John surgery. That ended his season and his Twins career, as the team later declined his $9 million option for 2012. He signed an incentive-laden one-year deal with the Cubs, but could never really get healthy. Baker threw just 107 innings after leaving the Twins and was finished as a big leaguer at age 33.

Post-surgery, Baker revealed that he'd been dealing with elbow problems for years, often pitching (and pitching well) through the pain. "It's something that I've been battling for a while," Baker said at a press conference. "I don't mind pitching through pain, as long as you don't have the chance to further the injury. But when it comes to a point where your velocity's not there and you don't have the ability to finish pitches like you know you're capable of doing, then something's got to be done."

Durability was never a strength for Baker, as he frequently spent stints on the disabled list and averaged 165 innings in five seasons as a full-time member of the Twins' rotation. Of course, when viewed within the context of lingering elbow issues that eventually required surgery, he was plenty tough to gut out that many innings. His solid performances are even more impressive within that context, as Baker went 63–48 with a 4.15 ERA for the Twins in an offense-driven era.

Only nine pitchers in Twins history have made more starts with a better adjusted ERA+ than Baker and his strikeout-to-walk ratio is the second-best in team history for starters behind only Johan Santana. He topped 180 innings just once, but 150–175 innings from Baker were more valuable than 180–200 innings from most pitchers. He did a fine job carrying the low-velocity, strike-throwing torch handed to him by

Radke in the mid-2000s and his departure coincided with the team's slippage in pitching quality.

He was by no means an ace, but Baker was certainly more capable of looking like an ace in a given start than most middle-of-the-rotation starters. In addition to nearly throwing a no-hitter against the Royals in 2007, he allowed zero earned runs in 20 of his 159 starts for the Twins and allowed two or fewer earned runs in 43 percent of his outings. While far from overpowering and almost always in the strike zone, Baker managed an above-average strikeout rate by getting hitters to chase high fastballs and bat-avoiding curves.

When he struggled, homers were usually to blame. Baker was one of the most extreme fly-ball pitchers in baseball throughout his career and served up more than his share of mammoth blasts into upper decks across the American League. However, his overall rate of allowing homers was barely above the MLB average at 27 per 200 innings. When he gave them up they tended to go very far, but Baker's reputation as a homer-prone pitcher is somewhat overblown. Baker and Radke both allowed 1.2 homers per nine innings.

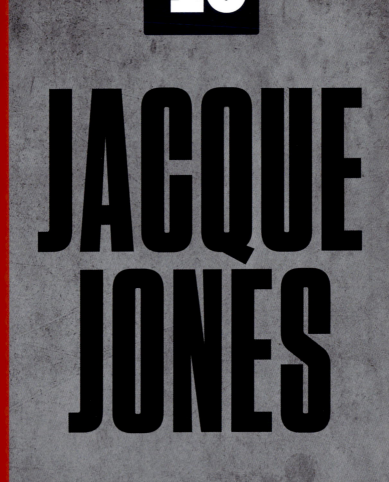

Jacque Jones starred at USC and was a member of the bronze medal–winning Olympic team in 1996 before the Twins picked him in the second round of the 1996 draft. He hit .297/.342/.464 with 15 homers, 24 steals, and a 110-to-33 strikeout-to-walk ratio in 131 games at Single-A in 1997 and nearly duplicated that by hitting .299/.350/.508 with 21 homers, 18 steals, and a 134-to-37 strikeout-to-walk ratio in 134 games at Double-A the next year.

Jones started 1999 at Triple-A and hit .298/.333/.444 in 52 games before the Twins called him up in June. He debuted with an 0-for-4 performance against the Reds on June 9, 1999, but became an immediate regular for the Twins and developed into a building block player as the team re-emerged as contenders in the early 2000s. Many of Jones' totals—132 homers, 476 RBIs, 189 doubles, 974 hits, 1,589 total bases—rank among the top 20 in team history, but few players had such a wide gap between their strengths and weaknesses.

Jones played for the Twins in a high-offense era and primarily played a key position for offense, left field, which makes his raw totals look somewhat better than they really are when compared to hitters from the 1960s, 1970s, and 1980s—or guys from various eras who hit well and played premium defensive positions. Another factor in any evaluation of Jones is that, because of the weaknesses in his game, he would've been more valuable for the Twins if only he'd have been utilized differently in a few key areas.

As a free-swinging left-handed hitter with plus power, Jones' strength was always his ability to hit right-handed pitching, but manager Ron Gardenhire wiped away much of that value by refusing to platoon him against lefties. The end result was relatively modest overall numbers for the era, but in seven seasons for the Twins he hit .294 with an .830 OPS off righties and .227 with a .616 OPS off lefties. Not once in seven seasons did he put together above-average production versus southpaws.

Because of that it would've been easy to squeeze the maximum value out of Jones as a hitter, letting him tee off on righties while shielding him versus most lefties, something Tom Kelly did regularly with several players. Gardenhire instead got the good hitting against righties and then let Jones erase many of those gains with his horrible work off lefties. Jones' time in Minnesota is a prime example of how not to get the most out of your players by not putting them in a position to succeed and maximize their talent.

His stint as a leadoff hitter is similar. Jones averaged 20 homers and 30 doubles per 150 games for the Twins, but also averaged just 35 walks with a middling .327 on-base percentage and poor base-stealing. If ever a player was meant to bat in a traditional RBI spot it was Jones, yet he batted leadoff in more than one-third of his Twins game. He did set the team record for leadoff homers with 20, but that isn't necessarily a good thing when it comes to lineup construction.

Gardenhire is at fault for refusing to platoon Jones and move him down in the order more, but the other main circumstance that could have added to Jones' value for the Twins can't really be pinned on anyone. Well, maybe Torii Hunter and whichever scout suggested that the Twins draft him back in 1993. In most organizations Jones would have spent seven seasons patrolling center field, where his defense would have been more important and his offense would have been more valuable.

However, with Hunter around Jones shifted first to left field and then to right field. His defense in both places was excellent—balancing spectacular range with a scattershot throwing arm—but his offense was really nothing special for a corner outfielder given the sluggers who usually patrol those spots. Interestingly, his hitting and Hunter's hitting were very similar while with the Twins. Hunter hit .268 with a .783 OPS. Jones hit .279 with a .776 OPS.

Almost identical overall numbers—albeit in different amounts of playing time—yet Hunter was a more valuable offensive player because his hitting was above average for center fielders while Jones' hitting was slightly below average for corner outfielders. If he were drafted by a team that didn't have an elite center fielder and played for a manager who knew the value of platooning, Jones would've been a superior player to the one the Twins got.

Of course, in ranking his place in Twins history, those points are little more than sidebars. Instead of being a platoon center fielder in a fantasy world, he was a strong defensive corner outfielder with a slugging-heavy bat that made him about average for the position. Multiply all of that by nearly 1,000 games spread over seven seasons and what you get is a very solid player—durable and productive even with the wild swings, helplessness versus lefties, and throws from the outfield that were either air-mailed past the catcher or launched directly into the turf.

MATT LAWTON

elected in the 13th round out of Mississippi Gulf Coast Community College just four months before the Twins' run to the World Series in 1991, Matt Lawton advanced slowly but surely up the minor-league ladder. After posting .400 on-base percentages in back-to-back seasons at Single-A and then batting .269/.361/.434 in 114 games at Double-A in 1995, Lawton made his major-league debut pinch-hitting for Pat Meares in a loss to the Tigers on September 5, 1995.

He whiffed against Mike Christopher, but notched his first hit off submarining southpaw Mike Myers the next day and ended up starting often down the stretch. Lawton hit .317/.414/.467 in 21 games as a 23-year-old and smacked his first homer against 245-game winner Dennis Martinez on September 28, 1995, which turned out to be a key date in team history: Martinez hit Kirby Puckett with a pitch in the first inning and the Hall of Famer never played again.

Lawton began 1996 as the everyday right fielder, but was sent down to Triple-A after hitting .205 in April. He returned in late June, but was demoted again with a .231 batting average in mid-July. After batting .297/.377/.481 in 53 games at Triple-A he was called up in early August and this time stayed for the rest of the year. He finished with a .258/.339/.365 line in 79 games, hitting .294 in the final two months to earn the team's confidence going into 1997.

With his days in the minors behind him for good, he split time among all three outfield spots in 1997 and hit .248/.366/.415 in 142 games. It was

The only hitters in Twins history with a higher on-base percentage than Matt Lawton are Rod Carew, Joe Mauer, Chuck Knoblauch, and Harmon Killebrew.

a modest campaign even for a 25-year-old, but along with Paul Molitor and Chuck Knoblauch he was one of only three Twins regulars with an adjusted OPS+ above the league average. As you might expect from a team with that little offense and a 5.02 ERA, the Twins finished 68–94 for their most losses since 1982.

The team continued to struggle in 1998, going 70–92, but Lawton had his first big year. Playing mostly right field and also filling in as the center fielder when Otis Nixon had his jaw broken by Felix Martinez, he batted .278/.387/.478 with 21 homers, 36 doubles, 86 walks, and 16 steals in 152 games. Lawton won team MVP honors and led the Twins in nearly every major offensive category, including homers, RBIs, runs, on-base percentage, slugging percentage, walks, and total bases.

Lawton got off to a slow start in 1999 and was batting just .262/.345/.406 when he was hit in the face by a Dennys Reyes pitch on June 8. A fractured eye socket sent him to the disabled list for more than a month. He returned in mid-July and continued to get on base at a good clip, but his power disappeared. Lawton hit five homers with a .406 slugging percentage prior to the injury, but had just two homers and a pitiful .299 slugging percentage after returning.

Lawton came back strong in 2000, bouncing back from what could have been a serious injury to put together arguably his best season. He hit .305/.405/.460 with 13 homers, 44 doubles, 91 walks, and 23 steals in 156 games, making his first All-Star team and winning another team MVP. The team continued to stink at 69–93, but unlike several of their token All-Stars from that period of losing, Lawton was deserving with a .330 first-half batting average.

After eight consecutive losing seasons the Twins got off to a 14–3 start in 2001, and carried a 55–32 record and five-game division lead over the Indians into the All-Star break. After winning the first game of the second half the Twins promptly went in the tank, losing 13 of the next 17 to fall into a tie with Cleveland atop the AL Central. On July 30, with the division slipping away, the Twins traded Lawton to the Mets for veteran starter Rick Reed.

It was a controversial move, in part because Lawton was the best hitter on a team that was relatively short on offense to begin with and in part because Reed was a 36-year-old former replacement player making $7 million. Lawton was hitting .293 at the time of the trade, while Reed had a 3.48 ERA over 135 innings in New York. After the deal Brian Buchanan and Dustan Mohr replaced Lawton in right field, Reed went 4–6 with a 5.19 ERA in 12 starts, and the Twins went 25–32 to fall out of contention.

It wasn't so much that picking up a veteran starter was a bad move—although certainly you could argue about Reed being the right guy—but rather that in order to get Reed the Twins had to take from an area that was far from a strength. That's typically not how contending teams bolster themselves for a stretch run and there was speculation that general manager Terry Ryan intended to swing a second deal for a hitter like Dmitri Young or Shannon Stewart to replace Lawton, but that fell through.

Reed went 15–7 with a 3.78 ERA in 2002 as the Twins made the playoffs for the first time since 1991, and then he was a mess in 2003 thanks to back problems. Meanwhile, Lawton batted just .246 for the Mets in 2001 following the trade and was dealt to the Indians for Roberto Alomar that winter. He spent three mediocre seasons in Cleveland while struggling through shoulder injuries and then bounced around with four different teams over his final two years while suspended for steroid use.

Lawton's strengths were drawing walks, lacing doubles, getting on base, and efficient running—skills that tend to be overlooked. He was productive in Minnesota, putting together three very good years and another solid season before the age of 30, and his name is plastered all over the team leaderboards. Lawton and Brad Radke were sort of the bridge from the Puckett/Hrbek/Knoblauch days to the Mauer/Morneau/Santana days. And as any Twins fan who grew up in the 1990s can tell you, it was an awfully long bridge.

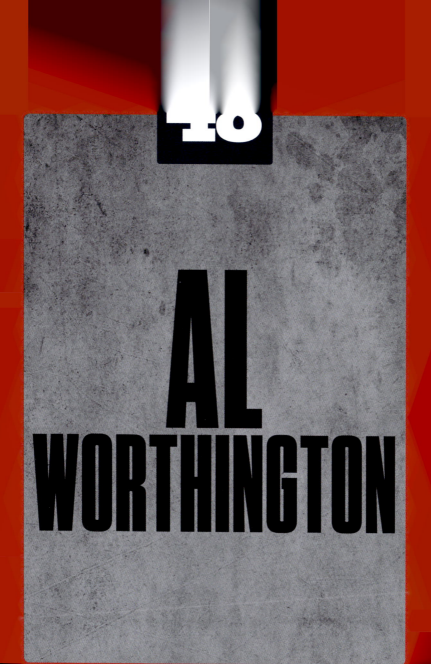

AL
WORTHINGTON

Originally signed out of the University of Alabama by the Cubs in 1951, Al Worthington made his major-league debut with the Giants in 1953 and amazingly pitched shutouts in each of his first two starts. He cooled down after that, finishing his rookie season at 4–8 with a 3.44 ERA in 102 innings. Worthington spent most of 1954 and all of 1955 pitching in the minors and returned to the Giants' rotation with a 7–14 record and 3.97 ERA across 166 innings in 1956.

He spent the next two seasons bouncing back and forth between the Giants' rotation and bullpen, and then posted a 3.68 ERA in 73 innings when they decided to use Worthington almost exclusively as a reliever in 1959. Just before the start of the 1960 season, San Francisco traded the 31-year-old Worthington to Boston for light-hitting first baseman Jim Marshall (not to be confused with the other, harder-hitting Vikings football player with the same name).

Worthington struggled with the Red Sox and was dealt to the White Sox that September. He lasted just four games in Chicago before leaving because he claimed they stole signs from teams and he was morally opposed. As you might expect, the White Sox felt he could use some time in the minor leagues. He threw a no-hitter while pitching for San Diego of the Pacific Coast League in 1961 and then went 15–4 with a 2.94 ERA for Indianapolis of the American Association in 1962.

According to a *New York Times* article in September 1962, then-Mets scout and Hall of Fame second baseman Rogers Hornsby identified Worthington as the minor leaguer most deserving of a shot in the majors and the Mets purchased his contract. Sure enough, he returned to the majors in 1963, but it wasn't with New York. Cincinnati snatched him up in the Rule 5 draft and watched as

Worthington went 4–4 with 10 saves and a 2.99 ERA in 81 innings out of the bullpen.

In a series of events that summed up Worthington's career to that point, he got off to a slow start in 1964 and the Reds gave up on him after just seven bad innings. They first sent him to Triple-A and then sold his contract to the Twins in June. Worthington was 35 years old and had been deemed washed up by seemingly every other team in baseball, but he immediately stepped in as the Twins' relief ace. Worthington made his Twins debut in relief of starter Dick Stigman against those sign-stealing White Sox on June 28, 1964.

Coming into a tie game with one out and the bases loaded in the sixth inning, he got out of the jam unscathed and then tossed three more scoreless innings to earn the win when Zoilo Versalles, Harmon Killebrew, and Bob Allison each homered off Chicago reliever Eddie Fisher late in the game. Despite not joining the Twins until three months into the season, Worthington threw 72 innings with a 1.37 ERA and team-high 14 saves. Decades later no pitcher in Twins history has thrown more innings in a season with a lower ERA.

He followed that up with 21 saves and a 2.13 ERA in 80 innings to help lead the Twins to the World Series in 1965, and pitched four scoreless innings against the Dodgers. He was then one of baseball's elite relievers from 1966 to '68, with ERAs of 2.46, 2.84, and 2.71 while saving 16, 16, and 18 games. Worthington gave up closer duties in 1969 at age 40, stepping aside in favor of Ron Perranoski and serving as a middle reliever in what would be his final season.

Worthington retired with a 2.62 ERA, 37 wins, and 88 saves in 473 career innings for the Twins, including a great five-year run as closer. His save totals aren't nearly as gaudy as those put up by the modern one-inning closers, but they're equally impressive considering the context. Not only did his 18 saves in 1968 lead the league, he ranked among the AL's top 10 in saves and games finished in each of those five years. Among all MLB pitchers, only Ted Abernathy had more saves than Worthington during that five-year span.

THE BIG 50

For whatever reason the Twins have likely had more than their fair share of top closers since 1961, from Perranoski, Mike Marshall, and Jeff Reardon to Rick Aguilera, Eddie Guardado, Joe Nathan, and Glen Perkins. You wouldn't necessarily know it based on his save totals, because he pitched before the dawn of modern closer usage, but Worthington leads off that list and the remarkable manner in which he ended up closing games in Minnesota is one of the more interesting career paths in team history.

DAVE
BOSWELL

After winning the 1963 bidding war for 18-year-old Dave Boswell, the Twins gave the 6'3" right-hander a then-large $15,000 bonus to sign straight out of high school. His minor-league career lasted under two seasons and Boswell made his major-league debut on September 18, 1964, lasting just three innings in a no-decision against Boston four months before his 20th birthday. He ended up making four September starts, going 2–0 with a 4.24 ERA.

Boswell made the team as a long man out of spring training in 1965, and after seven shutout innings in relief of Dick Stigman on May 11 was given a shot in the rotation. He pitched well, going 5–3 with a 3.53 ERA in 12 starts, but was shifted back to the bullpen in the second half after coming down with mononucleosis. He made one appearance in the World Series defeat to the Dodgers, throwing 2.2 innings of relief after Jim Kaat was knocked around in Game 5.

A full-fledged member of the rotation in 1966, he was 12–5 with a 3.14 ERA in 169 innings and led the league with a .706 winning percentage while ranking second with 9.2 strikeouts per nine innings. At just 21 the future looked bright, and sure enough over the next three seasons Boswell was among the most durable pitchers in the league. He went 44–37 with a 3.27 ERA in 669 innings from 1967 to '69, striking out 537 batters while allowing just 525 hits.

He was at his best in 1969, teaming with Jim Perry to give the Twins a pair of 20-game winners on the way to a division title. Boswell ranked among the league leaders in wins (20), innings (256), and strikeouts (190), but along with the overpowering raw stuff he also had significant trouble with his control. He handed out 99 walks, plunked another eight batters, and uncorked 10 wild pitches to rank among the American League's top 10 in each category.

Boswell stepped up in the playoffs as the Twins faced a 109-win Baltimore team that led the league in runs allowed and ranked second to the Twins in runs scored. He somehow managed to keep a lineup headed by Frank Robinson and Boog Powell—who finished second and third to Harmon Killebrew in the MVP balloting—off the scoreboard for 10.2 innings in Game 2, all while 20-game winner Dave McNally blanked the Twins for 11 frames.

With two runners on and two outs in the bottom of the 11th, manager Billy Martin yanked Boswell in favor of

TWINS' LOWEST OPPONENTS' BATTING AVERAGE

minimum 750 innings:

.217	Dave Boswell
.221	Johan Santana
.233	Camilo Pascual
.242	Jim Perry
.246	Bert Blyleven

closer Ron Perranoski, who'd saved an AL-high 31 games with a 2.11 ERA. Orioles skipper Earl Weaver responded by pinch-hitting Curt Motton for Elrod Hendricks and Motton delivered a walk-off single to right field. Not only was Boswell's amazing game wasted, he was tagged with a loss despite recording 32 outs without actually allowing a run to score.

Boswell didn't get another chance against the Orioles, as Baltimore finished off the three-game sweep with a blowout victory in Game 3 before eventually losing to the "Miracle Mets" in the World Series. And while no one knew it at the time, that extra-inning loss to the Orioles in the ALCS essentially marked the end of Boswell's days as an effective big-league pitcher despite the fact that he didn't turn 25 years old until a few months later.

Boswell was 3–7 with a ghastly 6.42 ERA in 69 innings in 1970 and didn't make an appearance in the Twins' second consecutive three-game ALCS sweep at the hands of the Orioles. He was released by the Twins before throwing a single inning in 1971 and immediately signed with the Tigers, who cut him loose following three poor relief outings. Boswell then latched on with the Orioles and finished his career by going 1–2 with a 4.38 ERA in 25 innings as a mop-up man.

It's hard to pin Boswell's early decline on that 10.2-inning ALCS start alone, because pitching past the ninth inning was relatively routine in 1969. In fact, that start wasn't even Boswell's longest of the season—he lasted 12 innings in a victory over the White Sox in mid-July—and across baseball there were 67 other starts of more than nine innings. Still, he likely threw more than 150 pitches in both the July win and ALCS loss, and that type of workload for a 24-year-old is certainly difficult to ignore given how his career fizzled.

Would he have lasted past his 27th birthday had he not logged nearly a thousand innings, completed 37 games, and had those marathon starts through age 24? Perhaps, but while his workload was obscene by today's standards it wasn't particularly out of the ordinary back then. Interestingly, the Twins fired Martin as manager after one division-winning year not because he worked Boswell so hard on the mound, but because he reportedly knocked Boswell out in a bar fight that August.

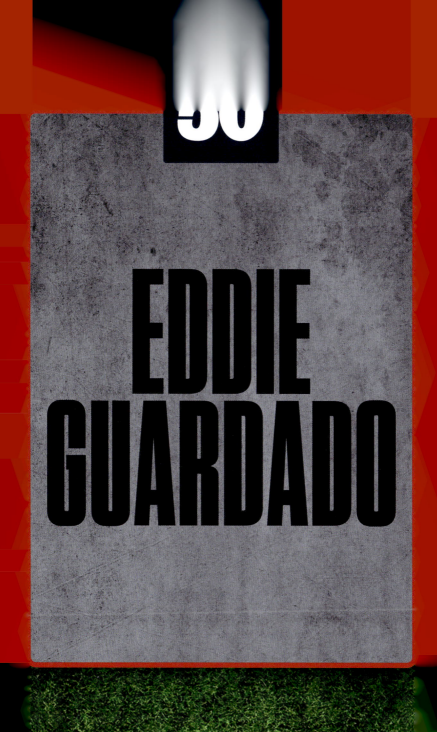

Taken by the Twins in the 21st round of the 1990 draft, Eddie Guardado debuted in 1991 and had a 1.86 ERA in rookie-ball, throwing a no-hitter in his final outing. He moved up to low Single-A in 1992 and struggled, but still received a late-season promotion to high Single-A and was nearly unhittable there by winning all seven starts with a 1.64 ERA. Guardado began 1993 at Double-A and went 4–0 with a 1.24 ERA in 10 starts, posting a nifty 57-to-10 strikeout-to-walk ratio in 65 innings.

Combined with his great work at high Single-A the previous season, Guardado was 11–0 with a 1.41 ERA in the span of 17 minor-league starts. That was enough to convince the Twins he was ready and Guarardo made his debut on June 13, 1993. Starting against the last-place A's at the Metrodome, his first pitch was to Hall of Famer Rickey Henderson. His second batter was native Minnesotan and former University of Minnesota star Terry Steinbach, who welcomed Guardado to the big leagues by homering.

Guardado went on to appear in a total of 19 games for the Twins in 1993, including 16 starts, and was 3–8 with a 6.18 ERA. That earned him a trip back to the minors in 1994, and Guardado was 12–7 with a 4.84 ERA in 24 starts at Triple-A before the Twins called him back up in July. He wasn't any better, posting an 8.47 ERA in four starts before the strike ended the season in mid-August. Guardado began the strike-shortened 1995 season in the Twins' bullpen as a long reliever but was moved back to the rotation in late May.

He again struggled as a starter, going 0–5 with a ghastly 9.28 ERA in five starts, which combined with his numbers from 1993 and 1994 gave him the following career stats as a major-league starting pitcher: 25 starts, 3–15 record, 6.95 ERA. As a starter, Guardado's so-so stuff barely missed any bats and he gave up hits in bunches. However, lost in his pathetic numbers as a starter is that Guardado had a 3.86 ERA in 70 innings as a reliever, with 65 strikeouts.

The attempt to turn him into a starter failed horribly, but in the process the Twins found one of the most durable relievers in team history. During the next eight years "Everyday Eddie" appeared in at least 60 games per season, including a league-high 83 in 1996. He was initially used as a lefty specialist, logging 233 innings in 294 games from 1996-99 for an average of just 0.8 innings per appearance. Then in 2000, the Twins started using him as a more typical one-inning setup man and that's when Guardado began to thrive.

He went 7–4 with nine saves and a 3.94 ERA in 62 innings, holding opponents to a .238 average. Minnesota began the 2001 season with LaTroy Hawkins as closer and Guardado as his primary setup man, and it worked for a while. The team shocked the baseball world by leading the AL Central at the All-Star break and Hawkins saved 23 games with a 3.48 ERA. However, as the team fell apart in the second half, so did Hawkins. In his 18 post-break innings he gave up 21 earned runs on the way to a 0–3 record and 10.70 ERA.

While it didn't occur until it was too late, the Twins eventually took away Hawkins' closer job and handed it to Guardado. He converted all but one of the 10 save opportunities he was given down the stretch to finish 7–1 with 12 saves and a 3.51 ERA in 67 innings. He entered 2002 as the full-time closer, and the Twins began a string of three straight division titles. And unlike Hawkins the year before, Guardado was fantastic from April all the way through September.

Guardado converted 14 consecutive saves to begin the year and ended up saving an AL-high 45 with a 2.93 ERA while making his first All-Star team and finishing 15th in the MVP voting. Trusted with ninth-inning duties again in 2003, he had another great and similar season, notching 41 saves with a 2.89 ERA. He was shaky at times, wriggling out of jams rather than abruptly slamming the door, but in two-plus seasons as Twins closer, Guardado converted 95 saves in 106 chances for a success rate of 90 percent.

Even in the playoffs, where his ERA was 9.00 in three series, he converted all three save chances and found a way to escape a potentially disastrous ninth inning against the A's in Game 5 of the 2002 ALDS. Following 14 seasons in the Twins organization, Guardado became a free agent in the winter of 2003. Guardado and the team spoke of wanting him to return, but the Twins used the money they would have needed to re-sign him to bring back Shannon Stewart, and then brilliantly found Guardado's replacement in Joe Nathan.

Guardado signed a three-year, $13 million deal with the Mariners and the Twins used one of the draft picks they received as compensation to select Glen Perkins. Guardado pitched well in his first two seasons in Seattle but struggled through injuries on last-place teams. He lost the closer job in early 2006 and was traded to Cincinnati, where he saved eight games with a 1.29 ERA before blowing out his elbow. After undergoing surgery he made a comeback with the Rangers in 2008, emerging as Texas' primary setup man at age 37.

He had a nice-looking 3.65 ERA in 49 innings, but a poor 28/17 K/BB ratio hinted that Guardado was running out of gas and he struggled after a mid-August trade to the Twins, finishing a second go-around in Minnesota with a 7.71 ERA. He's the Twins' leader with 648 appearances, out-pacing second-place Rick Aguilera by 32 percent and is third in team history in saves behind Aguilera and Nathan. And after moving to the bullpen, Guardado was one of the league's most consistent, durable, and valuable relievers for nine years.

Plus, those chants of "Eddie! Eddie! Eddie!" sure were a lot of fun.

[About the Author]

Aaron Gleeman was born and raised in St. Paul and now lives in Minneapolis with his girlfriend and (she insists he add) their cat. He's the Editor-In-Chief of Baseball Prospectus, co-hosts the Twins-centric "Gleeman and The Geek" radio show/podcast on KFAN, and has been writing about the Twins on AaronGleeman.com since 2002.